The (
Supernatural and Weird Fiction of Wilkie Collins
Volume 1

The Collected Supernatural and Weird Fiction of Wilkie Collins Volume 1

Contains one novel 'The Haunted Hotel',
one novella 'Mad Monkton',
three novelettes 'Mr Percy and the Prophet',
'The Biter Bit' and 'The Dead Alive'
and eight short stories to chill the blood

Wilkie Collins

LEONAUR

The Collected
Supernatural and Weird
Fiction of Wilkie Collins
Volume 1
Contains one novel 'The Haunted Hotel',
one novella 'Mad Monkton',
three novelettes 'Mr Percy and the Prophet',
'The Biter Bit' and 'The Dead Alive'
and eight short stories to chill the blood

by Wilkie Collins

FIRST EDITION

Leonaur is an imprint
of Oakpast Ltd

ISBN: 978-1-84677-822-3 (hardcover)
ISBN: 978-1-84677-821-6 (softcover)

http://www.leonaur.com

Publisher's Notes

In the interests of authenticity, the spellings, grammar and place names used have been retained from the original editions.

The opinions of the authors represent a view of events in which he was a participant related from his own perspective, as such the text is relevant as an historical document.

The views expressed in this book are not necessarily those of the publisher.

Contents

The Haunted Hotel

The First Part

Chapter 1

In the year 1860, the reputation of Doctor Wybrow as a London physician reached its highest point. It was reported on good authority that he was in receipt of one of the largest incomes derived from the practice of medicine in modern times.

One afternoon, toward the close of the London season, the Doctor had just taken his luncheon after a specially hard morning's work in his consulting-room, and with a formidable list of visits to patients at their own houses to fill up the rest of his day—when the servant announced that a lady wished to speak to him.

"Who is she?" the Doctor asked. "A stranger?"

"Yes, sir."

"I see no strangers out of consulting-hours. Tell her what the hours are, and send her away."

"I have told her, sir."

"Well?"

"And she won't go."

"Won't go?" The Doctor smiled as he repeated the words. He was a humorist in his way; and there was an absurd side to the situation which rather amused him. "Has this obstinate lady given you her name?" he inquired.

"No, sir. She refused to give any name—she said she wouldn't keep you five minutes, and the matter was too important to wait till tomorrow. There she is in the consulting-room; and how to get her out again is more than I know."

Doctor Wybrow considered for a moment. His knowledge of women (professionally speaking) rested on the ripe experience of more than thirty years; he had met with them in all their varieties—especially the variety which knows nothing of the value of time, and never hesitates at sheltering itself behind the privileges of its sex. A glance at his watch informed him that he must soon begin his rounds among the patients who were waiting for him at their own houses. He decided forthwith on taking the only wise course that was open under the circumstances. In other words, he decided on taking to flight.

"Is the carriage at the door?" he asked.

"Yes, sir."

"Very well. Open the house door for me without making any noise, and leave the lady in undisturbed possession of the consulting-room. When she gets tired of waiting, you know what to tell her. If she asks when I am expected to return, say that I dine at my club, and spend the evening at the theatre. Now then, softly, Thomas! If your shoes creak, I am a lost man."

He noiselessly led the way into the hall, followed by the servant on tip-toe.

Did the lady in the consulting-room suspect him? Or did Thomas's shoes creak, and was her sense of hearing unusually keen? Whatever the explanation may be, the event that actually happened was beyond all doubt. Exactly as Doctor Wybrow passed his consulting-room, the door opened—the lady appeared on the threshold—and laid her hand on his arm.

"I entreat you, sir, not to go away without letting me speak to you first."

The accent was foreign; the tone was low and firm. Her fingers closed gently and yet resolutely, on the Doctor's arm.

Neither her language nor her action had the slightest effect in inclining him to grant her request. The influence that instantly stopped him, on the way to his carriage, was the silent influence of her face. The startling contrast between the corpse-like pallor of her complexion and the overpowering life and light, the glittering metallic brightness in her large black eyes, held him literally spellbound. She was dressed in dark colours, with perfect taste; she was of middle height, and (apparently) of middle age say a year or two over thirty. Her lower features—the nose, mouth, and chin—possessed the fineness and delicacy of form which is oftener seen among women of foreign races than among women of English birth.

She was unquestionably a handsome person—with the one serious drawback of her ghastly complexion, and with the less noticeable defect of a total want of tenderness in the expression of her eyes. Apart from his first emotion of surprise, the feeling she produced in the Doctor may be described as an overpowering feeling of professional curiosity. The case might prove to be something entirely new in his professional experience. "It looks like it," he thought; "and it's worth waiting for."

She perceived that she had produced a strong impression of some kind upon him, and dropped her hold on his arm.

"You have comforted many miserable women in your time," she said. "Comfort one more, today."

"Without waiting to be answered, she led the way back into the room.

The Doctor followed her, and closed the door. He placed her in the patients' chair, opposite the windows. Even in London the sun, on that summer afternoon, was dazzlingly bright. The radiant light flowed in on her. Her eyes met it unflinchingly, with the steely steadiness of the eyes of an eagle. The smooth pallor of her unwrinkled skin looked more fearfully white than ever. For the first time, for many a long year past, the Doctor felt his pulse quicken its beat in the presence of a patient.

Having possessed herself of his attention, she appeared, strangely enough, to have nothing to say to him. A curious apathy seemed to have taken possession of this resolute woman. Forced to speak first, the Doctor merely inquired, in the conventional phrase, what he could do for her.

The sound of his voice seemed to rouse her. Still looking straight at the light, she said, abruptly: "I have a painful question to ask."

"What is it?"

Her eyes travelled slowly from the window to the doctor's face. Without the slightest outward appearance of agitation, she put the "painful question" in these extraordinary words:

"I want to know, if you please, whether I am in danger of going mad?"

Some men might have been amused, and some might have been alarmed. Doctor Wybrow was only conscious of a sense of disappointment. Was this the rare case that he had anticipated, judging rashly by appearances? Was the new patient only a hypochondriacal woman, whose malady was a disordered stomach and whose misfortune was a weak brain? "Why do you come to me?" he asked, sharply. "Why don't you consult a doctor whose special employment is the treatment of the insane?"

She had her answer ready on the instant.

"I don't go to a doctor of that sort," she said, "for the very reason that he is a specialist: he has the fatal habit of judging everybody by lines and rules of his own laying down. I come to you, because my case is outside of all lines and rules, and because you are famous in your profession for the discovery of mysteries in disease. Are you satisfied?"

He was more than satisfied—his first idea bad been the right idea, after all. Besides, she was correctly informed as to his professional position. The capacity which had raised him to fame and fortune was his capacity (unrivalled among his brethren) for the discovery of remote disease.

"I am at your disposal," he answered. "Let me try if I can find out what is the matter with you."

He put his medical questions. They were promptly and plainly answered; and they led to no other conclusion than that the strange lady was, mentally and physically, in excellent health. Not satisfied with questions, he carefully examined the great organs of life. Neither his hand nor his stethoscope could discover anything that was amiss. With the admirable patience and devotion to his art which had distinguished him from the time when he was a student, he still subjected her to one test after another.

The result was always the same. Not only was there no tendency to brain disease—there was not even a perceptible derangement of the nervous system. "I can find nothing the matter with you," he said. "I can't even account for the extraordinary pallor of your complexion. You completely puzzle me."

"The pallor of my complexion is nothing," she answered, a little impatiently. "In my early life I had a narrow escape from death by poisoning. I have never had a complexion—since and my skin is so delicate, I cannot paint without producing a hideous rash. But that is of no importance. I wanted your opinion given positively. I believed in you, and you have disappointed me." Her head dropped on her breast. "And so it ends!" she said to herself bitterly.

The Doctor's sympathies were touched. Perhaps it might be more correct to say that his professional pride was a little hurt. "It may end in the right way yet," he remarked, "if you choose to help me."

She looked up again with flashing eyes. "Speak plainly," she said. "How can I help you?"

"Plainly, madam, you come to me as an enigma and you leave me to make the right guess by the unaided efforts of my art. My art will do much, but not all. For example, something must have occurred—something quite unconnected with the state of your bodily health—to frighten you about yourself, or you would never have come here to consult me. Is that true?"

She clasped her hands in her lap. "That is true!" she said, eagerly. "I begin to believe in you again."

"Very well. You can't expect me to find out the moral cause which has alarmed you. I can positively discover that there is no physical cause of alarm; and (unless you admit me to your confidence) I can do no more."

She rose, and took a turn in the room. "Suppose I tell you?" she said. "But, mind, I shall mention no names!"

"There is no need to mention names. The facts are all I want."

"The facts are nothing," she rejoined. "I have only my own impressions to confess—and you will very likely think me a fanciful fool when you hear what they are. No matter. I will do my best to content you—I will begin with the facts that you want. Take my word for it, they won't do much to help you."

She sat down again. In the plainest possible words, she began the strangest and wildest confession that had ever reached the Doctor's ears.

Chapter 2

"It is one fact, sir, that I am a widow," she said. "It is another fact that I am going to be married again."

There she paused, and smiled at some thought that occurred to her. Doctor Wybrow was not favourably impressed by her smile—there was something at once sad and cruel in it. It came slowly, and it went away suddenly. He began to doubt whether he had been wise in acting on his first impression. His mind reverted to the commonplace patients and the discoverable maladies that were waiting for him, with a certain tender regret.

The lady went on.

"My approaching marriage," she said, "has one embarrassing circumstance connected with it. The gentleman whose wife I am to be, was engaged to another lady when he happened to meet with me, abroad: that lady, mind, being of his own blood and family, related to him as his cousin. I have innocently robbed her of her lover, and destroyed her prospects in life. Innocently, I say—because he told me nothing of his engagement until after I had accepted him.

"When we next met in England—and when there was danger, no doubt, of the affair coming to my knowledge—he told me the truth. I was naturally indignant. He had his excuse ready; he showed me a letter from the lady herself, releasing him from his engagement. A more noble, a more high-minded letter, I never read in my life. I cried over it—I who have no tears in me for sorrows of my own!

"If the letter had left him any hope of being forgiven, I

would have positively refused to marry him. But the firmness of it—without anger, without a word of reproach, with heartfelt wishes even for his happiness—the firmness of it, I say, left him no hope. He appealed to my compassion; he appealed to his love for me. You know what women are. I too was soft-hearted—I said, Very well; yes! In a week more (I tremble as I think of it) we are to be married."

She did really tremble—she was obliged to pause and compose herself, before she could go on. The Doctor, waiting for more facts, began to fear that he stood committed to a long story. "Forgive me for reminding you that I have suffering persons waiting to see me," he said. "The sooner you can come to the point, the better for my patients and for me."

The strange smile—at once so sad and so cruel—showed itself again on the lady's lips. "Every word I have said is to the point," she answered. "You will see it yourself in a moment more."

She resumed her narrative.

"Yesterday—you need fear no long story, sir; only yesterday—I was among the visitors at one of your English luncheon parties. A lady, a perfect stranger to me, came in late—after we had left the table, and had retired to the drawing-room. She happened to take a chair near me; and we were presented to each other. I knew her by name, as she knew me.

"It was the woman whom I had robbed of her lover, the woman who had written the noble letter. Now listen! You were impatient with me for not interesting you in what I said just now. I said it to satisfy your mind that I had no enmity of feeling toward the lady, on my side. I admired her, I felt for her—I had no cause to reproach myself. This is very important, as you will presently see.

"On her side, I have reason to be assured that the circumstances had been truly explained to her, and that she understood I was in no way to blame. Now, knowing all these necessary things as you do, explain to me, if you can, why, when I rose and met that woman's eyes looking at me, I turned cold from head to foot, and shuddered, and shivered, and knew what a deadly panic of fear was, for the first time in my life."

The Doctor began to feel interested at last.

"Was there anything remarkable in the lady's personal appearance?" he asked.

"Nothing whatever!" was the vehement reply. "Here is the true description of her:—The ordinary English lady; the clear cold blue eyes, the fine rosy complexion, the inanimately polite manner, the large good-humoured mouth, the too plump cheeks and chin; these, and nothing more."

"Was there anything in her expression, when you first looked at her, that took you by surprise?"

"There was natural curiosity to see the woman who had been preferred to her; and perhaps some astonishment also, not to see a more engaging and more beautiful person; both those feelings restrained within the limits of good breeding, and both not lasting for more than a few moments—so far as I could see. I say, 'so far,' because the horrible agitation that she communicated to me disturbed my judgment. If I could have got to the door, I would have run out of the room, she frightened me so! I was not even able to stand up—I sank back in my chair; I stared horror-struck at the calm blue eyes that were only looking at me with a gentle surprise.

"To say they affected me like the eyes of a serpent is to say nothing. I felt her soul in them, looking into mine—looking, if such a thing can be, unconsciously to her own mortal self. I tell you my impression, in all its horror and in all its folly! That woman is destined (without knowing it herself) to be the evil genius of my life Her innocent eyes saw hidden capabilities of wickedness in me that I was not aware of myself, until I felt them stirring under her look.

"If I commit faults in my life to come—if I am even guilty of crimes—she will bring the retribution, without (as I firmly believe) any conscious exercise of her own will. In one indescribable moment I felt all this—and I suppose my face showed it. The good artless creature was inspired by a sort of gentle alarm for me. 'I am afraid the heat of the room is too much for you; will you try my smelling-bottle?' I heard her say those kind words; and I remember nothing else—I fainted. When I recovered my senses, the company had all gone; only the lady of the house was with me. For the moment I could say nothing to her; the dreadful impression that I have tried to describe to you came back to me with the coming back of my life.

"As soon as I could speak, I implored her to tell me the whole truth about the woman whom I had supplanted. You see, I had a faint hope that her good character might not really be deserved, that her noble letter was a skilful piece of hypocrisy—in short, that she secretly hated me, and was cunning enough to hide it. No! the lady had been her friend from her girlhood, was as familiar with her as if they had been sisters—knew her positively to be as good, as innocent, as incapable of hating anybody, as the greatest saint that ever lived.

"My one last hope, that I had only felt an ordinary forewarning of danger in the presence of an ordinary enemy, was a hope destroyed forever. There was one more effort I could make, and I made it. I went next to the man whom I am to marry. I implored him to release me from my promise. He refused. I declared I would break my engagement. He showed me letters from his sisters, letters from his brothers, and his dear friends—all entreating him to think again before he made me his wife; all repeating reports of me in Paris, Vienna, and London, which are so many vile lies.

"'If you refuse to marry me,' he said, 'you admit that these reports are true—you admit that you are afraid to face society in the character of my wife.' What could I answer? There was no contradicting him—he was plainly right; if I persisted in my refusal, the utter destruction of my reputation would be the result. I consented to let the wedding take place as we had arranged it—and left him. The night has passed. I am here, with my fixed conviction—that innocent woman is ordained to have a fatal influence over my life.

"I am here with my one question to put, to the one man who can answer it. For the last time, sir, what am I—a demon who has seen the avenging angel? Or only a poor mad woman, misled by the delusion of a deranged mind?"

Doctor Wybrow rose from his chair, determined to close the interview.

He was strongly and painfully impressed by what he had heard. The longer he had listened to her, the more irresistibly the conviction of the woman's wickedness had forced itself on him. He tried vainly to think of her as a person to be pitied—a person with a morbidly sensitive imagination, conscious of the capacities for evil which lie dormant in us all, and striving earnestly to open her heart to the counter-influence of her own better nature; the effort was beyond him. A perverse instinct; in him said, as if in words, Beware how you believe in her!

"I have already given you my opinion," he said. "There is no sign of your intellect being deranged, or being likely to be deranged, that medical science can discover—as I understand it. As for the impressions you have confided to me, I can only say that yours is a case (as I venture to think) for spiritual rather than for medical advice. Of one thing be assured: what you have said to me in this room shall not pass out of it. Your confession is safe in my keeping."

She heard him, with a certain dogged resignation, to the end.

"Is that all?" she asked.

"That is all," he answered.

She put a little paper packet of money on the table. "Thank you, sir. There is your fee."

With those words she rose. Her wild black eyes looked upward, with an expression of despair so defiant and so horrible in its silent agony that the Doctor turned away his head, unable to endure the sight of it. The bare idea of taking anything from her—not money only, but anything even that she had touched—suddenly revolted him. Still without looking at her, he said, "Take it back; I don't want my fee."

She neither heeded nor heard him. Still looking upward, she said slowly to herself, "Let the end come. I have done with the struggle: I submit."

She drew her veil over her face, bowed to the Doctor, and left the room.

He rang the bell, and followed her into the hall. As the servant closed the door on her, a sudden impulse of curiosity—utterly unworthy of him, and at the same time utterly irresistible-sprang up in the Doctor's mind. Blushing like a boy, he said to the servant, "Follow her home, and find out her name." For one moment the man looked at his master, doubting if his own ears had not deceived him. Doctor Wybrow looked back at him in silence. The submissive servant knew what that silence meant-he took his hat and hurried into the street.

The Doctor went back to the consulting-room. A sudden revulsion of feeling swept over his mind. Had the woman left an infection of wickedness in the house, and had he caught it? What devil had possessed him to degrade himself in the eyes of his own servant? He had behaved infamously—he had asked an honest man, a man who had served him faithfully for years, to turn spy!

Stung by the bare thought of it, he ran out into the hall again, and opened the door. The servant had disappeared; it was too late to call him back. But one refuge from his con- tempt for himself was now open to him—the refuge of work. He got into his carriage and went his rounds among his patients.

If the famous physician could have shaken his own reputation, he would have done it that after- noon. Never before had he made himself so little welcome at the bedside. Never before had he put off until tomorrow the prescription which ought to have been written, the opinion which ought to have been given, today. He went home earlier than usual—unutterably dissatisfied with himself.

The servant had returned. Dr. Wybrow was ashamed to question him. The man reported the result of his errand, without waiting to be asked.

"The lady's name is the Countess Narona. She lives at—"

Without waiting to hear where she lived, the Doctor acknowledged the all-important discovery of her name by a silent bend of the head, and entered his consulting-room. The fee that he had vainly refused still lay in its little white paper covering on the table. He sealed it up in an envelope; addressed it to the "Poor-box" of the nearest police-court; and, calling the servant in, directed him to take it to the magistrate the next morning. Faithful to his duties, the servant waited to ask the customary question, "Do you dine at home today, sir?"

After a moment's hesitation he said, "No: I shall dine at the club."

The most easily deteriorated of all the moral qualities is the quality called "conscience." In one state of a man's mind, his conscience is the severest judge that can pass sentence on him. In another state, he and his conscience are on the best possible terms with each other in the comfortable capacity of accomplices. When Doctor Wybrow left his house for the second time, he did not even attempt to conceal from himself that his sole object, in dining at the club, was to hear what the world said of the Countess Narona.

Chapter 3

There was a time when a man in search of the pleasures of gossip sought the society of ladies. The man knows better now. He goes to the smoking-room of his club.

Doctor Wybrow lighted his cigar, and looked round him at his brethren in social conclave assembled. The room was well filled; but the flow of talk was still languid. The Doctor innocently applied the stimulant that was wanted. When he inquired if anybody knew the Countess Narona, he was answered by something like a shout of astonishment.

Never (the conclave agreed) had such an absurd question been asked before! Every human creature, with the slightest claim to a place in society, knew the Countess Narona. An adventuress with a European reputation of the blackest possible colour—such was the general description of the woman with the deathlike complexion and the glittering eyes.

Descending to particulars, each member of the club contributed his own little stock of scandal to the memoirs of the Countess. It was doubtful whether she was really, what she called herself, a Dalmatian lady. It was doubtful whether she had ever been married to the Count whose widow she assumed to be. It was doubtful whether the man who accompanied her in her travels (under the name of Baron Rivar, and in the character of her brother) was her brother at all.

Report pointed to the Baron as a gambler at every "table" on the Continent. Report whispered that his so-called sister had narrowly escaped being implicated in a famous trial for poisoning at Vienna—that she had been known at Milan as a spy in the interests of Austria—that her "apartment" in Paris had been denounced to the police as nothing less than a private gambling-house—and that her present appearance in England was the natural result of the discovery.

Only one member of the assembly in the smoking-room took the part of this much-abused woman, and declared that her character had been most cruelly and most unjustly assailed. But as the man was a lawyer, his interference went for nothing; it was naturally attributed to the spirit of contradiction inherent in his profession. He was asked derisively what he thought of the circumstances under which the Countess had become engaged to be married; and he made the characteristic answer, that he thought the circumstances highly creditable to both parties, and that he looked on the lady's future husband as a most enviable man.

Hearing this, the Doctor raised another shout of astonishment by inquiring the name of the gentleman whom the Countess was about to marry.

His friends in the smoking-room decided unanimously that the celebrated physician must be a second "Rip-van-Winkle," and that he had just awakened from a supernatural sleep of twenty years. It was all very well to say that he was devoted to his profession, and that he had neither time nor inclination to pick up fragments of gossip at dinner-parties and balls. A man who did not know that the Countess Narona had borrowed money at Homberg of no less a person than Lord Montbarry, and had then deluded him into making her a proposal of marriage, was a man who had probably never heard of Lord Montbarry himself. The younger members of the club, humouring the joke, sent a waiter for the *Peerage*; and read aloud the memoir of the nobleman in question, for the Doctor's benefit—with illustrative morsels of information interpolated by themselves.

> Herbert John Westwick. First Baron Montbarry, of Montbarry, King's County, Ireland. Created a Peer for distinguished military services in India. Born, 1812. Forty-eight years old, Doctor, at the present time. Not married. Will be married next week, Doctor, to the delightful creature we have been talking about. Heir presumptive, his lordship's next brother, Stephen Robert, married to Ella, youngest daughter of the Reverend Silas Marden, Rector of Runnigate, and has issue, three daughters. Younger brothers of his lordship, Francis and Henry, unmarried. Sisters of his lordship, Lady Barville, married to Sir Theodore Barville, Bart.; and Anne, widow of the late Peter Norbury, Esq., of Norbury Cross. Bear his lordship's relations well in mind, Doctor. Three brothers Westwick, Stephen, Francis, and Henry; and two sisters, Lady Barville and Mrs. Norbury. Not one of the five will be present at the marriage; and not one of the five will leave a stone unturned to stop it, if the Countess will only give them a chance. Add to these hostile members of the family another offended relative not mentioned in the *Peerage*, a young lady—

A sudden outburst of protest in more than one part of the room stopped the coming disclosure, and released the Doctor from further persecution.

"Don't mention the poor girl's name; it's too bad to make a joke of that part of the business; she has behaved nobly under shameful provocation; there is but one excuse for Montbarry—he is either a madman or a fool."

In these terms the protest expressed itself on all sides. Speaking confidentially to his next neighbour, the Doctor discovered that the lady referred to was already known to him (through the Countess's confession) as the lady deserted by Lord Montbarry. Her name was Agnes Lockwood. She was described as being the superior of the Countess in personal attraction, and as being also by some years the younger woman of the two.

Making all allowance for the follies that men committed every day in their relations with women, Montbarry's delusion was still the most monstrous delusion on record. In this expression of opinion every man present agreed—the lawyer even included. Not one of them could call to mind the innumerable instances in which the sexual influence has proved irresistible in the persons of women without even the pretension to beauty.

The very members of the club whom the Countess (in spite of her personal disadvantages) could have most easily fascinated, if she had thought it worth her while, were the members who wondered most loudly at Montbarry's choice of a wife.

While the topic of the Countess's marriage was still the one topic of conversation, a member of the club entered the smoking-room whose appearance instantly produced a dead silence. Doctor Wybrow's next neighbour whispered to him, "Montbarry's brother—Henry Westwick!"

The newcomer looked round him slowly, with a bitter smile.

"You are all talking of my brother," he said. "Don't mind me. Not one of you can despise him more heartily than I do. Go on, gentlemen—go on!"

But one man present took the speaker at his word. That man was the lawyer who had already undertaken the defence of the Countess.

"I stand alone in my opinion," he said, "and I am not ashamed of repeating it in anybody's hearing. I consider the Countess Narona to be a cruelly-treated woman. Why shouldn't she be Lord Montbarry's wife? Who can say she has a mercenary motive in marrying him?"

Montbarry's brother turned sharply on the speaker. "I say it!" he answered .

The reply might have shaken some men. The lawyer stood on his ground as firmly as ever.

"I believe I am right," he rejoined, "in stating that his lordship's income is not more than sufficient to support his station in life; also that it is an income derived almost entirely from landed property in Ireland, every acre of which is entailed."

Montbarry's brother made a sign, admitting that he had no objection to offer so far.

"If his lordship dies first," the lawyer proceeded, "I have been informed that the only provision he can make for his widow consists in a rent-charge on the property of no more than four hundred a year. His retiring pension and allowances, it is well known, die with him. Four hundred a year is therefore all that he can leave to the Countess, if he leaves her a widow."

"Four hundred a year is not all," was the reply to this. "My brother has insured his life for ten thousand pounds; and he has settled the whole of it on the Countess, in the event of his death."

This announcement produced a strong sensation. Men looked at each other and repeated the three startling words, "Ten thousand pounds!" Driven fairly to the wall, the lawyer made a last effort to defend his position.

"May I ask who made that settlement a condition of the marriage?" he said. "Surely it was not the Countess herself?"

Henry Westwick answered, "It was the Countess's brother;" and added, "Which comes to the same thing."

After that, there was no more to be said—so long, at least, as Montbarry's brother was present. The talk flowed into other channels; and the Doctor went home.

But his morbid curiosity about the Countess was not set at rest yet. In his leisure moments he found himself wondering whether Lord Montbarry's family would succeed in stopping the marriage after all. And more than this, he was conscious of a growing desire to see the infatuated man himself. Every day during the brief interval before the wedding, he looked in at the club, on the chance of hearing some news. Nothing had happened, so far as the club knew. The Countess's position was secure; Montbarry's resolution to be her husband was unshaken. They were both Roman Catholics, and they were to be married at the chapel in Spanish Place. So much the Doctor discovered about them—and no more.

On the day of the wedding, after a feeble struggle with himself, he actually sacrificed his patients and their guineas, and slipped away secretly to see the marriage. To the end of his life, he was angry with anybody who reminded him of what he had done on that day !

The wedding was strictly private. A close carriage stood at the church door; a few people, mostly of the lower class, and mostly old women, were scattered about the interior of the building. Here and there Doctor Wybrow detected the faces of some of his brethren of the club, attracted by curiosity, like himself. Four persons only stood before the altar—the bride and bridegroom and their two witnesses. One of these last was an elderly woman, who might have been the Countess's companion or maid; the other was undoubtedly her brother, Baron Rivar.

The bridal party (the bride herself included) wore their ordinary morning costume. Lord Montbarry, personally viewed, was a middle-aged military man of the ordinary type: nothing in the least remarkable distinguished him either in face or figure. Baron Rivar, again, in his way was another conventional representative of another well known type. One sees his finely-pointed moustache, his bold eyes, his crisply-curling hair, and his dashing carriage of the head, repeated hundreds of times over on the Boulevards of Paris.

The only noteworthy point about him was of the negative sort—he was not in the least like his sister. Even the officiating priest was only a harmless, humble-looking old man, who went through his duties resignedly, and felt visible rheumatic difficulties every time he bent his knees. The one remarkable person, the Countess herself, only raised her veil at the beginning of the ceremony, and presented nothing in her plain dress that was worth a second look. Never, on the face of it, was there a less interesting and less romantic marriage than this.

From time to time the Doctor glanced round at the door or up at the galleries, vaguely anticipating the appearance of some protesting stranger, in possession of some terrible secret, commissioned to forbid the progress of the service. Nothing in the shape of an event occurred—nothing extraordinary, nothing dramatic. Bound fast together as man and wife, the two disappeared, followed by their witnesses, to sign the registers; and still Doctor Wybrow waited, and still he cherished the obstinate hope that something worth seeing must certainly happen yet.

The interval passed, and the married couple, returning to the church, walked together down the nave to the door. Doctor Wybrow drew back as they approached. To his confusion and surprise, the Countess discovered him. He heard her say to her husband, "One moment; I see a friend."

Lord Montbarry bowed and waited. She stepped up to the Doctor, took his hand, and wrung it hard. He felt her overpowering black eyes looking at him through her veil. "One step more, you see, on the way to the end!" She whispered those strange words, and returned to her husband. Before the Doctor could recover himself and follow her, Lord and Lady Montbarry had stepped into their carriage and had driven away.

Outside the church door stood the three or four members of the club who, like Doctor Wybrow, had watched the ceremony out of curiosity. Near them was the bride's brother, waiting alone. He was evidently bent on seeing the man whom his sister had spoken to, in broad daylight. His bold eyes rested on the Doctor's face, with a momentary flash of suspicion in them. The cloud suddenly cleared away; the Baron smiled with charming courtesy, lifted his hat to his sister's friend, and walked off.

The members constituted themselves into a club conclave on the church steps. They began with the Baron. "Damned ill-looking rascal!"

They went on with Montbarry. "Is he going to take that horrid woman with him to Ireland?"

"Not he! He can't face the tenantry; they know about Agnes Lockwood."

"Well, but where is he going?"

"To Scotland."

"Does she like that?"

"It's only for a fortnight; they come back to London, and go abroad."

"And they will never return to England, eh?"

"Who can tell? Did you see how she looked at Montbarry, when she had to lift her veil at the beginning of the service? In his place, I should have bolted. Did you see her, Doctor?"

By this time, Doctor Wybrow, had remembered his patients and had heard enough of the club gossip. He followed the example of Baron Rivar, and walked off.

"One step more, you see, on the way to the end," he repeated to himself, on his way home. "What end?"

Chapter 4

On the day of the marriage Agnes Lockwood sat alone in the little drawing-room of her London lodgings, burning the letters which had been written to her by Montbarry in the bygone time.

The Countess's maliciously smart description of her, addressed to Doctor Wybrow, had not even hinted at the charm that most distinguished Agnes—the artless expression of goodness and purity which instantly attracted everyone who approached her. She looked by many years younger than she really was. "With her fair complexion and. her shy manner, it seemed only natural to speak of her as "a girl," although she was now really advancing toward thirty years of age.

She lived alone with an old nurse devoted to her, on a modest little income which was just enough to support the two. There were none of the ordinary signs of grief in her face, as she slowly tore the letters of her false lover in two, and threw the pieces into the small fire which had been lighted to consume them.

Unhappily for herself, she was one of those women who feel too deeply to find relief in tears. Pale and quiet, with cold trembling fingers, she destroyed the letters one by one without daring to read them again. She had torn the last of the series, and was still shrinking from throwing it after the rest into the swiftly destroying flame, when the old nurse came in, and asked if she would see "Master Henry"—meaning that youngest member of the Westwick family, who had publicly declared his contempt for his brother in the smoking-room of the club.

Agnes hesitated. A faint tinge of colour stole over her face.

There had been a long past time when Henry Westwick had owned that he loved her. She had made her confession to him, acknowledging that her heart was given to his eldest brother. He had submitted to his disappointment; and they had met thenceforth as cousins and friends. Never before had she associated the idea of him with embarrassing recollections.

But now, on the very day when his brother's marriage to another woman had consummated his brother's treason toward her, there was something vaguely repellent in the prospect of seeing him. The old nurse (who remembered them both in their cradles) observed her hesitation; and sympathizing of course with the man, put in a timely word for Henry.

"He says, he's going away, my dear; and he only wants to shake hands, and say goodbye." This plain statement of the case had its effect. Agnes decided on receiving her cousin.

He entered the room so rapidly that he surprised her in the act of throwing the fragments of Montbarry's last letter into the fire. She hurriedly spoke first.

"You are leaving London very suddenly, Henry. Is it business? Or pleasure?"

Instead of answering her, he pointed to the flaming letter, and to some black ashes of burned paper lying lightly in the lower part of the fireplace.

"Are you burning letters?"

"Yes."

"His letters?"

"Yes."

He took her hand gently. "I had no idea I was intruding on you, at a time when you must wish to be alone. Forgive me, Agnes—I shall see you when I return."

She signed to him, with a faint smile, to take a chair.

"We have known one another since we were children," she said. "Why should I feel a foolish pride about myself in your presence? Why should I have any secrets from you? I sent back all your brother's gifts to me some time ago. I have been advised to do more, to keep nothing that can remind me of him—in short, to burn his letters. I have taken the advice; but I own I shrank a little from destroying the last of the letters. No—not because it was the last, but because it had this in it." She opened her hand, and showed him a lock of Montbarry's hair, tied with a morsel of golden cord. "Well! Well! Let it go with the rest."

She dropped it into the flame. For a while, she stood with her back to Henry, leaning on the mantel-piece, and looking into the fire. He took the chair to which she had pointed, with a strange contradiction of expression in his face: the tears were in his eyes, while the brows above were knit close in an angry frown. He muttered to himself, "Damn him!"

She rallied her courage, and looked at him again when she spoke. "Well, Henry, and why are you going away?"

"I am out of spirits, Agnes, and I want a change."

She paused before she spoke again. His face told her plainly that he was thinking of her when he made that reply. She was grateful to him, but her mind was not with him: her mind was still with the man who had deserted her. She turned round again to the fire.

"Is it true," she asked, after a long silence, "that they have been married today?"

He answered ungraciously in the one necessary word:- "Yes."

"Did you go to the church?"

He resented the question with an expression of indignant surprise. "Go to the church?" he repeated. "I would as soon go to —" He checked himself there. "How can you ask?" he added in lower tones. "I have never spoken to Montbarry, I have not even seen him, since he treated you like the scoundrel and the fool that he is."

She looked at him suddenly, without saying a word. He understood her, and begged her pardon. But he was still angry. "The reckoning comes to some men," he said, "even in this world. He will live to rue the day when he married that woman!"

Agnes took a chair by his side, and looked at him with a gentle surprise.

"Is it quite reasonable to be so angry with her, because your brother preferred her to me?" she asked.

Henry turned on her sharply. "Do you defend the Countess, of all the people in the world?"

"Why not?" Agnes answered. "I know nothing against her. On the only occasion when we met, she appeared to be a singularly timid, nervous person, looking dreadfully ill; and being indeed so ill that she fainted under the heat of the room. "Why should we not do her justice? We know that she was innocent of any intention to wrong me; we know that she was not aware of my engagement—"

Henry lifted his hand impatiently and stopped her. "There is such a thing as being too just and too forgiving!" he interposed. "I can't bear to hear you talk in that patient way, after the scandalously cruel manner in which you have been treated. Try to forget them both, Agnes. I wish to God I could help you to do it!"

Agnes laid her hand on his arm. "You are very good to me, Henry; but you don't quite understand me. I was thinking of myself and my trouble in quite a different way, when you came in. I was wondering whether anything which has so entirely filled my heart, and so absorbed all that is best and truest in me, as my feeling for your brother, can really pass away as if it had never existed. I have destroyed the last visible things that remind me of him. In this world I shall see him no more. But is the tie that once bound us completely broken? Am I as entirely parted from the good and evil fortune of his life as if we had never met and never loved? "What do you think, Henry? I can hardly believe it."

"If you could bring the retribution on him that he has deserved," Henry Westwick answered, sternly, "I might be inclined to agree with you."

As that reply passed his lips, the old nurse appeared again at the door, announcing another visitor.

"I'm sorry to disturb you, my dear. But here is little Mrs. Ferrari wanting to know when she may say a few words to you."

Agnes turned to Henry, before she replied. "You remember Emily Bidwell, my favourite pupil years ago at the village school, and afterward my maid? She left me, to marry an Italian courier, named Ferrari—and I am afraid it has not turned out very well. Do you mind my having her in here for a minute or two?"

Henry rose to take his leave. "I should be glad to see Emily again at any other time," he said. "But it is best that I should go now. My mind is disturbed, Agnes; I might say things to you, if I stayed here any longer, which—which are better not said now. I shall cross the Channel by the mail tonight, and see how a few weeks' change will help me."

He took her hand. "Is there anything in the world that I can do for you?" he asked very earnestly. She thanked him, and tried to release her hand. He held it with a tremulous lingering grasp.

"God bless you, Agnes!" he said, in faltering tones, with his eyes on the ground. Her face flushed again, and the next instant turned paler than ever; she knew his heart as well as he knew it himself—she was too distressed to speak. He lifted her hand to his lips, kissed it fervently, and, without looking at her again, left the room. The nurse hobbled after him to the head of the stairs: she had not forgotten the time when the younger brother had been the unsuccessful rival of the older for the hand of Agnes.

"Don't be down-hearted, Master Henry," whispered the old woman, with the unscrupulous commonsense of persons in the lower rank of life. "Try her again, when you come back!"

Left alone for a few moments, Agnes took a turn in the room, trying to compose herself. She paused before a little watercolour drawing on the wall, which had belonged to her mother: it was her own portrait when she was a child. "How much happier we should be," she thought to herself sadly, "If we never grew up!"

The courier's wife was shown in—a little meek, melancholy woman, with white eyelashes, and watery eyes, who curtseyed deferentially and was troubled with a small chronic cough. Agnes shook hands with her kindly. "Well, Emily, what can I do for you?"

The courier's wife made rather a strange answer: "I'm afraid to tell you, miss."

"Is it such a very difficult favour to grant? Sit down, and let me hear how you are going on. Perhaps the petition will slip out while we are talking. How does your husband behave to you?"

Emily's light gray eyes looked more watery than ever. She shook her head and sighed resignedly. "I have no positive complaint to make against him, miss. But I'm afraid he doesn't care about me; and he seems to take no interest in his home—I may almost say he's tired of his home. It might be better for both of us, miss, if he went travelling for a while—not to mention the money, which is beginning to be wasted sadly." She put her handkerchief to her eyes, and sighed again more resignedly than ever.

"I don't quite understand," said Agnes. "I thought your husband had an engagement to take some ladies to Switzerland and Italy?"

"That was his ill-luck, miss. One of the ladies fell ill—and the others wouldn't go without her. They paid him a month's salary as compensation. But they had engaged him for the autumn and winter—and the loss is serious."

"I am sorry to hear it, Emily. Let us hope he will soon have another chance."

"It's not his turn, miss, to be recommended when the next applications come to the couriers' office. You see, there are so many of them out of employment just now. If he could be privately recommended—" She stopped, and left the unfinished sentence to speak for itself.

Agnes understood her directly. "You want my recommendation," she rejoined. "Why couldn't you say so at once?"

Emily blushed. "It would be such a chance for my husband, "she answered confusedly. "A letter, inquiring for a good courier (a six months' engagement, miss!) came to the office this morning. It's another man's turn to be chosen—and the secretary will recommend him. If my husband could only send his testimonials by the same post—with just a word in your name, miss—it might turn the scale, as they say. A private recommendation between gentlefolks goes so far." She stopped again, and sighed again, and looked down at the carpet, as if she had some private reason for feeling a little ashamed of herself.

Agnes began to be rather weary of the persistent tone of mystery in which her visitor spoke.

"If you want my interest with any friend of mine," she said, "why can't you tell me the name?"

The courier's wife began to cry. "I'm ashamed to tell you, miss."

For the first time, Agnes spoke sharply. "Nonsense, Emily! Tell me the name directly—or drop the subject—whichever you like best."

Emily made a last desperate effort. She wrung her handkerchief hard in her lap, and let off the name as if she had been letting off a loaded gun: "Lord Montbarry!"

Agnes rose and looked at her.

"You have disappointed me," she said very quietly, but with a look which the courier's wife had never seen in her face before. "Knowing what you know, you ought to be aware that it is impossible for me to communicate with Lord Montbarry. I always supposed you had some delicacy of feeling. I am sorry to find that I have been mistaken."

Weak as she was, Emily had spirit enough to feel the reproof. She walked in her meek, noiseless way to the door. "I beg your pardon, miss. I am not quite so bad as you think me. But I beg your pardon, all the same."

She opened the door. Agnes called her back. There was something in the woman's apology that appealed irresistibly to her just and generous nature. "Come," she said; "we must not part in this way. Let me not misunderstand you. What is it that you expected me to do?"

Emily was wise enough to answer this time without any reserve. "My husband will send his testimonials, miss, to Lord Montbarry in Scotland. I only wanted you to let him say in his letter that his wife has been known to you since she was a child, and that you feel some little interest in his welfare on that account. I don't ask it now, miss. You have made me understand that I was wrong."

Had she really been wrong? Past remembrances, as well as present troubles, pleaded powerfully with Agnes for the courier's wife. "It seems only a small favour to ask," she said, speaking under the impulse of kindness which was the strongest impulse in her nature. "But I am not sure that I ought to allow my name to be mentioned in your husband's letter. Let me hear again exactly what he wishes to say." Emily repeated the words—and then offered one of those suggestions, which have a special value of their own to persons unaccustomed to the use of their pens. "Suppose you try, miss, how it looks in writing?"

Childish as the idea was, Agnes tried the experiment. "If I let you mention me," she said, "we must at least decide what you are to say." She wrote the words in the briefest and plainest form:

"I venture to state that my wife has been known from her childhood to Miss Agnes Lockwood, who feels some little interest in my welfare on that account."

Reduced to this one sentence, there was surely nothing in the reference to her name which implied that Agnes had permitted it, or that she was even aware of it. After a last struggle with herself, she handed the written paper to Emily.

"Your husband must copy it exactly, without altering anything," she stipulated. "On that condition, I grant your request."

Emily was not only thankful—she was really touched. Agnes hurried the little woman out of the room. "Don't give me time to repent and take it back again," she said. Emily vanished.

"Is the tie that once bound us completely broken? Am I as entirely parted from the good and evil fortune of his life as if we had never met and never loved?" Agnes looked at the clock on the mantelpiece. Not ten minutes since, those serious questions had been on her lips. It almost shocked her to think of the commonplace manner in which they had already met with their reply. The mail of that night would appeal once more to Montbarry's remembrance of her in the choice of a servant.

Two days later, the post brought a few grateful lines from Emily. Her husband had got the place. Ferrari was engaged, for six months certain, as Lord Montbarry's courier.

The Second Part

Chapter 5

After only one week of travelling in Scotland, my lord and my lady returned unexpectedly to London. Introduced to the mountains and lakes of the Highlands, her ladyship positively declined to improve her acquaintance with them. When she was asked for her reason, she answered with a Roman brevity: "I have seen Switzerland."

For a week more the newly-married couple remained in London, in the strictest retirement. On one day in that week the nurse returned in a state of most uncustomary excitement from an errand on which Agnes had sent her. Passing the door of a fashionable dentist, she had met Lord Montbarry himself just leaving the house. The good woman's report described him, with malicious pleasure, as looking wretchedly ill. "His cheeks are getting hollow, my dear, and his beard is turning gray. I hope the dentist hurt him!"

Knowing how heartily her faithful old servant hated the man who had deserted her, Agnes made due allowance for a large infusion of exaggeration in the picture presented to her. The main impression produced on her mind was an impression of nervous uneasiness. If she trusted herself in the streets by daylight while Lord Montbarry remained in London, how could she be sure that his next chance-meeting might not be a meeting with herself? She waited at home, privately ashamed of her own undignified conduct, for the next two days. On the third day the fashionable intelligence of the newspapers announced the departure of Lord and Lady Montbarry for Paris, on their way to Italy.

Mrs. Ferrari, calling the same evening, informed Agnes that her husband had left her with all reasonable expression of conjugal kindness; his temper being improved by the prospect of going abroad. But one other servant accompanied the travellers—Lady Montbarry's maid, rather a silent, unsociable woman, so far as Emily had heard. Her ladyship's brother, Baron Rivar, was already on the Continent. It had been arranged that he was to meet his sister and her husband at Rome.

One by one the dull weeks succeeded each other in the life of Agnes. She faced her position with admirable courage, seeing her friends, keeping herself occupied in her leisure hours with reading and drawing, leaving no means untried of diverting her mind from the melancholy remembrance of the past. But she had loved too faithfully, she had been wounded too deeply, to feel in any adequate degree the influence of the moral remedies which she employed.

Persons who met with her in the ordinary relations of life, deceived by her outward serenity of manner, agreed that "Miss Lockwood seemed to be getting over her disappointment." But an old friend and school companion who happened to see her during a brief visit to London, was inexpressibly distressed by the change that she detected in Agnes. This lady was Mrs. Westwick, the wife of that brother of Lord Montbarry who came next to him in age, and who was described in the *Peerage* as presumptive heir to the title. He was then away, looking after his interests in some mining property which he possessed in America. Mrs. Westwick insisted on taking Agnes back with her to her home in Ireland.

"Come and keep me company while my husband is away. My three little girls will make you their playfellow, and the only stranger you will meet is the governess, whom I answer for your liking beforehand. Pack up your things, and I will call for you tomorrow on my way to the train." In those hearty terms the invitation was given.

Agnes thankfully accepted it. For three happy months she lived under the roof of her friend. The girls hung round her in tears at her departure; the youngest of them wanted to go back with Agnes to London. Half in jest, half in earnest, she said to her old friend at parting, "If your governess leaves you, keep the place open for me." Mrs. Westwick laughed. The wiser children took it seriously, and promised to let Agnes know.

On the very day when Miss Lockwood returned to London, she was recalled to those associations with the past which she was most anxious to forget. After the first kissings and greetings were over, the old nurse (who had been left in charge at the lodgings) had some startling information to communicate, derived from the courier's wife.

"Here has been little Mrs. Ferrari, my dear, in a dreadful state of mind; inquiring when you would be back. Her husband has left Lord Montbarry, without a word of warning—and nobody knows what has become of him."

Agnes looked at her in astonishment. "Are you sure of what you are saying?" she asked.

The nurse was quite sure. "Why, Lord bless you! The news comes from the couriers' office in Golden Square—from the secretary, Miss Agnes, the secretary himself!" Hearing this, Agnes began to feel alarmed as well as surprised. It was still early in the evening. She at once sent a message to Mrs. Ferrari, to say that she had returned.

In an hour more the courier's wife appeared, in a state of

agitation which it was not easy to control. Her narrative, when she was at last able to speak connectedly, entirely confirmed the nurse's report of it.

After hearing from her husband with tolerable regularity from Paris, Rome, and Venice, Emily had twice written to him afterward—and had received no reply. Feeling uneasy, she had gone to the office in Golden Square, to inquire if he had been heard of there. The post of the morning had brought a letter to the secretary from a courier then at Venice. It contained startling news of Ferrari. His wife had been allowed to take a copy of it, which she now handed to Agnes to read.

The writer stated that he had recently arrived in Venice. He had previously heard that Ferrari was with Lord and Lady Montbarry, at one of the old Venetian palaces which they had hired for a term. Being a friend of Ferrari, he had gone to pay him a visit. Ringing at the door that opened on the canal, and failing to make any one hear him, he had gone round to a side entrance opening on one of the narrow lanes of Venice. Here, standing at the door (as if she was waiting for him to try that way next), he found a pale woman with magnificent dark eyes, who proved to be no other than Lady Montbarry herself.

She asked, in Italian, what he wanted. He answered that he wanted to see the courier Ferrari, if it was quite convenient. She at once informed him that Ferrari had left the palace, without assigning any reason, and without even leaving an address at which his monthly salary (then due to him) could be paid. Amazed at this reply, the courier inquired if any person had offended Ferrari, or quarrelled with him. The lady answered, "To my knowledge, certainly not. I am Lady Montbarry; and I can positively assure you that Ferrari was treated with the greatest kindness in this house. We are as much astonished as you are at his extraordinary disappearance. If you should hear of him, pray let us know, so that we may at least pay him the money which is due."

After one or two more questions (quite readily answered) relating to the date and the time of day at which Ferrari had left the palace, the courier took his leave.

He at once entered on the necessary investigations—without the slightest result so far as Ferrari was concerned. Nobody had seen him. Nobody appeared to have been taken into his confidence. Nobody knew anything (that is to say, anything of the slightest importance) even about persons so distinguished as Lord and Lady Montbarry.

It was reported that her ladyship's English maid had left her, before the disappearance of Ferrari, to return to her relatives in her own country, and that Lady Montbarry had taken no steps to supply her place. His lordship was described as being in delicate health. He lived in the strictest retirement—nobody was admitted to him, not even his own countrymen.

A stupid old woman was discovered who did the housework at the palace, arriving in the morning and going away again at night. She had never seen the lost courier—she had never even seen Lord Montbarry, who was then confined to his room. Her ladyship, "a most gracious and adorable mistress," was in constant attendance on her noble husband. There was no other servant then in the house (so far as the old woman knew) but herself. The meals were sent in from a restaurant. My lord, it was said, disliked strangers. My lord's brother-in-law, the Baron, was generally shut up in a remote part of the palace, occupied (the gracious mistress said) with experiments in chemistry.

The experiments sometimes made a nasty smell. A doctor had latterly been called in to his lordship—an Italian doctor, long resident in Venice. Inquiries being addressed to this gentleman (a physician of undoubted capacity and respectability), it turned out that he also had never seen Ferrari, having been summoned to the palace (as his memorandum-book showed) at a date subsequent to the courier's disappearance.

The doctor described Lord Montbarry's malady as bronchitis. So far, there was no reason to feel any anxiety, though the attack was a sharp one. If alarming symptoms should appear, he had arranged with her ladyship to call in another physician. For the rest, it was impossible to speak too highly of my lady; night and day she was at her lord's bedside.

"With these particulars began and ended the discoveries made by Ferrari's courier-friend. The police were on the look-out for the lost man—and that was the only hope which could be held forth for the present, to Ferrari's wife.

"What do you think of it, miss?" the poor woman asked, eagerly. "What would you advise me to do?"

Agnes was at a loss how to answer her; it was an effort even to listen to what Emily was saying. The references in the courier's letter to Montbarry—the report of his illness, the melancholy picture of his secluded life—had reopened the old wound. She was not even thinking of the lost Ferrari; her mind was at Venice, by the sick man's bedside.

"I hardly know what to say," she answered. "I have had no experience in serious matters of this kind."

"Do you think it would help you, miss, if you read my husband's letters to me? There are only three of them—they won't take long to read."

Agnes compassionately read the letters.

They were not written in a very tender tone. "Dear Emily," and "Yours affectionately"—these conventional phrases were the only phrases of endearment which they contained. In the first letter, Lord Montbarry was not very favourably spoken of:

> "We leave Paris tomorrow. I don't much like my lord. He is proud and cold, and, between ourselves, stingy in money matters. I have had to dispute such trifles as a few *centimes* in the hotel bill; and twice already, some sharp remarks have passed between the newly-married couple, in consequence of her ladyship's freedom in purchasing pretty tempting things at the shops in Paris. 'I can't afford it; you must keep to your allowance.' She has had to hear those words already. For my part, I like her. She has the nice, easy foreign manners—she talks to me as if I was a human being like herself."

The second letter was dated from Rome.

"My lord's *caprices*" (Ferrari wrote) "have kept us perpetually on the move. He is becoming incurably restless I suspect he is uneasy in his mind. Painful recollections, I should say—I find him constantly reading old letters, when her ladyship is not present. We were to have stopped at Genoa, but he hurried us on. The same thing at Florence. Here, at Rome, my lady insists on resting. Her brother has met us at this place. There has been a quarrel already (the lady's maid tells me) between my lord and the Baron. The latter wanted to borrow money of the former. His lordship refused in language which offended Baron Rivar. My lady pacified them, and made them shake hands."

The third, and last letter, was from Venice.

"More of my lord's economy! Instead of staying at the hotel, we have hired a damp, mouldy, rambling old palace. My lady insists on having the best suites of rooms wherever we go—and the palace comes cheaper for a two months' term. My lord tried to get it for longer; he says the quiet of Venice is good for his nerves. But a foreign speculator has secured the palace, and is going to turn it into a hotel. The Baron is still with us, and there have been more disagreements about money matters.

"I don't like the Baron—and I don't find the attractions of my lady grow on me. She was much nicer before the Baron joined us. My lord is a punctual paymaster; it's a matter of honour with him; he hates parting with his money, but he does it because he has given his word. I receive my salary regularly at the end of each month not a *franc* extra, though I have done many things which are not part of a courier's proper work. Fancy the Baron trying to borrow money of me! He is an inveterate gambler.

"I didn't believe it when my lady's maid first told me so—but I have seen enough since to satisfy me that she was right.—I have seen other things besides, which—well! Which don't increase my respect for my lady and the

Baron. The maid says she means to give warning to leave. She is a respectable British female, and doesn't take things quite so easily as I do. It is a dull life here. No going into company—no company at home—not a creature sees my lord—not even the consul, or the banker.

"When he goes out, he goes alone, and generally toward nightfall. Indoors, he shuts himself up in his own room with his books, and sees as little of his wife and the Baron as possible. I fancy things are coming to a crisis here. If my lord's suspicions are once awakened, the consequences will be terrible. Under certain provocations, the noble Montbarry is a man who would stick at nothing. However, the pay is good—and I can't afford to talk of leaving the place, like my lady's maid."

Agnes handed back the letters—so suggestive of the penalty paid already for his own infatuation by the man who had deserted her!—with feelings of shame and distress, which made her no fit counsellor for the helpless woman who depended on her advice.

"The one thing I can suggest," she said, after first speaking some kind words of comfort and hope, "is that we should consult a person of greater experience than ours. Suppose I write and ask my lawyer (who is also my friend and trustee) to come and advise us tomorrow after his business hours?"

Emily eagerly and gratefully accepted the suggestion. An hour was arranged for the meeting on the next day; the correspondence was left under the care of Agnes; and the courier's wife took her leave.

Weary and heartsick, Agnes lay down on the sofa, to rest and compose herself. The careful nurse brought in a reviving cup of tea. Her quaint gossip about herself and her occupations while Agnes had been away, acted as a relief to her mistress's overburdened mind. They were still talking quietly, when they were startled by a loud knock at the house door. Hurried footsteps ascended the stairs. The door of the sitting-room was thrown open violently; the courier's wife rushed in like a mad woman.

"He's dead! they've murdered him!" Those wild words were all she could say. She dropped on her knees at the foot of the sofa-held out her hand with something clasped in it—and fell back in a swoon.

The nurse, signing to Agnes to open the window, took the necessary measures to restore the fainting woman. "What's this?" she exclaimed.

"Here's a letter in her hand. See what it is, miss."

The open envelope was addressed (evidently in a feigned handwriting) to "Mrs. Ferrari." The post-mark was "Venice." The contents of the envelope were a sheet of foreign note-paper and a folded inclosure.

On the note-paper one line only was written. It was again in a feigned handwriting, and it contained these words :

"To console you for the loss of your husband."

Agnes opened the inclosure next.

It was a Bank of England note for a thousand pounds.

Chapter 6

The next day, the friend and legal adviser of Agnes Lockwood, Mr. Troy, called on her by appointment in the evening.

Mrs. Ferrari—still persisting in the conviction of her husband's death—had sufficiently recovered to be present at the consultation. Assisted by Agnes, she told the lawyer the little that was known relating to Ferrari's disappearance, and then produced the correspondence connected with that event. Mr. Troy read (first) the three letters addressed by Ferrari to his wife; (secondly) the letter written by Ferrari's courier-friend, describing his visit to the palace and his interview with Lady Montbarry; and (thirdly) the one line of anonymous writing which had accompanied the extraordinary gift of a thousand pounds to Ferrari's wife.

Well known, at a later period, as the lawyer who acted for Lady Lydiard in the case of theft, generally described as the case of "My Lady's Money," Mr. Troy was not only a man of learning and experience in his profession—he was also a man who had seen something of society at home and abroad. He possessed a keen eye for character, a quaint humour, and a kindly nature which had not been deteriorated even by a lawyer's professional experience of mankind. With all these personal advantages it is a question, nevertheless, whether he was the fittest adviser whom Agnes could have chosen under the circumstances. Little Mrs. Ferrari, with many domestic merits, was an essentially commonplace woman. Mr. Troy was the last person living who was likely to attract her sympathies—he was the exact opposite of a commonplace man.

"She looks very ill, poor thing!" In these words the lawyer opened the business of the evening, referring to Mrs. Ferrari as unceremoniously as if she had been out of the room.

"She has suffered a terrible shock," Agnes answered.

Mr. Troy turned to Mrs. Ferrari, and looked at her again, with the interest due to the victim of a shock. He drummed absently with his fingers on the table. At last he spoke to her.

"My good lady, you don't really believe that your husband is dead?"

Mrs. Ferrari put her handkerchief to her eyes. The word "dead" was ineffectual to express her feelings. "Murdered !" she said, sternly, behind her handkerchief.

"Why? And by whom?" Mr. Troy asked.

Mrs. Ferrari seemed to have some difficulty in answering. "You have read my husband's letters, sir," she began. "I believe he discovered—" She got as far as that, and there she stopped.

"What did he discover?"

There are limits to human patience—even the patience of a bereaved wife. This cool question irritated Mrs. Ferrari into expressing herself plainly at last.

"He discovered Lady Montbarry and the Baron!" she answered, with a burst of hysterical vehemence. "The Baron is no more that vile woman's brother than I am. The wickedness of those two wretches came to my poor dear husband's knowledge. The lady's maid left her place on account of it. If Ferrari had gone away too, he would have been alive at this moment. They have killed him. I say they have killed him, to prevent it from getting to Lord Montbarry's ears." So, in short, sharp sentences, and in louder and louder accents, Mrs. Ferrari stated her opinion of the case.

Still keeping his own view in reserve, Mr. Troy listened with an expression of satirical approval.

"Very strongly stated, Mrs. Ferrari," he said. "You build up your sentences well; you clinch your conclusions in a workmanlike manner. If you had been a man, you would have made a good lawyer—you would have taken juries by the scruff of their necks. Complete the case, my good lady—complete the case. Tell us next who sent you this letter, inclosing the banknote. The 'two wretches' who murdered Mr. Ferrari would hardly put their hands in their pockets and send you a thousand pounds.. Who is it—eh? I see the postmark on the letter is 'Venice.' Have you any friend in that interesting city, with a large heart, and a purse to correspond, who has been let into the secret and who wishes to console you anonymously?"

It was not easy to reply to this. Mrs. Ferrari began to feel the first inward approaches of something like hatred toward Mr. Troy. "I don't understand you, sir," she answered. "I don't think this is a joking matter."

Agnes interfered, for the first time. She drew her chair a little nearer to her legal counsellor and friend.

"What is the most probable explanation, in your opinion?" she asked.

"I shall offend Mrs. Ferrari if I tell you," Mr. Troy answered.

"No, sir, you won't!" cried Mrs Ferrari, hating Mr. Troy undisguisedly by this time.

The lawyer leaned back in his chair. "Very well," he said, in his most good-humoured manner. "Let's have it out. Observe, madam, I don't dispute your view of the position of affairs at the palace in Venice. You have your husband's letters to justify you; and you have also the significant fact that Lady Montbarry's maid did really leave the house. We will say, then, that Lord Montbarry has presumably been made the victim of a foul wrong—that Mr. Ferrari was the first to find it out—and that the guilty persons had reason to fear, not only that he would acquaint Lord Montbarry with his discovery, but that he would be a principal witness against them if the scandal was made public in a court of law.

"Now mark! Admitting all this, I draw a totally different conclusion from the conclusion at which you have arrived. Here is your husband left in this miserable household of three, under very awkward circumstances for him. "What does he do? But for the banknote and the written message sent to you with it, I should say that he had wisely withdrawn himself from association with a disgraceful discovery and exposure, by taking secretly to flight.

"The money modifies this view—unfavourably so far as Mr. Ferrari is concerned. I still believe he is keeping out of the way. But I now say he is paid for keeping out of the way—and that banknote there on the table is the price of his absence, sent by the guilty persons to his wife."

Mrs. Ferrari's watery gray eyes brightened suddenly; Mrs. Ferrari's dull drab-coloured complexion became enlivened by a glow of brilliant red.

"It's false!" she cried. "It's a burning shame to speak of my husband in that way!"

"I told you I should offend you!" said Mr. Troy.

Agnes interposed once more—in the interests of peace. She took the offended wife's hand; she appealed to the lawyer to reconsider that side of his theory which reflected harshly on Ferrari. While she was still speaking, the servant interrupted her by entering the room with a visiting-card. It was the card of Henry Westwick; and there was an ominous request written on it in pencil. "I bring bad news. Let me see you for a minute downstairs." Agnes immediately left the room.

Alone with Mrs. Ferrari, Mr. Troy permitted his natural kindness of heart to show itself on the surface at last. He tried to make his peace with the courier's wife.

"You have every claim, my good soul, to resent a reflection

cast upon your husband," he began. "I may even say that I respect you for speaking so warmly in his defence. At the same time, remember that I am bound, in such a serious matter as this, to tell you what is really in my mind.

"I can have no intention of offending you, seeing that I am a total stranger to you and to Mr. Ferrari. A thousand pounds is a large sum of money; and a poor man may excusably be tempted by it to do nothing worse than to keep out of the way for a while. My only interest, acting on your behalf, is to get at the truth. If you will give me time, I see no reason to despair of finding your husband yet."

Ferrari's wife listened, without being convinced: her narrow little mind, filled to its extreme capacity by her unfavourable opinion of Mr. Troy, had no room left for the process of correcting its first impression. "I am much obliged to you, sir," was all she said. Her eyes were more communicative—her eyes added, in their language, "You may say what you please; I will never forgive you to my dying day."

Mr. Troy gave it up. He composedly wheeled his chair round, put his hands in his pockets, and looked out of window.

After an interval of silence, the drawing-room door was opened.

Mr. Troy wheeled round again briskly to the table, expecting to see Agnes. To his surprise there appeared, in her place, a perfect stranger to him—a gentleman, in the prime of life, with a marked expression of pain and embarrassment on his handsome face.

He looked at Mr. Troy, and bowed gravely.

"I am so unfortunate as to have brought news to Miss Agnes Lockwood which has greatly distressed her," he said. "She has retired to her room. I am requested to make her excuses, and to speak to you in her place."

Having introduced himself in those terms, he noticed Mrs. Ferrari, and held out his hand to her kindly. "It is some years since we last met, Emily," he said. "I am afraid you have almost forgotten the 'Master Henry' of old times." Emily, in some little confusion, made her acknowledgments, and begged to know if she could be of any use to Miss Lockwood.

"The old nurse is with her," Henry answered; "they will be better left together." He turned once more to Mr. Troy.

"I ought to tell you," he said, "that my name is Henry Westwick. I am the younger brother of the late Lord Montbarry."

"The late Lord Montbarry!" Mr. Troy exclaimed.

"My brother died at Venice yesterday evening. There is the telegram." With that startling answer, he handed the paper to Mr. Troy.

The message was in these words :

"Lady Montbarry, Venice. To Stephen Robert Westwick, Newbury's Hotel, London. It is useless to take the journey. Lord Montbarry died of bronchitis, at 8:40 this evening. All needful details by post."

"Was this expected, sir?" the lawyer asked.

"I cannot say that it has taken us entirely by surprise," Henry answered. "My brother Stephen (who is now the head of the family) received a telegram three days since, informing him that alarming symptoms had declared themselves, and that a second physician had been called in. He telegraphed back to say that he had left Ireland for London, on his way to Venice, and to direct that any further message might be sent to his hotel.

"The reply came in a second telegram. It announced that Lord Montbarry was in a state of insensibility, and that, in his brief intervals of consciousness, he recognized nobody. My brother was advised to wait in London for later information. The third telegram is now in your hands. That is all I know, up to the present time."

Happening to look at the courier's wife, Mr. Troy was struck by the expression of blank fear which showed itself in the woman's face.

"Mrs. Ferrari," he said, "have you heard what Mr. Westwick has just told me?"

"Every word of it, sir."

"Have you any questions to ask?"

"No, sir."

"You seem to be alarmed," the lawyer persisted. "Is it still about your husband?"

"I shall never see my husband again, sir. I have thought so all along, as you know. I feel sure of it now."

"Sure of it, after what you have just heard?"

"Yes, sir."

"Can you tell me why?"

"No, sir. It's a feeling I have. I can't tell why."

"Oh, a feeling?" Mr. Troy repeated, in a tone of compassionate contempt. "When it comes to feelings, my good soul!—" He left the sentence unfinished, and rose to take his leave of Mr. Westwick. The truth is, he began to feel puzzled himself, and he did not choose to let Mrs. Ferrari see it. "Accept the expression of my sympathy, sir, "he said to Mr. Westwick politely. "I wish you good-evening."

Henry turned to Mrs. Ferrari as the lawyer closed the door. "I have heard of your trouble, Emily, from Miss Lockwood. Is there anything I can do to help you?"

"Nothing, sir, thank you. Perhaps, I had better go home after what has happened? I will call tomorrow, and see if I can be of any use to Miss Agnes. I am very sorry for her." She stole away, with her formal curtsey, her noiseless step, and her obstinate resolution to take the gloomiest view of her husband's case.

Henry Westwick looked round him in the solitude of the little drawing-room. There was nothing to keep him in the house, and yet he lingered in it. It was something to be even near Agnes—to see the things belonging to her that were scattered about the room. There, in one corner, was her chair, with her embroidery on the work-table by its side. On the little easel near the window was her last drawing, not quite finished yet.

The book she had been reading lay on the sofa, with her tiny pencil-case in it to mark the place at which she had left off. One after another, he looked at the objects that reminded him of the woman whom he loved—took them up tenderly—and laid them down again with a sigh. Ah, how far, how unattainably far from him, she was still! "She will never forget Montbarry," he thought to himself as he took up his hat to go. "Not one of us feels his death as she feels it. Miserable, miserable wretch—how she loved him!"

In the street, as Henry closed the house-door, he was stopped by a passing acquaintance—a wearisome inquisitive man—doubly unwelcome to him, at that moment. "Sad news, Westwick, this about your brother. Rather an unexpected death, wasn't it? We never heard at the club that Montbarry's lungs were weak. What will the insurance offices, do?"

Henry started; he had never thought of his brother's life insurance. What could the offices do but pay? A death by bronchitis, certified by two physicians, was surely the least disputable of all deaths. "I wish you hadn't put that question into my head!" he broke out irritably. "Ah!" said his friend, "you think the widow will get the money? So do I! so do I!"

Chapter 7

Some days later, the insurance offices (two in number) "received the formal announcement of Lord Montbarry's death, from her ladyship's London solicitors. The sum insured in each office was five thousand pounds—on which one year's premium only had been paid. In the face of such a pecuniary emergency as this, the Directors thought it desirable to consider their position.

The medical advisers of the two offices, who had recommended the insurance of Lord Montbarry's life, were called into council over their own reports. The result excited some interest among persons connected with the business of life insurance. Without absolutely declining to pay the money, the two offices (acting in concert) decided on sending a commission of inquiry to Venice, "for the purpose of obtaining further information."

Mr. Troy received the earliest intelligence of what was going on. He wrote at once to communicate his news to Agnes; adding, what he considered to be a valuable hint, in these words :

"You are intimately acquainted, I know, with Lady Barville,

the late Lord Montbarry's eldest sister. The solicitors employed by her husband are also the solicitors to one of the two insurance offices. There may possibly be something in the report of the commission of inquiry touching on Ferrari's disappearance.

"Ordinary persons would not be permitted, of course, to see such a document. But a sister of the late lord is so near a relative as to be an exception to general rules. If Sir Theodore Barville puts it on that footing, the lawyers, even if they do not allow his wife to look at the report, will at least answer any discreet questions she may ask referring to it. Let me hear what you think of this suggestion, at your earliest convenience."

The reply was received by return of post. Agnes declined to avail herself of Mr. Troy's proposal.

"My interference, innocent as it was," she wrote, "has already been productive of such deplorable results, that I cannot and dare not stir any further in the case of Ferrari. If I had not consented to let that unfortunate man refer to me by name, the late Lord Montbarry would never have engaged him, and his wife would have been spared the misery and suspense from which she is suffering now.

"I would not even look at the report to which you allude if it was placed in my hands—I have heard more than enough already of that hideous life in the palace at Venice. If Mrs. Ferrari chooses to address herself to Lady Barville (with your assistance), that is of course quite another thing. But, even in this case, I must make it a positive condition that my name shall not be mentioned. Forgive me, dear Mr. Troy! I am very unhappy, and very unreasonable—but I am only a woman, and you must not expect too much from me."

Foiled in this direction, the lawyer next advised making the attempt to discover the present address of Lady Montbarry's English maid. This excellent suggestion had one drawback; it could only be carried out by spending money—and there was no money to spend. Mrs. Ferrari shrank from the bare idea of making any use of the thousand-pound note. It had been deposited in the safe keeping of a bank. If it was even mentioned in her hearing, she shuddered and referred to it, with melodramatic fervour, as "my husband's blood-money!"

So, under stress of circumstances, the attempt to solve the mystery of Ferrari's disappearance was suspended for a while.

It was the last month of the year 1860. The commission of inquiry was already at work; having begun its investigations on December 6. On the 10th, the term for which the late Lord Montbarry had hired the Venetian palace, expired. News by telegram reached the insurance offices that Lady Montbarry had been advised by her lawyers to leave for London with as little delay as possible. Baron Rivar, it was believed, would accompany her to England, but would not remain in that country, unless his services were absolutely required by her ladyship. The Baron, "well known as an enthusiastic student of chemistry," had heard of certain recent discoveries in connection with that science in the United States, and was anxious to investigate them personally.

These items of news, collected by Mr. Troy, were duly communicated to Mrs. Ferrari, whose anxiety about her husband made her a frequent, a too frequent, visitor at the lawyer's office. She attempted to relate what she had heard to her good friend and protectress. Agnes steadily refused to listen, and positively forbade any further conversation relating to Lord Montbarry's wife, now that Lord Montbarry was no more.

"You have Mr. Troy to advise you," she said; "and you are welcome to what little money I can spare, if money is wanted. All I ask in return is that you will not distress me. I am trying to separate myself from remembrances—" her voice faltered; she paused to control herself—"from remembrances," she resumed, "which are sadder than ever since I have heard of Lord Montbarry's death. Help me by your silence to recover my spirits, if I can. Let me hear nothing more, until I can rejoice with you that your husband is found."

Time advanced to the 13th of the month; and more information of the interesting sort reached Mr. Troy. The labours of the insurance commission had come to an end—the report had been received from Venice on that day.

Chapter 8

On the 14th the Directors and their legal advisers met for the reading of the report, with, closed doors. These were the terms in which the Commissioners related the results of their inquiry :

Private and Confidential:—

We have the honour to inform our Directors that we arrived in Venice on December 6, 1860. On the same day we proceeded to the palace inhabited by Lord Montbarry at the time of his last illness and death.

We were received with all possible courtesy by Lady Montbarry's brother, Baron Rivar. 'My sister was her husband's only attendant throughout his illness,' the Baron informed us. 'She is overwhelmed by grief and fatigue—or she would have been here to receive you personally. What are your wishes, gentlemen? and what can I do for you, in her ladyship's place?'

In accordance with our instructions, we answered that the death and burial of Lord Montbarry abroad made it desirable to obtain more complete information relating to his illness, and to the circumstances which had attended it, than could be conveyed in writing. We explained that the law provided for the lapse of a certain interval of time before the payment of the sum assured, and we expressed our wish to conduct the inquiry with the most respectful consideration for her ladyship's feelings, and for the convenience of any other members of the family inhabiting the house.

To this the Baron replied, 'I am the only member of the family living here, and I and the palace are entirely at your disposal.' From first to last we found this gentleman perfectly straightforward, and most amiably willing to assist us.

With the one exception of her ladyship's room, we went over the whole of the palace the same day. It is an immense place only partially furnished. The first floor and part of the second floor were the portions of it that had been inhabited by Lord Montbarry and the members of the household. We saw the bedchamber, at one extremity of the palace, in which his lordship died, and the small room communicating with it, which he used as a study. Next to this was a large apartment or hall, the doors of which he habitually kept locked, his object being (as we were informed) to pursue his studies uninterruptedly in perfect solitude.

On the other side of the large hall were the bedchamber occupied by her ladyship, and the dressing-room in which the maid slept previous to her departure for England. Beyond these were the dining and reception rooms, opening into an antechamber, which gave access to the grand staircase of the palace.

The only inhabited rooms on the second floor were the sitting-room and bedroom occupied by Baron Rivar, and another room at some distance from it, which had been the bedroom of the courier Ferrari.

The rooms on the third floor and on the basement were completely unfurnished, and in a condition of great neglect. We inquired if there was anything to be seen below the basement-and we were at once informed that there were vaults beneath, which we were at perfect liberty to visit.

We went down, so as to leave no part of the palace unexplored. The vaults were, it was believed, used as dungeons in the old times—say, some centuries since. Air and light were only partially admitted to these dismal places by two long shafts of winding construction, which communicated with the back yard of the palace, and the openings of which, high above the ground, were protected by iron gratings. The stone stairs leading down into the vaults could be closed at will by a heavy trapdoor in the back hall, which we found open.

The Baron himself led the way down the stairs. We remarked that it might be awkward if that trapdoor fell down and closed the opening behind us. The Baron smiled at the idea. 'Don't be alarmed, gentlemen,' he said: 'the door is safe I had an interest in seeing to it myself, when we first inhabited the palace. My favourite study is the study of experimental chemistry—and my workshop, since we have been in Venice, is down here.'

These last words explained a curious smell in the vaults, which we noticed the moment we entered them. We can only describe the smell by saying that it was of a twofold sort—faintly aromatic, as it were, in its first effect, but with some after-odour very sickening in our nostrils. The Baron's furnaces and retorts, and other things, were all there to speak for themselves, together with some packages of chemicals, having the name and address of the person who had supplied them plainly visible on their labels. 'Not a pleasant place for study,'

Baron Rivar observed, 'but my sister is timid. She has a horror of chemical smells and explosions—and she has banished me to these lower regions, so that my experiments may neither be smelled nor heard.' He held out his hands, on which we had noticed that he wore gloves in the house. 'Accidents will happen sometimes,' he said, 'no matter how careful a man may be. I burned my hands severely in trying a new combination the other day, and they are only recovering now.'

We mention these otherwise unimportant incidents, in order to show that our exploration of the palace was not impeded by any attempt at concealment. We were even admitted to her ladyship's own room—on a subsequent occasion, when she went out to take the air. Our instructions recommended us to examine his lordship's residence, because the extreme privacy of his life at Venice, and the remarkable departure of the only two servants in the house, might have some suspicious connection with the nature of his death. We found nothing to justify suspicion.

As to his lordship's retired way of life, we have conversed on the subject with the consul and the banker—the only two strangers who held any communication with him. He called once at the bank to obtain money on his letter of credit, and excused himself from accepting an invitation to visit the banker at his private residence, on the ground of delicate health. His lordship wrote to the same effect on sending his card to the consul, to excuse himself from personally returning that gentleman's visit to the palace.

We have seen the letter, and we beg to offer the following copy of it.

> 'Many years passed in India have injured my constitution. I have ceased to go into society; the one occupation of my life now is the study of Oriental literature. The air of Italy is better for me than the air of England, or I should never have left home. Pray accept the apologies of a student and an invalid. The active part of my life is at an end.'

The self-seclusion of his lordship seems to us to be explained in these brief lines. We have not, however, on that account spared our inquiries in other directions. Nothing to excite a suspicion of anything wrong has come to our knowledge.

As to the departure of the lady's maid, we have seen the woman's receipt for her wages, in which it is expressly stated that she left Lady Montbarry's service because she disliked the Continent, and wished to get back to her own country. This is not an uncommon result of taking English servants to foreign parts. Lady Montbarry has informed us that she abstained from engaging another maid in consequence of the extreme dislike which his lordship expressed to having strangers in the house, in the state of his health at that time.

The disappearance of the courier Ferrari is, in itself, unquestionably a suspicious circumstance. Neither her ladyship nor the Baron can explain it; and no investigation that we could make has thrown the smallest light on this event, or has justified us in associating it, directly or indirectly, with the object of our inquiry. We have even gone the length of examining the portmanteau which Ferrari left behind him. It contains nothing but clothes and linen—no money, and not even a scrap of paper in the pockets of the clothes. The portmanteau remains in charge of the police.

We have also found opportunities of speaking privately to the old woman who attends to the rooms occupied by her ladyship and the Baron. She was recommended to fill this situation by the keeper of the restaurant who has supplied the meals to the family throughout the period of their residence at the palace. Her character is most favourably spoken of. Unfortunately, her limited intelligence makes her of no value as a witness. We were patient and careful in questioning her, and we found her perfectly willing to answer us; but we could elicit nothing which is worth including in the present report.

On the second day of our inquiries, we had the honour of an interview with Lady Montbarry. Her ladyship looked miserably worn and ill, and seemed to be quite at a loss to understand what we wanted with her. Baron Rivar, who introduced us, explained the nature of our errand in Venice, and took pains to assure her that it was a purely formal duty on which we were engaged. Having satisfied her ladyship on this point, he discreetly left the room.

The questions which we addressed to Lady Montbarry related mainly, of course, to his lordship's illness. The answers, given with great nervousness of manner, but without the slightest appearance of reserve, informed us of the facts that follow :

Lord Montbarry had been out of order for some time past—nervous and irritable. He first complained of having taken cold on November 13 last; he passed a wakeful and feverish night, and remained in bed the next day. Her ladyship proposed sending for medical advice. He refused to allow her to do this, saying that he could quite easily be his own doctor in such a trifling matter as a cold.

Some hot lemonade was made at his request, with a view to producing perspiration. Lady Montbarry's maid having left her at that time, the courier Ferrari (then the only servant in the house) went out to buy the lemons. Her ladyship made the drink with her own hands. It was successful in producing perspiration—and Lord Montbarry had some hours of sleep afterward.

Later in the day, having need of Ferrari's services, Lady Montbarry rang for him. The bell was not answered. Baron Rivar searched for the man, in the palace and out of it, in vain. From that time forth not a trace of Ferrari could be discovered. This happened on November 14.

On the night of the 14th, the feverish symptoms accompanying his lordship's cold returned. They were in part perhaps attributable to the annoyance and alarm caused by Ferrari's mysterious disappearance. It had been impossible to conceal the circumstance, as his lordship rang repeatedly for the courier; insisting that the man should relieve Lady Montbarry and the Baron by taking their places during the night at his bedside.

On the 15th (the day on which the old woman first came to do the housework), his lordship complained of sore throat, and of a feeling of oppression on the chest. On this day, and again on the 16th, her ladyship and the Baron entreated him to see a doctor. He still refused. 'I don't want strange faces about me; my cold will run its course, in spite of the doctor'—that was his answer. On the 17th he was so much worse that it was decided to send for medical help whether he liked it or not. Baron Rivar, after inquiry at the consul's, secured the services of Doctor Bruno, well known as an eminent physician in Venice; with the additional recommendation of having resided in England, and having made himself acquainted with English forms of medical practice.

Thus far our account of his lordship's illness has been derived from statements made by Lady Montbarry. The narrative will now be most fitly continued in the language of the doctor's own report, herewith subjoined.

> 'My medical diary informs me that I first saw the English Lord Montbarry, on November 17. He was suffering from a sharp attack of bronchitis. Some precious time had been lost, through his obstinate objection to the presence of a medical man at his bedside. Generally speaking, he appeared to be in a delicate state of health. His nervous system was out of order—he was at once timid and contradictory.
>
> 'When I spoke to him in English, he answered in Italian; and when I tried him in Italian, he went back to Eng-

lish. It mattered little—the malady had already made such progress that he could only speak a few words at a time, and those in a whisper.

'I at once applied the necessary remedies. Copies of my prescriptions (with translation into English) accompany the present statement, and are left to speak for themselves.

'For the next three days I was in constant attendance on my patient. He answered to the remedies employed—improving slowly, but decidedly. I could conscientiously assure Lady Montbarry that no danger was to be apprehended thus far. She was indeed a most devoted wife. I vainly endeavoured to induce her to accept the services of a competent nurse; she would allow nobody to attend on her husband but herself.

'Night and day this estimable woman was at his bedside. In her brief intervals of repose, her brother watched the sick man in her place. This brother was, I must say, very good company, in the intervals when we had time for a little talk. He dabbled in chemistry, down in the horrid underwater vaults of the palace; and he wanted to show me some of his experiments.. I have enough of chemistry in writing prescriptions—and I declined. He took it quite good-humouredly.

'I am straying away from my subject. Let me return to the sick lord.

'Up to the 20th, then, things went well enough. I was quite unprepared for the disastrous change that showed itself, when I paid Lord Montbarry my morning visit on the 21st. He had relapsed and seriously relapsed. Examining him to discover the cause, I found symptoms of pneumonia—that is to say, in unmedical language, inflammation of the substance of the lungs. He breathed with difficulty, and was only partially able to relieve himself by coughing.

'I made the strictest inquiries, and was assured that his

medicine had been administered as carefully as usual, and that he had not been exposed to any changes of temperature. It was with great reluctance that I added to Lady Montbarry's distress; but I felt bound, when she suggested a consultation with another physician, to own that I too thought there was really need for it.

'Her ladyship instructed me to spare no expense, and to get the best medical opinion in Italy. The best opinion was happily within our reach. The first and foremost of Italian physicians is Torello of Padua. I sent a special messenger for the great man. He arrived on the evening of the 21st, and confirmed my opinion that pneumonia had set in and that our patient's life was in danger. I told him what my treatment of the case had been, and he approved of it in every particular. He made some valuable suggestions, and (at Lady Montbarry's express request) he consented to defer his return to Padua until the following morning.

'We both saw the patient at intervals in the course of the night. The disease, steadily advancing, set our utmost resistance at defiance. In the morning Doctor Torello took his leave. "I can be of no further use," he said to me. "The man is past all help—and he ought to know it."

'Later in the day I warned my lord, as gently as I could, that his time had come. I am informed that there are serious reasons for my stating what passed between us on this occasion, in detail, and without any reserve. I comply with the request.

'Lord Montbarry received the intelligence of his approaching death with becoming composure, but with a certain doubt. He signed to me to put my ear to his mouth. He whispered faintly, "Are you sure?"

It was no time to deceive him; I said, "Positively sure."

He waited a little, gasping for breath, and then he whispered again, "Feel under my pillow." I found under his pillow a letter, sealed and stamped, ready for the post.

His next words were just audible and no more—"Post it

yourself." I answered of course that I would do so—and I did post the letter with my own hand. I looked at the address. It was directed to a lady in London. The street I cannot remember. The name I can perfectly recall: it was an Italian name—"Mrs. Ferrari."

'That night my lord nearly died of asphyxia. I got him through it for the time; and his eyes showed that he understood me when I told him, the next morning, that I had posted the letter. This was his last effort of consciousness. When I saw him again he was sunk in apathy. He lingered in a state of insensibility, supported by stimulants, until the 25th, and died (unconscious to the last) on the evening of that day.

'As to the cause of his death, it seems (if I may be excused for saying so) simply absurd to ask the question. Bronchitis, terminating in pneumonia—there is no more doubt that this, and this only, was the malady of which he expired, than that two and two make four. Doctor Torello's own note of the case is added here to a duplicate of my certificate, in order (as I am informed) to satisfy some English offices in which his lordship's life was insured. The English offices must have been founded by that celebrated saint and doubter, mentioned in the New Testament, whose name was Thomas!'

Doctor Bruno's evidence ends here.

Reverting for a moment to our inquiries addressed to Lady Montbarry, we have to report that she can give us no information on the subject of the letter which the doctor posted at Lord Montbarry's request. "When his lordship wrote it? what it contained? why he kept it a secret from Lady Montbarry (and from the Baron also); and why he should write at all to the wife of his courier? these are questions to which we find it simply impossible to obtain any replies.

It seems even useless to say that the matter is open to suspicion. Suspicion implies conjecture of some kind—and the letter under my lord's pillow baffles all conjecture. Application to

Mrs. Ferrari may perhaps clear up the mystery. Her residence in London will be easily discovered at the Italian Couriers' Office, Golden Square.

Having arrived at the close of the present report, we have now to draw your attention to the conclusion which is justified by the results of our investigation.

The plain question before our Directors and ourselves appears to be this: Has the inquiry revealed any extraordinary circumstances which render the death of Lord Montbarry open to suspicion? The inquiry has revealed extraordinary circumstances beyond all doubt—such as the disappearance of Ferrari, the remarkable absence of the customary establishment of servants in the house, and the mysterious letter which his lordship asked the doctor to post.

But where is the proof that any one of these circumstances is associated—suspiciously and directly associated—with the only event which concerns us, the event of Lord Montbarry's death? In the absence of any such proof, and in the face of the evidence of two eminent physicians, it is impossible to dispute the statement on the certificate that his lordship died a natural death. We are bound, therefore, to report, that there are no valid grounds for refusing the payment of the sum for which the late Lord Montbarry's life was assured.

We shall send these lines to you by the post of tomorrow, December 10; leaving time to receive your further instructions (if any), in reply to our telegram of this evening announcing the conclusion of the inquiry.

Chapter 9

"Now, my good creature, whatever you have to say to me, out with it at once! I don't want to hurry you needlessly; but these are business hours, and I have other people's affairs to attend to besides yours."

Addressing Ferrari's wife with his usual blunt good-humour, in these terms, Mr. Troy registered the lapse of time by a glance at the watch on his desk, and then waited to hear what his client had to say to him.

"It's something more, sir, about the letter with the thousand-pound note," Mrs. Ferrari began. "I have found out who sent it to me."

Mr. Troy started. "This is news, indeed!" he said. "Who sent you the letter?"

"Lord Montbarry sent it, sir."

It was not easy to take Mr. Troy by surprise. But Mrs. Ferrari threw him completely off his balance. For a while he could only look at her in silent surprise. "Nonsense!" he said, as soon as he had recovered himself. "There is some mistake—it can't be!"

"There is no mistake," Mrs. Ferrari rejoined, in her most positive manner. "Two gentlemen from the insurance offices called on me this morning, to see the letter. They were completely puzzled—especially when they heard of the banknote inside. But they know who sent the letter. His lordship's doctor in Venice posted it at his lordship's request. Go to the gentlemen yourself, sir, if you don't believe me. They were polite enough to ask if I could account for Lord Montbarry writing to me and sending me the money. I gave them my opinion directly—I said it was like his lordship's kindness."

"Like his lordship's kindness?" Mr. Troy repeated, in blank amazement.

"Yes, sir! Lord Montbarry knew me, like all the other members of the family, when I was at school on the estate in Ireland. If he could have done it, he would have protected my poor dear husband. But he was helpless himself in the hands of my lady and the Baron—and the only kind thing he could do was to provide for me in my widowhood, like the true nobleman he was!"

"A very pretty explanation!" said Mr. Troy.

"What did your visitors from the insurance offices think of it?"

"They asked if I had any proof of my husband's death."

"And what did you say?"

"I said, 'I give you better than proof, gentlemen; I give you my positive opinion.'"

"That satisfied them, of course?"

"They didn't say so in words, sir. They looked at each other-and wished me good-morning."

"Well, Mrs. Ferrari, unless you have some more extraordinary news for me, I think I shall wish you good-morning, too. I can take a note of your information (very startling information, I own); and, in the absence of proof, I can do no more."

"I can provide you with proof, sir—if that is all you want," said Mrs. Ferrari, with great dignity. "I only wish to know, first, whether the law justifies me in doing it. You may have seen in the fashionable intelligence of the newspapers that Lady Montbarry has arrived in London, at Newbury 's Hotel. I propose to go and see her."

"The deuce you do! May I ask for what purpose?"

Mrs. Ferrari answered in a mysterious whisper. "For the purpose of catching her in a trap! I shan't send in my name—I shall announce myself as a person on business, and the first words I say to her will be these: 'I come, my lady, to acknowledge the receipt of the money sent to Ferrari's widow.' Ah! you may well start, Mr. Troy! It almost takes you off your guard, doesn't it? Make your mind easy, sir; I shall find the proof that everybody asks me for in her guilty face. Let her only change colour by the shadow of a shade—let her eyes only drop for half an instant—I shall discover her! The one thing I want to know is, does the law permit it?"

"The law permits it," Mr. Troy answered, gravely; "but whether her ladyship will permit it, is quite another question. Have you really courage enough, Mrs Ferrari, to carry out this notable scheme of yours? You have been described to me, by Miss Lockwood, as rather a nervous, timid sort of person—and, if I may trust my own observation, I should say you justify the description."

"If you had lived in the country, sir, instead of living in London," Mrs. Ferrari replied, "you would sometimes have seen even a sheep turn on a dog. I am far from saying that I am a bold woman—quite the reverse. But when I stand in that wretch's presence, and think of my murdered husband, the one of us two who is likely to be frightened is not me. I am going there now, sir. You shall hear how it ends. I wish you good-morning."

"With those brave words the courier's wife gathered her mantle about her, and walked out of the room.

Mr. Troy smiled—not satirically, but compassionately. "The little simpleton!" he thought to himself. "If half of what they say of Lady Montbarry is true, Mrs. Ferrari and her trap have but a poor prospect before them. I wonder how it will end?"

All Mr. Troy's experience failed to forewarn him of how it did end.

Chapter 10

In the meantime, Mrs. Ferrari held to her resolution. She went straight from Mr. Troy's office to Newbury's Hotel.

Lady Montbarry was at home, and alone. But the authorities of the hotel hesitated to disturb her when they found that the' visitor declined to mention her name. Her ladyship's new maid happened to cross the hall while the matter was still in debate. She was a Frenchwoman, and, on being appealed to, she settled the question in the swift, easy, rational French way. "*Madame's* appearance was perfectly respectable. *Madame* might have reasons for not mentioning her name which Miladi might approve. In any case, there being no orders forbidding the introduction of a strange lady, the matter clearly rested between *Madame* and Miladi. Would *Madame*, therefore, be good enough to follow Miladi's maid up the stairs?"

In spite of her resolution, Mrs. Ferrari's heart beat as if it would burst out of her bosom, when her conductress led her into an ante-room, and knocked at a door opening into a room beyond. But it is remarkable that persons of sensitively-nervous organization are the very persons who are capable of forcing themselves (apparently by the exercise of a spasmodic effort of will) into the performance of acts of the most audacious courage.

A low, grave voice from the inner room said, "Come in." The maid, opening the door, announced: "A person to see you, Miladi, on business," and immediately retired. In the one instant while these events passed, timid little Mrs. Ferrari mastered her own throbbing heart; stepped over the threshold, conscious of her clammy hands, dry lips, and burning head; and stood in the presence of Lord Montbarry's widow, to all outward appearance as supremely self-possessed as her ladyship herself.

It was still early in the afternoon, but the light in the room was dim. The blinds were drawn down. Lady Montbarry sat with her back to the windows, as if even the subdued daylight were disagreeable to her. She had altered sadly for the worse in her personal appearance, since the memorable day when Doctor Wybrow had seen her in his consulting-room. Her beauty was gone—her face had fallen away to mere skin and bone; the contrast between her ghastly complexion and her steely glittering black eyes was more startling than ever.

Robed in dismal black, relieved only by the brilliant whiteness of her widow's cap—reclining in a panther-like suppleness of attitude on a little green sofa—she looked at the stranger who had intruded on her with a moment's languid curiosity, then dropped her eyes again to the hand-screen which she held between her face and the fire. "I don't know you," she said. "What do you want with me?"

Mrs. Ferrari tried to answer. Her first burst of courage had already worn itself out. The bold words that she had determined to speak were living words still in her mind, but they dried on her lips.

There was a moment of silence. Lady Montbarry looked round again at the speechless stranger. "Are you deaf?" she asked. There was another pause. Lady Montbarry quietly looked back again at the screen, and put another question. "Do you want money?"

"Money!" That one word roused the sinking spirit of the courier's wife. She recovered her courage; she found her voice. "Look at me, my lady, if you please," she said, with a sudden outbreak of audacity.

Lady Montbarry looked round for the third time. The fatal words passed Mrs. Ferrari's lips.

"I come, my lady, to acknowledge the receipt of the money sent to Ferrari's widow."

Lady Montbarry's glittering black eyes rested with steady attention on the woman who had addressed her in those terms. Not the faintest expression of confusion or alarm, not even a momentary flutter of interest stirred the deadly stillness of her face. She reposed as quietly, she held the screen as composedly as ever. The test had been tried, and had utterly failed.

There was another silence. Lady Montbarry considered with herself. The smile that came slowly and went away suddenly the smile at once so sad and so cruel—showed itself on her thin lips. She lifted her screen, and pointed with it to a seat at the further end of the room. "Be so good as to take that chair," she said.

Helpless under her first bewildering sense of failure—not knowing what to say or what to do next—Mrs. Ferrari mechanically obeyed. Lady Montbarry, rising on the sofa for the first time, watched her with undisguised scrutiny as she crossed the room—then sank back into a reclining position once more. "No," she said to herself, "the woman walks steadily; she is not intoxicated—the only other possibility is that she may be mad."

She had spoken loud enough to be heard. Stung by the insult, Mrs. Ferrari instantly answered her: "I am no more drunk or mad than you are!"

"No?" said Lady Montbarry. "Then you are only insolent? The ignorant English mind (I have observed) is apt to be insolent in the exercise of unrestrained English liberty. This is very noticeable to us foreigners among you people in the streets. Of course I can't be insolent to you, in return. I hardly know what to say to you. My maid was imprudent in admitting you so easily to my room. I suppose your respectable appearance misled her. I wonder who you are? You mentioned the name of a courier who left us very strangely. Was he married by any chance? Are you his wife? And do you know where he is?"

Mrs. Ferrari's indignation burst its way through all restraints. She advanced to the sofa; she feared nothing, in the fervour and rage of her reply.

"I am his widow—and you know it, you wicked woman! Ah! it was an evil hour when Miss Lockwood recommended my husband to be his lordship's courier—!"

Before she could add another word, Lady Montbarry sprang from the sofa with the stealthy suddenness of a cat—seized her by both shoulders—and shook her with the strength and frenzy of a madwoman. "You lie! you lie! you lie!" She dropped her hold at the third repetition of the accusation, and threw up her hands wildly with a gesture of despair.

"Oh, *Jesu Maria*! is it possible?" she cried. "Can the courier have come to me through that woman?" She turned like lightning on Mrs. Ferrari and stopped her as she was escaping from the room.

"Stay here, you fool—stay here, and answer me! If you cry out, as sure as the heavens are above you, I'll strangle you with my own hands. Sit down again—and fear nothing. Wretch! It is I who am frightened—frightened out of my senses. Confess that you lied, when you used Miss Lockwood's name just now! No! I don't believe you on your oath; I will believe nobody but Miss Lockwood herself. Where does she live? Tell me that, you noxious, stinging little insect—and you may go."

Terrified as she was, Mrs. Ferrari hesitated. Lady Montbarry lifted her hands threateningly, with the long, lean, yellow-white fingers outspread and crooked at the tips. Mrs. Ferrari shrank at the sight of them and gave the address. Lady Montbarry pointed contemptuously to the door—then changed her mind. "No! not yet! you will tell Miss Lockwood what has happened, and she may refuse to see me. I will go there at once, and you shall go with me. As far as the house—not inside of it. Sit down again. I am going to ring for my maid. Turn your back to the door-your cowardly face is not fit to be seen!"

She rang the bell. The maid appeared.

"My cloak and bonnet—instantly!"

The maid produced the cloak and bonnet from the bedroom.

"A cab at the door—before I can count ten!"

The maid vanished. Lady Montbarry surveyed herself in the glass, and wheeled round again, with her cat-like suddenness, to Mrs. Ferrari.

"I look more than half dead already, don't I?" she said with a grim outburst of irony. "Give me your arm."

She took Mrs. Ferrari's arm and left the room. "You have nothing to fear, so long as you obey," she whispered, on the way downstairs. "You leave me at Miss Lockwood's door, and never see me again."

In the hall they were met by the landlady of the hotel. Lady Montbarry graciously presented her companion. "My good friend, Mrs. Ferrari; I am so glad to have seen her." The landlady accompanied them to the door. The cab was waiting. "Get in first, good Mrs. Ferrari," said her ladyship; "and tell the man where to go."

They were driven away. Lady Montbarry's variable humour changed again. With a low groan of misery, she threw herself back in the cab. Lost in her own dark thoughts, as careless of the woman whom she had bent to her iron will as if no such person sat by her side, she preserved a sinister silence, until they reached the house where Miss Lockwood lodged. In an instant, she roused herself to action. She opened the door of the cab, and closed it again on Mrs. Ferrari, before the driver could get off his box.

"Take that lady a mile further on her way home!" she said as she paid the man his fare. The next moment she had knocked at the house-door. "Is Miss Lockwood at home?"

"Yes, ma'am." She stepped over the threshold—the door closed on her.

"Which way, ma'am?" asked the driver of the cab.

Mrs. Ferrari put her hand to her head, and tried to collect her thoughts. Could she leave her friend and benefactress helpless at Lady Montbarry's mercy? She was still vainly endeavouring to decide on the course that she ought to follow—when a gentleman, stopping at Miss Lockwood's door, happened to look toward the cab-window, and saw her.

"Are you going to call on Miss Agnes, too?" he asked.

It was Henry Westwick. Mrs. Ferrari clasped her hands in gratitude as she recognized him.

"Go in, sir!" she cried. "Go in, directly. That dreadful woman is with Miss Agnes. Go and protect her!"

"What woman?" Henry asked.

The answer literally struck him speechless. With amazement and indignation in his face, he looked at Mrs. Ferrari as she pronounced the hated name of "Lady Montbarry."

"I'll see to it," was all he said. He knocked at the house-door; and he too, in his turn, was let in.

Chapter 11

"Lady Montbarry, miss."

Agnes was writing a letter when the servant astonished her by announcing the visitor's name. Her first impulse was to refuse to see the woman who had intruded on her. But Lady Montbarry had taken care to follow close on the servant's heels. Before Agnes could speak, she had entered the room.

"I beg to apologize for my intrusion, Miss Lockwood. I have a question to ask you, in which I am very much interested. No one can answer me but yourself." In low, hesitating tones, with her glittering black eyes bent modestly on the ground, Lady Montbarry opened the interview in those words.

Without answering, Agnes pointed to a chair. She could do this, and, for the time, she could do no more. All that she had read of the hidden and sinister life in the palace at Venice; all that she had heard of Montbarry's melancholy death and burial in a foreign land; all that she knew of the mystery of Ferrari's disappearance, rushed into her mind, when the black-robed figure confronted her, standing just inside the door.

The strange conduct of Lady Montbarry added a new perplexity to the doubts and misgivings that troubled her. There stood the adventuress whose character had left its mark on society all over Europe—the Fury who had terrified Mrs. Ferrari at the hotel—inconceivably transformed into a timid, shrinking woman! Lady Montbarry had not once ventured to look at Agnes since she had made her way into the room.

Advancing to take the chair that had been pointed out to her, she hesitated, put her hand on the rail to support herself, and still remained standing. "Please give me a moment to compose myself," she said faintly. Her head sank on her bosom: she stood before Agnes like a conscious culprit before a merciless judge.

The silence that followed was, literally, the silence of fear on both sides. In the midst of it, the door was opened once more-and Henry Westwick appeared.

He looked at Lady Montbarry with a moment's steady attention—bowed to her with formal politeness—and passed on in silence. At the sight of her husband's brother, the sinking spirit of the woman sprang to life again. Her drooping figure became erect. Her eyes met Westwick's look, brightly defiant. She returned his bow with an icy smile of contempt.

Henry crossed the room to Agnes.

"Is Lady Montbarry here by your invitation?" he asked, quietly.

"No."

"Do you wish to see her?"

"It is very painful to me to see her."

He turned and looked at his sister-in-law. "Do you hear that?" he asked, coldly.

"I hear it," she answered, more coldly still.

"Your visit is, to say the least of it, ill-timed."

"Your interference is, to say the least of it, out of place."

With that retort, Lady Montbarry approached Agnes. The presence of Henry Westwick seemed at once to relieve and embolden her. "Permit me to ask my question, Miss Lockwood," she said, with graceful courtesy. "It is nothing to embarrass you. When the courier Ferrari applied to my late husband for employment, did you—" Her resolution failed her, before she could say more. She sank trembling into the nearest chair, and, after a moment's struggle, composed herself again. "Did you permit Ferrari," she resumed, "to make sure of being chosen for our courier by using your name?"

Agnes did not reply with her customary directness. Trifling as it was, the reference to Montbarry, proceeding from that woman of all others, confused and agitated her.

"I have known Ferrari's wife for many years, "she began. "And I take an interest—"

Lady Montbarry abruptly lifted her hands with a gesture of entreaty. "Ah, Miss Lockwood, don't waste time by talking of his wife! Answer my plain question, plainly!"

"Let me answer her," Henry whispered. "I will undertake to speak plainly enough."

Agnes refused by a gesture. Lady Montbarry's interruption had roused her sense of what was due to herself. She resumed her reply in plainer terms.

"When Ferrari wrote to the late Lord Montbarry," she said, "he did certainly mention my name."

Even now, she had innocently failed to see the object which her visitor had in view. Lady Montbarry's impatience became ungovernable. She started to her feet, and advanced to Agnes.

"Was it with your knowledge and permission that Ferrari used your name?" she asked. "The whole soul of my question is in that. For God's sake answer me—Yes, or No!"

"Yes."

That one word struck Lady Montbarry as a blow might have struck her. The fierce life that had animated her face the instant before, faded out of it suddenly, and left her like a woman turned to stone. She stood, mechanically confronting Agnes, with a stillness so rapt and perfect that not even the breath she drew was perceptible to the two persons who were looking at her.

Henry spoke to her roughly. "Rouse yourself," he said. "You have received your answer."

She looked round at him. "I have received my Sentence," she rejoined—and turned slowly to leave the room.

To Henry's astonishment, Agnes stopped her. "Wait a moment, Lady Montbarry. I have something to ask on my side. "You have spoken of Ferrari. I wish to speak of him, too."

Lady Montbarry bent her head in silence. Her hand trembled as she took out her handkerchief and passed it over her forehead. Agnes detected the trembling, and shrank back a step. "Is the subject painful to you?" she asked, timidly.

Still silent, Lady Montbarry invited her by a wave of the hand to go on. Henry approached, attentively watching his sister-in-law. Agnes went on.

"No trace of Ferrari has been discovered in England," she said. "Have you any news of him? And will you tell me (if you have heard anything), in mercy to his wife?"

Lady Montbarry's thin lips suddenly relaxed into their sad and cruel smile.

"Why do you ask me about the lost courier?" she said. "You will know what has become of him, Miss Lockwood, when the time is ripe for it."

Agnes started. "I don't understand you," she said. "How shall I know? Will someone tell me?"

"Someone will tell you."

Henry could keep silence no longer. "Perhaps your ladyship may be the person?" he interrupted, with ironical politeness.

She answered him with contemptuous ease. "You may be right, Mr. Westwick. One day or another, I may be the person who tells Miss Lockwood what has become of Ferrari, if—" She stopped; with her eyes fixed on Agnes.

"If what?" Henry asked.

"If Miss Lockwood forces me to it."

Agnes listened in astonishment. "Force you to it?" she repeated. "How can I do that? Do you mean to say my will is stronger than yours?"

"Do you mean to say that the candle doesn't burn the moth, when the moth flies into it?" Lady Montbarry rejoined. "Have you ever heard of such a thing as the fascination of terror? I am drawn to you by a fascinate on of terror. I have no right to visit you, I have no wish to visit you: you are my enemy. For the first time in my life, against my own will, I submit to my enemy. See! I am waiting because you told me to wait—and the fear of you (I swear it!) creeps through me while I stand here. Oh, don't let me excite your curiosity or your pity! Follow the example of Mr. Westwick. Be hard and brutal and unforgiving, like him. Grant me my release. Tell me to go."

The frank and simple nature of Agnes could discover but one intelligible meaning in this strange outbreak.

"You are mistaken in thinking me your enemy," she said. "The wrong you did me when you gave your hand to Lord Montbarry was not intentionally done. I forgave you my sufferings in his lifetime. I forgive you even more freely now that he has gone."

Henry heard her with mingled emotions of admiration and distress. "Say no more!" he exclaimed. "You are too good to her; she is not worthy of it."

The interruption passed unheeded by Lady Montbarry. The simple words in which Agnes had replied seemed to have absorbed the whole attention of this strangely-changeable woman. As she listened, her face settled slowly into an expression of hard and tearless sorrow. There was a marked change in her voice when she spoke next. It expressed that last worst resignation which has done with hope.

"You good innocent creature," she said, "what does your amiable forgiveness matter? What are your poor little wrongs, in the reckoning for greater wrongs which is demanded of me? I am not trying to frighten you; I am only miserable about myself. Do you know what it is to have a firm presentiment of calamity that is coming to you—and yet to hope that your own positive conviction will not prove true? When I first met you, before my marriage, and first felt your influence over me, I had that hope. It was a starveling sort of hope that lived a lingering life in me until today. You struck it dead, when you answered my question about Ferrari."

"How have I destroyed your hopes?" Agnes asked. "What

connection is there between my permitting Ferrari to use my name to Lord Montbarry, and the strange and dreadful things you are saying to me now?"

"The time is near, Miss Lockwood, when you will discover that for yourself. In the meanwhile, you shall I know what my fear of you is, in the plainest words I can find. On the day when I took your hero from you and blighted your life—I am firmly persuaded of it!—you were made the instrument of the retribution that my sins of many years had deserved.

"Oh, such things have happened before today! One person has, before now, been the means of innocently ripening the growth of evil in another. You have done that already—and you have more to do yet. You have still to bring me to the day of discovery, and to the punishment that is my doom. We shall meet again here in England,—or there in Venice where my husband died—and meet for the last time."

In spite of her better sense, in spite of her natural superiority to superstitions of all kinds, Agnes was impressed by the terrible earnestness with which those words were spoken. She turned pale as she looked at Henry. "Do you understand her?" she asked.

"Nothing is easier than to understand her," he replied, contemptuously. "She knows what has become of Ferrari; and she is confusing you in a cloud of nonsense, because she daren't own the truth. Let her go!"

If a dog had been under one of the chairs, and had barked, Lady Montbarry could not have proceeded more impenetrably with the last words she had to say to Agnes.

"Advise your interesting Mrs. Ferrari to wait a little longer," she said. "You will know what has become of her husband, and you will tell her. There will be nothing to alarm you. Some trifling event will bring us together the next time—as trifling, I daresay, as the engagement of Ferrari. Sad nonsense, Mr. Westwick, is it not? But you make allowances for women; we all talk nonsense. Good-morning, Miss Lockwood."

She opened the door—suddenly, as if she was afraid of being

called back for the second time—and left them.

CHAPTER 12

"Do you think, she is mad?" Agnes asked.

"I think she is simply wicked. False, superstitious, inveterately cruel—but not mad. I believe her main motive in coming here was to enjoy the luxury of frightening you."

"She has frightened me. I am ashamed to own it—but so it is."

Henry looked at her, hesitated for a moment, and seated himself on the sofa by her side.

"I am very anxious about you, Agnes," he said. "But for the fortunate chance which led me to call here today—who knows what that vile woman might not have said or done, if she had found you alone? My dear, you are leading a sadly unprotected solitary life. I don't like to think of it; I want to see it changed-especially after what has happened today.

"No! no! it is useless to tell me that you have your old nurse. She is too old: she is not in your rank of life—there is no sufficient protection in the companionship of such a person for a lady in your position. Don't mistake me, Agnes! what I say, I say in the sincerity of my devotion to you." He paused and took her hand. She made a feeble effort to withdraw it—and yielded. "Will the day never come," he pleaded, "when the privilege of protecting you may be mine? when you. will be the pride and joy of my life, as long as my life lasts?" He pressed her hand gently. She made no reply. The colour came and went on her face; her eyes were turned away from him. "Have I been so unhappy as to offend you?" he asked.

She answered that—she said, almost in a whisper, "No."

"Have I distressed you?"

"You have made me think of the sad days that are gone." She said no more, she only tried to withdraw her hand from his for the second time. He still held it; he lifted it to his lips.

"Can I never make you think of other days than those—of the happier days to come? Or, if you must think of the time that is passed, can you not look back to the time when I first loved you?"

She sighed as he put the question. "Spare me, Henry," she answered, sadly. "Say no more!"

The colour again rose in her cheeks; her hand trembled in his. She looked lovely, with her yes cast down and her bosom heaving gently. At that moment he would have given everything he had in the world to take her in his arms and kiss her. Some mysterious sympathy, passing from his hand to hers, seemed to tell her what was in his mind. She snatched her hand away and suddenly looked up at him. The tears were in her eyes. She said nothing; she let her eyes speak for her. They warned him-without anger, without unkindness—but still they warned him to press her no further that day.

"Only tell me that I am forgiven," he said, as he rose from the sofa.

"Yes," she answered, quietly, "you are forgiven."

"I have not lowered myself in your estimation, Agnes?"

"Oh, no!"

"Do you wish me to leave you?"

She rose, in her turn, from the sofa, and walked to her writing-table before she replied. The unfinished letter which she had been writing when Lady Montbarry interrupted her, lay open on the blotting-book. As she looked at the letter, and then looked at Henry, the smile that charmed everybody showed itself in her face.

"You must not go just yet," she said: "I have something to tell you. I hardly know how to express it. The shortest way perhaps will be to let you find it out for yourself. You have been speaking of my lonely, unprotected life here. It is not a very happy life, Henry—I own that."

She paused, observing the growing anxiety of his expression as he looked at her, with a shy satisfaction that perplexed him. "Do you know that I have anticipated your idea?" she went on. "I am going to make a great change in my life—if your brother Stephen and his wife will only consent to it." She opened the desk of the writing-table while she spoke, took a letter out, and handed it to Henry.

He received it from her mechanically. Vague doubts, which he hardly understood himself, kept him silent. It was impossible that the "change in her life" of which she had spoken could mean that she was about to be married—and yet he was conscious of a perfectly unreasonable reluctance to open the letter. Their eyes met; she smiled again. "Look at the address," she said. "You ought to know the handwriting—but I daresay you don't."

He looked at the address. It was in the large, irregular, uncertain writing of a child. He opened the letter instantly.

> "Dear Aunt Agnes—Our governess is going away. She has had money left to her, and a house of her own. We have had cake and wine to drink her health. You promised to be our governess if we wanted another. We want you. Mamma knows nothing about this. Please come before Mamma can get another governess. Your loving Lucy, who writes this. Clara and Blanche have tried to write too. But they are too young to do it. They blot the paper."

"Your eldest niece," Agnes explained, as Henry looked at her in amazement. "The children used to call me aunt when I was staying with their mother in Ireland, in the autumn. The three girls were my inseparable companions—they are the most charming children I know. It is quite true that I offered to be their governess, if they ever wanted one, on the day when I left them to return to London. I was writing to propose it to their mother, just before you came."

"Not seriously!" Henry exclaimed.

Agnes placed her unfinished letter in his hand. Enough of it had been written to show that she did seriously propose to enter the household of Mr. and Mrs. Stephen Westwick as governess to their children! Henry's bewilderment was not to be expressed in words.

"They won't believe you are in earnest," he said.

"Why not?" Agnes asked quietly.

"You are my brother Stephen's cousin; you are his wife's old friend."

"All the more reason, Henry, for trusting me with the charge of their children."

"But you are their equal; you are not obliged to get your living by teaching. There is something absurd in your entering their service as a governess!"

"What is there absurd in it? The children love me; the mother loves me; the father has shown me innumerable instances of his true friendship and regard. I am the very woman for the place—and, as to my education, I must have completely forgotten it indeed, if I am not fit to teach three children, the eldest of whom is only eleven years old. You say I am their equal. Are there no other women who serve as governesses, and who are the equals of the persons whom they serve?

"Besides, I don't know that I am their equal. Have I not heard that your brother Stephen was the next heir to the title? Will he not be the new lord? Never mind answering me! We won't dispute whether I am right or wrong in turning governess—we will wait the event. I am weary of my lonely useless existence here, and eager to make my life more happy and more useful, in the household of all others in which I should like most to have a place. If you will look again, you will see that I have these personal considerations still to urge before I finish my letter. You don't know your brother and his wife as well as I do, if you doubt their answer. I believe they have courage enough and heart enough to say Yes."

Henry submitted without being convinced.

He was a man who disliked all eccentric departures from custom and routine; and he felt especially suspicious of the change proposed in the life of Agnes. With new interests to occupy her mind, she might be less, favourably disposed to listen to him, on the next occasion when he urged his suit. The influence of the "lonely useless existence" of which she complained, was distinctly an influence in his favour.

While her heart was empty, her heart was accessible. But with his nieces in full possession of it, the clouds of doubt overshadowed his prospects. He knew the sex well enough to keep these purely selfish perplexities to himself. The waiting policy was especially the policy to pursue with a woman as sensitive as Agnes. If he once offended her delicacy he was lost. For the moment he wisely controlled himself and changed the subject.

"My little niece's letter has had an effect," he said, "which the child never contemplated in writing it. She has just reminded me of one of the objects that I had in calling on you today."

Agnes looked at the child's letter. "How does Lucy do that?" she asked.

"Lucy's governess is not the only lucky person who has had money left her, "Henry answered. "Is your old nurse in the house."

"You don't mean to say that nurse has got a legacy?"

"She has got a hundred pounds. Send for her, Agnes, while I show you the letter."

He took a handful of letters from his pocket, and looked through them, while Agnes rang the bell. Returning to him, she noticed a printed letter among the rest, which lay open on the table. It was a "prospectus," and the title of it was "Palace Hotel Company of Venice (Limited)." The two words, "Palace" and "Venice," instantly recalled her mind to the unwelcome visit of Lady Montbarry. "What is that?" she asked, pointing to the title.

Henry suspended his search, and glanced at the prospectus. "A really promising speculation," he said. "Large hotels always pay well, if they are well managed. I know the man who is appointed to be manager of this hotel when it is opened to the public; and I have such entire confidence in him that I have become one of the shareholders of the Company."

The reply did not appear to satisfy Agnes. "Why is the hotel called the 'Palace Hotel'?" she inquired.

Henry looked at her, and at once penetrated her motive for asking the question. "Yes," he said, "it is the palace that Montbarry hired at Venice; and it has been purchased by the Company to be changed into an hotel."

Agnes turned away in silence, and took a chair at the further end of the room. Henry had disappointed her. His income as a younger son stood in need, as she well knew, of all the additions that he could make to it by successful speculation. But she was unreasonable enough, nevertheless, to disapprove of his attempting to make money already out of the house in which his brother had died.

Incapable of understanding this purely sentimental view of a plain matter of business, Henry returned to his papers, in some perplexity at the sudden change in the manner of Agnes toward him. Just as he found the letter of which he was in search, the nurse made her appearance. He glanced at Agnes, expecting that she would speak first. She never even looked up when the nurse came in. It was left to Henry to tell the old woman why the bell had summoned her to the drawing-room.

"Well, nurse," he said, "you have had a windfall of luck. You have had a legacy left you of a hundred pounds."

The nurse showed no outward signs of exultation. She waited a little to get the announcement of the legacy well settled in her mind—and then she said quietly, "Master Henry, who gives me that money, if you please?"

"My late brother, Lord Montbarry, gives it to you." (Agnes instantly looked up, interested in the matter for the first time. Henry went on.) "His will leaves legacies to the surviving old servants of the family. There is a letter from his lawyers, authorizing you to apply to them for the money."

In every class of society, gratitude is the rarest of all human virtues. In the nurse's class it is extremely rare. Her opinion of the man who had deceived and deserted her mistress remained the same opinion still, perfectly undisturbed by the passing circumstance of the legacy.

"I wonder who reminded my lord of the old servants?" she said. "He would never have heart enough to remember them himself!"

Agnes suddenly interposed. Nature, always abhorring monotony, institutes reserves of temper as elements in the composition of the gentlest women living. Even Agnes could, on rare occasions, be angry. The nurse's view of Montbarry's character seemed to have provoked her beyond endurance.

"If you have any sense of shame in you," she broke out, "you ought to be ashamed of what you have just said! Your ingratitude disgusts me. I leave you to speak with her, Henry—you won't mind it!" With this significant intimation that he too had dropped out of his customary place in her good opinion, she left the room.

The nurse received the smart reproof administered to her with every appearance of feeling rather amused by it than not When the door had closed, this female philosopher winked at Henry.

"There's a power of obstinacy in young women," she remarked. "Miss Agnes wouldn't give my lord up as a bad one, even when he jilted her. And now she's sweet on him after he's head. Say a word against him and she fires up as you see. All obstinacy! It will wear out with time. Stick to her, Master Henry-stick to her!"

"She doesn't seem to have offended you," said Henry.

"She?" the nurse repeated in amazement—"she offend me? I like her in her tantrums; it reminds me of her when she was a baby. Lord bless you! when I go to bid her goodnight, she'll give me a big kiss, poor dear—and say, Nurse, I didn't mean it! About this money, Master Henry? If I was younger I should spend it in dress and jewellery. But I'm too old for that. What shall I do with my legacy when I have got it?"

"Put it out at interest," Henry suggested. "Get so much a year for it, you know."

"How much shall I get?" the nurse asked.

"If you put your hundred pounds into the Funds, you will get between three and four pounds a year."

The nurse shook her head. "Three or four pounds a year? That won't do! I want more than that. Look here, Master Henry.

I don't care about this bit of money—I never did like the man who has left it to me, though he was your brother. If I lost it all tomorrow, I shouldn't break my heart; I'm well enough off, as it is, for the rest of my days. They say you're a speculator. Put me in for a good thing, there's a dear! Neck-or-nothing—and that for the Funds!" She snapped her fingers to express her contempt for security of investment at three *per cent.*

Henry produced the prospectus of the Venetian Hotel Company. "You're a funny old woman," he said. "There, you dashing speculator—there is neck-or-nothing for you! You must keep it a secret from Miss Agnes, mind. I'm not at all sure that she would approve of my helping you to this investment."

The nurse took out her spectacles. "Six *per cent*, guaranteed," she read; "and the Directors have every reason to believe that ten *per cent*, or more, will be ultimately realized to the shareholders by the hotel." "Put me into that, Master Henry! And, wherever you go for heaven's sake recommend the hotel to your friends!"

So the nurse, following Henry's mercenary example, had her pecuniary interest, too, in the house in which Lord Montbarry had died.

Three days passed before Henry was able to visit Agnes again. In that time, the little cloud between them had entirely passed away. Agnes received him with even more than her customary kindness. She was in better spirits than usual. Her letter to Mrs. Stephen Westwick had been answered by return of post; and her proposal had been joyfully accepted, with one modification. She was to visit the Westwicks for a month—and, if she really liked teaching the children, she was then to be governess, aunt, and cousin, all in one—and was only to go away in an event which her friends in Ireland persisted in contemplating, the event of her marriage.

"You see I was right," she said to Henry.

He was still incredulous. "Are you really going?" he asked.

"I am going next week."

"When shall I see you again?"

"You know you are always welcome at your brother's house. You can see me when you like." She held out her hand. "Pardon me for leaving you—I am beginning to pack up already."

Henry tried to kiss her at parting. She drew back directly.

"Why not? I am your cousin," he said.

"I don't like it," she answered.

Henry looked at her, and submitted. Her refusal to grant him his privilege as a cousin was a good sign—it was indirectly an act of encouragement to him in the character of her lover.

On the first day in the new week, Agnes left London on her way to Ireland. As the event proved, this was not destined to be the end of her journey. The way to Ireland was only the first stage on a roundabout road—the road that led to the palace at Venice.

The Third Part

Chapter 13

In the spring of the year 1861, Agnes was established at the country-seat of her two friends—now promoted (on the death of the first lord, without offspring) to be the new Lord and Lady Montbarry. The old nurse was not separated from her mistress. A place, suited to her time of life, had been found for her in the pleasant Irish household. She was perfectly happy in her new sphere; and she spent her first half-year's dividend from the Venice Hotel Company, with characteristic prodigality, in presents for the children.

Early in the year, also, the Directors of the life insurance offices submitted to circumstances and paid the ten thousand pounds. Immediately afterward, the widow of the first Lord Montbarry (otherwise, the dowager Lady Montbarry) left England, with Baron Rivar, for the United States. The Baron's object was announced, in the scientific columns of the newspapers, to be investigation into the present state of experimental chemistry in the great American republic. His sister informed inquiring friends that she accompanied him, in the hope of finding consolation in change of scene after the bereavement that had fallen on her.

Hearing this news from Henry Westwick (then paying a visit at his brother's house), Agnes was conscious of a certain sense of relief. "With the Atlantic between us," she said, "surely I have done with that terrible woman now!"

Barely a week passed after those words had been spoken, before an event happened which reminded Agnes of "the terrible woman" once more.

On that day, Henry's engagements had obliged him to return to London. He had ventured, on the morning of his departure, to press his suit once more on Agnes; and the children, as he had anticipated, proved to be innocent obstacles in the way of his success. On the other hand, he had privately secured a firm ally in his sister-in-law. "Have a little patience," the new Lady Montbarry had said, "and leave me to turn the influence of the children in the right direction. If they can persuade her to listen to you—they shall!"

The two ladies had accompanied Henry, and some other guests who went away at the same time, to the railway station, and had just driven back to the house, when the servant announced that "a person of the name of Holland was waiting to see her ladyship."

"Is it a woman?"

"Yes, my lady."

Young Lady Montbarry turned to Agnes.

"This is the very person," she said, "whom your lawyer thought likely to help him, when he was trying to trace the lost courier."

"You don't mean the English maid who was with Lady Montbarry at Venice?"

"My dear! don't speak of Montbarry's horrid widow by the name which is my name now. Stephen and I have arranged to call her by her foreign title, before she was married. I am 'Lady Montbarry,' and she is 'the Countess.' In that way there will be no confusion.—Yes, Mrs. Rolland was in my service before she became the Countess's maid. She was a perfectly trustworthy person, with one defect that obliged me to send her away—a sullen temper which led to perpetual complaints of her in the servants' hall. Would you like to see her?"

Agnes accepted the proposal, in the faint hope of getting some information for the courier's wife. The complete defeat of every attempt to trace the lost man had been accepted as final by Mrs. Ferrari. She had deliberately arrayed herself in widow's mourning; and was earning her livelihood in an employment which the unwearied kindness of Agnes had procured for her in London. The last chance of penetrating the mystery of Ferrari's disappearance seemed to rest now on what Ferrari's former fellow-servant might be able to tell. With highly-wrought expectations, Agnes followed her friend into the room in which Mrs. Rolland was waiting.

A tall, bony woman, in the autumn of life, with sunken eyes and iron-gray hair, rose stiffly from her chair, and saluted the ladies with stern submission as they opened the door. A person of unblemished character, evidently—but not without visible drawbacks. Big bushy eyebrows, an awfully deep and solemn voice, a harsh, unbending manner, a complete absence in her figure of the undulating lines characteristic of the sex, presented Virtue in this excellent person under its least alluring aspect. Strangers, on a first introduction to her, were accustomed to wonder why she was not a man.

"Are you pretty well, Mrs. Rolland?"

"I am as well as I can expect to be, my lady, at my time of life."

"Is there anything I can do for you?"

"Your ladyship can do me a great favour, if you will please speak to my character while I was in your service. I am offered a place, to wait on an invalid lady who has lately come to live in this neighbourhood."

"Ah, yes—I have heard of her. A Mrs. Carbury, with a very pretty niece, I am told. But, Mrs. Rolland, you left my service some time ago. Mrs. Carbury will surely expect you to refer to the last mistress by whom you were employed."

A flash of virtuous indignation irradiated Mrs. Holland's sunken eyes. She coughed before she answered, as if her "last mistress" stuck in her throat.

"I have explained to Mrs. Carbury, my lady, that the person I last served—I really cannot give her her title in your ladyship's presence!—has left England for America. Mrs. Carbury knows that I quitted the person of my own free will, and knows why, and approves of my conduct so far. A word from your ladyship will be amply sufficient to get me the situation."

"Very well, Mrs. Holland, I have no objection to be your reference, under the circumstances. Mrs. Carbury will find me at home tomorrow until two o'clock."

"Mrs. Carbury is not well enough to leave the house, my lady. Her niece, Miss Haldane, will call and make the inquiries, if your ladyship has no objection."

"I have not the least objection. The pretty niece carries her own welcome with her. Wait a minute, Mrs. Rolland. This lady is Miss Lockwood—my husband's cousin, and my friend. She is anxious to speak to you about the courier who was in the late Lord Montbarry's service at Venice."

Mrs. Rolland's bushy eyebrows frowned in stern disapproval of the new topic of conversation. "I regret to hear it, my lady," was all she said.

"Perhaps you have not been informed of what happened after you left Venice?" Agnes ventured to add. "Ferrari left the palace secretly; and he has never been heard of since."

Mrs. Rolland mysteriously closed her eyes as if to exclude some vision of the lost courier which was of a nature to disturb a respectable woman. "Nothing that Mr. Ferrari could do would surprise me," she replied in her deepest bass tones.

"You speak rather harshly of him," said Agnes.

Mrs. Rolland suddenly opened her eyes again. "I speak harshly of nobody without reason," she said. "Mr. Ferrari behaved to me, Miss Lockwood, as no man living has ever behaved—before or since."

"What did he do?"

Mrs. Rolland answered, with a stony stare of horror :

"He took liberties with me."

Young Lady Montbarry suddenly turned aside, and put her handkerchief over her mouth in convulsions of suppressed laughter.

Mrs. Rolland went on, with a grim enjoyment of the bewilderment which her reply had produced on Agnes: "And when I insisted on an apology, miss, he had the audacity to say that the life at the palace was dull, and he didn't know how else to amuse himself!"

"I am afraid I have hardly made myself understood," said Agnes. "I am not speaking to you out of any interest in Ferrari. Are you aware that he is married?"

"I pity his wife," said Mrs. Rolland.

"She is naturally in great grief about him," Agnes proceeded.

"She ought to thank God she is rid of him," Mrs. Rolland interposed.

Agnes still persisted. "I have known Mrs. Ferrari from her childhood, and I am sincerely anxious to help her in this matter. Did you notice anything, while you were at Venice, that would account for her husband's extraordinary disappearance? On what sort of terms, for instance, did he live with his master and mistress?"

"On terms of familiarity with his mistress," said Mrs. Holland, "which were simply sickening to a respectable English servant. She used to encourage him to talk to her about all his affairs-how he got on with his wife, and how pressed he was for money, and such like—just as if they were equals. Contemptible—that's what I call it."

"And his master?" Agnes continued. "How did Ferrari get on with Lord Montbarry?"

"My lord used to live shut up with his studies and his sorrows," Mrs. Rolland answered, with a hard solemnity expressive of respect for his lordship's memory. "Mr. Ferrari got his money when it was due; and he cared for nothing else. 'If I could afford it, I would leave the place, too; but I can't afford it.' Those were the last words he said to me, on the morning when I left the palace. I made no reply. After what had happened (on that other occasion) I was naturally not on speaking terms with Mr. Ferrari."

"Can you really tell me nothing which will throw any light on this matter?"

"Nothing," said Mrs. Rolland, with an undisguised relish of the disappointment that she was inflicting.

"There was another member of the family at Venice," Agnes resumed, determined to sift the question to the bottom while she had the chance. "There was Baron Rivar."

Mrs. Rolland lifted her large hands, covered with rusty black gloves, in mute protest against the introduction of Baron Rivar as a subject of inquiry. "Are you aware, miss," she began, "that I left my place in consequence of what I observed—?"

Agnes stopped her there. "I only wanted to ask," she explained, "if anything was said or done by Baron Rivar which might account for Ferrari's strange conduct."

"Nothing that I know of," said Mrs. Rolland. "The Baron and Mr. Ferrari (if I may use such an expression) were 'birds of a feather,' so far as I could see—I mean, one was as unprincipled as the other. I am a just woman; and I will give you an example. Only the day before I left, I heard the Baron say (through the open door of his room while I was passing along the corridor), 'Ferrari, I want a thousand pounds. "What would you do for a thousand pounds?' And I heard Mr. Ferrari answer, 'Anything, sir, as long as I was not found out.' And then they both burst out laughing. I heard no more than that. Judge for yourself, miss."

Agnes reflected for a moment. A thousand pounds was the sum that had been sent to Mrs. Ferrari in the anonymous letter. Was that inclosure in any way connected, as a result, with the conversation between the Baron and Ferrari? It was useless to press any more inquiries on Mrs. Holland. She could give no further information which was of the slightest importance to the object in view. There was no alternative but to grant her her dismissal. One more effort had been made to find a trace of the lost man, and once again the effort had failed.

They were a family party at the dinner-table that day. The only guest left in the house was a nephew of the new Lord Montbarry the eldest son of his sister, Lady Barville. Lady Montbarry could not resist telling the story of the first (and last) attack made on the virtue of Mrs. Rolland, with a comically-exact imitation of Mrs. Rolland's deep and dismal voice.

Being asked by her husband what was the object which had brought that formidable person to the house, she naturally mentioned the expected visit of Miss Haldane. Arthur Barville, unusually silent and preoccupied so far, suddenly struck into the conversation with a burst of enthusiasm. "Miss Haldane is the most charming girl in all Ireland!" he said. "I caught sight of her yesterday, over the wall of her garden, as I was riding by. What time is she coming tomorrow? Before two? I'll look into the drawing-room by accident—I am dying to be introduced to her!"

Agnes was amused by his enthusiasm. "Are you in love with Miss Haldane already?" she asked.

Arthur answered gravely: "It's no joking matter. I have been all day at the garden wall, waiting to see her again! It depends on Miss Haldane to make me the happiest or the wretchedest man living."

"You foolish boy! How can you talk such nonsense?"

He was talking nonsense undoubtedly. But, if Agnes had only known it, he was doing something more than that. He was innocently leading her another stage nearer on the way to Venice.

Chapter 14

As the summer months advanced, the transformation of the Venetian palace into the modern hotel proceeded rapidly toward completion.

The outside of the building, with its fine Palladian front looking on the canal, was wisely left unaltered. Inside, as a matter of necessity, the rooms were almost rebuilt—so far at least as the size and the arrangement of them were concerned. The vast saloons were partitioned off into "apartments" containing three or four rooms each. The broad corridors in the upper regions afforded spare space enough for rows of little bedchambers, devoted to servants and to travellers with limited means.

Nothing was spared but the solid floors and the finely-carved ceilings. These last, in excellent preservation as to workmanship, merely required cleaning, and regilding here and there, to add greatly to the beauty and importance of the best rooms in the hotel. The only exception to the complete reorganization of the interior was at one extremity of the edifice, on the first and second floors. Here there happened, in each case, to be rooms of such comparatively moderate size, and so attractively decorated, that the architect suggested leaving them as they were.

It was afterward discovered that these were no other than the apartments formerly occupied by Lord Montbarry (on the first floor), and by Baron Rivar (on the second). The room in which Montbarry had died was still fitted up as a bedroom, and was now distinguished as Number Fourteen. The room above it, in which the Baron had slept, took its place on the hotel-register as Number Thirty-eight. With the ornaments on the walls and ceilings cleaned and brightened up, and with the heavy old-fashioned beds, chairs, and tables replaced by bright, pretty and luxurious modern furniture, these two promised to be at once the most attractive and the most comfortable bedchambers in the hotel.

As for the once-desolate and disused ground floor of the building, it was now transformed, by means of splendid dining-rooms, reception-rooms, billiard-rooms and smoking-rooms, into a palace by itself. Even the dungeon-like vaults beneath, now lighted and ventilated on the most approved modern plan, had been turned as if by magic into kitchens, servants' offices, ice-rooms, and wine cellars, worthy of the splendour of the grandest hotel in Italy, in the now bygone period of seventeen years since.

Passing from the lapse of the summer months at Venice, to the lapse of the summer months in Ireland, it is next to be recorded that Mrs. Rolland obtained the situation of attendant on the invalid Mrs. Carbury; and that the fair Miss Haldane, like a female Caesar, came, saw, and conquered, on her first day's visit to the new Lord Montbarry's house.

The ladies were as load in their praises as Arthur Barville himself. Lord Montbarry declared that she was the only perfectly pretty woman he had ever seen, who was really unconscious of her own attractions. The old nurse said she looked as if she had just stepped out of a picture, and wanted nothing but a gilt frame round her to make her complete. Miss Haldane, on her side, returned from her first visit to the Montbarrys charmed with her new acquaintances.

Later on the same day, Arthur called with an offering of fruit and flowers for Mrs. Carbury, and with instructions to ask if she was well enough to receive Lord and Lady Montbarry and Miss Lockwood on the morrow. In a week's time, the two households were on the friendliest terms. Mrs. Carbury, confined to the sofa by a spinal malady, had been hitherto dependent on her niece for one of the few pleasures she could enjoy, the pleasure of having the best new novels read to her as they came out. Discovering this, Arthur volunteered to relieve Miss Haldane, at intervals, in the office of reader.

He was clever at mechanical contrivances of all sorts, and he introduced improvements in Mrs. Carbury's couch, and in the means of conveying her from the bedchamber to the drawing-room, which alleviated the poor lady's sufferings and brightened her gloomy life. With these claims on the gratitude of the aunt, aided by the personal advantages which he unquestionably possessed, Arthur advanced rapidly in the favour of the charming niece. She was, it is needless to say, perfectly well aware that he was in love with her, while he was himself modestly reticent on the subject—so far as words went.

But she was not equally quick in penetrating the nature of her own feelings toward Arthur. Watching the two young people with keen powers of observation, necessarily concentrated on them by the complete seclusion of her life, the invalid lady discovered signs of roused sensibility in Miss Haldane, when Arthur was present, which had never yet shown themselves in her social relations with other admirers eager to pay their addresses to her. Having drawn her own conclusions in private, Mrs. Carbury took the first favourable opportunity (in Arthur's interests) of putting them to the test.

"I don't know what I shall do," she said one day, "when Arthur goes away."

Miss Haldane looked up quickly from her work. "Surely he is not going to leave us!" she exclaimed.

"My dear! he has already stayed at his uncle's house a month longer than he intended. His father and mother naturally expect to see him at home again."

Miss Haldane met this difficulty with a suggestion, which could only have proceeded from a judgment already disturbed by the ravages of the tender passion. "Why can't his father and mother go and see him at Lord Montbarry's?" she asked. "Sir Theodore's place is only thirty miles away, and Lady Barville is Lord Montbarry's sister. They needn't stand on ceremony."

"They may have other engagements," Mrs. Carbury remarked.

"My dear aunt, we don't know that! Suppose you ask Arthur?"

"Suppose you ask him?"

Miss Haldane bent her head again over her work. Suddenly as it was done, her aunt had seen her face—and her face betrayed her.

When Arthur came the next day, Mrs. Carbury said a word to him in private, while her niece was in the garden. The last new novel lay neglected on the table. Arthur followed Miss Haldane into the garden. The next day he wrote home, inclosing in his letter a photograph of Miss Haldane. Before the end of the week Sir Theodore and Lady Barville arrived at Lord Montbarry's, and formed their own judgment of the fidelity of the portrait. They had themselves married early in life—and, strange to say, they did not object on principle to the early marriages of other people.

The question of age being thus disposed of, the course of true love had no other obstacles to encounter. Miss Haldane was an only child, and was possessed of an ample fortune. Arthur's career at the university had been creditable, but certainly not brilliant enough to present his withdrawal in the light of a disaster. As Sir Theodore's eldest son, his position was already made for him. He was two-and-twenty years of age; and the young lady was eighteen. There was really no producible reason for keeping the lovers waiting, and no excuse for deferring the wedding-day beyond the first week in September.

In the interval, while the bride and bridegroom would be necessarily absent on the inevitable tour abroad, a sister of Mrs Carbury volunteered to stay with her during the temporary separation from her niece. On the conclusion of the honeymoon, the young couple were to return to Ireland, and were to establish themselves in Mrs. Carbury's spacious and comfortable house.

These arrangements were decided upon early in the month of August. About the same date, the last alterations in the old palace at Venice were completed. The rooms were dried by steam; the cellars were stocked; the manager collected round him his army of skilled servants; and the new hotel was advertised all over Europe to open in October.

Chapter 15

(Miss Agnes Lockwood To Mrs. Ferrari.)

I promised to give you some account, dear Emily, of .the marriage of Mr. Arthur Barville and Miss Haldane. It took place ten days since. But I have had so many things to look after in the absence of the master and mistress of this house, that I am only able to write to you today.

The invitations to the wedding were limited to members of the families on either side, in consideration of the ill health of Miss Haldane's aunt. On the side of the Montbarry family, there were present, besides Lord and Lady Montbarry, Sir Theodore and Lady Barville; Mrs. Norbury (whom you may remember as his lordship's second sister); and Mr. Francis Westwick, and Mr. Henry Westwick.

The three children and I attended the ceremony as bridesmaids. We were joined by two young ladies, cousins of the bride and very agreeable girls. Our dresses were white, trimmed with green in honour of Ireland; and we each had a handsome gold bracelet given to us as a present from the bridegroom. If you add to the persons whom I have already mentioned, the elder members of Mrs. Carbury's family, and the old servants in both houses—privileged to drink the healths of the married pair at the lower end of the room—you will have the list of the company at the wedding breakfast complete.

The weather was perfect, and the ceremony (with music) was beautifully performed. As for the bride, no words can describe how lovely she looked, or how well she went through it all. We were very merry at the breakfast, and the speeches went off on the whole quite well enough. The last speech, before the party broke up, was made by Mr. Henry Westwick, and was the best of all. He offered a happy suggestion, at the end, which has produced a very unexpected change in my life here.

As well as I remember, he concluded in these words:—

'On one point, we are all agreed we are sorry that the parting hour is near, and we should be glad to meet again. Why should we not meet again? This is the autumn time of the year; we are most of us leaving home for the holidays. What do you say (if you have no engagements that will prevent it) to joining our young married friends before the close of their tour, and renewing the social success of this delightful breakfast by another festival in honour of the honeymoon? The bride and bridegroom are going to Germany and the Tyrol, on their way to Italy. I propose that we allow them a month to themselves, and that we arrange to meet them afterward in the North of Italy—say at Venice.'

This proposal was received with great applause, which was changed into shouts of laughter by no less a person than my dear old nurse. The moment Mr. Westwick pronounced the word 'Venice,' she started up among the servants at the lower end of the room, and called out at the top of her voice, 'Go to our hotel, ladies and gentlemen! We get six *per cent* on our money already; and if you will only crowd the place and call for the best of everything, it will be ten per cent in our pockets in no time. Ask Master Henry!'

Appealed to in this irresistible manner, Mr. Westwick had no choice but to explain that he was concerned as a shareholder in a new Hotel Company at Venice, and that he had invested a small sum of money for the nurse (not very considerately, as I think) in the speculation. Hearing this, the company, by way of humouring the joke, drank a new toast:—Success to the nurse's hotel, and a speedy rise in the dividend !

When the conversation returned in due time to the more serious question of the proposed meeting at Venice, difficulties began to present themselves, caused of course by invitations for the autumn which many of the guests had already accepted. Only two members of Mrs. Carbury 's family were at liberty to keep the proposed appointment. On our side we were more at leisure to do as we pleased. Mr. Henry Westwick decided to go to Venice in advance of the rest, to test the accommodation of the new hotel on the opening day.

Mrs. Norbury and Mr. Francis Westwick volunteered to follow him; and, after some persuasion, Lord and Lady Montbarry consented to a species of compromise. His

> lordship could not conveniently spare time enough for the journey to Venice, but he and Lady Montbarry arranged to accompany Mrs. Norbury and Mr. Francis Westwick as far on their way to Italy as Paris. Five days since, they took their departure to meet their travelling companions in London; leaving me here in charge of the three dear children. They begged hard, of course, to be taken with papa and mamma. But it was thought better not to interrupt the progress of their education, and not to expose them (especially the two younger girls) to the fatigues of travelling.
>
> I have had a charming letter from the bride, this morning, dated Cologne. You cannot think how artlessly and prettily she assures me of her happiness. Some people, as they say in Ireland, are born to good luck—and I think Arthur Barville is one of them.
>
> When you next write, I hope to hear that you are in better health and spirits, and that you continue to like your employment. Believe me, sincerely your friend. A. L.

Agnes had just closed and directed her letter, when the eldest of her three pupils entered the room with the startling announcement that Lord Montbarry's travelling-servant had arrived from Paris! Alarmed by the idea that some misfortune had happened, she ran out to meet the man in the hall. Her face told him how seriously he had frightened her, before she could speak. "There's nothing wrong, miss," he hastened to say. "My lord and my lady are enjoying themselves at Paris. They only want you and the young ladies to be with them." Saying these amazing words, he handed to Agnes a letter from Lady Montbarry.

> "Dearest Agnes" (she read), "I am so charmed with the delightful change in my life—it is six years, remember, since I last travelled on the Continent—that I have exerted all my fascinations to persuade Lord Montbarry to go on to Venice. And, what is more to the purpose, I have actually succeeded! He has just gone to his room to

write the necessary letters of excuse in time for the post to England. May you have as good a husband, my dear, when your time comes! In the meanwhile, the one thing wanting now to make my happiness complete, is to have you and the darling children with us. Montbarry is just as miserable without them as I am—though he doesn't confess it so freely. You will have no difficulties to trouble you. Louis will deliver these hurried lines, and will take care of you on the journey to Paris. Kiss the children for me a thousand times—and never mind their education for the present! Pack up instantly, my dear, and I will be fonder of you than ever.

Your affectionate friend, Adela Montbarry.

Agnes folded up the letter; and feeling the need of composing herself, took refuge for a few minutes in her own room.

Her first natural sensations of surprise and excitement at the prospect of going to Venice were succeeded by impressions of a less agreeable kind. With the recovery of her customary composure came the unwelcome remembrance of the parting words spoken to her by Montbarry's widow: "We shall meet again-here in England, or there in Venice where my husband died-and meet for the last time."

It was an odd coincidence, to say the least of it, that the march of events should be unexpectedly taking Agnes to Venice, after those words had been spoken! Was the woman of the mysterious warnings and the wild black eyes still thousands of miles away in America? Or was the march of events taking her unexpectedly, too, on the journey to Venice? Agnes started out of her chair, ashamed of even the momentary concession to superstition which was implied by the mere presence of such questions as these in her mind.

She rang the bell, and sent for her little pupils, and announced their approaching departure to the household. The noisy delight of the children, the inspiriting effort of packing up in a hurry, roused all her energies. She dismissed her own absurd misgivings from consideration, with the contempt that they deserved. She worked as only women can work, when their hearts are in what they do. The travellers reached Dublin that day, in time for the boat to England. Two days later, they were with Lord and Lady Montbarry at Paris.

The Fourth Part

Chapter 16

It was only the twentieth of September, when Agnes and the children reached Paris. Mrs. Norbury and her brother Francis had then already started on their journey to Italy—at least three weeks before the date at which the new hotel was to open for the reception of travellers.

The person answerable for this premature departure was Francis Westwick.

Like his younger brother Henry, he had increased his pecuniary resources by his own enterprise and ingenuity; with this difference, that his speculations were connected with the Arts. He had made money, in the first instance, by a weekly newspaper; and he had then invested his profits in a London Theatre. This latter enterprise, admirably conducted, had been rewarded by the public with steady and liberal encouragement. Pondering over a new form of theatrical attraction for the coming winter season, Francis had determined to revive the languid public taste for the "ballet" by means of an entertainment of his own invention, combining dramatic interest with dancing.

He was now, accordingly, in search of the best dancer (possessed of the indispensable personal attractions) who was to be found in the theatres of the Continent. Hearing from his foreign correspondents of two women who had made successful first appearances, one at Milan and one at Florence, he had arranged to visit those cities, and to judge of the merits of the dancers for himself, before he joined the bride and bridegroom. His widowed sister, having friends at Florence whom she was anxious to see, readily accompanied him. The Montbarrys remained at Paris, until it was time to present themselves at the family meeting in Venice. Henry found them still in the French capital, when he arrived from London on his way to the opening of the new hotel.

Against Lady Montbarry's advice, he took the opportunity of renewing his addresses to Agnes. He could hardly have chosen a more unpropitious time for pleading his cause with her. The gayeties of Paris (quite incomprehensibly to herself as well as to everyone about her) had a depressing effect on her spirits. She had no illness to complain of; she shared willingly in the ever-varying succession of amusements offered to strangers by the ingenuity of the liveliest people in the world—but nothing roused her: she remained persistently dull and weary through it all.

In this frame of mind and body, she was in no humour to receive Henry's ill-timed addresses with favour, or even with patience: she plainly and positively refused to listen to him. "Why do you remind me of what I have suffered?" she asked petulantly. "Don't you see that it has left its mark on me for life?"

"I thought I knew something of women by this time," Henry said, appealing privately to Lady Montbarry for consolation. "But Agnes completely puzzles me. It is a year since Montbarry's death; and she remains as devoted to his memory as if he had died faithful to her—she still feels the loss of him, as none of us feel it!"

"She is the truest woman that ever breathed the breath of life," Lady Montbarry answered. "Remember that, and you will understand her. Can such a woman as Agnes give her love or refuse it, according to circumstances? Because the man was unworthy of her, was he less the man of her choice? The truest and best friend to him (little as he deserved it) in his lifetime, she naturally remains the truest and best friend to his memory now. If you really love her, wait; and trust to your two best friends—to time and to me. There is my advice; let your own experience decide whether it is not the best advice that I can offer. Resume your journey to Venice tomorrow; and when you take leave of Agnes, speak to her as cordially as if nothing had happened."

Henry wisely followed this advice. Thoroughly understanding him, Agnes made the leave-taking friendly and pleasant on her side. When he stopped at the door for a last look at her, she hurriedly turned her head so that her face was hidden from him. Was that a good sign? Lady Montbarry, accompanying Henry down the stairs, said, "Yes, decidedly! Write when you get to Venice. We shall wait here to receive letters from Arthur and his wife, and we shall time our departure for Italy accordingly."

A week passed, and no letter came from Henry. Some days later, a telegram was received from him. It was dispatched from Milan, instead of from Venice; and it brought this strange message:—

> I have left the hotel. Will return on the arrival of Arthur and his wife. Address, meanwhile, Albergo Reale, Milan.

Preferring Venice before all other cities of Europe, and having arranged to remain there until the family meeting took place, what unexpected event had led Henry to alter his plans? and why did he state the bare fact, without adding a word of explanation? Let the narrative follow him—and find the answer to those questions at Venice.

Chapter 17

The Palace Hotel, appealing for encouragement mainly to English and American travellers, celebrated the opening of its doors, as a matter of course, by the giving of a grand banquet, and the delivery of a long succession of speeches.

Delayed on his journey, Henry Westwick only reached Venice in time to join the guests over their coffee and cigars. Observing the splendour of the reception rooms, and taking note especially of the artful mixture of comfort and luxury in the bedchambers, he began to share the old nurse's view of the future, and to contemplate seriously the coming dividend of ten per cent. The hotel was beginning well, at all events.

So much interest in the enterprise had been aroused, at home and abroad, by profuse advertising, that the whole accommodation of the building had been secured by travellers of all nations for the opening night. Henry only obtained one of the small rooms on the upper floor, by a lucky accident—the absence of the gentleman who had written to engage it. He was quite satisfied, and was on his way to bed, when another accident altered his prospects for the night, and moved him into another and a better room.

Ascending on his way to the higher regions as far as the first floor of the hotel, Henry's attention was attracted by an angry voice protesting, in a strong New England accent, against one of the greatest hardships that can be inflicted on a citizen of the United States—the hardship of sending him to bed without gas in his room.

The Americans are not only the most hospitable people to be found on the face of the earth—they are (under certain conditions) the most patient and good-tempered people as well. But they are human; and the limit of American endurance is found in the obsolete institution of a bedroom candle. The American traveller, in the present case, declined to believe that his bedroom was in a completely finished state without a gas-burner. The manager pointed to the fine antique decorations (renewed and regilded) on the walls and the ceiling, and explained that the emanations of burning gas-light would certainly spoil them in the course of a few months.

To this the traveller replied that it was possible, but that he did not understand decorations. A bedroom with gas in it was what he was used to, was what he wanted, and was what he was determined to have. The compliant manager volunteered to ask some other gentleman, housed on the inferior upper story (which was lighted throughout with gas), to change rooms. Hearing this, and being quite willing to exchange a small bedchamber for a large one, Henry volunteered to be the other gentleman. The excellent American shook hands with him on the spot. "You are a cultured person, sir," he said; "and you will no doubt understand the decorations."

Henry looked at the number of the room on the door as he opened it. The number was Fourteen.

Tired and sleepy, he naturally anticipated a good night's rest. In the thoroughly healthy state of his nervous system, he slept as well in a bed abroad as in a bed at home. Without the slightest assignable reason, however, his just expectations were disappointed. The luxurious bed, the well-ventilated room, the delicious tranquillity of Venice by night, all were in favour of his sleeping well. He never slept at all.

An indescribable sense of depression and discomfort kept him waking through darkness and daylight alike. He went down to the coffee-room as soon as the hotel was astir, and ordered some breakfast. Another unaccountable change in himself appeared with the appearance of the meal. He was absolutely without appetite. An excellent omelette, and cutlets cooked to perfection, he sent away untasted—he, whose appetite never failed him, whose digestion was still equal to any demands on it!

The day was bright and fine. He sent for a gondola, and was rowed to the Lido.

Out on the airy Lagoon, he felt like a new man. He had not left the hotel ten minutes before he was fast asleep in the gondola. Waking, on reaching the landing-place, he crossed the Lido, and enjoyed a morning's swim in the Adriatic. There was only a poor restaurant on the island, in those days; but his appetite was now ready for anything; he eat whatever was offered to him, like a famished man. He could hardly believe, when he reflected on it, that he had sent away untasted his excellent breakfast at the hotel.

Returning to Venice, he spent the rest of the day in the picture-galleries and the churches. Toward six o'clock his gondola took him back, with another fine appetite, to meet some travelling acquaintances with whom he had engaged to dine at the *table d'hôte*.

The dinner was deservedly rewarded with the highest approval by every guest in the hotel but one. To Henry's astonishment, the appetite with which he had entered the house mysteriously and completely left him when he sat down to table. He could drink some wine, but he could literally eat nothing. "What in the world is the matter with you?" his travelling acquaintances asked. He could honestly answer: "I know no more than you do."

When night came, he gave his comfortable and beautiful bedroom another trial. The result of the second experiment was a repetition of the result of the first Again he felt the all-pervading sense of depression and discomfort. Again he passed a sleepless night. And once more, when he tried to eat his breakfast, his appetite completely failed him !

This personal experience of the new hotel was too extraordinary to be passed over in silence. Henry mentioned it to his friends in the public room, in the hearing of the manager. The manager, naturally zealous in defence of the hotel, was a little hurt at the implied reflection cast on Number Fourteen. He invited the travellers present to judge for themselves whether Mr. Westwick's bedroom was to blame for Mr. Westwick's sleepless nights; and he especially appealed to a gray-headed gentleman, a guest at the breakfast-table of an English traveller, to take the lead in the investigation. "This is Doctor Bruno, our first physician in Venice," he explained. "I appeal to him to say if there are any unhealthy influences in Mr. Westwick's room."

Introduced to Number Fourteen, the doctor looked round him with a certain appearance of interest which was noticed by everyone present. "The last time I was in this room," he said, "was on a melancholy occasion. It was before the palace was changed into a hotel. I was in professional attendance on an English nobleman who died here." One of the persons present inquired the name of the nobleman. Doctor Bruno answered (without the slightest suspicion that he was speaking before a brother of the dead man), "Lord Montbarry."

Henry quietly left the room, without saying a word to anybody.

He was not, in any sense of the term, a superstitious man. But he felt, nevertheless, an insurmountable reluctance to remaining in the hotel. He decided on leaving Venice. To ask for another room would be, as he could plainly see, an offense in the eyes of the manager. To remove to another hotel would be to openly abandon an establishment in the success of which he had a pecuniary interest. Leaving a note for Arthur Barville, on his arrival in Venice, in which he merely mentioned that he had gone to look at the Italian lakes, and that a line addressed to his hotel at Milan would bring him back again, he took the afternoon train to Padua— and dined with his usual appetite, and slept as well as ever that night.

The next day a gentleman and his wife (perfect strangers to the Montbarry family), returning to England by way of Venice, arrived at the hotel and occupied Number Fourteen.

Still mindful of the slur that had been cast on one of his best bedchambers, the manager took occasion to ask the travellers the next morning how they liked their room. They left him to judge for himself how well they were satisfied, by remaining a day longer in Venice than they had originally planned to do, solely for the purpose of enjoying the excellent accommodation offered to them by the new hotel, "We have met with nothing like it in Italy," they said; "you may rely on our recommending you to all our friends."

On the day when Number Fourteen was again vacant, an English lady travelling alone with her maid arrived at the hotel, saw the room, and at once engaged it.

The lady was Mrs. Norbury. She had left Francis West wick at Milan, occupied in negotiating for the appearance at his theatre of the new dancer at the Scala. Not having heard to the contrary, Mrs. Norbury supposed that Arthur Barville and his wife had already arrived at Venice. She was more interested in meeting the young married couple than in awaiting the result of the hard bargaining which delayed the engagement of the new dancer; and she volunteered to make her brother's apologies, if his theatrical business caused him to be late in keeping his appointment at the honeymoon festival.

Mrs. Norbury's experience of Number Fourteen differed entirely from her brother Henry's experience of the room.

Falling asleep as readily as usual, her repose was disturbed by a succession of frightful dreams; the central figure in every one of them, being the figure of her dead brother, the first Lord Montbarry. She saw him starving in a loathsome prison; she saw him pursued by assassins, and dying under their knives; she saw him drowning in immeasurable depths of dark water; she saw him in a bed on fire, burning to death in the flames; she saw him tempted by a shadowy creature to drink, and dying of the poisonous draught.

The reiterated horror of these dreams had such an effect on her that she rose with the dawn of day, afraid to trust herself again in bed. In the old times, she had been noted in the family as the one member of it who lived on affectionate terms with Montbarry. His other sister and his brothers were constantly quarrelling with him. Even his mother owned that her eldest son was of all her children the child whom she least liked. Sensible and resolute woman as she was, Mrs. Norbury shuddered with terror as she sat at the window of her room, watching the sunrise and 'thinking of her dreams.

She made the first excuse that occurred to her, when her maid came in at the usual hour, and noticed how ill she looked. The woman was of so superstitious a temperament that it would have been in the last degree indiscreet to trust her with the truth. Mrs. Norbury merely remarked that she had not founds the bed quite to her liking, on account of the large size of it. She was accustomed at home, as her maid knew, to sleep in a small bed.

Informed of this objection later in the day the manager regretted that he could only offer to the lady the choice of one other bedchamber, numbered Thirty-eight, and situated immediately over the bedchamber which she desired to leave. Mrs. Norbury accepted the proposed change of quarters. She was now about to pass her second night in the room occupied in the old days of the palace by Baron Rivar.

Once more she fell asleep as usual. And, once more, the frightful dreams of the first night terrified her; following each other in the same succession. This time her nerves, already shaken, were not equal to the renewed torture of terror inflicted on them. She threw on her dressing-gown, and rushed out of her room in the middle of the night. The porter, alarmed by the banging of the door, met her hurrying headlong down the stairs, in search of the first human being she could find to keep her company.

Considerably surprised at this last new manifestation of the famous "English eccentricity," the man looked at the hotel register, and led the lady upstairs again to the room occupied by her maid. The maid was not asleep, and, more wonderful still, was not even undressed. She received her mistress quietly. When they were alone, and when Mrs. Norbury had, as a matter of necessity, taken her attendant into her confidence, the woman made a very strange reply.

"I have been asking about the hotel, at the servants' supper tonight," she said. "The valet of one of the gentlemen staying here has heard that the late Lord Montbarry was the last person who lived in the palace, before it was made into a hotel. The room he died in, ma'am, was the room you slept in last night. Your room tonight is the room just above it. I said nothing for fear of frightening you. For my own part, I have passed the night as you see, keeping my light in, and reading my Bible. In my opinion, no member of your family can hope to be happy or comfortable in this house."

"What do you mean?"

"Please to let me explain myself, ma'am. "When Mr. Henry Westwick was here (I have this from the valet, too) he occupied the room his brother died in (without knowing it), like you. For two nights he never closed his eyes. Without any reason for it (the valet heard him tell the gentlemen in the coffee-room) he could not sleep; he felt so low and so wretched in himself. And what is more, when daytime came, he couldn't even eat while he was under this roof.

"You may laugh at me, ma'am—but even a servant may draw

her own conclusions. It's my conclusion that something happened to my lord, which we none of us know about, when he died in this house. His ghost walks in torment until he can tell it—and the living persons related to him are the persons who feel he is near them. Those persons may yet see him in the time to come. Don't, pray don't stay any longer in this dreadful place! I wouldn't stay another night here myself—no, not for anything that could be offered me!"

Mrs. Norbury at once set her servant's mind at ease on this last point.

"I don't think about it as you do," she said, gravely. "But I should like to speak to my brother of what has happened. We will go back to Milan."

Some hours necessarily elapsed before they could leave the hotel, by the first train in the forenoon.

In that interval, Mrs. Norbury's maid found an opportunity of confidentially informing the valet of what had passed between her mistress and herself. The valet had other friends to whom he related the circumstances in his turn. In due course of time, the narrative, passing from mouth to mouth, reached the ears of the manager. He instantly saw that the credit of the hotel was in danger, unless something was done to retrieve the character of the room numbered Fourteen.

English travellers, well acquainted with the peerage of their native country, informed him that Henry Westwick and Mrs. Norbury were by no means the only members of the Montbarry family. Curiosity might bring more of them to the hotel, after hearing what had happened. The manager's ingenuity easily hit on the obvious means of misleading them, in this case. The numbers of all the rooms were enamelled in blue, on white china plates, screwed to the doors.

He ordered a new plate to be prepared, bearing the number, "13 A"; and he kept the room empty, after its tenant for the time being had gone away, until the plate was ready. He then renumbered the room; placing the removed Number Fourteen on the door of his own room (on the second floor), which, not being to let, had not previously been numbered at all. By this device, Number Fourteen disappeared at once and forever from the books of the hotel, as the number of a bedroom to let.

Having warned the servants to beware of gossiping with travellers, on the subject of the changed numbers, under penalty of being dismissed, the manager composed his mind with the reflection that he had done his duty to his employers. "Now," he thought to himself, with an excusable sense of triumph, "let the whole family come here if they like! The hotel is a match for them."

Chapter 18

Before the end of the week, the manager found himself in relations with "the family" once more. A telegram from Milan announced that Mr. Francis Westwick would arrive in Venice on the next day; and would be obliged if Number Fourteen, on the first floor, could be reserved for him, in the event of its being vacant at the time.

The manager paused to consider, before he issued his directions.

The renumbered room had been last let to a French gentleman. It would be occupied on the day of Mr. Francis Westwick's arrival, but it would be empty again on the day after. Would it be well to reserve the room for the special occupation of Mr. Francis? and when he had passed the night unsuspiciously and comfortably in "No. 13 A," to ask him in the presence of witnesses how he liked his bedchamber? In this case, if the reputation of the room happened to be called in question again, the answer would vindicate it, on the evidence of a member of the very family which had first given Number Fourteen a bad name. After a little reflection, the manager decided on trying the experiment, and directed that "13 A" should be reserved accordingly.

On the next day, Francis Westwick arrived in excellent spirits.

He had signed agreements with the most popular dancer in Italy; he had transferred the charge of Mrs. Norbury to his brother Henry, who had joined him in Milan; and he was now at full liberty to amuse himself by testing in every possible way the extraordinary influence exercised over his relatives by the new hotel. When his brother and sister first told him what their experience had been, he instantly declared that he would go to Venice in the interest of his theatre. The circumstances related to him contained invaluable hints for a ghost-drama. The title occurred to him in the railway: *The Haunted Hotel*. Post that in red letters six feet high, on a black ground, all over London—and trust the excitable public to crowd into the theatre!

Received with the politest attention by the manager, Francis met with a disappointment on entering the hotel. "Some mistake, sir. No such room on the first floor as Number Fourteen. The room bearing that number is on the second floor, and has been occupied by me, from the day when the hotel opened. Perhaps you meant number 13 A, on the first floor? It will be at your service tomorrow—a charming room. In the meantime, we will do the best we can for you, tonight."

A man who is the successful manager of a theatre is probably the last man in the civilized universe who is capable of being impressed with favourable opinions of his fellow-creatures. Francis privately set the manager down as a humbug, and the story about the numbering of the rooms as a lie.

On the day of his arrival, he dined by himself in the restaurant, before the hour of the *table d'hôte*, for the express purpose of questioning the waiter, without being overheard by anybody. The answer led him to the conclusion that "13 A" occupied the situation in the hotel which had been described by his brother and sister as the situation of "14." He asked next for the Visitors' List; and found that the French gentleman who then occupied "13 A," was the proprietor of a theatre in Paris, personally well known to him.

Was the gentleman then in the hotel? He had gone out, but would certainly return for the *table d'hôte*. When the public dinner was over, Francis entered the room, and was welcomed by his Parisian colleague, literally, with open arms. "Come and have a cigar in my room," said the friendly Frenchman. "I want to hear whether you have really engaged that woman at Milan or not." In this easy way, Francis found his opportunity of comparing the interior of the room with the description which he had heard of it at Milan.

Arriving at the door, the Frenchman bethought himself of his travelling companion. "My scene-painter is here with me," he said, "on the look- out for materials. An excellent fellow, who will take it as a kindness if we ask him to join us. I'll tell the porter to send him up when he comes in." He handed the key of his room to Francis. "I will be back in a minute. It's at the end of the corridor—13 A."

Francis entered the room alone. There were the decorations on the walls and the ceiling, exactly as they had been described to him! He had just time to perceive this at a glance, before his attention was diverted to himself and his own sensations, by a grotesquely disagreeable occurrence which took him completely by surprise.

He became conscious of a mysteriously offensive odour in the room, entirely new in his experience of revolting smells. It was composed (if such a thing could be) of two mingling exhalations, which were separately-discoverable exhalations nevertheless. This strange blending of odours consisted of something faintly and unpleasantly aromatic, mixed with another underlying smell, so unutterably sickening that he threw open the window, and put his head out into the fresh air, unable to endure the horribly infected atmosphere for a moment longer.

The French proprietor joined his English friend, with his cigar already lighted. He started back in dismay at a sight terrible to his countrymen in general—the sight of an open window. "You English people are perfectly mad on the subject of fresh air!" he exclaimed. "We shall catch our deaths of cold."

Francis turned, and looked at him in astonishment. "Are you really not aware of the smell there is in the room?" he asked.

"Smell!" repeated his brother-manager. "I smell my own good cigar. Try one yourself. And for heaven's sake shut the window!"

Francis declined the cigar by a sign. "Forgive me," he said. "I will leave you to close the window. I feel faint and giddy—I had better go out. "He put his handkerchief over his nose and mouth, and crossed the room to the door.

The Frenchman followed the movements of Francis, in such a state of bewilderment that he actually forgot to seize the opportunity of shutting out the fresh air. "Is it so nasty as that?" he asked, with a broad stare of amazement.

"Horrible! "Francis muttered behind his handkerchief. "I never smelled anything like it in my life!"

There was a knock at the door. The scene-painter appeared. His employer instantly asked him if he smelled. anything.

"I smell your cigar. Delicious! Give me one directly!"

"Wait a minute. Besides my cigar, do you smell anything else—vile, abominable, overpowering, indescribable, never-never-never-smelled before?"

The scene-painter appeared to be puzzled by the vehement energy of the language addressed to him. "The room is as fresh and sweet as a room can be," he answered. As he spoke, he looked back with astonishment at Francis Westwick, standing outside in the corridor, and eying the interior of the bedchamber with an expression of undisguised disgust.

The Parisian director approached his English colleague, and looked at him with grave and anxious scrutiny.

"You see, my friend, here are two of us, with as good noses as yours, who smell nothing. If you want evidence from more noses, look there!" He pointed to two little English girls, at play in the corridor. "The door of my room is wide open—and you know how fast a smell can travel. Now listen, while I appeal to these innocent noses, in the language of their own dismal island. My little loves, do you sniff a nasty smell here—ha?" The children burst out laughing, and answered emphatically, "No."

"My good Westwick," the Frenchman resumed, in his own language, "the conclusion is surely plain? There is something wrong, very wrong, with your own nose. I recommend you to see a medical man."

Having given that advice, he returned to his room, and shut out the horrid fresh air with a loud exclamation of relief. Francis left the hotel, by the lanes that led to the Square of St. Mark. The night-breeze soon revived him. He was able to light a cigar, and to think quietly over what had happened.

Chapter 19

Avoiding the crowd under the colonnades, Francis walked slowly up and down the noble open space of the square, bathed in the light of the rising moon.

Without being aware of it himself, he was a thorough materialist. The strange effect produced on him by the room—following on the other strange effects produced on the other relatives of his dead brother—exercised no perplexing influence over the mind of this sensible man.

"Perhaps," he reflected, "my temperament is more imaginative than I supposed it to be—and this is a trick played on me by my own fancy? Or, perhaps, my friend is right; something is physically amiss with me? I don't feel ill, certainly. But that is no safe criterion sometimes. I am not going to sleep in that abominable room tonight—I can well wait till tomorrow to decide whether I shall speak to a doctor or not. In the meantime, the hotel doesn't seem likely to supply me with the subject of a piece. A terrible smell from an invisible ghost is a perfectly new idea. But it has one drawback. If I realize it on the stage, I shall drive the audience out of the theatre."

As his strong common sense arrived at this facetious conclusion, he became aware of a lady, dressed entirely in black, who was observing him with marked attention. "Am I right in supposing you to be Mr. Francis Westwick?" the lady asked, at the moment when he looked at her.

"That is my name, madam. May I inquire to whom I have the honour of speaking?"

"We have only met once," she answered a little evasively, "when your late brother introduced me to the members of his family. I wonder if you have quite forgotten my big black eyes and my hideous complexion?" She lifted her veil as she spoke, and turned so that the moonlight rested on her face.

Francis recognized at a glance the woman of all others whom he most cordially disliked—the widow of his dead brother, the first Lord Montbarry. He frowned as he looked at her. His experience on the stage, gathered at innumerable rehearsals with actresses who had sorely tried his temper, had accustomed him to speak roughly to women who were distasteful to him. "I remember you," he said. "I thought you were in America!"

She. took no notice of his ungracious tone and manner; she simply stopped him when he lifted his hat, and turned to leave her.

"Let me walk with you for a few minutes," she quietly replied. "I have something to say to you."

He showed her his cigar. "I am smoking," he said.

"I don't mind smoking."

After that, there was nothing to be done (short of downright brutality) but to yield. He did it with the worst possible grace. "Well?" he resumed. "What do you want of me?"

"You shall hear directly, Mr. Westwick. Let me first tell you what my position is. I am alone in the world. To the loss of my husband has now been added another bereavement, the loss of my companion in America, my brother—Baron Rivar."

The reputation of the Baron, and the doubt which scandal had thrown on his assumed relationship to the Countess, were well known to Francis. "Shot in a gambling-saloon?" he asked brutally.

"The question is a perfectly natural one on your part," she said, with the impenetrably ironical manner which she could assume on certain occasions. "As a native of horseracing England, you belong to a nation of gamblers. My brother died no extraordinary death, Mr. Westwick. He sank, with many other unfortunate people, under a fever prevalent in a Western city which we happened to visit. The calamity of his loss made the United States unendurable to me. I left by the first steamer that sailed from New York—a French vessel which brought me to Havre. I continued my lonely journey to the South of France. And then I went on to Venice."

"What does all this matter to me?" Francis thought to himself. She paused, evidently expecting him to say something. "So you have come to Venice?" he said carelessly. "Why?"

"Because I couldn't help it," she answered.

Francis looked at her with cynical curiosity.

"That sounds odd," he remarked. "Why couldn't you help it?"

"Women are accustomed to act on impulse," she explained. "Suppose we say that an impulse has directed my journey? And yet, this is the last place in the world that I wish to find myself in. Associations that I detest are connected with it in my mind. If I had a will of my own, I would never see it again. I hate Venice. As you see, however, I am here. When did you meet with such an unreasonable woman before? Never, I am sure!" She stopped, eyed him for a moment, and suddenly altered her tone. "When is Miss Agnes Lockwood expected to be in Venice?" she asked.

It was not easy to throw Francis off his balance, but that extraordinary question did it, "How the devil did you know that Miss Lockwood was coming to Venice?" he exclaimed.

She laughed—a bitter mocking laugh. "Say, I guessed it!"

Something in her tone, or perhaps something in the audacious defiance of her eyes as they rested on him, roused the quick temper that was in Francis Westwick. "Lady Montbarry—!" he began.

"Stop there!" she interposed. "Your brother Stephen's wife calls herself Lady Montbarry now. I share my title with no woman. Call me by my name before I committed the fatal mistake of marrying your brother. Address me, if you please, as Countess Narona."

"Countess Narona," Francis resumed, "if your object in claiming my acquaintance is to mystify me, you have come to the wrong man. Speak plainly, or permit me to wish you good-evening."

"If your object is to keep Miss Lockwood's arrival in Venice a secret," she retorted, "speak plainly, Mr. Westwick, on your side, and say so."

Her intention was evidently to irritate him; and she succeeded. "Nonsense!" he broke out petulantly. "My brother's travelling arrangements are secrets to nobody. He brings Miss Lockwood here, with Lady Montbarry and the children. As you seem so well informed, perhaps you know why she is coming to Venice?"

The Countess had suddenly become grave and thoughtful. She made no reply. The two strangely associated companions, having reached one extremity of the square, were now standing before the church of St. Mark. The moonlight was bright enough to show the architecture of the grand cathedral in its wonderful variety of detail. Even the pigeons of St. Mark were visible, in dark closely packed rows, roosting in the archways of the great entrance doors.

"I never saw the old church look so beautiful by moonlight," the Countess said quietly; speaking, not to Francis, but to herself. "Goodbye, St. Mark's by moonlight! I shall not see you again."

She turned away from the church, and saw Francis listening to her with wondering looks. "No," she resumed, placidly picking up the lost thread of the conversation, "I don't know why Miss Lockwood is coming here, I only know that we are to meet in Venice."

"By previous appointment?"

"By Destiny," she answered, with her head on her breast, and her eyes on the ground. Francis burst out laughing. "Or, if you like it better," she instantly resumed, "by what fools call Chance."

Francis answered easily, out of the depths of his strong common sense. "Chance seems to be taking a queer way of bringing the meeting about," he said. "We have all arranged to meet at the Palace Hotel. How is it that your name is not on the Visitors' List? Destiny ought to have brought you to the Palace Hotel too."

She abruptly pulled down her veil. "Destiny may do that yet!" she said. "The Palace Hotel?" she repeated, speaking once more to herself. "The old hell, transformed into the new purgatory. The place itself! *Jesu Maria*! the place itself!" She paused and laid her hand on her companion's arm. "Perhaps Miss 'Lockwood is not going there with the rest of you?" she burst out with sudden eagerness. "Are you positively sure she will be at the hotel?"

"Positively! Haven't I told you that Miss Lockwood travels with Lord and Lady Montbarry? and don't you know that she is a member of the family? You will have to move, Countess, to our hotel."

She was perfectly impenetrable to the bantering tone in which he spoke. "Yes," she said faintly, "I shall have to move to your hotel." Her hand was still on his arm—he could feel her shivering from head to foot while she spoke. Heartily as he disliked and distrusted her, the common instinct of humanity obliged him to ask if she felt cold.

"Yes," she said. "Cold and faint."

"Cold and faint, Countess, on such a night as this?"

"The night has nothing to do with it, Mr. Westwick. How do you suppose the criminal feels on the scaffold, while the hangman is putting the rope round his neck? Cold and faint, too, I should think. Excuse my grim fancy. You see, Destiny has got the rope round my neck—and I feel it."

She looked about her. They were at that moment close to the famous cafe known as "Florian's." "Take me in there," she said; "I must have something to revive me. You had better not hesitate. You are interested in reviving me. I have not said what I wanted to say to you yet. It's business, and it's connected with your theatre."

Wondering inwardly what she could possibly want with his theatre, Francis reluctantly yielded to the necessities of the situation, and took her into the cafe. He found a quiet corner in which they could take their places without attracting notice. "What will you have?" he inquired resignedly.

She gave her own orders to the waiter, without troubling him to speak for her. "*Maraschino*. And a pot of tea." The waiter stared; Francis stared. The tea was a novelty (in connection with *maraschino*) to both of them. Careless whether she surprised them or not, she instructed the waiter, when her directions had been complied with, to pour a large wine-glassful of the liqueur into a tumbler, and to fill it up from the teapot.

"I can't do it for myself," she remarked, "my hand trembles so." She drank the strange mixture eagerly, hot as it was. "*Maraschino* punch—will you taste some of it?" she said. "I inherit the discovery of this drink. When your English Queen Caroline was on the Continent, my mother was attached to her Court. That much injured Royal Person invented, in her happier hours, *maraschino* punch. Fondly attached to her gracious mistress, my mother shared her tastes. And I, in my turn, learned from my mother. Now, Mr. Westwick, suppose I tell you what my business is. You are manager of a theatre. Do you want a new play?"

"I always want a new play—provided it's a good one."

"And you pay, if it's a good one?"

"I pay liberally—in my own interests."

"If I write the play, will you read it?"

Francis hesitated. "What has put writing a play into your head?" he asked.

"Mere accident," she answered. "I had once occasion to tell my late brother of a visit which I paid to Miss Lockwood, when I was last in England. He took no interest in what happened at the interview, but something struck him in my way of relating it. He said, 'You describe what passed between you and the lady with the point and contrast of good stage dialogue. You have the dramatic instinct—try if you can write a play. You might make money.' That put it into my head."

Those last words seemed to startle Francis. "Surely you don't want money!" he exclaimed.

"I always want money. My tastes are expensive. I have nothing but my poor little four hundred a year—and the wreck that is left of the other money: about two hundred pounds in circular notes—no more."

Francis knew that she was referring to the ten thousand pounds paid by the insurance offices. "All those thousands gone already!" he exclaimed.

She blew a little puff of air over her fingers. "Gone like that!" she answered coolly.

"Baron Rivar?"

She looked at him with a flash of anger in her hard black eyes.

"My affairs are my own secret, Mr. Westwick. I have made you a proposal—and you have not answered me yet. Don't say No, without thinking first. Remember what a life mine has been. I have seen more of the world than most people, playwrights included. I have had strange adventures; I have heard remarkable stories; I have observed; I have remembered. Are there no materials, here in my head, for writing a play—if the opportunity is granted to me?" She waited a moment, and suddenly repeated her strange question about Agnes.

"When is Miss Lockwood expected to be in Venice?"

"What has that to do with your new play, Countess?"

The Countess appeared to feel some difficulty in giving that question its fit reply. She mixed another tumblerful of the *maraschino* punch, and drank one good half of it before she spoke again.

"It has everything to do with my new play," was all she said. "Answer me." Francis answered her.

"Miss Lockwood may be here in a week. Or, for all I know to the contrary, sooner than that."

"Very well. If I am a living woman and a free woman in a week's time—or if I am in possession of my senses in a week's time (don't interrupt me; I know what I am talking about)—I shall have a sketch or outline of my play ready, as a specimen of what I can do. Once again, will you read it?"

"I will certainly read it. But, Countess, I don't understand—"

She held up her hand for silence, and finished the second tumbler of *maraschino* punch.

"I am a living enigma—and you want to know the right reading of me," she said. "Here is the reading, as your English phrase goes, in a nutshell. There is a foolish idea in the minds of many persons that the natives of the warm climates are imaginative people. There never was a greater mistake. You will find no such unimaginative people anywhere as you find in Italy, Spain, Greece, and the other Southern countries.

"To anything fanciful, to anything spiritual, their minds are deaf and blind by nature. Now and then, in the course of centuries, a great genius springs up among them; and he is the exception which proves the rule. Now see! I, though I am no genius—I am, in my little way (as I suppose), an exception too. To my sorrow, I have some of that imagination which is so common among the English and the Germans—so rare among the Italians, the Spaniards, and the rest of them! And what is the result? I think it has become a disease in me. I am filled with presentiments which make this wicked life of mine one long terror to. me. It doesn't matter, just now, what they are.

"Enough that they absolutely govern me—they drive me over land and sea at their own horrible will; they are in me, and torturing me, at this moment! Why don't I resist them? Ha! but I do resist them. I am trying (with the help of the good punch) to resist them now. At intervals I cultivate the difficult virtue of sound sense. Sometimes, sound sense makes a hopeful woman of me.

"At one time, I had the hope that what seemed reality to me was only mad delusion, after all—I even asked the question of an English doctor! At other times, other sensible doubts of myself beset me. Never mind dwelling on them now—it always ends in the old terrors and superstitions taking possession of me again. In a week's time, I shall know whether Destiny does indeed decide my future for me, or whether I decide it for myself. In the last case, my resolution is to absorb this self-tormenting fancy of mine in the occupation that I have told you of already. Do you understand me a little better now? And, our business being settled, dear Mr. Westwick, shall we get out of this hot room into the nice cool air again."

They rose to leave the cafe. Francis privately concluded that the *maraschino* punch offered the only discoverable explanation of what the Countess had said to him.

Chapter 20

"Shall I see you again?" she asked, as she held out her hand to take leave. "It is quite understood between us, I suppose, about the play?"

Francis recalled his extraordinary experience of that evening in the re-numbered room. "My stay in Venice is uncertain," he replied. "If you have anything more to say about this dramatic venture of yours, it may be as well to say it now. Have you decided on a subject already? I know the public taste in England better than you—do I might save you some waste of time and trouble, if you have not chosen your subject wisely."

"I don't care what subject I write about, so long as I write," she answered carelessly. "If you have got a subject in your head, give it to me. I answer for the characters and the dialogue."

"You answer for the characters and the dialogue," Francis repeated. "That's a bold way of speaking for a beginner! I wonder if I should shake your sublime confidence in yourself, if I suggested the most ticklish subject to handle which is known to the stage? What do you say, Countess, to entering the lists with Shakespeare, and trying a drama with a ghost in it? A true story, mind! founded on events in this very city in which you and I are interested."

She caught him by the arm, and drew him away from the crowded colonnade into the solitary middle space of the square. "Now tell me!" she said eagerly. "Here, where nobody is near us. How am I interested in it? How? how?"

Still holding his arm, she shook him in her impatience to hear the coming disclosure. For a moment he hesitated. Thus far, amused by her ignorant belief in herself, he had merely spoken in jest. Now, for the first time, impressed by her irresistible earnestness, he began to consider what he was about from a more serious point of view. With her knowledge of all that had passed in the old palace, before its transformation into a hotel, it was surely possible that she might suggest some explanation of what had happened to his brother and sister, and himself.

Or, failing to do this, she might accidentally reveal some event in her own experience which, acting as a hint to a competent dramatist, might prove to be the making of a play. The prosperity of his theatre was his one serious object in life. "I may be on the trace of another *Corsican Brothers*," he thought. "A new piece of that sort would be ten thousand pounds in my pocket, at least."

With these motives (worthy of the single-hearted devotion to dramatic business which made Francis a successful manager) he related, without further hesitation, what his own experience had been, and what the experience of his relatives had been, in the haunted hotel. He even described the outbreak of superstitious terror which had escaped Mrs. Norbury's ignorant maid.

"Sad stuff, if you look at it reasonably," he remarked. "But there is something dramatic in the notion of the ghostly influence making itself felt by the relations in succession, as they one after another enter the fatal room—until the one chosen relative comes who will see the Unearthly Creature, and know the terrible truth. Material for a play, Countess—first-rate material for a play!"

There he paused. She neither moved nor spoke. He stooped and looked closer at her.

What impression had he produced? It was an impression which his utmost ingenuity had failed to anticipate. She stood by his side—just as she had stood before Agnes when her question about Ferrari was plainly answered at last—like a woman turned to stone. Her eyes were vacant and rigid; all the life in her face had faded out of it. Francis took her by the hand. Her hand was as cold as the pavement that they were standing on. He asked her if she was ill.

Not a muscle in her moved. He might as well have spoken to the dead.

"Surely," he said, "you are not foolish enough to take what I have been telling you seriously?"

Her lips moved slowly. As it seemed, she was making an effort to speak to him.

"Louder," he said. "I can't hear you."

She struggled to recover possession of herself. A faint light began to soften the dull cold stare of her eyes. In a moment more she spoke so that he could hear her.

"I never thought of the other world," she murmured, in low dull tones, like a woman talking in her sleep.

Her mind had gone back to the day of her last memorable interview with Agnes; she was slowly recalling the confession that had escaped her, the warning words which she had spoken at that past time. Necessarily incapable of understanding this, Francis looked at her in perplexity. She went on in the same dull vacant tone, steadily following out her own train of thought, with her heedless eyes on his face, and her wandering mind far away from him.

"I said some trifling event would bring us together the next time. I was wrong. No trifling event will bring us together. I said I might be the person who told her what had become of Ferrari, if she forced me to it. Shall I feel some other influence than hers? Will he force me to it? When she sees him, shall I see him too?"

Her head sank a little; her heavy eyelids dropped slowly; she heaved a long low weary sigh. Francis put her arm in his, and made an attempt to rouse her.

"Come, Countess, you are weary and overwrought. We have had enough talking tonight. Let me see you safe back to your hotel. Is it far from here?"

She started when he moved, and obliged her to move with him, as if he had suddenly awakened her out of a deep sleep.

"Not far," she said faintly. "The old hotel on the quay. My mind's in a strange state; I have forgotten the name."

"Danieli's?"

"Yes!"

He led her on slowly. She accompanied him in silence as

far as the end of the *Piazzetta*. There, when the full view of the moonlit lagoon revealed itself, she stopped him as he turned toward the *Riva degli Schiavoni*. "I have something to ask you. I want to wait and think."

She recovered her lost idea, after a long pause.

"Are you going to sleep in the room tonight?" she asked.

He told her that another traveller was in possession of the room that night. "But the manager has reserved it for me tomorrow," he added, "if I wish to have it."

"No," she said. "You must give it up."

"To whom?"

"To me!"

He started. "After what I have told you, do you really wish to sleep in that room tomorrow night?"

"I must sleep in it."

"Are you not afraid?"

"I am horribly afraid."

"So I should have thought, after what I have observed in you tonight. "Why should you take the room? you are not obliged to occupy it, unless you like."

"I was not obliged to go to Venice, when I left America," she answered. "And yet I came here. I must take the room, and keep the room, until—" She broke off at those words. "Never mind the rest," she said. "It doesn't interest you."

It was useless to dispute with her. Francis changed the subject. "We can do nothing tonight," he said. "I will call on you tomorrow morning, and hear what you think of it then."

They moved on again to the hotel. As they approached the door, Francis asked if she was staying in Venice under her own name.

She shook her head. "As your brother's widow, I am known here. As Countess Narona, I am known here. I want to be unknown, this time, to strangers in Venice; I am travelling under a common English name." She hesitated, and stood still. "What has come to me?" she muttered to herself. "Some things I remember; and some I forget. I forgot Danieli's—and now I forget my English name." She drew him hurriedly into the hall of the hotel, on the wall of which hung a list of visitors' names. Running her finger slowly down the list, she pointed to the English name that she had assumed—"Mrs. James."

"Remember that when you call tomorrow," she said. "My head is heavy. Goodnight."

Francis went back to his own hotel, wondering what the events of the next day would bring forth. A new turn in his affairs had taken place in his absence. As he crossed the hall, he was requested by one of the servants to walk into the private office. The manager was waiting there with a gravely preoccupied manner, as if he had something serious to say. He regretted to hear that Mr. Francis Westwick had, like other members of the family, discovered mysterious sources of discomfort in the new hotel. He had been informed in strict confidence of Mr. Westwick's extraordinary objection to the atmosphere of the bedroom upstairs. Without presuming to discuss the matter, he must beg to be excused from reserving the room for Mr. Westwick after what had happened.

Francis answered sharply, a little ruffled by the tone in which the manager had spoken to him. "I might, very possibly, have declined to sleep in the room, if you had reserved it," he said. "Do you wish me to leave the hotel?"

The manager saw the error that he had committed, and hastened to repair it. "Certainly not, sir! We will do our best to make you comfortable while you stay with us. I beg your pardon, if I have said anything to offend you. The reputation of an establishment like this is a matter of very serious importance. May I hope that you will do us the great favour to say nothing about what has happened upstairs? The two French gentlemen have kindly promised to keep it a secret."

This apology left Francis no polite alternative but to grant the manager's request. "There is an end to the Countess's wild scheme," he thought to himself, as he retired for the night. "So much the better for the Countess!"

He rose late the next morning. Inquiring for his Parisian

friends, he was informed that both the French gentlemen had left for Milan. As he crossed the hall, on his way to the restaurant, he noticed the head porter chalking the numbers of the rooms on some articles of luggage which were waiting to go upstairs. One trunk attracted his attention by the extraordinary number of old travelling labels left on it.

The porter was marking it at the moment—and the number was, "13 A." Francis instantly looked at the card fastened on the lid. It bore the common English name, "Mrs. James!" He at once inquired about the lady. She had arrived early that morning, and she was then in the Reading Room. Looking into the room, he discovered a lady in it alone. Advancing a little nearer, he found himself face to face with the Countess.

She was seated in a dark corner, with her head down and her arms crossed over her bosom. "Yes," she said, in a tone of weary impatience, before Francis could speak to her. "I thought it best not to wait for you—I determined to get here before anybody else could take the room"

"Have you taken it for long?" Francis asked.

"You told me Miss Lockwood would be here in a week's time. I have taken it for a week."

"What has Miss Lockwood to do with it?"

"She has everything to do with it—she must sleep in the room. I shall give the room up to her when she comes here."

Francis began to understand the superstitious purpose that she had in view. "Are you (an educated woman) really of the same opinion as my sister's maid!" he exclaimed. "Assuming your absurd superstition to be a serious thing, you are taking the wrong means to prove it true. If I and my brother and sister have seen nothing, how should Agnes Lockwood discover what was not revealed to Us? She is only distantly related to the Montbarrys—she is only our cousin."

"She was nearer to the heart of the Montbarry who is dead than any of you," the Countess answered, sternly. "To the last day of his life, my miserable husband repented his desertion of her. She will see what none of you have seen—she shall have the room."

Francis listened, utterly at a loss to account for the motives that animated her. "I don't see what interest you have in trying this extraordinary experiment," he said.

"It is my interest not to try it! It is my interest to fly from Venice, and never set eyes on Agnes Lockwood or any of your family again!"

"What prevents you from doing that?"

She started to her feet and looked at him wildly. "I know no more what prevents me than you do!" she burst out. "Some will that is stronger than mine drives me on to my destruction, in spite of my own self!" She suddenly sat down again and waved her hand for him to go. "Leave me," she said. "Leave me to my thoughts."

Francis left her, firmly persuaded by this time that she was out of her senses. For the rest of the day he saw nothing of her. The night, so far as he knew, passed quietly. The next morning he breakfasted early, determining to wait in the restaurant for the appearance of the Countess. She came in and ordered her breakfast quietly, looking dull and worn and self-absorbed, as she had looked when he last saw her. He hastened to her table, and asked if anything had happened in the night.

"Nothing," she answered.

"You have rested as well as usual?"

"Quite as well as usual. Have you had any letters this morning? Have you heard when she is coming?"

"I have had no letters. Are you really going to stay here? Has your experience of last night not altered the opinion which you expressed to me yesterday?"

"Not in the least."

The momentary gleam of animation which had crossed her face when she questioned him about Agnes, died out of it again when he answered her. She looked, she spoke, she eat her breakfast, with a vacant resignation, like a woman who had done with hopes, done with interests, done with everything but the mechanical movements and instincts of life.

Francis went out, on the customary travellers' pilgrimage to the shrines of Titian and Tintoret. After some hours of absence, he found a letter waiting for him when he got back to the hotel. It was written by his brother Henry, and it recommended him to return to Milan immediately. The proprietor of a French theatre, recently arrived from Venice, was trying to induce the famous dancer whom Francis had engaged to break faith with him and accept a higher salary.

Having made this startling announcement, Henry proceeded to inform his brother that Lord and Lady Montbarry, with Agnes and the children, would arrive in Venice in three days more. "They know nothing of our adventures at the hotel," Henry wrote; "and they have telegraphed to the manager for the accommodation that they want. There would be something absurdly superstitious in our giving them a warning which would frighten the ladies and children out of the best hotel in Venice. We shall be a strong party this time—too strong a party for ghosts! I shall meet the travellers on their arrival, of course, and try my luck again at what you call the Haunted Hotel. Arthur Barville and his wife have already got as far on their way as Trent; and two of the lady's relations have arranged to accompany them on the journey to Venice."

Naturally indignant at the conduct of his Parisian colleague, Francis made his preparations for returning to Milan by the train of that day.

On his way out, he asked the manager if his brother's telegram had been received. The telegram had arrived, and, to the surprise of Francis, the rooms were already reserved. "I thought you would refuse to let any more of the family into the house," he said, satirically. The manager answered (with the due dash of respect) in the same tone. "Number 13 A is safe, sir, in the occupation of a stranger. I am the servant of the Company; and I dare not turn money out of the hotel."

Hearing this, Francis said goodbye—and said nothing more. He was ashamed to acknowledge it to himself, but he felt an irresistible curiosity to know what would happen when Agnes arrived at the hotel. Besides, "Mrs. James" had reposed a confidence in him. He got into his gondola, respecting the confidence of "Mrs. James."

Toward evening on the third day, Lord Montbarry and his travelling companions arrived, punctual to their appointment.

"Mrs. James," sitting at the window of her room watching for them, saw the new lord land from the gondola first. He handed his wife to the steps. The three children were next committed to his care. Last of all, Agnes appeared in the little black doorway of the gondola cabin, and, taking Lord Montbarry's hand, passed in her turn to the steps. She wore no veil. As she ascended to the door of the hotel, the Countess (eying her through an opera-glass) noticed that she paused to look at the outside of the building, and that her face was very pale.

Chapter 21

Lord and Lady Montbarry were received by the housekeeper; the manager being absent for a day or two on business connected with the affairs of the hotel.

The rooms reserved for the travellers on the first floor were three in number; consisting of two bedrooms opening into each other, and communicating on the left with a drawing-room. Complete so far, the arrangements proved to be less satisfactory in reference to the third bedroom required for Agnes and for the eldest daughter of Lord Montbarry, who usually slept with her on their travels. The bedchamber on the right of the drawing-room was already occupied by an English widow lady. Other bedchambers at the other end of the corridor were also let in every case.

There was accordingly no alternative but to place at the disposal of Agnes a comfortable room on the second floor. Lady Montbarry vainly complained of this separation of one of the members of her travelling party from the rest. The housekeeper politely hinted that it was impossible for her to ask other travellers to give up their rooms. She could only express her regret, and assure Miss Lockwood that her bedchamber on the second floor was one of the best rooms in that part of the hotel.

On the retirement of the housekeeper, Lady Montbarry noticed that Agnes had seated herself apart, feeling apparently no interest in the question of the bedrooms. Was she ill? No; she felt a little unnerved by the railway journey, and that was all. Hearing this, Lord Montbarry proposed that she should go out with him, and try the experiment of half an hour's walk in the cool evening air. Agnes gladly accepted the suggestion. They directed their steps toward the square of St. Mark, so as to enjoy the breeze blowing over the lagoon.

It was the first visit of Agnes to Venice. The fascination of the wonderful city of the waters exerted its full influence over her sensitive nature. The proposed half-hour of the walk had passed away, and was fast expanding to half an hour more, before Lord Montbarry could persuade his companion to remember that dinner was waiting for them. As they returned, passing under the colonnade, neither of them noticed a lady in deep mourning, loitering in the open space of the square. She started as she recognized Agnes walking with the new Lord Montbarry-hesitated for a moment—and then followed them, at a discreet distance, back to the hotel.

Lady Montbarry received Agnes in high spirits—with news of an event which had happened in her absence.

She had not left the hotel more than ten minutes, before a little note in pencil was brought to Lady Montbarry by the housekeeper. The writer proved to be no less a person than the widow lady who occupied the room on the other side of the drawing-room, which her ladyship had vainly hoped to secure for Agnes. Writing under the name of Mrs. James, the polite widow explained that she had heard from the housekeeper of the disappointment experienced by Lady Montbarry in the matter of the rooms.

Mrs. James was quite alone; and as long as her bedchamber was airy and comfortable, it mattered nothing to her whether she slept on the first or the second floor of the house. She had accordingly much pleasure in proposing to change rooms with Miss Lockwood. Her luggage had already been removed, and Miss Lockwood had only to take possession of the room (Number 13 A), which was now entirely at her disposal.

"I immediately proposed to see Mrs. James," Lady Montbarry continued, "and to thank her personally for her extreme kindness. But I was informed that she had gone out, without leaving word at what hour she might be expected to return. I have written a little note of thanks, saying that we hope to have the pleasure of personally expressing our sense of Mrs. James's courtesy tomorrow. In the meantime, Agnes, I have ordered your boxes to be removed downstairs. Go!—and judge for yourself, my dear, if that good lady has not given up to you the prettiest room in the house!"

With those words, Lady Montbarry left Miss Lockwood to make a hasty toilet for dinner.

The new room at once produced a favourable impression on Agnes. The large window, opening into a balcony, commanded an admirable view of the canal. The decorations on the walls and ceiling were skilfully copied from the exquisitely graceful designs of Raphael in the Vatican. The massive wardrobe possessed compartments of unusual size, in which double the number of dresses that Agnes possessed might have been conveniently hung at full length.

In the inner corner of the room, near the head of the bedstead, there was a recess which had been turned into a little dressing-room, and which opened by a second door on the inferior staircase of the hotel, commonly used by the servants. Noticing these aspects of the room at a glance, Agnes made the necessary change in her dress, as quickly as possible. On her way back to the drawing-room she was addressed by a chambermaid in the corridor who asked for her key. "I will put your room tidy for the night, miss," the woman said, "and I will then bring the key back to you in the drawing-room."

While the chambermaid was at her work, a solitary lady, loitering about the corridor of the second story, was watching her over the banisters. After a while, the maid appeared, with her pail in her hand, leaving the room by way of the dressing-room and the back stairs. As she passed out of sight, the lady on the second floor (no other, it is needless to add, than the Countess herself), ran swiftly down the stairs, entered the bedchamber by the principal door, and hid herself in the empty side compartment of the wardrobe. The chambermaid returned, completed her work, locked the door of the dressing-room on the inner side, locked the principal entrance-door on leaving the room, and returned the key to Agnes in the drawing-room.

The travellers were just sitting down to their late dinner, when one of the children noticed that Agnes was not wearing her watch. Had she left it in her bedchamber in the hurry of changing her dress? She rose from the table at once in search of her watch; Lady Montbarry advising her, as she went out, to see to the security of her bedchamber, in the event of their being thieves in the house. Agnes found her watch, forgotten on the toilet table, as she had anticipated. Before leaving the room again she acted on Lady Montbarry's advice, and tried the key in the lock of the dressing-room door. It was properly secured. She left the bedchamber, locking the main door behind her.

Immediately on her departure, the Countess, oppressed by the confined air in the wardrobe, ventured on stepping out of her hiding-place into the empty room.

Entering the dressing-room, she listened at the door, until the silence outside informed her that the corridor was empty. Upon this, she unlocked the door, and, passing out, closed it again softly; leaving it to all appearance (when viewed on the inner side) as carefully secured as Agnes had seen it when she tried the key in the lock with her own hand.

While the Montbarrys were still at dinner, Henry Westwick joined them, arriving from Milan.

When he entered the room, and again when he advanced to shake hands with her, Agnes was conscious of a latent feeling which secretly reciprocated Henry's unconcealed pleasure on meeting her again. For a moment only, she returned his look; and in that moment her own observation told her that she had silently encouraged him to hope. She saw it in the sudden glow of happiness which overspread his face; and she confusedly took refuge in the usual conventional inquiries relating to the relatives whom he had left at Milan.

Taking his place at the table, Henry gave a most amusing account of the position of his brother Francis between the mercenary opera-dancer on one side, and the unscrupulous manager of the French theatre on the other. Matters had proceeded to such extremities, that the law had been called on to interfere, and had decided the dispute in favour of Francis.

On winning the victory the English manager had at once left Milan, recalled to London by the affairs of his theatre. He was accompanied on the journey back, as he had been accompanied on the journey out, by his sister. Resolved, after passing two nights of terror in the Venetian hotel, never to enter it again, Mrs. Norbury asked to be excused from appearing at the family festival on the ground of ill-health. At her age, travelling fatigued her, and she was glad to take advantage of her brother's escort to return to England.

While the talk of the dinner-table flowed easily onward, the evening-time advanced to night—and it became necessary to think of sending the children to bed.

As Agnes rose to leave the room, accompanied by the eldest girl, she observed with surprise that Henry's manner suddenly changed. He looked serious and preoccupied; and when his niece wished him goodnight, he abruptly said to her, "Marian, I want to know what part of the hotel you sleep in?" Marian, puzzled by the question, answered that she was going to sleep as usual, with "Aunt Agnes."

Not satisfied with that reply, Henry next inquired whether the bedroom was near the rooms occupied by the other members of the travelling party. Answering for the child, and wondering what Henry's object could possibly be, Agnes mentioned the polite sacrifice made to her convenience by Mrs. James. "Thanks to that lady's kindness, "she said," Marian and I are only on the other side of the drawing-room."

Henry made no remark; he looked incomprehensibly discontented as he opened the door for Agnes and her companion to pass out. After wishing them goodnight, he waited in the corridor until he saw them enter the fatal corner-room—and then he called abruptly to his brother, "Come out, Stephen, and let us smoke!"

As soon as the two brothers were at liberty to speak together privately, Henry explained the motive which had led to his strange inquiries about the bedrooms. Francis had informed him of the meeting with the Countess at Venice, and of all that had followed it; and Henry now carefully repeated the narrative to his brother in all its details. "I am not satisfied," he added, "about that woman's purpose in giving up her room. Without alarming the ladies by telling them what I have just told you, can you not warn Agnes to be careful in securing her door?"

Lord Montbarry replied, that the warning had been already given by his wife, and that Agnes might be trusted to take good care of herself and her little bed-fellow. For the rest, be looked upon the story of the Countess and her superstitions as a piece of theatrical exaggeration, amusing enough in itself, but unworthy of a moment's serious attention.

While the gentlemen were absent from the hotel, the room which had been already associated with so many startling circumstances became the scene of another strange event in which Lady Montbarry's eldest child was concerned.

Little Marian had been got ready for bed as usual, and had (so far) taken hardly any notice of the new room. As she knelt down to say her prayers, she happened to look up at that part of the ceiling above her which was just over the head of the bed. The next instant she alarmed Agnes by starting to her feet with a cry of terror, and pointing to a small brown spot on one of the white panelled spaces of the carved ceiling. "It's a spot of blood!" the child exclaimed. "Take me away! I won't sleep here!"

Seeing plainly that it would be useless to reason with her while she was in the room, Agnes hurriedly wrapped Marian in a dressing-gown, and carried her back to her mother in the drawing-room. Here, the ladies did their best to soothe and reassure the trembling girl. The effort proved to be useless; the impression that had been produced on the young and sensitive mind was not to be removed by persuasion.

Marian could give no explanation of the panic of terror that had seized her. She was quite unable to say why the spot on the ceiling looked like the colour of a spot of blood. She only knew that she should die of terror if she saw it again. Under these circumstances, but one alternative was left. It was arranged that the child should pass the night in the room occupied by her two younger sisters and the nurse.

In half an hour more, Marian was peacefully asleep with her arm round her sister's neck. Lady Montbarry went back with Agnes to her room to see the spot on the ceiling which had so strangely frightened the child. It was so small as to be only just perceptible, and it had in all probability been caused by the carelessness of a workman, or by a dripping from water accidentally spilled on the floor of the room above.

"I really cannot understand why Marian should place such a shocking interpretation on such a trifling thing," Lady Montbarry remarked.

"I suspect the nurse is in some way answerable for what has happened," Agnes suggested. "She may quite possibly have been telling Marian some tragic nursery story which has left its mischievous impression behind it. Persons in her position are sadly ignorant of the danger of exciting a child's imagination. You had better caution the nurse tomorrow."

Lady Montbarry looked round the room with admiration. "Is it not prettily decorated?" she said. "I suppose, Agnes, you don't mind sleeping here by yourself?"

Agnes laughed. "I feel so tired," she replied, "that I was thinking of bidding you goodnight, instead of going back to the drawing-room."

Lady Montbarry turned toward the door. "I see your jewel-case on the table," she resumed. "Don't forget to lock the other door there, in the dressing-room."

"I have already seen to it, and tried the key myself," said Agnes. "Can I be of any use to you before I go to bed?"

"No, my dear, thank you; I feel sleepy enough to follow your example. Good night, Agnes—and pleasant dreams on your first night in Venice."

CHAPTER 22

Having closed and secured the door on Lady Montbarry's departure, Agnes put on her dressing-gown, and, turning to her open boxes, began the business of unpacking. In the hurry of making her toilet for dinner, she had taken the first dress that lay uppermost in the trunk, and had thrown her travelling costume on the bed. She now opened the doors of the wardrobe for the first time, and began to hang her dresses on the hooks in the large compartment on one side.

After a few minutes only of this occupation, she grew weary of it, and decided on leaving the trunks as they were, until the next morning. The oppressive south wind, which had blown throughout the day, still prevailed at night. The atmosphere of the room felt close; Agnes threw a shawl over her head and shoulders, and, opening the window, stepped into the balcony to look at the view.

The night was heavy and overcast: nothing could be distinctly seen. The canal beneath the window looked like a black gulf; the opposite houses were barely visible as a row of shadows, dimly relieved against the starless and moonless sky. At long intervals, the warning cry of a belated gondolier was just audible, as he turned the corner of a distant canal, and called to invisible boats which might be approaching him in the darkness. Now and then, the nearer dip of an oar in the water told of the viewless passage of other gondolas bringing guests back to the hotel. Excepting these rare sounds, the mysterious night-silence of Venice was literally the silence of the grave.

Leaning on the parapet of the balcony, Agnes looked vacantly into the black void beneath. Her thoughts reverted to the miserable man who had broken his pledged faith to her, and who had died in that house. Some change seemed to have come over her since her arrival in Venice; some new influence appeared to be at work. For the first time in her experience of herself, compassion and regret were not the only emotions aroused in her by the remembrance of the dead Montbarry.

A keen sense of the wrong that she had suffered, never yet felt by that gentle and forgiving nature, was felt by it now. She found herself thinking of the bygone days of her humiliation almost as harshly as Henry Westwick had thought of them—she who had rebuked him the last time he had spoken slightingly of his brother in her presence! A sudden fear and doubt of herself, startled her physically as well as morally.

She turned from the shadowy abyss of the dark water as if the mystery and the gloom of it had been answerable for the emotions which had taken her by surprise. Abruptly closing the window, she threw aside her shawl, and lighted the candles on the mantelpiece, impelled by a sudden craving for light in the solitude of her room.

The cheering brightness round her, contrasting with the black gloom outside, restored her spirits. She felt herself enjoying the light like a child !

Would it be well (she asked herself) to get ready for bed? No! The sense of drowsy fatigue that she had felt half an hour since was gone. She returned to the dull employment of unpacking her boxes. After a few minutes only, the occupation became irksome to her once more. She sat down by the table and took up a guide-book. "Suppose I inform myself," she thought, "on the subject of Venice?"

Her attention wandered from the book, before she had turned the first page of it.

The image of Henry Westwick was the presiding image in her memory now. Recalling the minutest incidents and details of the evening, she could think of nothing which presented him under other than a favourable and interesting aspect. She smiled to herself softly, her colour rose by fine gradations, as she felt the full luxury of dwelling on the perfect truth and modesty of his devotion to her. Was the depression of spirits from which she had suffered so persistently on her travels attributable, by any chance, to their long separation from each other—embittered perhaps by her own vain regret when she remembered her harsh reception of him in Paris? Suddenly conscious of this bold question, and of the self-abandonment which it implied, she returned mechanically to her book, distrusting the unrestrained liberty of her own thoughts.

What lurking temptations to forbidden tenderness find their hiding-places in a woman's dressing-gown, when she is alone in her room at night! With her heart in the tomb of the dead Montbarry, could Agnes even think of another man, and think of love? How shameful! how unworthy of her! For the second time, she tried to interest herself in the guide-book—and once more she tried in vain. Throwing the book aside, she turned desperately to the one resource that was left, to her luggage-resolved to fatigue herself without mercy, until she was weary enough and sleepy enough to find a safe refuge in bed.

For some little time she persisted in the monotonous occupation of transferring her clothes from her trunk to the wardrobe. The large clock in the hall, striking midnight, reminded her that it was getting late. She sat down for a moment in an armchair by the bedside, to rest.

The silence in the house now caught her attention, and held it held it—disagreeably. Was everybody in bed and asleep but herself? Surely it was time for her to follow the general example? With a certain irritable nervous haste, she rose again and undressed herself. "I have lost two hours of rest," she thought, frowning at the reflection of herself in the glass, as she arranged her hair for the night. "I shall be good for nothing tomorrow!"

She lighted the night-light, and extinguished the candles-with one exception, which she removed to a little table, placed on the side of the bed opposite to the side occupied by the armchair. Having put her travelling-box of matches and the guide-book near the candle, in case she might be sleepless and might want to read, she blew out the light, and laid her head on the pillow.

The curtains of the bed were looped back to let the air pass freely over her. Lying on her left side, with her face turned away from the table, she could see the armchair by the dim night-light. It had a chintz covering—representing large bunches of roses scattered over a pale green ground. She tried to weary herself into drowsiness by counting over and over again the bunches of roses that were visible from her point of view.

Twice her attention was distracted from the counting, by sounds outside—by the clock chiming the half-hour past twelve; and then again, by the fall of a pair of boots on the upper floor, thrown out to be cleaned, with that barbarous disregard of the comfort of others which is observable in humanity when it inhabits a hotel. In the silence that followed these passing disturbances, Agnes went on counting the roses on the armchair, more and more slowly. Before long, she confused herself in the figures—tried to begin counting again—thought she would wait a little first—felt her eyelids drooping, and her head reclining lower and lower on the pillow—sighed faintly—and sank into sleep.

How long that first sleep lasted, she never knew. She could only remember, in the after-time, that she woke instantly.

Every faculty and perception in her passed the boundary line between insensibility and consciousness, so to speak, at a leap. Without knowing why, she sat up suddenly in the bed, listening for she knew not what. Her head was in a whirl; her heart beat furiously, without any assignable cause. But one trivial event had happened during the interval while she had been asleep. The night-light had gone out; and the room, as a matter of course, was in total darkness.

She felt for the matchbox, and paused after finding it. A vague sense of confusion was still in her mind. She was in no hurry to light the match. The pause in the darkness was, for the moment, agreeable to her.

In the quieter flow of her thoughts during this interval, she could ask herself the natural question: What cause had awakened her so suddenly, and had so strangely shaken her nerves? Had it been the influence of a dream? She had not dreamed at all—or, to speak more correctly, she had no waking remembrance of having dreamed. The mystery was beyond her fathoming: the darkness began to oppress her. She struck the match on the box and lighted her candle.

As the welcome light diffused itself over the room, she turned from the table and looked toward the other side of the bed.

In the moment when she turned, the chill of a sudden terror gripped her round the heart, as with the clasp of an icy hand.

She was not alone in her room!

There—in the chair at the bedside—there, suddenly revealed under the flow of light from the candle, was the figure of a woman, reclining.

Her head lay back over the chair. Her face, turned up to the ceiling, had the eyes closed, as if she was wrapped in a deep sleep.

The shock of the discovery held Agnes speechless and helpless. Her first conscious action, when she was in some degree mistress of herself again, was to lean over the bed, and to look closer at the woman who had so incomprehensibly stolen into her room in the dead of night. One glance was enough: she started back with a cry of amazement. The person in the chair was no other than the widow of the dead Montbarry—the woman who had warned her that they were to meet again, and that the place might be Venice !

Her courage returned to her, stung into action by the natural sense of indignation which the presence of the Countess provoked.

"Wake up!" she called out. "How dare you come here? How did you get in? Leave the room—or I will call for help!"

She raised her voice at the last words. It produced no effect. Leaning further over the bed, she boldly took the Countess by the shoulder and shook her. Not even this effort succeeded in rousing the sleeping woman. She still lay back in the chair, possessed by a torpor like the torpor of death—insensible to sound, insensible to touch. Was she really sleeping? Or had she fainted?

Agnes looked closer at her. She had not fainted . Her breathing was audible, rising and falling in deep heavy gasps. At intervals she ground her teeth savagely. Beads of perspiration stood thickly on her forehead. Her clinched hands rose and fell slowly from time to time on her lap. Was she in the agony of a dream? or was she spiritually conscious of something hidden in the room?

The doubt involved in that last question was unendurable. Agnes determined to rouse the servants who kept watch in the hotel at night.

The bell-handle was fixed to the wall, on the side of the bed by which the table stood.

She raised herself from the crouching position which she had assumed in looking close at the Countess; and, turning toward the other side of the bed, stretched out her hand to the bell. At the same instant, she stopped and looked upward. Her hand fell helplessly at her side. She shuddered, and sank back on the pillow.

What had she seen?

She had seen another intruder in her room.

Midway between her face and the ceiling, there hovered a human head—severed at the neck, like a head struck from the body by the guillotine.

Nothing visible, nothing audible, had given her any intelligible warning of its appearance. Silently and suddenly the head had taken its place above her. No supernatural change had passed over the room, or was perceptible in it now. The dumbly-tortured figure in the chair; the broad window opposite the foot of the bed, with the black night beyond it; the candle burning on the table—these, and all other objects in the room, remained unaltered. One object more, unutterably horrid, had been added to the rest. That was the only change—no more, no less.

By the yellow candlelight she saw the head distinctly, hovering in midair above her. She looked at it steadfastly, spellbound by the terror that held her.

The flesh of the face was gone. The shrivelled skin was darkened in hue, like the skin of an Egyptian mummy—except at the neck. There it was of a lighter colour; there it showed spots and splashes of the hue of that brown spot on the ceiling, which the child's fanciful terror had distorted into the likeness of a spot of blood. Thin remains of a discoloured moustache and whiskers, hanging over the upper lip, and over the hollows where the cheeks had once been, made the head just recognizable as the head of a man.

Over all the features death and time had done their obliterating work. The eyelids were closed. The hair on the skull, discoloured like the hair on the face, had been burned away in places. The bluish lips, parted in a fixed grin, showed the double row of teeth. By slow degrees, the hovering head (perfectly still when she first saw it) began to descend toward Agnes as she lay beneath.

By slow degrees, that strange doubly-blended odour, which the Commissioners had discovered in the vaults of the old palace—which had sickened Francis Westwick in the bedchamber of the new hotel—spread its fetid exhalations over the room. Downward and downward the hideous apparition made its slow progress, until it stopped close over Agnes—stopped, and turned slowly, so that the face of it confronted the upturned face of the woman in the chair.

There was a pause. Then, a supernatural movement disturbed the rigid repose of the dead face.

The closed eyelids opened slowly. The eyes revealed themselves, bright with the glassy film of death—and fixed their dreadful look on the woman in the chair.

Agnes saw that look; saw the eyelids of the living woman open slowly like the eyelids of the dead; saw her rise, as if in obedience to some silent command—and saw no more.

Her next conscious impression was of the sunlight pouring in at the window; of the friendly presence of Lady Montbarry at the bedside; and of the children's wondering faces peeping in at the door.

Chapter 23

"You have some influence over Agnes. Try what you can do, Henry, to make her take a sensible view of the matter. There is really nothing to make a fuss about. My wife's maid knocked at her door early in the morning, with the customary cup of tea. Getting no answer, she went round to the dressing-room—found the door on that side unlocked—and discovered Agnes on the bed in a fainting fit.

"With my wife's help, they brought her to herself again; and she told the extraordinary story which I have just repeated to you. You must have seen for yourself that she has been over-fatigued, poor thing, by our long railway journeys: her nerves are out of order—and she is just the person to be easily terrified by a dream. She obstinately refuses, however, to accept this rational view. Don't suppose that I have been severe with her!

"All that a man can do to humour her I have done. I have written to the Countess (in her assumed name) offering to restore the room to her. She writes back, positively declining to return to it. I have accordingly arranged (so as not to have the thing known in the hotel) to occupy the room for one or two nights, and to leave Agnes to recover her spirits under my wife's care. Is there anything more that I can do?

"Whatever questions Agnes has asked of me I have answered to the best of my ability; she knows all that you told me about Francis and the Countess last night. But try as I may I can't quiet her mind. I have given up the attempt in despair, and left her in the drawing-room. Go, like a good fellow, and try what you can do to compose her."

In those words, Lord Montbarry stated the case to his brother from the rational point of view. Henry made no remark, he went straight to the drawing-room.

He found Agnes walking rapidly backward and forward, flushed and excited. "If you come here to say what your brother has been saying to me," she broke out, before he could speak, "spare yourself the trouble. I don't want commonsense—I want a true friend who will believe in me."

"I am that friend, Agnes," Henry answered quietly, "and you know it."

"You really believe that I am not deluded by a dream?"

"I know that you are not deluded—in one particular, at least."

"In what particular?"

"In what you have said of the Countess. It is perfectly true—"

Agnes stopped him there. "Why do I only hear this morning that the Countess and Mrs. James are one and the same person?" she asked distrustfully. "Why was I not told of it last night?"

"You forget that you had accepted the exchange of rooms before I reached Venice," Henry replied. "I felt strongly tempted to tell you, even then—but your sleeping arrangements for the night were all made; I should only have inconvenienced and alarmed you. I waited till the morning, after hearing from my brother that you had yourself seen to your security from any intrusion. How that intrusion was accomplished it is impossible to say. I can only declare that the Countess's presence by your bedside last night was no dream of yours. On her own authority I can testify that it was a reality."

"On her own authority?" Agnes repeated eagerly. "Have you seen her this morning?"

"I have seen her not ten minutes since."

"What was she doing?"

"She was busily engaged in writing. I could not even get her to look at me until I thought of mentioning your name."

"She remembered me, of course?"

"She remembered you with some difficulty. Finding that she wouldn't answer me on any other terms, I questioned her as if I had come direct from you. Then she spoke. She not only admitted that she had the same superstitious motive for placing you in that room which she had acknowledged to Francis—she even owned that she had been by your bedside, watching through the night, 'to see what you saw,' as she expressed it. Hearing this, I tried to persuade her to tell me how she got into the room. Unluckily, her manuscript on the table caught her eye; she returned to her writing. 'The Baron wants money,' she said; 'I must get on with my play.'

"What she saw or dreamed, while she was in your room last night, it is at present impossible to discover. But judging by my brother's account of her, as well as by what I remember of her myself, some recent influence has been at work which has produced a marked change in this wretched woman for the worse. Her mind (since last night, perhaps) is partially deranged. One proof of it is that she spoke to me of the Baron as if he were still a living man.

"When Francis saw her, she declared that the Baron was dead, which is the truth. The United States Consul at Milan showed us the announcement of the death in an American newspaper. So far as I can see, such sense as she still possesses seems to be entirely absorbed in one absurd idea' the idea of writing a play for Francis to bring out at his theatre. He admits that he encouraged her to hope she might get money in this way. I think he did wrong. Don't you agree with me?"

"Without heeding the question, Agnes rose abruptly from her chair.

"Do me one more kindness, Henry," she said. "Take me to the Countess at once."

Henry hesitated. "Are you composed enough to see her, after the shock that you have suffered?" he asked.

She trembled, the flush on her face died away, and left it deadly pale. But she held to her resolution. "You have heard of what I saw last night?" she said faintly.

"Don't speak of it!" Henry interposed. "Don't uselessly agitate yourself."

"I must speak! My mind is full of horrid questions about it. I know I can't identify it—and yet I ask myself over and over again, in whose likeness did it appear? Was it in the likeness of Ferrari? or was it—?" she stopped, shuddering. "The Countess knows, I must see the Countess!" she resumed vehemently. "Whether my courage fails me or not, I must make the attempt. Take me to her before I have time to feel afraid of it!"

Henry looked at her anxiously. "If you are really sure of your own resolution," he said, "I agree with you—the sooner you see her the better. You remember how strangely she talked of your influence over her, when she forced her way into your room in London?"

"I remember it perfectly. Why do you ask?"

"For this reason. In the present state of her mind, I doubt if she will be much longer capable of realizing her wild idea of you as the avenging angel who is to bring her to a reckoning for her evil deeds. It may be well to try what your influence can do while she is still capable of feeling it."

He waited to hear what Agnes would say. She took his arm and led him in silence to the door.

They ascended to the second floor, and, after knocking, entered the Countess's room.

She was still busily engaged in writing. When she looked up from the paper, and saw Agnes, a vacant expression of doubt was the only expression in her wild black eyes. After a few moments, the lost remembrances and associations appeared to return slowly to her mind. The pen dropped from her hand. Haggard and trembling, she looked closer at Agnes, and recognized her at last. "Has the time come already?" she said in low awe-struck tones. "Give me a little longer respite, I haven't done my writing yet!"

She dropped on her knees, and held out her clasped hands entreatingly. Agnes was far from having recovered, after the shock that she had suffered in the night: her nerves were far from being equal to the strain that was now laid on them. She was so startled by the change in the Countess, that she was at a loss what to say or to do next. Henry was obliged to speak to her. "Put your questions while you have the chance," he said, lowering his voice. "See! the vacant look is coining over her face again."

Agnes tried to rally her courage. "You were in my room last

night—" she began. Before she could add a word more, the Countess lifted her hands, and wrung them above her head with a low moan of horror. Agnes shrank back, and turned as if to leave the room. Henry stopped her, and whispered to her to try again. She obeyed him after an effort. "I slept last night in the room that you gave up to me," she resumed. "I saw—"

The Countess suddenly rose to her feet. "No more of that," she cried. "Oh, *Jesu Maria*! do you think I want to be told what you saw? Do you think I don't know what it means for you and for me? Decide for yourself, miss. Examine your own mind. Are you well assured that the day of reckoning has come at last? Are you ready to follow me back, through the crimes of the past, to the secrets of the dead?"

She turned again to the writing table, without waiting to be answered. Her eyes flashed; she looked like her old self once more as she spoke. It was only for a moment. The old ardour and impetuosity were nearly worn out. Her head sank; she sighed heavily as she unlocked a desk which stood on the table. Opening a drawer in the desk she took out a leaf of vellum, covered with faded writing. Some ragged ends of silken thread were still attached to the leaf, as if it had been torn out of a book.

"Can you read Italian?" she asked, handing the leaf to Agnes.

Agnes answered silently by an inclination of her head.

"The leaf," the Countess proceeded, "once belonged to a book in the old library of the palace, while this building was still a palace. By whom it was torn out you have no need to know. For what purpose it was torn out you may discover for yourself, if you will. Read it first—at the fifth line from the top of the page."

Agnes felt the serious necessity of composing herself. "Give me a chair," she said to Henry; "and I will do my best." He placed himself behind her chair so that he could look over her shoulder and help her to understand the writing on the leaf. Rendered into English, it ran as follows:—

> I have now completed my literary survey of the first floor of the palace. At the desire of my noble and gracious pa-

tron, the lord of this glorious edifice, I next ascend to the second floor, and continue my catalogue or description of the pictures, decorations, and other treasures of art therein contained. Let me begin with the corner room at the western extremity of the palace, called the Room of the Caryatides, from the statues which support the mantelpiece.

This work is of comparatively recent execution: it dates from the eighteenth century only, and reveals the corrupt taste of the period in every part of it. Still, there is a certain interest which attaches to the mantelpiece: it conceals a cleverly constructed hiding-place, between the floor of the room and the ceiling of the room beneath, which was made during the last evil days of the Inquisition in Venice, and which is reported to have saved an ancestor of my gracious lord pursued by that terrible tribunal, The machinery of this curious place of concealment has been kept in good order by the present lord, as a species of curiosity. He condescended to show me the method of working it.

Approaching the two Caryatides, rest your hand on the forehead (midway between the eyebrows) of the figure which is on your left as you stand opposite to the fireplace, then press the head inward as if you were pushing it against the wall behind. By doing this, you set in motion the hidden machinery in the wall which turns the hearthstone on a pivot, and discloses the hollow place below. There is room enough in it for a man to lie easily at full length. The method of closing the cavity again is equally simple. Place both your hands on the temples of the figure; pull as if you were pulling it toward you—and the hearthstone will revolve into its proper position again.

"You need read no further," said the Countess. "Be careful to remember what you have read."

She put back the page of vellum in her writing-desk, locked it, and led the way to the door.

"Come!" she said; "and see what the mocking Frenchman called 'The beginning of the end.'"

Agnes was barely able to rise from her chair; she trembled from head to foot. Henry gave her his arm to support her. "Fear nothing," he whispered; "I shall be with you."

The Countess proceeded along the westward corridor, and stopped at the door numbered Thirty-eight. This was the room which had been inhabited by Baron Rivar in the old days of the palace; it was situated immediately over the bedchamber in which Agnes had passed the night. For the last two days the room had been empty. The absence of luggage in it, when they opened the door, showed that it had not yet been let.

"You see?" said the Countess, pointing to the carved figure at the fireplace; "and you know what to do. Have I deserved that you should temper justice with mercy?" she went on in lower tones. "Give me a few hours more to myself. The Baron wants money—I must get on with my play."

She smiled vacantly, and imitated the action of writing with her right hand as she pronounced the last words. The effort of concentrating her Weakened mind on other and less familiar topics than the constant want of money in the Baron's lifetime, and the vague prospect of gain from the still unfinished play, had evidently exhausted her poor reserves of strength. When her request had been granted she addressed no expressions of gratitude to Agnes; she only said, "Feel no fear, miss, of my attempting to escape you. Where you are, there I must be till the end comes."

Her eyes wandered round the room with a last weary and stupefied look. She returned to her writing with slow and feeble steps, like the steps of an old woman.

Chapter 24

Henry and Agnes were left alone in the Room of the Caryatides.

The person who had written the description of the palace-probably a poor author or artist—had correctly pointed out the defects of the mantelpiece. Bad taste, exhibiting itself on the most costly and splendid scale, was visible in every part of the work. It was nevertheless greatly admired by ignorant travellers of all classes; partly on account of its imposing size, and partly on account of the number of variously-coloured marbles which the sculptor had contrived to introduce into his design. Photographs of the mantelpiece were exhibited in the public rooms, and found a ready sale among English and American visitors to the hotel.

Henry led Agnes to the figure on the left, as they stood facing the empty fireplace. "Shall I try the experiment, " he asked, "or will you?" She abruptly drew her arm away from him and turned back to the door. "I can't even look at it," she said. "That merciless marble face frightens me!"

Henry put his hand on the forehead of the figure. "What is there to alarm you, my dear, in this conventionally classical face?" he asked jestingly. Before he could press the head inward, Agnes hurriedly opened the door. ' Wait till I am out of the room!" she cried. "The bare idea of what you may find there horrifies me!" She looked back into the room as she crossed the threshold. "I won't leave you altogether," she said, "I will wait outside."

She closed the door. Left by himself, Henry lifted his hand once more to the marble forehead of the figure.

For the second time, he was checked on the point of setting the machinery of the hiding-place in motion. On this occasion, the interruption came from an outbreak of friendly voices in the corridor. A woman's voice exclaimed "Dearest Agnes, how glad I am to see you again!" A man's voice followed, offering to introduce some friend to "Miss Lockwood."

A third voice (which Henry recognized as the voice of the manager of the hotel) became audible next, directing the housekeeper to show the ladies and gentlemen the vacant apartments at the other end of the corridor. "If more accommodation is wanted," the manager went on, "I have a charming room to let here." He opened the door as he spoke, and found himself face to face with Henry Westwick.

"This is indeed an agreeable surprise, sir!" said the manager cheerfully. "You are admiring our famous chimney-piece, I see. May I ask, Mr. Westwick, how you find yourself in the hotel, this time? Have the supernatural influences affected your appetite again?"

"The supernatural influences have spared me, this time," Henry answered. "Perhaps you may yet find that they have affected some other member of the family." He spoke gravely, resenting the familiar tone in which the manager had referred to his previous visit to the hotel. "Have you just returned?" he asked, by way of changing the topic.

"Just this minute, sir. I had the honour of travelling in the same train with friends of yours who have arrived at the hotel-Mr. and Mrs. Arthur Barville, and their travelling companions. Miss Lockwood is with them, looking at the roams. They will be here before long, if they find it convenient to have an extra room at their disposal."

This announcement decided Henry on exploring the hiding-place, before the interruption occurred. It had crossed his mind, when Agnes left him, that he ought perhaps to have a witness, in the not very probable event of some alarming discovery taking place. The too-familiar manager, suspecting nothing, was there at his disposal. He turned again to the Caryan figure, maliciously resolving to make the manager his witness.

"I am delighted to hear that our friends have arrived at last," he said. "Before I shake hands with them, let me ask you a question about this queer work of art here. I see photographs of it downstairs. Are they for sale?"

"Certainly, Mr. Westwick!"

"Do you think the chimney-piece is as solid as it looks?" Henry proceeded. "When you came in, I was just wondering whether this figure here had not accidentally got loosened from the wall behind it." He laid his hand on the marble forehead, for the third time. "To my eye, it looks a little out of the perpendicular. I almost fancied I could jog the head just now, when I touched it." He pressed the head inward as he said those words.

A sound of jarring iron was instantly audible behind the wall. The solid hearthstone in front of the fireplace turned slowly at the feet of the two men, and disclosed a dark cavity below. At the same moment, the strange and sickening combination of odours, hitherto associated with the vaults of the old palace and with the bedchamber beneath, now floated up from the open recess, and filled the room.

The manager started back. "Good God, Mr. Westwick!" he exclaimed, "what does this mean?"

Remembering, not only what his brother Francis had felt in the room beneath, but what the experience of Agnes had been on the previous night, Henry was determined to be on his guard. "I am as much surprised as you are," was his only reply.

"Wait for me one moment, sir," said the manager. "I must stop the ladies and gentlemen outside from coming in."

He hurried away—not forgetting to close the door after him. Henry opened the window, and waited there breathing the purer air. Vague apprehensions of the next discovery to come, filled his mind for the first time. He was doubly resolved, now, not to stir a step in the investigation without a witness.

The manager returned with a wax taper in his hand, which he lighted as soon as he entered the room.

"We need fear no interruption now," he said. "Be so kind, Mr. "Westwick, as to hold the light. It is my business to find out what this extraordinary discovery means."

Henry held the taper. Looking into the cavity, by the dim and flickering light, they both detected a dark object at the bottom of it. "I think I can reach the thing," the manager remarked, "if I lie down, and put my hand into the hole."

He knelt on the floor—and hesitated. "Might I ask you, sir, to give me my gloves?" he said. "They are in my hat, on the chair behind you."

Henry gave him the gloves. "I don't know what I may be going to take hold of," the manager explained, smiling rather uneasily as he put on his right glove.

He stretched himself at full length on the floor, and passed his right arm into the cavity. "I can't say exactly what I have got hold of," he said. "But I have got it."

Half raising himself, he drew his hand out.

The next instant, he started to his feet with a shriek of terror. A human head dropped from his nerveless grasp on the floor, and rolled to Henry's feet. It was the hideous head that Agnes had seen hovering above her, in the vision of the night !

The two men looked at each other, both struck speechless by the same emotion of horror. The manager was the first to control himself. "See to the door, for God's sake!" he said. "Some of the people outside may have heard me."

Henry moved mechanically to the door.

Even when he had his hand on the key, ready to turn it in the lock in case of necessity, he still looked back at the appalling object on the floor. There was no possibility of identifying those decayed and distorted features with any living creature whom he had seen—and yet, he was conscious of feeling a vague and awful doubt which shook him to the soul. The questions which had tortured the mind of Agnes, were now his questions too.

He asked himself, "In whose likeness might I have recognised it before the decay set in? The likeness of Ferrari? or the likeness of—?" He paused trembling, as Agnes had paused trembling before him. Agnes! The name, of all women's names the dearest to him, was a terror to him now! What was he to say to her? What might be the consequence if he trusted her with the terrible truth?

No footsteps approached the door; no voices were audible outside. The travellers were still occupied in the rooms at the eastern end of the corridor.

In the brief interval that had passed, the manager had sufficiently recovered himself to be able to think once more of the first and foremost interests of his life—the interests of the hotel. He approached Henry anxiously.

"If this frightful discovery becomes known," he said, "the closing of the hotel and the ruin of the Company will be the inevitable results. I feel sure that I can trust your discretion, sir, so far?"

"You can certainly trust me," Henry answered. "But surely discretion has its limits," he added, "after such a discovery as we have made?"

The manager understood that the duty which they owed to the community, as honest and law-abiding men, was the duty to which Henry now referred. "I will at once find the means," he said, "of conveying the remains privately out of the house, and I will myself place them in the care of the police authorities. Will you leave the room with me? or do you not object to keep watch here, and help me when I return?"

While he was speaking, the voices of the travellers made themselves heard again at the end of the corridor. Henry instantly consented to wait in the room. He shrank from facing the inevitable meeting with Agnes if he showed himself in the corridor at that moment.

The manager hastened his departure, in the hope of escaping notice. He was discovered by his guests before he could reach the head of the stairs. Henry heard the voices plainly as he turned the key. While the terrible drama of discovery was in progress on one side of the door, trivial questions about the amusements of Venice, and facetious discussions on the relative merits of French and Italian cookery, were proceeding on the other. Little by little, the sound of the talking grew fainter. The visitors, having arranged their plans of amusement for the day, were on their way out of the hotel. In a minute or two, there was silence once more.

Henry turned to the window, thinking to relieve his mind by looking at the bright view over the canal. He soon grew wearied of the familiar scene. The morbid fascination which seems to be exercised by all horrible sights, drew him back again to the ghastly object on the floor.

Dream or reality, how had Agnes survived the sight of it? As the question passed through his mind, he noticed for the first time something lying on the floor near the head. Looking closer, he perceived a thin little plate of gold, with three false teeth attached to it, which had apparently dropped out (loosened by the shock) when the manager let the head fall on the floor.

The importance of this discovery, and the necessity of not too readily communicating it to others, instantly struck Henry. Here surely was a chance—if any chance remained—of identifying the shocking relic of humanity which lay before him, the dumb witness of a crime! Acting on this idea, he took possession of the teeth, purposing to use them as a last means of inquiry when other attempts at investigation had been tried and had failed.

He went back again to the window: the solitude of the room began to weigh on his spirits. As he looked out again at the view, there was a soft knock at the door. He hastened to open it—and checked himself in the act. A doubt occurred to him. Was it the manager who had knocked? He called out, "Who is there?"

The voice of Agnes answered him. "Have you anything to tell me, Henry?"

He was hardly able to reply. "Not just now," he said, confusedly. "Forgive me if I don't open the door. I will speak to you a little later."

The sweet voice made itself heard again, pleading with him piteously. "Don't leave me alone, Henry! I can't go back to the happy people downstairs."

How could he resist that appeal? He heard her sigh—he heard the rustling of her dress as she moved away in despair. The very thing that he had shrunk from doing but a few minutes since was the thing that he did now! He joined Agnes in the corridor. She turned as she heard him, and pointed, trembling, in the direction of the closed room. "Is it so terrible as that?" she asked faintly.

He put his arm round her to support her. A thought came .to him as he looked at her, waiting in doubt and fear for his reply. "You shall know what I have discovered," he said, "if you will first put on your hat and cloak, and come out with me."

She was naturally surprised. "Can you tell me your object in going out?" she asked.

He owned what his object was unreservedly. "I want, before all things," he said, "to satisfy your mind and mine, on the subject of Montbarry's death. I am going to take you to the doctor who attended him in his illness, and to the consul who followed him to the grave."

Her eyes rested on Henry gratefully. "Oh, how well you understand me!" she said. The manager joined them at the same moment, on his way up the stairs. Henry gave him the key of the room, and then called to the servants in the hall to have a gondola ready at the steps. "Are you leaving the hotel?" the manager asked. "In search of evidence," Henry whispered, pointing to the key. "If the authorities want me, I shall be back in an hour."

Chapter 25

The day had advanced to evening. Lord Montbarry and the bridal party had gone to the Opera. Agnes alone, pleading the excuse of fatigue, remained at the hotel. Having kept up appearances by accompanying his friends to the theatre, Henry Westwick slipped away after the first act, and joined Agnes in the drawing-room.

"Have you thought of what I said to you earlier in the day?" he asked, taking a chair at her side. "Do you agree with me that the one dreadful doubt which oppressed us both is at least set at rest?"

Agnes shook her head sadly. "I wish I could agree with you, Henry—I wish I could honestly say that my mind is at ease."

The answer would have discouraged most men. Henry's patience (where Agnes was concerned) was equal to any demands on it.

"If you will only look back at the events of the day," he said, "you must surely admit that we have not been completely baffled. Remember how Dr. Bruno disposed of our doubts:- 'After thirty years of medical practice, do you think I am likely to mistake the symptoms of death by bronchitis?'

"If ever there was an unanswerable question, there it is! Was the consul's testimony doubtful in any part of it? He called at the palace to offer his services, after hearing of Lord Montbarry's death; he arrived at the time when the coffin was in the house; he himself saw the corpse placed in it, and the lid screwed down. The evidence of the priest is equally beyond dispute. He remained in the room with the coffin, reciting the prayers for the dead, until the funeral left the palace.

"Bear all these statements in mind, Agnes; and how can you deny that the question of Montbarry's death and burial is a question set at rest? We have really but one doubt left: we have still to ask ourselves whether the remains which I discovered are the remains of the lost courier, or not. There is the case, as I understand it. Have I stated it fairly?"

Agnes could not deny that he had stated it fairly.

"Then what prevents you from experiencing the same sense of relief that I feel?" Henry asked.

"What I saw last night prevents me," Agnes answered. "When we spoke of this subject, after our inquiries were over, you reproached me with taking what you called the superstitious view. I don't quite admit that—but I do acknowledge that I should find the superstitious view intelligible if I heard it expressed by some other person.

"Remembering what your brother and I once were to each other in the bygone time, I can understand the apparition making itself visible to Me, to claim the mercy of Christian burial, and the vengeance due to a crime. I can even perceive some faint possibility of truth in the explanation which you described as the mesmeric theory—that what I saw might be the result of magnetic influence communicated to me, as I lay between the remains of the murdered husband above me and the guilty wife suffering the tortures of remorse at my bedside.

"But what I do not understand is, that I should have passed through that dreadful ordeal; having no previous knowledge of the murdered man in his lifetime, or only knowing him (if you suppose that I saw the apparition of Ferrari) through the interest which I took in his wife. I can't dispute your reasoning, Henry. But I feel in my heart of hearts that you are deceived. Nothing will shake my belief that we are still as far from having discovered the dreadful truth as ever."

Henry made no further attempt to dispute with her. She had impressed him with a certain reluctant respect for her own opinion, in spite of himself.

"Have you thought of any better way of arriving at the truth?" he asked. "Who is to help us? No doubt there is the Countess, who has the clew to the mystery in her own hands. But, in the present state of her mind, is her testimony to be trusted—even if she were willing to speak? Judging by my own experience, I should say decidedly not."

"You don't mean that you have seen her again?" Agnes eagerly interposed.

"Yes. I disturbed her once more over her endless writing; and I insisted on her speaking out plainly."

"Then you told her what you found when you opened the hiding-place?"

"Of course I did!" Henry replied. "I said that I held her responsible for the discovery, though I had not mentioned her connection with it to the authorities as yet. She went on with her writing as if I had spoken in an unknown tongue! I was equally obstinate on my side. I told her plainly that the head had been placed under the care of the police, and that the manager and I had signed our declarations and given our evidence. She paid not the slightest heed to me.

"By way of tempting her to speak, I added that the whole investigation was to be kept a secret, and that she might depend on my discretion. For the moment I thought I had succeeded. She looked up from her writing with a passing flash of curiosity and said: 'What are they going to do with it?'—meaning, I suppose, the head. I answered that it was to be privately buried, after photographs of it had first been taken.

"I even went the length of communicating the opinion of the surgeon consulted, that some chemical means of arresting decomposition had been used and had only partially succeeded—and I asked her point-blank if the surgeon was right? The trap was not a bad one—but it completely failed. She said in the coolest manner: 'Now you are here, I should like to consult you about my play; I am at a loss for some new incidents.' Mind, there was nothing satirical in this.

"She was really eager to read her wonderful work to me—evidently supposing that I took a special interest in such things, because my brother is the manager of a theatre! I left her, making the first excuse that occurred to me. So far as I am concerned, I can do nothing with her. But it is possible that your influence may succeed with her again, as it has succeeded already. Will you make the attempt, to satisfy your own mind? She is still upstairs; and I am quite ready to accompany you."

Agnes shuddered at the bare suggestion of another interview with the Countess.

"I can't! I daren't!" she exclaimed. "After what has happened in that horrible room, she is more repellent to me than ever. Don't ask me to do it, Henry! Feel my hand—you have turned me as cold as death only with talking of it!"

She was not exaggerating the terror that possessed her. Henry hastened to change the subject.

"Let us talk of something more interesting," he said. "I have a question to ask you about yourself. Am I right in believing that the sooner you get away from Venice the happier you will be?"

"Right?" she repeated, excitedly. "You are more than right! No words can say how I long to be away from this horrible place. But you know how I am situated—you heard what Lord Montbarry said at dinner-time?"

"Suppose he has altered his plans, since dinner-time?" Henry suggested.

Agnes looked surprised. "I thought he had received letters from England which obliged him to leave Venice tomorrow," she said.

"Quite true," Henry admitted. "He had arranged to start for England tomorrow, and to leave you and Lady Montbarry and the children to enjoy your holiday in Venice, under my care. Circumstances have occurred, however, which have forced him to alter his plans. He must take you all back with him tomorrow because I am not able to assume the charge of you. I am obliged to give up my holiday in Italy and return to England, too."

Agnes looked at him in some little perplexity: she was not quite sure whether she understood him or not.

"Are you really obliged to go back?" she asked.

Henry smiled as he answered her. "Keep the secret," he said, "or Montbarry will never forgive me!"

She read the rest in his face. "Oh!" she exclaimed, blushing brightly, "you have not given up your pleasant holiday in Italy on my account?"

"I shall go back with you to England, Agnes. That will be holiday enough for me."

She took his hand in an irrepressible outburst of gratitude. "How good you are to me!" she murmured, tenderly. "What should I have done in the troubles that have come to me, without your sympathy? I can't tell you, Henry, how I feel your kindness."

She tried impulsively to lift his hand to her lips. He gently stopped her. "Agnes," he said, "are you beginning to understand how truly I love you?"

That simple question found its own way to her heart. She owned the whole truth, without saying a word. She looked at him and then looked away again.

He drew her nearer to him. "My own darling!" he whispered—and kissed her. Softly and tremulously, the sweet lips lingered and touched his lips in return. Then her head drooped. She put her arms round his neck, and hid her face on his bosom. They spoke no more.

The charmed silence had lasted but a little while, when it was mercilessly broken by a knock at the door.

Agnes started to her feet. She placed herself at the piano; the instrument being opposite to the door, it was impossible, when she seated herself on the music-stool, for any person entering the room to see her face. Henry called out irritably: "Come in."

The door was not opened. The person on the other side of it asked a strange question.

"Is Mr. Henry Westwick alone?"

Agnes instantly recognized the voice of the Countess. She hurried to a second door, which communicated with one of the bedrooms. "Don't let her come near me !" she whispered, nervously. "Goodnight, Henry! goodnight!"

If Henry could, by an effort of will, have transported the Countess to the uttermost ends of the earth, he would have made the effort without remorse. As it was, he only repeated, more irritably than ever, "Come in!"

She entered the room slowly, with her everlasting manuscript in her hand. Her step was unsteady; a dark flush appeared on her face, in place of its customary pallor; her eyes were bloodshot and widely dilated. In approaching Henry, she showed a strange incapability of calculating her distances—she struck against the table near which he happened to be sitting.

When she spoke, her articulation was confused, and her pronunciation of some of the longer words was hardly intelligible. Most men would have suspected her of being under the influence of some intoxicating liquor. Henry took a truer view—he said, as he placed a chair for her: "Countess, I am afraid you have been working too hard: you look as if you wanted rest."

She put her hand to her head. "My invention has gone, "she said. "I can't write my fourth act. It's all a blank all—a blank!"

Henry advised her to wait till the next day. "Go to bed," he suggested, "and try to sleep."

She waved her hand impatiently. "I must finish the play," she answered. "I only want a hint from you. You must know something about plays. Your brother has got a theatre. You must often have heard him talk about fourth and fifth acts—you must have seen rehearsals, and all the rest of it." She abruptly thrust the manuscript into Henry's hand. "I can't read it to you," she said; "I feel giddy when I look at my own writing. Just run your eye over it, there's a good fellow—and give me a hint."

Henry glanced at the manuscript. He happened to look at

the list of the persons of the drama. As he read the list he started and turned abruptly to the Countess, intending to ask her for some explanation. The words were suspended on his lips. It was but too plainly useless to speak to her. Her head lay back on the rail of the chair. She seemed to be half asleep already. The flush on her face had deepened: she looked like a woman who was in danger of having a fit.

He rang the bell, and directed the man who answered it to send one of the chambermaids upstairs. His voice seemed to partially rouse the Countess; she opened her eyes in a slow, drowsy way. "Have you read it?" she asked.

It was necessary as a mere act of humanity to humour her. "I will read it willingly," said Henry, "if you will go upstairs to bed. You shall hear what I think of it tomorrow morning. Our heads will be clearer, we shall be better able to make a fourth act in the morning."

The chambermaid came in while he was speaking. "I am afraid the lady is ill," Henry whispered. "Take her up to her room." The woman looked at the Countess, and whispered back, "Shall we send for a doctor, sir?"

Henry advised taking her upstairs first, and then asking the manager's opinion. There was great difficulty in persuading her to rise, and accept the support of the chambermaid's arm. It was only by reiterated promises to read the play that night, and to make the fourth act in the morning, that Henry prevailed on the Countess to return to her room.

Left to himself, he began to feel a certain languid curiosity in relation to the manuscript. He looked over the pages, reading a line here and a line there. Suddenly he changed colour as he read—and looked up from the manuscript like a man bewildered. "Good God! what does this mean?" he said to himself.

His eyes turned nervously to the door by which Agnes had left him. She might return to the drawing-room; she might want to see what the Countess had written. He looked back again at the passage which had startled him—considered with himself for a moment and, snatching up the unfinished play, suddenly and softly left the room.

Chapter 26

Entering his own room on the upper floor, Henry placed the manuscript on his table, open at the first leaf. His nerves were unquestionably shaken; his hand trembled as he turned the pages, he started at chance noises on the staircase of the hotel.

The *scenario*, or outline, of the Countess's play began with no formal prefatory phrases. She presented herself and her work with the easy familiarity of an old friend.

"Allow me, dear Mr. Francis Westwick, to introduce to you the persons in my proposed Play. Behold them, arranged symmetrically in a line.

"My Lord. The Baron. The Courier. The Doctor. The Countess.

"I don't trouble myself, you see, to invent fictitious family names. My characters are sufficiently distinguished by their social titles and by the striking contrast which they present one with another.

"The First Act opens—

"No! Before I open the First Act, I must announce, in justice to myself, that this Play is entirely the work of my own invention. I scorn to borrow from actual events; and, what is more extraordinary still, I have not stolen one of my ideas from the Modern French drama. As the manager of an English theatre, you will naturally refuse to believe this. It doesn't matter. Nothing matters—except the opening of my first act.

"We are at Homburg, in the famous *Salon d'Or*, at the height of the season. The Countess (exquisitely dressed) is seated at the green table. Strangers of all nations are standing behind the players, venturing their money or only looking on. My Lord is among the strangers. He is struck by the Countess's personal appearance, in which beauties and defects are fantastically mingled in the most attractive manner. He watches the Countess's game, and places his money where he sees her deposit her own little stake.

"She looks round at him and says, 'Don't trust to my colour; I have been unlucky the whole evening. Place your stake on the other colour, and you may have a chance of winning.' My Lord (a true Englishman) blushes, bows, and obeys. The Countess proves to be a prophet. She loses again. My Lord wins twice the sum that he has risked.

"The Countess rises from the table. She has no more money, and she offers my Lord her chair.

"Instead of taking it, he politely places his winnings in her hand, and begs her to accept the loan as a favour to himself. The Countess stakes again, and loses again. My Lord smiles superbly, and presses a second loan on her. From that moment her luck turns. She wins, and wins largely. Her brother, the Baron, trying his fortune in another room, hears of what is going on, and joins my Lord and the Countess.

"Pay attention, if you please, to the Baron. He is delineated as a remarkable and interesting character.

"This noble person has begun life with a single-minded devotion to the science of experimental chemistry, very surprising in a young and handsome man with a brilliant future before him. A profound knowledge of the occult sciences has persuaded the Baron that it is possible to solve the famous problem called the 'Philosopher's Stone.' His own pecuniary resources have long since been exhausted by his costly experiments. His sister has next supplied him with the small fortune at her disposal: reserving only the family jewels, placed in the charge of her banker and friend at Frankfort.

"The Countess's fortune also being swallowed up, the Baron has in a fatal moment sought for new supplies at the gaming-table. He proves, at starting on his perilous career, to be a favourite of fortune; wins largely, and, alas! profanes his noble enthusiasm for science by yielding his soul to the all-debasing passion of the gamester.

"At the period of the Play, the Baron's good fortune has deserted him. He sees his way to a crowning experiment in the fatal search after the secret of transmuting the baser metals into gold. But how is he to pay the preliminary expenses? Destiny, like a mocking echo, answers, How?

"Will his sister's winnings (with my Lord's money) prove large enough to help him? Eager for this result, he gives the Countess his advice how to play. From that disastrous moment the infection of his own adverse fortune spreads to his sister. She loses again and again—loses to the last farthing.

"The amiable and wealthy Lord offers a third loan; but the scrupulous Countess positively refuses to take it. On leaving the table, she presents her brother to my Lord. The gentlemen fall into pleasant talk. My Lord asks leave to pay his respects to the Countess, the next morning, at her hotel. The Baron hospitably invites him to breakfast. My Lord accepts, with a last admiring glance at the Countess which does not escape her brother's observation, and takes his leave for the night.

"Alone with his sister, the Baron speaks out plainly. 'Our affairs,' he says, 'are in a desperate condition, and must find a desperate remedy. Wait for me here, while I make inquiries about my Lord. You have evidently produced a strong impression of him. If we can turn that impression into money, no matter at what sacrifice, the thing must be done.'

"The Countess now occupies the stage alone, and indulges in a soliloquy which develops her character.

"It is at once a dangerous and attractive character. Immense capacities for good are implanted in her nature, side by side with equally remarkable capacities for evil. It rests with circumstances to develop either the one or the other. Being a person who produces a sensation wherever she goes, this noble lady is naturally made the subject of all sorts of scandalous reports.

"To one of these reports (which falsely and abominably points to the Baron as her lover instead of her brother) she now refers with just indignation. She has just expressed her desire to leave Homburg, as the place in which the vile calumny first took its rise, when the Baron returns, overhears her last words, and says to her, 'Yes, leave Homburg by all means; provided you leave it in the character of my Lord's betrothed wife!'

"The Countess is startled and shocked. She protests that she does not reciprocate my Lord's admiration for her. She even goes the length of refusing to see him again. The Baron answers, 'I must positively have command of money. Take your choice, between marrying my Lord's income, in the interest of my grand discovery—or leave me to sell myself and my title to the first rich woman of low degree who is ready to buy me.'

"The Countess listens in surprise and dismay. Is it possible that the Baron is in earnest? He is horribly in earnest. 'The woman who will buy me,' he says, 'is in the next room to us at this moment. She is the wealthy widow of a Jewish usurer. She has the money I want to reach the solution of the great problem. I have only to be that woman's husband, and to make myself master of untold millions of gold. Take five minutes to consider what I have said to you, and tell me on my return which of us is to marry for the money I want, you or I.'

"As he turns away, the Countess stops him.

"All the noblest sentiments in her nature are exalted to the highest pitch. 'Where is the true woman,' she exclaims, 'who wants time to consummate the sacrifice of herself, when the man to whom she is devoted demands it? She does not want five minutes—she does not want five seconds—she holds out her hand to him, and she says, Sacrifice me on the altar of your glory! Take as stepping-stones on the way to your triumph, my love, my liberty, and my life!'

"On this grand situation the curtain falls. Judging by my first act, Mr. Westwick, tell me truly, and don't be afraid of turning my head: Am I not capable of writing a good play?"

Henry paused between the First and Second Acts; reflecting, not on the merits of the Play, but on the strange resemblance which the incidents so far presented to the incidents that had attended the disastrous marriage of the first Lord Montbarry.

"Was it possible that the Countess, in the present condition of her mind, supposed herself to be exercising her invention when she was only exercising her memory?

The question involved considerations too serious to be made

the subject of a hasty decision. Reserving his opinion, Henry turned the page, and devoted himself to the reading of the next act. The manuscript proceeded as follows :

"The Second Act opens at Venice. An interval of four months has elapsed since the date of the scene at the gambling table. The action now takes place in the reception-room of one of the Venetian palaces.

"The Baron is discovered, alone, on the stage. He reverts to the events which have happened since the close of the First Act. The Countess has sacrificed herself; the mercenary marriage has taken place—but not without obstacles, caused by difference of opinion on the question of marriage settlements.

"Private inquiries, instituted in England, have informed the Baron that my Lord's income is derived chiefly from what is called entailed property. In case of accidents, he is surely bound to do something for his bride? Let him, for example, insure his life, for a sum proposed by the Baron, and let him so settle the money that his widow shall have it, if he dies first.

"My Lord hesitates. The Baron wastes no time in useless discussion. 'Let us by all means' (he says) 'consider the marriage as broken off.' My Lord shifts his ground, and pleads for a smaller sum than the sum proposed. The Baron briefly replies, 'I never bargain.' My Lord is in love; the natural result follows—he gives way.

"So far, the Baron has no cause to complain. But my Lord's turn comes, when the marriage has been celebrated and when the honeymoon is over. The Baron has joined the married pair at a palace which they have hired in Venice. He is still bent on solving the problem of the 'Philosopher's Stone.' His laboratory is set up in the vaults beneath the palace—so that smells from chemical experiments may not incommode the Countess, in the higher regions of the house.

"The one obstacle in the way of his grand discovery is, as usual, the want of money. His position at the present time has become truly critical. He owes debts of honour to gentlemen in his own rank of life, which must positively be paid; and he proposes, in his own friendly manner, to borrow the money of my Lord. My Lord positively refuses, in the rudest terms. The Baron applies to his sister to exercise her conjugal influence. She can only answer that her noble husband (being no longer distractedly in love with her) now appears in his true character, as one of the meanest men living. The sacrifice of the marriage has been made, and has already proved useless.

"Such is the state of affairs at the opening of the Second Act.

"The entrance of the Countess suddenly disturbs the Baron's reflections. She is in a state bordering on frenzy. Incoherent expressions of rage burst from her lips: it is some time before she can sufficiently control herself to speak plainly. She has been doubly insulted—first, by a menial person in her employment; secondly, by her husband. Her maid, an Englishwoman, has declared that she will serve the Countess no longer. She will give up her wages and return at once to England. Being asked her reason for this strange proceeding, she insolently hints that the Countess's service is no service for an honest woman, since the Baron has entered the house. The Countess does what any lady in her position would do; she indignantly dismisses the wretch on the spot.

"My Lord, hearing his wife's voice raised in anger, leaves the study in which he is accustomed to shut himself up over his books, and asks what this disturbance means. The Countess informs him of the outrageous language and conduct of her maid. My Lord not only declares his entire approval of the woman's conduct, but expresses his own abominable doubts of his wife's fidelity in language of such horrible brutality that no lady could pollute her lips by repeating it. 'If I had been a man,' the Countess says, 'and if I had had a weapon in my hand, I would have struck him dead at my feet!'

"The Baron, listening silently so far, now speaks. 'Permit me to finish the sentence for you,' he says. 'You would have struck your husband dead at your feet; and by that rash act, you would have deprived yourself of the insurance money settled on the widow—the very money which is wanted to relieve your brother from the unendurable pecuniary position which he now occupies!'

"The Countess gravely reminds the Baron that this is no joking matter. After what my Lord has said to her, she has little doubt that he will communicate his infamous suspicions to his lawyers in England. If nothing is done to prevent it, she may be divorced and disgraced, and thrown on the world, with no resource but the sale of her jewels to keep her from starving.

"At this moment, the Courier who has been engaged to travel with my Lord from England crosses the stage with a letter to take to the post. The Countess stops him and asks to look at the address on the letter. She takes it from him for a moment, and shows it to her brother. The handwriting is my Lord's; and the letter is directed to his lawyers in London.

"The Courier proceeds to the post-office. The Baron and the Countess look at each other in silence. No words are needed. They thoroughly understand the position in which they are placed; they clearly see the terrible remedy for it. What is the plain alternative before them? Disgrace and ruin—or, my Lord's death and the insurance money!

"The Baron walks backward and forward in great agitation, talking to himself. The Countess hears fragments of what he is saying. He speaks of my Lord's constitution, probably weakened in India—of a cold which my Lord has caught two or three days since—of the remarkable manner in which such slight things as colds sometimes end in serious illness and death.

"He observes that the Countess is listening to him, and asks if she has anything to propose. She is a woman who, with many defects, has the great merit of speaking out. 'Is there no such thing as a serious illness,' she asks, 'corked up in one of those bottles of yours in the vaults downstairs?'

"The Baron answers by gravely shaking his head. What is he afraid of?—a possible examination of the body after death? No: he can set any post-mortem examination at defiance. It is the process of administering the poison that he dreads. A man so distinguished as my Lord cannot be taken seriously ill without medical attendance. Where there is a Doctor, there is always danger of discovery. Then, again, there is the Courier, faithful to my Lord as long as my Lord pays him. Even if the Doctor sees nothing suspicious, the Courier may discover something.

"The poison, to do its work with the necessary secrecy, must be repeatedly administered in graduated doses. One trifling miscalculation or mistake may rouse suspicion. The insurance offices may hear of it, and may refuse to pay the money. As things are, the Baron will not risk it, and will not allow his sister to risk it in his place.

"My Lord himself is the next character who appears. He has repeatedly rung for the Courier, and the bell has not been answered. 'What does this insolence mean?'

"The Countess (speaking with quiet dignity—for why should her infamous husband have the satisfaction of knowing how deeply he has wounded her?) reminds my Lord that the Courier has gone to the post. My Lord asks suspiciously if she has looked at the letter. The Countess informs him coldly that she has no curiosity about his letters. Referring to the cold from which he is suffering, she inquires if he thinks of consulting a medical man. My Lord answers roughly that he is quite old enough to be capable of doctoring himself.

"As he makes this reply, the Courier appears, returning from the post. My Lord gives him orders to go out again and buy some lemons. He proposes to try hot lemonade as a means of inducing perspiration in bed. In that way he has formerly cured colds, and in that way he will cure the cold from which he is suffering now.

"The Courier obeys in silence. Judging by appearances, he goes very reluctantly on this second errand.

"My Lord turns to the Baron (who has thus far taken no part in the conversation) and asks him, in a sneering tone, how much longer he proposes to prolong his stay in Venice. The Baron answers quietly, 'Let us speak plainly to one another, my Lord. If you wish me to leave your house, you have only to say the word, and I go.' My Lord turns to his wife, and asks if she can support the calamity of her brother's absence—laying a grossly insulting emphasis on the word 'brother.' The Countess preserves her impenetrable composure; nothing in her betrays the deadly hatred with which she regards the titled ruffian who has insulted her. 'You are master in this house, my Lord,' is all she says. 'Do as you please.'

"My Lord looks at his wife; looks at the Baron—and suddenly alters his tone. Does he perceive in the composure of the Countess and her brother something lurking under the surface that threatens him? This is at least certain, he makes a clumsy apology for the language that he has used. (Abject wretch!)

"My Lord's excuses are interrupted by the return of the Courier with the lemons and hot water.

"The Countess observes for the first time that the man looks ill. His hands tremble as he places the tray on the table. My Lord orders his Courier to follow him, and make the lemonade in the bedroom. The Countess remarks that the Courier seems hardly capable of obeying his orders. Hearing this, the man admits that he is ill. He, too, is suffering from a cold; he has been kept waiting in a draught at the shop where he bought the lemons; he feels alternately hot and cold, and he begs permission to lie down for a little while on his bed.

"Feeling her humanity appealed to, the Countess volunteers to make the lemonade herself. My Lord takes the Courier by the arm, leads him aside, and whispers these words to him: 'Watch her, and see that she puts nothing into the lemonade; then bring it to me with your own hands; and, then, go to bed, if you like.'

"Without a word more to his wife, or to the Baron, my Lord leaves the room.

"The Countess makes the lemonade, and the Courier takes it to his master.

"Returning, on the way to his own room, he is so weak, and feels, he says, so giddy, that he is obliged to support himself by the backs of the chairs as he passes them. The Baron, always considerate to persons of low degree, offers his arm. 'I am afraid, my poor fellow,' he says, 'that you are really ill.' The Courier makes this extraordinary answer: 'It's all over with me, sir: I have caught my death.'

"The Countess is naturally startled. 'You are not an old man,' she says, trying to rouse the Courier's spirits. 'At your age, catching cold doesn't surely mean catching your death?' The Courier fixes his eyes despairingly on the Countess.

"'My lungs are weak, my Lady,' he says; 'I have already had two attacks of bronchitis. The second time, a great physician joined my own doctor in attendance on me. He considered my recovery almost in the light of a miracle. Take care of yourself,' he said. 'If you have a third attack of bronchitis, as certainly as two and two make four, you will be a dead man. I feel the same inward shivering, my Lady, that I felt on those two former occasions and I tell you again, I have caught my death in Venice.'

"Speaking some comforting words, the Baron leads him to his room. The Countess is left alone on the stage.

"She seats herself, and looks toward the door by which the Courier has been led out. 'Ah! my poor fellow,' she says, 'if you could only change constitutions with my Lord, what a happy result would follow for the Baron and for me! If you could only get cured of a trumpery cold with a little hot lemonade, and if he could only catch his death in your place—!'

"She suddenly pauses—considers for a while—and springs to her feet, with a cry of triumphant surprise: the wonderful, the unparalleled idea has crossed her mind like a flash of lightning. Make the two men change names and places—and the deed is done! Where are the obstacles? Remove my Lord (by fair means or foul) from his room; and keep him secretly prisoner in the palace, to live or die as future necessity may determine. Place the Courier in the vacant bed, and call in the doctor to see him—ill, in my Lord's character, and (if he dies) dying under my Lord's name!"

The manuscript dropped from Henry's hands. A sickening sense of horror overpowered him. The question which had occurred to his mind at the close of the First Act of the Play assumed a new and terrible interest now. As far as the scene of the Countess's soliloquy, the incidents of the Second Act had reflected the events of his late brother's life as faithfully as the incidents of the First Act. Was the monstrous plot, revealed in the lines which he had just read, the offspring of the Countess's morbid imagination? or had she, in this case also, deluded herself with the idea that she was inventing when she was really writing under the influence of her own guilty remembrances of the past?

If the latter interpretation were the true one, he had just read the narrative of the contemplated murder of his brother, planned in cold blood by a woman who was at that moment inhabiting the same house with him. While, to make the fatality complete, Agnes herself had innocently provided the conspirators with the one man who was fitted to be the passive agent of their crime.

Even the bare doubt that it might be so was more than he could endure. He left his room; resolved to force the truth out of the Countess, or to denounce her before the authorities as a murderess at large.

Arrived at her door, he was met by a person just leaving the room. The person was the manager. He was hardly recognizable; he looked and spoke like a man in a state of desperation.

"Oh, go in, if you like!" he said to Henry. "Mark this, sir! I am not a superstitious man; but I do begin to believe that crimes carry their own curse with them. This hotel is under a curse. What happens in the morning? We discover a crime committed in the old days of the palace. The night comes, and brings another dreadful event with it—a death; a sudden and shocking death, in the house. Go in, and see for yourself! I shall resign my situation, Mr. Westwick: I can't contend with the fatalities that pursue me here!"

Henry entered the room.

The Countess was stretched on her bed. The doctor on one side, and the chambermaid on the other, were standing looking at her. From time to time, she drew a heavy stertorous breath, like a person oppressed in sleeping. "Is she likely to die?" Henry asked.

"She is dead," the doctor answered. "Dead of the rupture of a blood-vessel on the brain. Those sounds that you hear are purely mechanical—they may go on for hours."

Henry looked at the chambermaid. She had little to tell. The Countess had refused to go to bed, and had placed herself at her desk to proceed with her writing. Finding it useless to remonstrate with her, the maid had left the room to speak to the manager. In the shortest possible time the doctor was summoned to the hotel, and found the Countess dead on the floor. There was this to tell—and no more.

Looking at the writing-table as he went out, Henry saw the sheet of paper on which the Countess had traced her last lines of writing. The characters were almost illegible. Henry could just distinguish the words, "First Act," and "Persons of the Drama." The lost wretch had been thinking of her Play to the last, and had begun it all over again!

Chapter 27

Henry returned to his room.

His first impulse was to throw aside the manuscript, and never to look at it again. The one chance of relieving his mind from the dreadful uncertainty that oppressed it, by obtaining positive evidence of the truth, was a chance annihilated by the Countess's death. What good purpose could be served, what relief could he anticipate, if he read more?

He walked up and down the room. After an interval, his thoughts took a new direction; the question of the manuscript presented itself under another point of view. Thus far, his reading had only informed him that the conspiracy had been planned. How did he know that the plan had been put in execution?

The manuscript lay just before him on the floor. He hesitated; then picked it up; and, returning to the table, read on as follows, from the point at which he had left off:

"While the Countess is still absorbed in the bold yet simple combination of circumstances which she has discovered, the

Baron returns. He takes a serious view of the case of the Courier; it may be necessary, he thinks, to send for medical advice. No servant is left in the palace, now the English maid has taken her departure. The Baron himself must fetch the doctor, if the doctor is really needed.

"'Let us have medical help, by all means,' his sister replies. 'But wait and hear something that I have to say to you first.' She then electrifies the Baron by communicating her idea to him. What danger of discovery have they to dread? My Lord's life in Venice has been a life of absolute seclusion: nobody but his banker knows him, even by personal appearance. He has presented his letter of credit as a perfect stranger; and he and his banker have never seen each other since that first visit. He has given no parties, and gone to no parties.

"On the few occasions when he has hired a gondola or taken a walk, he has always been alone. Thanks to the atrocious suspicion which makes him ashamed of being seen with his wife, he has led the very life which makes the proposed enterprise easy of accomplishment.

"The cautious Baron listens—but gives no positive opinion, as yet. 'See what you can do with the Courier,' he says; 'and I will decide when I hear the result. One valuable hint I may give you before you go. Your man is easily tempted by money—if you only offer him enough. The other day I asked him, in jest, what he would do for a thousand pounds. He answered, "Anything. "Bear that in mind; and offer your highest bid without bargaining.'

"The scene changes to the Courier's room, and shows the poor wretch with a photographic portrait of his wife in his hand, crying. The Countess enters.

"She wisely begins by sympathizing with her contemplated accomplice. He is duly grateful; he confides his sorrows to his gracious mistress. Now that he believes himself to be on his deathbed, he feels remorse for his neglectful treatment of his wife. He could resign himself to die; but despair overpowers him when he remembers that he has saved no money, and that he will leave his widow, without resources, to the mercy of the world.

"On this hint, the Countess speaks. 'Suppose you were asked to do a perfectly easy thing,' she says; 'and suppose you were rewarded for doing it by a present of a thousand pounds, as a legacy for your widow?'

"The Courier raises himself on his pillow and looks at the Countess with an expression of incredulous surprise. She can hardly be cruel enough (he thinks) to joke with a man in his miserable plight. Will she say plainly what this perfectly easy thing is, the doing of which will meet with such a magnificent reward?

"The Countess answers that question by confiding her project to the Courier, without the slightest reserve.

"Some minutes of silence follow when she has done. The Courier is not weak enough yet to speak without stopping to think first. Still keeping his eyes on the Countess, he makes a quaintly insolent remark on what he has just heard. 'I have not hitherto been a religious man; but I feel myself on the way to it. Since your ladyship has spoken to me, I believe in the Devil.'

"It is the Countess's interest to see the humorous side of this confession of faith. She takes no offense. She only says, 'I will give you half an hour by yourself, to think over my proposal. You are in danger of death. Decide, in your wife's interests, whether you will die worth nothing, or die worth a thousand pounds.'

"Left alone, the Courier seriously considers his position–and decides. He rises with difficulty; writes a few lines on a leaf taken from his pocketbook; and, with slow and faltering steps, leaves the room.

"The Countess, returning at the expiration of the half-hour's interval, finds the room empty. While she is wondering, the Courier opens the door. What has he been doing out of his bed? He answers: 'I have been protecting my own life, my lady, on the bare chance that I may recover from the bronchitis for the third time. If you or the Baron attempts to hurry me out of this world, or to deprive me of my thousand pounds reward, I shall tell the doctor where he will find a few lines of writing, which describe your ladyship's plot. I may not have strength enough, in the case supposed, to betray you by making a complete confession with my own lips; but I can employ my last breath to speak the half-dozen words which will tell the doctor where he is to look. Those words, it is needless to add, will be addressed to your Ladyship, if I find your engagements toward me faithfully kept.'

"With this audacious preface, he proceeds to state the conditions on which he will play his part in the conspiracy, and die (if he does die) worth a thousand pounds.

"Either the Countess or the Baron are to taste the food and drink brought to his bedside, in his presence, and even the medicines which the doctor may prescribe for him. As for the promised sum of money, it is to be produced in one banknote, folded in a sheet of paper, on which a line is to be written, dictated by the Courier. The two inclosures are then to be sealed up in an envelope, addressed to his wife, and stamped ready for the post.

"This done, the letter is to be placed under his pillow; the Baron or the Countess being at liberty to satisfy themselves, day by day, at their own time, that the letter remains in its place, with the seal unbroken, as long as the doctor has any hope of his patient's recovery. The last stipulation follows. The Courier has a conscience; and with a view to keeping it easy, insists that he shall be left in ignorance of that part of the plot which relates to the sequestration of my Lord. Not that he cares particularly what becomes of his miserly master—but he does dislike taking other people's responsibilities on his own shoulders.

"These conditions being agreed to, the Countess calls in the Baron, who has been waiting events in the next room.

"He is informed that the Courier has yielded to temptation; but he is still too cautious to make any compromising remarks. Keeping his back turned on the bed, he shows a bottle to the Countess. It is labelled 'Chloroform'. She understands that my Lord is to be removed from his room in a convenient state of insensibility. In what part of the palace is he to be hidden? As they open the door to go out, the Countess whispers that question to the Baron. The Baron whispers back, 'In the vaults!' The curtain falls."

Chapter 28

So the Second Act ended.

Turning to the Third Act, Henry looked wearily at the pages as he let them slip through his fingers. Both in mind and body, he began to feel the need of repose.

In one important respect, the later portion of the manuscript differed from the pages which he had just been reading. Signs of an overwrought brain showed themselves, here and there, as the outline of the Play approached its end.

The handwriting grew worse and worse. Some of the longer sentences were left unfinished. In the exchange of dialogue, questions and answers were not always attributed respectively to the right speaker. At certain intervals the writer's failing intelligence seemed to recover itself for a while; only to relapse again, and to lose the thread of the narrative more hopelessly than ever.

After reading one or two of the more coherent passages Henry recoiled from the ever-darkening horror of the story. He closed the manuscript, heartsick and exhausted, and threw himself on his bed to rest. The door opened almost at the same moment. Lord Montbarry entered the room.

"We have just returned from the Opera," he said; "and we have heard the news of that miserable woman's death. They say you spoke to her in her last moments; and I want to hear how it happened."

"You shall hear how it happened," Henry answered; "and more than that. You are now the head of the family, Stephen; and I feel bound, in the position which oppresses me, to leave you to decide what ought to be done."

With those introductory words, he told his brother how the Countess's Play had come into his hands. "Read the first few pages," he said. "I am anxious to know whether the same impression is produced on both of us."

Before Lord Montbarry had got half-way through the First Act, he stopped, and looked at his brother. "What does she mean by boasting of this as her own invention?" he asked. "Was she too crazy to remember that these things really happened?"

This was enough for Henry: the same impression had been produced on both of them. "You will do as you please," he said. "But if you will be guided by me, spare yourself the reading of those pages to come, which describe our brother's terrible expiation of his heartless marriage."

"Have you read it all, Henry?"

"Not all. I shrank from reading some of the latter part of it. Neither you nor I saw much of our elder brother after we left school; and, for my part, I felt, and never scrupled to express my feeling, that he behaved infamously to Agnes. But when I read that unconscious confession of the murderous conspiracy to which he fell a victim, I remembered, with something like remorse, that the same mother bore us. I have felt for him tonight, what I am ashamed to think I never felt for him before."

Lord Montbarry took his brother's hand.

"You are a good fellow, Henry, "he said; "but are you quite sure that you have not been needlessly distressing yourself? Because some of this crazy creature's writing accidentally tells what we know to be the truth, does it follow that all the rest is to be relied on to the end?"

"There is no possible doubt of it," Henry replied.

"No possible doubt?" his brother repeated. "I shall go on with my reading, Henry—and see what justification there may be for that confident conclusion of yours."

He read on steadily, until he had reached the end of the Second Act. Then he looked up.

"Do you really believe that the mutilated remains which you discovered this morning are the remains of our brother?" he asked. "And do you believe it on such evidence as this?"

Henry answered silently by a sign in the affirmative.

Lord Montbarry checked himself—evidently on the point of entering an indignant protest.

"You acknowledge that you have not read the later scenes of the piece," he said. "Don't be childish, Henry! If you persist in pinning your faith on such stuff as this, the least you can do is to make yourself thoroughly acquainted with it. Will you read the Third Act? No? Then I shall read it to you."

He turned to the Third Act, and ran over those fragmentary passages which were clearly enough written and expressed to be intelligible to the mind of a stranger.

"Here is a scene in the vaults of the palace," he began. "The victim of the conspiracy is sleeping on his miserable bed; and the Baron and the Countess are considering the position in which they stand. The Countess (as well as I can make it out) has raised the money that is wanted by borrowing on the security of her jewels at Frankfort; and the Courier upstairs is still declared by the Doctor to have a chance of recovery.

"What are the conspirators to do if the man does recover? The cautious Baron suggests setting the prisoner free. If he ventures to appeal to the law, it is easy to declare that he is subject to insane delusion, and to call his own wife as witness. On the other hand, if the Courier dies, how is the sequestrated and unknown nobleman to be put out of the way? Passively, by letting him starve in his prison? No: the Baron is a man of refined tastes; he dislikes needless cruelty.

"The active policy remains—say, assassination by the knife of a hired bravo? The Baron objects to trusting an accomplice; also to spending money on any one but himself. Shall they drop their prisoner into the canal? The Baron declines to trust water; water will show him on the surface. Shall they set his bed on fire? An excellent idea; but the smoke might be seen. No: the circumstances being now entirely altered, poisoning him presents the easiest way out of it. He has simply become a superfluous person. The cheapest poison will do.—Is it possible, Henry, that you believe this consultation really took place?"

Henry made no reply. The succession of the questions that had just been read to him, exactly followed the succession of the dreams that had terrified Mrs. Norbury, on the two nights which she had passed in the hotel. It was useless to point out this coincidence to his brother. He only said: "Go on."

Lord Montbarry turned the pages until he came to the next intelligible passage.

"Here," he proceeded, "is a double scene on the stage—so far as I can understand the sketch of it. The Doctor is upstairs, innocently writing his certificate of my Lord's disease, by the dead Courier's bedside. Down in the vaults, the Baron stands by the corpse of the poisoned lord, preparing the strong chemical acids which are to reduce it to a heap of ashes—Surely, it is not worthwhile to trouble ourselves with deciphering such melodramatic horrors as these? Let us get on! let us get on!"

He turned the leaves again; attempting vainly to discover the meaning of the confused scenes that followed. On the last page but one, he found the last intelligible sentences.

"The Third Act seems to be divided," he said, "into two Parts or Tableaux. I think I can read the writing at the beginning of the Second Part. The Baron and the Countess open the scene. The Baron's hands are mysteriously concealed by gloves. He has reduced the body to ashes by his own system of cremation, with the exception of the head—"

Henry interrupted his brother there. "Don't read any more!" he exclaimed.

"Let us do the Countess justice," Lord Montbarry persisted. "There are not half a dozen lines more that I can make out! The accidental breaking of his jar of acid has burned the Baron's hands severely. He is still unable to proceed to the destruction of the head—and the Countess is woman enough (with all her wickedness) to shrink from attempting to take his place when the first news is received of the coming arrival of the commission of inquiry dispatched by the insurance offices. The Baron feels no alarm.

"Inquire as the commission may, it is the natural death of the Courier (in my Lord's character) that they are blindly investigating. The head not being destroyed, the obvious alternative is to hide it—and the Baron is equal to the occasion. His studies in the old library have informed him of a safe place of concealment in the palace. The Countess may recoil from handling the acids and watching the process of cremation; but she can surely sprinkle a little disinfecting powder—"

"No more!" Henry reiterated. "No more!"

"There is no more that can be read, my dear fellow. The last page looks like sheer delirium. She may well have told you that her invention had failed her!"

"Face the truth honestly, Stephen, and say her memory."

Lord Montbarry rose from the table at which he had been sitting, and looked at his brother with pitying eyes.

"Your nerves are out of order, Henry," he said. "And no wonder, after that frightful discovery under the hearth-stone. We won't dispute about it; we will wait a day or two until you are quite yourself again. In the meantime, let us understand each other on one point at least. You leave the question of what is to be done with these pages of writing to me, as the head of the family?"

"I do."

Lord Montbarry quietly took up the manuscript and threw it into the fire. "Let this rubbish be of some use," he said, holding the pages down with the poker. "The room is getting chilly-the Countess's Play will set some of these charred logs flaming again." He waited a little at the fireplace, and returned to his brother.

"Now, Henry, I have a last word to say, and then I have done. I am ready to admit that you have stumbled, by an unlucky chance, on the proof of a crime committed in the old days of the palace, nobody knows how long ago. With that one concession, I dispute everything else. Rather than agree in the opinion you have formed, I won't believe anything that has happened. The supernatural influences that some of us felt when we first slept in this hotel—your loss of appetite, our sister's dreadful dreams, the smell that overpowered Francis, and the head that appeared to Agnes—I declare them all to be sheer delusions. I believe in nothing, nothing, nothing!" He opened the door to go out and looked back into the room. "Yes," he resumed, "there is one thing I believe in. My wife has committed a breach of confidence—I believe Agnes will marry you. Goodnight, Henry. We leave Venice the first thing tomorrow morning."

So Lord Montbarry disposed of the mystery of *The Haunted Hotel.*

Postscript

A last chance of deciding the difference of opinion between the two brothers remained in Henry's possession. He had his own idea of the use to which he might put the false teeth as a means of inquiry when he and his fellow-travellers returned to England.

The only surviving depositary of the domestic history of the family in past years, was Agnes Lockwood's old nurse. Henry took his first opportunity of trying to revive her personal recollections of the deceased Lord Montbarry. But the nurse had never forgiven the great man of the family for his desertion of Agnes; she flatly refused to consult her memory. "Even the bare sight of my lord, when I last saw him in London," said the old woman, "made my fingernails itch to set their mark on his face. I was sent on an errand by Miss Agnes; and I met him coming out of his dentist's door—and, thank God, that's the last I ever saw of him!"

Thanks to the nurse's quick temper and quaint way of expressing herself, the object of Henry's inquiries was gained already! He ventured on asking if she had noticed the situation of the house. She had noticed, and still remembered the situation—did Master Henry suppose she had lost the use of her senses, because she happened to be nigh on eighty years old? The same day he took the false teeth to the dentist, and set all further doubt (if doubt had still been possible) at rest forever. The teeth had been made for the first Lord Montbarry.

Henry never revealed the existence of this last link in the chain of discovery to any living creature, his brother Stephen included. He carried his terrible secret with him to the grave.

There was one other event in the memorable past on which he preserved the same compassionate silence. Little Mrs. Ferrari never knew that her husband had been—not, as she supposed, the Countess's victim—but the Countess's accomplice. She still believed that the late Lord Montbarry had sent her the thousand-pound note, and still recoiled from making use of a present which she persisted in declaring had "the stain of her husband's blood on it." Agnes, with the widow's entire approval, took the money to the Children's Hospital; and spent it in adding to the number of the beds.

In the spring of the new year the marriage took place. At the special request of Agnes, the members of the family were the only persons present at the ceremony. There was no wedding breakfast and the honeymoon was spent in the retirement of a cottage on the banks of the Thames.

During the last few days of the residence of the newly-married couple by the riverside, Lady Montbarry's children were invited to enjoy a day's play in the garden. The eldest girl overheard (and reported to her mother) a little conjugal dialogue which touched on the topic of The Haunted Hotel.

"Henry, I want you to give me a kiss."

"There it is, my dear."

"Now I am your wife, may I speak to you about something?"

"What is it?"

"Something that happened the day before we left Venice. You saw the Countess, during the last hours of her life. Won't you tell me whether she made any confession to you?"

"No conscious confession, Agnes—and therefore no confession that I need distress you by repeating."

"Did she say nothing about what she saw or heard, on that dreadful night in my room?"

"Nothing. We only know that her mind never recovered the terror of it."

Agnes was not quite satisfied. The subject troubled her. Even her own brief intercourse with her miserable rival of other days suggested questions that perplexed her. She remembered the Countess's prediction. "You have to bring me to the day of discovery, and to the punishment that is my doom." Had the prediction simply failed, like other mortal prophecies?—or had it been fulfilled on the terrible night when she had seen the apparition, and when she had innocently tempted the Countess to watch her in her room?

Let it, however, be recorded, among the other virtues of Mrs. Henry Westwick, that she never again attempted to persuade her husband into betraying his secrets. Other men's wives, hearing of this extraordinary conduct (and being trained in the modern school of morals and manners), naturally regarded her with compassionate contempt. They spoke of Agnes, from that time forth, as "rather an old-fashioned person."

Is that all?

That is all.

Is there no explanation of the mystery of The Haunted Hotel?

Ask yourself if there is any explanation of the mystery of your own life and death. Farewell.

Memoirs of an Adopted Son

1.—Circumstances which preceded his birth

[1]Towards the beginning of the eighteenth century there stood on a rock in the sea, near a fishing village on the coast of Brittany, a ruined Tower with a very bad reputation. No mortal was known to have inhabited it within the memory of living man. The one tenant whom Tradition associated with the occupation of the place, at a remote period, had moved into it from the infernal regions, nobody knew why—had lived in it, nobody knew how long—and had quitted possession, nobody knew when. Under such circumstances, nothing was more natural than that this unearthly Individual should give a name to his residence; for which reason the building was thereafter known to all the neighbourhood round as Satanstower.

Early in the year seventeen hundred, the inhabitants of the village were startled one night by seeing the reel gleam of a fire in the Tower, and by smelling, in the same direction, a preternaturally strong odour of fried fish. The next morning, the fishermen who passed by the building in their boats were amazed to find that a stranger had taken up his abode in it. Judging of him at a distance, he seemed to be a fine tall stout fellow: he was

1. The curious legend connected with the birth of this "Adopted Son," and the facts relating to his extraordinary career in after life, are derived from the "Records" of the French Police of the period. In this instance, and in the instances of those other papers in the present collection which deal with foreign incidents and characters, while the facts of each narrative exist in print, the form in which the narrative is cast is of my own devising. If these facts had been readily accessible to readers in general, the papers in question would not have been reprinted. But the scarce and curious books, from which my materials are derived, have been long since out of print, and are, in all human probability, never likely to be published again.

dressed in fisherman's costume, and he had a new boat of his own, moored comfortably in a cleft of the rock. If he had inhabited a place of decent reputation, his neighbours would have immediately made his acquaintance; but, as things were, all they could venture to do was to watch him in silence.

The first day passed, and, though it was fine weather, he made no use of his boat. The second day followed, with a continuance of the fine weather, and still he was as idle as before. On the third day, when a violent storm kept all the boats of the village on the beach—on the third day, in the midst of the tempest, away went the man of the Tower to make his first fishing experiment in strange waters!

He and his boat came back safe and sound, in a lull of the storm; and the villagers, watching on the cliff above, saw him carrying the fish up, by great basketsful, to his Tower. No such haul had ever fallen to the lot of any one of them—and the stranger had taken it in a whole gale of wind!

Upon this, the inhabitants of the village called a council. The lead in the debate was assumed by a smart young fellow, a fisherman named Poulailler, who stoutly declared that the stranger at the Tower was of infernal origin. "The rest of you may call him what you like," said Poulailler; "I call him The Fiend-Fisherman!"

The opinion thus expressed proved to be the opinion of the entire audience—with the one exception of the village priest. The priest said, "Gently, my sons. Don't make sure about the man of the Tower, before Sunday. "Wait and see if he comes to church."

"And if he doesn't come to church?" asked all the fishermen, in a breath.

"In that case," replied the priest, "I will excommunicate him—and then, my children, you may call him what you like."

Sunday came; and no sign of the stranger darkened the church doors. He was excommunicated, accordingly. The whole village forthwith adopted Poulailler's idea; and called the man of the Tower by the name which Poulailler had given him—"The Fiend-Fisherman."

These strong proceedings produced not the slightest apparent effect on the diabolical personage who had occasioned them. He persisted in remaining idle when the weather was fine; in going out to fish when no other boat in the place dare put to sea; and in coming back again to his solitary dwelling-place, with his nets full, his boat uninjured, and himself alive and hearty. He made no attempts to buy and sell with anybody; he kept steadily away from the village; he lived on fish of his own preternaturally strong frying; and he never spoke to a living soul—with the solitary exception of Poulailler himself.

One fine evening, when the young man was rowing home past the Tower, the Fiend-Fisherman darted out on to the rock—said, "Thank you, Poulailler, for giving me a name"—bowed politely—and darted in again. The young fisherman felt the words run cold down the marrow of his back; and whenever he was at sea again, he gave the Tower a wide berth from that day forth.

Time went on—and an important event occurred in Poulailler's life. He was engaged to be married. On the day when his betrothal was publicly made known, his friends clustered noisily about him on the fishing-jetty of the village to offer their congratulations. While they were all in full cry, a strange voice suddenly made itself heard through the confusion, which silenced everybody in an instant. The crowd fell back, and disclosed the Fiend-Fisherman sauntering up the jetty. It was the first time he had ever set foot—cloven foot—within the precincts of the village.

"Gentlemen," said the Fiend-Fisherman, "where is my friend Poulailler?" He put the question with perfect politeness; he looked remarkably well in his fisherman's costume; he exhaled a relishing odour of fried fish; he had a cordial nod for the men and a sweet smile for the women—but, with all these personal advantages, everybody fell back from him, and nobody answered his question. The coldness of the popular reception, however, did not in any way abash him. He looked about for Poulailler with searching eyes, discovered the place in which he was standing, and addressed him in the friendliest manner.

"So you are going to be married?" remarked the Fiend-Fisherman.

"What's that to you?' said Poulailler. He was inwardly terrified, but outwardly gruff—not an uncommon combination of circumstances with men of his class, in his mental situation.

"My friend," pursued the Fiend-Fisherman, "I have not forgotten your polite attention in giving me a name; and I come here to requite it. You will have a family, Poulailler; and your first child will be a boy. I propose to make that boy my Adopted Son."

The marrow of Poulailler's back became awfully cold—but he grew gruffer than ever, in spite of his back.

"You won't do anything of the sort," he replied. "If I have the largest family in France, no child of mine shall ever go near you."

"I shall adopt your firstborn for all that," persisted the Fiend-Fisherman. "Poulailler! I wish you good morning. Ladies and gentlemen! the same to all of you."

With those words, he withdrew from the jetty; and the marrow of Poulailler's back recovered its temperature.

The next morning was stormy; and all the village expected to see the boat from the Tower put out, as usual, to sea. Not a sign of it appeared. Later in the day, the rock on which the building stood was examined from a distance. Neither boat nor nets were in their customary places. At night, the red gleam of the fire was missed for the first time. The Fiend-Fisherman had gone! He had announced his intentions on the jetty, and had disappeared. What did this mean? Nobody knew.

On Poulailler's wedding-day, a portentous circumstance recalled the memory of the diabolical stranger, and, as a matter of course, seriously discomposed the bridegroom's back. At the moment when the marriage ceremony was complete, a relishing odour of fried fish stole into the nostrils of the company, and a voice from invisible lips said: "Keep up your spirits, Poulailler; I have not forgotten my promise!"

A year later, Madame Poulailler was in the hands of the midwife of the district, and a repetition of the portentous circumstance took place. Poulailler was waiting in the kitchen to hear how matters ended upstairs. The nurse came in with a baby. "Which is it?" asked the happy father; "girl or boy?" Before the nurse could answer, an odour of supernaturally fried fish filled the kitchen; and a voice from invisible lips replied: "A boy, Poulailler—and I've got him."

Such were the circumstances under which the subject of this *Memoir* was introduced to the joys and sorrows of mortal existence.

2.—His Boyhood and Early Life

When a boy is born under auspices which lead his parents to suppose that, while the bodily part of him is safe at home, the spiritual part is subjected to a course of infernal tuition elsewhere—what are his father and mother to do with him? They must do the best they can—which was exactly what Poulailler and his wife did with the hero of these pages.

In the first place, they had him christened instantly. It was observed with horror that his infant face was distorted with grimaces, and that his infant voice roared with a preternatural lustiness of tone the moment the priest touched him. The first thing he asked for, when he learnt to speak was "fried fish;" and the first place he wanted to go to, when he learnt to walk, was the diabolical Tower on the rock.

"He won't learn anything," said the master, when he was old enough to go to school.

"Thrash him," said Poulailler—and the master thrashed him.

"He won't come to his first communion," said the priest.

"Thrash him," said Poulailler—and the priest thrashed him.

The farmer's orchards were robbed; the neighbouring rabbit-warrens were depopulated; linen was stolen from the gardens, and nets were torn on the beach.

"The deuce take Poulailler's boy," was the general cry.

"The deuce has got him," was Poulailler's answer.

"And yet he is a nice-looking boy," said Madame Poulailler. And he was—as tall, as strong, as handsome a young fellow, as could be seen in all France.

"Let us pray for him," said Madame Poulailler.

"Let us thrash him," said her husband.

"Our son has been thrashed till all the sticks in the neighbourhood are broken," pleaded his mother.

"We will try him with the rope's end next," retorted his father; "he shall go to sea and live in an atmosphere of thrashing. Our son shall be a cabin-boy."

It was all one to Poulailler Junior—he knew who had adopted him, as well as his father—he had been instinctively conscious from infancy of the Fiend-Fisherman's interest in his welfare-he cared for no earthly discipline—and a cabin-boy he became at ten years old.

After two years of the rope's-end (applied quite ineffectually), the subject of this memoir robbed his captain, and ran away in an English port. London became the next scene of his adventures. At twelve years old, he persuaded society in the Metropolis that he was the forsaken natural son of a French duke. British benevolence, after blindly providing for him for four years, opened its eyes and found him out at the age of sixteen; upon which he returned to France, and entered the army in the capacity of drummer.

At eighteen he deserted, and had a turn with the gipsies. He told fortunes, he conjured, he danced on the tight-rope, he acted, he sold quack medicines, he altered his mind again, and returned to the army. Here he fell in love with the *vivandière* of his new regiment. The sergeant-major of the company, touched by the same amiable weakness, naturally resented his attentions to the lady. Poulailler (perhaps unjustifiably) asserted himself by boxing his officer's ears. Out flashed the swords on both sides, and in went Poulailler's blade through and through the tender heart of the sergeant-major. The frontier was close at hand. Poulailler wiped his sword, and crossed it.

Sentence of death was recorded against him in his absence. When society has condemned us to die, if we are men of any spirit, how are we to return the compliment? By condemning society to keep us alive—or, in other words, by robbing right and left for a living. Poulailler's destiny was now accomplished. He was picked out to be the Greatest Thief of his age; and when Fate summoned him to his place in the world, he stepped forward and took it. His life hitherto had been merely the life of a young scamp—he was now to do justice to the diabolical father who had adopted him, and to expand to the proportions of a full-grown Robber.

His first exploits were performed in Germany. They showed such novelty of combination, such daring, such dexterity, and, even in his most homicidal moments, such irresistible gaiety and good humour, that a band of congenial spirits gathered about him in no time. As commander-in-chief of the Thieves' army, his popularity never wavered.

His weaknesses—and what illustrious man is without them?—were three in number. First weakness—he was extravagantly susceptible to the charms of the fair sex. Second weakness—he was perilously fond of practical jokes. Third weakness (inherited from his adopted parent)—his appetite was insatiable in the matter of fried fish.

As for the merits to set against these defects, some have been noticed already, and others will appear immediately. Let it merely be premised, in this place, that he was one of the handsomest men of his time, that he dressed superbly, and that he was capable of the most exalted acts of generosity wherever a handsome woman was concerned—let this be understood, to begin with; and let us now enter on the narrative of his last exploit in Germany before he returned to France.

This adventure is something more than a mere specimen of

his method of workmanship—it proved, in the future, to be the fatal event of his life.

On a Monday in the week, he had stopped on the highway, and robbed of all his valuables and all his papers, an Italian nobleman—the Marquis Petrucci of Sienna. On Tuesday, he was ready for another stroke of business. Posted on the top of a steep hill, he watched the road which wound up to the summit on one side, while his followers were ensconced on the road which led down from it on the other. The prize expected, in this case, was the travelling carriage (with a large sum of money inside) of the Baron de Kirbergen.

Before long, Poulailler discerned the carriage afar off, at the bottom of the hill, and in advance of it, ascending the eminence, two ladies on foot. They were the Baron's daughters—Wilhelmina, a fair beauty; Frederica, a brunette—both lovely, both accomplished, both susceptible, both young. Poulailler sauntered down the hill to meet the fascinating travellers. He looked—bowed—introduced himself—and fell in love with Wilhelmina on the spot.

Both the charming girls acknowledged in the most artless manner that confinement to the carriage had given them the fidgets, and that they were walking up the hill to try the remedy of gentle exercise. Poulailler's heart was touched, and Poulailler's generosity to the sex was roused in the nick of time. With a polite apology to the young ladies, he ran back, by a short cut, to the ambush on the other side of the hill in which his men were posted.

"Gentlemen!" cried the generous thief, "in the charming name of Wilhelmina do Kirbergen, I charge you all, let the Baron's carriage pass free." The band was not susceptible—the band demurred. Poulailler knew them. He had appealed to their hearts in vain—he now appealed to their pockets.

"Gentlemen!" he resumed, "excuse my momentary misconception of your sentiments. Here is my one half share of the Marquis Petrucci's property. If I divide it among you, will you let the carriage pass free?"

The band knew the value of money—and accepted the terms. Poulailler rushed back up the hill, and arrived at the top just in time to hand the young ladies into the carriage. "Charming man!" said the white Wilhelmina to the brown Frederica, as they drove off. Innocent soul! What would she have said if she had known that her personal attractions had saved her father's property? Was she ever to see the charming man again? Yes: she was to see him the next day—and, more than that, Fate was hereafter to link her fast to the robber's life and the robber's doom.

Confiding the direction of the band to his first lieutenant, Poulailler followed the carriage on horseback, and ascertained the place of the Baron's residence that night.

The next morning a superbly-dressed stranger knocked at the door. "What name, sir?" said the servant. "The Marquis Petrucci of Sienna," replied Poulailler.

"How are the young ladies after their journey?" The Marquis was shown in, and introduced to the Baron. The Baron was naturally delighted to receive a brother nobleman—Miss Wilhelmina was modestly happy to see the charming man again—Miss Frederica was affectionately pleased on her sister's account. Not being of a disposition to lose time where his affections were concerned, Poulailler expressed his sentiments to the "beloved object that evening. The next morning he had an interview with the Baron, at which he produced the papers which proved him to be the Marquis.

Nothing could be more satisfactory to the mind of the most anxious parent—the two noblemen embraced. They were still in each other's arms, when a second stranger knocked at the door.

"What name, sir?" said the servant.

"The Marquis Petrucci of Sienna," replied the stranger.

"Impossible!" said the servant; "his lordship is now in the house."

"Show me in, scoundrel," cried the visitor. The servant submitted, and the two Marquises stood face to face. Poulailler's composure was not shaken in the least; he had come first to the house, and he had got the papers.

"You are the villain who robbed me!" cried the true Petrucci.

"You are drunk, mad, or an impostor," retorted the false Petrucci.

"Send to Florence, where I am known," exclaimed one of the Marquises, apostrophizing the Baron.

"Send to Florence by all means," echoed the other, addressing himself to the Baron also.

"Gentlemen," replied the noble Kirbergen, "I will do myself the honour of taking your advice"—and he sent to Florence accordingly.

Before the messenger had advanced ten miles on his journey, Poulailler had said two words in private to the susceptible Wilhelmina—and the pair eloped from the baronial residence that night. Once more the subject of this *Memoir* crossed the frontier, and re-entered France. Indifferent to the attractions of rural life, he forthwith established himself with the beloved object in Paris. In that superb city he met with his strangest adventures, performed his boldest achievements, committed his most prodigious robberies, and, in a word, did himself and his infernal patron the fullest justice, in the character of the Fiend-Fisherman's Adopted Son.

3.—His Career in Paris

Once established in the French metropolis, Poulailler planned and executed that vast system of perpetual robbery and occasional homicide which made him the terror and astonishment of all Paris. Indoors, as well as out, his good fortune befriended him. No domestic anxieties harassed his mind, and diverted him from the pursuit of his distinguished public career. The attachment of the charming creature with whom he had eloped from Germany survived the discovery that the Marquis Petrucci was

Poulailler the robber. True to the man of her choice, the devoted Wilhelmina shared his fortunes, and kept his house. And why not, if she loved him?—in the all-conquering name of Cupid, why not?

Joined by picked men from his German followers, and by new recruits gathered together in Paris, Poulailler now set society and its safeguards at flat defiance. Cartouche himself was his inferior in audacity and cunning.

In course of time, the whole city was panic-stricken by the new robber and his band—the very Boulevards were deserted after nightfall Monsieur Hérault, lieutenant of police of the period, in despair of laying hands on Poulailler by any other means, at last offered a reward of a hundred *pistoles* and a place in his office worth two thousand *livres* a-year to anyone who would apprehend the robber alive. The bills were posted all over Paris—and, the next morning, they produced the very last result in the world which the lieutenant of police could possibly have anticipated.

Whilst Monsieur Hérault was at breakfast in his study, the Count de Villeneuve was announced as wishing to speak to him. Knowing the Count by name only, as belonging to an ancient family in Provence, or in Languedoc, Monsieur Hérault ordered him to be shown in. A perfect gentleman appeared, dressed with an admirable mixture of magnificence and good taste. "I have something for your private ear, sir," said the Count. "Will you give orders that no one must be allowed to disturb us?"

Monsieur Hérault gave the orders.

"May I inquire, Count, what your business is?" he asked, when the door was closed.

"To earn the reward you offer for taking Poulailler," answered the Count. "I am Poulailler."

Before Monsieur Hérault could open his lips, the robber produced a pretty little dagger and some rose-coloured silk cord. "The point of this dagger is poisoned," he observed; "and one scratch of it, my dear sir, would be the death of you."

With these words Poulailler gagged the lieutenant of police, bound him to his chair with the rose-coloured cord, and lightened his writing-desk of one thousand *pistoles*. "I'll take money, instead of taking the place in the office which you kindly offer," said Poulailler. "Don't trouble yourself to see me to the door. Good morning."

A few weeks later, while Monsieur Hérault was still the popular subject of ridicule throughout Paris, business took Poulailler on the road to Lille and Cambrai. The only inside passenger in the coach besides himself, was the venerable Dean Potter of Brussels. They fell into talk on the one interesting subject of the time—not the weather, but Poulailler.

"It's a disgrace, sir, to the police," said the Dean, "that such a miscreant is still at large. I shall be returning to Paris, by this road, in ten days' time, and I shall call on Monsieur Hérault, to suggest a plan of my own for catching the scoundrel."

"May I ask what it is?" said Poulailler.

"Excuse me," replied the Dean; "you are a stranger, sir,—and, moreover, I wish to keep the merit of suggesting the plan to myself."

"Do you think the lieutenant of police will see you?" asked Poulailler; "he is not accessible to strangers, since the miscreant you speak of played him that trick at his own breakfast table."

"He will see Dean Potter of Brussels," was the reply, delivered with the slightest possible tinge of offended dignity.

"Oh, unquestionably!" said Poulailler,—"pray pardon me."

"Willingly, sir," said the Dean and the conversation flowed into other channels.

Nine days later the wounded pride of Monsieur Hérault was soothed by a very remarkable letter. It was signed by one of Poulailler's band, who offered himself as King's evidence, in the hope of obtaining a pardon. The letter stated that the venerable Dean Potter had been waylaid and murdered by Poulailler, and that the robber, with his customary audacity, was to re-enter Paris by the Lisle coach, the next day, disguised in the Dean's clothes, and furnished with the Dean's own papers.

Monsieur Hérault took his precautions without losing a moment. Picked men were stationed, with their orders, at the barrier through which the coach must pass to enter Paris; while the lieutenant of police waited at his office, in the company of two French gentlemen who could speak to the Dean's identity, in the event of Poulailler's impudently persisting in the assumption of his victim's name.

At the appointed hour the coach appeared, and out of it got a man in the Dean's costume. He was arrested in spite of his protestations; the papers of the murdered Potter were found on him, and he was dragged off to the police office in triumph. The door opened, and the *posse comitatus* entered with the prisoner. Instantly the two witnesses burst out with a cry of recognition, and turned indignantly on the lieutenant of police.

"Gracious Heaven, sir, what have you done?" they exclaimed in horror; "this is not Poulailler—here is our venerable friend; here is the Dean himself!"

At the same moment, a servant entered with a letter. "Dean Potter. To the care of Monsieur Hérault, Lieutenant of Police." The letter was expressed in these words:

> Venerable sir,—Profit by the lesson I have given you. Be a Christian for the future, and never again try to injure a man unless he tries to injure you. Entirely yours, Poulailler.

These feats of cool audacity were matched by others, in which his generosity to the sex asserted itself as magnanimously as ever.

Hearing, one day, that large sums of money were kept in the house of a great lady, one Madame de Brienne, whose door was guarded, in anticipation of a visit from the famous thief, by a porter of approved trustworthiness and courage, Poulailler undertook to rob her in spite of her precautions, and succeeded. With a stout pair of leather straps and buckles in his pocket, and with two of his band, disguised as a coachman, and footman, he followed Madame de Brienne one night to the theatre.

Just before the close of the performance, the lady's coachman and footman were tempted away for five minutes by Poulailler's disguised subordinates to have a glass of wine.

No attempt was made to detain them, or to drug, their liquor. But, in their absence, Poulailler had slipped under the carriage, had hung his leather straps round the pole—one to hold by, and one to support his feet—and, with these simple preparations, was now ready to wait for events. Madame de Brienne entered the carriage—the footman got up behind—Poulailler hung himself horizontally under the pole,, and was driven home with them, under those singular circumstances.

He was strong enough to keep his position after the carriage had been taken into the coach-house; and he only left it when the doors were locked for the night. Provided with food beforehand, he waited patiently, hidden in the coach-house, for two days and nights, watching his opportunity of getting into Madame de Brienne's *boudoir*.

On the third night the lady went to a grand ball—the servants relaxed in their vigilance while her back was turned—and Poulailler slipped into the room. He found two thousand *louis d'ors*, which was nothing like the sum he expected, and a pocketbook, which he took away with him to open at home. It contained some stock-warrants for a comparatively trifling amount. Poulailler was far too well off to care about taking them, and far too polite, where a lady was concerned, not to send them back again, under those circumstances. Accordingly, Madame de Brienne received her warrants, with a note of apology from the polite thief.

> "Pray excuse my visit to your charming *boudoir*," wrote Poulailler, "in consideration of the false reports of your wealth, which alone induced me to enter it. If I had known what your pecuniary circumstances really were, on the honour of a gentleman, Madam, I should have been incapable of robbing you. I cannot return your two thousand *louis d'ors* by post, as I return your warrants. But if you are at all pressed for money in future, I shall be proud

to assist so distinguished a lady by lending her, from my own ample resources, double the sum of which I regret to have deprived her on the present occasion."

This letter was shown to royalty at Versailles. It excited the highest admiration of the Court—especially of the ladies. Whenever the robber's name was mentioned, they indulgently referred to him as the Chevalier de Poulailler. Ah! that was the age of politeness, when good-breeding was recognized, even in a thief. Under similar circumstances, who would recognize it now? *O tempora*! *O mores*!

On another occasion, Poulailler was out one night, taking the air and watching his opportunities on the roofs of the houses; a member of the band being posted in the street below to assist him in case of necessity. While in this position, sobs and groans proceeding from an open back-garret window caught his ear. A parapet rose before the window, which enabled him to climb down and look in.

Starving children surrounding a helpless mother, and clamouring for food, was the picture that met his eye. The mother was young and beautiful; and Poulailler's hand impulsively clutched his purse, as a necessary consequence. Before the charitable thief could enter by the window, a man rushed in by the door, with a face of horror; and cast a handful of gold into the lovely mother's lap.

"My honour is gone," he cried; "but our children are saved! Listen to the circumstances. I met a man in the street below; he was tall and thin; he had a green patch over one eye; he was looking up suspiciously at this house, apparently waiting for somebody. I thought of you—I thought of the children—I seized the suspicious stranger by the collar. Terror overwhelmed him on the spot. 'Take my watch, my money, and my two valuable gold snuff-boxes,' he said—'but spare my life.' I took them."

"Noble-hearted man!" cried Poulailler, appearing at the window. The husband started; the wife screamed; the children hid themselves.

"Let me entreat you to be composed," continued Poulailler. "Sir! I enter on the scene for the purpose of soothing your uneasy conscience. From your vivid description, I recognize the man whose property is now in your wife's lap. Resume your mental tranquillity. You have robbed a robber—in other words, you have vindicated society. Accept my congratulations on your restored innocence. The miserable coward whose collar you seized, is one of Poulailler's band. He has lost his stolen property, as the fit punishment for his disgraceful want of spirit."

"Who are you?" exclaimed the husband.

"I am Poulailler," replied the illustrious man, with the simplicity of an ancient hero. "Take this purse; and set up in business with the contents. There is a prejudice, Sir, in favour of honesty. Give that prejudice a chance. There was a time when I felt it myself; I regret to feel it no longer. Under all varieties of misfortune, an honest man has his consolation still left. Where is it left? Here!" He struck his heart—and the family fell on their knees before him.

"Benefactor of your species!" cried the husband—"how can I show my gratitude?"

"You can permit me to kiss the hand of *madame*," answered Poulailler.

Madame started to her feet, and embraced the generous stranger. "What more can I do?" exclaimed this lovely woman eagerly—"Oh, Heavens! what more?"

"You can beg your husband to light me down stairs," replied Poulailler. He spoke, pressed their hands, dropped a generous tear, and departed. At that touching moment, his own adopted father would not have known him.

This last anecdote closes the record of Poulailler's career in Paris. The lighter and more agreeable aspects of that career have hitherto been designedly presented, in discreet remembrance of the contrast which the tragic side of the picture must now present. Comedy and Sentiment, twin sisters of French extraction, farewell! Horror enters next on the stage and enters welcome, in the name of the Fiend Fisherman's Adopted Son.

4.— His Exit from the Scene

The nature of Poulailler's more serious achievements in the art of robbery may be realized by reference to one terrible fact. In the police records of the period, more than one hundred and fifty men and women are reckoned up as having met their deaths at the hands of Poulailler and his band. It was not the practice of this formidable robber to take life as well as property, unless life happened to stand directly in his way—in which case he immediately swept off the obstacle without hesitation and without remorse.

His deadly determination to rob, which was thus felt by the population in general, was matched by his deadly determination to be obeyed, which was felt by his followers in particular. One of their number, for example, having withdrawn from his allegiance, and having afterwards attempted to betray his leader, was tracked to his hiding-place in a cellar, and was there walled up alive in Poulailler's presence; the robber composing the unfortunate wretch's epitaph, and scratching it on the wet plaster with his own hand.

Years afterwards the inscription was noticed, when the house fell into the possession of a new tenant, and was supposed to be nothing more than one of the many jests which the famous robber had practised in his time. When the plaster was removed, the skeleton fell out, and testified that Poulailler was in earnest.

To attempt the arrest of such a man as this by tampering with his followers, was practically impossible. No sum of money that could be offered would induce any one of the members of his band to risk the fatal chance of his vengeance.

Other means of getting possession of him had been tried, and tried in vain. Five times over, the police had succeeded in tracking him to different hiding-places; and on all five occasions, the women—who adored him for his gallantry, his generosity, and his good looks—had helped him to escape.

If he had not unconsciously paved the way to his own capture, first by eloping with Mademoiselle Wilhelmina de Kirbergen, and secondly by maltreating her, it is more than doubtful whether the long arm of the law would ever have reached far enough to fasten its grasp on him. As it was, the extremes of love and hatred met at last in the bosom of the devoted Wilhelmina; and the vengeance of a neglected woman accomplished what the whole police force of Paris had been powerless to achieve.

Poulailler, never famous for the constancy of his attachments, had wearied, at an early period, of the companion of his flight from Germany—but Wilhelmina was one of those women whose affections, once aroused, will not take "No" for an answer. She persisted in attaching herself to a man who had ceased to love her. Poulailler's patience became exhausted; he tried twice to rid himself of his unhappy mistress—once by the knife and once by poison—and failed on both occasions.

For the third and last time, by way of attempting an experiment of another kind, he established a rival to drive the German woman out of the house. From that moment his fate was sealed. Maddened by jealous rage, Wilhelmina cast the last fragments of her fondness to the winds. She secretly communicated with the police and Poulailler met his doom.

A night was appointed with the authorities; and the robber was invited by his discarded mistress to a farewell interview. His contemptuous confidence in her fidelity rendered him careless of his customary precautions. He accepted the appointment; and the two supped together, on the understanding that they were henceforth to be friends, and nothing more. Towards the close of the meal, Poulailler was startled by a ghastly change in the face of his companion.

"What is wrong with you?" he asked.

"A mere trifle," she answered, looking at her glass of wine. "I can't help loving you still, badly as you have treated me. You are a dead man, Poulailler—and I shall not survive you."

The robber started to his feet, and seized a knife on the table.

"You have poisoned me?" he exclaimed.

"No," she replied. "Poison is my vengeance on myself; not my vengeance on you. You will rise from this table as you sat down to it. But your evening will be finished in prison; and your life will be ended on the Wheel."

As she spoke the words, the door was burst open by the police, and Poulailler was secured. The same night the poison did its fatal work; and his mistress made atonement with her life for the first, last, act of treachery which had revenged her on the man she loved.

Once safely lodged in the hands of justice, the robber tried to gain time to escape in, by promising to make important disclosures. The manoeuvre availed him nothing. In those days, the Laws of the Land had not yet made acquaintance with the Laws of Humanity. Poulailler was put to the torture—was suffered to recover—was publicly broken on the Wheel—and was taken off it alive, to be cast into a blazing fire. By those murderous means, Society rid itself of a murderous man—and the idlers on the Boulevards took their evening stroll again in recovered security.

Paris had seen the execution of Poulailler—but, if legends are to be trusted, our old friends, the people of the fishing village in Brittany, saw the end of him afterwards. On the day and hour when he perished, the heavens darkened, and a terrible storm arose. Once more, and for a moment only, the gleam of the unearthly fire reddened the windows of the old Tower. Thunder pealed and struck the building into fragments.

Lightning flashed incessantly over the ruins; and, in the scorching glare of it, the boat which in former years had put off to sea whenever the storm rose highest, was seen to shoot out into the raging ocean from the cleft in the rock—and was discovered, on this final occasion, to be doubly manned. The Fiend-Fisherman sat at the helm; his Adopted Son tugged at the oars; and a clamour of diabolical voices, roaring awfully through the roaring storm, wished the pair of them a prosperous voyage.

My Black Mirror

Has everybody heard of Doctor Dee, the magician, and of the "black speculum" or mirror of cannel coal, in which he could see at will everything in the wide world, and many things beyond it? If so, I may introduce myself to my readers in the easiest manner possible. Although I cannot claim to be a descendant of Doctor Dee, I profess the occult art to the extent of keeping a black mirror, made exactly after the model of that possessed by the old astrologer. My speculum, like his, is constructed of an oval piece of cannel coal, highly polished, and set on a wooden back with a handle to hold it by.

Nothing can be simpler than its appearance; nothing more marvellous than its capacities—provided always that the person using it be a true adept. Any man who disbelieves nothing is a true adept. Let him get a piece of cannel coal, polish it highly, clean it before use with a white cambric handkerchief, retire to a private sitting-room, invoke the name of Doctor Dee, shut both eyes for a moment, and open them again suddenly on the black mirror. If he does not see anything he likes, after that—past, present, or future—then let him depend on it there is some speck or flaw of incredulity in his nature; and the sad termination of his career may be considered certain. Sooner or later, he will end in being nothing but a rational man.

I, who have not one morsel of rationality about me; I, who am as true an adept as if I had lived in the good old times ("the Ages of Faith," as another adept has very properly called them), find unceasing interest and occupation in my black mirror. For everything I want to know, and for everything I want to do, I consult it. This very day, for instance (being in the position of most of the other inhabitants of London, at the present season), I am thinking of soon going out of town.

My time for being away is so limited, and my wanderings have extended, at home and abroad, in so many directions, that I can hardly hope to visit any really beautiful scenes, or gather any really interesting experiences that are absolutely new to me. I must go to some place that I have visited before; and I must, in common regard to my own holiday interests, take care that it is a place where I have already thoroughly enjoyed myself, without a single drawback to my pleasure that is worth mentioning.

Under these circumstances, if I were a mere rational man, what should I do? Weary my memory to help mo to decide on a destination, by giving me my past travelling recollections in one long panorama—although I can tell by experience that of all my faculties memory is the least serviceable at the very time when I most want to employ it. As a true adept, I know better than to give myself any useless trouble of this sort. I retire to my private sitting-room, take up my black mirror, mention what I—want and, behold!

On the surface of the cannel coal the image of my former travels passes before me, in a succession of dream-scenes. I revive my past experiences by the evidence of my own eyes; and I may add, by that of my own ears also—for the figures in my magic landscapes move and speak!

Shall I go on the continent again? Yes. To what part of it? Suppose I revisit Austrian Italy, for the sake of renewing my familiarity with certain views, buildings, and pictures which once delighted me?[1] But let me first ascertain whether I had any serious drawbacks to complain of on making acquaintance with that part of the world. Black Mirror! Show me my first evening in Austrian Italy.

---

1. The reader is requested to bear in mind that this article was written before the year 1859—W. C.

A cloud rises on the magic surface—rests on it a little while—slowly disappears. My eyes are fixed on the cannel coal. I see nothing, hear nothing of the world about me. The first of the magic scenes grows visible. I behold it, as in a dream. Away with the ignorant Present. I am in Italy again—before Italy was one Kingdom.

The darkness is just coming on. I see myself looking out of the side window of a carriage. The hollow roll of the wheels has changed to a sharp rattle, and we have entered a town. We cross a vast square, illuminated by two lamps and a glimmer of reflected light from a coffee-shop window. We get on into a long street, with heavy stone arcades for foot-passengers to walk under. Everything looks dark and confused; grim visions of cloaked men flit by, all smoking; shrill female voices rise above the clatter of our wheels, then subside again in a moment.

We stop. The bells on the horses' necks ring their last tiny peal for the night. A greasy hand opens the carriage-door, and helps me down the steps. I am under an archway, with blank darkness before me, with a smiling man holding a flaming tallow candle by my side, with street spectators silently looking on behind me. They wear high-crowned hats and brown cloaks, mysteriously muffling them up to the chin. Brigands, evidently. Pass, Scene! I am a peaceable man, and I don't like the suspicion of a *stiletto*,, even in a dream.

Show me my sitting-room. Where did I dine, and how, on my first evening in Austrian Italy?

I am in the presence of two cheerful waiters, with two flaring candles. One is lighting lamps; the other is setting brushwood and logs in a blaze in a perfect cavern of a hearth. Where am I, now that there is plenty of light to see by? Apparently in a banqueting hall, fifty feet long by forty wide. This is my private sitting-room, and I am to eat my little bit of dinner in it all alone. Let me look about observantly, while the meal is preparing.

Above me is an arched painted ceiling, all alive with Cupids rolling about on clouds, and scattering perpetual roses on the heads of travellers beneath. Around me are classical landscapes of the school which treats the spectator to umbrella-shaped trees, calm green oceans, and foregrounds rampant with dancing goddesses. Beneath me is something elastic to tread upon, smelling very like old straw, which indeed it is, covered with a thin drugget.

This is humanely intended to protect me against the cold of the stone or brick floor, and is a concession to English prejudices on the subject of comfort. May I be grateful for it, and take no unfriendly notice of the fleas, though they are crawling up my legs from the straw and the drugget already!

What do I see next? Dinner on table. Drab-coloured soup, which will take a great deal of thickening with grated Parmesan cheese, and five dishes all round it. Trout fried in oil, rolled beef steeped in succulent brown gravy, roast chicken with water-cresses, square pastry cakes with mincemeat inside them, fried potatoes —all excellent. This is really good Italian cookery: it is more fanciful than the English and more solid than the French. It is not greasy, and none of the fried dishes taste in the slightest degree of lamp oil. The wine is good, too—effervescent, smacking of the Muscatel grape, and only eighteen-pence a bottle.

The second course more than sustains the character of the first. Small browned birds that look like larks, their plump breasts clothed succulently with a counterpane of fat bacon, their tender backs reposing on beds of savoury toast,—stewed pigeon,—a sponge cake pudding,—baked pears. Where could one find a better dinner or a pleasanter waiter to serve at table? He is neither servile nor familiar, and is always ready to occupy any superfluous attention I have to spare with all the small talk that is in him. He has, in fact, but one fault, and that consists in his very vexatious and unaccountable manner of varying the language in which he communicates with me.

I speak French and Italian, and he can speak French also as well as his own tongue. I naturally, however, choose Italian on first addressing him, because it is his native language. He understands what I say to him perfectly, but he answers me in French. I bethink myself, upon this, that he may be wishing, like the rest of us, to show off any little morsel of learning that he has picked up, or that he may fancy I understand French better than I do Italian, and may be politely anxious to make our colloquy as easy as possible to me.

Accordingly, I humour him, and change to French when I next speak. No sooner are the words out of my mouth than, with inexplicable perversity, he answers me in Italian. All through the dinner I try hard to make him talk the same language that I do; yet, excepting now and then a few insignificant phrases, I never succeed. What is the meaning of his playing this game of philological see-saw with me? Do the people here actually carry the national politeness so far as to flatter the stranger by according him an undisturbed monopoly of the language in which he chooses to talk to them?

I cannot explain it, and dessert surprises me in the midst of my perplexities. Four dishes again! Parmesan cheese, macaroons, pears, and green figs. With these and another bottle of the effervescent wine, how brightly the evening will pass away by the blazing wood fire! Surely, I cannot do better than go to Austrian Italy again, after having met with such a first welcome to the country as this. Shall I put down the cannel coal, and determine, without any more ado, on paying a second visit to the land that is cheered by my comfortable inn? No, not too hastily. Let me try the effect of one or two more scenes from my past travelling experience in this particular division of the Italian peninsula before I decide.

Black Mirror! How did I end my evening at the comfortable inn?

The cloud passes again, heavily and thickly this time, over the surface of the mirror—clears away slowly—shows me myself dozing luxuriously by the red embers with an empty bottle at my side. A suddenly opening door wakes me up; the landlord of the inn approaches, places a long, official-looking book on the table, and hands me pen and ink. I inquire peevishly what I am wanted to write at that time of night, when I am just digesting my dinner.

The landlord answers respectfully that I am required to give the police a full, true, and particular account of myself. I approach the table, thinking this demand rather absurd, for my passport is already in the hands of the authorities. However, as I am in a despotic country, I keep my thoughts to myself, open a blank page in the official looking book, see that it is divided into columns, with printed headings, and find that I no more understand what they mean than I understand an assessed tax-paper at home, to which, by-the-bye, the blank page bears a striking general resemblance. The headings are technical official words, which I now meet with as parts of Italian speech for the first time. I am obliged to appeal to the polite landlord; and, by his assistance, I get gradually to understand what it is the Austrian police want of me.

The police require to know, before they will let me go on peaceably tomorrow, first, what my name is in full! (Answered easily enough.) Second, what is my nation? (British, and delighted to cast it in the teeth of continental tyrants.) Third, where was I born? (In London—parish of Marylebone—and I wish my native vestry knew how the Austrian authorities were using me.) Fourth, where do I live? (In London, again—and I have half a mind to write to the *Times* about this nuisance before I go to bed.)

Fifth, how old am I? (My age is what it has been for the last seven years, and what it will remain till further notice—twenty-five exactly.) What next? By all that is inquisitive, here are the police wanting to know (Sixth) whether I am married or single! Landlord, what is the Italian for Bachelor? "Write Nubile, *signor.*" Nubile? That means marriageable. Permit me to remark, my good sir, that this is a woman's definition of a bachelor not a man's. No matter, let it pass. What next? (O distrustful despots! what next?)

Seventh, what is my condition! (First rate condition, to be sure,—full of rolled beef, toasted larks, and effervescent wine. Condition? What do they mean by that? Profession, is it? I have not got one. What shall I write? "Write Proprietor, *signor.*" Very well: but I don't know that I am proprietor of anything except the clothes I stand up in: even my trunk was borrowed of a friend.) Eighth, where do I come from? Ninth, where am I going to?

Tenth, when did I get my passport? Eleventh, where did I get my passport? Twelfth, who gave me my passport? Was there ever such a monstrous string of questions to address to a harmless, idle man, who only wants to potter about Italy quietly in a post-chaise! Do they catch Mazzini, landlord, with all these precautions? No: they only catch me.

There! There! Take your *Traveller's Book* back to the police. Surely such unfounded distrust of my character as the production of that volume at my dinner table implies, forms a serious drawback to the pleasure of travelling in Austrian Italy. Shall I give up at once all idea of going there, in my own innocent character again? No! Let me be deliberate in arriving at a decision,—let me patiently try the experiment of looking at one more scene from the past.

Black Mirror! How did I travel in Austrian Italy after I had paid my bill in the morning, and had left my comfortable inn?

The new dream scene shows me evening again. I have joined another English traveller in taking a vehicle that they call a *calèche*. It is a frowsy kind of sedan-chair on wheels, with greasy leather curtains and cushions. In the days of its prosperity it might have been a state coach, and might have earned Sir Robert Walpole to court, or the Abbé Dubois to a supper with the Regent Orleans.

It is driven by a tall, cadaverous, ruffianly postilion, with his clothes all in rags, and without a spark of mercy for his miserable horses. It smells badly, looks badly, goes badly; and jerks, and cracks, and totters as if it would break down altogether—when it is suddenly stopped on a rough stone pavement in front of a lonely post-house, just as the sun is sinking and the night is setting in.

The postmaster comes out to superintend the harnessing of fresh horses. He is tipsy, familiar, and confidential; he first apostrophizes the *calèche* with contemptuous curses, then takes me mysteriously aside, and declares that the whole high road onward to our morning's destination swarms with thieves. It seems, then, that the Austrian police reserve all their vigilance for innocent travellers, and leave local rogues entirely unmolested.

I make this reflection, and ask the postmaster what he recommends us to do for the protection of our portmanteaus, which are tied on to the roof of the *calèche*. He answers that, unless we take special precautions, the thieves will get up behind, on our crazy footboard, and will cut the trunks off the top of our frowsy travelling carriage, under cover of the night, while we are quietly seated inside, seeing and suspecting nothing.

We instantly express our readiness to take any precautions that any one may be kind enough to suggest. The postmaster winks, lays his finger archly on the side of his nose, and gives an unintelligible order in the *patois* of the district. Before I have time to ask what he is going to do, every idler about the post house who can climb scales the summit of the *calèche*, and every idler who cannot, stands roaring and gesticulating below with a lighted candle in his hand.

While the hubbub is at its loudest, a rival travelling carriage suddenly drives into the midst of us, in the shape of a huge barrel-organ on wheels, and bursts out awfully in the darkness with the grand march in Semiramide, played with the utmost fury of the drum, cymbal, and trumpet-stops. The noise is so bewildering that my travelling companion and I take refuge inside our carriage, and shut our eyes, and stop our ears, and abandon ourselves to despair.

After a time, our elbows are jogged, and a string apiece is given to us through each window. We are informed in shouts, accompanied fiercely by the grand march, that the strings are fastened to our portmanteaus above; that we are to keep the loose ends round our forefingers all night; and that the moment we feel a tug, we may be quite certain the thieves are at work, and may feel justified in stopping the carriage and fighting for our baggage without any more ado.

Under these agreeable auspices, we start again, with our strings round our forefingers. We feel like men about to ring the bell—or like men engaged in deep sea-fishing—or like men on the point of pulling the string of a shower-bath. Fifty times at least, during the next stage, each of us is certain that he feels a tug, and pops his head agitatedly out of window, and sees absolutely nothing, and falls back again exhausted with excitement in a corner of the *calèche*.

All through the night this wear and tear of our nerves goes on; and all through the night (thanks, probably, to the ceaseless popping of our heads out of the windows) not the ghost of a thief conies near us. We begin, at last, almost to feel that it would be a relief to be robbed—almost to doubt the policy of resisting any mercifully-larcenous hands stretched forth to rescue us from the incubus of our own baggage.

The morning dawn finds us languid and haggard, with the accursed portmanteau strings dangling unregarded in the bottom of the *calèche*. And this is taking our pleasure! This is an incident of travel in Austrian Italy! Faithful Black Mirror, accept my thanks. The warning of the two last dream-scenes that you have shown me shall not be disregarded. Whatever other direction I may take when I go out of town for the present season, one road at least I know that I shall avoid—the road that leads to Austrian Italy.

Shall I keep on the northern side of the Alps, and travel a little, let us say, in German-Switzerland? Black Mirror! How did I get on when I was last in that country? Did I like my introductory experience at my first inn?

The vision changes, and takes me again to the outside of a house of public entertainment; a great white, clean, smooth-fronted, opulent looking hotel—a very different building from my dingy, cavernous Italian inn. At the street door stands the landlord. He is a little, lean, rosy man, dressed all in black, and looking like a master undertaker. I observe that he neither steps forward nor smiles when I get out of the carriage and ask for a bedroom.

He gives me the shortest possible answer, growls guttural instructions to a waiter, then looks out into the street again, and, before I have so much as turned my back on him, forgets my existence immediately. The vision changes again, and takes me inside the hotel. I am following a waiter upstairs—the man looks unaffectedly sorry to see me. In the bedroom corridor we find a chambermaid asleep with her head on a table. She is woke up; opens a door with a groan, and scowls at me reproachfully when I say that the room will do.

I descend to dinner. Two waiters attend on me, under protest, and look as if they were on the point of giving warning every time I require them to change my plate. At the second course the landlord comes in, and stands and stares at me intently and silently with his hands in his pockets. This may be his way of seeing that my dinner is well served; but it looks much more like his way of seeing that I do not abstract any spoons from his table. I become irritated by the boorish staring and frowning of everybody about me, and express myself strongly on the subject of my reception at the hotel to an English traveller dining near me.

The English traveller is one of those exasperating men who are always ready to put up with injuries, and he coolly accounts for the behaviour of which I complain, by telling me that it is the result of the blunt honesty of the natives, who cannot pretend to take an interest in me which they do not really feel. What do I care about the feelings of the stolid landlord and the sulky waiters? I require the comforting outward show from them—the inward substance is not of the smallest consequence to me.

When I travel in civilized countries, I want such a reception at my inn as shall genially amuse and gently tickle all the region round about my organ of self-esteem. Blunt honesty, which is too offensively truthful to pretend to be glad to see me, shows no corresponding integrity—as my own experience informs me at this very hotel—about the capacities of its wine bottles, but gives me a pint and charges me for a quart in the bill, like the rest of the world.

Blunt honesty, although it is too brutally sincere to look civilly distressed and sympathetic when I say that I am tired after my journey, does not hesitate to warm up, and present before me as newly dressed a Methuselah of a duck that has been cooked several times over, several days ago, and paid for, though not eaten, by my travelling predecessors.

Blunt honesty fleeces me according to every established predatory law of the landlord's code, yet shrinks from the amiable duplicity of fawning affectionately before me all the way up stairs when I first present myself to be swindled. Away with such detestable sincerity as this! Away with the honesty which brutalizes a landlord's manners without reforming his bottles or his bills! Away with my German-Swiss hotel, and the extortionate cynic who keeps it! Let ethers pay tribute if they will to that boor in innkeeper's clothing, the colour of my money he shall never see again.

Suppose I avoid German-Switzerland, and try Switzerland Proper? Mirror! How did I travel when I last found myself on the Swiss side of the Alps?

The new vision removes me even from the most distant view of an hotel of any kind, and places me in a wild mountain country, where the end of a rough road is lost in the dry bed of a torrent. I am seated in a queer little box on wheels, called a *Char*, drawn by a mule and a mare, and driven by a jovial coachman in a blue blouse. I have hardly time to look down alarmedly at the dry bed of the torrent, before the *Char* plunges into it.

Rapidly and recklessly we thump along over rocks and stones, acclivities and declivities that would shake down the stoutest English travelling carriage, knock up the best bred English horses, nonplus the most knowing English coachman. Jovial Blue Blouse, singing like a nightingale, drives ahead regardless of every obstacle—the mule and mare tear along as if the journey was the great enjoyment of the day to them—the *Char* cracks, rends, sways, bumps, and totters, but scorns, as becomes a hardy little mountain vehicle, to overturn or come to pieces.

When we are not among the rocks we are rolling and heaving in sloughs of black mud and sand, like a Dutch herring boat in a ground swell. It is all one to Blue Blouse and the mule and mare. They are just as ready to drag through sloughs as to jolt over rocks; and when we do come occasionally to a bit of unencumbered ground, they always indemnify themselves for past hardship and fatigue by galloping like mad.

As for my own sensations in the character of passenger in the *Char*, they are not, physically speaking, of the pleasantest possible kind. I can only keep myself inside my vehicle by dint of holding tight with both hands by anything I can find to grasp at; and I am so shaken throughout my whole anatomy that my very jaws clatter again, and my feet play a perpetual tattoo on the bottom of the *Char*. Did I hit on no method of travelling more composed and deliberate than this, I wonder, when I was last in Switzerland? Must I make up my mind to be half shaken to pieces if I am bold enough to venture on going there again?

The surface of the Black Mirror is once more clouded over. It clears, and the vision is now of a path along the side of a precipice. A mule is following the path, and I am the adventurous traveller who is astride on the beast's back. The first observation that occurs to me in my new position is, that mules thoroughly deserve their reputation for obstinacy, and that, in regard to the particular animal on which I am riding, the less I interfere with him and the more I conduct myself as if I was a pack-saddle on his back, the better we are sure to get on together.

Carrying pack-saddles is his main business in life; and though he saw me get on his back, he persists in treating me as if I was a bale of goods, by walking on the extreme edge of the precipice, so as not to run any risk of rubbing his load against the safe, or mountain, side of the path. In this and in other things I find that he is the victim of routine, and the slave of habit. He has a way of stopping short, placing himself in a slanting position, and falling into a profound "meditation" at some of the most awkward turns in the wild mountain-roads.

I imagine at first that he may be halting in this abrupt and inconvenient manner to take breath; but then he never exerts himself so as to tax his lungs in the smallest degree, and he stops on the most unreasonably irregular principles, sometimes twice in ten minutes,—sometimes not more than twice in two hours—evidently just as his new ideas happen to absorb his attention or not.

It is part of his exasperating character at these times always to become immersed in reflection where the muleteer's staff has not room to reach him with the smallest effect; and where, loading him with blows being out of the question, loading him with abusive language is the only other available process for getting him on. I find that he generally turns out to be susceptible to the influence of injurious epithets after he has heard himself insulted five or six times.

Once, his obdurate nature gave way, even, at the third appeal. He has just stopped with me on his back, to amuse himself, at a dangerous part of the road, with a little hard thinking in a steeply slanting position; and it becomes therefore urgently necessary to abuse him into proceeding forthwith. First, the muleteer calls him a Serpent—he never stirs an inch. Secondly, the muleteer calls him a Frog—he goes on imperturbably with his meditation.

Thirdly, the muleteer roars out indignantly, *Ah, sacré nom d'un Butor*! (which, interpreted by the help of my Anglo-French dictionary, means apparently, Ah, sacred name of a Muddlehead!); and at this extraordinary abjuration the beast instantly jerks up his nose, shakes his ears, and goes on his way indignantly.

Mule-riding, under these circumstances, is certainly an adventurous and amusing method of travelling, and well worth trying for once in a way; but I am not at all sure that I should enjoy a second experience of it, and I have my doubts on this account—to say nothing of my dread of a second jolting journey in a *Char*—about the propriety of undertaking another visit to Switzerland during the present sultry season.

It will be wisest, perhaps, to try the effect of a new scene from the past, representing some former visit to some other locality, before I venture on arriving as a decision. I have rejected Austrian Italy and German Switzerland, and I am doubtful about Switzerland Proper. Suppose I do my duty as a patriot, and give the attractions of any own country a fair chance of appealing to any past influences of the agreeable kind, which they may have exercised over me? Black Mirror! When I was last a tourist at home, how did I travel about from place to place?

The cloud on the magic surface rises slowly and grandly, like the lifting of a fog at sea, and discloses a tiny drawing, zoom, with a skylight window, and a rose-coloured curtain drawn over it to keep out the sun. A bright book shelf runs all round this little fairy chamber, just below the ceiling, where the cornice would be in loftier rooms. Sofas extend along the wall on either side, and mahogany cupboards full of good things ensconce themselves snugly in the four corners.

The table is brightened with nosegays; the mantel-shelf has a smart railing all round it; and the looking-glass above is just large enough to reflect becomingly the face and shoulders of any lady who will give herself the trouble of looking into it. The present inhabitants of the room are three gentlemen with novels and newspapers in their hands, taking their ease in blouses, dressing-gowns, and slippers. They are reposing on the sofas with fruit and wine within easy reach—and one of the party looks to me very much like the enviable possessor of the Black Mirror. They exhibit a spectacle of luxury which would make an ancient Spartan shudder with disgust; and, in an adjoining apartment, their band is attending on them, in the shape of a musical box which is just now playing the last scene in *Lucia di Lammermoor.*

Hark! What sounds are those mingling with the notes of Donizetti's lovely music—now rising over it sublimely, now dying away under it, gently and more gently still? Our sweet opera air shall come to its close, our music shall play for its short destined time and then be silent again; but those more glorious sounds shall go on with us day and night, shall still swell and sink inexhaustibly, long after we and all who know and love and remember us have passed from this earth forever.

It is the wash of the waves that now travels along with us grandly wherever we go. We are at sea in a schooner yacht, and are taking our pleasure along the southern shores of the English coast.

Yes, this to every man who can be certain of his own stomach, this is the true luxury of travelling, the true secret for thoroughly enjoying all the attractions of moving about from place to place. Wherever we now go, we carry our elegant and comfortable home along with us. We can stop where we like, see what we like, and always come back to our favourite corner on the sofa, always carry on our favourite occupations and amusements, and still be travelling, still be getting forward to new scenes all the time.

Here is no hurrying to accommodate yourself to other people's hours for starting, no scrambling for places, no wearisome watchfulness over baggage. Here are no anxieties about strange beds,—for have we not each of us our own sweet little cabin to nestle in at night?—no agitating dependence at the dinner hour upon the vagaries of strange cooks—for have we not our own sumptuous larder always to return to, our own accomplished and faithful culinary artist always waiting to minister to our special tastes? We can walk and sleep, stand up or lie down, just as we please, in our floating travelling-carriage. We can make our own road, and trespass nowhere.

The bores we dread, the letters we don't want to answer, cannot follow and annoy us. We are the freest travellers: under Heaven; and we find something to interest and attract us through every hour of the day. The ships we meet, the trimming of our sails, the varying of the weather, the everlasting innumerable changes of the ocean, afford constant occupation for eye and ear. Sick, indeed, must that libellous traveller have been who first called the sea monotonous—sick to death, and perhaps, born brother also to that other traveller of evil renown, the first man who journeyed from Dan to Beersheba, and found all barren.

Rest then awhile unemployed, my faithful Black Mirror! The

last scene you have shown me is sufficient to answer the purpose for which I took you up. Towards what point of the compass I may turn after leaving London is more than I can tell; but this I know, that my next post horses shall be the winds, my next stages coast towns, my next road over the open waves. I will be a sea-traveller once more, and will put off resuming my land journeyings until the arrival of that most obliging of all convenient periods of time—a future opportunity.

Miss Jéromette and the Clergyman

1

My brother, the clergyman, looked over my shoulder before I was aware of him, and discovered that the volume which completely absorbed my attention was a collection of famous Trials, published in a new edition and in a popular form.

He laid his finger on the Trial which I happened to be reading at the moment. I looked up at him; his face startled me. He had turned pale. His eyes were fixed on the open page of the book with an expression which puzzled and alarmed me.

"My dear fellow," I said, "what in the world is the matter with you?"

He answered in an odd absent manner, still keeping his finger on the open page.

"I had almost forgotten," he said. "And this reminds me."

"Reminds you of what?" I asked. "You don't mean to say you know anything about the Trial?"

"I know this," he said. "The prisoner was guilty."

"Guilty?" I repeated. "Why, the man was acquitted by the jury, with the full approval of the judge! What can you possibly mean?"

"There are circumstances connected with that Trial," my brother answered, "which were never communicated to the judge or the jury—which were never so much as hinted or whispered in court. I know—of my own knowledge, by my own personal experience. They are very sad, very strange, very terrible. I have mentioned them to no mortal creature. I have done my best to forget them. You—quite innocently—have brought them back to my mind. They oppress, they distress me. I wish I had found you reading any book in your library, except that book!"

My curiosity was now strongly excited. I spoke out plainly.

"Surely," I suggested, "you might tell your brother what you are unwilling to mention to persons less nearly related to you. We have followed different professions, and have lived in different countries, since we were boys at school. But you know you can trust me."

He considered a little with himself.

"Yes," he said. "I know I can trust you." He waited a moment; and then he surprised me by a strange question.

"Do you believe," he asked, "that the spirits of the dead can return to earth, and show themselves to the living?"

I answered cautiously—adopting as my own the words of a great English writer, touching the subject of ghosts.

"You ask me a question," I said, "which, after five thousand years, is yet undecided. On that account alone, it is a question not to be trifled with."

My reply seemed to satisfy him.

"Promise me," he resumed, "that you will keep what I tell you a secret as long as I live. After my death I care little what happens. Let the story of my strange experience be added to the published experience of those other men who have seen what I have seen, and who believe what I believe.

"The world will not be the worse, and may be the better, for knowing one day what I am now about to trust to your ear alone."

My brother never again alluded to the narrative which he had confided to me, until the later time when I was sitting by his deathbed. He asked if I still remembered the story of Jéromette. "Tell it to others," he said, "as I have told it to you."

I repeat it after his death—as nearly as I can in his own words.

2

On a fine summer evening, many years since, I left my chambers in the Temple, to meet a fellow-student, who had proposed to me a night's amusement in the public gardens at Cremorne.

You were then on your way to India; and I had taken my degree at Oxford. I had sadly disappointed my father by choosing the Law as my profession, in preference to the Church. At that time, to own the truth, I had no serious intention of following any special vocation. I simply wanted an excuse for enjoying the pleasures of a London life. The study of the Law supplied me with that excuse. And I chose the Law as my profession accordingly.

On reaching the place at which we had arranged to meet, I found that my friend had not kept his appointment. After waiting vainly for ten minutes, my patience gave way and I went into the Gardens by myself.

I took two or three turns round the platform devoted to the dancers without discovering my fellow-student, and without seeing any other person with whom I happened to be acquainted at that time.

For some reason which I cannot now remember, I was not in my usual good spirits that evening. The noisy music jarred on my nerves, the sight of the gaping crowd round the platform irritated me, the blandishments of the painted ladies of the profession of pleasure saddened and disgusted me. I opened my cigar-case, and turned aside into one of the quiet by-walks of the Gardens.

A man who is habitually careful in choosing his cigar has this advantage over a man who is habitually careless. He can always count on smoking the best cigar in his case, down to the last. I was still absorbed in choosing my cigar, when I heard these words behind me—spoken in a foreign accent and in a woman's voice:

"Leave me directly, sir! I wish to have nothing to say to you."

I turned round and discovered a little lady very simply and

tastefully dressed, who looked both angry and alarmed as she rapidly passed me on her way to the more frequented part of the Gardens. A man (evidently the worse for the wine he had drunk in the course of the evening) was following her, and was pressing his tipsy attentions on her with the coarsest insolence of speech and manner. She was young and pretty, and she cast one entreating look at me as she went by, which it was not in manhood-perhaps I ought to say, in young-manhood—to resist.

I instantly stepped forward to protect her, careless whether I involved myself in a discreditable quarrel with a blackguard or not. As a matter of course, the fellow resented my interference, and my temper gave way. Fortunately for me, just as I lifted my hand to knock him down, a policeman appeared who had noticed that he was drunk, and who settled the dispute officially by turning him out of the Gardens.

I led her away from the crowd that had collected. She was evidently frightened—I felt her hand trembling on my arm-but she had one great merit; she made no fuss about it.

"If I can sit down for a few minutes," she said in her pretty foreign accent, "I shall soon be myself again, and I shall not trespass any further on your kindness. I thank you very much, sir, for taking care of me."

We sat down on a bench in a retired part of the Gardens, near a little fountain. A row of lighted lamps ran round the outer rim of the basin. I could see her plainly.

I have said that she was "a little lady." I could not have described her more correctly in three words.

Her figure was slight and small: she was a well-made miniature of a woman from head to foot. Her hair and her eyes were both dark. The hair curled naturally; the expression of the eyes was quiet, and rather sad; the complexion, as I then saw it, very pale; the little mouth perfectly charming. I was especially attracted, I remembered, by the carriage of her head; it was strikingly graceful and spirited; it distinguished her, little as she was and quiet as she was, among the thousands of other women in the Gardens, as a creature apart.

Even the one marked defect in her a slight "cast" in the left eye—seemed to add, in some strange way, to the quaint attractiveness of her face. I have already spoken of the tasteful simplicity of her dress. I ought now to add that it was not made of any costly material, and that she wore no jewels or ornaments of any sort. My little lady was not rich; even a man's eye could see that.

She was perfectly unembarrassed and unaffected. We fell as easily into talk as if we had been friends instead of strangers.

I asked how it was that she had no companion to take care of her."You are too young and too pretty," I said in my blunt English way, "to trust yourself alone in such a place as this."

She took no notice of the compliment. She calmly put it away from her as if it had not reached her ears

"I have no friend to take care of me," she said simply. "I was sad and sorry this evening, all by myself, and I thought I would go to the Gardens and hear the music, just to amuse me. It is not much to pay at the gate; only a shilling."

"No friend to take care of you?" I repeated. "Surely there must be one happy man who might have been here with you tonight?"

"What man do you mean?" she asked.

"The man," I answered thoughtlessly, "whom we call, in England, a Sweetheart."

I would have given worlds to have recalled those foolish words the moment they passed my lips. I felt that I had taken a vulgar liberty with her. Her face saddened; her eyes dropped to the ground. I begged her pardon.

"There is no need to beg my pardon," she said. "If you wish to know, sir—yes, I had once a sweetheart, as you call it in England. He has gone away and left me. No more of him, if you please. I am rested now. I will thank you again, and go home."

She rose to leave me.

I was determined not to part with her in that way. I begged to be allowed to see her safely back to her own door. She hesitated. I took a man's unfair advantage of her, by appealing to her fears. I said, "Suppose the blackguard who annoyed you should be waiting outside the gates?" That decided her. She took my arm. We went away together by the bank of the Thames, in the balmy summer night.

A walk of half an hour brought us to the house in which she lodged—a shabby little house in a by-street, inhabited evidently by very poor people.

She held out her hand at the door, and wished me goodnight. I was too much interested in her to consent to leave my little foreign lady without the hope of seeing her again. I asked permission to call on her the next day. We were standing under the light of the street-lamp. She studied my face with a grave and steady attention before she made any reply.

"Yes," she said at last. "I think I do know a gentleman when I see him. You may come, sir, if you please, and call upon me tomorrow."

So we parted. So I entered—doubting nothing, foreboding nothing—on a scene in my life which I now look back on with unfeigned repentance and regret.

3

I am speaking at this later time in the position of a clergyman, and in the character of a man of mature age. Remember that; and you will understand why I pass as rapidly as possible over the events of the next year of my life—why I say as little as I can of the errors and the delusion of my youth.

I called on her the next day. I repeated my visits during the days and weeks that followed, until the shabby little house in the by-street had become a second and (I say it with shame and self-reproach) a dearer home to me.

All of herself and her story which she thought fit to confide to me under these circumstances may be repeated to you in few words.

The name by which letters were addressed to her was "Mademoiselle Jéromette." Among the ignorant people of the house and the small tradesmen of the neighbourhood—who found her name not easy of pronunciation by the average English tongue—she was known by the friendly nickname of "The French Miss." When I knew her, she was resigned to her lonely life among strangers. Some years had elapsed since she had lost her parents, and had left France.

Possessing a small, very small, income of her own, she added to it by colouring miniatures for the photographers. She had relatives still living in France; but she had long since ceased to correspond with them. "Ask me nothing more about my family," she used to say. "I am as good as dead in my own country and among my own people."

This was all—literally all—that she told me of herself, I have never discovered more of her sad story from that day to this.

She never mentioned her family name—never even told me what part of France she came from, or how long she had lived in England. That she was by birth and breeding a lady, I could entertain no doubt; her manners, her accomplishments, her ways of thinking and speaking, all proved it. Looking below the surface, her character showed itself in aspects not common among young women in these days.

In her quiet way, she was an incurable fatalist, and a firm believer in the ghostly reality of apparitions from the dead. Then again in the matter of money, she had strange views of her own. Whenever my purse was in my hand, she held me resolutely at a distance from first to last. She refused to move into better apartments; the shabby little house was clean inside, and the poor people who lived in it were kind to her—and that was enough.

The most expensive present that she ever permitted me to offer her was a little enamelled ring, the plainest and cheapest thing of the kind in the jeweller's shop. In all relations with me she was sincerity itself. On all occasions, and under all circumstances, she spoke her mind (as the phrase is) with the same uncompromising plainness.

"I like you," she said to me; "I respect you; I shall always be faithful to you while you are faithful to me. But my love has gone from me. There is another man who has taken it away with him, I know not where."

Who was the other man?

She refused to tell me. She kept his rank and his name strict secrets from me. I never discovered how he had met with her, or why he had left her, or whether the guilt was his of making of her an exile from her country and her friends. She despised herself for still loving him; but the passion was too strong for her—she owned it and lamented it with the frankness which was so pre-eminently a part of her character.

More than this, she plainly told me, in the early days of our acquaintance, that she believed he would return to her. It might be tomorrow, or it might be years hence. Even if he failed to repent of his own cruel conduct, the man would still miss her, as something lost out of his life; and, sooner or later, he would come back.

"And will you receive him if he does come back?" I asked.

"I shall receive him," she replied, "against my own better judgment—in spite of my own firm persuasion that the day of his return to me will bring with it the darkest days of my life."

I tried to remonstrate with her.

"You have a will of your own," I said. "Exert it if he attempts to return to you."

"I have no will of my own," she answered quietly, "where he is concerned. It is my misfortune to love him." Her eyes rested for a moment on mine, with the utter self-abandonment of despair. "We have said enough about this," she added abruptly. "Let us say no more."

From that time we never spoke again of the unknown man. During the year that followed our first meeting, she heard nothing of him directly or indirectly. He might be living, or he might be dead. There came no word of him, or from him. I was fond enough of her to be satisfied with this—he never disturbed us.

4

The year passed—and the end came. Not the end as you may have anticipated it, or as I might have foreboded it.

You remember the time when your letters from home informed you of the fatal termination of our mother's illness? It is the time of which I am now speaking. A few hours only before she breathed her last, she called me to her bedside, and desired that we might be left together alone. Reminding me that her death was near, she spoke of my prospects in life; she noticed my want of interest in the studies which were then supposed to be engaging my attention, and she ended by entreating me to reconsider my refusal to enter the Church.

"Your father's heart is set upon it," she said. "Do what I ask of you, my dear, and you will help to comfort him when I am gone."

Her strength failed her: she could say no more. Could I refuse the last request she would ever make to me? I knelt at the bedside, and took her wasted hand in mine, and solemnly promised her the respect which a son owes to his mother's last wishes.

Having bound myself by this sacred engagement, I had no choice but to accept the sacrifice which it imperatively exacted from me. The time had come when I must tear myself free from all unworthy associations. No matter what the effort cost me, I must separate myself at once and forever from the unhappy woman who was not, who never could be, my wife.

At the close of a dull foggy day I set forth with a heavy heart to say the words which were to part us forever.

Her lodging was not far from the banks of the Thames. As I drew near the place the darkness was gathering, and the broad surface of the river was hidden from me in a chill white mist. I stood for a while, with my eyes fixed on the vaporous shroud that brooded over the flowing water—I stood and asked myself in despair the one dreary question: "What am I to say to her?"

The mist chilled me to the bones. I turned from the riverbank, and made my way to her lodgings hard by. "It must be done!" I said to myself, as I took out my key and opened the house door.

She was not at her work, as usual, when I entered her little sitting-room. She was standing by the fire, with her head down and with an open letter in her hand.

The instant she turned to meet me, I saw in her face that something was wrong. Her ordinary manner was the manner of an unusually placid and self-restrained person. Her temperament had little of the liveliness which we associate in England with the French nature. She was not ready with her laugh; and in all my previous experience, I had never yet known her to cry. Now, for the first time, I saw the quiet face disturbed; I saw tears in the pretty brown eyes. She ran to meet me, and laid her head on my breast, and burst into a passionate fit of weeping that shook her from head to foot.

Could she by any human possibility have heard of the coming change in my life? Was she aware, before I had opened my lips, of the hard necessity which had brought me to the house?

It was simply impossible; the thing could not be.

I waited until her first burst of emotion had worn itself out. Then I asked—with an uneasy conscience, with a sinking heart—what had happened to distress her.

She drew herself away from me, sighing heavily, and gave me the open letter which I had seen in her hand.

"Read that," she said. "And remember I told you what might happen when we first met."

I read the letter.

It was signed in initials only; but the writer plainly revealed himself as the man who had deserted her. He had repented; he had returned to her. In proof of his penitence he was willing to do her the justice which he had hitherto refused—he was willing to marry her, on the condition that she would engage to keep the marriage a secret, so long as his parents lived.

Submitting this proposal, he waited to know whether she would consent, on her side, to forgive and forget.

I gave her back the letter in silence. This unknown rival had done me the service of paving the way for our separation. In offering her the atonement of marriage, he had made it, on my part, a matter of duty to her, as well as to myself, to say the parting words. I felt this instantly. And yet, I hated him for helping me!

She took my hand, and led me to the sofa. We sat down, side by side. Her face was composed to a sad tranquillity. She was quiet; she was herself again.

"I have refused to see him," she said, "until I had first spoken to you. You have read his letter. What do you say?"

I could make but one answer. It was my duty to tell her what my own position was in the plainest terms. I did my duty-leaving her free to decide on the future for herself. Those sad words said, it was useless to prolong the wretchedness of our separation. I rose, and took her hand for the last time.

I see her again now, at that final moment, as plainly as if it had happened yesterday. She had been suffering from an affection of the throat; and she had a white silk handkerchief tied loosely round her neck. She wore a simple dress of purple merino, with a black silk apron over it. Her face was deadly pale; her fingers felt icily cold as they closed round my hand.

"Promise me one thing," I said, "before I go. While I live, I am your friend—if I am nothing more. If you are ever in trouble, promise that you will let me know it."

She started, and drew back from me as if I had struck her with a sudden terror.

"Strange!" she said, speaking to herself. "He feels as I feel. He is afraid of what may happen to me, in my life to come."

I attempted to reassure her. I tried to tell her what was indeed the truth—that I had only been thinking of the ordinary chances and changes of life, when I spoke.

She paid no heed to me; she came back and put her hands on my shoulders and thoughtfully and sadly looked up in my face.

"My mind is not your mind in this matter," she said. "I once owned to you that I had my forebodings, when we first spoke of this man's return, I may tell you now, more than I told you then. I believe I shall die young, and die miserably. If I am right, have you interest enough still left in me to wish to hear of it?"

She paused, shuddering—and added these startling words:

"You shall hear of it."

The tone of steady conviction in which she spoke alarmed and distressed me. My face showed her how deeply and how painfully I was affected.

"There, there!" she said, returning to her natural manner; "don't take what I say too seriously. A poor girl who has led a lonely life like mine thinks strangely and talks strangely—sometimes. Yes; I give you my promise. If I am ever in trouble, I will let you know it. God bless you—you have been very kind to me—goodbye!"

A tear dropped on my face as she kissed me. The door closed between us. The dark street received me.

It was raining heavily. I looked up at her window, through the drifting shower. The curtains were parted: she was standing in the gap, dimly lit by the lamp on the table behind her, waiting for our last look at each other. Slowly lifting her hand, she waved her farewell at the window, with the unsought native grace which had charmed me on the night when we first met. The curtain fell again—she disappeared—nothing was before me, nothing was round me, but the darkness and the night.

5

In two years from that time, I had redeemed the promise given to my mother on her deathbed. I had entered the Church.

My father's interest made my first step in my new profession an easy one. After serving my preliminary apprenticeship as a curate, I was appointed, before I was thirty years of age, to a living in the West of England.

My new benefice offered me every advantage that I could possibly desire—with the one exception of a sufficient income. Although my wants were few, and although I was still an unmarried man, I found it desirable, on many accounts, to add to my resources. Following the example of other young clergymen in my position, I determined to receive pupils who might stand in need of preparation for a career at the Universities. My relatives exerted themselves; and my good fortune still befriended me.

I obtained two pupils to start with. A third would complete the number which I was at present prepared to receive. In course of time, this third pupil made his appearance, under circumstances sufficiently remarkable to merit being mentioned in detail.

It was the summer vacation; and my two pupils had gone home. Thanks to a neighbouring clergyman, who kindly undertook to perform my duties for me, I too obtained a fortnight's holiday, which I spent at my father's house in London.

During my sojourn in the metropolis, I was offered an opportunity of preaching in a church, made famous by the eloquence of one of the popular pulpit-orators of our time. In accepting the proposal, I felt naturally anxious to do my best, before the unusually large and unusually intelligent congregation which would be assembled to hear me.

At the period of which I am now speaking, all England had been startled by the discovery of a terrible crime, perpetrated under circumstances of extreme provocation. I chose this crime as the main subject of my sermon. Admitting that the best among us were frail mortal creatures, subject to evil promptings and provocations like the worst among us, my object was to show how a Christian man may find his certain refuge from temptation in the safeguards of his religion.

I dwelt minutely on the hardship of the Christian's first struggle to resist the evil influence—on the help which his Christianity inexhaustibly held out to him in the worst relapses of the weaker and viler part of his nature—on the steady and certain gain which was the ultimate reward of his faith and his firmness—and on the blessed sense of peace and happiness which accompanied the final triumph. Preaching to this effect, with the fervent conviction which I really felt, I may say for myself, at least, that I did no discredit to the choice which had placed me in the pulpit. I held the attention of my congregation, from the first word to the last.

While I was resting in the vestry on the conclusion of the service, a note was brought to me written in pencil. A member of my congregation—a gentleman—wished to see me, on a matter of considerable importance to himself. He would call on me at any place, and at any hour, which I might choose to appoint. If I wished to be satisfied of his respectability, he would beg leave to refer me to his father, with whose name I might possibly be acquainted.

The name given in the reference was undoubtedly familiar to me, as the name of a man of some celebrity and influence in the world of London. I sent back my card, appointing an hour for the visit of my correspondent on the afternoon of the next day.

6

The stranger made his appearance punctually. I guessed him to be some two or three years younger than myself. He was undeniably handsome; his manners were the manners of a gentleman—and yet, without knowing why, I felt a strong dislike to him the moment he entered the room.

After the first preliminary words of politeness had been exchanged between us, my visitor informed me as follows of the object which he had in view.

"I believe you live in the country, sir?" he began.

"I live in the West of England," I answered.

"Do you make a long stay in London?"

"No. I go back to my rectory tomorrow."

"May I ask if you take pupils?"

"Yes."

"Have you any vacancy?"

"I have one vacancy."

"Would you object to let me go back with you tomorrow, as your pupil?"

The abruptness of the proposal took me by surprise. I hesitated.

In the first place (as I have already said) I disliked him. In the second place, he was too old to be a fit companion for my other two pupils—both lads in their teens. In the third place, he had asked me to receive him at least three weeks before the vacation came to an end. I had my own pursuits and amusements in prospect during that interval, and saw no reason why I should inconvenience myself by setting them aside.

He noticed my hesitation, and did not conceal from me that I had disappointed him.

"I have it very much at heart," he said, "to repair without delay the time that I have lost. My age is against me, I know. The truth is—I have wasted my opportunities since I left school, and I am anxious, honestly anxious, to mend my ways, before it is too late. I wish to prepare myself for one of the Universities—I wish to show, if I can, that I am not quite unworthy to inherit my father's famous name.

"You are the man to help me, if I can only persuade you to do it. I was struck by your sermon yesterday; and, if I may venture to make the confession in your presence, I took a strong liking to you. Will you see my father, before you decide to say No? He will be able to explain whatever may seem strange in my present application; and he will be happy to see you this afternoon, if you can spare the time. As to the question of terms, I am quite sure it can be settled to your entire satisfaction."

He was evidently in earnest—gravely, vehemently in earnest. I unwillingly consented to see his father.

Our interview was a long one. All my questions were answered fully and frankly.

The young man had led an idle and desultory life. He was weary of it, and ashamed of it. His disposition was a peculiar one. He stood sorely in need of a guide, a teacher, and a friend, in whom he was disposed to confide. If I disappointed the hopes which he had centred in me, he would be discouraged, and he would relapse into the aimless and indolent existence of which he was now ashamed. Any terms for which I might stipulate were at my disposal if I would consent to receive him, for three months to begin with, on trial.

Still hesitating, I consulted my father and my friends.

They were all of opinion (and justly of opinion so far) that the new connection would be an excellent one for me. They all reproached me for taking a purely capricious dislike to a well-born and well-bred young man, and for permitting it to influence me, at the outset of my career, against my own interests. Pressed by these considerations, I allowed myself to be persuaded to give the new pupil a fair trial. He accompanied me, the next day, on my way back to the rectory.

7

Let me be careful to do justice to a man whom I personally disliked. My senior pupil began well: he produced a decidedly favourable impression on the persons attached to my little house hold.

The women, especially, admired his beautiful light hair, his crisply-curling beard, his delicate complexion, his clear blue eyes, and his finely shaped hands and feet. Even the inveterate reserve in his manner, and the downcast, almost sullen, look which had prejudiced me against him, aroused a common feeling of romantic enthusiasm in my servants' hall. It was decided, on the high authority of the housekeeper herself, that "the new gentleman" was in love—and, more interesting still, that he was the victim of an unhappy attachment which had driven him away from his friends and his home.

For myself, I tried hard, and tried vainly, to get over my first dislike to the senior pupil.

I could find no fault with him. All his habits were quiet and regular; and he devoted himself conscientiously to his reading. But, little by little, I became satisfied that his heart was not in his studies. More than this, I had my reasons for suspecting that he was concealing something from me, and that he felt painfully the reserve on his own part which he could not, or dared not, break through. There were moments when I almost doubted whether he had not chosen my remote country rectory as a safe place of refuge from some person or persons of whom he stood in dread.

For example, his ordinary course of proceeding, in the matter of his correspondence, was, to say the least of it, strange.

He received no letters at my house. They waited for him at

the village post office. He invariably called for them himself, and invariably forbore to trust any of my servants with his own letters for the post.

Again, when we were out walking together, I more than once caught him looking furtively over his shoulder, as if he suspected some person of following him, for some evil purpose. Being constitutionally a hater of mysteries, I determined, at an early stage of our intercourse, on making an effort to clear matters up. There might be just a chance of my winning the senior pupil's confidence, if I spoke to him while the last days of the summer vacation still left us alone together in the house.

"Excuse me for noticing it," I said to him one morning, while we were engaged over our books—"I cannot help observing that you appear to have some trouble on your mind. Is it indiscreet, on my part, to ask if I can be of any use to you?"

He changed colour—looked up at me quickly looked down again at his book—struggled hard with some secret fear or secret reluctance that was in him and suddenly burst out with this extraordinary question:

"I suppose you were in earnest when you preached that sermon in London?"

"I am astonished that you should doubt it," I replied.

He paused again; struggled with himself again; and startled me by a second outbreak, even stranger than the first.

"I am one of the people you preached at in your sermon," he said. "That's the true reason why I asked you to take me for your pupil. Don't turn me out! When you talked to your congregation of tortured and tempted people, you talked of Me."

I was so astonished by the confession, that I lost my presence of mind. For the moment, I was unable to answer him,

"Don't turn me out!" he repeated. "Help me against myself. I am telling you the truth. As God is my witness, I am telling you the truth!"

"Tell me the whole truth," I said; "and rely on my consoling and helping you—rely on my being your friend."

In the fervour of the moment, I took his hand. It lay cold and still in mine; it mutely warned me that I had a sullen and a secret nature to deal with.

"There must be no concealment between us," I resumed. "You have entered my house, by your own confession, under false pretences. It is your duty to me, and your duty to yourself, to speak out."

The man's inveterate reserve—cast off for the moment only—renewed its hold on him. He considered, carefully considered, his next words before he permitted them to pass his lips.

"A person is in the way of my prospects in life," he began slowly, with his eyes cast down on his book. "A person provokes me horribly. I feel dreadful temptations (like the man you spoke of in your sermon) when I am in the person's company. Teach me to resist temptation! I am afraid of myself, if I see the person again. You are the only man who can help me. Do it while you can."

He stopped, and passed his handkerchief over his forehead.

"Will that do?" he asked—still with his eyes on his book.

"It will not do," I answered. "You are so far from really opening your heart to me, that you won't even let me know whether it is a man or a woman who stands in the way of your prospects in life. You used the word 'person,' over and over again—rather than say 'he' or 'she' when you speak of the provocation which is trying you. How can I help a man who has so little confidence in me as that?"

My reply evidently found him at the end of his resources. He tried, tried desperately, to say more than he had said yet. No! The words seemed to stick in his throat. Not one of them would pass his lips.

"Give me time," he pleaded piteously. "I can't bring myself to it, all at once. I mean well. Upon my soul, I mean well. But I am slow at this sort of thing. Wait till tomorrow."

Tomorrow came—and again he put it off.

"One more day!" he said. "You don't know how hard it is to speak plainly. I am half afraid; I am half ashamed. Give me one more day."

I had hitherto only disliked him. Try as I might (and did) to make merciful allowance for his reserve, I began to despise him now.

8

The day of the deferred confession came, and brought an event with it, for which both he and I were alike unprepared. Would he really have confided in me but for that event? He must either have done it, or have abandoned the purpose which had led him into my house.

We met as usual at the breakfast-table. My housekeeper brought in my letters of the morning. To my surprise, instead of leaving the room again as usual, she walked round to the other side of the table, and laid a letter before my senior pupil—the first letter, since his residence with me, which had been delivered to him under my roof.

He started, and took up the letter. He looked at the address. A spasm of suppressed fury passed across his face; his breath came quickly; his hand trembled as it held the letter. So far, I said nothing. I waited to see whether he would open the envelope in my presence or not.

He was afraid to open it in my presence. He got on his feet; he said, in tones so low that I could barely hear him: "Please excuse me for a minute"—and left the room.

I waited for half an hour—for a quarter of an hour after that—and then I sent to ask if he had forgotten his breakfast.

In a minute more, I heard his footstep in the hall. He opened the breakfast-room door, and stood on the threshold, with a small travelling-bag in his hand.

"I beg your pardon," he said, still standing at the door. "I must ask for leave of absence for a day or two. Business in London."

"Can I be of any use?" I asked. "I am afraid your letter has brought you bad news?"

"Yes," he said shortly. "Bad news. I have no time for breakfast."

"Wait a few minutes," I urged. "Wait long enough to treat

me like your friend—to tell me what your trouble is before you go."

He made no reply. He stepped into the hall and closed the door—then opened it again a little way, without showing himself.

"Business in London," he repeated—as if he thought it highly important to inform me of the nature of his errand. The door closed for the second time. He was gone.

I went into my study, and carefully considered what had happened.

The result of my reflections is easily described. I determined on discontinuing my relations with my senior pupil. In writing to his father (which I did, with all due courtesy and respect, by that day's post), I mentioned as my reason for arriving at this decision:—First, that I had found it impossible to win the confidence of his son. Secondly, that his son had that morning suddenly and mysteriously left my house for London, and that I must decline accepting any further responsibility toward him, as the necessary consequence.

I had put my letter in the postbag, and was beginning to feel a little easier after having written it, when my housekeeper appeared in the study, with a very grave face, and with something hidden apparently in her closed hand.

"Would you please look, sir, at what we have found in the gentleman's bedroom, since he went away this morning?"

I knew the housekeeper to possess a woman's full share of that amiable weakness of the sex which goes by the name of "Curiosity." I had also, in various indirect ways, become aware that my senior pupil's strange departure had largely increased the disposition among the women of my household to regard him as the victim of an unhappy attachment. The time was ripe, as it seemed to me, for checking any further gossip about him, and any renewed attempts at prying into his affairs in his absence.

"Your only business in my pupil's bedroom," I said to the housekeeper, "is to see that it is kept clean, and that it is properly aired. There must be no interference, if you please, with his letters, or his papers, or with anything else that he has left behind him. Put back directly whatever you may have found in his room."

The housekeeper had her full share of a woman's temper as well as of a woman's curiosity. She listened to me with a rising colour, and a just perceptible toss of the head.

"Must I put it back, sir, on the floor, between the bed and the wall?" she inquired, with an ironical assumption of the humblest deference to my wishes. "That's where the girl found it when she was sweeping the room. Anybody can see for themselves," pursued the housekeeper indignantly, "that the poor gentleman has gone away broken-hearted. And there, in my opinion, is the hussy who is the cause of it!"

With those words, she made me a low curtsey, and laid a small photographic portrait on the desk at which I was sitting.

I looked at the photograph.

In an instant, my heart was beating wildly my head turned giddy—the housekeeper, the furniture, the walls of the room, all swayed and whirled round me.

The portrait that had been found in my senior pupil's bedroom was the portrait of Jéromette!

9

I had sent the housekeeper out of my study. I was alone, with the photograph of the Frenchwoman on my desk.

There could surely be little doubt about the discovery that had burst upon rue. The man who had stolen his way into my house, driven by the terror of a temptation that he dared not reveal, and the man who had been my unknown rival in the bygone time, were one and the same!

Recovering self-possession enough to realize this plain truth, the inferences that followed forced their way into my mind as a matter of course. The unnamed person who was the obstacle to my pupil's prospects in life, the unnamed person in whose company he was assailed by temptations which made him tremble for himself, stood revealed to me now as being, in all human probability, no other than Jéromette. Had she bound him in the fetters of the marriage which he had himself proposed? Had she discovered his place of refuge in my house? And was the letter that had been delivered to him of her writing?

Assuming these questions to be answered in the affirmative, what, in that case, was his "business in London"? I remembered how he had spoken to me of his temptations, I recalled the expression that had crossed his face when he recognized the handwriting on the letter—and the conclusion that followed literally shook me to the soul. Ordering my horse to be saddled, I rode instantly to the railway-station.

The train by which he had travelled to London had reached the terminus nearly an hour since. The one useful course that I could take, by way of quieting the dreadful misgivings crowding one after another on my mind, was to telegraph to Jéromette at the address at which I had last seen her. I sent the subjoined message—prepaying the reply:

> If you are in any trouble, telegraph to me. I will be with you by the first train. Answer, in any case.

There was nothing in the way of the immediate dispatch of my message. And yet the hours passed, and no answer was received. By the advice of the clerk, I sent a second telegram to the London office, requesting an explanation. The reply came back in these terms:

> Improvements in street. Houses pulled down. No trace of person named in telegram.

I mounted my horse, and rode back slowly to the rectory.

"The day of his return to me will bring with it the darkest days of my life."

"I shall die young, and die miserably. Have you interest enough still left in me to wish to hear of it?"

"You shall hear of it."

Those words were in my memory while I rode home in the cloudless moonlight night. They were so vividly present to me that I could hear again her pretty foreign accent, her quiet clear tones, as she spoke them. For the rest, the emotions of that memorable day had worn me out. The answer from the telegraph-office had struck me with a strange and stony despair. My mind was a blank. I had no thoughts. I had no tears.

I was about half-way on my road home, and I had just heard the clock of a village church strike ten, when I became conscious, little by little, of a chilly sensation slowly creeping through and through me to the bones. The warm, balmy air of a summer night was abroad. It was the month of July. In the month of July, was it possible that any living creature (in good health) could feel cold? It was not possible—and yet, the chilly sensation still crept through and through me to the bones.

I looked up. I looked all round me.

My horse was walking along an open high-road. Neither trees nor waters were near me. On either side, the flat fields stretched away bright and broad in the moonlight.

I stopped my horse, and looked round me again.

Yes: I saw it. With my own eyes I saw it. A pillar of white mist—between five and six feet high, as well as I could judge-was moving beside me at the edge of the road, on my left hand. When I stopped, the white mist stopped. When I went on, the white mist went on. I pushed my horse to a trot—the pillar of mist was with me. I urged him to a gallop—the pillar of mist was with me. I stopped him again—the pillar of mist stood still.

The white colour of it was the white colour of the fog which I had seen over the river on the night when I had gone to bid her farewell. And the chill which had then crept through me to the bones was the chill that was creeping through me now.

I went on again slowly. The white mist went on again slowly—with the clear bright night all round it.

I was awed rather than frightened. There was one moment, and one only, when the fear came to me that my reason might be shaken. I caught myself keeping time to the slow tramp of the horse's feet with the slow utterances of these words, repeated over and over again: "Jéromette is dead. Jéromette is dead." But my will was still my own: I was able to control myself, to impose silence on my own muttering lips. And I rode on quietly. And the pillar of mist went quietly with me.

My groom was waiting for my return at the rectory gate. I pointed to the mist, passing through the gate with me.

"Do you see anything there?" I said.

The man looked at me in astonishment.

I entered the rectory. The housekeeper met me in the hall. I pointed to the mist, entering with me.

"Do you see anything at my side?" I asked.

The housekeeper looked at me as the groom had looked at me.

"I am afraid you are not well, sir," she said. "Your colour is all gone—you are shivering. Let me get you a glass of wine."

I went into my study, on the ground-floor, and took the chair at my desk. The photograph still lay where I had left it. The pillar of mist floated round the table, and stopped opposite to me, behind the photograph.

The housekeeper brought in the wine. I put the glass to my lips, and set it down again. The chill of the mist was in the wine. There was no taste, no reviving spirit in it, The presence of the housekeeper oppressed me. My dog had followed her into the room. The presence of the animal oppressed me. I said to the woman: "Leave me by myself, and take the dog with you."

They went out, and left me alone in the room.

I sat looking at the pillar of mist, hovering opposite to me.

It lengthened slowly, until it reached to the ceiling. As it lengthened, it grew bright and luminous. A time passed, and a shadowy appearance showed itself in the centre of the light. Little by little, the shadowy appearance took the outline of a human form. Soft brown eyes, tender and melancholy, looked at me through the unearthly light in the mist.

The head and the rest of the face broke next slowly on my view. Then the figure gradually revealed itself, moment by moment, downward and downward to the feet. She stood before me as I had last seen her, in her purple-merino dress, with the black-silk apron, with the white handkerchief tied loosely round her neck. She stood before me, in the gentle beauty that I remembered so well; and looked at me as she had looked when she gave me her last kiss—when her tears had dropped on my cheek.

I fell on my knees at the table. I stretched out my hands to her imploringly. I said: "Speak to me—O, once again speak to me, Jéromette."

Her eyes rested on me with a divine compassion in them. She lifted her hand, and pointed to the photograph on my desk, with a gesture which bade me turn the card. I turned it. The name of the man who had left my house that morning was inscribed on it, in her own handwriting.

I looked up at her again, when I had read it.

She lifted her hand once more, and pointed to the handkerchief round her neck. As I looked at it, the fair white silk changed horribly in colour—the fair white silk became darkened and drenched in blood.

A moment more—and the vision of her began to grow dim. By slow degrees, the figure, then the face, faded back into the shadowy appearance that I had first seen. The luminous inner light died out in the white mist. The mist itself dropped slowly downward—floated a moment in airy circles on the floor—vanished. Nothing was before me but the familiar wall of the room, and the photograph lying face downward on my desk.

10

The next day, the newspapers reported the discovery of a murder in London. A Frenchwoman was the victim. She had been killed by a wound in the throat. The crime had been discovered between ten and eleven o'clock on the previous night.

I leave you to draw your conclusion from what I have related. My own faith in the reality of the apparition is immovable. I say, and believe, that Jéromette kept her word with me. She died young, and died miserably. And I heard of it from herself.

Take up the Trial again, and look at the circumstances that

were revealed during the investigation in court. His motive for murdering her is there.

You will see that she did indeed marry him privately; that they lived together contentedly, until the fatal day when she discovered that his fancy had been caught by another woman; that violent quarrels took place between them, from that time to the time when my sermon showed him his own deadly hatred toward her, reflected in the case of another man; that she discovered his place of retreat in my house, and threatened him by letter with the public assertion of her conjugal rights; lastly, that a man, variously described by different witnesses, was seen leaving the door of her lodgings on the night of the murder.

The Law—advancing no further than this—may have discovered circumstances of suspicion, but no certainty. The Law, in default of direct evidence to convict the prisoner, may have rightly decided in letting him go free.

But I persisted in believing that the man was guilty. I declare that he, and he alone, was the murderer of Jéromette. And now, you know why.

Mr. Percy and the Prophet

Part 1.—The Prediction

Chapter 1
The Quack

The disasters that follow the hateful offense against Christianity, which men call war, were severely felt in England during the peace that ensued on the overthrow of Napoleon at Waterloo. With rare exceptions, distress prevailed among all classes of the community. The starving nation was ripe and ready for a revolutionary rising against its rulers, who had shed the people's blood and wasted the people's substance in a war which had yielded to the popular interests absolutely nothing in return.

Among the unfortunate persons who were driven, during the disastrous early years of this century, to strange shifts and devices to obtain the means of living, was a certain obscure medical man, of French extraction, named Lagarde. The Doctor (duly qualified to bear the title) was an inhabitant of London; living in one of the narrow streets which connect the great thoroughfare of the Strand with the bank of the Thames.

The method of obtaining employment chosen by poor Lagarde, as the one alternative left in the face of starvation, was, and is still considered by the medical profession to be, the method of a quack. He advertised in the public journals.

Addressing himself especially to two classes of the community, the Doctor proceeded in these words:

"I have the honour of inviting to my house, in the first place: Persons afflicted with maladies which ordinary medical practice has failed to cure—and, in the second place: Persons interested in investigations, the object of which is to penetrate the secrets of the future. Of the means by which I endeavour to alleviate suffering and to enlighten doubt, it is impossible to speak intelligibly within the limits of an advertisement.

"I can only offer to submit my system to public inquiry, without exacting any preliminary fee from ladies and gentlemen who may honour me with a visit. Those who see sufficient reason to trust me, after personal experience, will find a money-box fixed on the waiting-room table, into which they can drop their offerings according to their means Those whom I am not fortunate enough to satisfy will be pleased to accept the expression of my regret, and will not be expected to give anything. I shall be found at home every evening between the hours of six and ten."

Toward the close of the year 1816 this strange advertisement became a general topic of conversation among educated people in London. For some weeks the Doctor's invitations were generally accepted—and, all things considered, were not badly remunerated. A faithful few believed in him, and told wonderful stories of what he had pronounced and prophesied in the sanctuary of his consulting-room. The majority of his visitors simply viewed him in the light of a public amusement, and wondered why such a gentleman-like man should have chosen to gain his living by exhibiting himself as a quack.

Chapter 2
The Numbers

On a raw and snowy evening toward the latter part of January, 1817, a gentleman, walking along the Strand, turned into the street in which Doctor Lagarde lived, and knocked at the physician's door.

He was admitted by an elderly male servant to a waiting-room on the first floor. The light of one little lamp, placed on a bracket fixed to the wall, was so obscured by a dark green shade as to make it difficult, if not impossible, for visitors meeting by accident to recognize each other. The metal money-box fixed to the table was just visible. In the flickering light of a small fire, the stranger perceived the figures of three men seated, apart and silent, who were the only occupants of the room beside himself.

So far as objects were to be seen, there was nothing to attract attention in the waiting-room. The furniture was plain and neat, and nothing more. The elderly servant handed a card, with a number inscribed on it, to the new visitor, said in a whisper, "Your number will be called, sir, in your turn," and disappeared. For some minutes nothing disturbed the deep silence but the faint ticking of a clock.

After a while a bell rang from an inner room, a door opened, and a gentleman appeared, whose interview with Doctor Lagarde had terminated. His opinion of the sitting was openly expressed in one emphatic word—"Humbug!" No contribution dropped from his hand as he passed the moneybox, on his way out.

The next number (being Number Fifteen) was called by the elderly servant, and the first incident occurred in the strange series of events destined to happen in the Doctor's house that night.

One after another the three men who had been waiting rose, examined their cards under the light of the lamp, and sat down again surprised and disappointed.

The servant advanced to investigate the matter. The numbers possessed by the three visitors, instead of being Fifteen, Sixteen and Seventeen, proved to be Sixteen, Seventeen and Eighteen. Turning to the stranger who had arrived the last, the servant said:

"Have I made a mistake, sir? Have I given you Number Fifteen instead of Number Eighteen?"

The gentleman produced his numbered card.

A mistake had certainly been made, but not the mistake that the servant supposed. The card held by the latest visitor turned out to be the card previously held by the dissatisfied stranger who had just left the room—Number Fourteen! As to the card numbered Fifteen, it was only discovered the next morning lying in a corner, dropped on the floor!

Acting on his first impulse, the servant hurried out, calling to the original holder of Fourteen to come back and bear his testimony to that fact. The street-door had been opened for him by the landlady of the house. She was a pretty woman—and the gentleman had fortunately lingered to talk to her. He was induced, at the intercession of the landlady, to ascend the stairs again.

On returning to the waiting-room, he addressed a characteristic question to the assembled visitors. "More humbug?" asked the gentleman who liked to talk to a pretty woman.

The servant—completely puzzled by his own stupidity attempted to make his apologies.

"Pray forgive me, gentlemen," he said. "I am afraid I have confused the cards I distribute with the cards returned to me. I think I had better consult my master."

Left by themselves, the visitors began to speak jestingly of the strange situation in which they were placed. The original holder of Number Fourteen described his experience of the Doctor in his own pithy way. "I applied to the fellow to tell my fortune. He first went to sleep over it, and then he said he could tell me nothing. I asked why. 'I don't know,' says he. 'I do,' says I—'humbug!' I'll bet you the long odds, gentlemen, that you find it humbug, too."

Before the wager could be accepted or declined, the door of the inner room was opened again. The tall, spare, black figure of a new personage appeared on the threshold, relieved darkly against the light in the room behind him. He addressed the visitors in these words:

"Gentlemen, I must beg your indulgence. The accident—as we now suppose it to be—which has given to the last comer the number already held by a gentleman who has unsuccessfully consulted me, may have a meaning which we can none of us at present see. If the three visitors who have been so good as to wait will allow the present holder of Number Fourteen to consult me out of his turn—and if the earlier visitor who left me dissatisfied with his consultation will consent to stay here a little longer something may happen which will justify a trifling sacrifice of your own convenience. Is ten minutes' patience too much to ask of you?"

The three visitors who had waited longest consulted among themselves, and (having nothing better to do with their time) decided on accepting the Doctor's proposal. The visitor who believed it all to be "humbug" coolly took a gold coin out of his pocket, tossed it into the air, caught it in his closed hand, and walked up to the shaded lamp on the bracket.

"Heads, stay," he said, "Tails, go" He opened his hand, and looked at the coin. "Heads! Very good. Go on with your hocus-pocus, Doctor—I'll wait."

"You believe in chance," said the Doctor, quietly observing him. "That is not my experience of life."

He paused to let the stranger who now held Number Fourteen pass him into the inner room—then followed, closing the door behind him.

Chapter 3
The Consultation

The consulting-room was better lighted than the waiting-room, and that was the only difference between the two. In the one, as in the other, no attempt was made to impress the imagination. Everywhere, the commonplace furniture of a London lodging-house was left without the slightest effort to alter or improve it by changes of any kind.

Seen under the clearer light, Doctor Lagarde appeared to be the last person living who would consent to degrade himself by an attempt at imposture of any kind. His eyes were the dreamy eyes of a visionary; his look was the prematurely-aged look of a student, accustomed to give the hours to his book which ought to have been given to his bed. To state it briefly, he was a man who might easily be deceived by others, but who was incapable of consciously practicing deception himself.

Signing to his visitor to be seated, he took a chair on the opposite side of the small table that stood between them waited a moment with his face hidden in his hands, as if to collect himself—and then spoke.

"Do you come to consult me on a case of illness?" he inquired, "or do you ask me to look to the darkness which hides your future life?"

The answer to these questions was frankly and briefly expressed. "I have no need to consult you about my health. I come to hear what you can tell me of my future life."

"I can try," pursued the Doctor; "but I cannot promise to succeed."

"I accept your conditions," the stranger rejoined. "I never believe nor disbelieve. If you will excuse me speaking frankly, I mean to observe you closely, and to decide for myself."

Doctor Lagarde smiled sadly.

"You have heard of me as a charlatan who contrives to amuse a few idle people," he said. "I don't complain of that; my present position leads necessarily to misinterpretation of myself and my motives. Still, I may at least say that I am the victim of a sincere avowal of my belief in a great science. Yes! I repeat it, a great science! New, I dare say, to the generation we live in, though it was known and practiced in the days when pyramids were built.

"The age is advancing; and the truths which it is my misfortune to advocate, before the time is ripe for them, are steadily forcing their way to recognition. I am resigned to wait. My sincerity in this matter has cost me the income that I derived from my medical practice. Patients distrust me; doctors refuse to consult with me. I could starve if I had no one to think of but myself. But I have another person to consider, who is very dear to me; and I am driven, literally driven, either to turn beggar in the streets, or do what I am doing now."

He paused, and looked round toward the corner of the room behind him. "Mother," he said gently, "are you ready?"

An elderly lady, dressed in deep mourning, rose from her seat in the corner. She had been, thus far, hidden from notice by the high back of the easy-chair in which her son sat. Excepting some folds of fine black lace, laid over her white hair so as to form a head-dress at once simple and picturesque, there was nothing remarkable in her attire. The visitor rose and bowed. She gravely returned his salute, and moved so as to place herself opposite to her son.

"May I ask what this lady is going to do?" said the stranger.

"To be of any use to you," answered Doctor Lagarde, "I must be thrown into the magnetic trance. The person who has the strongest influence over me is the person who will do it to-night."

He turned to his mother. "When you like," he said.

Bending over him, she took both the Doctor's hands, and looked steadily into his eyes. No words passed between them; nothing more took place. In a minute or two, his head was resting against the back of the chair, and his eyelids had closed.

"Are you sleeping?" asked Madame Lagarde.

"I am sleeping," he answered.

She laid his hands gently on the arms of the chair, and turned to address the visitor.

"Let the sleep gain on him for a minute or two more," she said. "Then take one of his hands, and put to him what questions you please."

"Does he hear us now, madam?"

"You might fire off a pistol, sir, close to his ear, and he would not hear it. The vibration might disturb him; that is all. Until you or I touch him, and so establish the nervous sympathy, he is as lost to all sense of our presence here, as if he were dead."

"Are you speaking of the thing called Animal Magnetism, madam?"

"Yes, sir."

"And you believe in it, of course?"

"My son's belief, sir, is my belief in this thing as in other things. I have heard what he has been saying to you. It is for me that he sacrifices himself by holding these exhibitions; it is in my poor interests that his hardly-earned money is made. I am in infirm health; and, remonstrate as I may, my son persists in providing for me, not the bare comforts only, but even the luxuries of life. Whatever I may suffer, I have my compensation; I can still thank God for giving me the greatest happiness that a woman can enjoy, the possession of a good son."

She smiled fondly as she looked at the sleeping man. "Draw your chair nearer to him," she resumed, "and take his hand. You may speak freely in making your inquiries. Nothing that happens in this room goes out of it."

With those words she returned to her place, in the corner behind her son's chair.

The visitor took Doctor Lagarde's hand. As they touched each other, he was conscious of a faintly-titillating sensation in his own hand—a sensation which oddly reminded him of bygone experiments with an electrical machine, in the days when he was a boy at school!

"I wish to question you about my future life," he began. "How ought I to begin?"

The Doctor spoke his first words in the monotonous tones of a man talking in his sleep.

"Own your true motive before you begin," he said. "Your interest in your future life is centred in a woman. You wish to know if her heart will be yours in the time that is to come—and there your interest in your future life ends."

This startling proof of the sleeper's capacity to look, by sympathy, into his mind, and to see there his most secret thoughts, instead of convincing the stranger, excited his suspicions. "You have means of getting information," he said, "that I don't understand."

The Doctor smiled, as if the idea amused him.

Madame Lagarde rose from her seat and interposed.

"Hundreds of strangers come here to consult my son," she said quietly. "If you believe that we know who those strangers are, and that we have the means of inquiring into their private lives before they enter this room, you believe in something much more incredible than the magnetic sleep!"

This was too manifestly true to be disputed. The visitor made his apologies.

"I should like to have some explanation," he added. "The thing is so very extraordinary. How can I prevail upon Doctor Lagarde to enlighten me?"

"He can only tell you what he sees," Madame Lagarde answered; "ask him that, and you will get a direct reply. Say to him: 'Do you see the lady?'"

The stranger repeated the question. The reply followed at once, in these words:

"I see two figures standing side by side. One of them is your figure. The other is the figure of a lady. She only appears dimly. I can discover nothing but that she is taller than women generally are, and that she is dressed in pale blue."

The man to whom he was speaking started at those last words. "Her favourite colour!" he thought to himself—forgetting that, while he held the doctor's hand, the doctor could think with his mind.

"Yes," added the sleeper quietly, "her favourite colour, as you know. She fades and fades as I look at her," he went on. "She is gone. I only see you, under a new aspect. You have a pistol in your hand. Opposite to you, there stands the figure of another man. He, too, has a pistol in his hand. Are you enemies? Are you meeting to fight a duel? Is the lady the cause? I try, but I fail to see her."

"Can you describe the man?"

"Not yet. So far, he is only a shadow in the form of a man."

There was another interval. An appearance of disturbance showed itself on the sleeper's face. Suddenly, he waved his free hand in the direction of the waiting-room.

"Send for the visitors who are there," he said. "They are all to come in. Each one of them is to take one of my hands in turn-while you remain where you are, holding the other hand. Don't let go of me, even for a moment. My mother will ring."

Madame Lagarde touched a bell on the table. The servant received his orders from her and retired. After a short absence, he appeared again in the consulting-room, with one visitor only waiting on the threshold behind him.

Chapter 4
The Man

"The other three gentlemen have gone away, madam," the servant explained, addressing Madame Lagarde. "They were tired of waiting. I found this gentleman fast asleep; and I am afraid he is angry with me for taking the liberty of waking him."

"Sleep of the common sort is evidently not allowed in this house." With that remark the gentleman entered the room, and stood revealed as the original owner of the card numbered Fourteen.

Viewed by the clear lamplight, he was a tall, finely-made man, in the prime of life, with a florid complexion, golden-brown hair, and sparkling blue eyes. Noticing Madame Lagarde, he instantly checked the flow of his satire, with the instinctive good-breeding of a gentleman. "I beg your pardon," he said; "I have a great many faults, and a habit of making bad jokes is one of them. Is the servant right, madam, in telling me that I have the honour of presenting myself here at your request?"

Madame Lagarde briefly explained what had passed.

The florid gentleman (still privately believing it to be all "humbug") was delighted to make himself of any use. "I congratulate you, sir," he said, with his easy humour, as he passed the visitor who had become possessed of his card. "Number Fourteen seems to be a luckier number in your keeping than it was in mine."

As he spoke, he took Doctor Lagarde's disengaged hand. The instant they touched each other the sleeper started. His voice rose; his face flushed. "You are the man !" he exclaimed. "I see you plainly now!"

"What am I doing?"

"You are standing opposite to the gentleman here who is

holding my other hand; and (as I have said already) you have met to fight a duel."

The unbeliever cast a shrewd look at his companion in the consultation.

"Considering that you and I are total strangers, sir," he said, "don't you think the Doctor had better introduce us, before he goes any further? We have got to fighting a duel already, and we may as well know who we are, before the pistols go off." He turned to Doctor Lagarde. "Dramatic situations don't amuse me out of the theatre," he resumed. "Let me put you to a very commonplace test. I want to be introduced to this gentleman. Has he told you his name?"

"No."

"Of course, you know it, without being told."

"Certainly. I have only to look into your own knowledge of yourselves, while I am in this trance, and while you have got my hands, to know both your names as well as you do."

"Introduce us, then!" retorted the jesting gentleman. "And take my name first."

"Mr. Percy Linwood," replied the Doctor; "I have the honour of presenting you to Captain Bervie, of the Artillery."

"With one accord, the gentlemen both dropped Dr. Lagarde's hands, and looked at each other in blank amazement.

"Of course he has discovered our names somehow!" said Mr. Percy Linwood, explaining the mystery to his own perfect satisfaction in that way.

Captain Bervie had not forgotten what Madame Lagarde had said to him, when he too had suspected a trick. He now repeated it (quite ineffectually) for Mr. Linwood's benefit. "If you don't feel the force of that argument as I feel it," he added, "perhaps, as a favour to me, sir? you will not object to our each taking the Doctor's hand again, and hearing what more he can tell us while he remains in the state of trance?"

"With the greatest pleasure!" answered good-humoured Mr. Linwood. "Our friend is beginning to amuse me; I am as anxious as you are to know what he is going to see next."

Captain Bervie put the next question.

"You have seen us ready to fight a duel—can you tell us the result?"

"I can tell you nothing more than I have told you already. The figures of the duellists have faded away, like the other figures I saw before them. What I see now looks like the winding gravel-path of a garden. A man and a woman are walking toward me. The man stops, and places a ring on the woman's finger, and kisses her."

Captain Bervie opened his lips to continue his inquiries-turned pale—and checked himself. Mr. Linwood put the next question.

"Who is the happy man?" he asked.

"You are the happy man," was the instantaneous reply.

"Who is the woman?" cried Captain Bervie, before Mr. Linwood could speak again.

"The same woman whom I saw before; dressed in the same colour, in pale blue."

Captain Bervie positively insisted on receiving clearer information than this. "Surely you can see something of her personal appearance?" he said.

"I can see that she has long dark-brown hair, falling below her waist. I can see that she has lovely dark-brown eyes. She has the look of a sensitive nervous person. She is quite young. I can see no more."

"Look again at the man who is putting the ring on her finger," said the Captain. "Are you sure that the face you see. is the face of Mr. Percy Linwood?"

"I am absolutely sure."

Captain Bervie rose from his chair.

"Thank you, madam," he said to the Doctor's mother. "I have heard enough."

He walked to the door. ' Mr. Percy Linwood dropped Doctor Lagarde's hand, and appealed to the retiring Captain with a broad stare of astonishment.

"You don't really believe this?" he said.

"I only say I have heard enough," Captain Bervie answered.

Mr. Linwood could hardly fail to see that any further attempt to treat the matter lightly might lead to undesirable results.

"It is difficult to speak seriously of this kind of exhibition," he resumed quietly. "But I suppose I may mention a mere matter of fact? without meaning or giving offense. The description of the lady, I can positively declare, does not apply in any single particular to any one whom I know."

Captain Bervie turned round at the door. His patience was in some danger of failing him. Mr. Linwood's unruffled composure, assisted in its influence by the presence of Madame Lagarde, reminded him of the claims of politeness. He restrained the rash words as they rose to his lips. "You may make new acquaintances, sir," was all that he said. "You have the future before you."

Upon that, he went out. Percy Linwood waited a little,, reflecting on the Captain's conduct.

Had Doctor Lagarde's description of the lady accidentally answered the description of a living lady whom Captain Bervie knew? Was he by any chance in love with her? and had the Doctor innocently reminded him that his love was not returned? Assuming this to be likely, was it really possible that he believed in prophetic revelations offered to him under the fantastic influence of a trance? Could any man in the possession of his senses go to those lengths? The Captain's conduct was simply incomprehensible.

Pondering these questions, Percy decided on returning to his place by the Doctor's chair. "Of one thing I am certain, at any rate," he thought to himself. "I'll see the whole imposture out before I leave the house."

He took Doctor Lagarde's hand "Now, then! what is the next discovery?" he asked.

The sleeper seemed to find some difficulty in answering the question.

"I indistinctly see the man and the woman again," he said.

"Am I the man still?" Percy inquired.

"No. The man, this time, is the Captain. The woman is agitated by something that he is saying to her. He seems to be trying to persuade her to go away with him. She hesitates. He whispers something in her ear. She yields. He leads her away. The darkness gathers behind them. I look and look, and I can see no more."

"Shall we wait a while?" Percy suggested, "and then try again?"

Doctor Lagarde sighed, and reclined in his chair. "My head is heavy," he said; "my spirits are dull. The darkness baffles me. I have toiled long enough for you. Drop my hand and leave me to rest."

Hearing those words, Madame Lagarde approached her son's chair.

"It will be useless, sir, to ask him any more questions tonight," she said. "He has been weak and nervous all day, and he is worn out by the effort he has made. Pardon me, if I ask you to step aside for a moment, while I give him the repose that he needs."

She laid her right hand gently on the Doctor's head, and kept it there for a minute or so. "Are you at rest now?" she asked.

"I am at rest," he answered, in faint, drowsy tones.

Madame Lagarde returned to Percy. "If you are not yet satisfied," she said, "my son will be at your service tomorrow evening, sir."

"Thank you, madam, I have only one more question to ask, and you can no doubt answer it. When your son wakes, will he remember what he has said to Captain Bervie and to myself?"

"My son will be as absolutely ignorant of everything that he has seen, and of everything that he has said in the trance, as if he had been at the other end of the world."

Percy Linwood swallowed this last outrageous assertion with an effort which he was quite unable to conceal. "Many thanks, madam," he said; "I wish you goodnight."

Returning to the waiting-room, he noticed the money-box fixed to the table. "These people look poor," he thought to himself, "and I feel really indebted to them for an amusing evening. Besides, I can afford to be liberal, for I shall certainly never go back." He dropped a five-pound note into the moneybox, and left the house.

Walking toward his club, Percy's natural serenity of mind was a little troubled by the remembrance of Captain Bervie's language and conduct. The Captain had interested the young man in spite of himself. His first idea was to write to Bervie, and mention what had happened at the renewed consultation with Doctor Lagarde. On second thoughts, he saw reason to doubt how the Captain might receive such an advance as this, on the part of a stranger.

"After all," Percy decided, "the whole thing is too absurd to be worth thinking about seriously. Neither he nor I are likely to meet again, or to see the Doctor again—and there's an end of it."

He never was more mistaken in his life. The end of it was not to come for many a long day yet.

Part 2.—The Fulfilment

Chapter 5
The Ballroom

While the consultation at Doctor Lagarde's was still fresh in the memory of the persons present at it, Chance or Destiny, occupied in sowing the seeds for the harvest of the future, discovered as one of its fit instruments a retired military officer named Major Mulvany.

The Major was a smart little man, who persisted in setting up the appearance of youth as a means of hiding the reality of fifty. Being still a bachelor, and being always ready to make himself agreeable, he was generally popular in the society of women. In the ballroom he was a really welcome addition to the company. The German waltz had then been imported into England little more than three years since. The outcry raised against the dance, by persons skilled in the discovery of latent impropriety, had not yet lost its influence in certain quarters. Men who could waltz were scarce. The Major had successfully grappled with the difficulties of learning the dance in mature life; and the young ladies rewarded him nobly for the effort. That is to say, they took the assumption of youth for granted in the palpable presence of fifty.

Knowing everybody and being welcome everywhere, playing a good hand at whist, and having an inexhaustible fancy in the invention of a dinner, Major Mulvany naturally belonged to all the best clubs of his time. Percy Linwood and he constantly met in the billiard-room or at the dinner table. The Major approved of the easy, handsome, pleasant-tempered young man. "I have lost the first freshness of youth," he used to say, with pathetic resignation, "and I see myself revived, as it were, in Percy. Naturally I like Percy."

About three weeks after the memorable evening at Doctor Lagarde's, the two friends encountered each other on the steps of a club.

"Have you got anything to do tonight?" asked the Major.

"Nothing that I know of," said Percy, "unless I go to the theatre."

"Let the theatre wait, my boy. My old regiment gives a ball at Woolwich tonight. I have got a ticket to spare; and I know several sweet girls who are going. Some of them waltz, Percy! Gather your rosebuds while you may. Come with me."

The invitation was accepted as readily as it was given. The Major found the carriage, and Percy paid for the post-horses. They entered the ballroom among the earlier guests; and the first person whom they met, waiting near the door, was—Captain Bervie.

Percy bowed a little uneasily. "I feel some doubt," he said, laughing, "whether we have been properly introduced to one another or not."

"Not properly introduced!" cried Major Mulvany. "I'll soon set that right. My dear friend, Percy Linwood; my dear friend, Arthur Bervie—be known to each other! esteem each other!"

Captain Bervie acknowledged the introduction by a cold salute. Percy, yielding to the good-natured impulse of the moment, alluded to what had happened in Doctor Lagarde's consulting-room.

"You missed something worth hearing when you left the Doctor the other night," he said.

We continued the sitting; and you turned up again among the persons of the drama, in a new character—"

"Excuse me for interrupting you," said Captain Bervie. "I am a member of the committee, charged with the arrangements of the ball, and I must really attend to my duties."

He withdrew without waiting for a reply. Percy looked round wonderingly at Major Mulvany. "Strange!" he said, "I feel rather attracted toward Captain Bervie; and he seems to have taken such a dislike to me that he can hardly behave with common civility. What does it mean?"

"I'll tell you," answered the Major, confidentially. "Arthur Bervie is madly in love—madly is really the word—with a Miss Bowmore. And (this is between ourselves) the young lady doesn't feel it quite in the same way. A sweet girl; I've often had her on my knee when she was a child. Her father and mother are old friends of mine. She is coming to the ball tonight. That's the true reason why Arthur left you just now. Look at him—waiting to be the first to speak is her.

"If he could have his way, he wouldn't let another man come near the poor girl all through the evening; he really persecutes her. I'll introduce you to Miss Bowmore; and you will see how he looks at us for presuming to approach her. It's a great pity; she will never marry him. Arthur Bervie is a man in a thousand; but he's fast becoming a perfect bear under the strain on his temper. What's the matter? You don't seem to be listening to me."

This last remark was perfectly justified. In telling the Captain's love-story, Major Mulvany had revived his young friend's memory of the lady in the blue dress, who had haunted the visions of Doctor Lagarde.

"Tell me," said Percy, "what is Miss Bowmore like? Is there

anything remarkable in her personal appearance? I have a reason for asking."

As he spoke, there arose among the guests in the rapidly-filling ballroom a low murmur of surprise and admiration. The Major laid one hand on Percy's shoulder, and, lifting the other, pointed to the door.

"What is Miss Bowmore like?" he repeated. "There she is! Let her answer for herself."

Percy turned toward the lower end of the room.

A young lady was entering, dressed in plain silk, and the colour of it was a pale blue! Excepting a white rose at her breast, she wore no ornament of any sort. Doubly distinguished by the perfect simplicity of her apparel, and by her tall, supple, commanding figure, she took rank at once as the most remarkable woman in the room.

Moving nearer to her through the crowd, under the guidance of the complaisant Major, young Linwood gained a clearer view of her hair, her complexion, and the colour of her eyes. In every one of these particulars she was the living image of the woman described by Doctor Lagarde!

While Percy was absorbed over this strange discovery, Major Mulvany had got within speaking distance of the young lady and of her mother, as they stood together in conversation with Captain Bervie. "My dear Mrs. Bowmore, how well you are looking! My dear Miss Charlotte, what a sensation you have made already! The glorious simplicity (if I may so express myself) of your dress is—is—what was I going to say?—the ideas come thronging on me; I merely want words."

Miss Bowmore's magnificent brown eyes, wandering from the Major to Percy, rested on the young man with a modest and momentary interest, which Captain Bervie's jealous attention instantly detected.

"They are forming a dance," he said, pressing forward impatiently to claim his partner. "If we don't take our places we shall be too late."

"Stop! stop!" cried the Major. "There is a time for everything, and this is the time for presenting my dear friend here, Mr. Percy Linwood. He is like me, Miss Charlotte—he has been struck by your glorious simplicity, and he wants words."

At this part of the presentation, he happened to look toward the irate Captain, and instantly gave him a hint on the subject of his temper. "I say, Arthur Bervie! we are all good-humoured people here. What have you got on your eyebrows? It looks like a frown; and it doesn't become you. Send for a skilled waiter, and have it brushed off and taken away directly!"

"May I ask, Miss Bowmore, if you are disengaged for the next dance?" said Percy, the moment the Major gave him an opportunity of speaking.

"Miss Bowmore is engaged to me for the next dance," said the angry Captain, before the young lady could answer.

"The third dance, then?" Percy persisted, with his brightest smile.

"With pleasure, Mr. Linwood," said Miss Bowmore. She would have been no true woman if she had not resented the open exhibition of Arthur's jealousy; it was like asserting a right over her to which he had not the shadow of a claim. She threw a look at Percy as her partner led her away, which was the severest punishment she. could inflict on the man who ardently loved her.

The third dance stood in the programme as a waltz.

In jealous distrust of Percy, the Captain took the conductor of the band aside, and used his authority as committeeman to substitute another dance. He had no sooner turned his back on the orchestra than the wife of the Colonel of the regiment, who had heard him, spoke to the conductor in her turn, and insisted on the original programme being retained.

"Quote the Colonel's authority," said the lady, "if Captain Bervie ventures to object." In the meantime, the Captain, on his way to rejoin Charlotte, was met by one of his brother officers, who summoned him officially to an impending debate of the committee charged with the administrative arrangements of the supper-table. Bervie had no choice but to follow his brother officer to the committee-room.

Barely a minute later the conductor appeared at his desk, and the first notes of the music rose low and plaintive, introducing the third dance.

"Percy, my boy!" cried the Major, recognizing the melody, "you're in luck's way—it's going to be a waltz!"

Almost as he spoke, the notes of the symphony glided by subtle modulations into the inspiriting air of the waltz. Percy claimed his partner's hand. Miss Charlotte hesitated, and looked at her mother.

"Surely you waltz?" said Percy.

"I have learned to waltz," she answered, modestly; "but this is such a large room, and there are so many people!"

"Once round," Percy pleaded; "only once round!"

Miss Bowmore looked again at her mother. Her foot was keeping time with the music, under her dress; her heart was beating with a delicious excitement; kind-hearted Mrs. Bowmore smiled and said: "Once round, my dear, as Mr. Linwood suggests."

In another moment Percy's arm took possession of her waist, and they were away on the wings of the waltz!

Could words describe, could thought realize, the exquisite enjoyment of the dance? Enjoyment? It was more—it was an epoch in Charlotte's life—it was the first time she had waltzed with a man. What a difference between the fervent clasp of Percy's arm and the cold, formal contact of the mistress who had taught her! How brightly his eyes looked down into hers; admiring her with such a tender restraint, that there could surely be no harm in looking up at him now and then in return.

Round and round they glided, absorbed in the music and in themselves. Occasionally her bosom just touched him, at those critical moments when she was most in need of support. At other intervals, she almost let her head sink on his shoulder in trying to hide from him the smile which acknowledged his admiration too boldly.

"Once round," Percy had suggested; "once round," her mother had said. They had been ten, twenty, thirty times round; they had never stopped to rest like other dancers; they had centred the eyes of the whole room on them—including the eyes of Captain Bervie—without knowing it; her delicately pale complexion had changed to rosy-red; the neat arrangement of her hair had become disturbed; her bosom was rising and falling faster and faster in the effort to breathe—before fatigue and heat overpowered her at last, and forced her to say to him faintly, "I'm very sorry—I can't dance anymore!"

Percy led her into the cooler atmosphere of the refreshment-room, and revived her with a glass of lemonade. Her arm still rested on his she was just about to thank him for the care he had taken of her—when Captain Bervie entered the room.

"Mrs. Bowmore wishes me to take you back to her," he said to Charlotte. Then, turning to Percy, he added: "Will you kindly wait here while I take Miss Bowmore to the ballroom? I have a word to say to you—I will return directly."

The Captain spoke with perfect politeness—but his face betrayed him. It was pale with the sinister whiteness of suppressed rage.

Percy sat down to cool and rest himself. With his experience of the ways of men, he felt no surprise at the marked contrast between Captain Bervie's face and Captain Bervie's manner. "He has seen us waltzing, and he is coming back to pick a quarrel with me." Such was the interpretation which Mr. Linwood's knowledge of the world placed on Captain Bervie's politeness. In a minute or two more the Captain returned to the refreshment-room, and satisfied Percy that his anticipations had not deceived him.

Chapter 6
Love

Four days had passed since the night of the ball.

Although it was no later in the year than the month of February, the sun was shining brightly, and the air was as soft as the air of a day in spring. Percy and Charlotte were walking together in the little garden at the back of Mr. Bowmore's cottage, near the town of Dartford, in Kent.

"Mr. Linwood," said the young lady, "you were to have paid us your first visit the day after the ball. Why have you kept us waiting? Have you been too busy to remember your new friends?"

"I have counted the hours since we parted, Miss Charlotte. If I had not been detained by business—"

"I understand! For three days business has controlled you. On the fourth day, you have controlled business—and here you are? I don't believe one word of it, Mr. Linwood!"

There was no answering such a declaration as this. Guiltily conscious that Charlotte was right in refusing to accept his well-worn excuse, Percy made an awkward attempt to change the topic of conversation.

They happened, at the moment, to be standing near a small conservatory at the end of the garden. The glass door was closed, and the few plants and shrubs inside had a lonely, neglected look. "Does nobody ever visit this secluded place?" Percy asked, jocosely, "or does it hide discoveries in the rearing of plants which are forbidden mysteries to a stranger?"

"Satisfy your curiosity, Mr. Linwood, by all means," Charlotte answered in the same tone. "Open the door, and I will follow you."

Percy obeyed. In passing through the doorway, he encountered the bare hanging branches of some creeping plant, long since dead, and detached from its fastenings on the woodwork of the roof. He pushed aside the branches so that Charlotte could easily follow him in, without being aware that his own forced passage through them had a little deranged the folds of spotless white cambric which a well-dressed gentleman wore round his neck in those days. Charlotte seated herself, and directed Percy's attention to the desolate conservatory with a saucy smile.

"The mystery which your lively imagination has associated with this place," she said, "means, being interpreted, that we are too poor to keep a gardener. Make the best of your disappointment, Mr. Linwood, and sit here by me. We are out of hearing and out of sight of mamma's other visitors. You have no excuse now for not telling me what has really kept you away from us."

She fixed her eyes on him as she said those words. Before Percy could think of another excuse, her quick observation detected the disordered condition of his cravat, and discovered the upper edge of a black plaster attached to one side of his neck.

"You have been hurt in the neck!" she said. "That is why you have kept away from us for the last three days!"

"A mere trifle," he answered, in great confusion; "please don't notice it."

Her eyes, still resting on his face, assumed an expression of suspicious inquiry, which Percy was entirely at a loss to understand. Suddenly, she started to her feet, as if a new idea had occurred to her. "Wait here," she said, flushing with excitement, "till I come back: I insist on it!"

Before Percy could ask for an explanation she had left the conservatory.

In a minute or two, Miss Bowmore returned, with a newspaper in her hand. "Read that," she said, pointing to a paragraph distinguished by a line drawn round it in ink.

The passage that she indicated contained an account of a duel which had recently taken place in the neighbourhood of London. The names of the duellists were not mentioned. One was described as an officer, and the other as a civilian. They had quarrelled at cards, and had fought with pistols. The civilian had had a narrow escape of his life. His antagonist's bullet had passed near enough to the side of his neck to tear the flesh, and had missed the vital parts, literally, by a hairbreadth.

Charlotte's eyes, riveted on Percy, detected a sudden change of colour in his face the moment he looked at the newspaper. That was enough for her. "You are the man!" she cried. "Oh, for shame, for shame! To risk your life for a paltry dispute about cards!"

"I would risk it again," said Percy, "to hear you speak as if you set some value on it."

She looked away from him without a word of reply. Her

mind seemed to be busy again with its own thoughts. Did she meditate returning to the subject of the duel? Was she not satisfied with the discovery which she had just made?

No such doubts as these troubled the mind of Percy Linwood. Intoxicated by the charm of her presence, emboldened by her innocent betrayal of the interest that she felt in him, he opened his whole heart to her as unreservedly as if they had known each other from the days of their childhood. There was but one excuse for him. Charlotte was his first love.

"You don't know how completely you have become a part of my life, since we met at the ball," he went on. "That one delightful dance seemed, by some magic which I can't explain, to draw us together in a few minutes as if we had known each other for years. Oh, dear! I could make such a confession of what I felt—only I am afraid of offending you by speaking too soon. Women are so dreadfully difficult to understand.

"How is a man to know at what time it is considerate toward them to conceal his true feelings; and at what time it is equally considerate to express his true feelings? One doesn't know whether it is a matter of days or weeks or months—there ought to be a law to settle it.

"Dear Miss Charlotte, when a poor fellow loves you at first sight, as he has never loved any other woman, and when he is tormented by the fear that some other man may be preferred to him, can't you forgive him if he lets out the truth a little too soon?" He ventured, as he put that very downright question, to take her hand. "It really isn't my fault," he said, simply. "My heart is so full of you I can talk of nothing else."

To Percy's delight, the first experimental pressure of his hand, far from being resented, was softly returned. Charlotte looked at him again, with a new resolution in her face.

"I'll forgive you for talking nonsense, Mr. Linwood," she said; "and I will even permit you to come and see me again,—on one condition that you tell the whole truth about the duel. If you conceal the smallest circumstance, our acquaintance is at an end."

"Haven't I owned everything already?" Percy inquired, in great perplexity. "Did I say No, when you told me I was the man?"

"Could you say No, with that plaster on your neck?" was the ready rejoinder. "I am determined to know more than the newspaper tells me. Will you declare, on your word of honour, that Captain Bervie had nothing to do with the duel? Can you look me in the face, and say that the real cause of the quarrel was a disagreement at cards?

"When you were talking with me just before I left the ball, how did you answer a gentleman who asked you to make one at the whist-table? You said, 'I don't play at cards.' Ah! You thought I had forgotten that? Don't kiss my hand! Trust me with the whole truth, or say goodbye forever."

"Only tell me what you wish to know, Miss Charlotte," said Percy humbly. "If you will put the questions, I will give the answers—as well as I can."

On this understanding, Percy's evidence was extracted from him as follows:

"Was it Captain Bervie who quarrelled with you?"

"Yes,"

"Was it about me?"

"Yes."

"What did he say?"

"He said I had committed an impropriety in waltzing with you."

"Why?"

"Because your parents disapproved of your waltzing in a public ballroom."

"That's not true! What did he say next?"

"He said I had added tenfold to my offense, by waltzing with you in such a manner as to make you the subject of remark to the whole room."

"Oh! did you let him say that?"

"No; I contradicted him instantly. And I said, besides, 'It's an insult to Miss Bowmore, to suppose that she would permit any impropriety.'"

"Quite right! And what did he say?"

"Well, he lost his temper; I would rather not repeat what he said when he was mad with jealousy. There was nothing to be done with him but to give him his way."

"Give him his way? Does that mean fight a duel with him?"

"Don't be angry—it does."

"And you kept my name out of it, by pretending to quarrel at the card-table?"

"Yes. "We managed it when the card-room was emptying at supper-time, and nobody was present but Major Mulvany and another friend as witnesses."

"And when did you fight the duel?"

"The next morning."

"You never thought of me, I suppose?"

"Indeed, I did; I was very glad that you had no suspicion of what we were at."

"Was that all?"

"No; I had your flower with me, the flower you gave me out of your nosegay, at the ball."

"Well?"

"Oh, never mind, it doesn't matter."

"It does matter. What did you do with my flower?"

"I gave it a sly kiss while they were measuring the ground; and (don't tell anybody!) I put it next to my heart to bring me luck."

"Was that just before he shot at you?"

"Yes."

"How did he shoot?"

"He walked (as the seconds had arranged it) ten paces forward; and then he stopped, and lifted his pistol—"

"Don't tell me anymore! Oh, to think of my being the miserable cause of such horrors! I'll never dance again as long as I live. Did you think he had killed you, when the bullet wounded your poor neck!"

"No; I hardly felt it at first."

"Hardly felt it? How he talks! And when the wretch had done his best to kill you, and when it came to your turn, what did you do?"

"Nothing."

"What! You didn't walk your ten paces forward?"

"No."

"And you never shot at him in return?"

"No; I had no quarrel with him, poor fellow; I just stood where I was, and fired in the air—"

Before he could stop her, Charlotte seized his hand, and kissed it with an hysterical fervour of admiration, which completely deprived him of his presence of mind.

"Why shouldn't I kiss the hand of a hero?" she cried, with tears of enthusiasm sparkling in her eyes. "Nobody but a hero would have given that man his life; nobody but a hero would have pardoned him, while the blood was streaming from the wound that he had inflicted. I respect you, I admire you. Oh, don't think me bold! I can't control myself when I hear of anything noble and good. You will understand me better when we get to be old friends—won't you?"

She spoke in low sweet tones of entreaty. Percy's arm stole softly round her.

"Are we never to be nearer and dearer to each other than old friends?" he asked in a whisper. "I am not a hero—your goodness overrates me, dear Miss Charlotte. My one ambition is to be the happy man who is worthy enough to win you. At your own time! I wouldn't distress you, I wouldn't confuse you, I wouldn't for the whole world take advantage of the compliment which your sympathy has paid to me. If it offends you, I won't even ask if I may hope,"

She sighed as he said the last words; trembled a little, and silently looked at him.

Percy read his answer in her eyes. Without meaning it on either side their heads drew nearer together; their cheeks, then their lips, touched. She started back from him, and rose to leave the conservatory. At the same moment, the sound of slowly-approaching footsteps became audible on the gravel walk of the garden. Charlotte hurried to the door.

"My father!" she exclaimed, turning to Percy. "Come, and be introduced to him."

Percy followed her into the garden.

CHAPTER 7
POLITICS

Judging by appearances, Mr. Bowmore looked like a man prematurely wasted and worn by the cares of a troubled life. His eyes presented the one feature in which his daughter resembled him. In shape and colour they were exactly reproduced in Charlotte; the difference was in the expression. The father's look was habitually restless, eager, and suspicious. Not a trace was to be seen in it of the truthfulness and gentleness which made the charm of the daughter's expression.

A man whose bitter experience of the world had soured his temper and shaken his faith in the his fellow-creatures such was Mr. Bowmore as he presented himself on the surface. He received Percy politely—but with a preoccupied air. Every now and then, his restless eyes wandered from the visitor to an open letter in his hand. Charlotte observing him, pointed to the letter.

"Have you any bad news there, papa?" she asked.

"Dreadful news!" Mr. Bowmore answered. "Dreadful news, my child, to every Englishman who respects the liberties which his ancestors won. My correspondent is a man who is in the confidence of the Ministers," he continued, addressing Percy. "What do you think is the remedy that the Government proposes for the universal distress among the population, caused by an infamous and needless war? Despotism, Mr. Linwood; despotism in this free country is the remedy! In one week more, sir, Ministers will bring in a Bill for suspending the *Habeas Corpus* Act!"

Before Percy could do justice in words to the impression produced on him, Charlotte innocently asked a question which shocked her father.

"What is the *Habeas Corpus* Act, papa?"

"Good God!" cried Mr. Bowmore, "is it possible that a child of mine has grown up to womanhood, in ignorance of the palladium of English liberty? Oh, Charlotte! Charlotte!"

"I am very sorry, papa. If you will only tell me, I will never forget it."

Mr. Bowmore reverently uncovered his head, saluting an invisible *Habeas Corpus* Act. He took his daughter by the hand, with a certain parental sternness; his voice trembled with emotion as he spoke his next words:

"The *Habeas Corpus* Act, my child, forbids the imprisonment of an English subject, unless that imprisonment can be first justified by law. Not even the will of the reigning monarch can prevent us from appearing before the judges of the land, and summoning them to declare whether our committal to prison is legally just."

He put on his hat again. "Never forget what I have told you, Charlotte!" he said solemnly. "I would not remove my hat, sir," he continuing, turning to Percy, "in the presence of the proudest autocrat that ever sat on a throne. I uncover, in homage to the grand law which asserts the sacredness of human liberty. When Parliament has sanctioned the infamous Bill now before it, English patriots may be imprisoned, may even be hanged, on warrants privately obtained by the paid spies and informers of the men who rule us. Perhaps I weary you, sir. You are a young man; the conduct of the Ministry may not interest you."

"On the contrary," said Percy, "I have the strongest personal interest in the conduct of the Ministry."

"How? in what way?" cried Mr. Bowmore eagerly.

"My late father had a claim on Government," Percy answered, "for money expended in foreign service. As his heir, I inherit the claim, which has been formally recognized by the present Ministers. My petition for a settlement will be presented by friends of mine who can advocate my interests in the House of Commons."

Mr. Bowmore took Percy's hand, and shook it warmly.

"In such a matter as this you cannot have too many friends to help you," he said. "I myself have some influence, as representing opinion outside the House; and I am entirely at your service. Come tomorrow, and let us talk over the details of your claim at my humble dinner-table. Today I must attend a meeting of the Branch-Hampden-Club, of which I am vice-president, and to which I am now about to communicate the alarming news which my letter contains. Excuse me for leaving you and count on a hearty welcome when we see you tomorrow."

The amiable patriot saluted his daughter with a smile, and disappeared.

"I hope you like my father?" said Charlotte. "All our friends say he ought to be in Parliament. He has tried twice. The expenses were dreadful; and each time the other man defeated him. The agent says he would be certainly elected, if he tried again; but there is no money, and we mustn't think of it."

A man of a suspicious turn of mind might have discovered, in those artless words, the secret of Mr, Bowmore's interest in the success of his young friend's claim on the Government. One British subject, with a sum of ready money at his command, may be an inestimably useful person to another British subject (without ready money) who cannot sit comfortably unless he sits in Parliament. But honest Percy Linwood was not a man of a suspicious turn of mind. He had just opened his lips to echo Charlotte's filial glorification of her father, when a shabbily dressed man-servant met them with a message, for which they were both alike unprepared:

"Captain Bervie has called, miss, to say goodbye, and my mistress requests your company in the parlour."

Chapter 8
The Warning

Having delivered his little formula of words, the shabby servant cast a look of furtive curiosity at Percy and withdrew. Charlotte turned to her lover, with indignation sparkling in her eyes and flushing on her cheeks at the bare idea of seeing Captain

Bervie again. "Does he think I will breathe the same air," she exclaimed, "with the man who attempted to take your life!"

Percy gently remonstrated with her.

"You are sadly mistaken," he said. "Captain Bervie stood to receive my fire as fairly as I stood to receive his. When I discharged my pistol in the air, he was the first man who ran up to me, and asked if I was seriously hurt. They told him my wound was a trifle; and he fell on his knees and thanked God for preserving my life from his guilty hand.

"'I am no longer the rival who hates you,' he said. 'Give me time to try if change of scene will quiet my mind; and I will be your brother, and her brother.' Whatever his faults may be, Charlotte, Arthur Bervie has a great heart. Go in, I entreat you, and be friends with him as I am."

Charlotte listened with downcast eyes and changing colour. "You believe him?" she asked in low and trembling tones.

"I believe him as I believe You," Percy answered.

She secretly resented the comparison, and detested the Captain more heartily than ever. "I will go in and see him, if you wish it," she said. "But not by myself. I want you to come with me."

"Why?" Percy asked.

"I want to see what his face says, when you and he meet."

"Do you still doubt him, Charlotte?"

She made no reply. Percy had done his best to convince her, and had evidently failed.

They went together into the cottage. Fixing her eyes steadily on the Captain's face, Charlotte saw it turn pale when Percy followed her into the parlour. The two men greeted one another cordially. Charlotte sat down by her mother, preserving her composure so far as appearances went. "I hear you have called to bid us goodbye," she said to Bervie. "Is it to be a long absence?"

"I have got two months' leave," the Captain answered, without looking at her while he spoke.

"Are you going abroad?"

"Yes. I think so."

She turned away to her mother. Bervie seized the opportunity of speaking to Percy. "I have a word of advice for your private ear." At the same moment, Charlotte whispered to her mother: "Don't encourage him to prolong his visit."

The Captain showed no intention to prolong his visit. To Charlotte's surprise, when he took leave of the ladies, Percy also rose to go. "His carriage," he said, "was waiting at the door; and he had offered to lake Captain Bervie back to London."

Charlotte instantly suspected an arrangement between the two men for a confidential interview. Her obstinate distrust of Bervie strengthened tenfold. She reluctantly gave him her hand, as he parted from her at the parlour-door. The effort of concealing her true feeling toward him gave a colour and a vivacity to her face which made her irresistibly beautiful.

Bervie looked at the woman whom he had lost with an immeasurable sadness in his eyes. "When we meet again," he said, "you will see me in a new character." He hurried out of the gate, as if he feared to trust himself for a moment longer in her presence.

Charlotte followed Percy into the passage. "I shall be here to-morrow, dearest!" he said, and tried to raise her hand to his lips. She abruptly drew it away. "Not that hand !" she answered. "Captain Bervie has just touched it. Kiss the other!"

"Do you still doubt the Captain?" said Percy, amused by her petulance.

She put her arm over his shoulder, and touched the plaster on his neck gently with her finger. "There's one thing I don't doubt," she said: "the Captain did that!"

Percy left her, laughing. At the front gate of the cottage he found Arthur Bervie in conversation with the same shabbily-dressed man-servant who had announced the Captain's visit to Charlotte.

"What has become of the other servant?" Bervie asked. "I mean the old man who has been with Mr. Bowmore for so many years."

"He has left his situation, sir."

"Why?"

"As I understand, sir, he spoke disrespectfully to the master."

"Oh! And how came the master to hear of you?"

"I advertised; and Mr. Bowmore answered my advertisement."

Bervie looked hard at the man for a moment, and then joined Percy at the carriage door. The two gentlemen started for London.

"What do you think of Mr. Bowmore's new servant?" asked the Captain as they drove away from the cottage. "I don't like the look of the fellow."

"I didn't particularly notice him," Percy answered.

There was a pause. When the conversation was resumed, it turned on commonplace subjects. The Captain looked uneasily out of the carriage window. Percy looked uneasily at the Captain.

They had left Dartford about two miles behind them, when Percy noticed an old gabled house, sheltered by magnificent trees, and standing on an eminence well removed from the high-road. Carriages and saddle-horses were visible on the drive in front, and a flag was hoisted on a staff placed in the middle of the lawn.

"Something seems to be going on there," Percy remarked. "A fine old house! Who does it belong to?"

Bervie smiled. "It belongs to my father," he said. "He is chairman of the bench of local magistrates, and he receives his brother justices today, to celebrate the opening of the sessions."

He stopped and looked at Percy with some embarrassment. "I am afraid I have surprised and disappointed you," he resumed, abruptly changing the subject. "I told you when we met just now at Mr. Bowmore's cottage that I had something to say to you; and I have not yet said it. The truth is, I don't feel sure whether I have been long enough your friend to take the liberty of advising you."

"Whatever your advice is," Percy answered, "trust me to take it kindly on my side."

Thus encouraged, the Captain spoke out.

"You will probably pass much of your time at the cottage," he began, "and you will be thrown a great deal into Mr. Bowmore's society. I have known him for many years. Speaking from that knowledge, I most seriously warn you against him as a thoroughly unprincipled and thoroughly dangerous man."

This was strong language—and, naturally enough, Percy said so. The Captain justified his language.

"Without alluding to Mr. Bowmore's politics," he went on, "I can tell you that the motive of everything he says and does is vanity. To the gratification of that one passion he would sacrifice you or me, his wife or his daughter, without hesitation and without remorse. His one desire is to get into Parliament. You are wealthy, and you can help him. He will leave no effort untried to reach that end; and, if he gets you into political difficulties, he will desert you without scruple."

Percy made a last effort to take Mr. Bowmore's part—for the one irresistible reason that he was Charlotte's father.

"Pray don't think I am unworthy of your kind interest in my welfare," he pleaded. "Can you tell me of any facts which justify what you have just said?"

"I can tell you of three facts," Bervie said. "Mr. Bowmore belongs to one of the most revolutionary clubs in England; he has spoken in the ranks of sedition at public meetings; and his name is already in the black book at the Home Office. So much for the past. As to the future, if the rumour be true that Ministers mean to stop the insurrectionary risings among the population by suspending the *Habeas Corpus* Act, Mr. Bowmore will certainly be in danger; and it may be my father's duty to grant the warrant that apprehends him.

"Write to my father to verify what I have said, and I will forward your letter by way of satisfying him that he can trust you. In the meantime, refuse to accept Mr. Bowmore's assistance in the matter of your claim on Parliament; and, above all things, stop him at the outset, when he tries to steal his way into your intimacy. I need not caution you to say nothing against him to his wife and daughter. His wily tongue has long since deluded them. Don't let him delude you! Have you thought any more of our evening at Doctor Lagarde's?" he asked, abruptly changing the subject.

"I hardly know," said Percy, still under the impression of the formidable warning which he had just received.

"Let me jog your memory," the other continued. "You went on with the consultation by yourself, after I had left the Doctor's house. It will be really doing me a favour if you can call to mind what Lagarde saw in the trance—in my absence?"

Thus entreated Percy roused himself. His memory of events were still fresh enough to answer the call that his friend had made on it. In describing what had happened, he accurately repeated all that the Doctor had said.

Bervie dwelt on the words with alarm in his face as well as surprise.

"A man like me, trying to persuade a woman like—" he checked himself, as if he was afraid to let Charlotte's name pass his lips. "Trying to induce a woman to go away with me," he resumed, "and persuading her at last? Pray, go on! What did the Doctor see next?"

"He was too much exhausted, he said, to see any more."

"Surely you returned to consult him again?"

"No; I had had enough of it."

"When we get to London," said the Captain, "we shall pass along the Strand, on the way to your chambers. Will you kindly drop me at the turning that leads to the Doctor's lodgings?"

Percy looked at him in amazement. "You still take it seriously?" he said.

"Is it not serious?" Bervie asked. "Have you and I, so far, not done exactly what this man saw us doing? Did we not meet, in the days when we were rivals (as he saw us meet), with the pistols in our hands? Did you not recognise his description of the lady when you met her at the ball, as I recognized it before you?"

"Mere coincidences!" Percy answered, quoting Charlotte's

opinion when they had spoken together of Doctor Lagarde, but taking care not to cite his authority. "How many thousand men have been crossed in love? How many thousand men have fought duels for love? How many thousand women choose blue for their favourite colour, and answer to the vague description of the lady whom the Doctor pretended to see?"

"Say that it is so," Bervie rejoined. "The thing is remarkable, even from your point of view. And if more coincidences follow, the result will be more remarkable still."

Arrived at the Strand, Percy set the Captain down at the turning which led to the Doctor's lodgings. "You will call on me or write me word, if anything remarkable happens?" he said.

"You shall hear from me without fail," Bervie replied.

That night, the Captain's pen performed the Captain's promise, in few and startling words.

> Melancholy news! Madame Lagarde is dead. Nothing is known of her son but that he has left England, I have found out that he is a political exile. If he has ventured back to France, it is barely possible that I may hear something of him. I have friends at the English embassy in Paris who will help me to make inquiries; and I start for the Continent in a day or two. Write to me while I am away, to the care of my father, at 'The Manor House, near Dartford.' He will always know my address abroad, and will forward your letters. For your own sake, remember the warning I gave you this afternoon!
>
> Your faithful friend, A. B.

Chapter 9

Official Secrets

There was a more serious reason than Bervie was aware of, at the time, for the warning which he had thought it his duty to address to Percy Linwood. The new footman who had entered Mr. Bowmore's service was a Spy.

Well practiced in the infamous vocation that he followed, the wretch had been chosen by the Department of Secret Service at the Home Office, to watch the proceedings of Mr. Bowmore and his friends, and to report the result to his superiors. It may not be amiss to add that the employment of paid spies and informers, by the English Government of that time, was openly acknowledged in the House of Lords, and was defended as a necessary measure in the speeches of Lord Redesdale and Lord Liverpool.[1]

The reports furnished by the Home Office Spy, under these circumstances, begin with the month of March, and take the form of a series of notes introduced as follows:

"Mr. Secretary Since I entered Mr. Bowmore's service, I have the honour to inform you that my eyes and ears have been kept in a state of active observation; and I can further certify that my means of making myself useful in the future to my honourable employers are in no respect diminished. Not the slightest suspicion of my true character is felt by any person in the house.

First Note

The young gentleman now on a visit to Mr. Bowmore is, as you have been correctly informed, Mr. Percy Linwood. Although he is engaged to be married to Miss Bowmore, he is not discreet enough to conceal a certain want of friendly feeling, on his part, toward her father. The young lady has noticed this, and has resented it. She accuses her lover of having allowed himself to be prejudiced against Mr. Bowmore by some slanderous person unknown.

"Mr. Percy's clumsy defence of himself led (in my hearing) to a quarrel! Nothing but his prompt submission prevented the marriage engagement from being broken off. 'If you showed a want of confidence in Me' (I heard Miss Charlotte say), 'I might forgive it. But when you show a want of confidence in a man so noble as my father, I have no mercy on you.' After such an expression of filial sentiment as this, Mr. Percy wisely took the readiest way

1. Readers who may desire to test the author's authority for this statement, are referred to *The Annual Register* for 1817, Chapters 1. and 3.; and, further on, to page 66 in the same volume.

of appealing to the lady's indulgence. The young man has a demand on Parliament for moneys due to his father's estate; and he pleased and flattered Miss Charlotte by asking Mr. Bowmore to advise him as to the best means of asserting his claim. By way of advancing his political interests. Mr. Bowmore introduced him to the local Hampden Club; and Miss Charlotte rewarded him with a generosity which must not be passed over in silence. Her lover was permitted to put an engagement ring on her finger, and to kiss her afterward to his heart's content."

Second Note

Mr. Percy has paid more visits to the Republican Club; and Justice Bervie (father of the Captain) has heard of it, and has written to his son. The result that might have been expected has followed. Captain Bervie announces his return to England, to exert his influence for political good against the influence of Mr. Bowmore for political evil.

In the meanwhile, Mr. Percy's claim has been brought before the House of Commons, and has been adjourned for further consideration in six months' time. Both the gentlemen are indignant—especially Mr. Bowmore. He has called a meeting of the Club to consider his young friend's wrongs, and has proposed the election of Mr. Percy as a member of that revolutionary society.

Third Note

Mr. Percy has been elected. Captain Bervie has tried to awaken his mind to a sense of the danger that threatens him, if he persists in associating with his republican friends—and has utterly failed. Mr. Bowmore and Mr. Percy have made speeches at the Club, intended to force the latter gentleman's claim on the immediate attention of Government. Mr. Bowmore's flow of frothy eloquence has its influence (as you know from our shorthand writers' previous reports) on thousands of ignorant people. As it seems to me, the reasons for at once putting this man in prison are beyond dispute. Whether it is desirable to include Mr. Percy in the order of arrest, I must not venture to decide. Let me only hint that his seditious speech rivals the more elaborate efforts of Mr. Bowmore himself.

So much for the present. I may now respectfully direct your attention to the future.

On the second of April next the Club assembles a public meeting, 'in aid of British liberty,' in a field near Dartford. Mr. Bowmore is to preside, and is to be escorted afterward to Westminster Hall on his way to plead Mr. Percy's cause, in his own person, before the House of Commons. He is quite serious in declaring that 'the minions of Government dare not touch a hair of his head.' Miss Charlotte agrees with her father. And Mr. Percy agrees with Miss Charlotte. Such is the state of affairs at the house in which I am acting the part of domestic servant. "I inclose shorthand reports of the speeches recently delivered at the Hampden Club, and have the honour of waiting for further orders.

Fourth Note.

Your commands have reached me by this morning's post. I immediately waited on Justice Bervie (in plain clothes, of course), and gave him your official letter, instructing me to arrest Mr. Bowmore and Mr. Percy Linwood.

The venerable magistrate hesitated.

He quite understood the necessity for keeping the arrest a strict secret, in the interests of Government. The only reluctance he felt in granting the warrant related to his son's intimate friend. But for the peremptory tone of your letter, I really believe he would have asked you to give Mr. Percy time for consideration.

Not being rash enough to proceed to such an extreme as this, he slyly consulted the young man's interests by declining, on formal grounds, to date the warrant earlier than the second of April. Please note that my visit to him was paid at noon, on the thirty-first of March.

If the object of this delay (to which I was obliged to submit) is to offer a chance of escape to Mr. Percy, the same chance necessarily includes Mr. Bowmore, whose name is also in the warrant. Trust me to keep a watchful eye on both these gentlemen; especially on Mr. Bowmore. He is the most dangerous man of the two, and the most likely, if he feels any suspicions, to slip through the fingers of the law.

I have also to report that I discovered three persons in the hall of Justice Bervie's house, as I went out.

"One of them was his son, the Captain; one was his daughter, Miss Bervie; and the third was that smooth-tongued old soldier, Major Mulvany. If the escape of Mr. Bowmore and Mr. Linwood is in contemplation, mark my words: the persons whom I have just mentioned will be concerned in it—and perhaps Miss Charlotte herself as well.

At present, she is entirely unsuspicious of any misfortune hanging over her head; her attention being absorbed in the preparation of her bridal finery. As an admirer myself of the fair sex, I must own that it seems hard on the girl to have her lover clapped into prison, before the wedding-day.

I will bring you word of the arrest myself. There will be plenty of time to catch the afternoon coach to London.

Here—unless something happens which it is impossible to foresee my report may come to an end."

Chapter 10
The Elopement

On the evening of the first of April, Mrs. Bowmore was left alone with the servants. Mr. Bowmore and Percy had gone out together to attend a special meeting of the Club. Shortly afterward Miss Charlotte had left the cottage, under very extraordinary circumstances.

A few minutes only after the departure of her father and

Percy, she received a letter, which appeared to cause her the most violent agitation. She said to Mrs. Bowmore:

"Mamma, I must see Captain Bervie for a few minutes in private, on a matter of serious importance to all of us. He is waiting at the front gate, and he will come in if I show myself at the hall door."

Upon this, Mrs. Bowmore had asked for an explanation.

"There is no time for explanation," was the only answer she received; "I ask you to leave me for five minutes alone with the Captain."

Mrs. Bowmore still hesitated. Charlotte snatched up her garden hat, and declared, wildly, that she would go out to Captain Bervie, if she was not permitted to receive him at home. In the face of this declaration, Mrs. Bowmore yielded, and left the room.

In a minute more the Captain made his appearance.

Although she had given way, Mrs. Bowmore was not disposed to trust her daughter, without supervision, in the society of a man whom Charlotte herself had reviled as a slanderer and a false friend. She took up her position in the veranda outside the parlour, at a safe distance from one of the two windows of the room which had been left partially open to admit the fresh air. Here she waited and listened The conversation was for some time carried on in whispers.

As they became more and more excited, both Charlotte and Bervie ended in unconsciously raising their voices.

"I swear it to you on my faith as a Christian!" Mrs. Bowmore heard the Captain say. "I declare before God who hears me that I am speaking the truth!"

And Charlotte had answered, with a burst of tears:

"I can't believe you! I daren't believe you! Oh, how can you ask me to do such a thing? Let me go! let me go!"

Alarmed at those words, Mrs. Bowmore advanced to the window and looked in.

Bervie had put her daughter's arm on his arm, and was trying to induce her to leave the parlour with him. She resisted, and implored him to release her. He dropped her arm, and whispered in her ear. She looked at him—and instantly made up her mind.

"Let me tell my mother where I am going," she said; "and I will consent."

"Be it so!" he answered. "And remember one thing: every minute is precious; the fewest words are the best."

Mrs. Bowmore re-entered the cottage by the adjoining room, and met them in the passage. In few words, Charlotte spoke.

"I must go at once to Justice Bervie's house. Don't be afraid, mamma! I know what I am about, and I know I am right."

"Going to Justice Bervie's!" cried Mrs. Bowmore, in the utmost extremity of astonishment. "What will your father say, what will Percy think, when they come back from the Club?"

"My sister's carriage is waiting for me close by," Bervie answered. "It is entirely at Miss Bowmore's disposal. She can easily get back, 'if she wishes to keep her visit a secret, before Mr. Bowmore and Mr. Linwood return."

He led her to the door as he spoke. She ran back and kissed her mother tenderly. Mrs. Bowmore called to them to wait.

"I daren't let you go," she said to her daughter, "without your father's leave!"

Charlotte seemed not to hear, the Captain seemed not to hear. They ran across the front garden, and through the gate-and were out of sight in less than a minute.

More than two hours passed; the sun sank below the horizon, and still there were no signs of Charlotte's return.

Feeling seriously uneasy, Mrs. Bowmore crossed the room to ring the bell, and send the man-servant to Justice Bervie's house to hasten her daughter's return.

As she approached the fireplace, she was startled by a sound of stealthy footsteps in the hall, followed by a loud noise as of some heavy object that had dropped on the floor. She rang the bell violently, and opened the door of the parlour. At the same moment, the spy-footman passed her, running out, apparently in pursuit of somebody, at the top of his speed. She followed him, as rapidly as she could, across the little front garden, to the gate.

Arrived in the road, she was in time to see him vault upon the luggage-board at the back of a post-chaise before the cottage, just as the postilion started the horses on their way to London. The spy saw Mrs. Bowmore looking at him, and pointed, with an insolent nod of his head, first to the inside of the vehicle, and then over it to the highroad; signing to her that he designed to accompany the person in the post-chaise to the end of the journey.

Turning to go back, Mrs. Bowmore saw her own bewilderment reflected in the faces of the two female servants, who had followed her out.

"Who can the footman be after, ma'am?" asked the cook. "Do you think it's a thief?"

The housemaid pointed to the post-chaise, barely visible in the distance.

"Simpleton!" she said. "Do thieves travel in that way? I wish my master had come back," she proceeded, speaking to herself: "I'm afraid there's something wrong."

Mrs. Bowmore, returning through the garden-gate, instantly stopped and looked at the woman.

"What makes you mention your master's name, Amelia, when you fear that something is wrong?" she asked.

Amelia changed colour, and looked confused.

"I am loath to alarm you, ma'am," she said; "and I can't rightly see what it is my duty to do."

Mrs. Bowmore's heart sank within her under the cruellest of all terrors, the terror of something unknown. "Don't keep me in suspense," she said faintly. "Whatever it is, let me know it."

She led the way back to the parlour. The housemaid followed her. The cook (declining to be left alone) followed the housemaid.

"It was something I heard early this afternoon, ma'am," Amelia began. "Cook happened to be busy—"

The cook interposed: she had not forgiven the housemaid for calling her a simpleton. "No? Amelia, if you must bring me into it—not busy. Uneasy in my mind on the subject of the soup."

"I don't know that your mind makes much difference," Amelia resumed. "What it comes to is this it was I, and not you, who went into the kitchen-garden for the vegetables."

"Not by my wish, Heaven knows!" persisted the cook.

"Leave the room !" said Mrs. Bowmore. Even her patience had given way at last.

The cook looked as if she declined to believe her own ears. Mrs. Bowmore pointed to the door. The cook said "Oh?"—accenting it as a question. Mrs. Bowmore's finger still pointed. The cook, in solemn silence, yielded to circumstances, and banged the door.

"I was getting the vegetables, ma'am," Amelia proceeded, "when I heard voices on the other side of the paling. The wood is so old that one can see through the cracks easy enough. I saw my master, and Mr. Linwood, and Captain Bervie. The Captain seemed to have stopped the other two on the pathway that leads to the field; he stood, as it might be, between them and the back way to the house—and he spoke severely, that he did!"

"What did Captain Bervie say?"

"He said these words, ma'am: 'For the last time, Mr. Bowmore,' says he, 'will you understand that you are in danger, and that Mr. Linwood is in danger, unless you both leave this neighbourhood tonight?' My master made light of it.

"'For the last time,' says he, 'will you refer us to a proof of what you say, and allow us to judge for ourselves?'

"'I have told you already,' says the Captain, 'I am bound by my duty toward another person to keep what I know a secret.'

"'Very well,' says my master, 'I am bound by my duty to my country. And I tell you this,' says he, in his high and mighty way, 'neither Government, nor the spies of Government dare touch a hair of my head: they know it, sir, for the head of the people's friend!'"

"That's quite true," said Mrs. Bowmore, still believing in her husband as firmly as ever.

Amelia went on:

"Captain Bervie didn't seem to think so," she said. "He lost his temper. 'What stuff!' says he; 'there's a Government spy in your house at this moment, disguised as your footman.'

"My master looked at Mr. Linwood, and burst out laughing. 'You won't beat that, Captain,' says he, 'if you talk till doomsday.' He turned about without a word more, and went home.

"The Captain caught Mr. Linwood by the arm, as soon as they were alone. 'For God's sake,' says he, 'don't follow that madman's example!'"

Mrs. Bowmore was shocked. "Did he really call my husband a madman?" she asked.

"He did, indeed, ma'am—and he was in earnest about it, too. 'If you value your liberty,' he says to Mr. Linwood; 'if you hope to become Charlotte's husband, consult your own safety. I can give you a passport. Escape to France and wait till this trouble is over.' Mr. Linwood was not in the best of tempers—Mr. Linwood shook him off.

"'Charlotte's father will soon be my father,' says he, 'do you think I will desert him? My friends at the Club have taken up my claim; do you think I will forsake them at the meeting tomorrow? You ask me to be unworthy of Charlotte, and unworthy of my friends—you insult me, if you say more.' He whipped round on his heel, and followed my master."

"And what did the Captain do?"

"Lifted up his hands, ma'am, to the heavens, and looked—I declare it turned my blood to see him. If there's truth in mortal man, it's my firm belief—"

What the housemaid's belief was, remained unexpressed. Before she could get to her next word, a shriek of horror from the hall announced that the cook's powers of interruption were not exhausted yet.

Mistress and servant both hurried out in terror of they knew not what. There stood the cook, alone in the hall, confronting the stand on which the overcoats and hats of the men of the family were placed.

"Where's the master's travelling coat?" cried the cook, staring wildly at an unoccupied peg. "And where's his cap to match! Oh Lord, he's off in the post-chaise! and the footman's after him!"

Simpleton as she was, the woman had blundered on a very serious discovery.

Coat and cap—both made after a foreign pattern, and both strikingly remarkable in form and colour to English eyes—had unquestionably disappeared. It was equally certain that they were well known to the footman, whom the Captain had declared to be a spy, as the coat and cap which his master used in travelling. Had Mr. Bowmore discovered (since the afternoon) that he was really in danger? Had the necessities of instant flight only allowed him time enough to snatch his coat and cap out of the hall?

And had the treacherous man-servant seen him as he was making his escape to the post-chaise? The cook's conclusions answered all these questions in the affirmative—and, if Captain Bervie's words of warning had been correctly reported, the cook's conclusion for once was not to be despised.

Under this last trial of her fortitude, Mrs. Bowmore's feeble reserves of endurance completely gave way. The poor lady turned faint and giddy. Amelia placed her on a chair in the hall, and told the cook to open the front door, and let in the fresh air.

The cook obeyed; and instantly broke out with a second terrific scream; announcing nothing less, this time, than the appearance of Mr. Bowmore himself, alive and hearty, returning with Percy from the meeting at the Club!

The inevitable inquiries and explanations followed.

Fully assured, as he had declared himself to be of the sanctity of his person (politically speaking), Mr. Bowmore turned pale, nevertheless, when he looked at the unoccupied peg on his clothes stand. Had some man unknown personated him? And had a post-chaise been hired to lead an impending pursuit of him in the wrong direction?

What did it mean? Who was the friend to whose services he was indebted? As for the proceedings of the man-servant, but one interpretation could now be placed on them. They distinctly justified what Captain Bervie had said of him. Mr. Bowmore thought of the Captain's other assertion, relating to the urgent necessity for making his escape; and looked at Percy in silent dismay; and turned paler than ever.

Percy's thoughts, diverted for the moment only from the lady of his love, returned to her with renewed fidelity. "Let us hear what Charlotte thinks of it," he said. "Where is she?"

It was impossible to answer this question plainly and in few words.

Terrified at the effect which her attempt at explanation produced on Percy, helplessly ignorant when she was called upon to account for her daughter's absence, Mrs. Bowmore could only shed tears and express a devout trust in Providence. Her husband looked at the new misfortune from a political point of view. He sat down and slapped his forehead theatrically with the palm of his hand. "Thus far," said the patriot, I 'my political assailants have only struck at me through the newspapers. Now they strike at me through my child!"

Percy made no speeches. There was a look in his eyes which boded ill for Captain Bervie if the two met. "I am going to fetch her," was all he said, "as fast as a horse can carry me."

He hired his horse at an inn in the town, and set forth for Justice Bervie's house at a gallop.

During Percy's absence, Mr. Bowmore secured the front and back entrances to the cottage with his own hands.

These first precautions taken, he ascended to his room and packed his travelling bag. "Necessaries for my use in prison," he remarked. "The bloodhounds of Government are after me."—

"Are they after Percy, too?" his wife ventured to ask.

Mr. Bowmore looked up impatiently, and cried "Pooh!"—as if Percy was of no consequence. Mrs. Bowmore thought otherwise: the good woman privately packed a bag for Percy, in the sanctuary of her own room.

For an hour, and more than an hour, no event of any sort occurred.

Mr. Bowmore stalked up and down the parlour, meditating. At intervals, ideas of flight presented themselves attractively to his mind. At intervals, ideas of the speech that he had prepared for the public meeting on the next day took their place. "If I fly tonight," he wisely observed, "what will become of my speech? I will not fly tonight! The people shall hear me."

He sat down and crossed his arms fiercely. As he looked at his wife to see what effect he had produced on her, the sound of heavy carriage-wheels and the trampling of horses penetrated to the parlour from the garden-gate.

Mr. Bowmore started to his feet, with every appearance of having suddenly altered his mind on the question of flight. Just as he reached the hall, Percy's voice was heard at the front door. "Let me in. Instantly! Instantly!"

Mrs. Bowmore drew back the bolts before the servants could help her. "Where is Charlotte?" she cried; seeing Percy alone on the doorstep.

"Gone!" Percy answered furiously. "Eloped to Paris with Captain Bervie! Read her own confession. They were just sending the messenger with it, when I reached the house."

He handed a note to Mrs. Bowmore, and turned aside to speak to her husband while she read it. Charlotte wrote to her mother very briefly; promising to explain everything on her return. In the meantime, she had left home under careful protection—she had a lady for her companion on the journey—and she would write again from Paris. So the letter, evidently written in great haste, began and ended.

Percy took Mr. Bowmore to the window, and pointed to a carriage and four horses waiting at the garden-gate.

"Do you come with me, and back me with your authority as her father?" he asked, sternly. "Or do you leave me to go alone?"

Mr. Bowmore was famous among his admirers for his "happy replies." He made one now.

"I am not Brutus," he said. "I am only Bowmore. My daughter before everything. Fetch my travelling-bag."

While the travellers' bags were being placed in the chaise, Mr. Bowmore was struck by an idea.

He produced from his coat-pocket a roll of many papers thickly covered with writing. On the blank leaf in which they were tied up, he wrote in the largest letters: "Frightful domestic calamity! Vice-President Bowmore obliged to leave England! Welfare of a beloved daughter! His speech will be read at the meeting by Secretary Joskin, of the Club. (Private to Joskin. Have these lines printed and posted everywhere. And, when you read my speech, for God's sake don't drop your voice at the ends of the sentences.")

He threw down the pen and embraced Mrs. Bowmore in the most summary manner. The poor woman was ordered to send the roll of paper to the Club, without a word to comfort and sustain her from her husband's lips. Percy spoke to her hopefully and kindly, as he kissed her cheek at parting.

On the next morning, a letter, addressed to Mrs. Bowmore, was delivered at the cottage by private messenger.

Opening the letter, she recognized the handwriting of her husband's old friend, and her old friend—Major Mulvany. In breathless amazement, she read these lines:

> Mrs. Bowmore In matters of importance, the golden rule is never to waste words. I have performed one of the great actions of my life—I have saved your husband.
>
> How I discovered that my friend was in danger, I must not tell you at present. Let it be enough if I say that I have been a guest under Justice Bervie's hospitable roof, and that I know of a Home Office spy who has taken you unawares, under pretence of being your footman. If I had not circumvented him, the scoundrel would have imprisoned your husband, and another dear friend of mine. This is how I did it.
>
> I must begin by appealing to your memory.
>
> Do you happen to remember that your husband and I are as near as may be of about the same height? Very good, so far. Did you, in the next place, miss Bowmore's travelling

coat and cap from their customary peg? I am the thief, dearest lady; I put them on my own humble self. Did you hear a sudden noise in the hall? Oh, forgive me—I made the noise! And it did just what I wanted of it, It brought the spy up from the kitchen, suspecting that something might be wrong.

What did the wretch see when he got into the hall? His master, in travelling costume, running out. What did he find when he reached the garden? His master escaping, in a post-chaise, on the road to London. What did he do, the born blackguard that he was? Jumped up behind the chaise to make sure of his prisoner. It was dark when we got to London. In a hop, skip, and jump, I was out of the carriage, and in at my own door, before he could look me in the face.

The date of the warrant, you must know, obliged him to wait till the morning. All that night, he and the Bow Street runners kept watch. They came in with the sunrise—and who did they find? Major Mulvany snug in his bed, and as innocent as the babe unborn. Oh, they did their duty! Searched the place from the kitchen to the garrets—and gave it up. There's but one thing I regret—I let the spy off without a good thrashing. No matter. I'll do it yet, one of these days.

Let me know the first good news of our darling fugitives, and I shall be more than rewarded for what little I have done.

Your always devoted,

Terence Mulvany."

Chapter 11
Pursuit And Discovery

Feeling himself hurried away on the road to Dover, as fast; as four horses could carry him, Mr. Bowmore had leisure to criticise Percy's conduct, from his own purely selfish point of view.

"If you had listened to my advice," he said, "you would have treated that man Bervie like the hypocrite and villain that he is. But no! you trusted to your own crude impressions. Having given him your hand after the duel (I would have given him the contents of my pistol!) you hesitated to withdraw it again, when that slanderer appealed to your friendship not to cast him off. Now you see the consequence!"

"Wait till we get to Paris!" All the ingenuity of Percy's travelling companion failed to extract from him any other answer than that.

Foiled so far, Mr. Bowmore began to start difficulties next. Had they money enough for the journey? Percy touched his pocket, and answered shortly, "Plenty." Had they passports? Percy sullenly showed a letter. "There is the necessary voucher from a magistrate," he said.

"The consul at Dover will give us our passports. Mind this!" he added, in warning tones, "I have pledged my word of honour to Justice Bervie that we have no political object in view in travelling to France. Keep your politics to yourself, on the other side of the Channel."

Mr. Bowmore listened in blank amazement. Charlotte's lover was appearing in a new character—the character of a man who had lost his respect for Charlotte's father!

It was useless to talk to him. He deliberately checked any further attempts at conversation by leaning back in the carriage, and closing his eyes. The truth is, Mr. Bowmore's own language and conduct were insensibly producing the salutary impression on Percy's mind which Bervie had vainly tried to convey, under the disadvantage of having Charlotte's influence against him. Throughout the journey, Percy did exactly what Bervie had once entreated him to do—he kept Mr. Bowmore at a distance.

At every stage, they inquired after the fugitives. At every stage, they were answered by a more or less intelligible description of Bervie and Charlotte, and of the lady who accompanied them. No disguise had been attempted; no person had in any case been bribed to conceal the truth.

When the first tumult of his emotions had in some degree

subsided, this strange circumstance associated itself in Percy's mind with the equally unaccountable conduct of Justice Bervie, on his arrival at the manor house.

The old gentleman met his visitor in the hall, without expressing, and apparently without feeling, any indignation at his son's conduct. It was even useless to appeal to him for information. He only said, "I am not in Arthur's confidence; he is of age, and my daughter (who has volunteered to accompany him) is of age. I have no claim to control them. I believe they have taken Miss Bowmore to Paris; and that is all I know about it."

He had shown the same dense insensibility in giving his official voucher for the passports. Percy had only to satisfy him on the question of politics; and the document was drawn out as a matter of course. Such had been the father's behaviour; and the conduct of the son now exhibited the same shameless composure. To what conclusion did this discovery point? Percy abandoned the attempt to answer that question in despair.

They reached Dover toward two o'clock in the morning.

At the pier-head they found a coastguardsman on duty, and received more information.

In 1817 the communication with France was still by sailing-vessels. Arriving long after the departure of the regular packet, Bervie had hired a lugger, and had sailed with the two ladies for Calais, having a fresh breeze in his favour. Percy's first angry impulse was to follow him instantly. The next moment he remembered the insurmountable obstacle of the passports. The Consul would certainly not grant those essentially necessary documents at two in the morning!

The only alternative was to wait for the regular packet, which sailed some hours later—between eight and nine o'clock in the forenoon. In this case, they might apply for their passports before the regular office hours, if they explained the circumstances, backed by the authority of the magistrate's letter.

Mr. Bowmore followed Percy to the nearest inn that was open, sublimely indifferent to the delays and difficulties of the journey. He ordered refreshments with the air of a man who was performing a melancholy duty to himself, in the name of humanity.

"When I think of my speech," he said, at supper, "my heart bleeds for the people. In a few hours more, they will assemble in their thousands, eager to hear me. And what will they see? Joskin in my place! Joskin with a manuscript in his hand! Joskin, who drops his voice at the ends of his sentences! I will never forgive Charlotte. Waiter, another glass of brandy and water."

After an unusually quick passage across the Channel, the travellers landed on the French coast, before the defeated spy had returned from London to Dartford by stagecoach. Continuing their journey by post as far as Amiens, they reached that city in time to take their places by the diligence to Paris.

Arrived in Paris, they encountered another incomprehensible proceeding on the part of Captain Bervie.

Among the persons assembled in the yard to see the arrival of the diligence was a man with a morsel of paper in his hand, evidently on the lookout for some person whom he expected to discover among the travellers.

After consulting his bit of paper, he looked with steady attention at Percy and Mr. Bowmore, and suddenly approached them. "If you wish to see the Captain," he said, in broken English, "you will find him at that hotel." He handed a printed card to Percy, and disappeared among the crowd before it was possible to question him.

Even Mr. Bowmore gave way to human weakness, and condescended to feel astonished in the face of such an event as this. "What next?" he exclaimed.

"Wait till we get to the hotel," said Percy.

In half an hour more the landlord had received them, and the waiter had led them to the right door. Percy pushed the man aside, and burst into the room.

Captain Bervie was alone, reading a newspaper. Before the first furious words had escaped Percy's lips, Bervie silenced him by pointing to a closed door on the right of the fireplace.

" She is in that room," he said; "speak quietly, or you may

frighten her. I know what you are going to say," he added, as Percy stepped nearer to him. "Will you hear me in my own defence, and then decide whether I am the greatest scoundrel living, or the best friend you ever had?"

He put the question kindly, with something that was at once grave and tender in his look and manner. The extraordinary composure with which he acted and spoke had its tranquilizing influence over Percy. He felt himself surprised into giving Bervie a hearing.

"I will tell you first what I have done," the Captain proceeded, "and next why I did it. I have taken it on myself, Mr. Linwood, to make an alteration in your wedding arrangements. Instead of being married at Dartford church, you will be married (if you see no objection) at the chapel of the embassy in Paris, by my old college friend the chaplain."

This was too much for Percy's self-control. "Your audacity is beyond belief," he broke out.

"And beyond endurance," Mr. Bowmore added. "Understand this, sir! Whatever your defence may be, I object, under any circumstances, to be made the victim of a trick."

"You are the victim of your own obstinate refusal to profit by a plain warning," Bervie rejoined. "At the eleventh hour, I entreated you, and I entreated Mr, Linwood, to provide for your own safety; and I spoke in vain."

Percy's patience gave way once more.

"To use your own language," he said, "I have still to decide whether you have behaved toward me like a 'scoundrel or a friend. You have said nothing to justify yourself yet."

"Very well put," Mr. Bowmore chimed in. "Come to the point, sir! My daughter's reputation is in question."

"Miss Bowmore's reputation is not in question for a single instant," Bervie answered. "My sister has been the companion of her journey from first to last."

"Journey?" Mr, Bowmore repeated, indignantly. "I want to know, sir, what the journey means. As an outraged father, I ask one plain question. Why did you run away with my daughter?"

Bervie took a slip of paper from his pocket, and handed it to Percy with a smile.

It was a copy of the warrant which Justice Bervie's duty had compelled him to issue for the "arrest of Orlando Bowmore and Percy Linwood." There was no danger in divulging the secret now. British warrants were waste paper in France, in those days.

"I ran away with the bride," Bervie said, coolly, "in the certain knowledge that you and Mr. Bowmore would run after me. If I had not forced you both to follow me out of England on the first of April, you would have been made State prisoners on the second. What do you say to my conduct now?"

"Wait, Percy, before you answer him," Mr. Bowmore interposed. "He is ready enough at excusing himself. But, observe-he hasn't a word to say in justification of my daughter's readiness to run away with him."

"Have you quite done?" Bervie asked, as quietly as ever.

Mr. Bowmore reserved the right of all others which he most prized, the right of using his tongue. "For the present," he answered in his loftiest manner, "I have done."

Bervie proceeded: "Your daughter consented to run away with me, because I took her to my father's house, and prevailed upon him to trust her with the secret of the coming arrests. She had no choice left but to let her obstinate father and her misguided lover go to prison—or to take her place with my sister and me in the travelling-carriage." He appealed once more to Percy. "My friend, you remember the day when you spared my life. Have I remembered it, too?"

For once, there was an Englishman who was not contented to express the noblest emotions that humanity can feel by the commonplace ceremony of shaking hands. Percy's heart overflowed. In an outburst of unutterable gratitude he threw himself on Bervie's breast. As brothers the two men embraced. As brothers they loved and trusted one another, from that day forth.

The door on the right was softly opened from within. A charming face—the dark eyes bright with happy tears, the rosy lips just opening into a smile—peeped into the room. A low sweet voice, with an undernote of trembling in it, made this modest protest, in the form of an inquiry:

"When you have quite done, Percy, with our good friend, perhaps you will have something to say to ME?"

Last Words

The persons immediately interested in the marriage of Percy and Charlotte were the only persons present at the ceremony.

At the little breakfast afterward, in the French hotel, Mr. Bowmore insisted on making a speech to a select audience of six; namely, the bride and bridegroom, the bridesmaid, the Chaplain, the Captain, and Mrs. Bowmore. But what does a small audience matter? The English frenzy for making speeches is not to be cooled by such a trifle as that. At the end of the world, the expiring forces of Nature will hear a dreadful voice—the voice of the last Englishman delivering the last speech.

Percy wisely made his honeymoon a long one; he determined to be quite sure of his superior influence over his wife before he trusted her within reach of her father again.

Mr. and Mrs. Bowmore accompanied Captain Bervie and Miss Bervie on their way back to England, as far as Boulogne. In that pleasant town the banished patriot set up his tent. It was a cheaper place to live in than Paris, and it was conveniently close to England, when he had quite made up his mind whether to be an exile on the Continent, or to go back to his own country and be a martyr in prison. In the end, the course of events settled that question for him.

Mr. Bowmore returned to England, with the return of the *Habeas Corpus* Act.

The years passed. Percy and Charlotte (judged from the romantic point of view) became two uninteresting married people. Bervie (always remaining a bachelor) rose steadily in his profession, through the higher grades of military rank. Mr. Bowmore, wisely overlooked by a new Government, sank back again into the obscurity from which shrewd Ministers would never have assisted him to emerge.

The one subject of interest left, among the persons of this little drama, was now represented by Doctor Lagarde. Thus far, not a trace had been discovered of the French physician, who had so strangely associated the visions of his magnetic sleep with the destinies of the two men who had consulted him.

Steadfastly maintaining his own opinion of the prediction and the fulfilment, Bervie persisted in believing that he and Lagarde (or Percy and Lagarde) were yet destined to meet, and resume the unfinished consultation at the point where it had been broken off. Persons, happy in the possession of "sound common sense," who declared the prediction to be skilled guesswork, and the fulfilment manifest coincidence, ridiculed the idea of finding Doctor Lagarde as closely akin to that other celebrated idea of finding the needle in the bottle of hay. But Bervie's obstinacy was proverbial. Nothing shook his confidence in his own convictions.

More than thirteen years had elapsed since the consultation at the Doctor's lodgings, when Bervie went to Paris to spend a summer holiday with his friend, the chaplain at the English embassy. His last words to Percy and Charlotte when he took his leave were: "Suppose I meet with Doctor Lagarde?"

It was then the year 1830. Bervie arrived at his friend's rooms on the 24th of July. On the 27th of the month the famous revolution broke out which dethroned Charles the Tenth in three days.

On the second day, Bervie and his host ventured into the streets, watching the revolution (like other reckless Englishmen) at the risk of their lives. In the confusion around them they were separated. Bervie, searching for his companion, found his progress stopped by a barricade, which had been desperately attacked, and desperately defended. Men in blouses and men in uniform lay dead and dying together: the tricolored flag waved over them, in token of the victory of the people.

Bervie had just revived a poor wretch with a drink from an overthrown bowl of water, which still had a few drops left in it, when he felt a hand laid on his shoulder from behind. He turned and discovered a National Guard, who had been watching his charitable action. "Give a helping hand to that poor fellow," said the citizen-soldier, pointing to a workman standing near, grimed with blood and gunpowder. The tears were rolling down the man's cheeks. "I can't see my way, sir, for crying," he said.

"Help me to carry that sad burden into the next street." He pointed to a rude wooden litter, on which lay a dead or wounded man, his face and breast covered with an old cloak. "There is the best friend the people ever had," the workman said. "He cured us, comforted us, respected us, loved us. And there he lies, shot dead while he was binding up the wounds of friends and enemies alike!"

"Whoever he is, he has died nobly," Bervie answered. "May I look at him?"

The workman signed that he might look.

Bervie lifted the cloak—and met with Doctor Lagarde once more.

Nine o'Clock!

The Night of the 30th of June, 1793, is memorable in the prison annals of Paris, as the last night in confinement of the leaders of the famous Girondin party in the first French revolution. On the morning of the 31st, the twenty-one deputies who represented the department of the Gironde, were guillotined to make way for Robespierre and the Reign of Terror.

With these men fell the last revolutionists of that period who shrank from founding a republic on massacre; who recoiled from substituting for a monarchy of corruption, a monarchy of bloodshed. The elements of their defeat lay as much in themselves, as in the events of their time. They were not, as a party, true to their own convictions; they temporized; they fatally attempted to take a middle course amid the terrible emergencies of a terrible epoch, and they fell—fell before worse men, because those men were in earnest.

Condemned to die, the Girondins submitted nobly to their fate; their great glory was the glory of their deaths. The speech of one of them on hearing his sentence pronounced, was a prophecy of the future, fulfilled to the letter.

'I die,' he said to the Jacobin judges, the creatures of Robespierre, who tried him. 'I die at a time when the people have lost their reason; you will die on the day when they recover it.' Valazé was the only member of the condemned party who displayed a momentary weakness; he stabbed himself on hearing his sentence pronounced. But the blow was not mortal—he died on the scaffold, and died bravely with the rest.

On the night of the 30th the Girondins held their famous banquet in the prison; celebrated, with the ferocious stoicism of the time, their last social meeting before the morning on which they were to die. Other men, besides the twenty-one, were present at this supper of the condemned. They were prisoners who held Girondin opinions, but whose names were not illustrious enough for history to preserve.

Though sentenced to confinement they were not sentenced to death. Some of their number, who had protested most boldly against the condemnation of the deputies, were ordered to witness the execution on the morrow, as a timely example to terrify them into submission. More than this, Robespierre and his colleagues did not, as yet, venture to attempt: the Reign of Terror was a cautious reign at starting.

The supper-table of the prison was spread; the guests, twenty-one of their number stamped already with the seal of death, were congregated at the last Girondin banquet; toast followed toast; the *Marseillaise* was sung; the desperate triumph of the feast was rising fast to its climax, when a new and ominous subject of conversation was started at the lower end of the table, and spread electrically, almost in a moment , to the top.

This subject (by whom originated no one knew) was simply a question as to the hour in the morning at which the execution was to take place. Every one of the prisoners appeared to be in ignorance on this point; and the gaolers either could not, or would not, enlighten them. Until the cart for the condemned rolled into the prison-yard, not one of the Girondins could tell whether he was to be called out to the guillotine soon after sunrise, or not till near noon.

This uncertainty was made a topic for discussion, or for jesting on all sides. It was eagerly seized on as a pretext for raising to the highest pitch the ghastly animation and hilarity of the evening. In some quarters, the recognised hour of former executions was quoted as precedent sure to be followed by the executioners of the morrow; in others, it was asserted that Robespierre and his party would purposely depart from established customs in this, as in previous instances.

Dozens of wild schemes were suggested for guessing the hour by fortune-telling rules on the cards; bets were offered and accepted among the prisoners who were not condemned to death, and witnessed in stoical mockery by the prisoners who were. Jests were exchanged about early rising and hurried toilets; in short, every man contributed an assertion, with one solitary exception. That exception was the Girondin, Duprat, one of the deputies who was sentenced to die by the guillotine.

He was a younger man than the majority of his brethren, and was personally remarkable by his pale, handsome, melancholy face, and his reserved yet gentle manners. Throughout the evening, he had spoken but rarely; there was something of the silence and serenity of a martyr in his demeanour. That he feared death as little as any of his companions was plainly visible in his bright, steady eye; in his unchanging complexion; in his firm, calm voice, when he occasionally addressed those who happened to be near him.

But he was evidently out of place at the banquet; his temperament was reflective, his disposition serious; feasts were at no time a sphere in which he was calculated to shine.

His taciturnity, while the hour of the execution was under discussion, had separated him from most of those with whom he sat, at the lower end of the table. They edged up towards the top, where the conversation was most general and most animated. One of his friends, however, still kept his place by Duprat's side, and thus questioned him anxiously, but in low tones, on the cause of his immovable silence:

'Are you the only man of the company, Duprat, who has neither a guess nor a joke to make about the time of the execution?'

'I never joke, Marginy,' was the answer, given with a slight smile which had something of the sarcastic in it; 'and as for guessing at the time of the execution, I never guess at things which I know.'

'Know! You know the hour of the execution! Then why not

communicate your knowledge to your friends around you?'

'Because not one of them would believe what I said.'

'But, surely, you could prove it. Somebody must have told you.'

'Nobody has told me.'

'You have seen some private letter, then; or you have managed to get sight of the execution-order; or —'

'Spare your conjectures, Marginy. I have not read, as I have not been told, what is the hour at which we are to die tomorrow.'

'Then how on earth can you possibly know it?'

'I do not know when the execution will begin, or when it will end. I only know that it will be going on at nine o'clock tomorrow morning. Out of the twenty-one who are to suffer death, one will be guillotined exactly at that hour. Whether he will be the first whose head falls, or the last, I cannot tell.'

'And pray who may this man be, who is going to die exactly at nine o'clock? Of course, prophetically knowing so much, you know that!'

'I do know it. I am the man whose death by the guillotine will take place exactly at the hour I have mentioned.'

'You said just now, Duprat, that you never joked. Do you expect me to believe that what you have just spoken is spoken in earnest?'

'I repeat that I never joke; and I answer that I expect you to believe me. I know the hour at which my death will take place tomorrow, just as certainly as I know the fact of my own existence tonight.'

'But how? My dear friend, can you really lay claim to supernatural intuition, in this eighteenth century of the world, in this renowned Age of reason?'

'No two men, Marginy, understand that word, supernatural, exactly in the same sense; you and I differ about its meaning, or, in other words, differ about the real distinction between the doubtful and the true. We will not discuss the subject: I wish to be understood, at the outset, as laying claim to no superior intuitions whatever; but I tell you, at the same time, that even in this Age of Reason, I have reason for what I have said. My father and my brother both died at nine o'clock in the morning, and were both warned very strangely of their deaths. I am the last of my family; I was warned last night, as they were warned; and I shall die by the guillotine, as they died in their beds, at the fatal hour of nine.'

'But, Duprat, why have I never heard of this before? As your oldest and, I am sure, your dearest friend, I thought you had long since trusted me with all your secrets.'

'And you shall know this secret; I only kept it from you till the time when I would be certain that my death would substantiate my words, to the very letter. Come! You are as bad supper-company as I am; let us slip away from the table unperceived, while our friends are all engaged in conversation. Yonder end of the hall is dark and quiet—we can speak there uninterruptedly, for some hours to come.'

He led the way from the supper-table, followed by Marginy. Arrived at one of the darkest and most retired corners of the great hall of the prison, Duprat spoke again:

'I believe, Marginy,' he said, 'that you are one of those who have been ordered by our tyrants to witness my execution, and the execution of my brethren, as a warning spectacle for an enemy to the Jacobin cause?'

'My dear, dear friend! It is too true; I am ordered to witness the butchery which I cannot prevent—our last awful parting will be at the foot of the scaffold. I am among the victims who are spared—mercilessly spared—for a little while yet.'

'Say the martyrs! We die as martyrs, calmly, hopefully, innocently. When I am placed under the guillotine tomorrow morning, listen, my friend, for the striking of the church clocks; listen for the hour while you look your last on me. Until that time, suspend your judgement on the strange chapter of family history which I am now about to relate.'

Marginy took his friend's hand, and promised compliance with the request. Duprat then began as follows:

'You knew my brother Alfred, when he was quite a youth, and you knew something of what people flippantly termed, the eccentricities of his character. He was three years my junior; but from childhood, he showed far less of a child's innate levity and happiness than his elder brother.

He was noted for his seriousness and thoughtfulness as a boy; showed little inclination for a boy's usual lessons, and less still for a boy's usual recreations,—in short, he was considered by everybody (my father included) as deficient in intellect; as a vacant dreamer, and an inveterate idler, whom it was hopeless to improve.

Our tutor tried to lead him to various studies, and tried in vain. It was the same when the cultivation of his mind was given up, and the cultivation of his body was next attempted. The fencing-master could make nothing of him; and the dancing-master, after the first three lessons, resigned in despair. Seeing that it was useless to set others to teach him, my father made a virtue of necessity, and left him, if he chose, to teach himself.

'To the astonishment of everyone, he had not been long consigned to his own guidance, when he was discovered in the library, reading every old treatise on astrology which he could lay his hands on. He had rejected all useful knowledge for the most obsolete of obsolete sciences—the old, abandoned delusion of divination by stars!

'My father laughed heartily over the strange study to which his idle son had at last applied himself, but made no attempt to oppose his new caprice, and sarcastically presented him with a telescope on his next birthday. I should remind you here, of what you may perhaps have forgotten, that my father was a philosopher of the Voltaire school, who believed that the summit of human wisdom was to arrive at the power of sneering at all enthusiasms, and doubting of all truths.

'Apart from his philosophy, he was a kind-hearted, easy man, of quick, rather than profound intelligence. He could see nothing in my brother's new occupation, but the evidence of a new idleness, a fresh caprice which would be abandoned in a few months. My father was not the man to appreciate those yearnings towards the poetical and the spiritual, which were part of Alfred's temperament, and which gave to his peculiar studies of the stars and their influences, a certain charm altogether unconnected with the more practical attractions of scientific investigation.

'This idle caprice of my brother's, as my father insisted on terming it, had lasted more than a twelvemonth, when there occurred the first of a series of mysterious and—as I consider them—supernatural events, with all of which Alfred was very remarkably connected. I was myself a witness of the strange circumstance, which I am now about to relate to you.

'One day—my brother being then sixteen years of age—I happened to go into my father's study, during his absence, and found Alfred there, standing close to a window, which looked into the garden. I walked up to him, and observed a curious expression of vacancy and rigidity in his face, especially in his eyes.

'Although I knew him to be subject to what are called fits of absence, I still thought it rather extraordinary that he never moved, and never noticed me when I was close to him. I took his hand, and asked if he was unwell. His flesh felt quite cold; neither my touch nor my voice produced the smallest sensation in him. Almost at the same moment when I noticed this, I happened to be looking accidentally towards the garden. There was my father walking along one of the paths, and there, by his side, walking with him, was another Alfred!—Another, yet exactly the same as the Alfred by whose side I was standing, whose hand I still held in mine!

'Thoroughly panic-stricken, I dropped his hand, and uttered a cry of terror. At the loud sound of my voice, the statue-like presence before me immediately began to show signs of animation. I looked round again at the garden. The figure of my brother, which I had beheld there, was gone, and I saw to my horror, that my father was looking for it—looking in all directions for the companion (spectre, or human being?) of his walk!

'When I turned towards Alfred once more, he had (if I may so express it) come to life again, and was asking, with his usual gentleness of manner and kindness of voice, why I was looking so pale? I evaded the question by making some excuse, and in my turn inquired of him, how long he had been in my father's study.

'"Surely you ought to know best," he answered with a laugh, "for you must have been here before me. It is not many minutes ago since I was walking in the garden with —"

'Before he could complete the sentence my father entered the room.

'"Oh! Here you are, Master Alfred," said he. "May I ask for what purpose you took it into your wise head to vanish in that extraordinary manner? Why you slipped away from me in an instant, while I was picking a flower! On my word, sir, you're a better player at hide-and-seek than your brother,—he would only have run into the shrubbery, you have managed to run in here, though how you did it in the time passes my poor comprehension. I was not a moment picking the flower, yet in that moment you were gone!"

'Alfred glanced suddenly and searchingly at me; his face became deadly pale, and, without speaking a word, he hurried from the room.

'"Can you explain this?" said my father, looking very much astonished.

'I hesitated a moment, and then told him what I had seen. He took a pinch of snuff—a favourite habit with him when he was going to be sarcastic, in imitation of Voltaire.

'"One visionary in a family is enough," said he; "I recommend you not to turn yourself into a bad imitation of your brother Alfred! Send your ghost after me, my good boy! I am going back into the garden, and should like to see him again!"

'Ridicule, even much sharper than this, would have had little effect on me. If I was certain of anything in the world, I was certain that I had seen my brother in the study—nay, more, had touched him,—and equally certain that I had seen his double-his exact similitude, in the garden. As far as any man could know that he was in possession of his own senses, I knew myself to be in possession of mine.

'Left alone to think over what I had beheld, I felt a supernatural terror creeping through me—a terror which increased, when I recollected that, on one or two occasions friends had said they had seen Alfred out of doors, when we all knew him to be at home. These statements, which my father had laughed at, and had taught me to laugh at, either as a trick, or a delusion on the part of others, now recurred to my memory as startling corroborations of what I had just seen myself. The solitude of the study oppressed me in a manner which I cannot describe. I left the apartment to seek Alfred, determined to question him, with all possible caution, on the subject of his strange trance, and his sensations at the moment when I had awakened him from it.

'I found him in his bedroom, still pale, and now very thoughtful. As the first words in reference to the scene in the study passed my lips, he started violently, and entreated me, with very unusual warmth of speech and manner, never to speak to him on that subject again,—never, if I had any love or regard for him! Of course, I complied with his request. The mystery, however, was not destined to end here.

'About two months after the event which I have just related, we had arranged, one evening, to go to the theatre. My father had insisted that Alfred should be of the party, otherwise he would certainly have declined accompanying us; for he had no inclination whatever for public amusements of any kind. However, with his usual docility, he prepared to obey my father's desire, by going upstairs to put on his evening dress. It was wintertime, so he was obliged to take a candle with him.

'We waited in the drawing-room for his return a very long time, so long, that my father was on the point of sending upstairs to remind him of the lateness of the hour, when Alfred reappeared without the candle which he had taken with him from the room. The ghostly alteration over his face—the hideous, death-look that distorted his features I shall never forget,—I shall see it tomorrow on the scaffold!

'Before either my father or I could utter a word, my brother said: "I have been taken suddenly ill; but I am better now. Do you still wish me to go to the theatre?"

'"Certainly not, my dear Alfred," answered my father; "we must send for the doctor immediately."

'"Pray do not call in the doctor, sir; he would be of no use. I will tell you why, if you will let me speak to you alone."

'My father, looking seriously alarmed, signed to me to leave the room. For more than half an hour I remained absent, suffering almost unendurable suspense and anxiety on my brother's account. When I was recalled, I observed that Alfred was quite calm, though still deadly pale. My father's manner displayed an agitation which I had never observed in it before. He rose from his chair when I re-entered the room, and left me alone with my brother.

'"Promise me," said Alfred, in answer to my entreaties to know what had happened, "promise that you will not ask me to tell you more than my father has permitted me to tell. It is his desire that I should keep certain things a secret from you."

'I gave the required promise, but gave it most unwillingly. Alfred then proceeded.

'"When I left you to go and dress for the theatre, I felt a sense of oppression all over me, which I cannot describe. As soon as I was alone, it seemed as if some part of the life within me was slowly wasting away. I could hardly breathe the air around me, big drops of perspiration burst out on my forehead, and then a feeling of terror seized me which I was utterly unable to control. Some of those strange fancies of seeing my mother's spirit, which used to influence me at the time of her death, came back again to my mind. I ascended the stairs slowly and painfully, not daring to look behind me, for I heard—yes, heard!—something following me.

'"When I got into my room, and had shut the door, I began to recover my self-possession a little. But the sense of oppression was still as heavy on me as ever, when I approached the wardrobe to get out my clothes. Just as I stretched forth my hand to turn the key, I saw, to my horror, the two doors of the wardrobe opening of themselves, opening slowly and silently.

'"The candle went out at the same moment, and the whole inside of the wardrobe became to me like a great mirror, with a bright light shining in the middle of it. Out of that light there came a figure, the exact counterpart of myself. Over its breast hung an open scroll, and on that I read the warning of my own death, and a revelation of the destinies of my father and his race. Do not ask me what were the words on the scroll, I have given my promise not to tell you. I may only say that, as soon as I had read all, the room grew dark, and the vision disappeared."

'Forgetful of my promise, I entreated Alfred to repeat to me the words on the scroll. He smiled sadly, and refused to speak on the subject any more. I next sought out my father, and begged him to divulge the secret. Still sceptical to the last, he answered that one diseased imagination in the family was enough, and that he would not permit me to run the risk of being infected by Alfred's mental malady.

'I passed the whole of that day and the next in a state of agitation and alarm which nothing could tranquilise. The sight I had seen in the study gave a terrible significance to the little that my brother had told me. I was uneasy if he was a moment out of my sight. There was something in his expression,—calm and even cheerful as it was,—which made me dread the worst.

'On the morning of the third day after the occurrence I have just related, I rose very early, after a sleepless night, and went into Alfred's bedroom. He was awake, and welcomed me with more than usual affection and kindness. As I drew a chair to his bedside, he asked me to get pen, ink, and paper, and write down something from his dictation.

'I obeyed, and found to my terror and distress, that the idea of death was more present to his imagination than ever. He employed me in writing a statement of his wishes in regard to the disposal of all his own little possessions, as keepsakes to be given, after he was no more, to my father, myself, the house-servants, and one or two of his own most intimate friends. Over and over again I entreated him to tell me whether he really believed that his death was near. He invariably replied that I should soon know, and then led the conversation to indifferent topics. As the morning advanced, he asked to see my father, who came, accompanied by the doctor, the latter having been in attendance for the last two days.

'Alfred took my father's hand, and begged his forgiveness of any offence, any disobedience of which he had ever been guilty. Then, reaching out his other hand, and taking mine, as I stood on the opposite side of the bed, he asked what the time was. A clock was placed on the mantelpiece of the room, but not in a position in which he could see it, as he now lay. I turned round to look at the dial, and answered that, it was just on the stroke of nine.

'"Farewell!" said Alfred, calmly; "in this world, farewell forever!"

'The next instant the clock struck. I felt his fingers tremble in mine, then grow quite still. The doctor seized a hand-mirror that lay on the table, and held it over his lips. He was dead—dead, as the last chime of the hour echoed through the awful silence of the room!

'I pass over the first days of our affliction. You, who have suffered the loss of a beloved sister, can well imagine their misery. I pass over these days, and pause for a moment at the time when we could speak with some calmness and resignation on the subject of our bereavement. On the arrival of that period, I ventured, in conversation with my father, to refer to the vision which had been seen by our dear Alfred in his bedroom, and to the prophecy which he described himself as having read upon the supernatural scroll.

'Even yet my father persisted in his scepticism; but now, as it seemed to me, more because he was afraid, than because he was unwilling, to believe. I again recalled to his memory what I myself had seen in the study. I asked him to recollect how certain Alfred had been beforehand, and how fatally right, about the day and hour of his death. Still I could get but one answer; my brother had died of a nervous disorder (the doctor said so); his imagination had been diseased from his childhood; there was only one way of treating the vision which he described himself as having seen, and that was, not to speak of it again between ourselves; never to speak of it at all to our friends.

'We were sitting in the study during this conversation. It was evening. As my father uttered the last words of his reply to me, I saw his eye turn suddenly and uneasily towards the further end of the room. In dead silence, I looked in the same direction, and saw the door opening of itself. the vacant space beyond was filled with a bright, steady glow, which hid all outer objects in the hall, and which I cannot describe to you by likening it to any light that we are accustomed to behold either by day or night. In my terror, I caught my father by the arm, and asked him, in a whisper, whether he did not see something extraordinary in the direction of the doorway?

'"Yes," he answered, in tones as low as mine, "I see, or fancy I see, a strange light.

The subject on which we have been speaking has impressed our feelings as it should not. Our nerves are still unstrung by the shock of the bereavement we have suffered: our senses are deluding us. Let us look away towards the garden."

'"But the opening of the door, father; remember the opening of the door!"

'"Ours is not the first door which has accidentally flown open of itself."

'"Then why not shut it again?"

'"Why not, indeed. I will close it at once." He rose, advanced a few paces, then stopped, and came back to his place. "It is a warm evening," he said, avoiding my eyes, which were eagerly fixed on him, "the room will be all the cooler, if the door is suffered to remain open."

'His face grew quite pale as he spoke. The light lasted for a few minutes longer, then suddenly disappeared. For the rest of the evening my father's manner was very much altered. He was silent and thoughtful, and complained of a feeling of oppression and languor, which he tried to persuade himself was produced by the heat of the weather. At an unusually hour he retired to his room.

'The next morning, when I got down stairs, I found, to my astonishment, that the servants were engaged in preparations for the departure of somebody from the house. I made inquiries of one of them who was hurriedly packing a trunk. "My master, sir, starts for Lyons the first thing this morning," was the reply. I immediately repaired to my father's room, and found him there with an open letter in his hand, which he was reading. His face, as he looked up at me on my entrance, expressed the most violent emotions of apprehension and despair.

'"I hardly know whether I am awake or dreaming; whether I am the dupe of a terrible delusion, or the victim of a supernatural reality more terrible still," he said in low awestruck tones as I approached him. "One of the prophecies which Alfred told me in private that he had read upon the scroll, has come true! He predicted the loss of the bulk of my fortune—here is the letter, which informs me that the merchant at Lyons in whose hands my money was placed, has become bankrupt.

'"Can the occurrence of this ruinous calamity be the chance fulfilment of a mere guess? Or was the doom of my family really revealed to my dead son? I go to Lyons immediately to know the truth: this letter may have been written under false information; it may be the work of an impostor. And yet, Alfred's prediction—I shudder to think of it!"

'"The light, father!" I exclaimed, "The light we saw last night in the study!"

'"Hush! Don't speak of it! Alfred said that I should be warned of the truth of the prophecy, and of its immediate fulfilment, by the shining of the same supernatural light that he had seen—I tried to disbelieve what I beheld last night—I hardly know whether I dare believe it even now! This prophecy is not the last: there are others yet to be fulfilled—but let us not speak, let us not think of them! I must start at once for Lyons; I must be on the spot, if this horrible news is true, to save what I can from the wreck. The letter—give me back the letter!—I must go directly!"

'He hurried back from the room. I followed him; and, with some difficulty, obtained permission to be the companion of his momentous journey. When we arrived at Lyons, we found that the statement in the letter was true. My father's fortune was gone: a mere pittance, derived from a small estate that had belonged to my mother, was all that was left to us.

'My father's health gave way under this misfortune. He never referred again to Alfred's prediction, and I was afraid to mention the subject; but I saw that it was affecting his mind quite as painfully as the loss of his property. Over, and over again, he checked himself very strangely when he was on the point of speaking to me about my brother. I saw that there was some secret pressing heavily on his mind, which he was afraid to disclose to me.

'It was useless to ask for his confidence. His temper had become irritable under disaster; perhaps, also, under the dread uncertainties which were now evidently tormenting him in secret. My situation was a very sad, and a very dreary one, at that time: I had no remembrances of the past that were not mournful and affrighting remembrances; I had no hopes for the future that were not darkened by a vague presentiment of troubles and perils to come; and I was expressly forbidden by my father to say a word about the terrible events which had cast an unnatural gloom over my youthful career, to any of the friends (yourself included) whose counsel and whose sympathy might have guided and sustained me in the day of trial.

'We returned to Paris; sold our house there; and retired to live on the small estate, to which I have referred, as the last possession left us. We had not been many days in our new abode, when my father imprudently exposed himself to a heavy shower of rain, and suffered in consequence from a violent attack of cold. This temporary malady was not dreaded by the medical attendant; but it was soon aggravated by a fever, produced as much by the anxiety and distress of mind from which he continued to suffer, as by any other cause.

Still the doctor gave hope; but still he grew daily worse—so much worse, that I removed my bed into his room, and never quitted him night or day.

'One night I had fallen asleep, overpowered by fatigue and anxiety, when I was awakened by a cry from my father. I instantly trimmed the light, and ran to his side. He was sitting up in bed, with his eyes fixed on the door, which had been left ajar to ventilate the room. I saw nothing in that direction, and asked what was the matter. He murmured some expressions of affection towards me, and begged me to sit by his bedside till the morning; but gave no definite answer to my question.

'Once or twice, I thought he wandered a little; and I observed that he occasionally moved his hand under the pillow, as if searching for something there. However, when the morning came, he appeared to be calm and self-possessed. The doctor arrived; and pronouncing him to be better, retired to the dressing-room to write a prescription.

'The moment his back was turned, my father laid his weak hand on my arm, and whispered faintly: "Last night I saw the supernatural light again—the second prediction—true, true—my death this time—the same hour as Alfred's—nine—nine o'clock, this morning." He paused a moment through weakness; then added: "Take that sealed paper—under the pillow—when I am dead, read it—now go into the dressing-room—my watch is there—I have heard the church clock strike eight; let me see how long it is now till nine—go—go quickly!"

'Horror-stricken, moving and acting like a man in a trance, I silently obeyed him. The doctor was still in the dressing-room: despair made me catch eagerly at any chance of saving my father; I told his medical attendant what I had just heard, and entreated advice and assistance without delay.

'"He is a little delirious," said the doctor—"don't be alarmed: we can cheat him out of his dangerous idea, and so perhaps save his life. Where is the watch?" (I produced it)—"See: it is ten minutes to nine. I will put back the hands one hour; that will give good time for a composing draught to operate. There! Take him the watch, and let him see the false time with his own eyes. He will be comfortably asleep before the hour hand gets round again to nine."

'I went back with the watch to my father's bedside. "Too slow," he murmured, as he looked at the dial—"too slow by an hour—the church clock—I counted eight."

'"Father! Dear father! You are mistaken," I cried, "I counted also: it was only seven."

'"Only seven!" he echoed faintly, "another hour then—another hour to live!" He evidently believed what I had said to him. In spite of the fatal experiences of the past, I now ventured to hope the best for our stratagem, as I resumed my place by his side.

'The doctor came in; but my father never noticed him. He kept his eyes fixed on the watch, which lay between us, on the coverlid. When the minute hand was within a few seconds of indicating the false hour of eight, he looked round at me, murmured very feebly and doubtingly, "another hour to live!" and then gently closed his eyes. I looked at the watch, and saw that it was just eight o'clock, according to our alteration of the right time. At the same moment, I heard the doctor, whose hand had been on my father's pulse, exclaim, "My God! It's stopped! He has died at nine o'clock!"

'The fatality, which no human stratagem or human science could turn aside, was accomplished! I was alone in the world!

'In the solitude of our little cottage, on the day of my father's burial, I opened the sealed letter, which he had told me to take from the pillow of his death-bed. In preparing to read it, I knew that I was preparing for the knowledge of my own doom; but I neither trembled nor wept. I was beyond grief: despair such as mine was then, is calm and self-possessed to the last.

'The letter ran thus:

> '"After your father and brother have fallen under the fatality that pursues our house, it is right, my dear son, that you should be warned how you are included in the last

of the predictions which still remains unaccomplished. Know then, that the final lines read by our dear Alfred on the scroll, prophesied that you should die, as we have died, at the fatal hour of nine; but by a bloody and violent death, the day of which was not foretold.

'"My beloved boy! You know not, you never will know, what I suffered in the possession of this terrible secret, as the truth of the former prophecies forced itself more and more plainly on my mind! Even now, as I write, I hope against all hope; believe vainly and desperately against all experience, that this last, worst doom may be avoided. Be cautious; be patient; look well before you at each step of your career.

'"The fatality by which you are threatened is terrible; but there is a Power above fatality; and before that Power my spirit and my child's spirit now pray for you. Remember this when your heart is heavy, your path through life grows dark. Remember that the better world is still before you, the world where we shall all meet! Farewell!"

'When I first read those lines, I read them with the gloomy, immovable resignation of the Eastern fatalists; and that resignation never left me afterwards.

Here, in this prison, I feel it, calm as ever. I bowed patiently to my doom, when it was only predicted: I bow to it as patiently now, when it is on the eve of accomplishment. You have often wondered, my friend, at the tranquil, equable sadness of my manner: after what I have just told you, can you wonder any longer?

'But let me return for a moment to the past. Though I had no hope of escaping the fatality which had overtaken my father and my brother, my life, after my double bereavement, was the existence of all others which might seem most likely to evade the accomplishment of my predicted doom. Yourself and one other friend excepted, I saw no society; my walks were limited to the cottage garden and the neighbouring fields, and my everyday, unvarying occupation was confined to that hard and resolute course of study, by which alone I could hope to prevent my mind from dwelling on what I had suffered in the past, or on what I might still be condemned to suffer in the future. Never was there a life more quiet and more uneventful than mine!

'You know how I awoke to an ambition, which irresistibly impelled me to change this mode of existence. News from Paris penetrated even to my obscure retreat, and disturbed my self-imposed tranquillity. I heard of the last errors and weaknesses of Louis the Sixteenth; I heard of the assembling of the States-General; and I knew that the French Revolution had begun. The tremendous emergencies of that epoch drew men of all characters from private to public pursuits, and made politics the necessity rather than the choice of every Frenchman's life. The great change preparing for the country acted universally on individuals, even to the humblest, and it acted on me.

'I was elected a deputy, more for the sake of the name I bore, than on account of any little influence which my acquirements and my character might have exercised in the neighbourhood of my country abode. I removed to Paris, and took my seat in the Chamber, little thinking at that time, of the crime and the bloodshed to which our revolution, so moderate in its beginning, would lead; little thinking that I had taken the first, irretrievable steps towards the bloody and violent death which was lying in store for me.

'Need I go on? You know how warmly I joined the Girondin party; you know how we have been sacrificed; you know what the death is which I and my brethren are to suffer tomorrow. On now ending, I repeat what I said at beginning: Judge not of my narrative till you have seen with your own eyes what really takes place in the morning. I have carefully abstained from all comment, I have simply related events as they happened, forbearing to add my own views of their significance, my own ideas on the explanation of which they admit.

'You may believe us to have been a family of nervous visionaries, witnesses of certain remarkable contingencies; victims of curious, but not impossible chances, which we have fancifully and falsely interpreted into supernatural events. I leave you undisturbed in this conviction (if you really feel it); tomorrow you will think differently; tomorrow you will be an altered man. In the mean time, remember what I now say, as you would remember my dying words: Last night I saw the supernatural radiance which warned my father and my brother; and which warns me, that, whatever the time when the execution begins, whatever the order in which the twenty-one Girondins are chosen for death, I shall be the man who kneels under the guillotine, as the clock strikes nine!'

It was morning. Of the ghastly festivities of the night no sign remained. The prison-hall wore an altered look, as the twenty-one condemned men (followed by those who were ordered to witness their execution) were marched out to the carts appointed to take them from the dungeon to the scaffold.

The sky was cloudless, the sun warm and brilliant, as the Girondin leaders and their companions were drawn slowly through the streets to the place of execution. Duprat and Marginy were placed in separate vehicles: the contrast in their demeanour at that awful moment was strongly marked. The features of the doomed man still preserved their noble and melancholy repose; his glance was steady; his colour never changed. The face of Marginy, on the contrary, displayed the strongest agitation; he was pale even to his lips.

The terrible narrative he had heard, the anticipation of the final and appalling proof by which its truth was now to be tested, had robbed him, for the first time in his life, of all his self-possession. Duprat had predicted truly; the morrow had come, and he was an altered man already.

The carts drew up at the foot of the scaffold which was soon to be stained with the blood of twenty-one human beings. The condemned deputies mounted it; and ranged themselves at the end opposite the guillotine. The prisoners who were to behold the execution remained in their cart. Before Duprat ascended the steps, he held his friend's hand for the last time: 'Farewell!' he said, calmly. 'Farewell! I go to my father, and my brother!

Remember my words of last night.'

With straining eyes, and bloodless cheeks, Marginy saw Duprat take his position in the middle row of his companions, who stood in three ranks of seven each. Then the awful spectacle of the execution began. After the first seven deputies had suffered there was a pause; the horrible traces of the judicial massacre were being removed.

When the execution proceeded, Duprat was the third taken from the middle rank of the condemned. As he came forward, he stood for an instant erect under the guillotine, he looked with a smile on his friend, and repeated in a clear voice the word, 'Remember!'—then bowed himself on the block. The blood stood still at Marginy's heart, as he looked and listened, during the moment of silence that followed. That moment past, the church clocks of Paris struck. He dropped down in the cart, and covered his face with his hands; for through the heavy beat of the hour he heard the fall of the fatal steel.

'Pray, sir, was it nine or ten that struck just now?' said one of Marginy's fellow-prisoners to an officer of the guard who stood near the cart.

The person addressed referred to his watch, and answered—

'Nine O'Clock!'

Brother Owen's Story of

The Siege of the Black Cottage

To begin at the beginning, I must take you back to the time after my mother's death, when my only brother had gone to sea, when my sister was out at service, and when I lived alone with my father in the midst of a moor in the west of England.

The moor was covered with great limestone rocks, and intersected here and there by streamlets. The nearest habitation to ours was situated about a mile and a half off, where a strip of the fertile land stretched out into the waste like a tongue. Here the outbuildings of the great Moor Farm, then in the possession of my husband's father, began. The farm-lands stretched down gently into a beautiful rich valley, lying nicely sheltered by the high platform of the moor.

When the ground began to rise again, miles and miles away, it led up to a country house called Holme Manor, belonging to a gentleman named Knifton. Mr. Knifton had lately married a young lady whom my mother had nursed, and whose kindness and friendship for me, her foster-sister, I shall remember gratefully to the last day of my life. These and other slight particulars it is necessary to my story that I should tell you, and it is also necessary that you should be especially careful to bear them well in mind.

My father was by trade a stone-mason. His cottage stood a mile and a half from the nearest habitation. In all other directions we were four or five times that distance from neighbours. Being very poor people, this lonely situation had one great attraction for us—we lived rent free on it. In addition to that advantage, the stones, by shaping which my father gained his livelihood, lay all about him at his very door, so that he thought his position, solitary as it was, quite an enviable one. I can hardly say that I agreed with him, though I never complained. I was very fond of my father, and managed to make the best of my loneliness with the thought of being useful to him. Mrs. Knifton wished to take me into her service when she married, but I declined, unwillingly enough, for my father's sake. If I had gone away, he would have had nobody to live with him; and my mother made me promise on her death-bed that he should never be left to pine away alone in the midst of the bleak moor.

Our cottage, small as it was, was stoutly and snugly built, with stone from the moor as a matter of course. The walls were lined inside and fenced outside with wood, the gift of Mr. Knifton's father to my father. This double covering of cracks and crevices, which would have been superfluous in a sheltered position, was absolutely necessary, in our exposed situation, to keep out the cold winds which, excepting just the summer months, swept over us continually all the year round. The outside boards, covering our roughly-built stone walls, my father protected against the wet with pitch and tar. This gave to our little abode a curiously dark, dingy look, especially when it was seen from a distance; and so it had come to be called in the neighbourhood, even before I was born, the Black Cottage.

I have now related the preliminary particulars which it is desirable that you should know, and may proceed at once to the pleasanter task of telling you my story.

One cloudy autumn day, when I was rather more than eighteen years old, a herdsman walked over from Moor Farm with a letter which had been left there for my father. It came from a builder living at our county town, half a day's journey off, and it invited my father to come to him and give his judgment about an estimate for some stonework on a very large scale. My father's expenses for loss of time were to be paid, and he was to have his share of employment afterwards in preparing the stone. He was only too glad, therefore, to obey the directions which the letter contained, and to prepare at once for his long walk to the county town.

Considering the time at which he received the letter, and the necessity of resting before he attempted to return, it was impossible for him to avoid being away from home for one night, at least. He proposed to me, in case I disliked being left alone in the Black Cottage, to lock the door and to take me to Moor Farm to sleep with any one of the milkmaids who would give me a share of her bed. I by no means liked the notion of sleeping with a girl whom I did not know, and I saw no reason to feel afraid of being left alone for only one night; so I declined.

No thieves had ever come near us; our poverty was sufficient protection against them; and of other dangers there were none that even the most timid person could apprehend. Accordingly, I got my father's dinner, laughing at the notion of my taking refuge under the protection of a milkmaid at Moor Farm. He started for his walk as soon as he had done, saying he should try and be back by dinner-time the next day, and leaving me and my cat Polly to take care of the house.

I had cleared the table and brightened up the fire, and had sat down to my work with the cat dozing at my feet, when I heard the trampling of horses, and, running to the door, saw Mr. and Mrs. Knifton, with their groom behind them, riding up to the Black Cottage. It was part of the young lady's kindness never to neglect an opportunity of coming to pay me a friendly visit, and her husband was generally willing to accompany her for his wife's sake. I made my best courtesy, therefore, with a great deal of pleasure, but with no particular surprise at seeing them.

They dismounted and entered the cottage, laughing and talking in great spirits. I soon heard that they were riding to the same county town for which my father was bound and that they intended to stay with some friends there for a few days, and to return home on horseback, as they went out.

I heard this, and I also discovered that they had been having an argument, in jest, about money-matters, as they rode along to our cottage. Mrs. Knifton had accused her husband of inveterate extravagance, and of never being able to go out with money in his pocket without spending it all, if he possibly could, before he got home again. Mr. Knifton had laughingly defended himself by declaring that all his pocket-money went in presents for his wife, and that, if he spent it lavishly, it was under her sole influence and superintendence.

"We are going to Cliverton now," he said to Mrs. Knifton, naming the county town, and warming himself at our poor fire just as pleasantly as if he had been standing on his own grand hearth. "You will stop to admire every pretty thing in every one of the Cliverton shop-windows; I shall hand you the purse, and you will go in and buy. When we have reached home again, and you have had time to get tired of your purchases, you will clasp your hands in amazement, and declare that you are quite shocked at my habits of inveterate extravagance. I am only the banker who keeps the money; you, my love, are the spendthrift who throws it all away!"

"Am I, sir?" said Mrs. Knifton, with a look of mock indignation. "We will see if I am to be misrepresented in this way with impunity. Bessie, my dear" (turning to me), "you shall judge how far I deserve the character which that unscrupulous man has just given to me. I am the spendthrift, am I? And you are only the banker? Very well. Banker, give me my money at once, if you please!"

Mr. Knifton laughed, and took some gold and silver from his waistcoat pocket.

"No, no," said Mrs. Knifton, "you may want what you have got there for necessary expenses. Is that all the money you have about you? What do I feel here?" and she tapped her husband on the chest, just over the breast-pocket of his coat.

Mr. Knifton laughed again, and produced his pocketbook. His wife snatched it out of his hand, opened it, and drew out some bank-notes, put them back again immediately, and, closing the pocketbook, stepped across the room to my poor mother's little walnut-wood book-case, the only bit of valuable furniture we had in the house.

"What are you going to do there?" asked Mr. Knifton, following his wife.

Mrs. Knifton opened the glass door of the book-case, put the pocketbook in a vacant place on one of the lower shelves, closed and locked the door again, and gave me the key.

"You called me a spendthrift just now," she said. "There is my answer. Not one farthing of that money shall you spend at Cliverton on me. Keep the key in your pocket, Bessie, and, whatever Mr. Knifton may say, on no account let him have it until we call again on our way back. No, sir, I won't trust you with that money in your pocket in the town of Cliverton. I will make sure of your taking it all home again, by leaving it here in more trustworthy hands than yours until we ride back. Bessie, my dear, what do you say to that as a lesson in economy inflicted on a prudent husband by a spendthrift wife?"

She took Mr. Knifton's arm while she spoke, and drew him away to the door. He protested and made some resistance, but she easily carried her point, for he was far too fond of her to have a will of his own in any trifling matter between them. Whatever the men might say, Mr. Knifton was a model husband in the estimation of all the women who knew him.

"You will see us as we come back, Bessie. Till then, you are our banker, and the pocketbook is yours," cried Mrs. Knifton, gaily, at the door. Her husband lifted her into the saddle, mounted himself, and away they both galloped over the moor as wild and happy as a couple of children.

Although my being trusted with money by Mrs. Knifton was no novelty (in her maiden days she always employed me to pay her dress-maker's bills), I did not feel quite easy at having a pocketbook full of bank-notes left by her in my charge. I had no positive apprehensions about the safety of the deposit placed in my hands, but it was one of the odd points in my character then (and I think it is still) to feel an unreasonably strong objection to charging myself with money responsibilities of any kind, even to suit the convenience of my dearest friends.

As soon as I was left alone, the very sight of the pocketbook behind the glass door of the book-case began to worry me, and instead of returning to my work, I puzzled my brains about finding a place to lock it up in, where it would not be exposed to the view of any chance passers-by who might stray into the Black Cottage.

This was not an easy matter to compass in a poor house like ours, where we had nothing valuable to put under lock and key. After running over various hiding-places in my mind, I thought of my tea-caddy, a present from Mrs. Knifton, which I always kept out of harm's way in my own bedroom. Most unluckily-as it afterward turned out—instead of taking the pocketbook to the tea-caddy, I went into my room first to take the tea-caddy to the pocketbook. I only acted in this roundabout way from sheer thoughtlessness, and severely enough I was punished for it, as you will acknowledge yourself when you have read a page or two more of my story.

I was just getting the unlucky tea-caddy out of my cupboard, when I heard footsteps in the passage, and, running out immediately, saw two men walk into the kitchen—the room in which I had received Mr. and Mrs. Knifton. I inquired what they wanted sharply enough, and one of them answered immediately that they wanted my father. He turned toward me, of course, as he spoke, and I recognized him as a stone-mason, going among his comrades by the name of Shifty Dick. He bore a very bad character for everything but wrestling, a sport for which the working men of our parts were famous all through the county.

Shifty Dick was champion, and he had got his name from some tricks of wrestling, for which he was celebrated. He was a tall, heavy man, with a lowering, scarred face, and huge hairy hands—the last visitor in the whole world that I should have been glad to see under any circumstances. His companion was a stranger, whom he addressed by the name of Jerry—a quick, dapper, wicked-looking man, who took off his cap to me with mock politeness, and showed, in so doing, a very bald head, with some very ugly-looking knobs on it. I distrusted him worse than I did Shifty Dick, and managed to get between his leering eyes and the book-case, as I told the two that my father was gone out, and that I did not expect him back till the next day.

The words were hardly out of my mouth before I repented that my anxiety to get rid of my unwelcome visitors had made me incautious enough to acknowledge that my father would be away from home for the whole night.

Shifty Dick and his companion looked at each other when I unwisely let out the truth, but made no remark except to ask me if I would give them a drop of cider. I answered sharply that I had no cider in the house, having no fear of the consequences of refusing them drink, because I knew that plenty of men were at work within hail, in a neighbouring quarry.

The two looked at each other again when I denied having any cider to give them; and Jerry (as I am obliged to call him, knowing no other name by which to distinguish the fellow) took off his cap to me once more, and, with a kind of blackguard gentility upon him, said they would have the pleasure of calling the next day, when my father was at home. I said good-afternoon as ungraciously as possible, and, to my great relief, they both left the cottage immediately afterward.

As soon as they were well away, I watched them from the door. They trudged off in the direction of Moor Farm; and, as it was beginning to get dusk, I soon lost sight of them.

Half an hour afterward I looked out again.

The wind had lulled with the sunset, but the mist was rising, and a heavy rain was beginning to fall. Never did the lonely prospect of the moor look so dreary as it looked to my eyes that evening. Never did I regret any slight thing more sincerely than I then regretted the leaving of Mr. Knifton's pocketbook in my charge. I cannot say that I suffered under any actual alarm, for I felt next to certain that neither Shifty Dick nor Jerry had got a chance of setting eyes on so small a thing as the pocketbook while they were in the kitchen; but there was a kind of vague distrust troubling me—a suspicion of the night—a dislike of being left by myself, which I never remember having experienced before.

This feeling so increased after I had closed the door and gone back to the kitchen, that, when I heard the voices of the quarrymen as they passed our cottage on their way home to the village in the valley below Moor Farm, I stepped out into the passage with a momentary notion of telling them how I was situated, and asking them for advice and protection.

I had hardly formed this idea, however, before I dismissed it. None of the quarrymen were intimate friends of mine. I had a nodding acquaintance with them, and believed them to be honest men, as times went. But my own common sense told me that what little knowledge of their characters I had was by no means sufficient to warrant me in admitting them into my confidence in the matter of the pocketbook.

I had seen enough of poverty and poor men to know what a terrible temptation a large sum of money is to those whose whole lives are passed in scraping up sixpences by weary hard work. It is one thing to write fine sentiments in books about incorruptible honesty, and another thing to put those sentiments in practice when one day's work is all that a man has to set up in the way of an obstacle between starvation and his own fireside.

The only resource that remained was to carry the pocketbook with me to Moor Farm, and ask permission to pass the night there. But I could not persuade myself that there was any real necessity for taking such a course as this; and, if the truth must be told, my pride revolted at the idea of presenting myself in the character of a coward before the people at the farm.

Timidity is thought rather a graceful attraction among ladies, but among poor women it is something to be laughed at. A woman with less spirit of her own than I had, and always shall have, would have considered twice in my situation before she made up her mind to encounter the jokes of plowmen and the jeers of milkmaids. As for me, I had hardly considered about going to the farm before I despised myself for entertaining any such notion.

"No, no," thought I, "I am not the woman to walk a mile and a half through rain, and mist, and darkness to tell a whole kitchenful of people that I am afraid. Come what may, here I stop till father gets back."

Having arrived at that valiant resolution, the first thing I did was to lock and bolt the back and front doors, and see to the security of every shutter in the house.

That duty performed, I made a blazing fire, lighted my candle, and sat down to tea, as snug and comfortable as possible. I could hardly believe now, with the light in the room, and the sense of security inspired by the closed doors and shutters, that I had ever felt even the slightest apprehension earlier in the day. I sang as I washed up the tea-things; and even the cat seemed to catch the infection of my good spirits. I never knew the pretty creature so playful as she was that evening.

The tea-things put by, I took up my knitting, and worked away at it so long that I began at last to get drowsy. The fire was so bright and comforting that I could not muster resolution enough to leave it and go to bed. I sat staring lazily into the blaze, with my knitting on my lap—sat till the splashing of the rain outside and the fitful, sullen sobbing of the wind grew fainter and fainter on my ear. The last sounds I heard before I fairly dozed off to sleep were the cheerful crackling of the fire and the steady purring of the cat, as she basked luxuriously in the warm light on the hearth. Those were the last sounds before I fell asleep. The sound that woke me was one loud bang at the front door.

I started up, with my heart (as the saying is) in my mouth, with a frightful momentary shuddering at the roots of my hair—I started up breathless, cold and motionless, waiting in the silence I hardly knew for what, doubtful at first whether I had dreamed about the bang at the door, or whether the blow had really been struck on it.

In a minute or less there came a second bang, louder than the first. I ran out into the passage.

"Who's there?"

"Let us in," answered a voice, which I recognised immediately as the voice of Shifty Dick.

"Wait a bit, my dear, and let me explain," said a second voice, in the low, oily, jeering tones of Dick's companion—the wickedly clever little man whom he called Jerry. "You are alone in the house, my pretty little dear. You may crack your sweet voice with screeching, and there's nobody near to hear you. Listen to reason, my love, and let us in. We don't want cider this time—we only want a very neat-looking pocketbook which you happen to have, and your late excellent mother's four silver teaspoons, which you keep so nice and clean on the chimney-piece. If you let us in we won't hurt a hair of your head, my cherub, and we promise to go away the moment we have got what we want, unless you particularly wish us to stop to tea. If you keep us out, we shall be obliged to break into the house and then—"

"And then," burst in Shifty Dick, "we'll mash you!"

"Yes," said Jerry, "we'll mash you, my beauty. But you won't drive us to doing that, will you? You will let us in?"

This long parley gave me time to recover from the effect which the first bang at the door had produced on my nerves. The threats of the two villains would have terrified some women out of their senses, but the only result they produced on me was violent indignation. I had, thank God, a strong spirit of my own, and the cool, contemptuous insolence of the man Jerry effectually roused it.

"You cowardly villains!" I screamed at them through the door. "You think you can frighten me because I am only a poor girl left alone in the house. You ragamuffin thieves, I defy you both! Our bolts are strong, our shutters are thick. I am here to keep my father's house safe, and keep it I will against an army of you!"

You may imagine what a passion I was in when I vapoured and blustered in that way. I heard Jerry laugh and Shifty Dick swear a whole mouthful of oaths. Then there was a dead silence for a minute or two, and then the two ruffians attacked the door.

I rushed into the kitchen and seized the poker, and then heaped wood on the fire, and lighted all the candles I could find;

for I felt as though I could keep up my courage better if I had plenty of light.

Strange and improbable as it may appear, the next thing that attracted my attention was my poor pussy, crouched up, panic-stricken, in a corner. I was so fond of the little creature that I took her up in my arms and carried her into my bedroom and put her inside my bed. A comical thing to do in a situation of deadly peril, was it not? But it seemed quite natural and proper at the time.

All this while the blows were falling faster and faster on the door. They were dealt, as I conjectured, with heavy stones picked up from the ground outside. Jerry sang at his wicked work, and Shifty Dick swore. As I left the bedroom after putting the cat under cover, I heard the lower panel of the door begin to crack.

I ran into the kitchen and huddled our four silver spoons into my pocket; then took the unlucky book with the bank-notes and put it in the bosom of my dress. I was determined to defend the property confided to my care with my life. Just as I had secured the pocketbook I heard the door splintering, and rushed into the passage again with my heavy kitchen poker lifted in both hands.

I was in time to see the bald head of Jerry, with the ugly-looking knobs on it, pushed into the passage through a great rent in one of the lower panels of the door.

"Get out, you villain, or I'll brain you on the spot!" I screeched, threatening him with the poker.

Mr. Jerry took his head out again much faster than he put it in.

The next thing that came through the rent was a long pitch-fork, which they darted at me from the outside, to move me from the door. I struck at it with all my might, and the blow must have jarred the hand of Shifty Dick up to his very shoulder, for I heard him give a roar of rage and pain. Before he could catch at the fork with his other hand I had drawn it inside. By this time even Jerry lost his temper and swore more awfully than

Dick himself.

Then there came another minute of respite. I suspected they had gone to get bigger stones, and I dreaded the giving way of the whole door.

Running into the bedroom as this fear beset me, I laid hold of my chest of drawers, dragged it into the passage, and threw it down against the door. On the top of that I heaped my father's big tool chest, three chairs, and a scuttleful of coals; and last, I dragged out the kitchen table and rammed it as hard as I could against the whole barricade. They heard me as they were coming up to the door with fresh stones. Jerry said: "Stop a bit!" and then the two consulted together in whispers. I listened eagerly, and just caught these words:

"Let's try it the other way."

Nothing more was said, but I heard their footsteps retreating from the door.

Were they going to besiege the back door now?

I had hardly asked myself that question when I heard their voices at the other side of the house. The back door was smaller than the front, but it had this advantage in the way of strength-it was made of two solid oak boards joined lengthwise, and strengthened inside by heavy cross pieces. It had no bolts like the front door, but was fastened by a bar of iron running across it in a slanting direction, and fitting at either end into the wall.

"They must have the whole cottage down before they can break in at that door!" I thought to myself. And they soon found out as much for themselves. After five minutes of banging at the back door they gave up any further attack in that direction and cast their heavy stones down with curses of fury awful to hear.

I went into the kitchen and dropped on the window-seat to rest for a moment. Suspense and excitement together were beginning to tell upon me. The perspiration broke out thick on my forehead, and I began to feel the bruises I had inflicted on my hands in making the barricade against the front door. I had not lost a particle of my resolution, but I was beginning to lose strength. There was a bottle of rum in the cupboard, which my brother the sailor had left with us the last time he was ashore. I drank a drop of it. Never before or since have I put anything down my throat that did me half so much good as that precious mouthful of rum!

I was still sitting in the window-seat drying my face, when I suddenly heard their voices close behind me.

They were feeling the outside of the window against which I was sitting. It was protected, like all the other windows in the cottage, by iron bars. I listened in dreadful suspense for the sound of filing, but nothing of the sort was audible. They had evidently reckoned on frightening me easily into letting them in, and had come unprovided with house-breaking tools of any kind. A fresh burst of oaths informed me that they had recognized the obstacle of the iron bars. I listened breathlessly for some warning of what they were going to do next, but their voices seemed to die away in the distance. They were retreating from the window. Were they also retreating from the house altogether? Had they given up the idea of effecting an entrance in despair?

A long silence followed—a silence which tried my courage even more severely than the tumult of their first attack on the cottage.

Dreadful suspicions now beset me of their being able to accomplish by treachery what they had failed to effect by force. Well as I knew the cottage, I began to doubt whether there might not be ways of cunningly and silently entering it against which I was not provided. The ticking of the clock annoyed me; the crackling of the fire startled me. I looked out twenty times in a minute into the dark corners of the passage, straining my eyes, holding my breath, anticipating the most unlikely events, the most impossible dangers. Had they really gone, or were they still prowling about the house? Oh, what a sum of money I would have given only to have known what they were about in that interval of silence!

I was startled at last out of my suspense in the most awful manner. A shout from one of them reached my ears on a sudden down the kitchen chimney. It was so unexpected and so horrible in the stillness that I screamed for the first time since the attack on the house. My worst forebodings had never suggested to me that the two villains might mount upon the roof.

"Let us in, you she-devil!" roared a voice down the chimney.

There was another pause. The smoke from the wood fire, thin and light as it was in the red state of the embers at that moment, had evidently obliged the man to take his face from the mouth of the chimney. I counted the seconds while he was, as I conjectured, getting his breath again. In less than half a minute there came another shout:

"Let us in, or we'll burn the place down over your head!"

Burn it? Burn what? There was nothing easily combustible but the thatch on the roof; and that had been well soaked by the heavy rain which had now fallen incessantly for more than six hours. Burn the place over my head? How?

While I was still casting about wildly in my mind to discover what possible danger there could be of fire, one of the heavy stones placed on the thatch to keep it from being torn up by high winds came thundering down the chimney. It scattered the live embers on the hearth all over the room. A richly-furnished place, with knickknacks and fine muslin about it, would have been set on fire immediately. Even our bare floor and rough furniture gave out a smell of burning at the first shower of embers which the first stone scattered.

For an instant I stood quite horror-struck before this new proof of the devilish ingenuity of the villains outside. But the dreadful danger I was now in recalled me to my senses immediately. There was a large canful of water in my bedroom, and I ran in at once to fetch it. Before I could get back to the kitchen a second stone had been thrown down the chimney, and the floor was smouldering in several places.

I had wit enough to let the smouldering go on for a moment or two more, and to pour the whole of my canful of water over the fire before the third stone came down the chimney. The live embers on the floor I easily disposed of after that. The man on the roof must have heard the hissing of the fire as I put it out, and have felt the change produced in the air at the mouth of the chimney, for after the third stone had descended no more followed it. As for either of the ruffians themselves dropping down by the same road along which the stones had come, that was not to be dreaded. The chimney, as I well knew by our experience in cleaning it, was too narrow to give passage to any one above the size of a small boy.

I looked upward as that comforting reflection crossed my mind—I looked up, and saw, as plainly as I see the paper I am now writing on, the point of a knife coming through the inside of the roof just over my head. Our cottage had no upper story, and our rooms had no ceilings. Slowly and wickedly the knife wriggled its way through the dry inside thatch between the rafters. It stopped for a while, and there came a sound of tearing. That, in its turn, stopped too; there was a great fall of dry thatch on the floor; and I saw the heavy, hairy hand of Shifty Dick, armed with the knife, come through after the fallen fragments. He tapped at the rafters with the back of the knife, as if to test their strength. Thank God, they were substantial and close together! Nothing lighter than a hatchet would have sufficed to remove any part of them.

The murderous hand was still tapping with the knife when I heard a shout from the man Jerry, coming from the neighbourhood of my father's stone-shed in the back yard. The hand and knife disappeared instantly. I went to the back door and put my ear to it, and listened.

Both men were now in the shed. I made the most desperate efforts to call to mind what tools and other things were left in it which might be used against me. But my agitation confused me. I could remember nothing except my father's big stone-saw, which was far too heavy and unwieldy to be used on the roof of the cottage. I was still puzzling my brains, and making my head swim to no purpose, when I heard the men dragging something out of the shed. At the same instant that the noise caught my ear, the remembrance flashed across me like lightning of some beams of wood which had lain in the shed for years past. I had hardly time to feel certain that they were removing one of these beams before I heard Shifty Dick say to Jerry.

"Which door?"

"The front," was the answer. "We've cracked it already; we'll have it down now in no time."

Senses less sharpened by danger than mine would have understood but too easily, from these words, that they were about to use the beam as a battering-ram against the door. When that conviction overcame me, I lost courage at last. I felt that the door must come down. No such barricade as I had constructed could support it for more than a few minutes against such shocks as it was now to receive.

"I can do no more to keep the house against them," I said to myself, with my knees knocking together, and the tears at last beginning to wet my cheeks. "I must trust to the night and the thick darkness, and save my life by running for it while there is yet time."

I huddled on my cloak and hood, and had my hand on the bar of the back door, when a piteous mew from the bedroom reminded me of the existence of poor Pussy. I ran in, and huddled the creature up in my apron. Before I was out in the passage again, the first shock from the beam fell on the door.

The upper hinge gave way. The chairs and coal-scuttle, forming the top of my barricade, were hurled, rattling, on to the floor, but the lower hinge of the door, and the chest of drawers and the tool-chest still kept their places.

"One more!" I heard the villains cry—"one more run with the beam, and down it comes!"

Just as they must have been starting for that "one more run," I opened the back door and fled into the night, with the bookful of banknotes in my bosom, the silver spoons in my pocket, and the cat in my arms. I threaded my way easily enough through the familiar obstacles in the backyard, and was out in the pitch darkness of the moor before I heard the second shock, and the crash which told me that the whole door had given way.

In a few minutes they must have discovered the fact of my flight with the pocketbook, for I heard shouts in the distance as if they were running out to pursue me. I kept on at the top of my speed, and the noise soon died away. It was so dark that twenty thieves instead of two would have found it useless to follow me.

How long it was before I reached the farmhouse—the nearest place to which I could fly for refuge—I cannot tell you. I remember that I had just sense enough to keep the wind at my back (having observed in the beginning of the evening that it blew toward Moor Farm), and to go on resolutely through the darkness. In all other respects I was by this time half crazed by what I had gone through. If it had so happened that the wind had changed after I had observed its direction early in the evening, I should have gone astray, and have probably perished of fatigue and exposure on the moor.

Providentially, it still blew steadily as it had blown for hours past, and I reached the farmhouse with my clothes wet through, and my brain in a high fever. When I made my alarm at the door, they had all gone to bed but the farmer's eldest son, who was sitting up late over his pipe and newspaper. I just mustered strength enough to gasp out a few words, telling him what was the matter, and then fell down at his feet, for the first time in my life in a dead swoon.

That swoon was followed by a severe illness. When I got strong enough to look about me again, I found myself in one of the farmhouse beds—my father, Mrs. Knifton, and the doctor were all in the room—my cat was asleep at my feet, and the pocketbook that I had saved lay on the table by my side.

There was plenty of news for me to hear as soon as I was fit to listen to it. Shifty Dick and the other rascal had been caught, and were in prison, waiting their trial at the next assizes. Mr. and Mrs. Knifton had been so shocked at the danger I had run—for which they blamed their own want of thoughtfulness in leaving the pocketbook in my care—that they had insisted on my father's removing from our lonely home to a cottage on their land, which we were to inhabit rent free. The bank-notes that I had saved were given to me to buy furniture with, in place of the things that the thieves had broken.

These pleasant tidings assisted so greatly in promoting my recovery, that I was soon able to relate to my friends at the farmhouse the particulars that I have written here. They were all surprised and interested, but no one, as I thought, listened to me with such breathless attention as the farmer's eldest son. Mrs. Knifton noticed this too, and began to make jokes about it, in her light-hearted way, as soon as we were alone.

I thought little of her jesting at the time; but when I got well, and we went to live at our new home, "the young farmer," as he was called in our parts, constantly came to see us, and constantly managed to meet me out of doors. I had my share of vanity, like other young women, and I began to think of Mrs. Knifton's jokes with some attention. To be brief, the young farmer managed one Sunday—I never could tell how—to lose his way with me in returning from church, and before we found out the right road home again he had asked me to be his wife.

His relations did all they could to keep us asunder and break off the match, thinking a poor stonemason's daughter no fit wife for a prosperous yeoman. But the farmer was too obstinate for them. He had one form of answer to all their objections. "A man, if he is worth the name, marries according to his own notions, and to please himself," he used to say.

"My notion is, that when I take a wife I am placing my character and my happiness—the most precious things I have to trust—in one woman's care. The woman I mean to marry had a small charge confided to her care, and showed herself worthy of it at the risk of her life. That is proof enough for me that she is worthy of the greatest charge I can put into her hands. Rank and riches are fine things, but the certainty of getting a good wife is something better still. I'm of age, I know my own mind, and I mean to marry the stone-mason's daughter."

And he did marry me. Whether I proved myself worthy or not of his good opinion is a question which I must leave you to ask my husband. All that I had to relate about myself and my doings is now told. Whatever interest my perilous adventure may excite, ends, I am well aware, with my escape to the farmhouse. I have only ventured on writing these few additional sentences because my marriage is the moral of my story. It has brought me the choicest blessings of happiness and prosperity, and I owe them all to my night-adventure in The Black Cottage.

Brother Morgan's Story of

The Dream-Woman

Chapter 1

I had not been settled much more than six weeks in my country practice when I was sent for to a neighbouring town, to consult with the resident medical man there on a case of very dangerous illness.

My horse had come down with me at the end of a long ride the night before, and had hurt himself, luckily, much more than he had hurt his master. Being deprived of the animal's services, I started for my destination by the coach (there were no railways at that time), and I hoped to get back again, toward the afternoon, in the same way.

After the consultation was over, I went to the principal inn of the town to wait for the coach. When it came up it was full inside and out. There was no resource left me but to get home as cheaply as I could by hiring a gig. The price asked for this accommodation struck me as being so extortionate, that I determined to look out for an inn of inferior pretensions, and to try if I could not make a better bargain with a less prosperous establishment.

I soon found a likely-looking house, dingy and quiet, with an old-fashioned sign, that had evidently not been repainted for many years past. The landlord, in this case, was not above making a small profit, and as soon as we came to terms he rang the yard-bell to order the gig.

"Has Robert not come back from that errand?" asked the landlord, appealing to the waiter who answered the bell.

"No, sir, he hasn't."

"Well, then, you must wake up Isaac."

"Wake up Isaac!" I repeated; "that sounds rather odd. Do your ostlers go to bed in the daytime?"

"This one does," said the landlord, smiling to himself in rather a strange way.

"And dreams too," added the waiter; "I shan't forget the turn it gave me the first time I heard him."

"Never you mind about that," retorted the proprietor; "you go and rouse Isaac up. The gentleman's waiting for his gig."

The landlord's manner and the waiter's manner expressed a great deal more than they either of them said. I began to suspect that I might be on the trace of something professionally interesting to me as a medical man, and I thought I should like to look at the ostler before the waiter awakened him.

"Stop a minute," I interposed; "I have rather a fancy for seeing this man before you wake him up. I'm a doctor; and if this queer sleeping and dreaming of his comes from anything wrong in his brain, I may be able to tell you what to do with him."

"I rather think you will find his complaint past all doctoring, sir," said the landlord; "but, if you would like to see him, you're welcome, I'm sure."

He led the way across a yard and down a passage to the stables, opened one of the doors, and, waiting outside himself, told me to look in.

I found myself in a two-stall stable. In one of the stalls a horse was munching his corn; in the other an old man was lying asleep on the litter.

I stooped and looked at him attentively. It was a withered, woe-begone face. The eyebrows were painfully contracted; the mouth was fast set, and drawn down at the corners.

The hollow wrinkled cheeks, and the scanty grizzled hair, told their own tale of some past sorrow or suffering. He was drawing his breath convulsively when I first looked at him, and in a moment more he began to talk in his sleep.

"Wake up!" I heard him say, in a quick whisper, through his

clinched teeth. "Wake up there! Murder!"

He moved one lean arm slowly till it rested over his throat, shuddered a little, and turned on his straw. Then the arm left his throat, the hand stretched itself out, and clutched at the side toward which he had turned, as if he fancied himself to be grasping at the edge of something. I saw his lips move, and bent lower over him. He was still talking in his sleep.

"Light gray eyes," he murmured, "and a droop in the left eyelid; flaxen hair, with a gold-yellow streak in it—all right, mother—fair white arms, with a down on them—little lady's hand, with a reddish look under the finger nails. The knife—always the cursed knife—first on one side, then on the other. Aha! you she-devil, where's the knife?"

At the last word his voice rose, and he grew restless on a sudden. I saw him shudder on the straw; his withered face became distorted, and he threw up both his hands with a quick hysterical gasp. They struck against the bottom of the manger under which he lay, and the blow awakened him. I had just time to slip through the door and close it before his eyes were fairly open, and his senses his own again.

"Do you know anything about that man's past life?" I said to the landlord.

"Yes, sir, I know pretty well all about it," was the answer, "and an uncommon queer story it is. Most people don't believe it. It's true, though, for all that. Why, just look at him," continued the landlord, opening the stable door again. "Poor devil! he's so worn out with his restless nights that he's dropped back into his sleep already."

"Don't wake him," I said; "I'm in no hurry for the gig. Wait till the other man comes back from his errand; and, in the meantime, suppose I have some lunch and a bottle of sherry, and suppose you come and help me to get through it?"

The heart of mine host, as I had anticipated, warmed to me over his own wine. He soon became communicative on the subject of the man asleep in the stable, and by little and little I drew the whole story out of him. Extravagant and incredible as the events must appear to everybody, they are related here just as I heard them and just as they happened.

Chapter 2

Some years ago there lived in the suburbs of a large seaport town on the west coast of England a man in humble circumstances, by name Isaac Scatchard. His means of subsistence were derived from any employment that he could get as an ostler, and occasionally, when times went well with him, from temporary engagements in service as stable-helper in private houses.

Though a faithful, steady, and honest man, he got on badly in his calling. His ill luck was proverbial among his neighbours. He was always missing good opportunities by no fault of his own, and always living longest in service with amiable people who were not punctual payers of wages. "Unlucky Isaac" was his nickname in his own neighbourhood, and no one could say that he did not richly deserve it.

With far more than one man's fair share of adversity to endure, Isaac had but one consolation to support him, and that was of the dreariest and most negative kind. He had no wife and children to increase his anxieties and add to the bitterness of his various failures in life. It might have been from mere insensibility, or it might have been from generous unwillingness to involve another in his own unlucky destiny, but the fact undoubtedly was, that he had arrived at the middle term of life without marrying, and, what is much more remarkable, without once exposing himself, from eighteen to eight-and-thirty, to the genial imputation of ever having had a sweetheart.

When he was out of service he lived alone with his widowed mother. Mrs. Scatchard was a woman above the average in her lowly station as to capacity and manners. She had seen better days, as the phrase is, but she never referred to them in the presence of curious visitors; and, though perfectly polite to everyone who approached her, never cultivated any intimacies among her neighbours. She contrived to provide, hardly enough, for her simple wants by doing rough work for the tailors, and always managed to keep a decent home for her son to return to whenever his ill luck drove him out helpless into the world.

One bleak autumn when Isaac was getting on fast toward forty and when he was as usual out of place through no fault of his own, he set forth, from his mother's cottage on a long walk inland to a gentleman's seat where he had heard that a stable-helper was required.

It wanted then but two days of his birthday; and Mrs. Scatchard, with her usual fondness, made him promise, before he started, that he would be back in time to keep that anniversary with her, in as festive a way as their poor means would allow. It was easy for him to comply with this request, even supposing he slept a night each way on the road.

He was to start from home on Monday morning, and, whether he got the new place or not, he was to be back for his birthday dinner on Wednesday at two o'clock.

Arriving at his destination too late on the Monday night to make application for the stable-helper's place, he slept at the village inn, and in good time on the Tuesday morning presented himself at the gentleman's house to fill the vacant situation. Here again his ill luck pursued him as inexorably as ever. The excellent written testimonials to his character which he was able to produce availed him nothing; his long walk had been taken in vain: only the day before the stable-helper's place had been given to another man.

Isaac accepted this new disappointment resignedly and as a matter of course. Naturally slow in capacity, he had the bluntness of sensibility and phlegmatic patience of disposition which frequently distinguish men with sluggishly-working mental powers. He thanked the gentleman's steward with his usual quiet civility for granting him an interview, and took his departure with no appearance of unusual depression in his face or manner.

Before starting on his homeward walk he made some inquiries at the inn, and ascertained that he might save a few miles on his return by following the new road. Furnished with full instructions, several times repeated, as to the various turnings he was to take, he set forth on his homeward journey and walked on all day with only one stoppage for bread and cheese.

Just as it was getting toward dark, the rain came on and the wind began to rise, and he found himself, to make matters worse, in a part of the country with which he was entirely unacquainted, though he knew himself to be some fifteen miles from home. The first house he found to inquire at was a lonely roadside inn, standing on the outskirts of a thick wood. Solitary as the place looked, it was welcome to a lost man who was also hungry, thirsty, footsore and wet. The landlord was civil and respectable-looking, and the price he asked for a bed was reasonable enough. Isaac therefore decided on stopping comfortably at the inn for that night.

He was constitutionally a temperate man. His supper consisted of two rashers of bacon, a slice of home-made bread and a pint of ale. He did not go to bed immediately after this moderate meal, but sat up with the landlord, talking about his bad prospects and his long run of ill-luck, and diverging from these topics to the subjects of horse-flesh and racing. Nothing was said either by himself, his host, or the few labourers who strayed into the tap-room, which could, in the slightest degree, excite the very small and very dull imaginative faculty which Isaac Scatchard possessed.

At a little after eleven the house was closed. Isaac went round with the landlord and held the candle while the doors and lower windows were being secured. He noticed with surprise the strength of the bolts and bars, and iron-sheathed shutters.

"You see, we are rather lonely here," said the landlord. "We never have had any attempts made to break in yet, but it's always as well to be on the safe side. When nobody is sleeping here, I am the only man in the house. My wife and daughter are timid, and the servant-girl takes after her missuses. Another glass of ale before you turn in? No! Well, how such a sober man as you comes to be out of place is more than I can make out, for one. Here's where you're to sleep. You're our only lodger tonight, and I think you'll say my missus has done her best to make you comfortable. You're quite sure you won't have another glass of ale? Very well. Goodnight."

It was half-past eleven by the clock in the passage as they went upstairs to the bedroom, the window of which looked on to the wood at the back of the house.

Isaac locked the door, set his candle on the chest of drawers, and wearily got ready for bed.

The bleak autumn wind was still blowing, and the solemn, monotonous, surging moan of it in the wood was dreary and awful to hear through the night-silence. Isaac felt strangely wakeful. He resolved, as he lay down in bed, to keep the candle alight until he began to grow sleepy, for there was something unendurably depressing in the bare idea of lying awake in the darkness, listening to the dismal, ceaseless moaning of the wind in the wood.

Sleep stole on him before he was aware of it. His eyes closed, and he fell off insensibly to rest without having so much as thought of extinguishing the candle.

The first sensation of which he was conscious after sinking into slumber was a strange shivering that ran through him suddenly from head to foot, and a dreadful sinking pain at the heart, such as he had never felt before. The shivering only disturbed his slumbers; the pain woke him instantly. In one moment he passed from a state of sleep to a state of wakefulness—his eyes wide open—his mental perceptions cleared on a sudden, as if by a miracle.

The candle had burned down nearly to the last morsel of tallow, but the top of the unsnuffed wick had just fallen off, and the light in the little room was, for the moment, fair and full.

Between the foot of his bed and the closed door there stood a woman with a knife in her hand, looking at him.

He was stricken speechless with terror, but he did not lose the preternatural clearness of his faculties, and he never took his eyes off the woman. She said not a word as they stared each other in the face, but she began to move slowly toward the left-hand side of the bed.

His eyes followed her. She was a fair, fine woman, with yellowish flaxen hair and light gray eyes, with a droop in the left eyelid. He noticed those things and fixed them on his mind before she was round at the side of the bed. Speechless, with no expression in her face, with no noise following her footfall, she came closer and closer—stopped—and slowly raised the knife. He laid his right arm over his throat to save it; but, as he saw the knife coming down, threw his hand across the bed to the right side, and jerked his body over that way just as the knife descended on the mattress within an inch of his shoulder.

His eyes fixed on her arm and hand as she slowly drew her knife out of the bed: a white, well-shaped arm, with a pretty down lying lightly over the fair skin—a delicate lady's hand, with the crowning beauty of a pink flush under and round the finger-nails.

She drew the knife out, and passed back again slowly to the foot of the bed; stopped there for a moment looking at him; then came on—still speechless, still with no expression on the blank, beautiful face, still with no sound following the stealthy footfalls—came on to the right side of the bed, where he now lay.

As she approached, she raised the knife again, and he drew himself away to the left side. She struck, as before, right into the mattress, with a deliberate, perpendicularly downward action of the arm. This time his eyes wandered from her to the knife. It was like the large clasp-knives which he had often seen labouring men use to cut their bread and bacon with. Her delicate little fingers did not conceal more than two-thirds of the handle: he noticed that it was made of buck-horn, clean and shining as the blade was, and looking like new.

For the second time she drew the knife out, concealed it in the wide sleeve of her gown, then stopped by the bedside, watching him. For an instant he saw her standing in that position, then the wick of the spent candle fell over into the socket; the flame diminished to a little blue point, and the room grew dark.

A moment, or less, if possible, passed so, and then the wick flamed up, smokingly, for the last time. His eyes were still looking eagerly over the right-hand side of the bed when the final flash of light came, but they discovered nothing. The fair woman with the knife was gone.

The conviction that he was alone again weakened the hold of the terror that had struck him dumb up to this time. The preternatural sharpness which the very intensity of his panic had mysteriously imparted to his faculties left them suddenly. His brain grew confused—his heart beat wildly—his ears opened for the first time since the appearance of the woman to a sense of the woeful ceaseless moaning of the wind among the trees. With the dreadful conviction of the reality of what he had seen still strong within him, he leaped out of bed, and screaming "Murder! Wake up, there! wake up!" dashed headlong through the darkness to the door.

It was fast locked, exactly as he had left it on going to bed.

His cries on starting up had alarmed the house. He heard the terrified, confused exclamations of women; he saw the master of the house approaching along the passage with his burning rush-candle in one hand and his gun in the other.

"What is it?" asked the landlord, breathlessly.

Isaac could only answer in a whisper. "A woman, with a knife in her hand," he gasped out. "In my room—a fair, yellow-haired woman; she jobbed at me with the knife twice over."

The landlord's pale cheeks grew paler. He looked at Isaac eagerly by the flickering light of his candle, and his face began to get red again; his voice altered, too, as well as his complexion.

"She seems to have missed you twice," he said.

"I dodged the knife as it came down," Isaac went on, in the same scared whisper. "It struck the bed each time."

The landlord took his candle into the bedroom immediately. In less than a minute he came out again into the passage in a violent passion.

"The devil fly away with you and your woman with the knife! There isn't a mark in the bedclothes anywhere. What do you mean by coming into a man's place and frightening his family out of their wits about a dream?"

"I'll leave your house," said Isaac, faintly. "Better out on the road, in rain and dark, on my road home, than back again in that room, after what I've seen in it. Lend me a light to get my clothes by, and tell me what I'm to pay."

"Pay!" cried the landlord, leading the way with his light sulkily into the bedroom. "You'll find your score on the slate when you go downstairs. I wouldn't have taken you in for all the money you've got about you if I'd known your dreaming, screeching ways beforehand. Look at the bed. Where's the cut of a knife in it? Look at the window—is the lock bursted? Look at the door (which I heard you fasten yourself)—is it broke in? A murdering woman with a knife in my house! You ought to be ashamed of yourself!"

Isaac answered not a word. He huddled on his clothes, and then they went downstairs together.

"Nigh on twenty minutes past two!" said the landlord, as they passed the clock. "A nice time in the morning to frighten honest people out of their wits!"

Isaac paid his bill, and the landlord let him out at the front door, asking, with a grin of contempt, as he undid the strong fastenings, whether "the murdering woman got in that way."

They parted without a word on either side. The rain had ceased, but the night was dark, and the wind bleaker than ever. Little did the darkness, or the cold, or the uncertainty about the way home matter to Isaac. If he had been turned out into a wilderness in a thunder-storm it would have been a relief after what he had suffered in the bedroom of the inn.

What was the fair woman with the knife? The creature of a dream, or that other creature from the unknown world called among men by the name of ghost?

He could make nothing of the mystery—had made nothing of it, even when it was midday on Wednesday, and when he stood, at last, after many times missing his road, once more on the doorstep of home.

Chapter 3

His mother came out eagerly to receive him. His face told her in a moment that something was wrong.

"I've lost the place; but that's my luck. I dreamed an ill dream last night, mother—or maybe I saw a ghost. Take it either way, it scared me out of my senses, and I'm not my own man again yet."

"Isaac, your face frightens me. Come in to the fire—come in, and tell mother all about it."

He was as anxious to tell as she was to hear; for it had been his hope, all the way home, that his mother, with her quicker capacity and superior knowledge, might be able to throw some light on the mystery which he could not clear up for himself. His memory of the dream was still mechanically vivid, though his thoughts were entirely confused by it.

His mother's face grew paler and paler as he went on. She never interrupted him by so much as a single word; but when he had done, she moved her chair close to his, put her arm round his neck, and said to him:

"Isaac, you dreamed your ill dream on this Wednesday morning. What time was it when you saw the fair woman with the knife in her hand?"

Isaac reflected on what the landlord had said when they had passed by the clock on his leaving the inn; allowed as nearly as he could for the time that must have elapsed between the unlocking of his bedroom door and the paying of his bill just before going away, and answered:

"Somewhere about two o'clock in the morning."

His mother suddenly quitted her hold of his neck, and struck her hands together with a gesture of despair.

"This Wednesday is your birthday, Isaac, and two o'clock in the morning was the time when you were born."

Isaac's capacities were not quick enough to catch the infection of his mother's superstitious dread. He was amazed, and a little startled, also, when she suddenly rose from her chair, opened her old writing-desk, took pen, ink and paper, and then said to him:

"Your memory is but a poor one, Isaac, and, now I'm an old woman, mine's not much better. I want all about this dream of yours to be as well known to both of us, years hence, as it is now. Tell me over again all you told me a minute ago, when you spoke of what the woman with the knife looked like."

Isaac obeyed, and marvelled much as he saw his mother carefully set down on paper the very words that he was saying.

"Light gray eyes," she wrote, as they came to the descriptive part, "with a droop in the left eyelid; flaxen hair, with a gold-yellow streak in it; white arms, with a down upon them; little lady's hand, with a reddish look about the finger nails; clasp-knife with a buck-horn handle, that seemed as good as new." To these particulars Mrs. Scatchard added the year, month, day of the week, and time in the morning when the woman of the dream appeared to her son. She then locked up the paper carefully in her writing-desk.

Neither on that day nor on any day after could her son induce her to return to the matter of the dream. She obstinately kept her thoughts about it to herself, and even refused to refer again to the paper in her writing-desk. Ere long Isaac grew weary of attempting to make her break her resolute silence; and time, which sooner or later wears out all things, gradually wore out the impression produced on him by the dream. He began by thinking of it carelessly, and he ended by not thinking of it at all.

The result was the more easily brought about by the advent of some important changes for the better in his prospects which commenced not long after his terrible night's experience at the inn. He reaped at last the reward of his long and patient suffering under adversity by getting an excellent place, keeping it for seven years, and leaving it, on the death of his master, not only with an excellent character, but also with a comfortable annuity bequeathed to him as a reward for saving his mistress's life in a carriage accident. Thus it happened that Isaac Scatchard returned to his old mother, seven years after the time of the dream at the inn, with an annual sum of money at his disposal sufficient to keep them both in ease and independence for the rest of their lives.

The mother, whose health had been bad of late years, profited so much by the care bestowed on her and by freedom from money anxieties, that when Isaac's birthday came round she was able to sit up comfortably at table and dine with him.

On that day, as the evening drew on, Mrs. Scatchard discovered that a bottle of tonic medicine which she was accustomed to take, and in which she had fancied that a dose or more was still left, happened to be empty. Isaac immediately volunteered to go to the chemist's and get it filled again. It was as rainy and bleak an autumn night as on the memorable past occasion when he lost his way and slept at the road-side inn.

On going into the chemist's shop he was passed hurriedly by a poorly-dressed woman coming out of it. The glimpse he had of her face struck him, and he looked back after her as she descended the door-steps.

"You're noticing that woman?" said the chemist's apprentice behind the counter. "It's my opinion there's something wrong with her. She's been asking for laudanum to put to a bad tooth. Master's out for half an hour, and I told her I wasn't allowed to sell poison to strangers in his absence. She laughed in a queer way, and said she would come back in half an hour. If she expects master to serve her, I think she'll be disappointed. It's a case of suicide, sir, if ever there was one yet."

These words added immeasurably to the sudden interest in the woman which Isaac had felt at the first sight of her face. After he had got the medicine-bottle filled, he looked about anxiously for her as soon as he was out in the street. She was walking slowly up and down on the opposite side of the road. With his heart, very much to his own surprise, beating fast, Isaac crossed over and spoke to her.

He asked if she was in any distress. She pointed to her torn shawl, her scanty dress, her crushed, dirty bonnet; then moved under a lamp so as to let the light fall on her stern, pale, but still most beautiful face.

"I look like a comfortable, happy woman, don't I?" she said, with a bitter laugh.

She spoke with a purity of intonation which Isaac had never heard before from other than ladies' lips. Her slightest actions seemed to have the easy, negligent grace of a thoroughbred woman. Her skin, for all its poverty-stricken paleness, was as delicate as if her life had been passed in the enjoyment of every social comfort that wealth can purchase. Even her small, finely-shaped hands, gloveless as they were, had not lost their whiteness.

Little by little, in answer to his questions, the sad story of the woman came out. There is no need to relate it here; it is told over and over again in police reports and paragraphs about attempted suicides.

"My name is Rebecca Murdoch," said the woman, as she ended. "I have nine pence left, and I thought of spending it at the chemist's over the way in securing a passage to the other world. Whatever it is, it can't be worse to me than this, so why should I stop here?"

Besides the natural compassion and sadness moved in his heart by what he heard, Isaac felt within him some mysterious influence at work all the time the woman was speaking which utterly confused his ideas and almost deprived him of his powers of speech. All that he could say in answer to her last reckless words was that he would prevent her from attempting her own life, if he followed her about all night to do it. His rough, trembling earnestness seemed to impress her.

"I won't occasion you that trouble," she answered, when he repeated his threat. "You have given me a fancy for living by speaking kindly to me. No need for the mockery of protestations and promises. You may believe me without them. Come to Fuller's Meadow tomorrow at twelve, and you will find me alive, to answer for myself—No!—no money. My nine pence will do to get me as good a night's lodging as I want."

She nodded and left him. He made no attempt to follow—he

felt no suspicion that she was deceiving him.

"It's strange, but I can't help believing her," he said to himself, and walked away, bewildered, toward home.

On entering the house, his mind was still so completely absorbed by its new subject of interest that he took no notice of what his mother was doing when he came in with the bottle of medicine. She had opened her old writing-desk in his absence, and was now reading a paper attentively that lay inside it. On every birthday of Isaac's since she had written down the particulars of his dream from his own lips, she had been accustomed to read that same paper, and ponder over it in private.

The next day he went to Fuller's Meadow.

He had done only right in believing her so implicitly. She was there, punctual to a minute, to answer for herself. The last-left faint defences in Isaac's heart against the fascination which a word or look from her began inscrutably to exercise over him sank down and vanished before her forever on that memorable morning.

When a man, previously insensible to the influence of women, forms an attachment in middle life, the instances are rare indeed, let the warning circumstances be what they may, in which he is found capable of freeing himself from the tyranny of the new ruling passion. The charm of being spoken to familiarly, fondly, and gratefully by a woman whose language and manners still retained enough of their early refinement to hint at the high social station that she had lost, would have been a dangerous luxury to a man of Isaac's rank at the age of twenty.

But it was far more than that—it was certain ruin to him—now that his heart was opening unworthily to a new influence at that middle time of life when strong feelings of all kinds, once implanted, strike root most stubbornly in a man's moral nature. A few more stolen interviews after that first morning in Fuller's Meadow completed his infatuation. In less than a month from the time when he first met her, Isaac Scatchard had consented to give Rebecca Murdoch a new interest in existence, and a chance of recovering the character she had lost by promising to make her his wife.

She had taken possession, not of his passions only, but of his faculties as well. All the mind he had he put into her keeping. She directed him on every point—even instructing him how to break the news of his approaching marriage in the safest manner to his mother.

"If you tell her how you met me and who I am at first," said the cunning woman, "she will move heaven and earth to prevent our marriage. Say I am the sister of one of your fellow-servants—ask her to see me before you go into any more particulars—and leave it to me to do the rest. I mean to make her love me next best to you, Isaac, before she knows anything of who I really am."

The motive of the deceit was sufficient to sanctify it to Isaac. The stratagem proposed relieved him of his one great anxiety, and quieted his uneasy conscience on the subject of his mother. Still, there was something wanting to perfect his happiness, something that he could not realize, something mysteriously untraceable, and yet something that perpetually made itself felt; not when he was absent from Rebecca Murdoch, but, strange to say, when he was actually in her presence!

She was kindness itself with him. She never made him feel his inferior capacities and inferior manners. She showed the sweetest anxiety to please him in the smallest trifles; but, in spite of all these attractions, he never could feel quite at his ease with her. At their first meeting, there had mingled with his admiration, when he looked in her face, a faint, involuntary feeling of doubt whether that face was entirely strange to him. No after familiarity had the slightest effect on this inexplicable, wearisome uncertainty.

Concealing the truth as he had been directed, he announced his marriage engagement precipitately and confusedly to his mother on the day when he contracted it. Poor Mrs. Scatchard showed her perfect confidence in her son by flinging her arms round his neck, and giving him joy of having found at last, in the sister of one of his fellow-servants, a woman to comfort and care for him after his mother was gone. She was all eagerness to see the woman of her son's choice, and the next day was fixed for the introduction.

It was a bright sunny morning, and the little cottage parlour was full of light as Mrs. Scatchard, happy and expectant, dressed for the occasion in her Sunday gown, sat waiting for her son and her future daughter-in-law.

Punctual to the appointed time, Isaac hurriedly and nervously led his promised wife into the room. His mother rose to receive her—advanced a few steps, smiling—looked Rebecca full in the eyes, and suddenly stopped. Her face, which had been flushed the moment before, turned white in an instant; her eyes lost their expression of softness and kindness, and assumed a blank look of terror; her outstretched hands fell to her sides, and she staggered back a few steps with a low cry to her son.

"Isaac," she whispered, clutching him fast by the arm when he asked alarmedly if she was taken ill, "Isaac, does that woman's face remind you of nothing?"

Before he could answer—before he could look round to where Rebecca stood, astonished and angered by her reception, at the lower end of the room, his mother pointed impatiently to her writing-desk, and gave him the key.

"Open it," she said, in a quick breathless whisper.

"What does this mean? Why am I treated as if I had no business here? Does your mother want to insult me?" asked Rebecca, angrily.

"Open it, and give me the paper in the left-hand drawer. Quick! quick, for Heaven's sake!" said Mrs. Scatchard, shrinking further back in terror.

Isaac gave her the paper. She looked it over eagerly for a moment, then followed Rebecca, who was now turning away haughtily to leave the room, and caught her by the shoulder-abruptly raised the long, loose sleeve of her gown, and glanced at her hand and arm. Something like fear began to steal over the angry expression of Rebecca's face as she shook herself free from the old woman's grasp. "Mad!" she said to herself; "and

Isaac never told me." With these few words she left the room.

Isaac was hastening after her when his mother turned and stopped his further progress. It wrung his heart to see the misery and terror in her face as she looked at him.

"Light gray eyes," she said, in low, mournful, awe-struck tones, pointing toward the open door; "a droop in the left eyelid; flaxen hair, with a gold-yellow streak in it; white arms, with a down upon them; little lady's hand, with a reddish look under the finger nails—The Dream-Woman, Isaac, the Dream-Woman!"

That faint cleaving doubt which he had never been able to shake off in Rebecca Murdoch's presence was fatally set at rest forever. He had seen her face, then, before—seven years before, on his birthday, in the bedroom of the lonely inn.

"Be warned! oh, my son, be warned! Isaac, Isaac, let her go, and do you stop with me!"

Something darkened the parlour window as those words were said. A sudden chill ran through him, and he glanced sidelong at the shadow. Rebecca Murdoch had come back. She was peering in curiously at them over the low window-blind.

"I have promised to marry, mother," he said, "and marry I must."

The tears came into his eyes as he spoke and dimmed his sight, but he could just discern the fatal face outside moving away again from the window.

His mother's head sank lower.

"Are you faint?" he whispered.

"Broken-hearted, Isaac."

He stooped down and kissed her. The shadow, as he did so, returned to the window, and the fatal face peered in curiously once more.

Chapter 4

Three weeks after that day Isaac and Rebecca were man and wife. All that was hopelessly dogged and stubborn in the man's moral nature seemed to have closed round his fatal passion, and to have fixed it unassailably in his heart.

After that first interview in the cottage parlour no consideration would induce Mrs. Scatchard to see her son's wife again or even to talk of her when Isaac tried hard to plead her cause after their marriage.

This course of conduct was not in any degree occasioned by a discovery of the degradation in which Rebecca had lived. There was no question of that between mother and son. There was no question of anything but the fearfully-exact resemblance between the living, breathing woman and the spectre-woman of Isaac's dream.

Rebecca on her side neither felt nor expressed the slightest sorrow at the estrangement between herself and her mother-in-law. Isaac, for the sake of peace, had never contradicted her first idea that age and long illness had affected Mrs. Scatchard's mind. He even allowed his wife to upbraid him for not having confessed this to her at the time of their marriage engagement, rather than risk anything by hinting at the truth. The sacrifice of his integrity before his one all-mastering delusion seemed but a small thing, and cost his conscience but little after the sacrifices he had already made.

The time of waking from this delusion—the cruel and the rueful time—was not far off. After some quiet months of married life, as the summer was ending, and the year was getting on toward the month of his birthday, Isaac found his wife altering toward him. She grew sullen and contemptuous; she formed acquaintances of the most dangerous kind in defiance of his objections, his entreaties, and his commands; and, worst of all, she learned, ere long, after every fresh difference with her husband, to seek the deadly self-oblivion of drink. Little by little, after the first miserable discovery that his wife was keeping company with drunkards, the shocking certainty forced itself on Isaac that she had grown to be a drunkard herself.

He had been in a sadly desponding state for some time before the occurrence of these domestic calamities. His mother's health, as he could but too plainly discern every time he went to see her at the cottage, was failing fast, and he upbraided himself in secret as the cause of the bodily and mental suffering she endured. When to his remorse on his mother's account was added the shame and misery occasioned by the discovery of his wife's degradation, he sank under the double trial—his face began to alter fast, and he looked what he was, a spirit-broken man.

His mother, still struggling bravely against the illness that was hurrying her to the grave, was the first to notice the sad alteration in him, and the first to hear of his last worst trouble with his wife. She could only weep bitterly on the day when he made his humiliating confession, but on the next occasion when he went to see her she had taken a resolution in reference to his domestic afflictions which astonished and even alarmed him. He found her dressed to go out, and on asking the reason received this answer:

"I am not long for this world, Isaac," she said, "and I shall not feel easy on my death-bed unless I have done my best to the last to make my son happy. I mean to put my own fears and my own feelings out of the question, and to go with you to your wife, and try what I can do to reclaim her. Give me your arm, Isaac, and let me do the last thing I can in this world to help my son before it is too late."

He could not disobey her, and they walked together slowly toward his miserable home.

It was only one o'clock in the afternoon when they reached the cottage where he lived. It was their dinner-hour, and Rebecca was in the kitchen. He was thus able to take his mother quietly into the parlour, and then prepare his wife for the interview. She had fortunately drunk but little at that early hour, and she was less sullen and capricious than usual.

He returned to his mother with his mind tolerably at ease. His wife soon followed him into the parlour, and the meeting between her and Mrs. Scatchard passed off better than he had ventured to anticipate, though he observed with secret apprehension that his mother, resolutely as she controlled herself in other respects, could not look his wife in the face when she spoke to her. It was a relief to him, therefore, when Rebecca began to lay the cloth.

She laid the cloth, brought in the bread-tray, and cut a slice from the loaf for her husband, then returned to the kitchen. At that moment, Isaac, still anxiously watching his mother, was startled by seeing the same ghastly change pass over her face which had altered it so awfully on the morning when Rebecca and she first met. Before he could say a word, she whispered, with a look of horror:

"Take me back—home, home again, Isaac. Come with me, and never go back again."

He was afraid to ask for an explanation; he could only sign to her to be silent, and help her quickly to the door. As they passed the bread-tray on the table she stopped and pointed to it.

"Did you see what your wife cut your bread with?" she asked, in a low whisper.

"No, mother—I was not noticing—what was it?"

"Look!"

He did look. A new clasp-knife with a buckhorn handle lay with the loaf in the bread-tray. He stretched out his hand shudderingly to possess himself of it; but, at the same time, there was a noise in the kitchen, and his mother caught at his arm.

"The knife of the dream! Isaac, I'm faint with fear. Take me away before she comes back."

He was hardly able to support her. The visible, tangible reality of the knife struck him with a panic, and utterly destroyed any faint doubts that he might have entertained up to this time in relation to the mysterious dream-warning of nearly eight years before. By a last desperate effort, he summoned self-possession enough to help his mother out of the house—so quietly that the "Dream-woman" (he thought of her by that name now) did not hear them departing from the kitchen.

"Don't go back, Isaac—don't go back!" implored Mrs. Scatchard, as he turned to go away, after seeing her safely seated again in her own room.

"I must get the knife," he answered, under his breath. His mother tried to stop him again, but he hurried out without another word.

On his return he found that his wife had discovered their secret departure from the house. She had been drinking, and was in a fury of passion. The dinner in the kitchen was flung under the grate; the cloth was off the parlour table. Where was the knife?

Unwisely, he asked for it. She was only too glad of the opportunity of irritating him which the request afforded her. "He wanted the knife, did he? Could he give her a reason why? No! Then he should not have it—not if he went down on his knees to ask for it." Further recriminations elicited the fact that she had bought it a bargain, and that she considered it her own especial property. Isaac saw the uselessness of attempting to get the knife by fair means, and determined to search for it, later in the day, in secret. The search was unsuccessful. Night came on, and he left the house to walk about the streets. He was afraid now to sleep in the same room with her.

Three weeks passed. Still sullenly enraged with him, she would not give up the knife; and still that fear of sleeping in the same room with her possessed him. He walked about at night, or dozed in the parlour, or sat watching by his mother's bedside. Before the expiration of the first week in the new month his mother died. It wanted then but ten days of her son's birthday. She had longed to live till that anniversary. Isaac was present at her death, and her last words in this world were addressed to him:

"Don't go back, my son, don't go back!"

He was obliged to go back, if it were only to watch his wife. Exasperated to the last degree by his distrust of her, she had revengefully sought to add a sting to his grief, during the last days of his mother's illness, by declaring that she would assert her right to attend the funeral. In spite of anything he could do or say, she held with wicked pertinacity to her word, and on the day appointed for the burial forced herself—inflamed and shameless with drink—into her husband's presence, and declared that she would walk in the funeral procession to his mother's grave.

This last worst outrage, accompanied by all that was most insulting in word and look, maddened him for the moment. He struck her.

The instant the blow was dealt he repented it. She crouched down, silent, in a corner of the room, and eyed him steadily; it was a look that cooled his hot blood and made him tremble. But there was no time now to think of a means of making atonement. Nothing remained but to risk the worst till the funeral was over. There was but one way of making sure of her. He locked her into her bedroom.

When he came back some hours after, he found her sitting, very much altered in look and bearing, by the bedside, with a bundle on her lap. She rose, and faced him quietly, and spoke with a strange stillness in her voice, a strange repose in her eyes, a strange composure in her manner.

"No man has ever struck me twice," she said, "and my husband shall have no second opportunity. Set the door open and let me go. From this day forth we see each other no more."

Before he could answer she passed him and left the room. He saw her walk away up the street.

Would she return?

All that night he watched and waited, but no footstep came near the house. The next night, overpowered by fatigue, he lay down in bed in his clothes, with the door locked, the key on the table, and the candle burning. His slumber was not disturbed. The third night, the fourth, the fifth, the sixth passed, and nothing happened.

He lay down on the seventh, still in his clothes, still with the door locked, the key on the table, and the candle burning, but easier in his mind.

Easier in his mind, and in perfect health of body when he fell off to sleep. But his rest was disturbed. He woke twice without any sensation of uneasiness. But the third time it was that never-to-be-forgotten shivering of the night at the lonely inn, that dreadful sinking pain at the heart, which once more aroused him in an instant.

His eyes opened toward the left-hand side of the bed, and there stood—

The Dream-Woman again? No! His wife; the living reality, with the dream-spectre's face, in the dream-spectre's attitude; the fair arm up, the knife clasped in the delicate white hand.

He sprang upon her almost at the instant of seeing her, and yet not quickly enough to prevent her from hiding the knife. Without a word from him—without a cry from her—he pinioned her in a chair. With one hand he felt up her sleeve, and there, where the Dream-Woman had hidden the knife, his wife had hidden it—the knife with the buckhorn handle, that looked like new.

In the despair of that fearful moment his brain was steady, his heart was calm. He looked at her fixedly with the knife in his hand, and said these last words:

"You told me we should see each other no more, and you have come back. It is my turn now to go, and to go forever. I say that we shall see each other no more, and my word shall not be broken."

He left her, and set forth into the night. There was a bleak wind abroad, and the smell of recent rain was in the air. The distant church-clocks chimed the quarter as he walked rapidly beyond the last houses in the suburb. He asked the first policeman he met what hour that was of which the quarter past had just struck.

The man referred sleepily to his watch, and answered, "Two o'clock." Two in the morning. What day of the month was this day that had just begun? He reckoned it up from the date of his mother's funeral. The fatal parallel was complete: it was his birthday!

Had he escaped the mortal peril which his dream foretold? or had he only received a second warning?

As that ominous doubt forced itself on his mind, he stopped, reflected, and turned back again toward the city. He was still resolute to hold to his word, and never to let her see him more; but there was a thought now in his mind of having her watched and followed. The knife was in his possession; the world was before him; but a new distrust of her—a vague, unspeakable, superstitious dread had overcome him.

"I must know where she goes, now she thinks I have left her," he said to himself, as he stole back wearily to the precincts of his house.

It was still dark. He had left the candle burning in the bed-chamber; but when he looked up to the window of the room now there was no light in it. He crept cautiously to the house door. On going away, he remembered to have closed it; on trying it now, he found it open.

He waited outside, never losing sight of the house, till day-light. Then he ventured indoors—listened, and heard nothing-looked into kitchen, scullery, parlour and found nothing; went up at last into the bedroom—it was empty. A picklock lay on the floor betraying how she had gained entrance in the night, and that was the only trace of her.

Whither had she gone? That no mortal tongue could tell him. The darkness had covered her flight; and when the day broke, no man could say where the light found her.

Before leaving the house and the town forever, he gave instructions to a friend and neighbour to sell his furniture for anything that it would fetch, and apply the proceeds to employing the police to trace her. The directions were honestly followed, and the money was all spent, but the inquiries led to nothing. The picklock on the bedroom floor remained the one last useless trace of the Dream-Woman.

At this point of the narrative the landlord paused, and, turning toward the window of the room in which we were sitting, looked in the direction of the stable-yard.

"So far," he said, "I tell you what was told to me. The little that remains to be added lies within my own experience. Between two and three months after the events I have just been relating, Isaac Scatchard came to me, withered and old-looking before his time, just as you saw him today. He had his testimonials to character with him, and he asked for employment here.

Knowing that my wife and he were distantly related, I gave him a trial in consideration of that relationship, and liked him in spite of his queer habits. He is as sober, honest, and willing a man as there is in England. As for his restlessness at night, and his sleeping away his leisure time in the day, who can wonder at it after hearing his story? Besides, he never objects to being roused up when he's wanted, so there's not much inconvenience to complain of, after all."

"I suppose he is afraid of a return of that dreadful dream, and of waking out of it in the dark?" said I.

"No," returned the landlord. "The dream comes back to him so often that he has got to bear with it by this time resignedly enough. It's his wife keeps him waking at night as he has often told me."

"What! Has she never been heard of yet?"

"Never. Isaac himself has the one perpetual thought about her, that she is alive and looking for him. I believe he wouldn't let himself drop off to sleep toward two in the morning for a king's ransom. Two in the morning, he says, is the time she will find him, one of these days. Two in the morning is the time all the year round when he likes to be most certain that he has got that clasp-knife safe about him. He does not mind being alone as long as he is awake, except on the night before his birthday, when he firmly believes himself to be in peril of his life. The birthday has only come round once since he has been here, and then he sat up along with the night-porter. 'She's looking for me,' is all he says when anybody speaks to him about the one anxiety of his life; 'she's looking for me.' He may be right. She may be looking for him. Who can tell?"

"Who can tell?" said I.

Brother Griffith's Story of

Mad Monkton

Chapter 1

The Monktons of Wincot Abbey bore a sad character for want of sociability in our county. They never went to other people's houses, and, excepting my father, and a lady and her daughter living near them, never received anybody under their own roof.

Proud as they all certainly were, it was not pride, but dread, which kept them thus apart from their neighbours. The family had suffered for generations past from the horrible affliction of hereditary insanity, and the members of it shrank from exposing their calamity to others, as they must have exposed it if they had mingled with the busy little world around them. There is a frightful story of a crime committed in past times by two of the Monktons, near relatives, from which the first appearance of the insanity was always supposed to date, but it is needless for me to shock any one by repeating it. It is enough to say that at intervals almost every form of madness appeared in the family, monomania being the most frequent manifestation of the affliction among them. I have these particulars, and one or two yet to be related, from my father.

At the period of my youth but three of the Monktons were left at the Abbey—Mr. and Mrs. Monkton and their only child Alfred, heir to the property. The one other member of this, the elder branch of the family, who was then alive, was Mr. Monkton's younger brother, Stephen. He was an unmarried man, possessing a fine estate in Scotland; but he lived almost entirely on the Continent, and bore the reputation of being a shameless profligate. The family at Wincot held almost as little communication with him as with their neighbours.

I have already mentioned my father, and a lady and her daughter, as the only privileged people who were admitted into Wincot Abbey.

My father had been an old school and college friend of Mr. Monkton, and accident had brought them so much together in later life that their continued intimacy at Wincot was quite intelligible. I am not so well able to account for the friendly terms on which Mrs. Elmslie (the lady to whom I have alluded) lived with the Monktons. Her late husband had been distantly related to Mrs. Monkton, and my father was her daughter's guardian. But even these claims to friendship and regard never seemed to me strong enough to explain the intimacy between Mrs. Elmslie and the inhabitants of the Abbey. Intimate, however, they certainly were, and one result of the constant interchange of visits between the two families in due time declared itself: Mr. Monkton's son and Mrs. Elmslie's daughter became attached to each other.

I had no opportunities of seeing much of the young lady; I only remember her at that time as a delicate, gentle, lovable girl, the very opposite in appearance, and apparently in character also, to Alfred Monkton. But perhaps that was one reason why they fell in love with each other. The attachment was soon discovered, and was far from being disapproved by the parents on either side. In all essential points except that of wealth, the Elmslies were nearly the equals of the Monktons, and want of money in a bride was of no consequence to the heir of Wincot. Alfred, it was well known, would succeed to thirty thousand a year on his father's death.

Thus, though the parents on both sides thought the young people not old enough to be married at once, they saw no reason why Ada and Alfred should not be engaged to each other, with the understanding that they should be united when young Monkton came of age, in two years' time. The person to be consulted in the matter, after the parents, was my father, in his capacity of Ada's guardian. He knew that the family misery had shown itself many years ago in Mrs. Monkton, who was her husband's cousin. The illness, as it was significantly called, had been palliated by careful treatment, and was reported to have passed away. But my father was not to be deceived. He knew where the hereditary taint still lurked; he viewed with horror the bare possibility of its reappearing one day in the children of his friend's only daughter; and he positively refused his consent to the marriage engagement.

The result was that the doors of the Abbey and the doors of Mrs. Elmslie's house were closed to him. This suspension of friendly intercourse had lasted but a very short time when Mrs. Monkton died. Her husband, who was fondly attached to her, caught a violent cold while attending her funeral. The cold was neglected, and settled on his lungs. In a few months' time he followed his wife to the grave, and Alfred was left master of the grand old Abbey and the fair lands that spread all around it.

At this period Mrs. Elmslie had the indelicacy to endeavour a second time to procure my father's consent to the marriage engagement. He refused it again more positively than before. More than a year passed away. The time was approaching fast when Alfred would be of age. I returned from college to spend the long vacation at home, and made some advances toward bettering my acquaintance with young Monkton.

They were evaded—certainly with perfect politeness, but still in such a way as to prevent me from offering my friendship to him again. Any mortification I might have felt at this petty repulse under ordinary circumstances was dismissed from my mind by the occurrence of a real misfortune in our household. For some months past my father's health had been failing, and, just at the time of which I am now writing, his sons had to mourn the irreparable calamity of his death.

This event, through some informality or error in the late Mr. Elmslie's will, left the future of Ada's life entirely at her mother's disposal. The consequence was the immediate ratification of the marriage engagement to which my father had so steadily refused his consent. As soon as the fact was publicly announced, some of Mrs. Elmslie's more intimate friends, who were acquainted with the reports affecting the Monkton family, ventured to mingle with their formal congratulations one or two significant references to the late Mrs. Monkton and some searching inquiries as to the disposition of her son.

Mrs. Elmslie always met these polite hints with one bold form of answer. She first admitted the existence of these reports about the Monktons which her friends were unwilling to specify distinctly, and then declared that they were infamous calumnies. The hereditary taint had died out of the family generations back.

Alfred was the best, the kindest, the sanest of human beings. He loved study and retirement; Ada sympathized with his tastes, and had made her choice unbiased; if any more hints were dropped about sacrificing her by her marriage, those hints would be viewed as so many insults to her mother, whose affection for her it was monstrous to call in question. This way of talking silenced people, but did not convince them. They began to suspect, what was indeed the actual truth, that Mrs. Elmslie was a selfish, worldly, grasping woman, who wanted to get her daughter well married, and cared nothing for consequences as long as she saw Ada mistress of the greatest establishment in the whole county.

It seemed, however, as if there was some fatality at work to prevent the attainment of Mrs. Elmslie's great object in life. Hardly was one obstacle to the ill-omened marriage removed by my father's death before another succeeded it in the shape of anxieties and difficulties caused by the delicate state of Ada's health. Doctors were consulted in all directions, and the result of their advice was that the marriage must be deferred, and that Miss Elmslie must leave England for a certain time, to reside in a warmer climate—the south of France, if I remember rightly.

Thus it happened that just before Alfred came of age Ada and her mother departed for the Continent, and the union of the two young people was understood to be indefinitely postponed.

Some curiosity was felt in the neighbourhood as to what Alfred Monkton would do under these circumstances. Would he follow his lady-love? would he go yachting? would he throw open the doors of the old Abbey at last, and endeavour to forget the absence of Ada and the postponement of his marriage in a round of gayeties? He did none of these things. He simply remained at Wincot, living as suspiciously strange and solitary a life as his father had lived before him.

Literally, there was now no companion for him at the Abbey but the old priest—the Monktons, I should have mentioned before, were Roman Catholics—who had held the office of tutor to Alfred from his earliest years. He came of age, and there was not even so much as a private dinner-party at Wincot to celebrate the event. Families in the neighbourhood determined to forget the offense which his father's reserve had given them, and invited him to their houses. The invitations were politely declined.

Civil visitors called resolutely at the Abbey, and were as resolutely bowed away from the doors as soon as they had left their cards. Under this combination of sinister and aggravating circumstances people in all directions took to shaking their heads mysteriously when the name of Mr. Alfred Monkton was mentioned, hinting at the family calamity, and wondering peevishly or sadly, as their tempers inclined them, what he could possibly do to occupy himself month after month in the lonely old house.

The right answer to this question was not easy to find. It was quite useless, for ex ample, to apply to the priest for it. He was a very quiet, polite old gentleman; his replies were always excessively ready and civil, and appeared at the time to convey an immense quantity of information; but when they came to be reflected on, it was universally observed that nothing tangible could ever be got out of them.

The housekeeper, a weird old woman, with a very abrupt

and repelling manner, was too fierce and taciturn to be safely approached. The few indoor servants had all been long enough in the family to have learned to hold their tongues in public as a regular habit. It was only from the farm-servants who supplied the table at the Abbey that any information could be obtained, and vague enough it was when they came to communicate it.

Some of them had observed the "young master" walking about the library with heaps of dusty papers in his hands. Others had heard odd noises in the uninhabited parts of the Abbey, had looked up, and had seen him forcing open the old windows, as if to let light and air into the rooms supposed to have been shut close for years and years, or had discovered him standing on the perilous summit of one of the crumbling turrets, never ascended before within their memories, and popularly considered to be inhabited by the ghosts of the monks who had once possessed the building.

The result of these observations and discoveries, when they were communicated to others, was of course to impress every one with a firm belief that "poor young Monkton was going the way that the rest of the family had gone before him," which opinion always appeared to be immensely strengthened in the popular mind by a conviction—founded on no particle of evidence—that the priest was at the bottom of all the mischief.

Thus far I have spoken from hearsay evidence mostly. What I have next to tell will be the result of my own personal experience.

Chapter 2

About five months after Alfred Monkton came of age I left college, and resolved to amuse and instruct myself a little by travelling abroad.

At the time when I quitted England young Monkton was still leading his secluded life at the Abbey, and was, in the opinion of everybody, sinking rapidly, if he had not already succumbed, under the hereditary curse of his family. As to the Elmslies, report said that Ada had benefited by her sojourn abroad, and that mother and daughter were on their way back to England to resume their old relations with the heir of Wincot.

Before they returned I was away on my travels, and wandered half over Europe, hardly ever planning whither I should shape my course beforehand. Chance, which thus led me everywhere, led me at last to Naples. There I met with an old school friend, who was one of the *attachés* at the English embassy, and there began the extraordinary events in connection with Alfred Monkton which form the main interest of the story I am now relating.

I was idling away the time one morning with my friend the *attaché*, in the garden of the Villa Reale, when we were passed by a young man, walking alone, who exchanged bows with my friend.

I thought I recognized the dark, eager eyes, the colourless cheeks, the strangely-vigilant, anxious expression which I remembered in past times as characteristic of Alfred Monkton's face, and was about to question my friend on the subject, when he gave me unasked the information of which I was in search.

"That is Alfred Monkton," said he; "he comes from your part of England. You ought to know him."

"I do know a little of him," I answered; "he was engaged to Miss Elmslie when I was last in the neighbourhood of Wincot. Is he married to her yet?"

"No, and he never ought to be. He has gone the way of the rest of the family—or, in plainer words, he has gone mad."

"Mad! But I ought not to be surprised at hearing that, after the reports about him in England."

"I speak from no reports; I speak from what he has said and done before me, and before hundreds of other people. Surely you must have heard of it?"

"Never. I have been out of the way of news from Naples or England for months past."

"Then I have a very extraordinary story to tell you. You know, of course, that Alfred had an uncle, Stephen Monkton. Well, some time ago this uncle fought a duel in the Roman

States with a Frenchman, who shot him dead. The seconds and the Frenchman (who was unhurt) took to flight in different directions, as it is supposed.

We heard nothing here of the details of the duel till a month after it happened, when one of the French journals published an account of it, taken from the papers left by Monkton's second, who died at Paris of consumption. These papers stated the manner in which the duel was fought, and how it terminated, but nothing more. The surviving second and the Frenchman have never been traced from that time to this. All that anybody knows, therefore, of the duel is that Stephen Monkton was shot; an event which nobody can regret, for a greater scoundrel never existed. The exact place where he died, and what was done with the body are still mysteries not to be penetrated."

"But what has all this to do with Alfred?"

"Wait a moment, and you will hear. Soon after the news of his uncle's death reached England, what do you think Alfred did? He actually put off his marriage with Miss Elmslie, which was then about to be celebrated, to come out here in search of the burial-place of his wretched scamp of an uncle; and no power on earth will now induce him to return to England and to Miss Elmslie until he has found the body, and can take it back with him, to be buried with all the other dead Monktons in the vault under Wincot Abbey Chapel.

"He has squandered his money, pestered the police, and exposed himself to the ridicule of the men and the indignation of the women for the last three months in trying to achieve his insane purpose, and is now as far from it as ever. He will not assign to anybody the smallest motive for his conduct. You can't laugh him out of it or reason him out of it. When we met him just now, I happen to know that he was on his way to the office of the police minister, to send out fresh agents to search and inquire through the Roman States for the place where his uncle was shot.

"And, mind, all this time he professes to be passionately in love with Miss Elmslie, and to be miserable at his separation from her. Just think of that! And then think of his self-imposed absence from her here, to hunt after the remains of a wretch who was a disgrace to the family, and whom he never saw but once or twice in his life. Of all the 'Mad Monktons,' as they used to call them in England, Alfred is the maddest. He is actually our principal excitement in this dull opera season; though, for my own part, when I think of the poor girl in England, I am a great deal more ready to despise him than to laugh at him."

"You know the Elmslies then?"

"Intimately. The other day my mother wrote to me from England, after having seen Ada. This escapade of Monkton's has outraged all her friends. They have been entreating her to break off the match, which it seems she could do if she liked. Even her mother, sordid and selfish as she is, has been obliged at last, in common decency, to side with the rest of the family; but the good, faithful girl won't give Monkton up.

"She humours his insanity; declares he gave her a good reason in secret for going away; says she could always make him happy when they were together in the old Abbey, and can make him still happier when they are married; in short, she loves him dearly, and will therefore believe in him to the last. Nothing shakes her. She has made up her mind to throw away her life on him, and she will do it."

"I hope not. Mad as his conduct looks to us, he may have some sensible reason for it that we cannot imagine. Does his mind seem at all disordered when he talks on ordinary topics?"

"Not in the least. When you can get him to say anything, which is not often, he talks like a sensible, well-educated man. Keep silence about his precious errand here, and you would fancy him the gentlest and most temperate of human beings; but touch the subject of his vagabond of an uncle, and the Monkton madness comes out directly.

"The other night a lady asked him, jestingly of course, whether he had ever seen his uncle's ghost. He scowled at her like a perfect fiend, and said that he and his uncle would answer her question together some day, if they came from hell to do it.

We laughed at his words, but the lady fainted at his looks, and we had a scene of hysterics and hartshorn in consequence. Any other man would have been kicked out of the room for nearly frightening a pretty woman to death in that way; but 'Mad Monkton,' as we have christened him, is a privileged lunatic in Neapolitan society, because he is English, good-looking, and worth thirty thousand a year.

"He goes out everywhere under the impression that he may meet with somebody who has been let into the secret of the place where the mysterious duel was fought. If you are introduced to him he is sure to ask you whether you know anything about it; but beware of following up the subject after you have answered him, unless you want to make sure that he is out of his senses. In that case, only talk of his uncle, and the result will rather more than satisfy you."

A day or two after this conversation with my friend the *attaché*, I met Monkton at an evening party.

The moment he heard my name mentioned, his face flushed up; he drew me away into a corner, and referring to his cool reception of my advance years ago toward making his acquaintance, asked my pardon for what he termed his inexcusable ingratitude with an earnestness and an agitation which utterly astonished me. His next proceeding was to question me, as my friend had said he would, about the place of the mysterious duel.

An extraordinary change came over him while he interrogated me on this point. Instead of looking into my face as they had looked hitherto, his eyes wandered away, and fixed themselves intensely, almost fiercely, either on the perfectly empty wall at our side, or on the vacant space between the wall and ourselves, it was impossible to say which.

I had come to Naples from Spain by sea, and briefly told him so, as the best way of satisfying him that I could not assist his inquiries. He pursued them no further; and, mindful of my friend's warning, I took care to lead the conversation to general topics. He looked back at me directly, and, as long as we stood in our corner, his eyes never wandered away again to the empty wall or the vacant space at our side.

Though more ready to listen than to speak, his conversation, when he did talk, had no trace of anything the least like insanity about it. He had evidently read, not generally only, but deeply as well, and could apply his reading with singular felicity to the illustration of almost any subject under discussion, neither obtruding his knowledge absurdly, nor concealing it affectedly.

His manner was in itself a standing protest against such a nickname as "Mad Monkton." He was so shy, so quiet, so composed and gentle in all his actions, that at times I should have been almost inclined to call him effeminate. We had a long talk together on the first evening of our meeting; we often saw each other afterward, and never lost a single opportunity of bettering our acquaintance.

I felt that he had taken a liking to me, and, in spite of what I had heard about his behaviour to Miss Elmslie, in spite of the suspicions which the history of his family and his own conduct had arrayed against him, I began to like "Mad Monkton" as much as he liked me. We took many a quiet ride together in the country, and sailed often along the shores of the Bay on either side. But for two eccentricities in his conduct, which I could not at all understand, I should soon have felt as much at my ease in his society as if he had been my own brother.

The first of these eccentricities consisted in the reappearance on several occasions of the odd expression in his eyes which I had first seen when he asked me whether I knew anything about the duel. No matter what we were talking about, or where we happened to be, there were times when he would suddenly look away from my face, now on one side of me, now on the other, but always where there was nothing to see, and always with the same intensity and fierceness in his eyes. This looked so like madness—or hypochondria at the least—that I felt afraid to ask him about it, and always pretended not to observe him.

The second peculiarity in his conduct was that he never referred, while in my company, to the reports about his errand at Naples, and never once spoke of Miss Elmslie, or of his life at

Wincot Abbey. This not only astonished me, but amazed those who had noticed our intimacy, and who had made sure that I must be the depositary of all his secrets. But the time was near at hand when this mystery, and some other mysteries of which I had no suspicion at that period, were all to be revealed.

I met him one night at a large ball, given by a Russian nobleman, whose name I could not pronounce then, and cannot remember now. I had wandered away from reception-room, ballroom, and card-room, to a small apartment at one extremity of the palace, which was half conservatory, half boudoir, and which had been prettily illuminated for the occasion with Chinese lanterns.

Nobody was in the room when I got there. The view over the Mediterranean, bathed in the bright softness of Italian moonlight, was so lovely that I remained for a long time at the window, looking out, and listening to the dance-music which faintly reached me from the ballroom. My thoughts were far away with the relations I had left in England, when I was startled out of them by hearing my name softly pronounced.

I looked round directly, and saw Monkton standing in the room. A livid paleness overspread his face, and his eyes were turned away from me with the same extraordinary expression in them to which I have already alluded.

"Do you mind leaving the ball early tonight?" he asked, still not looking at me.

"Not at all," said I. "Can I do anything for you? Are you ill?"

"No—at least nothing to speak of. Will you come to my rooms?"

"At once, if you like."

"No, not at once. I must go home directly; but don't you come to me for half an hour yet. You have not been at my rooms before, I know, but you will easily find them out; they are close by. There is a card with my address. I must speak to you tonight; my life depends on it. Pray come! for God's sake, come when the half hour is up!"

I promised to be punctual, and he left me directly.

Most people will be easily able to imagine the state of nervous impatience and vague expectation in which I passed the allotted period of delay, after hearing such words as those Monkton had spoken to me. Before the half hour had quite expired I began to make my way out through the ballroom.

At the head of the staircase my friend, the *attaché*, met me.

"What! going away already?" Said he.

"Yes; and on a very curious expedition. I am going to Monkton's rooms, by his own invitation."

"You don't mean it! Upon my honour, you're a bold fellow to trust yourself alone with 'Mad Monkton' when the moon is at the full."

"He is ill, poor fellow. Besides, I don't think him half as mad as you do."

"We won't dispute about that; but mark my words, he has not asked you to go where no visitor has ever been admitted before without a special purpose. I predict that you will see or hear something tonight which you will remember for the rest of your life."

We parted. When I knocked at the courtyard gate of the house where Monkton lived, my friend's last words on the palace staircase recurred to me, and, though I had laughed at him when he spoke them, I began to suspect even then that his prediction would be fulfilled.

Chapter 3

The porter who let me into the house where Monkton lived directed me to the floor on which his rooms were situated. On getting upstairs, I found his door on the landing ajar. He heard my footsteps, I suppose, for he called to me to come in before I could knock.

I entered, and found him sitting by the table, with some loose letters in his hand, which he was just tying together into a packet. I noticed, as he asked me to sit down, that his express ion looked more composed, though the paleness had not yet left his face. He thanked me for coming; repeated that he had something very important to say to me; and then stopped short, apparently too much embarrassed to proceed. I tried to set him at his ease by assuring him that, if my assistance or advice could be of any use, I was ready to place myself and my time heartily and unreservedly at his service.

As I said this I saw his eyes beginning to wander away from my face—to wander slowly, inch by inch, as it were, until they stopped at a certain point, with the same fixed stare into vacancy which had so often startled me on former occasions. The whole expression of his face altered as I had never yet seen it alter; he sat before me looking like a man in a death-trance.

"You are very kind," he said, slowly and faintly, speaking, not to me, but in the direction in which his eyes were still fixed. "I know you can help me; but—"

He stopped; his face whitened horribly, and the perspiration broke out all over it. He tried to continue—said a word or two—then stopped again. Seriously alarmed about him, I rose from my chair with the intention of getting him some water from a jug which I saw standing on a side-table.

He sprang up at the same moment. All the suspicions I had ever heard whispered against his sanity flashed over my mind in an instant, and I involuntarily stepped back a pace or two.

"Stop," he said, seating himself again; "don't mind me; and don't leave your chair. I want—I wish, if you please, to make a little alteration, before we say anything more. Do you mind sitting in a strong light?"

"Not in the least."

I had hitherto been seated in the shade of his reading-lamp, the only light in the room.

As I answered him he rose again, and, going into another apartment, returned with a large lamp in his hand; then took two candles from the side-table, and two others from the chimney piece; placed them all, to my amazement, together, so as to stand exactly between us, and then tried to light them. His hand trembled so that he was obliged to give up the attempt, and allow me to come to his assistance.

By his direction, I took the shade off the reading-lamp after I had lit the other lamp and the four candles. When we sat down again, with this concentration of light between us, his better and gentler manner began to return, and while he now addressed me he spoke without the slightest hesitation.

"It is useless to ask whether you have heard the reports about me," he said; "I know that you have. My purpose tonight is to give you some reasonable explanation of the conduct which has produced those reports. My secret has been hitherto confided to one person only; I am now about to trust it to your keeping, with a special object which will appear as I go on.

"First, however, I must begin by telling you exactly what the great difficulty is which obliges me to be still absent from England. I want your advice and your help; and, to conceal nothing from you, I want also to test your forbearance and your friendly sympathy, before I can venture on thrusting my miserable secret into your keeping. Will you pardon this apparent distrust of your frank and open character—this apparent ingratitude for your kindness toward me ever since we first met?"

I begged him not to speak of these things, but to go on.

"You know," he proceeded, "that I am here to recover the body of my Uncle Stephen, and to carry it back with me to our family burial-place in England, and you must also be aware that I have not yet succeeded in discovering his remains. Try to pass over, for the present, whatever may seem extraordinary and incomprehensible in such a purpose as mine is, and read this newspaper article where the ink-line is traced. It is the only evidence hitherto obtained on the subject of the fatal duel in which my uncle fell, and I want to hear what course of proceeding the perusal of it may suggest to you as likely to be best on my part."

He handed me an old French newspaper. The substance of what I read there is still so firmly impressed on my memory that I am certain of being able to repeat correctly at this distance of time all the facts which it is necessary for me to communicate to the reader.

The article began, I remember, with editorial remarks on the great curiosity then felt in regard to the fatal duel between the Count St. Lo and Mr. Stephen Monkton, an English gentleman. The writer proceeded to dwell at great length on the extraordinary secrecy in which the whole affair had been involved from first to last, and to express a hope that the publication of a certain manuscript, to which his introductory observations referred, might lead to the production of fresh evidence from other and better-informed quarters.

The manuscript had been found among the papers of Monsieur Foulon, Mr. Monkton's second, who had died at Paris of a rapid decline shortly after returning to his home in that city from the scene of the duel. The document was unfinished, having been left incomplete at the very place where the reader would most wish to find it continued. No reason could be discovered for this, and no second manuscript bearing on the all-important subject had been found, after the strictest search among the papers left by the deceased.

The document itself then followed.

It purported to be an agreement privately drawn up between Mr. Monkton's second, Monsieur Foulon, and the Count St. Lo's second, Monsieur Dalville, and contained a statement of all the arrangements for conducting the duel. The paper was dated "Naples, February 22nd," and was divided into some seven or eight clauses.

The first clause described the origin and nature of the quarrel—a very disgraceful affair on both sides, worth neither remembering nor repeating. The second clause stated that, the challenged man having chosen the pistol as his weapon, and the challenger (an excellent swordsman), having, on his side, thereupon insisted that the duel should be fought in such a manner as to make the first fire decisive in its results, the seconds, seeing that fatal consequences must inevitably follow the hostile meeting, determined, first of all, that the duel should be kept a profound secret from everybody, and that the place where it was to be fought should not be made known beforehand, even to the principals themselves.

It was added that this excess of precaution had been rendered absolutely necessary in consequence of a recent address from the Pope to the ruling powers in Italy commenting on the scandalous frequency of the practice of duelling, and urgently desiring that the laws against duellists should be enforced for the future with the utmost rigour.

The third clause detailed the manner in which it had been arranged that the duel should be fought.

The pistols having been loaded by the seconds on the ground, the combatants were to be placed thirty paces apart, and were to toss up for the first fire. The man who won was to advance ten paces—marked out for him beforehand—and was then to discharge his pistol. If he missed, or failed to disable his opponent, the latter was free to advance, if he chose, the whole remaining twenty paces before he fired in his turn. This arrangement insured the decisive termination of the duel at the first discharge of the pistols, and both principals and seconds pledged themselves on either side to abide by it.

The fourth clause stated that the seconds had agreed that the duel should be fought out of the Neapolitan States, but left themselves to be guided by circumstances as to the exact locality in which it should take place. The remaining clauses, so far as I remember them, were devoted to detailing the different precautions to be adopted for avoiding discovery.

The duellists and their seconds were to leave Naples in separate parties; were to change carriages several times; were to meet at a certain town, or, failing that, at a certain post-house on the high road from Naples to Rome; were to carry drawing-books, colour boxes, and camp-stools, as if they had been artists out on a sketching-tour; and were to proceed to the place of the duel on foot, employing no guides, for fear of treachery. Such general arrangements as these, and others for facilitating the flight of the survivors after the affair was over, formed the conclusion of this extraordinary document, which was signed, in initials only, by both the seconds.

Just below the initials appeared the beginning of a narrative, dated "Paris," and evidently intended to describe the duel itself with extreme minuteness. The hand-writing was that of the deceased second.

Monsieur Foulon, the gentleman in question, stated his belief that circumstances might transpire which would render an account by an eyewitness of the hostile meeting between St. Lo and Mr. Monkton an important document. He proposed, therefore, as one of the seconds, to testify that the duel had been fought in exact accordance with the terms of the agreement, both the principals conducting themselves like men of gallantry and honour(!).

And he further announced that, in order not to compromise any one, he should place the paper containing his testimony in safe hands, with strict directions that it was on no account to be opened except in a case of the last emergency.

After thus preamble, Monsieur Foulon related that the duel had been fought two days after the drawing up of the agreement, in a locality to which accident had conducted the duelling party. (The name of the place was not mentioned, nor even the neighbourhood in which it was situated.) The men having been placed according to previous arrangement, the Count St. Lo had won the toss for the first fire, had advanced his ten paces, and had shot his opponent in the body. Mr. Monkton did not immediately fall, but staggered forward some six or seven paces, discharged his pistol ineffectually at the count, and dropped to the ground a dead man.

Monsieur Foulon then stated that he tore a leaf from his pocketbook, wrote on it a brief description of the manner in which Mr. Monkton had died, and pinned the paper to his clothes; this proceeding having been rendered necessary by the peculiar nature of the plan organized on the spot for safely disposing of the dead body. What this plan was, or what was done with the corpse, did not appear, for at this important point the narrative abruptly broke off.

A footnote in the newspaper merely stated the manner in

which the document had been obtained for publication, and repeated the announcement contained in the editor's introductory remarks, that no continuation had been found by the persons intrusted with the care of Monsieur Foulon's papers. I have now given the whole substance of what I read, and have mentioned all that was then known of Mr. Stephen Monkton's death.

When I gave the newspaper back to Alfred he was too much agitated to speak, but he reminded me by a sign that he was anxiously waiting to hear what I had to say. My position was a very trying and a very painful one. I could hardly tell what consequences might not follow any want of caution on my part, and could think at first of no safer plan than questioning him carefully before I committed myself either one way or the other.

"Will you excuse me if I ask you a question or two before I give you my advice?" said I.

He nodded impatiently.

"Yes, yes—any questions you like."

"Were you at any time in the habit of seeing your uncle frequently?"

"I never saw him more than twice in my life—on each occasion when I was a mere child."

"Then you could have had no very strong personal regard for him?"

"Regard for him! I should have been ashamed to feel any regard for him. He disgraced us wherever he went."

"May I ask if any family motive is involved in your anxiety to recover his remains?"

"Family motives may enter into it among others—but why do you ask?"

"Because, having heard that you employ the police to assist your search, I was anxious to know whether you had stimulated their superiors to make them do their best in your service by giving some strong personal reasons at headquarters for the very unusual project which has brought you here."

"I give no reasons. I pay for the work I want done, and, in return for my liberality, I am treated with the most infamous indifference on all sides. A stranger in the country, and badly acquainted with the language, I can do nothing to help myself. The authorities, both at Rome and in this place, pretend to assist me, pretend to search and inquire as I would have them search and inquire, and do nothing more. I am insulted, laughed at, almost to my face."

"Do you not think it possible—mind, I have no wish to excuse the misconduct of the authorities, and do not share in any such opinion myself—but do you not think it likely that the police may doubt whether you are in earnest?"

"Not in earnest!" he cried, starting up and confronting me fiercely, with wild eyes and quickened breath. "Not in earnest! You think I'm not in earnest too. I know you think it, though you tell me you don't. Stop; before we say another word, your own eyes shall convince you. Come here—only for a minute-only for one minute!"

I followed him into his bedroom, which opened out of the sitting-room. At one side of his bed stood a large packing-case of plain wood, upward of seven feet in length.

"Open the lid and look in," he said, "while I hold the candle so that you can see."

I obeyed his directions, and discovered to my astonishment that the packing-case contained a leaden coffin, magnificently emblazoned with the arms of the Monkton family, and inscribed in old-fashioned letters with the name of "Stephen Monkton," his age and the manner of his death being added underneath.

"I keep his coffin ready for him," whispered Alfred, close at my ear. "Does that look like earnest?"

It looked more like insanity—so like that I shrank from answering him.

"Yes! yes! I see you are convinced," he continued quickly; "we may go back into the next room, and may talk without restraint on either side now."

On returning to our places, I mechanically moved my chair away from the table. My mind was by this time in such a state of confusion and uncertainty about what it would be best for me to say or do next, that I forgot for the moment the position he had assigned to me when we lit the candles. He reminded me of this directly.

"Don't move away," he said, very earnestly; "keep on sitting in the light; pray do! I'll soon tell you why I am so particular about that. But first give me your advice; help me in my great distress and suspense. Remember, you promised me you would."

I made an effort to collect my thoughts, and succeeded. It was useless to treat the affair otherwise than seriously in his presence; it would have been cruel not to have advised him as I best could.

"You know," I said, "that two days after the drawing up of the agreement at Naples, the duel was fought out of the Neapolitan States. This fact has of course led you to the conclusion that all inquiries about localities had better be confined to the Roman territory?"

"Certainly; the search, such as it is, has been made there, and there only. If I can believe the police, they and their agents have inquired for the place where the duel was fought (offering a large reward in my name to the person who can discover it) all along the high road from Naples to Rome.

"They have also circulated—at least so they tell me—descriptions of the duellists and their seconds; have left an agent to superintend investigations at the post-house, and another at the town mentioned as meeting-points in the agreement; and have endeavoured, by correspondence with foreign authorities, to trace the Count St. Lo and Monsieur Dalville to their place or places of refuge. All these efforts, supposing them to have been really made, have hitherto proved utterly fruitless."

"My impression is," said I, after a moment's consideration, "that all inquiries made along the high road, or anywhere near Rome, are likely to be made in vain.

"As to the discovery of your uncle's remains, that is, I think, identical with the discovery of the place where he was shot; for those engaged in the duel would certainly not risk detection by carrying a corpse any distance with them in their flight.

The place, then, is all that we want to find out. Now let us consider for a moment. The duelling-party changed carriages; travelled separately, two and two; doubtless took roundabout roads; stopped at the post-house and the town as a blind; walked, perhaps, a considerable distance unguided.

"Depend upon it, such precautions as these (which we know they must have employed) left them very little time out of the two days—though they might start at sunrise and not stop at nightfall—for straightforward travelling. My belief therefore is, that the duel was fought somewhere near the Neapolitan frontier; and, if I had been the police agent who conducted the search, I should only have pursued it parallel with the frontier, starting from west to east till I got up among the lonely places in the mountains. That is my idea; do you think it worth anything?"

His face flushed all over in an instant. "I think it an inspiration!" he cried. "Not a day is to be lost in carrying out our plan. The police are not to be trusted with it. I must start myself tomorrow morning; and you—"

He stopped; his face grew suddenly pale; he sighed heavily; his eyes wandered once more into the fixed look at vacancy; and the rigid, deathly expression fastened again upon all his features.

"I must tell you my secret before I talk of tomorrow," he proceeded, faintly. "If I hesitated any longer at confessing everything, I should be unworthy of your past kindness, unworthy of the help which it is my last hope that you will gladly give me when you have heard all."

I begged him to wait until he was more composed, until he was better able to speak; but he did not appear to notice what I said. Slowly, and struggling as it seemed against himself, he turned a little away from me, and, bending his head over the table, supported it on his hand.

The packet of letters with which I had seen him occupied when I came in lay just beneath his eyes. He looked down on it steadfastly when he next spoke to me.

Chapter 4

"You were born, I believe, in our county," he said; "perhaps, therefore, you may have heard at some time of a curious old prophecy about our family, which is still preserved among the traditions of Wincot Abbey?"

"I have heard of such a prophecy," I answered, "but I never knew in what terms it was expressed. It professed to predict the extinction of your family, or something of that sort, did it not?"

"No inquiries," he went on, "have traced back that prophecy to the time when it was first made; none of our family records tell us anything of its origin. Old servants and old tenants of ours remember to have heard it from their fathers and grandfathers. The monks, whom we succeeded in the Abbey in Henry the Eighth's time, got knowledge of it in some way, for I myself discovered the rhymes, in which we know the prophecy to have been preserved from a very remote period, written on a blank leaf of one of the Abbey manuscripts. These are the verses, if verses they deserve to be called:

When in Wincot vault a place
Waits for one of Monkton's race—
When that one forlorn shall lie
Graveless under open sky,
Beggared of six feet of earth,
Though lord of acres from his birth—
That shall be a certain sign
Of the end of Monkton's line.
Dwindling ever faster, faster,
Dwindling to the last-left master;
From mortal ken, from light of day,
Monkton's race shall pass away."

"The prediction seems almost vague enough to have been uttered by an ancient oracle," said I, observing that he waited, after repeating the verses, as if expecting me to say something.

"Vague or not, it is being accomplished," he returned. "I am now the 'last-left master'—the last of that elder line of our family at which the prediction points; and the corpse of Stephen Monkton is not in the vaults of Wincot Abbey. Wait before you exclaim against me. I have more to say about this. Long before the Abbey was ours, when we lived in the ancient manor-house near it (the very ruins of which have long since disappeared), the family burying-place was in the vault under the Abbey chapel.

"Whether in those remote times the prediction against us was known and dreaded or not, this much is certain: every one of the Monktons (whether living at the Abbey or on the smaller estate in Scotland) was buried in Wincot vault, no matter at what risk or what sacrifice. In the fierce fighting days of the olden time, the bodies of my ancestors who fell in foreign places were recovered and brought back to Wincot, though it often cost not heavy ransom only, but desperate bloodshed as well, to obtain them.

"This superstition, if you please to call it so, has never died out of the family from that time to the present day; for centuries the succession of the dead in the vault at the Abbey has been unbroken—absolutely unbroken—until now. The place mentioned in the prediction as waiting to be filled is Stephen Monkton's place; the voice that cries vainly to the earth for shelter is the spirit-voice of the dead. As surely as if I saw it, I know that they have left him unburied on the ground where he fell!"

He stopped me before I could utter a word in remonstrance by slowly rising to his feet, and pointing in the same direction toward which his eyes had wandered a short time since.

"I can guess what you want to ask me," he exclaimed, sternly and loudly; "you want to ask me how I can be mad enough to believe in a doggerel prophecy uttered in an age of superstition to awe the most ignorant hearers. I answer" (at those words his voice sank suddenly to a whisper), "I answer, because—Stephen Monkton himself stands there at this moment confirming me in my belief."

Whether it was the awe and horror that looked out ghastly from his face as he confronted me, whether it was that I had never hitherto fairly believed in the reports about his madness, and that the conviction of their truth now forced itself upon me on a sudden, I know not, but I felt my blood curdling as he spoke, and I knew in my own heart, as I sat there speechless, that I dare not turn round and look where he was still pointing close at my side.

"I see there," he went on, in the same whispering voice, "the figure of a dark-complexioned man standing up with his head uncovered. One of his hands, still clutching a pistol, has fallen to his side; the other presses a bloody handkerchief over his mouth. The spasm of mortal agony convulses his features; but I know them for the features of a swarthy man who twice frightened me by taking me up in his arms when I was a child at Wincot Abbey. I asked the nurses at the time who that man was, and they told me it was my uncle, Stephen Monkton.

"Plainly, as if he stood there living, I see him now at your side, with the death-glare in his great black eyes; and so have I ever seen him, since the moment when he was shot; at home and abroad, waking or sleeping, day and night, we are always together, wherever I go!"

His whispering tones sank into almost inaudible murmuring as he pronounced these last words. From the direction and expression of his eyes, I suspected that he was speaking to the apparition. If I had beheld it myself at that moment, it would have been, I think, a less horrible sight to witness than to see him, as I saw him now, muttering inarticulately at vacancy. My own nerves were more shaken than I could have thought possible by what had passed. A vague dread of being near him in his present mood came over me, and I moved back a step or two.

He noticed the action instantly.

"Don't go! pray—pray don't go! Have I alarmed you? Don't you believe me? Do the lights make your eyes ache? I only asked you to sit in the glare of the candles because I could not bear to see the light that always shines from the phantom there at dusk shining over you as you sat in the shadow. Don't go—don't leave me yet!"

There was an utter forlornness, an unspeakable misery in

his face as he spoke these words, which gave me back my self-possession by the simple process of first moving me to pity. I resumed my chair, and said that I would stay with him as long as he wished.

"Thank you a thousand times. You are patience and kindness itself," he said, going back to his former place and resuming his former gentleness of manner. "Now that I have got over my first confession of the misery that follows me in secret wherever I go, I think I can tell you calmly all that remains to be told. You see, as I said, my Uncle Stephen"—he turned away his head quickly, and looked down at the table as the name passed his lips—"my Uncle Stephen came twice to Wincot while I was a child, and on both occasions frightened me dreadfully. He only took me up in his arms and spoke to me—very kindly, as I afterward heard, for him,—but he terrified me, nevertheless.

"Perhaps I was frightened at his great stature, his swarthy complexion, and his thick black hair and moustache, as other children might have been; perhaps the mere sight of him had some strange influence on me which I could not then understand and cannot now explain. However it was, I used to dream of him long after he had gone away, and to fancy that he was stealing on me to catch me up in his arms whenever I was left in the dark.

"The servants who took care of me found this out, and used to threaten me with my Uncle Stephen whenever I was perverse and difficult to manage. As I grew up, I still retained my vague dread and abhorrence of our absent relative. I always listened intently, yet without knowing why, whenever his name was mentioned by my father or my mother—listened with an unaccountable presentiment that something terrible had happened to him, or was about to happen to me.

"This feeling only changed when I was left alone in the Abbey; and then it seemed to merge into the eager curiosity which had begun to grow on me, rather before that time, about the origin of the ancient prophecy predicting the extinction of our race. Are you following me?"

"I follow every word with the closest attention."

"You must know, then, that I had first found out some fragments of the old rhyme in which the prophecy occurs quoted as a curiosity in an antiquarian book in the library. On the page opposite this quotation had been pasted a rude old wood-cut, representing a dark-haired man, whose face was so strangely like what I remembered of my Uncle Stephen that the portrait absolutely startled me.

"When I asked my father about this—it was then just before his death—he either knew, or pretended to know, nothing of it; and when I afterward mentioned the prediction he fretfully changed the subject. It was just the same with our chaplain when I spoke to him. He said the portrait had been done centuries before my uncle was born, and called the prophecy doggerel and nonsense. I used to argue with him on the latter point, asking why we Catholics, who believed that the gift of working miracles had never departed from certain favoured persons, might not just as well believe that the gift of prophecy had never departed, either?

"He would not dispute with me; he would only say that I must not waste time in thinking of such trifles; that I had more imagination than was good for me, and must suppress instead of exciting it. Such advice as this only irritated my curiosity. I determined secretly to search throughout the oldest uninhabited part of the Abbey, and to try if I could not find out from forgotten family records what the portrait was, and when the prophecy had been first written or uttered. Did you ever pass a day alone in the long-deserted chambers of an ancient house?"

"Never! such solitude as that is not at all to my taste."

"Ah! what a life it was when I began my search. I should like to live it over again. Such tempting suspense, such strange discoveries, such wild fancies, such enthralling terrors, all belonged to that life.

"Only think of breaking open the door of a room which no living soul had entered before you for nearly a hundred years; think of the first step forward into a region of airless, awful stillness, where the light falls faint and sickly through closed windows and rotting curtains; think of the ghostly creaking of the old floor that cries out on you for treading on it, step as softly as you will; think of arms, helmets, weird tapestries of by-gone days, that seem to be moving out on you from the walls as you first walk up to them in the dim light; think of prying into great cabinets and iron-clasped chests, not knowing what horrors may appear when you tear them open; of poring over their contents till twilight stole on you and darkness grew terrible in the lonely place; of trying to leave it, and not being able to go, as if something held you; of wind wailing at you outside; of shadows darkening round you, and closing you up in obscurity within—only think of these things, and you may imagine the fascination of suspense and terror in such a life as mine was in those past days."

(I shrank from imagining that life: it was bad enough to see its results, as I saw them before me now.)

"Well, my search lasted months and months; then it was suspended a little; then resumed. In whatever direction I pursued it I always found something to lure me on. Terrible confessions of past crimes, shocking proofs of secret wickedness that had been hidden securely from all eyes but mine, came to light. Sometimes these discoveries were associated with particular parts of the Abbey, which have had a horrible interest of their own for me ever since; sometimes with certain old portraits in the picture-gallery, which I actually dreaded to look at after what I had found out.

"There were periods when the results of this search of mine so horrified me that I determined to give it up entirely; but I never could persevere in my resolution; the temptation to go on seemed at certain intervals to get too strong for me, and then I yielded to it again and again. At last I found the book that had belonged to the monks with the whole of the prophecy written in the blank leaf.

"This first success encouraged me to get back further yet in the family records. I had discovered nothing hitherto of the identity of the mysterious portrait; but the same intuitive conviction which had assured me of its extraordinary resemblance to my Uncle Stephen seemed also to assure me that he must be more closely connected with the prophecy, and must know more of it than anyone else. I had no means of holding any communication with him, no means of satisfying myself whether this strange idea of mine were right or wrong, until the day when my doubts were settled forever by the same terrible proof which is now present to me in this very room."

He paused for a moment, and looked at me intently and suspiciously; then asked if I believed all he had said to me so far. My instant reply in the affirmative seemed to satisfy his doubts, and he went on.

"On a fine evening in February I was standing alone in one of the deserted rooms of the western turret at the Abbey, looking at the sunset. Just before the sun went down I felt a sensation stealing over me which it is impossible to explain. I saw nothing, heard nothing, knew nothing. This utter self-oblivion came suddenly; it was not fainting, for I did not fall to the ground, did not move an inch from my place. If such a thing could be, I should say it was the temporary separation of soul and body without death; but all description of my situation at that time is impossible.

"Call my state what you will, trance or catalepsy, I know that I remained standing by the window utterly unconscious-dead, mind and body—until the sun had set. Then I came to my senses again; and then, when I opened my eyes, there was the apparition of Stephen Monkton standing opposite to me, faintly luminous, just as it stands opposite me at this very moment by your side."

"Was this before the news of the duel reached England?" I asked.

"Two weeks before the news of it reached us at Wincot. And even when we heard of the duel, we did not hear of the day on which it was fought. I only found that out when the document which you have read was published in the French newspaper. The date of that document, you will remember, is February

22nd, and it is stated that the duel was fought two days afterward. I wrote down in my pocketbook, on the evening when I saw the phantom, the day of the month on which it first appeared to me. That day was the 24th of February."

He paused again, as if expecting me to say something. After the words he had just spoken, what could I say? what could I think?

"Even in the first horror of first seeing the apparition," he went on, "the prophecy against our house came to my mind, and with it the conviction that I beheld before me, in that spectral presence, the warning of my own doom. As soon as I recovered a little, I determined, nevertheless, to test the reality of what I saw; to find out whether I was the dupe of my own diseased fancy or not. I left the turret; the phantom left it with me. I made an excuse to have the drawing-room at the Abbey brilliantly lighted up; the figure was still opposite me. I walked out into the park; it was there in the clear starlight.

"I went away from home, and travelled many miles to the seaside; still the tall dark man in his death agony was with me. After this I strove against the fatality no more. I returned to the Abbey, and tried to resign myself to my misery. But this was not to be. I had a hope that was dearer to me than my own life; I had one treasure belonging to me that I shuddered at the prospect of losing; and when the phantom presence stood a warning obstacle between me and this one treasure, this dearest hope, then my misery grew heavier than I could bear. You must know what I am alluding to; you must have heard often that I was engaged to be married?"

"Yes, often. I have some acquaintance myself with Miss Elmslie."

"You never can know all that she has sacrificed for me—never can imagine what I have felt for years and years past"—his voice trembled, and the tears came into his eyes—"but I dare not trust myself to speak of that; the thought of the old happy days in the Abbey almost breaks my heart now. Let me get back to the other subject. I must tell you that I kept the frightful vision which pursued me, at all times and in all places, a secret from everybody, knowing the vile reports about my having inherited madness from my family, and fearing that an unfair advantage would be taken of any confession that I might make.

"Though the phantom always stood opposite to me, and therefore always appeared either before or by the side of any person to whom I spoke, I soon schooled myself to hide from others that I was looking at it except on rare occasions, when I have perhaps betrayed myself to you. But my self-possession availed me nothing with Ada. The day of our marriage was approaching."

He stopped and shuddered. I waited in silence till he had controlled himself.

"Think," he went on, "think of what I must have suffered at looking always on that hideous vision whenever I looked on my betrothed wife! Think of my taking her hand, and seeming to take it through the figure of the apparition! Think of the calm angel-face and the tortured spectre-face being always together whenever my eyes met hers! Think of this, and you will not wonder that I betrayed my secret to her. She eagerly entreated to know the worst—nay, more, she insisted on knowing it.

"At her bidding I told all, and then left her free to break our engagement. The thought of death was in my heart as I spoke the parting words—death by my own act, if life still held out after our separation. She suspected that thought; she knew it, and never left me till her good influence had destroyed it forever. But for her I should not have been alive now; but for her I should never have attempted the project which has brought me here."

"Do you mean that it was at Miss Elmslie's suggestion that you came to Naples?" I asked, in amazement.

"I mean that what she said suggested the design which has brought me to Naples," he answered. "While I believed that the phantom had appeared to me as the fatal messenger of death, there was no comfort—there was misery, rather, in hearing her say that no power on earth should make her desert me, and that she would live for me, and for me only, through every trial. But it was far different when we afterward reasoned together about the purpose which the apparition had come to fulfil—far different when she showed me that its mission might be for good instead of for evil, and that the warning it was sent to give might be to my profit instead of to my loss.

"At those words, the new idea which gave the new hope of life came to me in an instant. I believed then, what I believe now, that I have a supernatural warrant for my errand here. In that faith I live; without it I should die. She never ridiculed it, never scorned it as insanity. Mark what I say! The spirit that appeared to me in the Abbey—that has never left me since—that stands there now by your side, warns me to escape from the fatality which hangs over our race, and commands me, if I would avoid it, to bury the unburied dead.

"Mortal loves and mortal interests must bow to that awful bidding. The spectre-presence will never leave me till I have sheltered the corpse that cries to the earth to cover it! I dare not return—I dare not marry till I have filled the place that is empty in Wincot vault."

His eyes flashed and dilated—his voice deepened—a fanatic ecstasy shone in his expression as he uttered these words. Shocked and grieved as I was, I made no attempt to remonstrate or to reason with him. It would have been useless to have referred to any of the usual commonplaces about optical delusions or diseased imaginations—worse than useless to have attempted to account by natural causes for any of the extraordinary coincidences and events of which he had spoken.

Briefly as he had referred to Miss Elmslie, he had said enough to show me that the only hope of the poor girl who loved him best and had known him longest of any one was in humouring his delusions to the last. How faithfully she still clung to the belief that she could restore him! How resolutely was she sacrificing herself to his morbid fancies, in the hope of a happy future that might never come! Little as I knew of Miss Elmslie, the mere thought of her situation, as I now reflected on it, made me feel sick at heart.

"They call me Mad Monkton!" he exclaimed, suddenly breaking the silence between us during the last few minutes, "Here and in England everybody believes I am out of my senses except Ada and you. She has been my salvation, and you will be my salvation too. Something told me that when I first met you walking in the Villa Peale. I struggled against the strong desire that was in me to trust my secret to you, but I could resist it no longer when I saw you tonight at the ball; the phantom seemed to draw me on to you as you stood alone in the quiet room.

"Tell me more of that idea of yours about finding the place where the duel was fought. If I set out tomorrow to seek for it myself, where must I go to first? where?" He stopped; his strength was evidently becoming exhausted, and his mind was growing confused. "What am I to do? I can't remember. You know everything—will you not help me? My misery has made me unable to help myself."

He stopped, murmured something about failing if he went to the frontier alone, and spoke confusedly of delays that might be fatal, then tried to utter the name of "Ada"; but, in pronouncing the first letter, his voice faltered, and, turning abruptly from me, he burst into tears.

My pity for him got the better of my prudence at that moment, and without thinking of responsibilities, I promised at once to do for him whatever he asked. The wild triumph in his expression as he started up and seized my hand showed me that I had better have been more cautious; but it was too late now to retract what I had said. The next best thing to do was to try if I could not induce him to compose himself a little, and then to go away and think coolly over the whole affair by myself.

"Yes, yes," he rejoined, in answer to the few words I now spoke to try and calm him, "don't be afraid about me. After what you have said, I'll answer for my own coolness and composure under all emergencies. I have been so long used to the apparition that I hardly feel its presence at all except on rare occasions. Besides, I have here in this little packet of letters the medicine for every malady of the sick heart.

"They are Ada's letters; I read them to calm me whenever my misfortune seems to get the better of my endurance. I wanted that half hour to read them in tonight before you came, to make myself fit to see you, and I shall go through them again after you are gone; so, once more, don't be afraid about me. I know I shall succeed with your help, and Ada shall thank you as you deserve to be thanked when we get back to England. If you hear the fools at Naples talk about my being mad, don't trouble yourself to contradict them; the scandal is so contemptible that it must end by contradicting itself."

I left him, promising to return early the next day.

When I got back to my hotel, I felt that any idea of sleeping after all that I had seen and heard was out of the question; so I lit my pipe, and, sitting by the window—how it refreshed my mind just then to look at the calm moonlight!—tried to think what it would be best to do. In the first place, any appeal to doctors or to Alfred's friends in England was out of the question.

I could not persuade myself that his intellect was sufficiently disordered to justify me, under existing circumstances, in disclosing the secret which he had intrusted to my keeping. In the second place, all attempts on my part to induce him to abandon the idea of searching out his uncle's remains would be utterly useless after what I had incautiously said to him. Having settled these two conclusions, the only really great difficulty which remained to perplex me was whether I was justified in aiding him to execute his extraordinary purpose.

Supposing that, with my help, he found Mr. Monkton's body, and took it back with him to England, was it right in me thus to lend myself to promoting the marriage which would most likely follow these events—a marriage which it might be the duty of every one to prevent at all hazards? This set me thinking about the extent of his madness, or to speak more mildly and more correctly, of his delusion. Sane he certainly was on all ordinary subjects; nay, in all the narrative parts of what he had said to me on this very evening he had spoken clearly and connectedly.

As for the story of the apparition, other men, with intellects as clear as the intellects of their neighbours had fancied themselves pursued by a phantom, and had even written about it in a high strain of philosophical speculation.

It was plain that the real hallucination in the case now before me lay in Monkton's conviction of the truth of the old prophecy, and in his idea that the fancied apparition was a supernatural warning to him to evade its denunciations; and it was equally clear that both delusions had been produced, in the first instance, by the lonely life he had led acting on a naturally excitable temperament, which was rendered further liable to moral disease by an hereditary taint of insanity.

Was this curable? Miss Elmslie, who knew him far better than I did, seemed by her conduct to think so. Had I any reason or right to determine offhand that she was mistaken? Supposing I refused to go to the frontier with him, he would then most certainly depart by himself, to commit all sorts of errors, and perhaps to meet with all sorts of accidents; while I, an idle man, with my time entirely at my own disposal, was stopping at Naples, and leaving him to his fate after I had suggested the plan of his expedition, and had encouraged him to confide in me.

In this way I kept turning the subject over and over again in my mind, being quite free, let me add, from looking at it in any other than a practical point of view. I firmly believed, as a derider of all ghost stories, that Alfred was deceiving himself in fancying that he had seen the apparition of his uncle before the news of Mr. Monkton's death reached England, and I was on this account, therefore, uninfluenced by the slightest infection of my unhappy friend's delusions when I at last fairly decided to accompany him in his extraordinary search.

Possibly my harum-scarum fondness for excitement at that time biased me a little in forming my resolution; but I must add, in common justice to myself, that I also acted from motives of real sympathy for Monkton, and from a sincere wish to allay, if I could, the anxiety of the poor girl who was still so faithfully waiting and hoping for him far away in England.

Certain arrangements preliminary to our departure, which I found myself obliged to make after a second interview with Alfred, betrayed the object of our journey to most of our Neapolitan friends. The astonishment of everybody was of course unbounded, and the nearly universal suspicion that I must be as mad in my way as Monkton himself showed itself pretty plainly in my presence. Some people actually tried to combat my resolution by telling me what a shameless profligate Stephen Monkton had been—as if I had a strong personal interest in hunting out his remains! Ridicule moved me as little as any arguments of this sort; my mind was made up, and I was as obstinate then as I am now.

In two days' time I had got everything ready, and had ordered the travelling carriage to the door some hours earlier than we had originally settled. We were jovially threatened with "a parting cheer" by all our English acquaintances, and I thought it desirable to avoid this on my friend's account; for he had been more excited, as it was, by the preparations for the journey than I at all liked. Accordingly, soon after sunrise, without a soul in the street to stare at us, we privately left Naples.

Nobody will wonder, I think, that I experienced some difficulty in realizing my own position, and shrank instinctively from looking forward a single day into the future, when I now found myself starting, in company with "Mad Monkton," to hunt for the body of a dead duellist all along the frontier line of the Roman States!

Chapter 5

I had settled it in my own mind that we had better make the town of Fondi, close on the frontier, our headquarters, to begin with, and I had arranged, with the assistance of the embassy, that the leaden coffin should follow us so far, securely nailed up in its packing-case. Besides our passports, we were well furnished with letters of introduction to the local authorities at most of the important frontier towns, and, to crown all, we had money enough at our command (thanks to Monkton's vast fortune) to make sure of the services of any one whom we wanted to assist us all along our line of search.

These various resources insured us every facility for action, provided always that we succeeded in discovering the body of the dead duellist. But, in the very probable event of our failing to do this, our future prospects—more especially after the responsibility I had undertaken—were of anything but an agreeable nature to contemplate. I confess I felt uneasy, almost hopeless, as we posted, in the dazzling Italian sunshine, along the road to Fondi.

We made an easy two days' journey of it; for I had insisted, on Monkton's account, that we should travel slowly.

On the first day the excessive agitation of my companion a little alarmed me; he showed, in many ways, more symptoms of a disordered mind than I had yet observed in him.

On the second day, however, he seemed to get accustomed to contemplate calmly the new idea of the search on which we were bent, and, except on one point, he was cheerful and composed enough. Whenever his dead uncle formed the subject of conversation, he still persisted—on the strength of the old prophecy, and under the influence of the apparition which he saw, or thought he saw always—in asserting that the corpse of Stephen Monkton, wherever it was, lay yet unburied. On every other topic he deferred to me with the utmost readiness and docility; on this he maintained his strange opinion with an obstinacy which set reason and persuasion alike at defiance.

On the third day we rested at Fondi. The packing-case, with the coffin in it, reached us, and was deposited in a safe place under lock and key. We engaged some mules, and found a man to act as guide who knew the country thoroughly. It occurred to me that we had better begin by confiding the real object of our journey only to the most trustworthy people we could find among the better-educated classes.

For this reason we followed, in one respect, the example of the fatal duelling-party, by starting, early on the morning of the fourth day, with sketch-books and colour-boxes, as if we were only artists in search of the picturesque.

After travelling some hours in a northerly direction within the Roman frontier, we halted to rest ourselves and our mules at a wild little village far out of the track of tourists in general.

The only person of the smallest importance in the place was the priest, and to him I addressed my first inquiries, leaving Monkton to await my return with the guide. I spoke Italian quite fluently, and correctly enough for my purpose, and was extremely polite and cautious in introducing my business, but in spite of all the pains I took, I only succeeded in frightening and bewildering the poor priest more and more with every fresh word I said to him.

The idea of a duelling-party and a dead man seemed to scare him out of his senses. He bowed, fidgeted, cast his eyes up to heaven, and piteously shrugging his shoulders, told me, with rapid Italian circumlocution, that he had not the faintest idea of what I was talking about. This was my first failure. I confess I was weak enough to feel a little dispirited when I rejoined Monkton and the guide.

After the heat of the day was over we resumed our journey.

About three miles from the village, the road, or rather cart-track, branched off in two directions. The path to the right, our guide informed us, led up among the mountains to a convent about six miles off. If we penetrated beyond the convent we should soon reach the Neapolitan frontier. The path to the left led far inward on the Roman territory, and would conduct us to a small town where we could sleep for the night.

Now the Roman territory presented the first and fittest field for our search, and the convent was always within reach, supposing we returned to Fondi unsuccessful. Besides, the path to the left led over the widest part of the country we were starting to explore, and I was always for vanquishing the greatest difficulty first; so we decided manfully on turning to the left.

The expedition in which this resolution involved us lasted a whole week, and produced no results. We discovered absolutely nothing, and returned to our headquarters at Fondi so completely baffled that we did not know whither to turn our steps next.

I was made much more uneasy by the effect of our failure on Monkton than by the failure itself. His resolution appeared to break down altogether as soon as we began to retrace our steps.

He became first fretful and capricious, then silent and desponding. Finally, he sank into a lethargy of body and mind that seriously alarmed me.

On the morning after our return to Fondi he showed a strange tendency to sleep incessantly, which made me suspect the existence of some physical malady in his brain. The whole day he hardly exchanged a word with me, and seemed to be never fairly awake. Early the next morning I went into his room, and found him as silent and lethargic as ever. His servant, who was with us, informed me that Alfred had once or twice before exhibited such physical symptoms of mental exhaustion as we were now observing during his father's lifetime at Wincot Abbey. This piece of information made me feel easier, and left my mind free to return to the consideration of the errand which had brought us to Fondi.

I resolved to occupy the time until my companion got better in prosecuting our search by myself. That path to the right hand which led to the convent had not yet been explored. If I set off to trace it, I need not be away from Monkton more than one night, and I should at least be able, on my return, to give him the satisfaction of knowing that one more uncertainty regarding the place of the duel had been cleared up. These considerations decided me. I left a message for my friend in case he asked where I had gone, and set out once more for the village at which we had halted when starting on our first expedition.

Intending to walk to the convent, I parted company with the guide and the mules where the track branched off, leaving them to go back to the village and await my return.

For the first four miles the path gently ascended through an open country, then became abruptly much steeper, and led me deeper and deeper among thickets and endless woods. By the time my watch informed me that I must have nearly walked my appointed distance, the view was bounded on all sides and the sky was shut out overhead by an impervious screen of leaves and branches. I still followed my only guide, the steep path; and in ten minutes, emerging suddenly on a plot of tolerably clear and level ground, I saw the convent before me.

It was a dark, low, sinister-looking place. Not a sign of life or movement was visible anywhere about it. Green stains streaked the once white façade of the chapel in all directions. Moss clustered thick in every crevice of the heavy scowling wall that surrounded the convent. Long lank weeds grew out of the fissures of roof and parapet, and, drooping far downward, waved wearily in and out of the barred dormitory windows. The very cross opposite the entrance-gate, with a shocking life-sized figure in wood nailed to it, was so beset at the base with crawling creatures, and looked so slimy, green, and rotten all the way up, that I absolutely shrank from it.

A bell-rope with a broken handle hung by the gate. I approached it—hesitated, I hardly knew why—looked up at the convent again, and then walked round to the back of the building, partly to gain time to consider what I had better do next, partly from an unaccountable curiosity that urged me, strangely to myself, to see all I could of the outside of the place before I attempted to gain admission at the gate.

At the back of the convent I found an outhouse, built on to the wall—a clumsy, decayed building, with the greater part of the roof fallen in, and with a jagged hole in one of its sides, where in all probability a window had once been. Behind the outhouse the trees grew thicker than ever. As I looked toward them I could not determine whether the ground beyond me rose or fell—whether it was grassy, or earthy, or rocky. I could see nothing but the all-pervading leaves, brambles, ferns, and long grass.

Not a sound broke the oppressive stillness. No bird's note rose from the leafy wilderness around me; no voices spoke in the convent garden behind the scowling wall; no clock struck in the chapel-tower; no dog barked in the ruined outhouse. The dead silence deepened the solitude of the place inexpressibly. I began to feel it weighing on my spirits—the more, because woods were never favourite places with me to walk in. The sort of pastoral happiness which poets often represent when they sing of life in the woods never, to my mind, has half the charm of life on the mountain or in the plain.

When I am in a wood, I miss the boundless loveliness of the sky, and the delicious softness that distance gives to the earthly view beneath. I feel oppressively the change which the free air suffers when it gets imprisoned among leaves, and I am always awed, rather than pleased, by that mysterious still light which shines with such a strange dim lustre in deep places among trees. It may convict me of want of taste and absence of due feeling for the marvellous beauties of vegetation, but I must frankly own that I never penetrate far into a wood without finding that the getting out of it again is the pleasantest part of my walk-the getting out on to the barest down, the wildest hill-side, the bleakest mountain top—the getting out anywhere, so that I can see the sky over me and the view before me as far as my eye can reach.

After such a confession as I have now made, it will appear surprising to no one that I should have felt the strongest possible inclination, while I stood by the ruined outhouse, to retrace my steps at once, and make the best of my way out of the wood. I had, indeed, actually turned to depart, when the remembrance of the errand which had brought me to the convent suddenly stayed my feet. It seemed doubtful whether I should be admitted into the building if I rang the bell; and more than doubtful, if I were let in, whether the inhabitants would be able to afford me any clew to the information of which I was in search. However, it was my duty to Monkton to leave no means of helping him in his desperate object untried; so I resolved to go round to the front of the convent again, and ring at the gate-bell at all hazards.

By the merest chance I looked up as I passed the side of the outhouse where the jagged hole was, and noticed that it was pierced rather high in the wall.

As I stopped to observe this, the closeness of the atmosphere in the wood seemed to be affecting me more unpleasantly than ever.

I waited a minute and untied my cravat.

Closeness? surely it was something more than that. The air was even more distasteful to my nostrils than to my lungs. There was some faint, indescribable smell loading it—some smell of which I had never had any previous experience—some smell which I thought (now that my attention was directed to it) grew more and more certainly traceable to its source the nearer I advanced to the outhouse.

By the time I had tried the experiment two or three times, and had made myself sure of this fact, my curiosity became excited. There were plenty of fragments of stone and brick lying about me. I gathered some of them together, and piled them up below the hole, then mounted to the top, and, feeling rather ashamed of what I was doing, peeped into the outhouse.

The sight of horror that met my eyes the instant I looked through the hole is as present to my memory now as if I had beheld it yesterday. I can hardly write of it at this distance of time without a thrill of the old terror running through me again to the heart.

The first impression conveyed to me, as I looked in, was of a long, recumbent object, tinged with a lightish blue colour all over, extended on trestles, and bearing a certain hideous, half-formed resemblance to the human face and figure. I looked again, and felt certain of it. There were the prominences of the forehead, nose, and chin, dimly shown as under a veil—there, the round outline of the chest and the hollow below it—there, the points of the knees, and the stiff, ghastly, upturned feet. I looked again, yet more attentively.

My eyes got accustomed to the dim light streaming in through the broken roof, and I satisfied myself, judging by the great length of the body from head to foot, that I was looking at the corpse of a man—a corpse that had apparently once had a sheet spread over it, and that had lain rotting on the trestles under the open sky long enough for the linen to take the livid, light-blue tinge of mildew and decay which now covered it.

How long I remained with my eyes fixed on that dread sight of death, on that tombless, terrible wreck of humanity, poisoning the still air, and seeming even to stain the faint descending light that disclosed it, I know not. I remember a dull, distant sound among the trees, as if the breeze were rising—the slow creeping on of the sound to near the place where I stood—the noiseless whirling fall of a dead leaf on the corpse below me, through the gap in the outhouse roof—and the effect of awakening my energies, of relaxing the heavy strain on my mind, which even the slight change wrought in the scene I beheld by the falling leaf produced in me immediately.

I descended to the ground, and, sitting down on the heap of stones, wiped away the thick perspiration which covered my face, and which I now became aware of for the first time. It was something more than the hideous spectacle unexpectedly offered to my eyes which had shaken my nerves as I felt that they were shaken now. Monkton's prediction that, if we succeeded in discovering his uncle's body, we should find it unburied, recurred to me the instant I saw the trestles and their ghastly burden.

I felt assured on the instant that I had found the dead man—the old prophecy recurred to my memory—a strange yearning sorrow, a vague foreboding of ill, an inexplicable terror, as I thought of the poor lad who was awaiting my return in the distant town, struck through me with a chill of superstitious dread, robbed me of my judgment and resolution, and left me when I had at last recovered myself, weak and dizzy, as if I had just suffered under some pang of overpowering physical pain.

I hastened round to the convent gate and rang impatiently at the bell—waited a little while and rang again—then heard footsteps.

In the middle of the gate, just opposite my face, there was a small sliding panel, not more than a few inches long; this was presently pushed aside from within. I saw, through a bit of iron grating, two dull, light gray eyes staring vacantly at me, and heard a feeble husky voice saying:

"What may you please to want?'

"I am a traveller—" I began.

"We live in a miserable place. We have nothing to show travellers here."

"I don't come to see anything. I have an important question to ask, which I believe someone in this convent will be able to answer. If you are not willing to let me in, at least come out and speak to me here."

"Are you alone?"

"Quite alone."

"Are there no women with you?"

"None."

The gate was slowly unbarred, and an old Capuchin, very infirm, very suspicious, and very dirty, stood before me. I was far too excited and impatient to waste any time in prefatory phrases; so, telling the monk at once how I had looked through the hole in the outhouse, and what I had seen inside, I asked him, in plain terms, who the man had been whose corpse I had beheld, and why the body was left unburied?

The old Capuchin listened to me with watery eyes that twinkled suspiciously. He had a battered tin snuff-box in his hand, and his finger and thumb slowly chased a few scattered grains of snuff round and round the inside of the box all the time I was speaking. When I had done, he shook his head and said: "That was certainly an ugly sight in their outhouse; one of the ugliest sights, he felt sure, that ever I had seen in all my life!"

"I don't want to talk of the sight," I rejoined, impatiently; "I want to know who the man was, how he died, and why he is not decently buried. Can you tell me?"

The monk's finger and thumb having captured three or four grains of snuff at last, he slowly drew them into his nostrils, holding the box open under his nose the while, to prevent the possibility of wasting even one grain, sniffed once or twice luxuriously—closed the box—then looked at me again with his eyes watering and twinkling more suspiciously than before.

"Yes," said the monk, "that's an ugly sight in our outhouse—a very ugly sight, certainly!"

I never had more difficulty in keeping my temper in my life than at that moment. I succeeded, however, in repressing a very disrespectful expression on the subject of monks in general, which was on the tip of my tongue, and made another attempt to conquer the old man's exasperating reserve. Fortunately for my chances of succeeding with him, I was a snuff-taker myself, and I had a box full of excellent English snuff in my pocket, which I now produced as a bribe. It was my last resource.

"I thought your box seemed empty just now," said I; "will you try a pinch out of mine?"

The offer was accepted with an almost youthful alacrity of gesture. The Capuchin took the largest pinch I ever saw held between any man's finger and thumb—inhaled it slowly without spilling a single grain—half closed his eyes—and, wagging his head gently, patted me paternally on the back.

"Oh, my son," said the monk, "what delectable snuff! Oh, my son and amiable traveller, give the spiritual father who loves you yet another tiny, tiny pinch!"

"Let me fill your box for you. I shall have plenty left for myself."

The battered tin snuff-box was given to me before I had done speaking; the paternal hand patted my back more approvingly than ever; the feeble, husky voice grew glib and eloquent in my praise. I had evidently found out the weak side of the old Capuchin, and, on returning him his box, I took instant advantage of the discovery.

"Excuse my troubling you on the subject again," I said, "but I have particular reasons for wanting to hear all that you can tell me in explanation of that horrible sight in the outhouse."

"Come in," answered the monk.

He drew me inside the gate, closed it, and then leading the way across a grass-grown courtyard, looking out on a weedy kitchen-garden, showed me into a long room with a low ceiling, a dirty dresser, a few rudely-carved stall seats, and one or two grim, mildewed pictures for ornaments. This was the sacristy.

"There's nobody here, and it's nice and cool," said the old Capuchin. It was so damp that I actually shivered. "Would you like to see the church?" said the monk; "a jewel of a church, if we could keep it in repair; but we can't. Ah! malediction and misery, we are too poor to keep our church in repair!"

Here he shook his head and began fumbling with a large bunch of keys.

"Never mind the church now," said I. "Can you, or can you not, tell me what I want to know?"

"Everything, from beginning to end—absolutely everything. Why, I answered the gate-bell—I always answer the gate-bell here," said the Capuchin.

"What, in Heaven's name, has the gate-bell to do with the unburied corpse in your house?"

"Listen, son of mine, and you shall know. Some time ago-some months—ah! me, I'm old; I've lost my memory; I don't know how many months—ah! miserable me, what a very old, old monk I am!" Here he comforted himself with another pinch of snuff.

"Never mind the exact time," said I. "I don't care about that."

"Good," said the Capuchin. "Now I can go on. Well, let us say it is some months ago—we in this convent are all at breakfast-wretched, wretched breakfasts, son of mine, in this convent!-we are at breakfast, and we hear bang! bang! twice over. 'Guns,' says I. 'What are they shooting for?' says Brother Jeremy. 'Game,' says Brother Vincent. 'Aha! game,' says Brother Jeremy. 'If I hear more, I shall send out and discover what it means,' says the father superior. We hear no more, and we go on with our wretched breakfasts."

"Where did the report of firearms come from?" I inquired.

"From down below—beyond the big trees at the back of the convent, where there's some clear ground—nice ground, if it wasn't for the pools and puddles. But, ah! misery, how damp we are in these parts! how very, very damp!"

"Well, what happened after the report of firearms?"

"You shall hear. We are still at breakfast, all silent—for what have we to talk about here? What have we but our devotions, our kitchen-garden, and our wretched, wretched bits of breakfasts and dinners? I say we are all silent, when there comes suddenly such a ring at the bell as never was heard before—a very devil of a ring—a ring that caught us all with our bits—our wretched, wretched bits!—in our mouths, and stopped us before we could swallow them. 'Go, brother of mine,' says the father superior to me, 'go; it is your duty—go to the gate.' I am brave—a very lion of a Capuchin. I slip out on tiptoe—I wait—I listen—I pull back our little shutter in the gate—I wait, I listen again—I peep through the hole—nothing, absolutely nothing that I can see.

"I am brave—I am not to be daunted. What do I do next? I open the gate. Ah! sacred Mother of Heaven, what do I behold lying all along our threshold? A man—dead!—a big man; bigger than you, bigger than me, bigger than anybody in this convent-buttoned up tight in a fine coat, with black eyes, staring, staring up at the sky, and blood soaking through and through the front of his shirt. What do I do? I scream once—I scream twice—and run back to the father superior!"

All the particulars of the fatal duel which I had gleaned from the French newspaper in Monkton's room at Naples recurred vividly to my memory. The suspicion that I had felt when I looked into the outhouse became a certainty as I listened to the old monk's last words.

"So far I understand," said I. "The corpse I have just seen in the outhouse is the corpse of the man whom you found dead outside your gate. Now tell me why you have not given the remains decent burial."

"Wait—wait—wait," answered the Capuchin. "The father superior hears me scream and comes out; we all run together to the gate; we lift up the big man and look at him close. Dead! dead as this (smacking the dresser with his hand). We look again, and see a bit of paper pinned to the collar of his coat. Aha! son of mine, you start at that. I thought I should make you start at last."

I had started, indeed. That paper was doubtless the leaf mentioned in the second's unfinished narrative as having been torn out of his pocketbook, and inscribed with the statement of how the dead man had lost his life. If proof positive were wanted to identify the dead body, here was such proof found.

"What do you think was written on the bit of paper?" continued the Capuchin "We read and shudder. This dead man has been killed in a duel—he, the desperate, the miserable, has died in the commission of mortal sin; and the men who saw the killing of him ask us Capuchins, holy men, servants of Heaven, children of our lord the Pope—they ask us to give him burial! Oh! but we are outraged when we read that; we groan, we wring our hands, we turn away, we tear our beards, we—"

"Wait one moment," said I, seeing that the old man was heating himself with his narrative, and was likely, unless I stopped him, to talk more and more fluently to less and less purpose-"wait a moment. Have you preserved the paper that was pinned to the dead man's coat; and can I look at it?"

The Capuchin seemed on the point of giving me an answer, when he suddenly checked himself. I saw his eyes wander away from my face, and at the same moment heard a door softly opened and closed again behind me.

Looking round immediately, I observed another monk in the sacristy—a tall, lean, black-bearded man, in whose presence my old friend with the snuff-box suddenly became quite decorous and devotional to look at. I suspected I was in the presence of the father superior, and I found that I was right the moment he addressed me.

"I am the father superior of this convent," he said, in quiet, clear tones, and looking me straight in the face while he spoke, with coldly attentive eyes. "I have heard the latter part of your conversation, and I wish to know why you are so particularly anxious to see the piece of paper that was pinned to the dead man's coat?"

The coolness with which he avowed that he had been listening, and the quietly imperative manner in which he put his concluding question, perplexed and startled me. I hardly knew at first what tone I ought to take in answering him. He observed my hesitation, and attributing it to the wrong cause, signed to the old Capuchin to retire. Humbly stroking his long gray beard, and furtively consoling himself with a private pinch of the "delectable snuff," my venerable friend shuffled out of the room, making a profound obeisance at the door just before he disappeared.

"Now," said the father superior, as coldly as ever, "I am waiting, sir, for your reply."

"You shall have it in the fewest possible words," said I, answering him in his own tone. "I find, to my disgust and horror, that there is an unburied corpse in an outhouse attached to your convent. I believe that corpse to be the body of an English gentleman of rank and fortune, who was killed in a duel. I have come into this neighbourhood with the nephew and only relation of the slain man, for the express purpose of recovering his remains; and I wish to see the paper found on the body, because I believe that paper will identify it to the satisfaction of the relative to whom I have referred. Do you find my reply sufficiently straightforward? And do you mean to give me permission to look at the paper?"

"I am satisfied with your reply, and see no reason for refusing you a sight of the paper," said the father superior; "but I have something to say first. In speaking of the impression produced on you by beholding the corpse, you used the words 'disgust' and 'horror.' This license of expression in relation to what you have seen in the precincts of a convent proves to me that you are out of the pale of the Holy Catholic Church. You have no right, therefore, to expect any explanation; but I will give you one, nevertheless, as a favour. The slain man died, unabsolved, in the commission of mortal sin. We infer so much from the paper which we found on his body; and we know, by the evidence of our own eyes and ears, that he was killed on the territories of the Church, and in the act of committing direct violation of those special laws against the crime of duelling, the strict enforcement of which the holy father himself has urged on the faithful throughout his dominions by letters signed with his own hand. Inside this convent the ground is consecrated, and we Catholics are not accustomed to bury the outlaws of our religion, the enemies of our holy father, and the violators of our most sacred laws in consecrated ground. Outside this convent we have no rights and no power; and, if we had both, we should remember that we are monks, not grave-diggers, and that the only burial with which we can have any concern is burial with the prayers of the Church. That is all the explanation I think it necessary to give. Wait for me here, and you shall see the paper." With those words the father superior left the room as quietly as he had entered it.

I had hardly time to think over this bitter and ungracious explanation, and to feel a little piqued by the language and manner of the person who had given it to me, before the father superior returned with the paper in his hand. He placed it before me on the dresser, and I read, hurriedly traced in pencil, the following lines:

> This paper is attached to the body of the late Mr. Stephen Monkton, an Englishman of distinction. He has been shot in a duel, conducted with perfect gallantry and honour on both sides. His body is placed at the door of this convent, to receive burial at the hands of its inmates, the survivors of the encounter being obliged to separate and secure their safety by immediate flight. I, the second of the slain man, and the writer of this explanation, certify, on my word of honour as a gentleman that the shot which killed my principal on the instant was fired fairly, in the strictest accordance with the rules laid down beforehand for the conduct of the duel. (Signed), F.

"F." I recognized easily enough as the initial letter of Monsieur Foulon's name, the second of Mr. Monkton, who had died of consumption at Paris.

The discovery and the identification were now complete. Nothing remained but to break the news to Alfred, and to get permission to remove the remains in the outhouse. I began almost to doubt the evidence of my own senses when I reflected that the apparently impracticable object with which we had left Naples was already, by the merest chance, virtually accomplished.

"The evidence of the paper is decisive," said I, handing it back. "There can be no doubt that the remains in the outhouse are the remains of which we have been in search. May I inquire if any obstacles will be thrown in our way should the late Mr. Monkton's nephew wish to remove his uncle's body to the family burial-place in England?"

"Where is this nephew?" asked the father superior.

"He is now awaiting my return at the town of Fondi."

"Is he in a position to prove his relationship?"

"Certainly; he has papers with him which will place it beyond a doubt."

"Let him satisfy the civil authorities of his claim, and he need expect no obstacle to his wishes from any one here."

I was in no humour for talking a moment longer with my sour-tempered companion than I could help. The day was wearing on me fast; and, whether night overtook me or not, I was resolved never to stop on my return till I got back to Fondi. Accordingly, after telling the father superior that he might expect to hear from me again immediately, I made my bow and hastened out of the sacristy.

At the convent gate stood my old friend with the tin snuff-box, waiting to let me out.

"Bless you, may son," said the venerable recluse, giving me a farewell pat on the shoulder, "come back soon to your spiritual father who loves you, and amiably favour him with another tiny, tiny pinch of the delectable snuff."

Chapter 6

I returned at the top of my speed to the village where I had left the mules, had the animals saddled immediately, and succeeded in getting back to Fondi a little before sunset.

While ascending the stairs of our hotel, I suffered under the most painful uncertainty as to how I should best communicate the news of my discovery to Alfred. If I could not succeed in preparing him properly for my tidings, the results, with such an organization as his, might be fatal. On opening the door of his room, I felt by no means sure of myself; and when I confronted him, his manner of receiving me took me so much by surprise that, for a moment or two, I lost my self-possession altogether.

Every trace of the lethargy in which he was sunk when I had last seen him had disappeared. His eyes were bright, his cheeks deeply flushed. As I entered, he started up, and refused my offered hand.

"You have not treated me like a friend," he said, passionately; "you had no right to continue the search unless I searched with you—you had no right to leave me here alone. I was wrong to trust you; you are no better than all the rest of them."

I had by this time recovered a little from my first astonishment, and was able to reply before he could say anything more. It was quite useless, in his present state, to reason with him or to defend myself. I determined to risk everything, and break my news to him at once.

"You will treat me more justly, Monkton, when you know that I have been doing you good service during my absence," I said. "Unless I am greatly mistaken, the object for which we have left Naples may be nearer attainment by both of us than—"

The flush left his cheeks almost in an instant. Some expression in my face, or some tone in my voice, of which I was not conscious, had revealed to his nervously-quickened perception more than I had intended that he should know at first. His eyes fixed themselves intently on mine; his hand grasped my arm; and he said to me in an eager whisper:

"Tell me the truth at once. Have you found him?"

It was too late to hesitate. I answered in the affirmative.

"Buried or unburied?"

His voice rose abruptly as he put the question, and his unoccupied hand fastened on my other arm.

"Unburied."

I had hardly uttered the word before the blood flew back into his cheeks; his eyes flashed again as they looked into mine, and he burst into a fit of triumphant laughter, which shocked and startled me inexpressibly.

"What did I tell you? What do you say to the old prophecy now?" he cried, dropping his hold on my arms, and pacing backward and forward in the room. "Own you were wrong. Own it, as all Naples shall own it, when once I have got him safe in his coffin!"

His laughter grew more and more violent. I tried to quiet him in vain. His servant and the landlord of the inn entered the room, but they only added fuel to the fire, and I made them go out again. As I shut the door on them, I observed lying on a table near at hand the packet of letters from Miss Elmslie, which my unhappy friend preserved with such care, and read and reread with such unfailing devotion.

Looking toward me just when I passed by the table, the letters caught his eye. The new hope for the future, in connection with the writer of them, which my news was already awakening in his heart, seemed to overwhelm him in an instant at sight of the treasured memorials that reminded him of his betrothed wife. His laughter ceased, his face changed, he ran to the table, caught the letters up in his hand, looked from them to me for one moment with an altered expression which went to my heart, then sank down on his knees at the table, laid his face on the letters, and burst into tears.

I let the new emotion have its way uninterruptedly, and quitted the room without saying a word. When I returned after a lapse of some little time, I found him sitting quietly in his chair, reading one of the letters from the packet which rested on his knee.

His look was kindness itself; his gesture almost womanly in its gentleness as he rose to meet me, and anxiously held out his hand.

He was quite calm enough now to hear in detail all that I had to tell him. I suppressed nothing but the particulars of the state in which I had found the corpse. I assumed no right of direction as to the share he was to take in our future proceedings, with the exception of insisting beforehand that he should leave the absolute superintendence of the removal of the body to me, and that he should be satisfied with a sight of M. Foulon's paper, after receiving my assurance that the remains placed in the coffin were really and truly the remains of which we had been in search.

"Your nerves are not so strong as mine," I said, by way of apology for my apparent dictation, "and for that reason I must beg leave to assume the leadership in all that we have now to do, until I see the leaden coffin soldered down and safe in your possession. After that I shall resign all my functions to you."

"I want words to thank you for your kindness," he answered. "No brother could have borne with me more affectionately, or helped me more patiently than you."

He stopped and grew thoughtful, then occupied himself in tying up slowly and carefully the packet of Miss Elmslie's letters, and then looked suddenly toward the vacant wall behind me with that strange expression the meaning of which I knew so well. Since we had left Naples I had purposely avoided exciting him by talking on the useless and shocking subject of the apparition by which he believed himself to be perpetually followed. Just now, however, he seemed so calm and collected—so little likely to be violently agitated by any allusion to the dangerous topic, that I ventured to speak out boldly.

"Does the phantom still appear to you," I asked, "as it appeared at Naples?"

He looked at me and smiled.

"Did I not tell you that it followed me everywhere?"

His eyes wandered back again to the vacant space, and he went on speaking in that direction as if he had been continuing the conversation with some third person in the room. "We shall part," he said, slowly and softly, "when the empty place is filled in Wincot vault. Then I shall stand with Ada before the altar in the Abbey chapel, and when my eyes meet hers they will see the tortured face no more."

Saying this, he leaned his head on his hand, sighed, and began repeating softly to himself the lines of the old prophecy:

When in Wincot vault a place
Waits for one of Monkton's race—
When that one forlorn shall lie
Graveless under open sky,
Beggared of six feet of earth,
Though lord of acres from his birth—
That shall be a certain sign
Of the end of Monktons line.
Dwindling ever faster, faster,
Dwindling to the last-left master;
From mortal ken, from light of day,
Monkton's race shall pass away.

Fancying that he pronounced the last lines a little incoherently, I tried to make him change the subject. He took no notice of what I said, and went on talking to himself.

"Monkton's race shall pass away," he repeated, "but not with me. The fatality hangs over my head no longer. I shall bury the unburied dead; I shall fill the vacant place in Wincot vault; and then—then the new life, the life with Ada!" That name seemed to recall him to himself. He drew his travelling desk toward him, placed the packet of letters in it, and then took out a sheet of paper. "I am going to write to Ada," he said, turning to me, "and tell her the good news. Her happiness, when she knows it, will be even greater than mine."

Worn out by the events of the day, I left him writing and went to bed. I was, however, either too anxious or too tired to sleep. In this waking condition, my mind naturally occupied itself with the discovery at the convent and with the events to which that discovery would in all probability lead. As I thought on the future, a depression for which I could not account weighed on my spirits. There was not the slightest reason for the vaguely melancholy forebodings that oppressed me.

The remains, to the finding of which my unhappy friend attached so much importance, had been traced; they would certainly be placed at his disposal in a few days; he might take them to England by the first merchant vessel that sailed from Naples; and, the gratification of his strange caprice thus accomplished, there was at least some reason to hope that his mind might recover its tone, and that the new life he would lead at Wincot might result in making him a happy man.

Such considerations as these were, in themselves, certainly not calculated to exert any melancholy influence over me; and yet, all through the night, the same inconceivable, unaccountable depression weighed heavily on my spirits—heavily through the hours of darkness—heavily, even when I walked out to breathe the first freshness of the early morning air.

With the day came the all-engrossing business of opening negotiations with the authorities.

Only those who have had to deal with Italian officials can imagine how our patience was tried by everyone with whom we came in contact. We were bandied about from one authority to the other, were stared at, cross-questioned, mystified—not in the least because the case presented any special difficulties or intricacies, but because it was absolutely necessary that every civil dignitary to whom we applied should assert his own importance by leading us to our object in the most roundabout manner possible. After our first day's experience of official life in Italy, I left the absurd formalities, which we had no choice but to perform, to be accomplished by Alfred alone, and applied myself to the really serious question of how the remains in the convent outhouse were to be safely removed.

The best plan that suggested itself to me was to write to a friend in Rome, where I knew that it was a custom to embalm the bodies of high dignitaries of the Church, and where, I consequently inferred, such chemical assistance as was needed in our emergency might be obtained. I simply stated in my letter that the removal of the body was imperative, then described the condition in which I had found it, and engaged that no expense on our part should be spared if the right person or persons could be found to help us.

Here, again, more difficulties interposed themselves, and more useless formalities were to be gone through, but in the end patience, perseverance, and money triumphed, and two men came expressly from Rome to undertake the duties we required of them.

It is unnecessary that I should shock the reader by entering into any detail in this part of my narrative. When I have said that the progress of decay was so far suspended by chemical means as to allow of the remains being placed in the coffin, and to insure their being transported to England with perfect safety and convenience, I have said enough. After ten days had been wasted in useless delays and difficulties, I had the satisfaction of seeing the convent outhouse empty at last; passed through a final ceremony of snuff-taking, or rather, of snuff-giving, with the old Capuchin, and ordered the travelling carriages to be ready at the inn door. Hardly a month had elapsed since our departure ere we entered Naples successful in the achievement of a design which had been ridiculed as wildly impracticable by every friend of ours who had heard of it.

The first object to be accomplished on our return was to obtain the means of carrying the coffin to England—by sea, as a matter of course. All inquiries after a merchant vessel on the point of sailing for any British port led to the most unsatisfactory results. There was only one way of insuring the immediate transportation of the remains to England, and that was to hire a vessel.

Impatient to return, and resolved not to lose sight of the coffin till he had seen it placed in Wincot vault, Monkton decided immediately on hiring the first ship that could be obtained. The vessel in port which we were informed could soonest be got ready for sea was a Sicilian brig, and this vessel my friend accordingly engaged. The best dock-yard artisans that could be got were set to work, and the smartest captain and crew to be picked up on an emergency in Naples were chosen to navigate the brig.

Monkton, after again expressing in the warmest terms his gratitude for the services I had rendered him, disclaimed any intention of asking me to accompany him on the voyage to England. Greatly to his surprise and delight, however, I offered of my own accord to take passage in the brig. The strange coincidences I had witnessed, the extraordinary discovery I had hit on since our first meeting in Naples, had made his one great interest in life my one great interest for the time being as well. I shared none of his delusions, poor fellow; but it is hardly an exaggeration to say that my eagerness to follow our remarkable adventure to its end was as great as his anxiety to see the coffin laid in Wincot vault. Curiosity influenced me, I am afraid, almost as strongly as friendship, when I offered myself as the companion of his voyage home.

We set sail for England on a calm and lovely afternoon.

For the first time since I had known him, Monkton seemed to be in high spirits. He talked and jested on all sorts of subjects, and laughed at me for allowing my cheerfulness to be affected by the dread of seasickness. I had really no such fear; it was my excuse to my friend for a return of that unaccountable depression under which I had suffered at Fondi. Everything was in our favour; everybody on board the brig was in good spirits. The captain was delighted with the vessel; the crew, Italians and Maltese, were in high glee at the prospect of making a short voyage on high wages in a well-provisioned ship. I alone felt heavy at heart. There was no valid reason that I could assign to myself for the melancholy that oppressed me, and yet I struggled against it in vain.

Late on our first night at sea, I made a discovery which was by no means calculated to restore my spirits to their usual equilibrium. Monkton was in the cabin, on the floor of which had been placed the packing-case containing the coffin, and I was on deck. The wind had fallen almost to a calm, and I was lazily watching the sails of the brig as they flapped from time to time against the masts, when the captain approached, and, drawing me out of hearing of the man at the helm, whispered in my ear:

"There's something wrong among the men forward. Did you observe how suddenly they all became silent just before sunset?"

I had observed it, and told him so.

"There's a Maltese boy on board," pursued the captain, "who is a smart enough lad, but a bad one to deal with. I have found out that he has been telling the men there is a dead body inside that packing-case of your friend's in the cabin."

My heart sank as he spoke. Knowing the superstitious irrationality of sailors—of foreign sailors especially—I had taken care to spread a report on board the brig, before the coffin was shipped, that the packing-case contained a valuable marble statue which Mr. Monkton prized highly, and was unwilling to trust out of his own sight. How could this Maltese boy have discovered that the pretended statue was a human corpse? As I pondered over the question, my suspicions fixed themselves on Monkton's servant, who spoke Italian fluently, and whom I knew to be an incorrigible gossip. The man denied it when I charged him with betraying us, but I have never believed his denial to this day.

"The little imp won't say where he picked up this notion of his about the dead body," continued the captain. "It's not my place to pry into secrets; but I advise you to call the crew aft, and contradict the boy, whether he speaks the truth or not. The men are a parcel of fools who believe in ghosts, and all the rest of it. Some of them say they would never have signed our articles if they had known they were going to sail with a dead man; others only grumble; but I'm afraid we shall have some trouble with them all, in case of rough weather, unless the boy is contradicted by you or the other gentleman.

"The men say that if either you or your friend tell them on

your words of honour that the Maltese is a liar, they will hand him up to be rope's-ended accordingly; but that if you won't, they have made up their minds to believe the boy."

Here the captain paused and awaited my answer. I could give him none. I felt hopeless under our desperate emergency. To get the boy punished by giving my word of honour to support a direct falsehood was not to be thought of even for a moment. What other means of extrication from this miserable dilemma remained? None that I could think of. I thanked the captain for his attention to our interests, told him I would take time to consider what course I should pursue, and begged that he would say nothing to my friend about the discovery he had made. He promised to be silent, sulkily enough, and walked away from me.

We had expected the breeze to spring up with the morning, but no breeze came. As it wore on toward noon the atmosphere became insufferably sultry, and the sea looked as smooth as glass. I saw the captain's eye turn often and anxiously to windward. Far away in that direction, and alone in the blue heaven, I observed a little black cloud, and asked if it would bring us any wind.

"More than we want," the captain replied, shortly; and then, to my astonishment, ordered the crew aloft to take in sail. The execution of this manoeuvre showed but too plainly the temper of the men; they did their work sulkily and slowly, grumbling and murmuring among themselves. The captain's manner, as he urged them on with oaths and threats, convinced me we were in danger. I looked again to windward. The one little cloud had enlarged to a great bank of murky vapour, and the sea at the horizon had changed in colour.

"The squall will be on us before we know where we are," said the captain. "Go below; you will be only in the way here."

I descended to the cabin, and prepared Monkton for what was coming. He was still questioning me about what I had observed on deck when the storm burst on us. We felt the little brig strain for an instant as if she would part in two, then she seemed to be swinging round with us, then to be quite still for a moment, trembling in every timber. Last came a shock which hurled us from our seats, a deafening crash, and a flood of water pouring into the cabin. We clambered, half drowned, to the deck. The brig had, in the nautical phrase, "broached to," and she now lay on her beam-ends.

Before I could make out anything distinctly in the horrible confusion except the one tremendous certainty that we were entirely at the mercy of the sea, I heard a voice from the fore part of the ship which stilled the clamouring and shouting of the rest of the crew in an instant. The words were in Italian, but I understood their fatal meaning only too easily. We had sprung a leak, and the sea was pouring into the ship's hold like the race of a mill-stream. The captain did not lose his presence of mind in this fresh emergency. He called for his axe to cut away the foremast, and, ordering some of the crew to help him, directed the others to rig out the pumps.

The words had hardly passed his lips before the men broke into open mutiny. With a savage look at me, their ringleader declared that the passengers might do as they pleased, but that he and his messmates were determined to take to the boat, and leave the accursed ship, and the dead man in her, to go to the bottom together. As he spoke there was a shout among the sailors, and I observed some of them pointing derisively behind me.

Looking round, I saw Monkton, who had hitherto kept close at my side, making his way back to the cabin. I followed him directly, but the water and confusion on deck, and the impossibility, from the position of the brig, of moving the feet without the slow assistance of the hands, so impeded my progress that it was impossible for me to overtake him. When I had got below he was crouched upon the coffin, with the water on the cabin floor whirling and splashing about him as the ship heaved and plunged. I saw a warning brightness in his eyes, a warning flush on his cheek, as I approached and said to him:

"There is nothing left for it, Alfred, but to bow to our misfortune, and do the best we can to save our lives."

"Save yours," he cried, waving his hand to me, "for you have a future before you. Mine is gone when this coffin goes to the bottom. If the ship sinks, I shall know that the fatality is accomplished, and shall sink with her."

I saw that he was in no state to be reasoned with or persuaded, and raised myself again to the deck. The men were cutting away all obstacles so as to launch the longboat placed amidships over the depressed bulwark of the brig as she lay on her side, and the captain, after having made a last vain exertion to restore his authority, was looking on at them in silence. The violence of the squall seemed already to be spending itself, and I asked whether there was really no chance for us if we remained by the ship.

The captain answered that there might have been the best chance if the men had obeyed his orders, but that now there was none. Knowing that I could place no dependence on the presence of mind of Monkton's servant, I confided to the captain, in the fewest and plainest words, the condition of my unhappy friend, and asked if I might depend on his help. He nodded his head, and we descended together to the cabin. Even at this day it costs me pain to write of the terrible necessity to which the strength and obstinacy of Monkton's delusion reduced us in the last resort. We were compelled to secure his hands, and drag him by main force to the deck. The men were on the point of launching the boat, and refused at first to receive us into it.

"You cowards!" cried the captain, "have we got the dead man with us this time? Isn't he going to the bottom along with the brig? Who are you afraid of when we get into the boat?"

This sort of appeal produced the desired effect; the men became ashamed of themselves, and retracted their refusal.

Just as we pushed off from the sinking ship Alfred made an effort to break from me, but I held him firm, and he never repeated the attempt. He sat by me with drooping head, still and silent, while the sailors rowed away from the vessel; still and silent when, with one accord, they paused at a little distance off, and we all waited and watched to see the brig sink; still and silent, even when that sinking happened, when the labouring hull plunged slowly into a hollow of the sea—hesitated, as it seemed, for one moment, rose a little again, then sank to rise no more.

Sank with her dead freight—sank, and snatched forever from our power the corpse which we had discovered almost by a miracle—those jealously-preserved remains, on the safe-keeping of which rested so strangely the hopes and the love-destinies of two living beings! As the last signs of the ship in the depths of the waters.

I felt Monkton trembling all over as he sat close at my side, and heard him repeating to himself, sadly, and many times over, the name of "Ada."

I tried to turn his thoughts to another subject, but it was useless. He pointed over the sea to where the brig had once been, and where nothing was left to look at but the rolling waves.

"The empty place will now remain empty forever in Wincot vault."

As he said these words, he fixed his eyes for a moment sadly and earnestly on my face, then looked away, leaned his cheek on his hand, and spoke no more.

We were sighted long before nightfall by a trading vessel, were taken on board, and landed at Cartagena in Spain. Alfred never held up his head, and never once spoke to me of his own accord the whole time we were at sea in the merchantman. I observed, however, with alarm, that he talked often and incoherently to himself—constantly muttering the lines of the old prophecy-constantly referring to the fatal place that was empty in Wincot vault—constantly repeating in broken accents, which it affected me inexpressibly to hear, the name of the poor girl who was awaiting his return to England.

Nor were these the only causes for the apprehension that I now felt on his account. Toward the end of our voyage he began to suffer from alternations of fever-fits and shivering-fits, which I ignorantly imagined to be attacks of ague. I was soon undeceived. We had hardly been a day on shore before he became so much worse that I secured the best medical assistance Cartagena could afford. For a day or two the doctors differed, as usual, about the nature of his complaint, but ere long alarming symptoms displayed themselves. The medical men declared that his life was in danger, and told me that his disease was brain fever.

Shocked and grieved as I was, I hardly knew how to act at first under the fresh responsibility now laid upon me. Ultimately I decided on writing to the old priest who had been Alfred's tutor, and who, as I knew, still resided at Wincot Abbey. I told this gentleman all that had happened, begged him to break my melancholy news as gently as possible to Miss Elmslie, and assured him of my resolution to remain with Monkton to the last.

After I had dispatched my letter, and had sent to Gibraltar to secure the best English medical advice that could be obtained, I felt that I had done my best, and that nothing remained but to wait and hope.

Many a sad and anxious hour did I pass by my poor friend's bedside. Many a time did I doubt whether I had done right in giving any encouragement to his delusion. The reasons for doing so which had suggested themselves to me after my first interview with him seemed, however, on reflection, to be valid reasons still. The only way of hastening his return to England and to Miss Elmslie, who was pining for that return, was the way I had taken. It was not my fault that a disaster which no man could foresee had overthrown all his projects and all mine. But, now that the calamity had happened and was irretrievable, how, in the event of his physical recovery, was his moral malady to be combated?

When I reflected on the hereditary taint in his mental organization, on that first childish fright of Stephen Monkton from which he had never recovered, on the perilously-secluded life that he had led at the Abbey, and on his firm persuasion of the reality of the apparition by which he believed himself to be constantly followed, I confess I despaired of shaking his superstitious faith in every word and line of the old family prophecy.

If the series of striking coincidences which appeared to attest its truth had made a strong and lasting impression on me (and this was assuredly the case), how could I wonder that they had produced the effect of absolute conviction on his mind, constituted as it was? If I argued with him, and he answered me, how could I rejoin? If he said, "The prophecy points at the last of the family: I am the last of the family. The prophecy mentions an empty place in Wincot vault; there is such an empty place there at this moment. On the faith of the prophecy I told you that Stephen Monkton's body was unburied, and you found that it was unburied"—if he said this, what use would it be for me to reply, "These are only strange coincidences after all?"

The more I thought of the task that lay before me, if he recovered, the more I felt inclined to despond. The oftener the English physician who attended on him said to me, "He may get the better of the fever, but he has a fixed idea, which never leaves him night or day, which has unsettled his reason, and which will end in killing him, unless you or some of his friends can remove it"—the oftener I heard this, the more acutely I felt my own powerlessness, the more I shrank from every idea that was connected with the hopeless future.

I had only expected to receive my answer from Wincot in the shape of a letter. It was consequently a great surprise, as well as a great relief, to be informed one day that two gentlemen wished to speak with me, and to find that of these two gentlemen the first was the old priest, and the second a male relative of Mrs. Elmslie.

Just before their arrival the fever symptoms had disappeared, and Alfred had been pronounced out of danger. Both the priest and his companion were eager to know when the sufferer would be strong enough to travel. They had come to Cartagena expressly to take him home with them, and felt far more hopeful than I did of the restorative effects of his native air. After all the questions connected with the first important point of the journey to England had been asked and answered, I ventured to make some inquiries after Miss Elmslie.

Her relative informed me that she was suffering both in body and in mind from excess of anxiety on Alfred's account. They had been obliged to deceive her as to the dangerous nature of his illness in order to deter her from accompanying the priest and her relation on their mission to Spain.

Slowly and imperfectly, as the weeks wore on, Alfred regained something of his former physical strength, but no alteration appeared in his illness as it affected his mind.

From the very first day of his advance toward recovery, it had been discovered that the brain fever had exercised the strangest influence over his faculties of memory. All recollection of recent events was gone from him. Everything connected with Naples, with me, with his journey to Italy, had dropped in some mysterious manner entirely out of his remembrance. So completely had all late circumstances passed from his memory that, though he recognized the old priest and his own servant easily on the first days of his convalescence, he never recognized me, but regarded me with such a wistful, doubting expression, that I felt inexpressibly pained when I approached his bedside. All his questions were about Miss Elmslie and Wincot Abbey, and all his talk referred to the period when his father was yet alive.

The doctors augured good rather than ill from this loss of memory of recent incidents, saying that it would turn out to be temporary, and that it answered the first great healing purpose of keeping his mind at ease. I tried to believe them—tried to feel as sanguine, when the day came for his departure, as the old friends felt who were taking him home. But the effort was too much for me. A foreboding that I should never see him again oppressed my heart, and the tears came into my eyes as I saw the worn figure of my poor friend half helped, half lifted into the travelling-carriage, and borne away gently on the road toward home.

He had never recognized me, and the doctors had begged that I would give him, for some time to come, as few opportunities as possible of doing so. But for this request I should have accompanied him to England. As it was, nothing better remained for me to do than to change the scene, and recruit as I best could my energies of body and mind, depressed of late by much watching and anxiety. The famous cities of Spain were not new to me, but I visited them again and revived old impressions of the Alhambra and Madrid. Once or twice I thought of making a pilgrimage to the East, but late events had sobered and altered me. That yearning, unsatisfied feeling which we call "homesickness" began to prey upon my heart, and I resolved to return to England.

I went back by way of Paris, having settled with the priest that he should write to me at my banker's there as soon as he could after Alfred had returned to Wincot. If I had gone to the East, the letter would have been forwarded to me. I wrote to prevent this; and, on my arrival at Paris, stopped at the banker's before I went to my hotel.

The moment the letter was put into my hands, the black border on the envelope told me the worst. He was dead.

There was but one consolation—he had died calmly, almost happily, without once referring to those fatal chances which had wrought the fulfilment of the ancient prophecy. "My beloved pupil," the old priest wrote, "seemed to rally a little the first few days after his return, but he gained no real strength, and soon suffered a slight relapse of fever. After this he sank gradually and gently day by day, and so departed from us on the last dread journey.

Miss Elmslie (who knows that I am writing this) desires me to express her deep and lasting gratitude for all your kindness to Alfred. She told me when we brought him back that she had waited for him as his promised wife, and that she would nurse him now as a wife should; and she never left him. His face was turned toward her, his hand was clasped in hers when he died. It will console you to know that he never mentioned events at Naples, or the shipwreck that followed them, from the day of his return to the day of his death."

Three days after reading the letter I was at Wincot, and heard all the details of Alfred's last moments from the priest. I felt a shock which it would not be very easy for me to analyze or explain when I heard that he had been buried, at his own desire, in the fatal Abbey vault.

The priest took me down to see the place—a grim, cold,

subterranean building, with a low roof, supported on heavy Saxon arches. Narrow niches, with the ends only of coffins visible within them, ran down each side of the vault. The nails and silver ornaments flashed here and there as my companion moved past them with a lamp in his hand. At the lower end of the place he stopped, pointed to a niche, and said, "He lies there, between his father and mother." I looked a little further on, and saw what appeared at first like a long dark tunnel. "That is only an empty niche," said the priest, following me. "If the body of Mr. Stephen Monkton had been brought to Wincot, his coffin would have been placed there."

A chill came over me, and a sense of dread which I am ashamed of having felt now, but which I could not combat then. The blessed light of day was pouring down gaily at the other end of the vault through the open door. I turned my back on the empty niche, and hurried into the sunlight and the fresh air.

As I walked across the grass glade leading down to the vault, I heard the rustle of a woman's dress behind me, and turning round, saw a young lady advancing, clad in deep mourning. Her sweet, sad face, her manner as she held out her hand, told me who it was in an instant.

"I heard that you were here," she said, "and I wished—" Her voice faltered a little. My heart ached as I saw how her lip trembled, but before I could say anything she recovered herself and went on: "I wished to take your hand, and thank you for your brotherly kindness to Alfred; and I wanted to tell you that I am sure in all you did you acted tenderly and considerately for the best. Perhaps you may be soon going away from home again, and we may not meet any more. I shall never, never forget that you were kind to him when he wanted a friend, and that you have the greatest claim of any one on earth to be gratefully remembered in my thoughts as long as I live."

The inexpressible tenderness of her voice, trembling a little all the while she spoke, the pale beauty of her face, the artless candour in her sad, quiet eyes, so affected me that I could not trust myself to answer her at first except by gesture. Before I recovered my voice she had given me her hand once more and had left me.

I never saw her again. The chances and changes of life kept us apart. When I last heard of her, years and years ago, she was faithful to the memory of the dead, and was Ada Elmslie still for Alfred Monkton's sake.

Brother Morgan's Story of

The Dead Hand

When this present nineteenth century was younger by a good many years than it is now, a certain friend of mine, named Arthur Holliday, happened to arrive in the town of Doncaster exactly in the middle of the race-week, or, in other words, in the middle of the month of September.

He was one of those reckless, rattle-pated, open-hearted, and open-mouthed young gentlemen who possess the gift of familiarity in its highest perfection, and who scramble carelessly along the journey of life, making friends, as the phrase is, wherever they go. His father was a rich manufacturer, and had bought landed property enough in one of the midland counties to make all the born squires in his neighbourhood thoroughly envious of him.

Arthur was his only son, possessor in prospect of the great estate and the great business after his father's death; well supplied with money, and not too rigidly looked after during his father's lifetime. Report, or scandal, whichever you please, said that the old gentleman had been rather wild in his youthful days, and that, unlike most parents, he was not disposed to be violently indignant when he found that his son took after him. This may be true or not. I myself only knew the elder Mr. Holliday when he was getting on in years, and then he was as quiet and as respectable a gentleman as ever I met with.

Well, one September, as I told you, young Arthur comes to Doncaster, having decided all of a sudden, in his hare-brained way, that he would go to the races. He did not reach the town till toward the close of evening, and he went at once to see about his dinner and bed at the principal hotel. Dinner they were ready enough to give him, but as for a bed, they laughed when he mentioned it.

In the race-week at Doncaster it is no uncommon thing for visitors who have not bespoken apartments to pass the night in their carriages at the inn doors. As for the lower sort of strangers, I myself have often seen them, at that full time, sleeping out on the doorsteps for want of a covered place to creep under. Rich as he was, Arthur's chance of getting a night's lodging (seeing that he had not written beforehand to secure one) was more than doubtful. He tried the second hotel, and the third hotel, and two of the inferior inns after that, and was met everywhere with the same form of answer. No accommodation for the night of any sort was left. All the bright golden sovereigns in his pocket would not buy him a bed at Doncaster in the race-week.

To a young fellow of Arthur's temperament, the novelty of being turned away into the street like a penniless vagabond, at every house where he asked for a lodging, presented itself in the light of a new and highly amusing piece of experience. He went on with his carpet-bag in his hand, applying for a bed at every place of entertainment for travellers that he could find in Doncaster, until he wandered into the outskirts of the town.

By this time the last glimmer of twilight had faded out, the moon was rising dimly in a mist, the wind was getting cold, the clouds were gathering heavily, and there was every prospect that it was soon going to rain!

The look of the night had rather a lowering effect on young Holliday's spirits. He began to contemplate the houseless situation in which he was placed from the serious rather than the humorous point of view, and he looked about him for another public house to inquire at with something very like downright anxiety in his mind on the subject of a lodging for the night.

The suburban part of the town toward which he had now strayed was hardly lighted at all, and he could see nothing of the houses as he passed them, except that they got progressively smaller and dirtier the further he went. Down the winding road before him shone the dull gleam of an oil lamp, the one faint lonely light that struggled ineffectually with the foggy darkness all round him. He resolved to go on as far as this lamp, and then, if it showed him nothing in the shape of an inn, to return to the central part of the town, and to try if he could not at least secure a chair to sit down on through the night at one of the principal hotels.

As he got near the lamp he heard voices, and, walking close under it, found that it lighted the entrance to a narrow court, on the wall of which was painted a long hand in faded flesh-colour, pointing, with a lean forefinger, to this inscription:

The Two Robins.

Arthur turned into the court without hesitation to see what The Two Robins could do for him. Four or five men were standing together round the door of the house, which was at the bottom of the court, facing the entrance from the street. The men were all listening to one other man, better dressed than the rest, who was telling his audience something, in a low voice, in which they were apparently very much interested.

On entering the passage, Arthur was passed by a stranger with a knapsack in his hand, who was evidently leaving the house.

"No," said the traveller with the knapsack, turning round and addressing himself cheerfully to a fat, sly-looking, bald-headed man, with a dirty white apron on, who had followed him down the passage, "no, Mr. Landlord, I am not easily scared by trifles; but I don't mind confessing that I can't quite stand that."

It occurred to young Holliday, the moment he heard these words, that the stranger had been asked an exorbitant price for a bed at The Two Robins, and that he was unable or unwilling to pay it. The moment his back was turned, Arthur, comfortably conscious of his own well-filled pockets, addressed himself in a great hurry, for fear any other benighted traveller should slip in and forestall him, to the sly-looking landlord with the dirty apron and the bald head.

"If you have got a bed to let," he said, "and if that gentleman who has just gone out won't pay your price for it, I will."

The sly landlord looked hard at Arthur. "Will you, sir?" he asked, in a meditative, doubtful way.

"Name your price," said young Holliday, thinking that the landlord's hesitation sprang from some boorish distrust of him. "Name your price, and I'll give you the money at once, if you like."

"Are you game for five shillings?" inquired the landlord, rubbing his stubby double chin and looking up thoughtfully at the ceiling above him.

Arthur nearly laughed in the man's face; but, thinking it prudent to control himself, offered the five shillings as seriously as he could. The sly landlord held out his hand, then suddenly drew it back again.

"You're acting all fair and aboveboard by me," he said, "and, before I take your money, I'll do the same by you. Look here; this is how it stands. You can have a bed all to yourself for five shillings, but you can't have more than a half share of the room it stands in. Do you see what I mean, young gentleman?"

"Of course I do," returned Arthur, a little irritably. "You mean that it is a double-bedded room, and that one of the beds is occupied?"

The land lord nodded his head, and rubbed his double chin harder than ever. Arthur hesitated, and mechanically moved back a step or two toward the door. The idea of sleeping in the same room with a total stranger did not present an attractive prospect to him. He felt more than half inclined to drop his five shillings into his pocket and to go out into the street once more.

"Is it yes or no?" asked the landlord. "Settle it as quick as you can, because there's lots of people wanting a bed at Doncaster tonight besides you."

Arthur looked toward the court and heard the rain falling heavily in the street outside. He thought he would ask a question or two before he rashly decided on leaving the shelter of The Two Robins.

"What sort of man is it who has got the other bed?" he inquired. "Is he a gentleman? I mean, is he a quiet, well-behaved person?"

"The quietest man I ever came across," said the landlord, rubbing his fat hands stealthily one over the other. "As sober as a judge, and as regular as clock-work in his habits. It hasn't struck nine, not ten minutes ago, and he's in his bed already. I don't know whether that comes up to your notion of a quiet man: it goes a long way ahead of mine, I can tell you."

"Is he asleep, do you think?" asked Arthur.

"I know he's asleep," returned the landlord; "and, what's more, he's gone off so fast that I'll warrant you don't wake him. This way, sir," said the landlord, speaking over young Holliday's shoulder, as if he was addressing some new guest who was approaching the house.

"Here you are," said Arthur, determined to be beforehand with the stranger, whoever he might be. "I'll take the bed." And he handed the five shillings to the landlord, who nodded, dropped the money carelessly into his waistcoat pocket, and lighted a candle.

"Come up and see the room," said the host ofThe Two Robins, leading the way to the staircase quite briskly, considering how fat he was.

They mounted to the second floor of the house. The landlord half opened a door fronting the landing, then stopped, and turned round to Arthur.

"It's a fair bargain, mind, on my side as well as on yours," he said. "You give me five shillings, and I give you in return a clean, comfortable bed; and I warrant, beforehand, that you won't be interfered with, or annoyed in anyway, by the man who sleeps in the same room with you." Saying those words, he looked hard, for a moment, in young Holliday's face, and then led the way into the room.

It was larger and cleaner than Arthur had expected it would be. The two beds stood parallel with each other, a space of about six feet intervening between them. They were both of the same medium size, and both had the same plain white curtains, made to draw, if necessary, all round them.

The occupied bed was the bed nearest the window. The curtains were all drawn round it except the half curtain at the bottom, on the side of the bed furthest from the window. Arthur saw the feet of the sleeping man raising the scanty clothes into a sharp little eminence, as if he was lying flat on his back. He took the candle, and advanced softly to draw the curtain—stopped half way, and listened for a moment—then turned to the landlord.

"He is a very quiet sleeper," said Arthur.

"Yes," said the landlord, "very quiet."

Young Holliday advanced with the candle, and looked in at the man cautiously.

"How pale he is," said Arthur.

"Yes," returned the landlord, "pale enough, isn't he?"

Arthur looked closer at the man. The bedclothes were drawn up to his chin, and they lay perfectly still over the region of his chest. Surprised and vaguely startled as he noticed this, Arthur stooped down closer over the stranger, looked at his ashy, parted lips, listened breathlessly for an instant, looked again at the strangely still face, and the motionless lips and chest, and turned round suddenly on the landlord with his own cheeks as pale for the moment as the hollow cheeks of the man on the bed.

"Come here," he whispered, under his breath. "Come here, for God's sake! The man's not asleep—he is dead."

"You have found that out sooner than I thought you would," said the landlord, composedly. "Yes, he's dead, sure enough. He died at five o'clock today."

"How did he die? Who is he?" asked Arthur, staggered for the moment by the audacious coolness of the answer.

"As to who is he," rejoined the landlord, "I know no more about him than you do. There are his books, and letters, and things all sealed up in that brown paper parcel for the coroner's inquest to open tomorrow or next day. He's been here a week, paying his way fairly enough, and stopping indoors, for the most part, as if he was ailing. My girl brought him up his tea at five today, and as he was pouring of it out, he fell down in a faint, or a fit, or a compound of both, for anything I know. We couldn't bring him to, and I said he was dead. And, the doctor couldn't bring him to, and the doctor said he was dead. And there he is. And the coroner's inquest's coming as soon as it can. And that's as much as I know about it."

Arthur held the candle close to the man's lips. The flame still burned straight up as steadily as ever. There was a moment of silence, and the rain pattered drearily through it against the panes of the window.

"If you haven't got nothing more to say to me," continued the landlord, "I suppose I may go. You don't expect your five shillings back, do you? There's the bed I promised you, clean and comfortable. There's the man I warranted not to disturb you, quiet in this world forever. If you're frightened to stop alone with him, that's not my lookout. I've kept my part of the bargain, and I mean to keep the money. I'm not Yorkshire myself, young gentleman, but I've lived long enough in these parts to have my wits sharpened, and I shouldn't wonder if you found out the way to brighten up yours next time you come among us."

With these words the landlord turned toward the door, and laughed to himself softly, in high satisfaction at his own sharpness.

Startled and shocked as he was, Arthur had by this time sufficiently recovered himself to feel indignant at the trick that had been played on him, and at the insolent manner in which the landlord exulted in it.

"Don't laugh," he said sharply, "till you are quite sure you have got the laugh against me. You shan't have the five shillings for nothing, my man. I'll keep the bed."

"Will you?" said the landlord. "Then I wish you a good night's rest." With that brief farewell he went out and shut the door after him.

A good night's rest! The words had hardly been spoken, the door had hardly been closed, before Arthur half repented the hasty words that had just escaped him. Though not naturally over-sensitive, and not wanting in courage of the moral as well as the physical sort, the presence of the dead man had an instantaneously chilling effect on his mind when he found himself alone in the room—alone, and bound by his own rash words to stay there till the next morning.

An older man would have thought nothing of those words, and would have acted, without reference to them, as his calmer sense suggested. But Arthur was too young to treat the ridicule even of his inferiors with contempt—too young not to fear the momentary humiliation of falsifying his own foolish boast more than he feared the trial of watching out the long night in the same chamber with the dead.

"It is but a few hours," he thought to himself, "and I can get away the first thing in the morning."

He was looking toward the occupied bed as that idea passed through his mind, and the sharp, angular eminence made in the clothes by the dead man's upturned feet again caught his eye. He advanced and drew the curtains, purposely abstaining, as he did so, from looking at the face of the corpse, lest he might unnerve himself at the outset by fastening some ghastly impression of it on his mind. He drew the curtain very gently, and sighed involuntarily as he closed it.

"Poor fellow," he said, almost as sadly as if he had known the man. "Ah! poor fellow!"

He went next to the window. The night was black, and he could see nothing from it. The rain still pattered heavily against the glass. He inferred, from hearing it, that the window was at the back of the house, remembering that the front was sheltered from the weather by the court and the buildings over it.

While he was still standing at the window—for even the dreary rain was a relief, because of the sound it made; a relief, also, because it moved, and had some faint suggestion, in consequence, of life and companionship in it—while he was standing at the window, and looking vacantly into the black darkness outside, he heard a distant church clock strike ten. Only ten!

How was he to pass the time till the house was astir the next morning?

Under any other circumstances he would have gone down to the public-house parlour, would have called for his grog, and would have laughed and talked with the company assembled as familiarly as if he had known them all his life. But the very thought of whiling away the time in this manner was now distasteful to him. The new situation in which he was placed seemed to have altered him to himself already.

Thus far his life had been the common, trifling, prosaic, surface-life of a prosperous young man, with no troubles to conquer and no trials to face. He had lost no relation whom he loved, no friend whom he treasured. Till this night, what share he had of the immortal inheritance that is divided among us all had lain dormant within him. Till this night, Death and he had not once met, even in thought.

He took a few turns up and down the room, then stopped. The noise made by his boots on the poorly-carpeted floor jarred on his ear. He hesitated a little, and ended by taking the boots off, and walking backward and forward noiselessly.

All desire to sleep or to rest had left him. The bare thought of lying down on the unoccupied bed instantly drew the picture on his mind of a dreadful mimicry of the position of the dead man. Who was he? What was the story of his past life? Poor he must have been, or he would not have stopped at such a place as the Two Robins Inn; and weakened, probably, by long illness, or he could hardly have died in the manner which the landlord had described. Poor, ill, lonely—dead in a strange place—dead, with nobody but a stranger to pity him. A sad story; truly, on the mere face of it, a very sad story.

While these thoughts were passing through his mind, he had stopped insensibly at the window, close to which stood the foot of the bed with the closed curtains. At first he looked at it absently; then he became conscious that his eyes were fixed on it; and then a perverse desire took possession of him to do the very thing which he had resolved not to do up to this time—to look at the dead man.

He stretched out his hand toward the curtains, but checked himself in the very act of undrawing them, turned his back sharply on the bed, and walked toward the chimney-piece, to see what things were placed on it, and to try if he could keep the dead man out of his mind in that way.

There was a pewter inkstand on the chimney-piece, with some mildewed remains of ink in the bottle. There were two coarse china ornaments of the commonest kind; and there was a square of embossed card, dirty and fly-blown, with a collection of wretched riddles printed on it, in all sorts of zigzag directions, and in variously coloured inks. He took the card and went away to read it at the table on which the candle was placed, sitting down with his back resolutely turned to the curtained bed.

He read the first riddle, the second, the third, all in one corner of the card, then turned it round impatiently to look at another. Before he could begin reading the riddles printed here the sound of the church clock stopped him.

Eleven.

He had got through an hour of the time in the room with the dead man.

Once more he looked at the card. It was not easy to make out the letters printed on it in consequence of the dimness of the light which the landlord had left him—a common tallow candle, furnished with a pair of heavy old-fashioned steel snuffers. Up to this time his mind had been too much occupied to think of the light. He had left the wick of the candle unsnuffed till it had risen higher than the flame, and had burned into an odd pent-house shape at the top, from which morsels of the charred cotton fell off from time to time in little flakes. He took up the snuffers now and trimmed the wick. The light brightened directly, and the room became less dismal.

Again he turned to the riddles, reading them doggedly and resolutely, now in one corner of the card, now in another. All his efforts, however, could not fix his attention on them. He pursued his occupation mechanically, deriving no sort of impression from what he was reading. It was as if a shadow from the curtained bed had got between his mind and the gaily printed letters—a shadow that nothing could dispel. At last he gave up the struggle, threw the card from him impatiently, and took to walking softly up and down the room again.

The dead man, the dead man, the hidden dead man on the bed!

There was the one persistent idea still haunting him. Hidden! Was it only the body being there, or was it the body being there—concealed,—that was preying on his mind? He stopped at the window with that doubt in him, once more listening to the pattering rain, once more looking out into the black darkness.

Still the dead man!

The darkness forced his mind back upon itself, and set his memory at work, reviving with a painfully vivid distinctness the momentary impression it had received from his first sight of the corpse. Before long the face seemed to be hovering out in the middle of the darkness, confronting him through the window, with the paleness whiter—with the dreadful dull line of light between the imperfectly-closed eyelids broader than he had seen it—with the parted lips slowly dropping further and further away from each other—with the features growing larger and moving closer, till they seemed to fill the window, and to silence the rain, and to shut out the night.

The sound of a voice shouting below stairs woke him suddenly from the dream of his own distempered fancy. He recognized it as the voice of the landlord.

"Shut up at twelve, Ben," he heard it say. "I'm off to bed."

He wiped away the damp that had gathered on his forehead, reasoned with himself for a little while, and resolved to shake his mind free of the ghastly counterfeit which still clung to it by forcing himself to confront, if it was only for a moment, the solemn reality. Without allowing himself an instant to hesitate, he parted the curtains at the foot of the bed, and looked through.

There was the sad, peaceful, white face, with the awful mystery of stillness on it, laid back upon the pillow. No stir, no change there! He only looked at it for a moment before he closed the curtains again, but that moment steadied him, calmed him, restored him—mind and body—to himself. He returned to his old occupation of walking up and down the room, persevering in it this time till the clock struck again.

Twelve.

As the sound of the clock-bell died away, it was succeeded by the confused noise downstairs of the drinkers in the taproom leaving the house. The next sound, after an interval of silence, was caused by the barring of the door and the closing of the shutters at the back of the inn. Then the silence followed again, and was disturbed no more.

He was alone now—absolutely, hopelessly alone with the dead man till the next morning.

The wick of the candle wanted trimming again. He took up the snuffers, but paused suddenly on the very point of using them, and looked attentively at the candle—then back, over his shoulder, at the curtained bed—then again at the candle. It had been lighted for the first time to show him the way upstairs, and three parts of it, at least, were already consumed. In another hour it would be burned out. In another hour, unless he called at once to the man who had shut up the inn for a fresh candle, he would be left in the dark.

Strongly as his mind had been affected since he had entered the room, his unreasonable dread of encountering ridicule and of exposing his courage to suspicion had not altogether lost its influence over him even yet.

He lingered irresolutely by the table, waiting till he could prevail on himself to open the door, and call from the landing, to the man who had shut up the inn. In his present hesitating frame of mind, it was a kind of relief to gain a few moments only by engaging in the trifling occupation of snuffing the candle. His hand trembled a little, and the snuffers were heavy and awkward to use. When he closed them on the wick, he closed them a hair-breadth too low. In an instant the candle was out, and the room was plunged in pitch darkness.

The one impression which the absence of light immediately produced on his mind was distrust of the curtained bed—distrust which shaped itself into no distinct idea, but which was powerful enough, in its very vagueness, to bind him down to his chair, to make his heart beat fast, and to set him listening intently. No sound stirred in the room, but the familiar sound of the rain against the window, louder and sharper now than he had heard it yet.

Still the vague distrust, the inexpressible dread possessed him, and kept him in his chair. He had put his carpet-bag on the table when he first entered the room, and he now took the key from his pocket, reached out his hand softly, opened the bag, and groped in it for his travelling writing-case, in which he knew that there was a small store of matches. When he had got one of the matches he waited before he struck it on the coarse wooden table, and listened intently again without knowing why. Still there was no sound in the room but the steady, ceaseless rattling sound of the rain.

He lighted the candle again without another moment of delay, and, on the instant of its burning up, the first object in the room that his eyes sought for was the curtained bed.

Just before the light had been put out he had looked in that direction, and had seen no change, no disarrangement of any sort in the folds of the closely-drawn curtains.

When he looked at the bed now, he saw hanging over the side of it a long white hand.

It lay perfectly motionless midway on the side of the bed, where the curtain at the head and the curtain at the foot met. Nothing more was visible. The clinging curtains hid everything but the long white hand.

He stood looking at it, unable to stir, unable to call out-feeling nothing, knowing nothing—every faculty he possessed gathered up and lost in the one seeing faculty. How long that first panic held him he never could tell afterward. It might have been only for a moment—it might have been for many minutes together. How he got to the bed—whether he ran to it headlong, or whether he approached it slowly—how he wrought himself up to unclose the curtains and look in, he never has remembered, and never will remember to his dying day. It is enough that he did go to the bed, and that he did look inside the curtains.

The man had moved. One of his arms was outside the clothes; his face was turned a little on the pillow; his eyelids were wide open. Changed as to position and as to one of the features, the face was otherwise fearfully and wonderfully unaltered. The dead paleness and the dead quiet were on it still.

One glance showed Arthur this—one glance before he flew breathlessly to the door and alarmed the house.

The man whom the landlord called "Ben" was the first to appear on the stairs. In three words Arthur told him what had happened, and sent him for the nearest doctor.

I, who tell you this story, was then staying with a medical friend of mine, in practice at Doncaster, taking care of his patients for him during his absence in London; and I, for the time being, was the nearest doctor. They had sent for me from the inn when the stranger was taken ill in the afternoon, but I was not at home, and medical assistance was sought for elsewhere. When the man from The Two Robins rang the night-bell, I was just thinking of going to bed. Naturally enough, I did not believe a word of his story about "a dead man who had come to life again." However, I put on my hat, armed myself with one or two bottles of restorative medicine, and ran to the inn, expecting to find nothing more remarkable, when I got there, than a patient in a fit.

My surprise at finding that the man had spoken the literal truth was almost, if not quite, equalled by my astonishment at finding myself face to face with Arthur Holliday as soon as I entered the bedroom. It was no time then for giving or seeking explanations. We just shook hands amazedly, and then I ordered everybody but Arthur out of the room, and hurried to the man on the bed.

The kitchen fire had not been long out. There was plenty of hot water in the boiler, and plenty of flannel to be had. With these, with my medicines, and with such help as Arthur could render under my direction, I dragged the man literally out of the jaws of death. In less than an hour from the time when I had been called in, he was alive and talking in the bed on which he had been laid out to wait for the coroner's inquest.

You will naturally ask me what had been the matter with him, and I might treat you, in reply, to a long theory, plentifully sprinkled with what the children call hard words. I prefer telling you that, in this case, cause and effect could not be satisfactorily joined together by any theory whatever.

There are mysteries in life and the conditions of it which human science has not fathomed yet; and I candidly confess to you that, in bringing that man back to existence, I was, morally speaking, groping haphazard in the dark. I know (from the testimony of the doctor who attended him in the afternoon) that the vital machinery, so far as its action is appreciable by our senses, had, in this case, unquestionably stopped, and I am equally certain (seeing that I recovered him) that the vital principle was not extinct. When I add that he had suffered from a long and complicated illness, and that his whole nervous system was utterly deranged, I have told you all I really know of the physical condition of my dead-alive patient at the Two Robins Inn.

When he "came to," as the phrase goes, he was a startling object to look at, with his colourless face, his sunken cheeks, his wild black eyes, and his long black hair. The first question he asked me about himself when he could speak made me suspect that I had been called in to a man in my own profession. I mentioned to him my surmise, and he told me that I was right.

He said he had come last from Paris, where he had been attached to a hospital; that he had lately returned to England, on his way to Edinburgh, to continue his studies; that he had been taken ill on the journey; and that he had stopped to rest and recover himself at Doncaster. He did not add a word about his name, or who he was, and of course I did not question him on the subject. All I inquired when he ceased speaking was what branch of the profession he intended to follow.

"Any branch," he said, bitterly, "which will put bread into the mouth of a poor man."

At this, Arthur, who had been hitherto watching him in silent curiosity, burst out impetuously in his usual good-humoured way:

"My dear fellow" (everybody was "my dear fellow" with Arthur), "now you have come to life again, don't begin by being down-hearted about your prospects. I'll answer for it I can help you to some capital thing in the medical line, or, if I can't, I know my father can."

The medical student looked at him steadily.

"Thank you," he said, coldly; then added, "May I ask who your father is?"

"He's well enough known all about this part of the country," replied Arthur. "He is a great manufacturer, and his name is Holliday."

My hand was on the man's wrist during this brief conversation. The instant the name of Holliday was pronounced I felt the pulse under my fingers flutter, stop, go on suddenly with a bound, and beat afterward for a minute or two at the fever rate.

"How did you come here?" asked the stranger, quickly, excitably, passionately almost.

Arthur related briefly what had happened from the time of his first taking the bed at the inn.

"I am indebted to Mr. Holliday's son, then, for the help that has saved my life," said the medical student, speaking to himself, with a singular sarcasm in his voice. "Come here!"

He held out, as he spoke, his long, white, bony right hand.

"With all my heart," said Arthur, taking his hand cordially. "I may confess it now," he continued, laughing, "upon my honour, you almost frightened me out of my wits."

The stranger did not seem to listen. His wild black eyes were fixed with a look of eager interest on Arthur's face, and his long bony fingers kept tight hold of Arthur's hand. Young Holliday, on his side, returned the gaze, amazed and puzzled by the medical student's odd language and manners. The two faces were close together; I looked at them, and, to my amazement, I was suddenly impressed by the sense of a likeness between them-not in features or complexion, but solely in expression. It must have been a strong likeness, or I should certainly not have found it out, for I am naturally slow at detecting resemblances between faces.

"You have saved my life," said the strange man, still looking hard in Arthur's face, still holding tightly by his hand. "If you had been my own brother, you could not have done more for me than that."

He laid a singularly strong emphasis on those three words "my own brother," and a change passed over his face as he pronounced them—a change that no language of mine is competent to describe.

"I hope I have not done being of service to you yet," said Arthur. "I'll speak to my father as soon as I get home."

"You seem to be fond and proud of your father," said the medical student. "I suppose, in return, he is fond and proud of you?"

"Of course he is," answered Arthur, laughing. "Is there anything wonderful in that? Isn't your father fond—"

The stranger suddenly dropped young Holliday's hand and turned his face away.

"I beg your pardon," said Arthur. "I hope I have not unintentionally pained you. I hope you have not lost your father?"

"I can't well lose what I have never had," retorted the medical student, with a harsh mocking laugh.

"What you have never had!"

The strange man suddenly caught Arthur's hand again, suddenly looked once more hard in his face.

"Yes," he said, with a repetition of the bitter laugh. "You have brought a poor devil back into the world who has no business there. Do I astonish you? Well, I have a fancy of my own for telling you what men in my situation generally keep a secret. I have no name and no father. The merciful law of society tells me I am nobody's son! Ask your father if he will be my father too, and help me on in life with the family name."

Arthur looked at me more puzzled than ever.

I signed to him to say nothing, and then laid my fingers again on the man's wrist. No. In spite of the extraordinary speech that he had just made, he was not, as I had been disposed to suspect, beginning to get light-headed. His pulse, by this time, had fallen back to a quiet, slow beat, and his skin was moist and cool. Not a symptom of fever or agitation about him.

Finding that neither of us answered him, he turned to me, and began talking of the extraordinary nature of his case, and asking my advice about the future course of medical treatment to which he ought to subject himself. I said the matter required careful thinking over, and suggested that I should send him a prescription a little later. He told me to write it at once, as he would most likely be leaving Doncaster in the morning before I was up. It was quite useless to represent to him the folly and danger of such a proceeding as this. He heard me politely and patiently, but held to his resolution, without offering any reasons or explanations, and repeated to me that, if I wished to give him a chance of seeing my prescription, I must write it at once.

Hearing this, Arthur volunteered the loan of a travelling writing-case, which he said he had with him, and, bringing it to the bed, shook the note-paper out of the pocket of the case forthwith in his usual careless way. With the paper there fell out on the counterpane of the bed a small packet of sticking-plaster, and a little water-colour drawing of a landscape.

The medical student took up the drawing and looked at it. His eye fell on some initials neatly written in cipher in one corner. He started and trembled; his pale face grew whiter than over; his wild black eyes turned on Arthur, and looked through and through him.

"A pretty drawing," he said, in a remarkably quiet tone of voice.

"Ah! and done by such a pretty girl," said Arthur. "Oh, such a pretty girl! I wish it was not a landscape—I wish it was a portrait of her!"

"You admire her very much?"

Arthur, half in jest, half in earnest, kissed his hand for answer.

"Love at first sight," said young Holliday, putting the drawing away again. "But the course of it doesn't run smooth. It's the old story. She's monopolized, as usual; trammelled by a rash engagement to some poor man who is never likely to get money enough to marry her. It was lucky I heard of it in time, or I should certainly have risked a declaration when she gave me that drawing. Here, doctor, here is pen, ink, and paper all ready for you."

"When she gave you that drawing? Gave it? gave it?"

He repeated the words slowly to himself, and suddenly closed his eyes. A momentary distortion passed across his face, and I saw one of his hands clutch up the bedclothes and squeeze them hard. I thought he was going to be ill again, and begged that there might be no more talking. He opened his eyes when I spoke, fixed them once more searchingly on Arthur, and said, slowly and distinctly:

"You like her, and she likes you. The poor man may die out of your way. Who can tell that she may not give you herself as well as her drawing, after all?"

Before young Holliday could answer he turned to me, and said in a whisper: "Now for the prescription." From that time, though he spoke to Arthur again, he never looked at him more.

When I had written the prescription, he examined it, approved of it, and then astonished us both by abruptly wishing us good-night. I offered to sit up with him, and he shook his head. Arthur offered to sit up with him, and he said, shortly, with his face turned away, "No." I insisted on having somebody left to watch him. He gave way when he found I was determined, and said he would accept the services of the waiter at the inn.

"Thank you both," he said, as we rose to go. "I have one last favour to ask—not of you, doctor, for I leave you to exercise your professional discretion, but of Mr. Holliday." His eyes, while he spoke, still rested steadily on me, and never once turned toward Arthur. "I beg that Mr. Holliday will not mention to any one, least of all to his father, the events that have occurred and the words that have passed in this room. I entreat him to bury me in his memory as, but for him, I might have been buried in my grave. I cannot give my reason for making this strange request. I can only implore him to grant it."

His voice faltered for the first time, and he hid his face on the pillow. Arthur, completely bewildered, gave the required pledge. I took young Holliday away with me immediately afterward to the house of my friend, determining to go back to the inn and to see the medical student again before he had left in the morning.

I returned to the inn at eight o'clock, purposely abstaining from waking Arthur, who was sleeping off the past night's excitement on one of my friend's sofas. A suspicion had occurred to me, as soon as I was alone in my bedroom, which made me resolve that Holliday and the stranger whose life he had saved should not meet again, if I could prevent it.

I have already alluded to certain reports or scandals which I knew of relating to the early life of Arthur's father. While I was thinking, in my bed, of what had passed at the inn; of the change in the student's pulse when he heard the name of Holliday; of the resemblance of expression that I had discovered between his face and Arthur's; of the emphasis he had laid on those three words, "my own brother," and of his incomprehensible acknowledgment of his own illegitimacy—while I was thinking of these things, the reports I have mentioned suddenly flew into my mind, and linked themselves fast to the chain of my previous reflections. Something within me whispered, "It is best that those two young men should not meet again." I felt it before I slept; I felt it when I woke; and I went as I told you, alone to the inn the next morning.

I had missed my only opportunity of seeing my nameless patient again. He had been gone nearly an hour when I inquired for him.

I have now told you everything that I know for certain in relation to the man whom I brought back to life in the double-bedded room of the inn at Doncaster. What I have next to add is matter for inference and surmise, and is not, strictly speaking, matter of fact.

I have to tell you, first, that the medical student turned out to be strangely and unaccountably right in assuming it as more than probable that Arthur Holliday would marry the young lady who had given him the water-colour drawing of the landscape. That marriage took place a little more than a year after the events occurred which I have just been relating.

The young couple came to live in the neighbourhood in which I was then established in practice. I was present at the wedding, and was rather surprised to find that Arthur was singularly reserved with me, both before and after his marriage, on the subject of the young lady's prior engagement. He only referred to it once when we were alone, merely telling me, on that occasion, that his wife had done all that honour and duty required of her in the matter, and that the engagement had been broken off with the full approval of her parents.

I never heard more from him than this. For three years he and his wife lived together happily. At the expiration of that time the symptoms of a serious illness first declared themselves in Mrs. Arthur Holliday. It turned out to be a long, lingering, hopeless malady. I attended her throughout. We had been great friends when she was well, and we became more attached to each other than ever when she was ill. I had many long and interesting conversations with her in the intervals when she suffered least. The result of one of those conversations I may briefly relate, leaving you to draw any inferences from it that you please.

The interview to which I refer occurred shortly before her death.

I called one evening as usual, and found her alone, with a look in her eyes which told me she had been crying. She only informed me at first that she had been depressed in spirits, but by little and little she became more communicative, and confessed to me that she had been looking over some old letters which had been addressed to her, before she had seen Arthur, by a man to whom she had been engaged to be married. I asked her how the engagement came to be broken off. She replied that it had not been broken off, but that it had died out in a very mysterious way.

The person to whom she was engaged—her first love, she called him—was very poor, and there was no immediate prospect of their being married. He followed my profession, and went abroad to study. They had corresponded regularly until the time when, as she believed, he had returned to England. From that period she heard no more of him. He was of a fretful, sensitive temperament, and she feared that she might have inadvertently done or said something to offend him.

However that might be, he had never written to her again, and after waiting a year she had married Arthur. I asked when the first estrangement had begun, and found that the time at which she ceased to hear anything of her first lover exactly corresponded with the time at which I had been called in to my mysterious patient at The Two Robins Inn.

A fortnight after that conversation she died. In course of time Arthur married again. Of late years he has lived principally in London, and I have seen little or nothing of him.

I have some years to pass over before I can approach to anything like a conclusion of this fragmentary narrative. And even when that later period is reached, the little that I have to say will not occupy your attention for more than a few minutes.

One rainy autumn evening, while I was still practicing as a country doctor, I was sitting alone, thinking over a case then under my charge, which sorely perplexed me, when I heard a low knock at the door of my room.

"Come in," I cried, looking up curiously to see who wanted me.

After a momentary delay, the lock moved, and a long, white, bony hand stole round the door as it opened, gently pushing it over a fold in the carpet which hindered it from working freely on the hinges. The hand was followed by a man whose face instantly struck me with a very strange sensation. There was something familiar to me in the look of him, and yet it was also something that suggested the idea of change.

He quietly introduced himself as "Mr. Lorn," presented to me some excellent professional recommendations, and proposed to fill the place, then vacant, of my assistant. While he was speaking I noticed it as singular that we did not appear to be meeting each other like strangers, and that, while I was certainly startled at seeing him, he did not appear to be at all startled at seeing me.

It was on the tip of my tongue to say that I thought I had met with him before. But there was something in his face, and something in my own recollections—I can hardly say what-which unaccountably restrained me from speaking and which as unaccountably attracted me to him at once, and made me feel ready and glad to accept his proposal.

He took his assistant's place on that very day. We got on together as if we had been old friends from the first; but, throughout the whole time of his residence in my house, he never volunteered any confidences on the subject of his past life, and I never approached the forbidden topic except by hints, which he resolutely refused to understand.

I had long had a notion that my patient at the inn might have been a natural son of the elder Mr. Holliday's, and that he might also have been the man who was engaged to Arthur's first wife. And now another idea occurred to me, that Mr. Lorn was the only person in existence who could, if he chose, enlighten me on both those doubtful points. But he never did choose, and I was never enlightened. He remained with me till I removed to London to try my fortune there as a physician for the second time, and then he went his way and I went mine, and we have never seen one another since.

I can add no more. I may have been right in my suspicion, or I may have been wrong. All I know is that, in those days of my country practice, when I came home late, and found my assistant asleep, and woke him, he used to look, in coming to, wonderfully like the stranger at Doncaster as he raised himself in the bed on that memorable night.

Brother Griffith's Story of

The Biter Bit

—Extracted from the Correspondence of the London Police.

From Chief Inspector Theakstone, of the Detective Police, to Sergeant Bulmer, of the Same Force.

London, 4th July, 18—.

Sergeant Bulmer—This is to inform you that you are wanted to assist in looking up a case of importance, which will require all the attention of an experienced member of the force. The matter of the robbery on which you are now engaged you will please to shift over to the young man who brings you this letter. You will tell him all the circumstances of the case, just as they stand; you will put him up to the progress you have made (if any) toward detecting the person or persons by whom the money has been stolen; and you will leave him to make the best he can of the matter now in your hands. He is to have the whole responsibility of the case, and the whole credit of his success if he brings it to a proper issue.

So much for the orders that I am desired to communicate to you.

A word in your ear, next, about this new man who is to take your place. His name is Matthew Sharpin, and he is to have the chance given him of dashing into our office at one jump—supposing he turns out strong enough to take it. You will naturally ask me how he comes by this privilege. I can only tell you that he has some uncommonly strong interest to back him in certain high quarters, which you and I had better not mention except under our breaths. He has been a lawyer's clerk, and he is wonderfully conceited in his opinion of himself, as well as mean and underhand, to look at. According to his own account, he leaves his old trade and joins ours of his own free will and preference.

You will no more believe that than I do. My notion is, that he has managed to ferret out some private information in connection with the affairs of one of his master's clients, which makes him rather an awkward customer to keep in the office for the future, and which, at the same time, gives him hold enough over his employer to make it dangerous to drive him into a corner by turning him away. I think the giving him this unheard-of chance among us is, in plain words, pretty much like giving him hush money to keep him quiet.

However that may be, Mr. Matthew Sharpin is to have the case now in your hands, and if he succeeds with it he pokes his ugly nose into our office as sure as fate. I put you up to this, sergeant, so that you may not stand in your own light by giving the new man any cause to complain of you at headquarters, and remain yours,

Francis Theakstone.

From Mr. Matthew Sharpin to Chief Inspector Theakstone.

London, 5th July, 18—.

Dear Sir—Having now been favoured with the necessary instructions from Sergeant Bulmer, I beg to remind you of certain directions which I have received relating to the report of my future proceedings which I am to prepare for examination at headquarters.

The object of my writing, and of your examining what I have written before you send it to the higher authorities, is, I am informed, to give me, as an untried hand, the benefit of your advice in case I want it (which I venture to think I shall not) at any stage of my proceedings. As the extraordinary circumstances of the case on which I am now engaged make it impossible for me to absent myself from the place where the robbery was committed until I have made some progress toward discovering the thief, I am necessarily precluded from consulting you personally. Hence the necessity of my writing down the various details, which might perhaps be better communicated by word of mouth.

This, if I am not mistaken, is the position in which we are now placed. I state my own impressions on the subject in writing, in order that we may clearly understand each other at the outset; and have the honour to remain your obedient servant,

Matthew Sharpin.

From Chief Inspector Theakstone to Mr. Matthew Sharpin.

London, 5th July, 18—.

Sir—You have begun by wasting time, ink, and paper. We both of us perfectly well knew the position we stood in toward each other when I sent you with my letter to Sergeant Bulmer. There was not the least need to repeat it in writing. Be so good as to employ your pen in future on the business actually in hand.

You have now three separate matters on which to write me. First, you have to draw up a statement of your instructions received from Sergeant Bulmer, in order to show us that nothing has escaped your memory, and that you are thoroughly acquainted with all the circumstances of the case which has been intrusted to you.

Secondly, you are to inform me what it is you propose to do. Thirdly, you are to report every inch of your progress (if you make any) from day to day, and, if need be, from hour to hour as well. This is your duty. As to what my duty may be, when I want you to remind me of it, I will write and tell you so.

In the meantime, I remain yours, Francis Theakstone.

From Mr. Matthew Sharpin to Chief Inspector Theakstone.

London, 6th July, 18—.

Sir—You are rather an elderly person, and as such, naturally inclined to be a little jealous of men like me, who are in the prime of their lives and their faculties. Under these circumstances, it is my duty to be considerate toward you, and not to bear too hardly on your small failings. I decline, therefore, altogether to take offense at the tone of your letter; I give you the full benefit of the natural generosity of my nature; I sponge the very existence of your surly communication out of my memory—in short, Chief Inspector Theakstone, I forgive you, and proceed to business.

My first duty is to draw up a full statement of the instructions I have received from Sergeant Bulmer. Here they are at your service, according to my version of them.

At Number Thirteen Rutherford Street, Soho, there is a stationer's shop. It is kept by one Mr. Yatman. He is a married man, but has no family. Besides Mr. and Mrs. Yatman, the other inmates in the house are a lodger, a young single man named Jay, who occupies the front room on the second floor—a shopman, who sleeps in one of the attics, and a servant-of-all-work, whose bed is in the back kitchen. Once a week a charwoman comes to help this servant. These are all the persons who, on ordinary occasions, have means of access to the interior of the house, placed, as a matter of course, at their disposal.

Mr. Yatman has been in business for many years, carrying on his affairs prosperously enough to realize a handsome independence for a person in his position. Unfortunately for himself, he endeavoured to increase the amount of his property by speculating. He ventured boldly in his investments; luck went against him; and rather less than two years ago he found himself a poor man again. All that was saved out of the wreck of his property was the sum of two hundred pounds.

Although Mr. Yatman did his best to meet his altered circumstances, by giving up many of the luxuries and comforts to which he and his wife had been accustomed, he found it impossible to retrench so far as to allow of putting by any money from the income produced by his shop. The business has been declining of late years, the cheap advertising stationers having done it injury with the public. Consequently, up to the last week, the only surplus property possessed by Mr. Yatman consisted of the two hundred pounds which had been recovered from the wreck of his fortune. This sum was placed as a deposit in a joint-stock bank of the highest possible character.

Eight days ago Mr. Yatman and his lodger, Mr. Jay, held a conversation on the subject of the commercial difficulties which are hampering trade in all directions at the present time. Mr. Jay (who lives by supplying the newspapers with short paragraphs relating to accidents, offenses, and brief records of remarkable occurrences in general—who is, in short, what they call a penny-a-liner) told his landlord that he had been in the city that day and heard unfavourable rumours on the subject of the joint-stock banks. The rumours to which he alluded had already reached the ears of Mr. Yatman from other quarters, and the confirmation of them by his lodger had such an effect on his mind-predisposed as it was to alarm by the experience of his former losses—that he resolved to go at once to the bank and withdraw his deposit. It was then getting on toward the end of the afternoon, and he arrived just in time to receive his money before the bank closed.

He received the deposit in bank-notes of the following amounts: one fifty-pound note, three twenty-pound notes, six ten-pound notes, and six five-pound notes. His object in drawing the money in this form was to have it ready to lay out immediately in trifling loans, on good security, among the small trades-people of his district, some of whom are sorely pressed for the very means of existence at the present time. Investments of this kind seemed to Mr. Yatman to be the most safe and the most profitable on which he could now venture.

He brought the money back in an envelope placed in his breast pocket, and asked his shopman, on getting home, to look for a small, flat, tin cash-box, which had not been used for years, and which, as Mr. Yatman remembered it, was exactly of the right size to hold the bank-notes. For some time the cash-box was searched for in vain. Mr. Yatman called to his wife to know if she had any idea where it was. The question was overheard by the servant-of-all-work, who was taking up the tea-tray at the time, and by Mr. Jay, who was coming downstairs on his way out to the theatre. Ultimately the cash-box was found by the shopman. Mr. Yatman placed the bank-notes in it, secured them by a padlock, and put the box in his coat pocket. It stuck out of the coat pocket a very little, but enough to be seen. Mr. Yatman remained at home, upstairs, all that evening. No visitors called. At eleven o'clock he went to bed, and put the cash-box under his pillow.

When he and his wife woke the next morning the box was gone. Payment of the notes was immediately stopped at the Bank of England, but no news of the money has been heard of since that time.

So far the circumstances of the case are perfectly clear. They point unmistakably to the conclusion that the robbery must have been committed by some person living in the house. Suspicion falls, therefore, upon the servant-of-all-work, upon the shopman, and upon Mr. Jay. The two first knew that the cash-box was being inquired for by their master, but did not know what it was he wanted to put into it. They would assume, of course, that it was money. They both had opportunities (the servant when she took away the tea, and the shopman when he came, after shutting up, to give the keys of the till to his master) of seeing the cash-box in Mr. Yatman's pocket, and of inferring naturally, from its position there, that he intended to take it into his bedroom with him at night.

Mr. Jay, on the other hand, had been told, during the afternoon's conversation on the subject of joint-stock banks, that his landlord had a deposit of two hundred pounds in one of them. He also knew that Mr. Yatman left him with the intention of drawing that money out; and he heard the inquiry for the cash-box afterward, when he was coming downstairs. He must, therefore, have inferred that the money was in the house, and that the cash-box was the receptacle intended to contain it. That he could have had any idea, however, of the place in which Mr. Yatman intended to keep it for the night is impossible, seeing that he went out before the box was found, and did not return till his landlord was in bed. Consequently, if he committed the robbery, he must have gone into the bedroom purely on speculation.

Speaking of the bedroom reminds me of the necessity of noticing the situation of it in the house, and the means that exist of gaining easy access to it at any hour of the night.

The room in question is the back room on the first floor. In consequence of Mrs. Yatman's constitutional nervousness on the subject of fire, which makes her apprehend being burned alive in her room, in case of accident, by the hampering of the lock if the key is turned in it, her husband has never been accustomed to lock the bedroom door. Both he and his wife are, by their own admission, heavy sleepers; consequently, the risk to be run by any evil-disposed persons wishing to plunder the bedroom was of the most trifling kind. They could enter the room by merely turning the handle of the door; and, if they moved with ordinary caution, there was no fear of their waking the sleepers inside. This fact is of importance. It strengthens our conviction that the money must have been taken by one of the inmates of the house, because it tends to show that the robbery, in this case, might have been committed by persons not possessed of the superior vigilance and cunning of the experienced thief.

Such are the circumstances, as they were related to Sergeant Bulmer, when he was first called in to discover the guilty parties, and, if possible, to recover the lost bank-notes. The strictest inquiry which he could institute failed of producing the smallest fragment of evidence against any of the persons on whom suspicion naturally fell. Their language and behaviour on being informed of the robbery was perfectly consistent with the language and behaviour of innocent people. Sergeant Bulmer felt from the first that this was a case for private inquiry and secret observation. He began by recommending Mr. and Mrs. Yatman to affect a feeling of perfect confidence in the innocence of the persons living under their roof, and he then opened the campaign by employing himself in following the goings and comings, and in discovering the friends, the habits, and the secrets of the maid-of-all-work.

Three days and nights of exertion on his own part, and on that of others who were competent to assist his investigations, were enough to satisfy him that there was no sound cause for suspicion against the girl.

He next practiced the same precaution in relation to the shopman. There was more difficulty and uncertainty in privately clearing up this person's character without his knowledge, but the obstacles were at last smoothed away with tolerable success; and, though there is not the same amount of certainty in this case which there was in the case of the girl, there is still fair reason for supposing that the shopman has had nothing to do with the robbery of the cash-box.

As a necessary consequence of these proceedings, the range of suspicion now becomes limited to the lodger, Mr. Jay.

When I presented your letter of introduction to Sergeant

Bulmer, he had already made some inquiries on the subject of this young man. The result, so far, has not been at all favourable. Mr. Jay's habits are irregular; he frequents public houses, and seems to be familiarly acquainted with a great many dissolute characters; he is in debt to most of the trades-people whom he employs; he has not paid his rent to Mr. Yatman for the last month; yesterday evening he came home excited by liquor, and last week he was seen talking to a prize-fighter; in short, though Mr. Jay does call himself a journalist, in virtue of his penny-a-line contributions to the newspapers, he is a young man of low tastes, vulgar manners, and bad habits. Nothing has yet been discovered in relation to him which redounds to his credit in the smallest degree.

I have now reported, down to the very last details, all the particulars communicated to me by Sergeant Bulmer. I believe you will not find an omission anywhere; and I think you will admit, though you are prejudiced against me, that a clearer statement of facts was never laid before you than the statement I have now made. My next duty is to tell you what I propose to do now that the case is confided to my hands.

In the first place, it is clearly my business to take up the case at the point where Sergeant Bulmer has left it. On his authority, I am justified in assuming that I have no need to trouble myself about the maid-of-all-work and the shopman. Their characters are now to be considered as cleared up. What remains to be privately investigated is the question of the guilt or innocence of Mr. Jay. Before we give up the notes for lost, we must make sure, if we can, that he knows nothing about them.

This is the plan that I have adopted, with the full approval of Mr. and Mrs. Yatman, for discovering whether Mr. Jay is or is not the person who has stolen the cash-box:

I propose today to present myself at the house in the character of a young man who is looking for lodgings. The back room on the second floor will be shown to me as the room to let, and I shall establish myself there tonight as a person from the country who has come to London to look for a situation in a respectable shop or office.

By this means I shall be living next to the room occupied by Mr. Jay. The partition between us is mere lath and plaster. I shall make a small hole in it, near the cornice, through which I can see what Mr. Jay does in his room, and hear every word that is said when any friend happens to call on him. Whenever he is at home, I shall be at my post of observation; whenever he goes out, I shall be after him. By employing these means of watching him, I believe I may look forward to the discovery of his secret—if he knows anything about the lost bank-notes—as to a dead certainty.

What you may think of my plan of observation I cannot undertake to say. It appears to me to unite the invaluable merits of boldness and simplicity. Fortified by this conviction, I close the present communication with feelings of the most sanguine description in regard to the future, and remain your obedient servant,

Matthew Sharpin.

From the Same to the Same.

7th July.

Sir—As you have not honoured me with any answer to my last communication, I assume that, in spite of your prejudices against me, it has produced the favourable impression on your mind which I ventured to anticipate. Gratified and encouraged beyond measure by the token of approval which your eloquent silence conveys to me, I proceed to report the progress that has been made in the course of the last twenty-four hours.

I am now comfortably established next door to Mr. Jay, and I am delighted to say that I have two holes in the partition instead of one. My natural sense of humour has led me into the pardonable extravagance of giving them both appropriate names. One I call my peep-hole, and the other my pipe-hole. The name of the first explains itself; the name of the second refers to a small tin pipe or tube inserted in the hole, and twisted so that the mouth of it comes close to my ear while I am standing at my post of observation. Thus, while I am looking at Mr. Jay through my peep-hole, I can hear every word that may be spoken in his room through my pipe-hole.

Perfect candour—a virtue which I have possessed from my childhood—compels me to acknowledge, before I go any further, that the ingenious notion of adding a pipe-hole to my proposed peep-hole originated with Mrs. Yatman. This lady—a most intelligent and accomplished person, simple, and yet distinguished in her manners, has entered into all my little plans with an enthusiasm and intelligence which I cannot too highly praise.

Mr. Yatman is so cast down by his loss that he is quite incapable of affording me any assistance. Mrs. Yatman, who is evidently most tenderly attached to him, feels her husband's sad condition of mind even more acutely than she feels the loss of the money, and is mainly stimulated to exertion by her desire to assist in raising him from the miserable state of prostration into which he has now fallen.

"The money, Mr. Sharpin," she said to me yesterday evening, with tears in her eyes, "the money may be regained by rigid economy and strict attention to business. It is my husband's wretched state of mind that makes me so anxious for the discovery of the thief. I may be wrong, but I felt hopeful of success as soon as you entered the house; and I believe that, if the wretch who robbed us is to be found, you are the man to discover him." I accepted this gratifying compliment in the spirit in which it was offered, firmly believing that I shall be found, sooner or later, to have thoroughly deserved it.

Let me now return to business—that is to say, to my peep-hole and my pipe-hole.

I have enjoyed some hours of calm observation of Mr. Jay. Though rarely at home, as I understand from Mrs. Yatman, on ordinary occasions, he has been indoors the whole of this day. That is suspicious, to begin with. I have to report, further, that he rose at a late hour this morning (always a bad sign in a young man), and that he lost a great deal of time, after he was up, in yawning and complaining to himself of headache. Like other debauched characters, he ate little or nothing for breakfast. His next proceeding was to smoke a pipe—a dirty clay pipe, which a gentleman would have been ashamed to put between his lips.

When he had done smoking he took out pen, ink and paper, and sat down to write with a groan—whether of remorse for having taken the bank-notes, or of disgust at the task before him, I am unable to say. After writing a few lines (too far away from my peep-hole to give me a chance of reading over his shoulder), he leaned back in his chair, and amused himself by humming the tunes of popular songs. I recognized "My Mary Anne," "Bobbin' Around," and "Old Dog Tray," among other melodies. Whether these do or do not represent secret signals by which he communicates with his accomplices remains to be seen.

After he had amused himself for some time by humming, he got up and began to walk about the room, occasionally stopping to add a sentence to the paper on his desk. Before long he went to a locked cupboard and opened it. I strained my eyes eagerly, in expectation of making a discovery. I saw him take something carefully out of the cupboard—he turned round—and it was only a pint bottle of brandy! Having drunk some of the liquor, this extremely indolent reprobate lay down on his bed again, and in five minutes was fast asleep.

After hearing him snoring for at least two hours, I was recalled to my peep-hole by a knock at his door. He jumped up and opened it with suspicious activity.

A very small boy, with a very dirty face, walked in, said: "Please, sir, they're waiting for you," sat down on a chair with his legs a long way from the ground, and instantly fell asleep! Mr. Jay swore an oath, tied a wet towel round his head, and, going back to his paper, began to cover it with writing as fast as his fingers could move the pen.

Occasionally getting up to dip the towel in water and tie it on again, he continued at this employment for nearly three hours; then folded up the leaves of writing, woke the boy, and gave them to him, with this remarkable expression: "Now, then, young sleepy-head, quick march! If you see the governor, tell him to have the money ready for me when I call for it." The boy grinned and disappeared. I was sorely tempted to follow "sleepy-head," but, on reflection, considered it safest still to keep my eye on the proceedings of Mr. Jay.

In half an hour's time he put on his hat and walked out. Of course I put on my hat and walked out also. As I went downstairs I passed Mrs. Yatman going up. The lady has been kind enough to undertake, by previous arrangement between us, to search Mr. Jay's room while he is out of the way, and while I am necessarily engaged in the pleasing duty of following him wherever he goes.

On the occasion to which I now refer, he walked straight to the nearest tavern and ordered a couple of mutton-chops for his dinner. I placed myself in the next box to him, and ordered a couple of mutton-chops for my dinner. Before I had been in the room a minute, a young man of highly suspicious manners and appearance, sitting at a table opposite, took his glass of porter in his hand and joined Mr. Jay. I pretended to be reading the newspaper, and listened, as in duty bound, with all my might.

"Jack has been here inquiring after you," says the young man.

"Did he leave any message?" asks Mr. Jay.

"Yes," says the other. "He told me, if I met with you, to say that he wished very particularly to see you tonight, and that he would give you a look in at Rutherford Street at seven o'clock."

"All right," says Mr. Jay. "I'll get back in time to see him."

Upon this, the suspicious-looking young man finished his porter, and saying that he was rather in a hurry, took leave of his friend (perhaps I should not be wrong if I said his accomplice?), and left the room.

At twenty-five minutes and a half past six—in these serious cases it is important to be particular about time-Mr. Jay finished his chops and paid his bill. At twenty-six minutes and three-quarters I finished my chops and paid mine. In ten minutes more I was inside the house in Rutherford Street, and was received by Mrs. Yatman in the passage. That charming woman's face exhibited an expression of melancholy and disappointment which it quite grieved me to see.

"I am afraid, ma'am," says I, "that you have not hit on any little criminating discovery in the lodger's room?"

She shook her head and sighed. It was a soft, languid, fluttering sigh—and, upon my life, it quite upset me. For the moment I forgot business, and burned with envy of Mr. Yatman.

"Don't despair, ma'am," I said, with an insinuating mildness which seemed to touch her. "I have heard a mysterious conversation—I know of a guilty appointment—and I expect great things from my peep-hole and my pipe-hole tonight. Pray don't be alarmed, but I think we are on the brink of a discovery."

Here my enthusiastic devotion to business got the better part of my tender feelings. I looked—winked—nodded—left her.

When I got back to my observatory, I found Mr. Jay digesting his mutton-chops in an armchair, with his pipe in his mouth. On his table were two tumblers, a jug of water, and the pint bottle of brandy. It was then close upon seven o'clock. As the hour struck the person described as "Jack" walked in.

He looked agitated—I am happy to say he looked violently agitated. The cheerful glow of anticipated success diffused itself (to use a strong expression) all over me, from head to foot. With breathless interest I looked through my peep-hole, and saw the visitor—the "Jack" of this delightful case—sit down, facing me, at the opposite side of the table to Mr. Jay. Making allowance for the difference in expression which their countenances just now happened to exhibit, these two abandoned villains were so much alike in other respects as to lead at once to the conclusion that they were brothers.

Jack was the cleaner man and the better dressed of the two. I admit that, at the outset. It is, perhaps, one of my failings to push justice and impartiality to their utmost limits. I am no Pharisee; and where Vice has its redeeming point, I say, let Vice have its due—yes, yes, by all manner of means, let Vice have its due.

"What's the matter now, Jack?" says Mr. Jay.

"Can't you see it in my face?" says Jack. "My dear fellow, delays are dangerous. Let us have done with suspense, and risk it, the day after tomorrow."

"So soon as that?" cries Mr. Jay, looking very much astonished. "Well, I'm ready, if you are. But, I say, Jack, is somebody else ready, too? Are you quite sure of that?"

He smiled as he spoke—a frightful smile—and laid a very strong emphasis on those two words, "Somebody else." There is evidently a third ruffian, a nameless desperado, concerned in the business.

"Meet us tomorrow," says Jack, "and judge for yourself. Be in the Regent's Park at eleven in the morning, and look out for us at the turning that leads to the Avenue Road."

"I'll be there," says Mr. Jay. "Have a drop of brandy-and-water? What are you getting up for? You're not going al-

ready?"
"Yes, I am," says Jack. "The fact is, I'm so excited and agitated that I can't sit still anywhere for five minutes together. Ridiculous as it may appear to you, I'm in a perpetual state of nervous flutter. I can't, for the life of me, help fearing that we shall be found out. I fancy that every man who looks twice at me in the street is a spy—"
At these words I thought my legs would have given way under me. Nothing but strength of mind kept me at my peep-hole—nothing else, I give you my word of honour.
"Stuff and nonsense!" cries Mr. Jay, with all the effrontery of a veteran in crime. "We have kept the secret up to this time, and we will manage cleverly to the end. Have a drop of brandy and water, and you will feel as certain about it as I do."
Jack steadily refused the brandy-and-water, and steadily persisted in taking his leave.
"I must try if I can't walk it off," he said. "Remember tomorrow morning—eleven o'clock, Avenue Road, side of the Regent's Park."
With those words he went out. His hardened relative laughed desperately and resumed the dirty clay pipe.
I sat down on the side of my bed, actually quivering with excitement.
It is clear to me that no attempt has yet been made to change the stolen bank-notes, and I may add that Sergeant Bulmer was of that opinion also when he left the case in my hands. What is the natural conclusion to draw from the conversation which I have just set down? Evidently that the confederates meet tomorrow to take their respective shares in the stolen money, and to decide on the safest means of getting the notes changed the day after.
Mr. Jay is, beyond a doubt, the leading criminal in this business, and he will probably run the chief risk—that of changing the fifty-pound note. I shall, therefore, still make it my business to follow him—attending at the Regent's

Park tomorrow, and doing my best to hear what is said there. If another appointment is made for the day after, I shall, of course, go to it. In the meantime, I shall want the immediate assistance of two competent persons (supposing the rascals separate after their meeting) to follow the two minor criminals. It is only fair to add that, if the rogues all retire together, I shall probably keep my subordinates in reserve. Being naturally ambitious, I desire, if possible, to have the whole credit of discovering this robbery to myself.

8th July.

I have to acknowledge, with thanks, the speedy arrival of my two subordinates—men of very average abilities, I am afraid; but, fortunately, I shall always be on the spot to direct them.

My first business this morning was necessarily to prevent possible mistakes by accounting to Mr. and Mrs. Yatman for the presence of two strangers on the scene. Mr. Yatman (between ourselves, a poor, feeble man) only shook his head and groaned. Mrs. Yatman (that superior woman) favoured me with a charming look of intelligence.

"Oh, Mr. Sharpin!" she said, "I am so sorry to see those two men! Your sending for their assistance looks as if you were beginning to be doubtful of success."

I privately winked at her (she is very good in allowing me to do so without taking offense), and told her, in my facetious way, that she laboured under a slight mistake.

"It is because I am sure of success, ma'am, that I send for them. I am determined to recover the money, not for my own sake only, but for Mr. Yatman's sake—and for yours."

I laid a considerable amount of stress on those last three words. She said: "Oh, Mr. Sharpin!" again, and blushed of a heavenly red, and looked down at her work. I could go to the world's end with that woman if Mr. Yatman would only die.

I sent off the two subordinates to wait until I wanted them

at the Avenue Road gate of the Regent's Park. Half-an-hour afterward I was following the same direction myself at the heels of Mr. Jay.

The two confederates were punctual to the appointed time. I blush to record it, but it is nevertheless necessary to state that the third rogue—the nameless desperado of my report, or, if you prefer it, the mysterious "somebody else" of the conversation between the two brothers—is—a woman! and, what is worse, a young woman! and, what is more lamentable still, a nice-looking woman! I have long resisted a growing conviction that, wherever there is mischief in this world, an individual of the fair sex is inevitably certain to be mixed up in it. After the experience of this morning, I can struggle against that sad conclusion no longer. I give up the sex—excepting Mrs. Yatman, I give up the sex.

The man named "Jack" offered the woman his arm. Mr. Jay placed himself on the other side of her. The three then walked away slowly among the trees. I followed them at a respectful distance. My two subordinates, at a respectful distance, also, followed me.

It was, I deeply regret to say, impossible to get near enough to them to overhear their conversation without running too great a risk of being discovered. I could only infer from their gestures and actions that they were all three talking with extraordinary earnestness on some subject which deeply interested them. After having been engaged in this way a full quarter of an hour, they suddenly turned round to retrace their steps.

My presence of mind did not forsake me in this emergency. I signed to the two subordinates to walk on carelessly and pass them, while I myself slipped dexterously behind a tree. As they came by me, I heard "Jack" address these words to Mr. Jay:

"Let us say half-past ten tomorrow morning. And mind you come in a cab. We had better not risk taking one in this neighbourhood."

Mr. Jay made some brief reply which I could not overhear. They walked back to the place at which they had met, shaking hands there with an audacious cordiality which it quite sickened me to see. They then separated. I followed Mr. Jay. My subordinates paid the same delicate attention to the other two.

Instead of taking me back to Rutherford Street, Mr. Jay led me to the Strand. He stopped at a dingy, disreputable-looking house, which, according to the inscription over the door, was a newspaper office, but which, in my judgment, had all the external appearance of a place devoted to the reception of stolen goods.

After remaining inside for a few minutes, he came out whistling, with his finger and thumb in his waistcoat pocket. Some men would now have arrested him on the spot. I remembered the necessity of catching the two confederates, and the importance of not interfering with the appointment that had been made for the next morning. Such coolness as this, under trying circumstances, is rarely to be found, I should imagine, in a young beginner, whose reputation as a detective policeman is still to make.

From the house of suspicious appearance Mr. Jay betook himself to a cigar-divan, and read the magazines over a cheroot. From the divan he strolled to the tavern and had his chops. I strolled to the tavern and had my chops. When he had done he went back to his lodging. When I had done I went back to mine. He was overcome with drowsiness early in the evening, and went to bed. As soon as I heard him snoring, I was overcome with drowsiness and went to bed also.

Early in the morning my two subordinates came to make their report.

They had seen the man named "Jack" leave the woman at the gate of an apparently respectable villa residence not far from the Regent's Park. Left to himself, he took a turning to the right, which led to a sort of suburban street, principally inhabited by shopkeepers. He stopped at the private door of one of the houses, and let himself in with his own key—looking about him as he opened the door, and staring suspiciously at my men as they lounged along on the opposite side of the way. These were all the particulars which the subordinates had to communicate. I kept them in my room to attend on me, if needful, and mounted to my peep-hole to have a look at Mr. Jay.

He was occupied in dressing himself, and was taking extraordinary pains to destroy all traces of the natural slovenliness of his appearance. This was precisely what I expected. A vagabond like Mr. Jay knows the importance of giving himself a respectable look when he is going to run the risk of changing a stolen banknote. At five minutes past ten o'clock he had given the last brush to his shabby hat and the last scouring with bread-crumb to his dirty gloves. At ten minutes past ten he was in the street, on his way to the nearest cab-stand, and I and my subordinates were close on his heels.

He took a cab and we took a cab. I had not overheard them appoint a place of meeting when following them in the Park on the previous day, but I soon found that we were proceeding in the old direction of the Avenue Road gate. The cab in which Mr. Jay was riding turned into the Park slowly. We stopped outside, to avoid exciting suspicion. I got out to follow the cab on foot. Just as I did so, I saw it stop, and detected the two confederates approaching it from among the trees. They got in, and the cab was turned about directly. I ran back to my own cab and told the driver to let them pass him, and then to follow as before.

The man obeyed my directions, but so clumsily as to excite their suspicions. We had been driving after them about three minutes (returning along the road by which we had advanced) when I looked out of the window to see how far they might be ahead of us. As I did this, I saw two hats popped out of the windows of their cab, and two faces looking back at me. I sank into my place in a cold sweat; the expression is coarse, but no other form of words can describe my condition at that trying moment.

"We are found out!" I said, faintly, to my two subordinates. They stared at me in astonishment. My feelings changed instantly from the depth of despair to the height of indignation.

"It is the cabman's fault. Get out, one of you," I said, with dignity—"get out, and punch his head."

Instead of following my directions (I should wish this act of disobedience to be reported at headquarters) they both looked out of the window. Before I could pull them back they both sat down again. Before I could express my just indignation, they both grinned, and said to me: "Please to look out, sir!"

I did look out. Their cab had stopped.

Where?

At a church door!

What effect this discovery might have had upon the ordinary run of men I don't know. Being of a strong religious turn myself, it filled me with horror. I have often read of the unprincipled cunning of criminal persons, but I never before heard of three thieves attempting to double on their pursuers by entering a church! The sacrilegious audacity of that proceeding is, I should think, unparalleled in the annals of crime.

I checked my grinning subordinates by a frown. It was easy to see what was passing in their superficial minds. If I had not been able to look below the surface, I might, on observing two nicely dressed men and one nicely dressed woman enter a church before eleven in the morning on a week day, have come to the same hasty conclusion at which my inferiors had evidently arrived. As it was, appearances had no power to impose on me. I got out, and, followed by one of my men, entered the church. The other man I sent round to watch the vestry door. You may catch a weasel asleep, but not your humble servant, Matthew Sharpin!

We stole up the gallery stairs, diverged to the organ-loft, and peered through the curtains in front. There they were, all three, sitting in a pew below—yes, incredible as it may appear, sitting in a pew below!

Before I could determine what to do, a clergyman made his appearance in full canonicals from the vestry door, followed by a clerk. My brain whirled and my eyesight grew dim. Dark remembrances of robberies committed in vestries floated through my mind. I trembled for the excellent man in full canonicals—I even trembled for the clerk.

The clergyman placed himself inside the altar rails. The three desperadoes approached him. He opened his book and began to read. What? you will ask.

I answer, without the slightest hesitation, the first lines of the Marriage Service.

My subordinate had the audacity to look at me, and then to stuff his pocket-handkerchief into his mouth. I scorned to pay any attention to him. After I had discovered that the man "Jack" was the bridegroom, and that the man Jay acted the part of father, and gave away the bride, I left the church, followed by my men, and joined the other subordinate outside the vestry door. Some people in my position would now have felt rather crestfallen, and would have begun to think that they had made a very foolish mistake. Not the faintest misgiving of any kind troubled me. I did not feel in the slightest degree depreciated in my own estimation. And even now, after a lapse of three hours, my mind remains, I am happy to say, in the same calm and hopeful condition.

As soon as I and my subordinates were assembled together outside the church, I intimated my intention of still following the other cab in spite of what had occurred. My reason for deciding on this course will appear presently. The two subordinates appeared to be astonished at my resolution. One of them had the impertinence to say to me:

"If you please, sir, who is it that we are after? A man who has stolen money, or a man who has stolen a wife?"

The other low person encouraged him by laughing. Both have deserved an official reprimand, and both, I sincerely trust, will be sure to get it.

When the marriage ceremony was over, the three got into their cab and once more our vehicle (neatly hidden round the corner of the church, so that they could not suspect it to be near them) started to follow theirs.

We traced them to the terminus of the South-western Railway. The newly-married couple took tickets for Richmond, paying their fare with a half sovereign, and so depriving me of the pleasure of arresting them, which I should certainly have done if they had offered a bank-note. They parted from Mr. Jay, saying: "Remember the address—14 Babylon Terrace. You dine with us tomorrow week."

Mr. Jay accepted the invitation, and added, jocosely, that he was going home at once to get off his clean clothes, and to be comfortable and dirty again for the rest of the day. I have to report that I saw him home safely, and that he is comfortable and dirty again (to use his own disgraceful language) at the present moment.

Here the affair rests, having by this time reached what I may call its first stage.

I know very well what persons of hasty judgment will be inclined to say of my proceedings thus far. They will assert that I have been deceiving myself all through in the most absurd way; they will declare that the suspicious conversations which I have reported referred solely to the difficulties and dangers of successfully carrying out a runaway match; and they will appeal to the scene in the church as offering undeniable proof of the correctness of their assertions. So let it be. I dispute nothing up to this point. But I ask a question, out of the depths of my own sagacity as a man of the world, which the bitterest of my enemies will not, I think, find it particularly easy to answer.

Granted the fact of the marriage, what proof does it afford me of the innocence of the three persons concerned in that clandestine transaction? It gives me none. On the contrary, it strengthens my suspicions against Mr. Jay and his confederates, because it suggests a distinct motive for their stealing the money. A gentleman who is going to spend his honeymoon at Richmond wants money; and a gentleman who is in debt to all his trades-people wants money. Is this an unjustifiable imputation of bad motives? In the name of outraged Morality, I deny it. These men have combined together, and have stolen a woman. Why should they not combine together and steal a cash-box? I take my stand on the logic of rigid Virtue, and I defy all the sophistry of Vice to move me an inch out of my position.

Speaking of virtue, I may add that I have put this view of the case to Mr. and Mrs. Yatman. That accomplished and charming woman found it difficult at first to follow the close chain of my reasoning. I am free to confess that she shook her head, and shed tears, and joined her husband in premature lamentation over the loss of the two hundred pounds. But a little careful explanation on my part, and a little attentive listening on hers, ultimately changed her opinion.

She now agrees with me that there is nothing in this unexpected circumstance of the clandestine marriage which absolutely tends to divert suspicion from Mr. Jay, or Mr. "Jack," or the runaway lady. "Audacious hussy" was the term my fair friend used in speaking of her; but let that pass. It is more to the purpose to record that Mrs. Yatman has not lost confidence in me, and that Mr. Yatman promises to follow her example, and do his best to look hopefully for future results.

I have now, in the new turn that circumstances have taken, to await advice from your office. I pause for fresh orders with all the composure of a man who has got two strings to his bow. When I traced the three confederates from the church door to the railway terminus, I had two motives for doing so. First, I followed them as a matter of official business, believing them still to have been guilty of the robbery.

Secondly, I followed them as a matter of private speculation, with a view of discovering the place of refuge to which the runaway couple intended to retreat, and of making my information a marketable commodity to offer to the young lady's family and friends. Thus, whatever happens, I may congratulate myself beforehand on not having wasted my time. If the office approves of my conduct, I have my plan ready for further proceedings.

If the office blames me, I shall take myself off, with my marketable information, to the genteel villa residence in the neighbourhood of the Regent's Park. Anyway, the affair puts money into my pocket, and does credit to my penetration as an uncommonly sharp man.

I have only one word more to add, and it is this: If any individual ventures to assert that Mr. Jay and his confederates are innocent of all share in the stealing of the cash-box, I, in return, defy that individual—though he may even be Chief Inspector Theakstone himself—to tell me who has committed the robbery at Rutherford Street, Soho.

Strong in that conviction, I have the honour to be your very obedient servant, Matthew Sharpin.

From Chief Inspector Theakstone to Sergeant Bulmer.

Birmingham, July 9th.

Sergeant Bulmer—That empty-headed puppy, Mr. Matthew Sharpin, has made a mess of the case at Rutherford

Street, exactly as I expected he would. Business keeps me in this town, so I write to you to set the matter straight. I inclose with this the pages of feeble scribble-scrabble which the creature Sharpin calls a report.

Look them over; and when you have made your way through all the gabble, I think you will agree with me that the conceited booby has looked for the thief in every direction but the right one. You can lay your hand on the guilty person in five minutes, now. Settle the case at once; forward your report to me at this place, and tell Mr. Sharpin that he is suspended till further notice.

Yours, Francis Theakstone.

From Sergeant Bulmer to Chief Inspector Theakstone.

London, July 10th.

Inspector Theakstone—Your letter and inclosure came safe to hand. Wise men, they say, may always learn something even from a fool. By the time I had got through Sharpin's maundering report of his own folly, I saw my way clear enough to the end of the Rutherford Street case, just as you thought I should. In half an hour's time I was at the house. The first person I saw there was Mr. Sharpin himself.

"Have you come to help me?" says he.

"Not exactly," says I. "I've come to tell you that you are suspended till further notice."

"Very good," says he, not taken down by so much as a single peg in his own estimation. "I thought you would be jealous of me. It's very natural and I don't blame you. Walk in, pray, and make yourself at home. I'm off to do a little detective business on my own account, in the neighbourhood of the Regent's Park. Ta-ta, sergeant, ta-ta!"

With those words he took himself out of the way, which was exactly what I wanted him to do.

As soon as the maid-servant had shut the door, I told her to inform her master that I wanted to say a word to him in private. She showed me into the parlour behind the shop, and there was Mr. Yatman all alone, reading the newspaper.

"About this matter of the robbery, sir," says I.

He cut me short, peevishly enough, being naturally a poor, weak, womanish sort of man.

"Yes, yes, I know," says he. "You have come to tell me that your wonderfully clever man, who has bored holes in my second floor partition, has made a mistake, and is off the scent of the scoundrel who has stolen my money."

"Yes, sir," says I. "That is one of the things I came to tell you. But I have got something else to say besides that."

"Can you tell me who the thief is?" says he, more pettish than ever.

"Yes, sir," says I, "I think I can."

He put down the newspaper, and began to look rather anxious and frightened.

"Not my shopman?" says he. "I hope, for the man's own sake, it's not my shopman."

"Guess again, sir," says I.

"That idle slut, the maid?" says he.

"She is idle, sir," says I, "and she is also a slut; my first inquiries about her proved as much as that. But she's not the thief."

"Then, in the name of Heaven, who is?" says he.

"Will you please to prepare yourself for a very disagreeable surprise, sir?" says I. "And, in case you lose your temper, will you excuse my remarking that I am the stronger man of the two, and that if you allow yourself to lay hands on me, I may unintentionally hurt you, in pure self-defence."

He turned as pale as ashes, and pushed his chair two or three feet away from me.

"You have asked me to tell you, sir, who has taken your money," I went on. "If you insist on my giving you an answer—"

"I do insist," he said, faintly. "Who has taken it?"

"Your wife has taken it," I said, very quietly, and very positively at the same time.

He jumped out of the chair as if I had put a knife into him, and struck his fist on the table so heavily that the wood cracked again.

"Steady, sir," says I. "Flying into a passion won't help you to the truth."

"It's a lie!" says he, with another smack of his fist on the table—"a base, vile, infamous lie! How dare you——"

He stopped, and fell back into the chair again, looked about him in a bewildered way, and ended by bursting out crying.

"When your better sense comes back to you, sir," says I, "I am sure you will be gentleman enough to make an apology for the language you have just used. In the meantime, please to listen, if you can, to a word of explanation. Mr. Sharpin has sent in a report to our inspector of the most irregular and ridiculous kind, setting down not only all his own foolish doings and sayings, but the doings and sayings of Mrs. Yatman as well. In most cases, such a document would have been fit only for the waste paper basket; but in this particular case it so happens that Mr. Sharpin's budget of nonsense leads to a certain conclusion, which the simpleton of a writer has been quite innocent of suspecting from the beginning to the end.

"Of that conclusion I am so sure that I will forfeit my place if it does not turn out that Mrs. Yatman has been practicing upon the folly and conceit of this young man, and that she has tried to shield herself from discovery by purposely encouraging him to suspect the wrong persons. I tell you that confidently; and I will even go further. I will undertake to give a decided opinion as to why Mrs. Yatman took the money, and what she has done with it, or with a part of it. Nobody can look at that lady, sir, without being struck by the great taste and beauty of her dress—"

As I said those last words, the poor man seemed to find

his powers of speech again. He cut me short directly as haughtily as if he had been a duke instead of a stationer. "Try some other means of justifying your vile calumny against my wife," says he. "Her milliner's bill for the past year is on my file of receipted accounts at this moment."

"Excuse me, sir," says I, "but that proves nothing. Milliners, I must tell you, have a certain rascally custom which comes within the daily experience of our office.

"A married lady who wishes it can keep two accounts at her dressmaker's; one is the account which her husband sees and pays; the other is the private account, which contains all the extravagant items, and which the wife pays secretly, by instalments, whenever she can. According to our usual experience, these instalments are mostly squeezed out of the housekeeping money. In your case, I suspect, no instalments have been paid; proceedings have been threatened; Mrs. Yatman, knowing your altered circumstances, has felt herself driven into a corner, and she has paid her private account out of your cash-box."

"I won't believe it," says he. "Every word you speak is an abominable insult to me and to my wife."

"Are you man enough, sir," says I, taking him up short, in order to save time and words, "to get that receipted bill you spoke of just now off the file, and come with me at once to the milliner's shop where Mrs. Yatman deals?"

He turned red in the face at that, got the bill directly, and put on his hat. I took out of my pocket-book the list containing the numbers of the lost notes, and we left the house together immediately.

Arrived at the milliner's (one of the expensive West-end houses, as I expected), I asked for a private interview, on important business, with the mistress of the concern. It was not the first time that she and I had met over the same delicate investigation. The moment she set eyes on me she sent for her husband. I mentioned who Mr. Yatman was, and what we wanted.

"This is strictly private?" inquires the husband. I nodded my head.

"And confidential?" says the wife. I nodded again.

"Do you see any objection, dear, to obliging the sergeant with a sight of the books?" says the husband.

"None in the world, love, if you approve of it," says the wife.

All this while poor Mr. Yatman sat looking the picture of astonishment and distress, quite out of place at our polite conference. The books were brought, and one minute's look at the pages in which Mrs. Yatman's name figured was enough, and more than enough, to prove the truth of every word that I had spoken.

There, in one book, was the husband's account which Mr. Yatman had settled; and there, in the other, was the private account, crossed off also, the date of settlement being the very day after the loss of the cash-box. This said private account amounted to the sum of a hundred and seventy-five pounds, odd shillings, and it extended over a period of three years. Not a single instalment had been paid on it. Under the last line was an entry to this effect:

"Written to for the third time, June 23rd."

I pointed to it, and asked the milliner if that meant "last June." Yes, it did mean last June; and she now deeply regretted to say that it had been accompanied by a threat of legal proceedings.

"I thought you gave good customers more than three years' credit?" says I.

The milliner looks at Mr. Yatman, and whispers to me, "Not when a lady's husband gets into difficulties."

She pointed to the account as she spoke. The entries after the time when Mr. Yatman's circumstances became involved were just as extravagant, for a person in his wife's situation, as the entries for the year before that period. If the lady had economized in other things, she had certainly not economized in the matter of dress.

There was nothing left now but to examine the cash-book, for form's sake. The money had been paid in notes, the amounts and numbers of which exactly tallied with the figures set down in my list.

After that, I thought it best to get Mr. Yatman out of the house immediately. He was in such a pitiable condition that I called a cab and accompanied him home in it. At first he cried and raved like a child; but I soon quieted him; and I must add, to his credit, that he made me a most handsome apology for his language as the cab drew up at his house door. In return, I tried to give him some advice about how to set matters right for the future with his wife. He paid very little attention to me, and went upstairs muttering to himself about a separation.

Whether Mrs. Yatman will come cleverly out of the scrape or not seems doubtful. I should say myself that she would go into screeching hysterics, and so frighten the poor man into forgiving her. But this is no business of ours. So far as we are concerned, the case is now at an end, and the present report may come to a conclusion along with it.

I remain, accordingly, yours to command,

Thomas Bulmer.

P.S. "I have to add that, on leaving Rutherford Street, I met Mr. Matthew Sharpin coming to pack up his things.

"Only think!" says he, rubbing his hands in great spirits, "I've been to the genteel villa residence, and the moment I mentioned my business they kicked me out directly. There were two witnesses of the assault, and it's worth a hundred pounds to me if it's worth a farthing."

"I wish you joy of your luck," says I.

"Thank you," says he. "When may I pay you the same compliment on finding the thief?"

"Whenever you like," says I, "for the thief is found."

"Just what I expected," says he. "I've done all the work, and now you cut in and claim all the credit"Mr. Jay, of course."

"No," says I.
"Who is it then?" says he.
"Ask Mrs. Yatman," says I. "She's waiting to tell you."
"All right! I'd much rather hear it from that charming woman than from you," says he, and goes into the house in a mighty hurry.
What do you think of that, Inspector Theakstone? Would you like to stand in Mr. Sharpin's shoes? I shouldn't, I can promise you.

From Chief Inspector Theakstone to Mr. Matthew Sharpin.

July 12th.

Sir—Sergeant Bulmer has already told you to consider yourself suspended until further notice. I have now authority to add that your services as a member of the Detective police are positively declined. You will please to take this letter as notifying officially your dismissal from the force.
I may inform you, privately, that your rejection is not intended to cast any reflections on your character. It merely implies that you are not quite sharp enough for our purposes. If we are to have a new recruit among us, we should infinitely prefer Mrs. Yatman.
Your obedient servant, Francis Theakstone.

Note on the Preceding Correspondence, Added by Mr. Theakstone.

The inspector is not in a position to append any explanations of importance to the last of the letters. It has been discovered that Mr. Matthew Sharpin left the house in Rutherford Street five minutes after his interview outside of it with Sergeant Bulmer, his manner expressing the liveliest emotions of terror and astonishment, and his left cheek displaying a bright patch of red, which looked as if it might have been the result of what is popularly termed a smart box on the ear.

He was also heard by the shopman at Rutherford Street to use a very shocking expression in reference to Mrs. Yatman, and was seen to clinch his fist vindictively as he ran round the corner of the street. Nothing more has been heard of him; and it is conjectured that he has left London with the intention of offering his valuable services to the provincial police.

On the interesting domestic subject of Mr. and Mrs. Yatman still less is known. It has, however, been positively ascertained that the medical attendant of the family was sent for in a great hurry on the day when Mr. Yatman returned from the milliner's shop. The neighbouring chemist received, soon afterward, a prescription of a soothing nature to make up for Mrs. Yatman.

The day after, Mr. Yatman purchased some smelling-salts at the shop, and afterward appeared at the circulating library to ask for a novel descriptive of high life that would amuse an invalid lady. It has been inferred from these circumstances that he has not thought it desirable to carry out his threat of separating from his wife, at least in the present (presumed) condition of that lady's sensitive nervous system.

The Fatal Cradle

OTHERWISE, THE HEART-RENDING STORY OF MR. HEAVYSIDES

There has never yet been discovered a man with a grievance who objected to mention it. I am no exception to this general human rule. I have got a grievance, and I don't object to mention it. Compose your spirits to hear a pathetic story, and kindly picture me in your own mind as a baby five minutes old.

Do I understand you to say that I am too big and too heavy to be pictured in anybody's mind as a baby? Perhaps I may be-but don't mention my weight again, if you please. My weight has been the grand misfortune of my life. It spoiled all my prospects (as you will presently hear) before I was two days old.

My story begins thirty-one years ago, at eleven o'clock in the forenoon, and starts with the great mistake of my first appearance in this world, at sea, on board the merchant ship *Adventure*, Captain Gillop, five hundred tons burden, coppered, and carrying an experienced surgeon.

In presenting myself to you (which I am now about to do) at that eventful period of my life when I was from five to ten minutes old, and in withdrawing myself again from your notice (so as not to trouble you with more than a short story) before the time when I cut my first tooth, I need not hesitate to admit that I speak on hearsay knowledge only. It is knowledge, however, that may be relied on, for all that.

My information comes from Captain Gillop, commander of the *Adventure* (who sent it to me in the form of a letter); from Mr. Jolly, experienced surgeon of the *Adventure* (who wrote it for me most unfeelingly, as I think—in the shape of a humorous narrative); and from Mrs. Drabble, stewardess of the *Adventure* (who told it me by word of mouth). Those three persons were, in various degrees, spectators—I may say astonished spectators-of the events which I have now to relate.

The *Adventure*, at the time I speak of, was bound out from London to Australia. I suppose you know without my telling you that thirty years ago was long before the time of the gold-finding and the famous clipper ships. Building in the new colony and sheep-farming far up inland were the two main employments of those days, and the passengers on board our vessel were consequently builders or sheep-farmers, almost to a man.

A ship of five hundred tons, well loaded with cargo, doesn't offer first-rate accommodation to a large number of passengers. Not that the gentlefolk in the cabin had any great reason to complain. There the passage money, which was a good round sum, kept them what you call select. One or two berths in this part of the ship were even empty and going a-begging, in consequence of there being only four cabin passengers. These are their names and descriptions:

Mr. Sims, a middle-aged man, going out on a building speculation; Mr. Purling, a weakly young gentleman, sent on a long sea-voyage, for the benefit of his health; and Mr. and Mrs. Smallchild, a young married couple, with a little independence, which Mr. Smallchild proposed to make a large one by sheep-farming.

This gentleman was reported to the captain as being very good company when on shore. But the sea altered him to a certain extent. When Mr. Smallchild was not sick, he was eating and drinking; and when he was not eating and drinking, he was fast asleep. He was perfectly patient and good-humoured, and wonderfully nimble at running into his cabin when the qualms took him on a sudden; but, as for his being good company, nobody heard him say ten words together all through the voyage. And no wonder. A man can't talk in the qualms; a man can't talk while he is eating and drinking; and a man can't talk when he is asleep. And that was Mr. Smallchild's life. As for Mrs. Smallchild, she kept her cabin from first to last. But you will hear more of her presently.

These four cabin passengers, as I have already remarked, were well enough off for their accommodation. But the miserable people in the steerage—a poor place at the best of times on board the *Adventure*—were all huddled together, men and women and children, higgledy-piggledy, like sheep in a pen, except that they hadn't got the same quantity of fine fresh air to blow over them. They were artisans and farm-labourers, who couldn't make it out in the Old Country.

I have no information either of their exact numbers or of their names. It doesn't matter; there was only one family among them which need be mentioned particularly—namely, the family of the Heavysides. To wit, Simon Heavysides, intelligent and well-educated, a carpenter by trade; Susan Heavysides, his wife; and seven little Heavysides, their unfortunate offspring. My father and mother and brothers and sisters, did I understand you to say? Don't be in a hurry! I recommend you to wait a little before you make quite sure of that circumstance.

Though I myself had not, perhaps, strictly speaking, come on board when the vessel left London, my ill luck, as I firmly believe, had shipped in the *Adventure* to wait for me—and decided the nature of the voyage accordingly.

Never was such a miserable time known. Stormy weather came down on us from all points of the compass, with intervals of light, baffling winds or dead calms. By the time the *Adventure* had been three months out, Captain Gillop's naturally sweet temper began to get soured. I leave you to say whether it was likely to be much improved by a piece of news which reached him from the region of the cabin on the morning of the ninety-first day. It had fallen to a dead calm again; and the ship was rolling about helpless, with her head all round the compass, when Mr. Jolly (from whose facetious narrative I repeat all conversations exactly as they passed) came on deck to the captain, and addressed him in these words:

"I have got some news that will rather surprise you," said Mr. Jolly, smiling and rubbing his hands. (Although the experienced surgeon has not shown much sympathy for my troubles, I won't deny that his disposition was as good as his name. To this day no amount of bad weather or hard work can upset Mr. Jolly's temper.)

"If it's news of a fair wind coming," grumbled the captain, "that would surprise me on board this ship, I can promise you!"

"It's not exactly a wind coming," said Mr. Jolly. "It's another cabin passenger."

The captain looked round at the empty sea, with the land thousands of miles away, and with not a ship in sight—turned sharply on the experienced surgeon—eyed him hard changed colour suddenly—and asked what he meant.

"I mean there's a fifth cabin passenger coming on board," persisted Mr. Jolly, grinning from ear to ear—"introduced by Mrs. Smallchild likely to join us, I should say, toward evening-size, nothing to speak of—sex, not known at present—manners and customs, probably squally."

"Do you really mean it?" asked the captain, backing away, and turning paler and paler.

"Yes, I do," answered Mr. Jolly, nodding hard at him.

"Then I'll tell you what," cried Captain Gillop, suddenly flying into a violent passion, "I won't have it! The infernal weather has worried me out of my life and soul already—and I won't have it! Put it off, Jolly—tell her there isn't room enough for that sort of thing on board my vessel. What does she mean by taking us all in in this way? Shameful! Shameful!"

"No! No!" remonstrated Mr. Jolly. "Don't look at it in that light. It's her first child, poor thing. How should she know? Give her a little more experience, and I dare say—"

"Where's her husband?" broke in the captain, with a threatening look. "I'll speak my mind to her husband, at any rate."

Mr. Jolly consulted his watch before he answered.

"Half-past eleven," he said. "Let me consider a little. It's Mr.

Smallchild's regular time just now for squaring accounts with the sea. He'll have done in a quarter of an hour. In five minutes more he'll be fast asleep. At one o'clock he'll eat a hearty lunch, and go to sleep again. At half-past two he'll square accounts as before—and so on till night. You'll make nothing out of Mr. Smallchild, captain. Extraordinary man—wastes tissue, and repairs it again perpetually, in the most astonishing manner. If we are another month at sea, I believe we shall bring him into port totally comatose.—Halloo! What do you want?"

The steward's mate had approached the quarter-deck while the doctor was speaking. Was it a curious coincidence? This man also was grinning from ear to ear, exactly like Mr. Jolly.

"You're wanted in the steerage, sir." said the steward's mate to the doctor. "A woman taken bad, name of Heavysides."

"Nonsense!" cried Mr. Jolly. "Ha, ha, ha! You don't mean eh?"

"That's it, sir, sure enough," said the steward's mate, in the most positive manner.

Captain Gillop looked all around him in silent desperation; lost his sea-legs for the first time these twenty years; staggered back till he was brought all standing by the side of his own vessel; dashed his fist on the bulwark, and found language to express himself in, at the same moment.

"This ship is bewitched," said the captain, wildly. "Stop!" he called out, recovering himself a little as the doctor bustled away to the steerage. "Stop! If it's true, Jolly, send her husband here aft to me. Damme, I'll have it out with one of the husbands!" said the captain, shaking his fist viciously at the empty air.

Ten minutes passed; and then there came staggering toward the captain, tottering this way and that with the rolling of the becalmed vessel, a long, lean, melancholy, light-haired man. with a Roman nose, a watery blue eye, and a complexion profusely spotted with large brown freckles. This was Simon Heavysides, the intelligent carpenter, with the wife and the family of seven small children on hoard.

"Oh! you're the man, are you?" said the captain.

The ship lurched heavily; and Simon Heavysides staggered away with a run to the opposite side of the deck, as if he preferred going straight overboard into the sea to answering the captain's question.

"You're the man—are you?" repeated the captain, following him, seizing him by the collar, and pinning him up fiercely against the bulwark. "It's your wife—is it? You infernal rascal! what do you mean by turning my ship into a lying-in hospital? You have committed an act of mutiny; or, if it isn't mutiny, it's next door to it. I've put a man in irons for less! I've more than half a mind to put you in irons! Hold up, you slippery lubber! What do you mean by bringing passengers I don't bargain for on board my vessel? What have you got to say for yourself, before I clap the irons on you?"

"Nothing, sir," answered Simon Heavysides, accepting the captain's strong language without a word of protest. "As for the punishment you mentioned just now, sir," continued Simon, "I wish to say—having seven children more than I know how to provide for, and an eighth coming to make things worse—I respectfully wish to say, sir, that my mind is in irons already; and I don't know as it will make much difference if you put my body in irons along with it."

The captain mechanically let go of the carpenter's collar; the mild despair of the man melted him in spite of himself.

"Why did you come to sea? Why didn't you wait ashore till it was all over?" asked the captain, as sternly as he could.

"It's no use waiting, sir," remarked Simon. "In our line of life, as soon as it's over it begins again. There's no end to it that I can see," said the miserable carpenter, after a moment's meek consideration—"except the grave."

"Who's talking about the grave?" cried Mr. Jolly, coming up at that moment. "It's births we've got to do with on board this vessel not burials. Captain Gillop, this woman, Mrs. Heavysides, can't be left in your crowded steerage in her present condition. She must be moved off into one of the empty berths—and the sooner the better, I can tell you!"

The captain began to look savage again. A steerage passenger in one of his "state-rooms" was a nautical anomaly subversive of all discipline. He eyed the carpenter once more, as if he was mentally measuring him for a set of irons.

"I'm very sorry, sir," Simon remarked, politely—"very sorry that any inadvertence of mine or Mrs. Heavysides—"

"Take your long carcass and your long tongue forward!" thundered the captain. "When talking will mend matters, I'll send for you again. Give your own orders, Jolly," he went on, resignedly, as Simon staggered off. "Turn the ship into a nursery as soon as you like!"

Five minutes later—so expeditious was Mr. Jolly—Mrs. Heavysides appeared horizontally on deck, shrouded in blankets and supported by three men. When this interesting procession passed the captain, he shrank aside from it with as vivid an appearance of horror as if a wild bull was being carried by him instead of a British matron.

The sleeping-berths below opened on either side out of the main cabin. On the left-hand side (looking toward the ship's bowsprit) was Mrs. Smallchild. On the right-hand side, opposite to her, the doctor established Mrs. Heavysides. A partition of canvas was next run up, entirely across the main cabin. The smaller of the two temporary rooms thus made lay nearest the stairs leading on deck, and was left free to the public. The larger was kept sacred to the doctor and his mysteries.

When an old clothes-basket, emptied, cleaned, and comfortably lined with blankets (to serve for a makeshift cradle), had been in due course of time carried into the inner cabin, and had been placed midway between the two sleeping-berths, so as to be easily producible when wanted, the outward and visible preparations of Mr. Jolly were complete; the male passengers had all taken refuge on deck; and the doctor and the stewardess were left in undisturbed possession of the lower regions.

While it was still early in the afternoon the weather changed for the better. For once in a way, the wind came from a fair quarter, and the *Adventure* bowled along pleasantly before it almost on an even keel. Captain Gillop mixed with the little group of male passengers on the quarter-deck, restored to his sweetest temper; and set them his customary example, after dinner, of smoking a cigar.

"If this fine weather lasts, gentlemen," he said, "we shall make out very well with our meals up here, and we shall have our two small extra cabin passengers christened on dry land in a week's time, if their mothers approve of it. How do you feel in your mind, sir, about your good lady?"

Mr. Smallchild (to whom the inquiry was addressed) had his points of external personal resemblance to Simon Heavysides. He was neither so tall nor so lean, certainly—but he, too, had a Roman nose, and light hair, and watery blue eyes. With careful reference to his peculiar habits at sea, he had been placed conveniently close to the bulwark, and had been raised on a heap of old sails and cushions, so that he could easily get his head over the ship's side when occasion required.

The food and drink which assisted in "restoring his tissue," when he was not asleep and not "squaring accounts with the sea," lay close to his hand. It was then a little after three o'clock; and the snore with which Mr. Smallchild answered the captain's inquiry showed that he had got round again, with the regularity of clock-work, to the period of the day when he recruited himself with sleep.

"What an insensible blockhead that man is!" said Mr. Sims, the middle-aged passenger, looking across the deck contemptuously at Mr. Smallchild.

"If the sea had the same effect on you that it has on him," retorted the invalid passenger, Mr. Purling, "you would just be as insensible yourself."

Mr. Purling (who was a man of sentiment) disagreed with Mr. Sims (who was a man of business) on every conceivable subject, all through the voyage. Before, however, they could continue the dispute about Mr. Smallchild, the doctor surprised them by appearing from the cabin.

"Any news from below, Jolly?" asked the captain, anxiously.

"None whatever," answered the doctor. "I've come to idle the afternoon away up here, along with the rest of you."

As events turned out, Mr. Jolly idled away an hour and a half exactly. At the end of that time Mrs. Drabble, the stewardess, appeared with a face of mystery, and whispered, nervously, to the doctor,

"Please to step below directly, sir."

"Which of them is it?" asked Mr. Jolly.

"Both of them," answered Mrs. Drabble, emphatically.

The doctor looked grave; the stewardess looked frightened. The two immediately disappeared together.

"I suppose, gentlemen," said Captain Gillop, addressing Mr. Purling, Mr. Sims, and the first mate, who had just joined the party—"I suppose it's only fit and proper, in the turn things have taken, to shake up Mr. Smallchild? And I don't doubt but what we ought to have the other husband handy, as a sort of polite attention under the circumstances. Pass the word forward there, for Simon Heavvsides. Mr. Smallchild, sir! rouse up! Here's your good lady—Hang me, gentlemen, if I know exactly how to put it to him."

"Yes. Thank you," said Mr. Smallchild, opening his eyes drowsily. "Biscuit and cold bacon, as usual—when I'm ready. I'm not ready yet. Thank you. Good-afternoon." Mr. Smallchild closed his eyes again, and became, in the doctor's phrase, "totally comatose."

Before Captain Gillop could hit on any new plan for rousing this imperturbable passenger, Simon Heavysides once more approached the quarter-deck.

"I spoke a little sharp to you, just now, my man," said the captain, "being worried in my mind by what's going on on board this vessel. But I'll make it up to you, never fear. Here's your wife in what they call an interesting situation. It's only right you should be within easy hail of her. I look upon you, Heavysides, as a steerage passenger in difficulties; and I freely give you leave to stop here along with us till it's all over."

"You are very good, sir," said Simon; "and I am indeed thankful to you and to these gentlemen. But please to remember, I have seven children already in the steerage—and there's nobody left to mind 'em but me. My wife has got over it uncommonly well, sir, on seven previous occasions—and I don't doubt but what she'll conduct herself in a similar manner on the eighth. It will be a satisfaction to her mind, Captain Gillop and gentlemen, if she knows I'm out of the way, and minding the children. For which reason, I respectfully take my leave." With those words Simon made his bow, and returned to his family.

"Well, gentlemen, these two husbands take it easy enough, at any rate!" said the captain. "One of them is used to it, to be sure; and the other is—"

Here a banging of cabin doors below, and a hurrying of footsteps, startled the speaker and his audience into momentary silence and attention.

"Ease her with the helm, Williamson!" said Captain Gillop, addressing the man who was steering the vessel. "In my opinion, gentlemen, the less the ship pitches the better, in the turn things are taking now."

The afternoon wore on into evening, and evening into night.

Mr. Smallchild performed the daily ceremonies of his nautical existence as punctually as usual. He was aroused to a sense of Mrs. Smallchild's situation when he took his biscuit and bacon; lost the sense again when the time came round for "squaring his accounts;" recovered it in the interval which ensued before he went to sleep; lost it again, as a matter of course, when his eyes closed once more—and so on through the evening and early night.

Simon Heavysides received messages occasionally (through the captain's care), telling him to keep his mind easy; returned messages mentioning that his mind was easy, and that the children were pretty quiet, but never approached the deck in his own person. Mr. Jolly now and then showed himself; said "All right—no news;" took a little light refreshment, and disappeared again as cheerful as ever. The fair breeze still held; the captain's temper remained unruffled; the man at the helm eased the vessel; from time to time, with the most anxious consideration.

Ten o'clock came; the moon rose and shone superbly; the nightly grog made its appearance on the quarter-deck; the captain gave the passengers the benefit of his company; and still nothing happened. Twenty minutes more of suspense slowly succeeded each other—and then, at last, Mr. Jolly was seen suddenly to ascend the cabin stairs.

To the amazement of the little group on the quarter-deck, the doctor held Mrs. Drabble, the stewardess, fast by the arm, and, without taking the slightest notice of the captain or the passengers, placed her on the nearest seat he could find. As he did this his face became visible in the moonlight, and displayed to the startled spectators an expression of blank consternation.

"Compose yourself, Mrs. Drabble," said the doctor, in tones of unmistakable alarm. "Keep quiet, and let the air blow over you. Collect yourself, ma'am—for Heaven's sake, collect yourself!"

Mrs. Drabble made no answer. She beat her hands vacantly on her knees, and stared straight before her, like a woman panic-stricken.

"What's wrong?" asked the captain, setting down his glass of grog in dismay. "Anything amiss with those two unfortunate women?"

"Nothing," said the doctor. "Both doing admirably well."

"Anything queer with their babies?" continued the captain. "Are there more than you bargained for, Jolly? Twins, for instance?"

"No! no!" replied Mr. Jolly, impatiently. "A baby apiece-both boys both in first-rate condition. Judge for yourselves," added the doctor, as the two new cabin passengers tried their lungs below for the first time, and found that they answered their purpose in the most satisfactory manner.

"What the devil's amiss, then, with you and Mrs. Drabble?" persisted the captain, beginning to lose his temper again.

"Mrs. Drabble and I are two innocent people, and we have

got into the most dreadful scrape that ever you heard of!" was Mr. Jolly's startling answer.

The captain, followed by Mr. Purling and Mr. Sims, approached the doctor with looks of horror. Even the man at the wheel stretched himself over it as far as he could to hear what was coming next. The only uninterested person present was Mr. Smallchild. His time had come round for going to sleep again, and he was snoring peacefully, with his biscuit and bacon close beside him.

"Let's hear the worst of it at once, Jolly," said the captain, a little impatiently.

The doctor paid no heed to his request. His whole attention was absorbed by Mrs. Drabble. "Are you better now, ma'am?" he asked, anxiously.

"No better in my mind," answered Mrs. Drabble, beginning to beat her knees again."

Worse, if anything."

"Listen to me," said Mr. Jolly, coaxingly. "I'll put the whole case over again to you, in a few plain questions. You'll find it all come back to your memory, if you only follow me attentively, and if you take time to think and collect yourself before you attempt to answer."

Mrs. Drabble bowed her head in speechless submission—and listened. Everybody else on the quarter-deck listened, except the impenetrable Mr. Smallchild.

"Now, ma'am!" said the doctor. "Our troubles began in Mrs. Heavysides's cabin, which is situated on the starboard side of the ship?"

"They did, sir," replied Mrs. Drabble.

"Good! We went backward and forward, an infinite number of times, between Mrs. Heavysides (starboard) and Mrs. Smallchild (larboard)—but we found that Mrs. Heavysides, having got the start, kept it—and when I called out, 'Mrs. Drabble! here's a chopping boy for you; come and take him!'—I called out starboard, didn't I?"

"Starboard, sir—I'll take my oath of it," said Mrs. Drabble.

"Good again! 'Here's a chopping boy,' I said. 'Take him, ma'am, and make him comfortable in the cradle.' And you took him, and made him comfortable in the cradle, accordingly? Now where was the cradle?"

"In the main cabin, sir," replied Mrs. Drabble.

"Just so! In the main cabin, because we hadn't got room for it in either of the sleeping- cabins. You put the starboard baby (otherwise Heavysides) in the clothes-basket cradle in the main cabin. Good once more. How was the cradle placed?"

"Crosswise to the ship, sir," said Mrs. Drabble.

"Crosswise to the ship? That is to say, with one side longwise toward the stern of the vessel, and one side longwise toward the bows. Bear that in mind and now follow me a little further. No! no! don't say you can't, and your head's in a whirl. My next question will steady it. Carry your mind on half an hour, Mrs. Drabble. At the end of half an hour you heard my voice again; and my voice called out, 'Mrs. Drabble! here's another chopping boy for you; come and take him!'—and you came and took him larboard, didn't you?"

"Larboard, sir, I don't deny it," answered Mrs. Drabble.

"Better and better! 'Here is another chopping boy,' I said. 'Take him, ma'am, and make him comfortable in the cradle, along with number one.' And you took the larboard baby (otherwise Smallchild), and made him comfortable in the cradle along with the starboard baby (otherwise Heavysides), accordingly? Now what happened after that?"

"Don't ask me, sir!" exclaimed Mrs. Drabble, losing her self-control, and wringing her hands desperately.

"Steady, ma'am! I'll put it to you as plain as print. Steady! and listen to me. Just as you had made the larboard baby comfortable I had occasion to send you into the starboard (or Heavysides) cabin to fetch something which I wanted in the larboard (or Smallchild) cabin; I kept you there a little while along with me; I left you and went into the Heavysides cabin, and called to you to bring me something I wanted out of the Smallchild cabin, but before you got half-way across the main cabin I said, 'No; stop where you are, and I'll come to you;' immediately after which Mrs. Smallchild alarmed you, and you came across to me of your own accord; and thereupon I stopped you in the main cabin, and said, 'Mrs. Drabble, your mind's getting confused; sit down and collect your scattered intellects;' and you sat down and tried to collect them—"

("And couldn't, sir," interposed Mrs. Drabble, parenthetically. "Oh, my head! My head!")

—"And tried to collect your scattered intellects, and couldn't?" continued the doctor. "And the consequence was, when I came out from the Smallchild cabin to see how you were getting on, I found you with the clothes-basket cradle hoisted up on the cabin table, staring down at the babies inside, with your mouth dropped open, and both your hands twisted in your hair?

"And when I said, 'Anything wrong with either of those two fine boys, Mrs. Drabble?' you caught me by the coat collar, and whispered in my right ear these words, 'Lord save us and help us, Mr. Jolly, I've confused the two babies in my mind, and I don't know which is which!'"

"And I don't know how!" cried Mrs. Drabble, hysterically. "Oh, my head! my head! I don't know now!"

"Captain Gillop and gentlemen," said Mr. Jolly, wheeling round and addressing his audience with the composure of sheer despair, "that is the Scrape—and, if you ever heard of a worse one, I'll trouble you to compose this miserable woman by mentioning it immediately."

Captain Gillop looked at Mr. Purling and Mr. Sims. Mr. Purling and Mr. Sims looked at Captain Gillop. They were all three thunderstruck—and no wonder.

"Can't you throw any light on it, Jolly?" inquired the captain, who was the first to recover himself.

"If you knew what I have had to do below, you wouldn't ask me such a question as that," replied the doctor. "Remember that I have had the lives of two women and two children to answer for—remember that I have been cramped up in two small sleeping-cabins, with hardly room to turn round in, and just light enough from two miserable little lamps to see my hand before me; remember the professional difficulties of the situation, the ship rolling about under me all the while, and the stewardess to compose into the bargain; bear all that in mind, will you, and then tell me how much spare time I had on my hands for comparing two boys together inch by inch—two boys born at night, within half an hour of each other, on board a ship at sea. Ha, ha! I only wonder the mothers and the boys and the doctor are all five of them alive to tell the story!"

"No marks on one or other of them that happened to catch your eye?" asked Mr. Sims.

"They must have been strongish marks to catch my eye in the light I had to work by, and in the professional difficulties I had to grapple with," said the doctor. "I saw they were both straight, well-formed children—and that's all I saw."

"Are their infant features sufficiently developed to indicate a family likeness?" inquired Mr. Purling. "Should you say they took after their fathers or their mothers?"

"Both of them have light eyes, and light hair—such as it is," replied Mr. Jolly, doggedly. "Judge for yourself."

"Mr. Smallchild has light eyes and light hair," remarked Mr. Sims.

"And Simon Heavysides has light eyes and light hair," rejoined Mr. Purling.

"I should recommend waking Mr. Smallchild, and sending for Heavysides, and letting the two fathers toss up for it," suggested Mr. Sims.

"The parental feeling is not to be trifled with in that heartless manner," retorted Mr. Purling.

"I should recommend trying the Voice of Nature."

"What may that be, sir?" inquired Captain Gillop, with great curiosity.

"The maternal instinct," replied Mr. Purling. "The mother's intuitive knowledge of her own child."

"Ay, ay!" said the captain, "Well thought of. What do you say, Jolly, to the Voice of Nature?"

The doctor held up his hand impatiently. He was engaged in resuming the effort to rouse Mrs. Drabble's memory by a system of amateur cross-examination, with the unsatisfactory result of confusing her more helplessly than ever.

Could she put the cradle back, in her own mind, into its original position? No. Could she remember whether she laid the starboard baby (otherwise Heavysides) on the side of the cradle nearest the stern of the ship, or nearest the bows? No. Could she remember any better about the larboard baby (otherwise Smallchild)? No.

Why did she move the cradle on to the cabin table, and so bewilder herself additionally, when she was puzzled already? Because it came over her, on a sudden, that she had forgotten, in the dreadful confusion of the time, which was which; and of course she wanted to look closer at them, and see; and she couldn't see; and to her dying day she should never forgive herself; and let them throw her overboard, for a miserable wretch, if they liked—and so on, till the persevering doctor was wearied out at last, and gave up Mrs. Drabble, and gave up, with her, the whole case.

"I see nothing for it but the Voice of Nature," said the captain, holding fast to Mr. Purling's idea. "Try it, Jolly—you can but try it."

"Something must be done," said the doctor. "I can't leave the women alone any longer, and the moment I get below they will both ask for their babies. Wait here till you're fit to be seen, Mrs. Drabble, and then follow me. Voice of Nature!" added Mr. Jolly, contemptuously, as he descended the cabin stairs. "Oh yes, I'll try it—much good the Voice of Nature will do us, gentlemen. You shall judge for yourselves."

Favoured by the night, Mr. Jolly cunningly turned down the dim lamps in the sleeping-cabins to a mere glimmer, on the pretext that the light was bad for his patients' eyes. He then took up the first of the two unlucky babies that came to hand, marked the clothes in which it was wrapped with a blot of ink, and carried it in to Mrs. Smallchild, choosing her cabin merely because he happened to be nearest to it.

The second baby (distinguished by having no mark) was taken by Mrs. Drabble to Mrs. Heavysides. For a certain time the two mothers and the two babies were left together. They were then separated again by medical order; and were afterward reunited, with the difference that the marked baby went on this occasion to Mrs. Heavysides, and the unmarked baby to Mrs. Smallchild—the result, in the obscurity of the sleeping-cabins, proving to be that one baby did just as well as the other, and that the Voice of Nature was (as Mr. Jolly had predicted) totally incompetent to settle the existing difficulty.

"While night serves us, Captain Gillop, we shall do very well," said the doctor, after he had duly reported the failure of Mr. Purling's suggested experiment. "But when morning comes, and daylight shows the difference between the children, we must be prepared with a course of some kind. If the two mothers below get the slightest suspicion of the case as it stands, the nervous shock of the discovery may do dreadful mischief. They must be kept deceived, in the interests of their own health. We must choose a baby for each of them when tomorrow comes, and then hold to the choice, till the mothers are well and up again. The question is, who's to take the responsibility? I don't usually stick at trifles—but I candidly admit that I'm afraid of it."

"I decline meddling in the matter, on the ground that I am a perfect stranger," said Mr. Sims.

"And I object to interfere, from precisely similar motives," added Mr. Purling, agreeing for the first time with a proposition that emanated from his natural enemy all through the voyage.

"Wait a minute, gentlemen," said Captain Gillop. "I've got this difficult matter, as I think, in its right bearings. We must make a clean breast of it to the husbands, and let them take the responsibility."

"I believe they won't accept it," observed Mr. Sims.

"And I believe they will," asserted Mr. Purling, relapsing into his old habits.

"If they won't," said the captain, firmly, "I'm master on board this ship—and, as sure as my name is Thomas Gillop, I'll take the responsibility!"

This courageous declaration settled all difficulties for the time being; and a council was held to decide on future proceedings. It was resolved to remain passive until the next morning, on the last faint chance that a few hours' sleep might compose Mrs. Brabble's bewildered memory. The babies were to be moved into the main cabin before the daylight grew bright—or, in other words, before Mrs. Smallchild or Mrs. Heavysides could identify the infant who had passed the night with her.

The doctor and the captain were to be assisted by Mr. Purling, Mr. Sims, and the first mate, in the capacity of witnesses; and the assembly so constituted was to meet, in consideration of the emergency of the case, at six o'clock in the morning, punctually. At six o'clock, accordingly, with the weather fine, and the wind still fair, the proceedings began. For the last time Mr. Jolly cross-examined Mrs. Drabble, assisted by the captain, and supervised by the witnesses. Nothing whatever was elicited from the unfortunate stewardess. The doctor pronounced her confusion to be chronic, and the captain and the witnesses unanimously agreed with him.

The next experiment tried was the revelation of the true state of the case to the husbands.

Mr. Smallchild happened, on this occasion, to be "squaring his accounts" for the morning; and the first articulate words which escaped him in reply to the disclosure were, "Devilled biscuit and anchovy paste."

Further perseverance merely elicited an impatient request that they would "pitch him overboard at once, and the two babies along with him." Serious remonstrance was tried next, with no better effect. "Settle it how you like," said Mr. Smallchild, faintly. "Do you leave it to me, sir, as commander of this vessel?" asked Captain Gillop. (No answer.) "Nod your head, sir, if you can't speak." Mr. Smallchild nodded his head round-wise on his pillow—and fell asleep. "Does that count for leave to me to act?" asked Captain Gillop of the witnesses. And the witnesses answered, decidedly, Yes.

The ceremony was then repeated with Simon Heavysides, who responded, as became so intelligent a man, with a proposal of his own for solving the difficulty

"Captain Gillop and gentlemen," said the carpenter, with fluent and melancholy politeness, "I should wish to consider Mr. Smallchild before myself in this matter. I am quite willing to part with my baby (whichever he is); and I respectfully propose that Mr. Smallchild should take both the children, and so make quite sure that he has really got possession of his own son."

The only immediate objection to this ingenious proposition was started by the doctor, who sarcastically inquired of Simon, "what he thought Mrs. Heavysides would say to it?" The carpenter confessed that this consideration had escaped him, and that Mrs. Heavysides was only too likely to be an irremovable obstacle in the way of the proposed arrangement. The witnesses all thought so too; and Heavysides and his idea were dismissed together, after Simon had first gratefully expressed his entire readiness to leave it all to the captain.

"Very well, gentlemen," said Captain Gillop. "As commander on board, I reckon next after the husbands in the matter of responsibility. I have considered this difficulty in all its bearings, and I'm prepared to deal with it. The Voice of Nature (which you proposed, Mr. Purling) has been found to fail. The tossing up for it (which you proposed, Mr. Sims) doesn't square altogether with my notions of what's right in a very serious business. No, sir! I've got my own plan; and I'm now about to try it. Follow me below, gentlemen, to the steward's pantry."

The witnesses looked round on one another in the profoundest astonishment—and followed.

"Pickerel," said the captain, addressing the steward, "bring out the scales."

The scales were of the ordinary kitchen sort, with a tin tray on one side to hold the commodity to be weighed, and a stout iron slab on the other to support the weights. Pickerel placed these scales upon a neat little pantry table, fitted on the ball-

and-socket principle, so as to save the breaking of crockery by swinging with the motion of the ship.

"Put a clean duster in the tray," said the captain. "Doctor," he continued, when this had been done, "shut the doors of the sleeping-berths (for fear of the women hearing anything), and oblige me by bringing those two babies in here."

"Oh, sir!" exclaimed Mrs. Drabble, who had been peeping guiltily into the pantry—"oh, don't hurt the little dears! If anybody suffers, let it be me!"

"Hold your tongue, if you please, ma'am," said the captain. "And keep the secret of these proceedings, if you wish to keep your place. If the ladies ask for their children, say they will have them in ten minutes' time."

The doctor came in, and set down the clothes-basket cradle on the pantry floor. Captain Gillop immediately put on his spectacles, and closely examined the two unconscious innocents who lay beneath him.

"Six of one and half a dozen of the other," said the captain. "I don't see any difference between them. Wait a bit, though! Yes, I do.' One's a bald baby. Very good. We'll begin with that one. Doctor, strip the bald baby, and put him in the scales."

The bald baby protested—in his own language—but in vain. In two minutes he was flat on his back in the tin tray, with the clean duster under him to take the chill off.

"Weigh him accurately, Pickerel," continued the captain. "Weigh him, if necessary, to an eighth of an ounce. Gentlemen! watch this proceeding closely; it's a very important one."

While the steward was weighing and the witnesses were watching, Captain Gillop asked his first mate for the log-book of the ship, and for pen and ink.

"How much, Pickerel?" asked the captain, opening the book.

"Seven pounds one ounce and a quarter," answered the steward.

"Right, gentlemen?" pursued the captain.

"Quite right," said the witnesses.

"Bald child—distinguished as Number One—weight, seven pounds one ounce and a quarter (*avoirdupois*)," repeated the captain, writing down the entry in the log-book. "Very good. We'll put the bald baby back now, doctor, and try the hairy one next."

The hairy one protested—also in his own language—and also in vain.

"How much, Pickerel?" asked the captain.

"Six pounds fourteen ounces and three-quarters," replied the steward.

"Right, gentlemen?" inquired the captain.

"Quite right," answered the witnesses.

"Hairy child—distinguished as Number Two—weight, six pounds fourteen ounces and three-quarters (*avoirdupois*)," repeated and wrote the captain. "Much obliged to you, Jolly-that will do. When you have got the other baby back in the cradle, tell Mrs. Drabble neither of them must be taken out of it till further orders; and then be so good as to join me and these gentlemen on deck. If anything of a discussion rises up among us, we won't run the risk of being heard in the sleeping-berths." With these words Captain Gillop led the way on deck, and the first mate followed with the log-book and the pen and ink.

"Now, gentlemen," began the captain, when the doctor had joined the assembly, "my first mate will open these proceedings by reading from the log a statement which I have written myself, respecting this business, from beginning to end. If you find it all equally correct with the statement of what the two children weigh, I'll trouble you to sign it, in your quality of witnesses, on the spot."

The first mate read the narrative, and the witnesses signed it, as perfectly correct. Captain Gillop then cleared his throat, and addressed his expectant audience in these words:

"You'll all agree with me, gentlemen, that justice is justice, and that like must to like. Here's my ship of five hundred tons, fitted with her spars accordingly. Say she's a schooner of a hundred and fifty tons, the veriest landsman among you, in that case, wouldn't put such masts as these into her. Say, on the other hand, she's an Indiaman of a thousand tons, would our spars (excellent good sticks as they are, gentlemen) be suitable for a vessel of that capacity? Certainly not. A schooner's spars to a schooner, and a ship's spars to a ship, in fit and fair proportion."

Here the captain paused, to let the opening of his speech sink well into the minds of the audience. The audience encouraged him with the parliamentary cry of "Hear! hear!" The captain went on:

"In the serious difficulty which now besets us, gentlemen, I take my stand on the principle which I have just stated to you. My decision is as follows: Let us give the heaviest of the two babies to the heaviest of the two women; and let the lightest then fall, as a matter of course, to the other. In a week's time, if- this weather holds, we shall all (please God) be in port; and if there's a better way out of this mess than my way, the parsons and lawyers ashore may find it, and welcome."

With those words the captain closed his oration; and the assembled council immediately sanctioned the proposal submitted to them, with all the unanimity of men who had no idea of their own to set up in opposition.

Mr. Jolly was next requested (as the only available authority) to settle the question of weight between Mrs. Smallchild and Mrs. Heavysides, and decided it, without a moment's hesitation, in favour of the carpenter's wife, on the indisputable ground that she was the tallest and stoutest woman of the two.

Thereupon the bald baby, "distinguished as Number One," was taken into Mrs. Heavysides' cabin; and the hairy baby, "distinguished as Number Two," was accorded to Mrs. Smallchild; the Voice of Nature, neither in the one case nor in the other, raising the slightest objection to the captain's principle of distribution.

Before seven o'clock Mr. Jolly reported that the mothers and sons, larboard and starboard, were as happy and comfortable as any four people on board ship could possibly wish to be; and the captain thereupon dismissed the council with these parting remarks:

"We'll get the studding-sails on the ship now, gentlemen, and make the best of our way to port. Breakfast, Pickerel, in half an hour, and plenty of it! I doubt if that unfortunate Mrs. Drabble has heard the last of this business yet. We must all lend a hand, gentlemen, and pull her through if we can. In other respects the job's over, so far as we are concerned; and the parsons and lawyers must settle it ashore."

The parsons and the lawyers did nothing of the sort, for the plain reason that nothing was to be done. In ten days the ship was in port, and the news was broken to the two mothers. Each one of the two adored her baby, after ten day's experience of it—and each one of the two was in Mrs. Drabble's condition of not knowing which was which.

Every test was tried. First, the test by the doctor, who only repeated what he had told the captain. Secondly, the test by personal resemblance; which failed in consequence of the light hair, blue eyes, and Roman noses shared in common by the fathers, and the light hair, blue eyes, and no noses worth mentioning shared in common by the children. Thirdly, the test of Mrs. Drabble, which began and ended in fierce talking on one side and floods of tears on the other.

Fourthly, the test by legal decision, which broke down through the total absence of any instructions for the law to act on. Fifthly, and lastly, the test by appeal to the husbands, which fell to the ground in consequence of the husbands knowing nothing about the matter in hand. The captain's barbarous test by weight remained the test still—and here am I, a man of the lower order, without a penny to bless myself with, in consequence.

Yes! I was the bald baby of that memorable period. My excess in weight settled my destiny in life. The fathers and mothers on either side kept the babies according to the captain's principle of distribution, in despair of knowing what else to do. Mr. Smallchild, who was sharp enough when not seasick, made his fortune. Simon Heavysides persisted in increasing his family, and died in the work-house.

Judge for yourself (as Mr. Jolly might say) how the two boys born at sea fared in afterlife. I, the bald baby, have seen nothing of the hairy baby for years past. He may be short, like Mr. Smallchild—but I happen to know that he is wonderfully like Heavysides, (deceased), in the face. I may be tall, like the carpenter—but I have the Smallchild eyes, hair, and expression, notwithstanding.

Make what you can of that! You will find it come, in the end, to the same thing. Smallchild, junior, prospers in the world, because he weighed six pounds, fourteen ounces and three-quarters. Heavysides, junior, fails in the world, because he weighed seven pounds one ounce and a quarter. Such is destiny, and such is life. I'll never forgive my destiny as long as I live. There is my grievance. I wish you good-morning.

The Dead Alive

Chapter 1
The Sick Man

"Heart all right," said the doctor. "Lungs all right. No organic disease that I can discover. Philip Lefrank, don't alarm yourself. You are not going to die yet. The disease you are suffering from is—overwork. The remedy in your case—is rest."

So the doctor spoke, in my chambers in the Temple (London); having been sent for to see me about half an hour after I had alarmed my clerk by fainting at my desk. I have no wish to intrude myself needlessly on the reader's attention; but it may be necessary to add, in the way of explanation, that I am a "junior" barrister in good practice. I come from the Channel Island of Jersey. The French spelling of my name (Lefranc) was Anglicized generations since—in the days when the letter "k" was still used in England at the end of words which now terminate in "c." We hold our heads high, nevertheless, as a Jersey family. It is to this day a trial to my father to hear his son described as a member of the English bar.

"Rest!" I repeated, when my medical adviser had done. "My good friend, are you aware that it is term-time? The courts are sitting. Look at the briefs waiting for me on that table! Rest means ruin in my case."

"And work," added the doctor, quietly, "means death."

I started. He was not trying to frighten me: he was plainly in earnest.

"It is merely a question of time," he went on. "You have a

fine constitution; you are a young man; but you cannot deliberately overwork your brain, and derange your nervous system, much longer. Go away at once. If you are a good sailor, take a sea-voyage. The ocean air is the best of all air to build you up again. No: I don't want to write a prescription. I decline to physic you. I have no more to say."

With these words my medical friend left the room. I was obstinate: I went into court the same day.

The senior counsel in the case on which I was engaged applied to me for some information which it was my duty to give him. To my horror and amazement, I was perfectly unable to collect my ideas; facts and dates all mingled together confusedly in my mind. I was led out of court thoroughly terrified about myself. The next day my briefs went back to the attorneys; and I followed my doctor's advice by taking my passage for America in the first steamer that sailed for New York.

I had chosen the voyage to America in preference to any other trip by sea, with a special object in view. A relative of my mother's had emigrated to the United States many years since, and had thriven there as a farmer. He had given me a general invitation to visit him if I ever crossed the Atlantic. The long period of inaction, under the name of rest, to which the doctor's decision had condemned me, could hardly be more pleasantly occupied, as I thought, than by paying a visit to my relation, and seeing what I could of America in that way. After a brief sojourn at New York, I started by railway for the residence of my host-Mr. Isaac Meadowcroft, of Morwick Farm.

There are some of the grandest natural prospects on the face of creation in America. There is also to be found in certain States of the Union, by way of wholesome contrast, scenery as flat, as monotonous, and as uninteresting to the traveller, as any that the earth can show. The part of the country in which M. Meadowcroft's farm was situated fell within this latter category. I looked round me when I stepped out of the railway-carriage on the platform at Morwick Station; and I said to myself, " If to be cured means, in my case, to be dull, I have accurately picked out the very place for the purpose."

I look back at those words by the light of later events; and I pronounce them, as you will soon pronounce them, to be the words of an essentially rash man, whose hasty judgment never stopped to consider what surprises time and chance together might have in store for him.

Mr. Meadowcroft's eldest son, Ambrose, was waiting at the station to drive me to the farm.

There was no forewarning, in the appearance of Ambrose Meadowcroft, of the strange and terrible events that were to follow my arrival at Morwick. A healthy, handsome young fellow, one of thousands of other healthy, handsome young fellows, said, "How d'ye do, Mr. Lefrank? Glad to see you, sir. Jump into the buggy; the man will look after your portmanteau." With equally conventional politeness I answered, "Thank you. How are you all at home?" So we started on the way to the farm.

Our conversation on the drive began with the subjects of agriculture and breeding. I displayed my total ignorance of crops and cattle before we had travelled ten yards on our journey. Ambrose Meadowcroft cast about for another topic, and failed to find it. Upon this I cast about on my side, and asked, at a venture, if I had chosen a convenient time for my visit. The young farmer's stolid brown face instantly brightened. I had evidently hit, hap-hazard, on an interesting subject.

"You couldn't have chosen a better time," he said. "Our house has never been so cheerful as it is now."

"Have you any visitors staying with you?"

"It's not exactly a visitor. It's a new member of the family who has come to live with us."

"A new member of the family! May I ask who it is?"

Ambrose Meadowcroft considered before he replied; touched his horse with the whip; looked at me with a certain sheepish hesitation; and suddenly burst out with the truth, in the plainest possible words:

"It's just the nicest girl, sir, you ever saw in your life."

"Ay, ay! A friend of your sister's, I suppose?"

"A friend? Bless your heart! It's our little American cousin, Naomi Colebrook."

I vaguely remembered that a younger sister of Mr. Meadowcroft's had married an American merchant in the remote past, and had died many years since, leaving an only child. I was now further informed that the father also was dead. In his last moments he had committed his helpless daughter to the compassionate care of his wife's relations at Morwick.

"He was always, a speculating man," Ambrose went on. "Tried one thing after another, and failed in all. Died, sir, leaving barely enough to bury him. My father was a little doubtful, before she came here, how his American niece would turn out. We are English, you know; and, though we do live in the United States, we stick fast to our English ways and habits. "We don't much like American women in general, I can tell you; but when Naomi made her appearance she conquered us all. Such a girl! Took her place as one of the family directly. Learned to make herself useful in the dairy in a week's time. I tell you this—she hasn't been with us quite two months yet, and we wonder already how we ever got on without her!"

Once started on the subject of Naomi Colebrook, Ambrose held to that one topic, and talked on it without intermission. It required no great gift of penetration to discover the impression which the American cousin had produced in this case. The young fellow's enthusiasm communicated itself, in a certain tepid degree, to me. I really felt a mild flutter of anticipation at the prospect of seeing Naomi, when we drew up, toward the close of evening, at the gates of Morwick Farm.

Chapter 2
The New Faces

Immediately on my arrival, I was presented to Mr. Meadowcroft, the father.

The old man had become a confirmed invalid, confined by chronic rheumatism to his chair. He received me kindly, and a little wearily as well. His only unmarried daughter (he had long since been left a widower) was in the room, in attendance on her father. She was a melancholy, middle-aged woman, without visible attractions of any sort—one of those persons who appear to accept the obligation of living under protest, as a burden which they would never have consented to bear if they had only been consulted first. We three had a dreary little interview in a parlour of bare walls; and then I was permitted to go upstairs, and unpack my portmanteau in my own room.

"Supper will be at nine o'clock, sir," said Miss Meadowcroft.

She pronounced those words as if "supper" was a form of domestic offense, habitually committed by the men, and endured by the women. I followed the groom up to my room, not over-well pleased with my first experience of the farm.

No Naomi, and no romance, thus far!

My room was clean—oppressively clean. I quite longed to see a little dust somewhere. My library was limited to the Bible and the Prayer-book. My view from the window showed me a dead flat in a partial state of cultivation, fading sadly from view in the waning light. Above the head of my spruce white bed hung a scroll, bearing a damnatory quotation from Scripture in emblazoned letters of red and black.

The dismal presence of Miss Meadowcroft had passed over my bedroom, and had blighted it. My spirits sank as I looked round me. Suppertime was still an event in the future. I lighted the candles and took from my portmanteau what I firmly believe to have been the first French novel ever produced at Morwick Farm. It was one of the masterly and charming stories of Dumas the elder. In five minutes I was in a new world, and my melancholy room was full of the liveliest French company. The sound of an imperative and uncompromising bell recalled me in due time to the regions of reality. I looked at my watch. Nine o'clock.

Ambrose met me at the bottom of the stairs, and showed me the way to the supper-room.

Mr. Meadowcroft's invalid chair had been wheeled to the head of the table. On his righthand side sat his sad and silent daughter. She signed to me, with a ghostly solemnity, to take the vacant place on the left of her father. Silas Meadowcroft came in at the same moment, and was presented to me by his brother. There was a strong family likeness between them, Ambrose being the taller and the handsomer man of the two. But there was no marked character in either face. I set them down as men with undeveloped qualities, waiting (the good and evil qualities alike) for time and circumstances to bring them to their full growth.

The door opened again while I was still studying the two brothers, without, I honestly confess, being very favourably impressed by either of them. A new member of the family circle, who instantly attracted my attention, entered the room.

He was short, spare, and wiry; singularly pale for a person whose life was passed in the country. The face was in other respects, besides this, a striking face to see. As to the lower part, it was covered with a thick black beard and moustache, at a time when shaving was the rule, and beards the rare exception, in America.

As to the upper part of the face, it was irradiated by a pair of wild, glittering brown eyes, the expression of which suggested to me that there was something not quite right with the man's mental balance. A perfectly sane person in all his sayings and doings, so far as I could see, there was still something in those wild brown eyes which suggested to me that, under exceptionally trying circumstances, he might surprise his oldest friends by acting in some exceptionally violent or foolish way. "A little cracked" that in the popular phrase was my impression of the stranger who now made his appearance in the supper-room.

Mr. Meadowcroft the elder, having not spoken one word thus far, himself introduced the newcomer to me, with a side-glance at his sons, which had something like defiance in it—a glance which, as I was sorry to notice, was returned with the defiance on their side by the two young men.

"Philip Lefrank, this is my overlooker, Mr. Jago," said the old man, formally presenting us. "John Jago, this is my young relative by marriage, Mr. Lefrank. He is not well: he has come over the ocean for rest, and change of scene. Mr. Jago is an American, Philip. I hope you have no prejudice against Americans. Make acquaintance with Mr. Jago. Sit together." He cast another dark look at his sons; and the sons again returned it. They pointedly drew back from John Jago as he approached the empty chair next to me, and moved round to the opposite side of the table. It was plain that the man with the beard stood high in the father's favour, and that he was cordially disliked for that or for some other reason by the sons.

The door opened once more. A young lady quietly joined the party at the supper-table.

Was the young lay Naomi Colebrook? I looked at Ambrose, and saw the answer in his face. Naomi Colebrook at last!

A pretty girl, and, so far as I could judge by appearances, a good girl too. Describing her generally, I may say that she had a small head, well carried, and well set on her shoulders; bright gray eyes, that looked at you honestly, and meant what they looked; a trim, slight little figure—too slight for our English notions of beauty; a strong American accent; and (a rare thing in America) a pleasantly toned voice, which made the accent agreeable to English ears.

Our first impressions of people are, in nine cases out of ten, the right impressions. I liked Naomi Colebrook at first sight; liked her pleasant smile; liked her hearty shake of the hand when we were presented to each other. "If I get on well with nobody else in this house," I thought to myself, "I shall certainly get on well with you."

For once in a way, I proved a true prophet. In the atmosphere of smouldering enmities at Morwick Farm, the pretty American girl and I remained firm and true friends from first to last. Ambrose made room for Naomi to sit between his brother and himself. She changed colour for a moment, and looked at him, with a pretty, reluctant tenderness, as she took her chair. I strongly suspected the young farmer of squeezing her hand privately, under cover of the tablecloth.

The supper was not a merry one. The only cheerful conversation was the conversation across the table between Naomi and me.

For some incomprehensible reason, John Jago seemed to be ill at ease in the presence of his young countrywoman. He looked up at Naomi doubtingly from his plate, and looked down again slowly with a frown. When I addressed him, he answered constrainedly. Even when he spoke to Mr. Meadowcroft, he was still on his guard—on his guard against the two young men, as I fancied by the direction which his eyes took on these occasions. When we began our meal, I had noticed for the first time that Silas Meadowcroft's left hand was strapped up with surgical plaster; and I now further observed that John Jago's wandering brown eyes, furtively looking at everybody round the table in turn, looked with a curious, cynical scrutiny at the young man's injured hand.

By way of making my first evening at the farm all the more embarrassing to me as a stranger, I discovered before long that the father and sons were talking indirectly at each other, through Mr. Jago and through me. When old Mr. Meadowcroft spoke disparagingly to his overlooker of some past mistake made in the cultivation of the arable land of the farm, old Mr. Meadowcroft's eyes pointed the application of his hostile criticism straight in the direction of his two sons.

When the two sons seized a stray remark of mine about animals in general, and applied it satirically to the mismanagement of sheep and oxen in particular, they looked at John Jago, while they talked to me. On occasions of this sort—and they happened frequently—Naomi struck in resolutely at the right moment, and turned the talk to some harmless topic. Every time she took a prominent part in this way in keeping the peace, melancholy Miss Meadowcroft looked slowly round at her in stern and silent disparagement of her interference.

A more dreary and more disunited family party I never sat at the table with. Envy, hatred, malice and uncharitableness are never so essentially detestable to my mind as when they are animated by a sense of propriety, and work under the surface.

But for my interest in Naomi, and my other interest in the little love-looks which I now and then surprised passing between her and Ambrose, I should never have sat through that supper. I should certainly have taken refuge in my French novel and my own room.

At last the unendurably long meal, served with ostentatious profusion, was at an end. Miss Meadowcroft rose with her ghostly solemnity, and granted me my dismissal in these words:

"We are early people at the farm, Mr. Lefrank. I wish you goodnight."

She laid her bony hands on the back of Mr. Meadowcroft's invalid-chair, cut him short in his farewell salutation to me, and wheeled him out to his bed as if she were wheeling him out to his grave.

"Do you go to your room immediately, sir? If not, may I offer you a cigar—provided the young gentlemen will permit it?"

So, picking his words with painful deliberation, and pointing his reference to "the young gentlemen" with one sardonic side-look at them, Mr. John Jago performed the duties of hospitality on his side. I excused myself from accepting the cigar. With studied politeness, the man of the glittering brown eyes wished me a good-night's rest, and left the room.

Ambrose and Silas both approached me hospitably, with their open cigar-cases in their hands.

"You were quite right to say 'No,'" Ambrose began. "Never smoke with John Jago. His cigars will poison you."

"And never believe a word John Jago says to you," added Silas. "He is the greatest liar in America, let the other be whom he may."

Naomi shook her forefinger reproachfully at them, as if the two sturdy young farmers had been two children.

"What will Mr. Lefrank think," she said, "if you talk in that way of a person whom your father respects and trusts? Go and smoke. I am ashamed of both of you."

Silas slunk away without a word of protest. Ambrose stood his ground, evidently bent on making his peace with Naomi before he left her.

Seeing that I was in the way, I walked aside toward a glass door at the lower end of the room. The door opened on the trim little farm-garden, bathed at that moment in lovely moonlight. I stepped out to enjoy the scene, and found my way to a seat under an elm-tree. The grand repose of nature had never looked so unutterably solemn and beautiful as it now appeared, after what I had seen and heard inside the house.

I understood, or thought I understood, the sad despair of humanity which led men into monasteries in the old times. The misanthropical side of my nature (where is the sick man who is not conscious of that side of him?) was fast getting the upper hand of me when I felt a light touch laid on my shoulder, and found myself reconciled to my species once more by Naomi Colebrook.

Chapter 3

The Moonlight Meeting

"I want to speak to you," Naomi began. "You don't think ill of me for following you out here? We are not accustomed to stand much on ceremony in America."

"You are quite right in America. Pray sit down."

She seated herself by my side, looking at me frankly and fearlessly by the light of the moon.

"You are related to the family here," she resumed, "and I am related too. I guess I may say to you what I couldn't say to a stranger. I am right glad you have come here, Mr. Lefrank; and for a reason, sir, which you don't suspect."

"Thank you for the compliment you pay me, Miss Colebrook, whatever the reason may be."

She took no notice of my reply; she steadily pursued her own train of thought.

"I guess you may do some good, sir, in this wretched house," the girl went on, with her eyes still earnestly fixed on my face. "There is no love, no trust, no peace, at Morwick Farm. They want somebody here, except Ambrose. Don't think ill of Ambrose; he is only thoughtless. I say, the rest of them want somebody here to make them ashamed of their hard hearts, and their horrid, false, envious ways. You are a gentleman; you know more than they know; they can't help themselves; they must look up to you. Try, Mr. Lefrank, when you have the opportunity—pray try, sir, to make peace among them. You heard what went on at supper-time; and you were disgusted with it. Oh yes, you were! I saw you frown to yourself; and I know what that means in you Englishmen."

There was no choice but to speak one's mind plainly to Naomi. I acknowledged the impression which had been produced on me at suppertime just as plainly as I have acknowledged it in these pages. Naomi nodded her head in undisguised approval of my candour.

"That will do; that's speaking out," she said. "But—oh my! You put it a deal too mildly, sir, when you say the men don't seem to be on friendly terms together here. They hate each other. That's the word, Mr. Lefrank—hate; bitter, bitter, bitter hate!" She clinched her little fists; she shook them vehemently, by way of adding emphasis to her last words; and then she suddenly remembered Ambrose. "Except Ambrose," she added, opening her hand again, and laying it very earnestly on my arm. "Don't go and misjudge Ambrose, sir. There is no harm in poor Ambrose."

The girl's innocent frankness was really irresistible.

"Should I be altogether wrong," I asked, "if I guessed that you were a little partial to Ambrose?"

An Englishwoman would have felt, or would at least have assumed, some little hesitation at replying to my question. Naomi did not hesitate for an instant.

"You are quite right, sir," she said with the most perfect composure. "If things go well, I mean to marry Ambrose."

"If things go well," I repeated. "What does that mean? Money?"

She shook her head.

"It means a fear that I have in my own mind," she answered-"a fear, Mr. Lefrank, of matters taking a bad turn among the men here—the wicked, hard-hearted, unfeeling men. I don't mean Ambrose, sir; I mean his brother Silas, and John Jago. Did you notice Silas's hand? John Jago did that, sir, with a knife."

"By accident?" I asked.

"On purpose," she answered. "In return for a blow."

This plain revelation of the state of things at Morwick Farm rather staggered me—blows and knives under the rich and respectable roof-tree of old Mr. Meadowcroft—blows and knives, not among the labourers, but among the masters! My first impression was like your first impression, no doubt. I could hardly believe it.

"Are you sure of what you say?" I inquired.

"I have it from Ambrose. Ambrose would never deceive me. Ambrose knows all about it."

My curiosity was powerfully excited. To what sort of household had I rashly voyaged across the ocean in search of rest and quiet?

"May I know all about it too?" I said.

"Well, I will try and tell you what Ambrose told me. But you must promise me one thing first, sir. Promise you won't go away and leave us when you know the whole truth. Shake hands on it, Mr. Lefrank; come, shake hands on it."

There was no resisting her fearless frankness. I shook hands on it. Naomi entered on her narrative the moment I had given her my pledge, without wasting a word by way of preface.

"When you are shown over the farm here," she began, "you will see that it is really two farms in one. On this side of it, as we look from under this tree, they raise crops: on the other side—on much the larger half of the land, mind—they raise cattle. When Mr. Meadowcroft got too old and too sick to look after his farm himself, the boys (I mean Ambrose and Silas) divided the work between them. Ambrose looked after the crops, and Silas after the cattle.

"Things didn't go well, somehow, under their management. I can't tell you why. I am only sure Ambrose was not in fault. The old man got more and more dissatisfied, especially about his beasts. His pride is in his beasts. Without saying a word to the boys, he looked about privately (I think he was wrong in that, sir; don't you?)—he looked about privately for help; and, in an evil hour, he heard of John Jago. Do you like John Jago, Mr. Lefrank?"

"So far, no. I don't like him."

"Just my sentiments, sir. But I don't know: it's likely we may be wrong. There's nothing against John Jago, except that he is so odd in his ways. They do say he wears all that nasty hair on his face (I hate hair on a man's face) on account of a vow he made when he lost his wife. Don't you think, Mr. Lefrank, a man must be a little mad who shows his grief at losing his wife by vowing that he will never shave himself again? Well, that's what they do say John Jago vowed.

"Perhaps it's a lie. People are such liars here! Anyway, it's truth (the boys themselves confess that), when John came to the farm, he came with a first-rate character. The old father here isn't easy to please; and he pleased the old father. Yes, that's so. Mr. Meadowcroft don't like my countrymen in general. He's like his sons—English, bitter English, to the marrow of his bones. Somehow, in spite of that, John Jago got round him; maybe because John does certainly know his business.

"Oh yes! Cattle and crops, John knows his business. Since he's been overlooker, things have prospered as they didn't prosper in the time of the boys. Ambrose owned as much to me himself. Still, sir, it's hard to be set aside for a stranger; isn't it? John gives the orders now. The boys do their work; but they have no voice in it when John and the old man put their heads together over the business of the farm. I have been long in telling you of it, sir; but now you know how the envy and the hatred grew among the men before my time.

"Since I have been here, things seem to get worse and worse. There's hardly a day goes by that hard words don't pass between the boys and John, or the boys and their father. The old man has an aggravating way, Mr. Lefrank—a nasty way, as we do call it—of taking John Jago's part. Do speak to him about it when you get the chance. The main blame of the quarrel between Silas and John the other day lies at his door, as I think. I don't want to excuse Silas, either. It was brutal of him—though he is Ambrose's brother—to strike John, who is the smaller and weaker man of the two. But it was worse than brutal in John, sir, to out with his knife and try to stab Silas. Oh, he did it! If Silas had not caught the knife in his hand (his hand's awfully cut, I can tell you; I dressed it myself), it might have ended, for anything I know, in murder—"

She stopped as the word passed her lips, looked back over her shoulder, and started violently.

I looked where my companion was looking. The dark figure of a man was standing, watching us, in the shadow of the elm-tree. I rose directly to approach him. Naomi recovered her self-possession, and checked me before I could interfere.

"Who are you?" she asked, turning sharply toward the stranger. "What do you want there?"

The man stepped out from the shadow into the moonlight, and stood revealed to us as John Jago.

"I hope I am not intruding?" he said, looking hard at me.

"What do you want?" Naomi repeated.

"I don't wish to disturb you, or to disturb this gentleman," he proceeded. "When you are quite at leisure, Miss Naomi, you would be doing me a favour if you would permit me to say a few words to you in private."

He spoke with the most scrupulous politeness; trying, and trying vainly, to conceal some strong agitation which was in possession of him. His wild brown eyes—wilder than ever in the moonlight—rested entreatingly, with a strange under- lying expression of despair, on Naomi's face. His hands, clasped lightly in front of him, trembled incessantly. Little as I liked the man, he did really impress me as a pitiable object at that moment.

"Do you mean that you want to speak to me tonight?" Naomi asked, in undisguised surprise.

"Yes, miss, if you please, at your leisure and at Mr. Lefrank's."

Naomi hesitated.

"Won't it keep till tomorrow?" she said.

"I shall be away on farm business tomorrow, miss, for the whole day. Please to give me a few minutes this evening." He advanced a step toward her; his voice faltered, and dropped timidly to a whisper. "I really have something to say to you, Miss Naomi. It would be a kindness on your part—a very, very great kindness—if you will let me say it before I rest tonight."

I rose again to resign my place to him. Once more Naomi checked me.

" No," she said. "Don't stir." She addressed John Jago very reluctantly: "If you are so much in earnest about it, Mr. John, I suppose it must be. I can't guess what you can possibly have to say to me which cannot be said before a third person. However, it wouldn't be civil, I suppose, to say 'No' in my place. You know it's my business to wind up the hall-clock at ten every night. If you choose to come and help me, the chances are that we shall have the hall to ourselves. Will that do?"

"Not in the hall, miss, if you will excuse me."

"Not in the hall!"

"And not in the house either, if I may make so bold."

"What do you mean?" She turned impatiently, and appealed to me. "Do you understand him?"

John Jago signed to me imploringly to let him answer for himself.

"Bear with me, Miss Naomi," he said. "I think I can make you understand me. There are eyes on the watch, and ears on the watch, in the house; and there are some footsteps—I won't say whose—so soft, that no person can hear them."

The last allusion evidently made itself understood. Naomi stopped him before he could say more.

"Well, where is it to be?" she asked, resignedly. "Will the garden do, Mr. John?"

"Thank you kindly, miss; the garden will do." He pointed to a gravel-walk beyond us, bathed in the full flood of the moonlight. "There," he said, "where we can see all round us, and be sure that nobody is listening. At ten o'clock." He paused, and addressed himself to me. "I beg to apologize, sir, for intruding myself on your conversation. Please to excuse me."

His eyes rested with a last anxious, pleading look on Naomi's face. He bowed to us, and melted away into the shadow of the tree. The distant sound of a door closed softly came to us through the stillness of the night. John Jago had re-entered the house.

Now that he was out of hearing, Naomi spoke to me very earnestly:

"Don't suppose, sir, I have any secrets with him," she said. "I know no more than you do what he wants with me. I have half a mind not to keep the appointment when ten o'clock comes. What would you do in my place?"

"Having made the appointment," I answered, "it seems to be due to yourself to keep it. If you feel the slightest alarm, I will wait in another part of the garden, so that I can hear if you call me."

She received my proposal with a saucy toss of the head, and a smile of pity for my ignorance.

"You are a stranger, Mr. Lefrank, or you would never talk to me in that way. In America, we don't do the men the honour of letting them alarm us. In America, the women take care of themselves. He has got my promise to meet him, as you say; and I must keep my promise. Only think," she added, speaking more to herself than to me, "of John Jago finding out Miss Meadowcroft's nasty, sly, underhand ways in the house! Most men would never have noticed her."

I was completely taken by surprise. Sad and severe Miss Meadowcroft a listener and a spy! What next at Morwick Farm?

"Was that hint at the watchful eyes and ears, and the soft footsteps, really an allusion to Mr. Meadowcroft's daughter?" I asked.

"Of course it was. Ah! She has imposed on you as she imposes on everybody else. The false wretch! She is secretly at the bottom of half the bad feeling among the men. I am certain of it—she keeps Mr. Meadowcroft's mind bitter toward the boys. Old as she is, Mr. Lefrank, and ugly as she is, she wouldn't object (if she could only make him ask her) to be John Jago's second wife. No, sir; and she wouldn't break her heart if the boys were not left a stick or a stone on the farm when the father dies, I have watched her, and I know it. Ah! I could tell you such things! But there's no time now—it's close on ten o'clock; we must say goodnight. I am right glad I have spoken to you, sir. I say again, at parting, what I have said already: Use your influence, pray use your influence, to soften them, and to make them ashamed of themselves, in this wicked house. We will have more talk about what you can do tomorrow, when you are shown over the farm. Say goodbye now. Hark! There is ten striking! And look! Here is John Jago stealing out again in the shadow of the tree! Goodnight, friend Lefrank; and pleasant dreams."

With one hand she took mine, and pressed it cordially; with the other she pushed me away without ceremony in the direction of the house. A charming girl—an irresistible girl! I was nearly as bad as the boys. I declare, I almost hated John Jago, too, as we crossed each other in the shadow of the tree.

Arrived at the glass door, I stopped and looked back at the gravel-walk.

They had met. I saw the two shadowy figures slowly pacing backward and forward in the moonlight, the woman a little in advance of the man. What was he saying to her? Why was he so anxious that not a word of it should be heard? Our presentiments are sometimes, in certain rare cases, the faithful prophecy of the future. A vague distrust of that moonlight meeting stealthily took a hold on my mind. "Will mischief come of it?" I asked myself as I closed the door and entered the house.

Mischief did come of it. You shall hear how.

Chapter 4

The Beechen Stick.

Persons of sensitive, nervous temperament, sleeping for the first time in a strange house, and in a bed that is new to them, must make up their minds to pass a wakeful night. My first night at Morwick Farm was no exception to this rule. The little sleep

I had was broken and disturbed by dreams. Toward six o'clock in the morning, my bed became unendurable to me. The sun was shining in brightly at the window. I determined to try the reviving influence of a stroll in the fresh morning air.

Just as I got out of bed, I heard footsteps and voices under my window.

The footsteps stopped, and the voices became recognizable. I had passed the night with my window open; I was able, without exciting notice from below, to look out.

The persons beneath me were Silas Meadowcroft, John Jago, and three strangers, whose dress and appearance indicated plainly enough that they were labourers on the farm. Silas was swinging a stout beechen stick in his hand, and was speaking to Jago, coarsely and insolently enough, of his moonlight meeting with Naomi on the previous night.

"Next time you go courting a young lady in secret," said Silas, "make sure that the moon goes down first, or wait for a cloudy sky. You were seen in the garden, Master Jago; and you may as well tell us the truth for once in a way. Did you find her open to persuasion, sir? Did she say 'Yes?'"

John Jago kept his temper.

"If you must have your joke, Mr. Silas," he said, quietly and firmly, "be pleased to joke on some other subject. You are quite wrong, sir, in what you suppose to have passed between the young lady and me."

Silas turned about, and addressed himself ironically to the three labourers.

"You hear him, boys? He can't tell the truth, try him as you may. He wasn't making love to Naomi in the garden last night-oh dear, no! He has had one wife already; and he knows better than to take the yoke on his shoulders for the second time!"

Greatly to my surprise, John Jago met this clumsy jesting with a formal and serious reply.

"You are quite right, sir," he said. "I have no intention of marrying for the second time. What I was saying to Miss Naomi doesn't matter to you. It was not at all what you choose to suppose; it was something of quite another kind, with which you have no concern. Be pleased to understand once for all, Mr. Silas, that not so much as the thought of making love to the young lady has ever entered my head. I respect her; I admire her good qualities; but if she was the only woman left in the world, and if I was a much younger man than I am, I should never think of asking her to be my wife." He burst out suddenly into a harsh, uneasy laugh. "No, no! Not my style, Mr. Silas—not my style!"

Something in those words, or in his manner of speaking them, appeared to exasperate Silas. He dropped his clumsy irony, and addressed himself directly to John Jago in a tone of savage contempt.

"Not your style?" he repeated. "Upon my soul, that's a cool way of putting it, for a man in your place! What do you mean by calling her 'not your style?' You impudent beggar! Naomi Colebrook is meat for your master!"

John Jago's temper began to give way at last. He approached defiantly a step or two nearer to Silas Meadowcroft.

"Who is my master?" he asked.

"Ambrose will show you, if you go to him," answered the other. "Naomi is his sweetheart, not mine. Keep out of his way, if you want to keep a whole skin on your bones."

John Jago cast one of his sardonic side-looks at the farmer's wounded left hand. "Don't forget your own skin, Mr. Silas, when you threaten mine! I have set my mark on you once, sir. Let me by on my business, or I may mark you for a second time."

Silas lifted his beechen stick. The labourers, roused to some rude sense of the serious turn which the quarrel was taking, got between the two men, and parted them. I had been hurriedly dressing myself while the altercation was proceeding; and I now ran downstairs to try what my influence could do toward keeping the peace at Morwick Farm.

The war of angry words was still going on when I joined the men outside.

"Be off with you on your business, you cowardly hound!" I heard Silas say. "Be off with you to the town! And take care you don't meet Ambrose on the way!"

"Take you care you don't feel my knife again before I go!" cried the other man.

Silas made a desperate effort to break away from the labourers who were holding him.

"Last time you only felt my fist!" he shouted. "Next time you shall feel this!"

He lifted the stick as he spoke. I stepped up and snatched it out of his hand.

"Mr. Silas," I said, "I am an invalid, and I am going out for a walk. Your stick will be useful to me. I beg leave to borrow it."

The labourers burst out laughing. Silas fixed his eyes on me with a stare of angry surprise. John Jago, immediately recovering his self-possession, took off his hat, and made me a deferential bow.

"I had no idea, Mr. Lefrank, that we were disturbing you," he said. "I am very much ashamed of myself, sir. I beg to apologize."

"I accept your apology, Mr. Jago," I answered, "on the understanding that you, as the older man, will set the example of forbearance, if your temper is tried on any future occasion as it has been tried today. And I have further to request," I added, addressing myself to Silas, "that you will do me a favour, as your father's guest. The next time your good spirits lead you into making jokes at Mr. Jago's expense, don't carry them quite so far. I am sure you meant no harm, Mr. Silas. "Will you gratify me by saying so yourself? I want to see you and Mr. Jago shake hands."

John Jago instantly held out his hand, with an assumption of good feeling which was a little overacted, to my thinking. Silas Meadowcroft made no advance of the same friendly sort on his side.

"Let him go about his business," said Silas. "I won't waste anymore words on him, Mr. Lefrank, to please you. But (saving your presence) I'm d—d if I take his hand!"

Further persuasion was plainly useless, addressed to such a

man as this. Silas gave me no further opportunity of remonstrating with him, even if I had been inclined to do so. He turned about in sulky silence, and, retracing his steps along the path, disappeared round the corner of the house. The labourers withdrew next, in different directions, to begin the day's work. John Jago and I were alone.

I left it to the man of the wild brown eyes to speak first.

"In half an hour's time, sir," he said, "I shall be going on business to Narrabee, our market-town here. Can I take any letters to the post for you? Or is there anything else that I can do in the town?"

I thanked him, and declined both proposals. He made me another deferential bow, and withdrew into the house. I mechanically followed the path in the direction which Silas had taken before me.

Turning the corner of the house, and walking on for a little way, I found myself at the entrance to the stables, and face to face with Silas Meadowcroft once more. He had his elbows on the gate of the yard, swinging it slowly backward and forward, and turning and twisting a straw between his teeth. When he saw me approaching him, he advanced a step from the gate, and made an effort to excuse himself, with a very ill grace.

"No offense, mister. Ask me what you will besides, and I'll do it for you. But don't ask me to shake hands with John Jago; I hate him too badly for that. If I touched him with one hand, sir, I tell you this, I should throttle him with the other."

"That's your feeling toward the man, Mr. Silas, is it?"

"That's my feeling, Mr. Lefrank; and I'm not ashamed of it either."

"Is there any such place as a church in your neighbourhood, Mr. Silas?"

"Of course there is."

"And do you ever go to it?"

"Of course I do."

"At long intervals, Mr. Silas?"

"Every Sunday, sir, without fail."

Some third person behind me burst out laughing; some third person had been listening to our talk. I turned round, and discovered Ambrose Meadowcroft.

"I understand the drift of your catechism, sir, though my brother doesn't," he said. "Don't be hard on Silas, sir. He isn't the only Christian who leaves his Christianity in the pew when he goes out of church. You will never make us friends with John Jago, try as you may. Why, what have you got there, Mr. Lefrank? May I die if it isn't my stick! I have been looking for it everywhere!"

The thick beechen stick had been feeling uncomfortably heavy in my invalid hand for some time past. There was no sort of need for my keeping it any longer. John Jago was going away to Narrabee, and Silas Meadowcroft's savage temper was subdued to a sulky repose. I handed the stick back to Ambrose. He laughed as he took it from me.

"You can't think how strange it feels, Mr. Lefrank, to be out without one's stick," he said. "A man gets used to his stick, sir; doesn't he? Are you ready for your breakfast?"

"Not just yet. I thought of taking a little walk first."

"All right, sir. I wish I could go with you; but I have got my work to do this morning, and Silas has his work too. If you go back by the way you came, you will find yourself in the garden. If you want to go further, the wicket-gate at the end will lead you into the lane."

Through sheer thoughtlessness, I did a very foolish thing. I turned back as I was told, and left the brothers together at the gate of the stable-yard.

Chapter 5
The News from Narrabee

Arrived at the garden, a thought struck me. The cheerful speech and easy manner of Ambrose plainly indicated that he was ignorant thus far of the quarrel which had taken place under my window. Silas might confess to having taken his brother's stick, and might mention whose head he had threatened with it. It was not only useless, but undesirable, that Ambrose should know of the quarrel. I retraced my steps to the stable-yard. Nobody was at the gate. I called alternately to Silas and to Ambrose. Nobody answered. The brothers had gone away to their work.

Returning to the garden, I heard a pleasant voice wishing me "Good-morning." I looked round. Naomi Colebrook was standing at one of the lower windows of the farm. She had her working apron on, and she was industriously brightening the knives for the breakfast-table on an old-fashioned board. A sleek black cat balanced himself on her shoulder, watching the flashing motion of the knife as she passed it rapidly to and fro on the leather-covered surface of the board.

"Come here," she said; "I want to speak to you."

I noticed, as I approached, that her pretty face was clouded and anxious. She pushed the cat irritably off her shoulder; she welcomed me with only the faint reflection of her bright customary smile.

"I have seen John Jago," she said. "He has been hinting at something which he says happened under your bedroom window this morning. When I begged him to explain himself, he only answered, 'Ask Mr. Lefrank; I must be off to Narrabee.' What does it mean? Tell me right away, sir! I'm out of temper, and I can't wait!"

Except that I made the best instead of the worst of it, I told her what had happened under my window as plainly as I have told it here. She put down the knife that she was cleaning, and folded her hands before her, thinking.

"I wish I had never given John Jago that meeting," she said. "When a man asks anything of a woman, the woman, I find, mostly repents it if she says 'Yes.'"

She made that quaint reflection with a very troubled brow. The moonlight meeting had left some unwelcome remembrances in her mind. I saw that as plainly as I saw Naomi herself.

What had John Jago said to her? I put the question with all needful delicacy, making my apologies beforehand.

"I should like to tell you," she began, with a strong emphasis on the last word.

There she stopped. She turned pale; then suddenly flushed again to the deepest red. She took up the knife once more, and went on cleaning it as industriously as ever.

"I mustn't tell you," she resumed, with her head down over the knife. "I have promised not to tell anybody. That's the truth. Forget all about it, sir, as soon as you can. Hush! Here's the spy who saw us last night on the walk, and who told Silas!"

Dreary Miss Meadowcroft opened the kitchen door. She carried an ostentatiously large prayer-book; and she looked at Naomi as only a jealous woman of middle age can look at a younger and prettier woman than herself.

"Prayers, Miss Colebrook," she said in her sourest manner. She paused, and noticed me standing under the window. "Prayers, Mr. Lefrank," she added, with a look of devout pity, directed exclusively to my address.

"We will follow you directly, Miss Meadowcroft," said Naomi.

"I have no desire to intrude on your secrets, Miss Colebrook."

With that acrid answer, our priestess took herself and her prayer-book out of the kitchen. I joined Naomi, entering the room by the garden door. She met me eagerly.

"I am not quite easy about something," she said. "Did you tell me that you left Ambrose and Silas together?"

"Yes."

"Suppose Silas tells Ambrose of what happened this morning?"

The same idea, as I have already mentioned, had occurred to my mind. I did my best to reassure Naomi.

"Mr. Jago is out of the way," I replied. "You and I can easily put things right in his absence."

She took my arm.

"Come in to prayers," she said. "Ambrose will be there, and I shall find an opportunity of speaking to him."

Neither Ambrose nor Silas was in the breakfast-room when

we entered it. After waiting vainly for ten minutes, Mr. Meadowcroft told his daughter to read the prayers. Miss Meadowcroft read, thereupon, in the tone of an injured woman taking the throne of mercy by storm, and insisting on her rights. Breakfast followed; and still the brothers were absent. Miss Meadow- croft looked at her father, and said, "From bad to worse, sir. What did I tell you?" Naomi instantly applied the antidote: "The boys are no doubt detained over their work, uncle." She turned to me. "You want to see the farm, Mr. Lefrank. Come and help me to find the boys."

For more than an hour we visited one part of the farm after another, without discovering the missing men. We found them at last near the outskirts of a small wood, sitting, talking together, on the trunk of a felled tree.

Silas rose as we approached, and walked away, without a word of greeting or apology, into the wood. As he got on his feet, I noticed that his brother whispered something in his ear; and I heard him answer, "All right."

"Ambrose, does that mean you have something to keep a secret from us?" asked Naomi, approaching her lover with a smile. "Is Silas ordered to hold his tongue?"

Ambrose kicked sulkily at the loose stones lying about him. I noticed, with a certain surprise, that his favourite stick was not in his hand, and was not lying near him.

"Business," he said in answer to Naomi, not very graciously—"business between Silas and me. That's what it means, if you must know."

Naomi went on, woman-like, with her questions, heedless of the reception which they might meet with from an irritated man.

"Why were you both away at prayers and breakfast-time?" she asked next.

"We had too much to do," Ambrose gruffly replied, "and we were too far from the house."

"Very odd," said Naomi. "This has never happened before since I have been at the farm."

"Well, live and learn. It has happened now."

The tone in which he spoke would have warned any man to let him alone. But warnings which speak by implication only are thrown away on women. The woman, having still something in her mind to say, said it.

"Have you seen anything of John Jago this morning?"

The smouldering ill-temper of Ambrose burst suddenly-why, it was impossible to guess—into a flame.

"How many more questions am I to answer?" he broke out violently. "Are you the parson putting me through my catechism? I have seen nothing of John Jago, and I have got my work to go on with. "Will that do for you?"

He turned with an oath, and followed his brother into the wood. Naomi's bright eyes looked up at me, flashing with indignation.

"What does he mean, Mr. Lefrank, by speaking to me in that way? Rude brute! How dare he do it?" She paused; her voice, look and manner suddenly changed. "This has never happened before, sir. Has anything gone wrong? I declare, I shouldn't know Ambrose again, he is so changed. Say, how does it strike you?"

I still made the best of a bad case.

"Something has upset his temper," I said. "The merest trifle, Miss Colebrook, upsets a man's temper sometimes. I speak as a man, and I know it. Give him time, and he will make his excuses, and all will be well again."

My presentation of the case entirely failed to reassure my pretty companion. We went back to the house. Dinnertime came, and the brothers appeared. Their father spoke to them of their absence from morning prayers with needless severity, as I thought. They resented the reproof with needless indignation on their side, and left the room. A sour smile of satisfaction showed itself on Miss Meadowcroft's thin lips. She looked at her father; then raised her eyes sadly to the ceiling, and said, "We can only pray for them, sir."

Naomi disappeared after dinner. When I saw her again, she had some news for me.

"I have been with Ambrose," she said, "and he has begged my pardon. We have made it up, Mr. Lefrank. Still—still"

"Still what, Miss Naomi?"

"He is not like himself, sir. He denies it; but I can't help thinking he is hiding something from me."

The day wore on; the evening came. I returned to my French novel. But not even Dumas himself could keep my attention to the story. What else I was thinking of I cannot say. Why I was out of spirits I am unable to explain. I wished myself back in England: I took a blind, unreasoning hatred to Morwick Farm.

Nine o'clock struck; and we all assembled again at supper, with the exception of John Jago. He was expected back to supper; and we waited for him a quarter of an hour, by Mr. Meadowcroft's own directions. John Jago never appeared.

The night wore on, and still the absent man failed to return. Miss Meadowcroft volunteered to sit up for him. Naomi eyed her, a little maliciously I must own, as the two women parted for the night. I withdrew to my room; and again I was unable to sleep. When sunrise came, I went out, as before, to breathe the morning air.

On the staircase I met Miss Meadowcroft ascending to her own room. Not a curl of her stiff gray hair was disarranged; nothing about the impenetrable woman betrayed that she had been watching through the night.

"Has Mr. Jago not returned?" I asked.

Miss Meadowcroft slowly shook her head, and frowned at me.

"We are in the hands of Providence, Mr. Lefrank. Mr. Jago must have been detained for the night at Narrabee."

The daily routine of the meals resumed its unalterable course. Breakfast-time came, and dinnertime came, and no John Jago darkened the doors of Morwick Farm. Mr. Meadowcroft and his daughter consulted together, and determined to send in search of the missing man. One of the more intelligent of the labourers was dispatched to Narrabee to make inquiries.

The man returned late in the evening, bringing startling news to the farm. He had visited all the inns, and all the places of business resort in Narrabee; he had made endless inquiries in every direction, with this result—no one had set eyes on John Jago. Everybody declared that John Jago had not entered the town.

We all looked at each other, excepting the two brothers, who were seated together in a dark corner of the room. The conclusion appeared to be inevitable. John Jago was a lost man.

Chapter 6
The Limekiln

Mr. Meadowcroft was the first to speak. "Somebody must find John," he said.

"Without losing a moment," added his daughter.

Ambrose suddenly stepped out of the dark corner of the room.

"I will inquire," he said.

Silas followed him.

"I will go with you," he added.

Mr. Meadowcroft interposed his authority.

"One of you will be enough; for the present, at least. Go you, Ambrose. Your brother may be wanted later. If any accident has happened (which God forbid !) we may have to inquire in more than one direction. Silas, you will stay at the farm."

The brothers withdrew together; Ambrose to prepare for his journey, Silas to saddle one of the horses for him. Naomi slipped out after them. Left in company with Mr. Meadowcroft and his daughter (both devoured by anxiety about the missing man, and both trying to conceal it under an assumption of devout resignation to circumstances), I need hardly add that I, too, retired, as soon as it was politely possible for me to leave the room.

Ascending the stairs on my way to my own quarters, I discovered Naomi half hidden by the recess formed by an old-fashioned window-seat on the first landing. My bright little friend was in sore trouble. Her apron was over her face, and she was crying bitterly. Ambrose had not taken his leave as tenderly as usual. She was more firmly persuaded than ever that "Ambrose was hiding something from her." We all waited anxiously for the next day. The next day made the mystery deeper than ever.

The horse which had taken Ambrose to Narrabee was ridden back to the farm by a groom from the hotel. He delivered a written message from Ambrose which startled us. Further inquiries had positively proved that the missing man had never been near Narrabee. The only attainable tidings of his whereabouts were tidings derived from vague report. It was said that a man like John Jago had been seen the previous day in a railway car, travelling on the line to New York. Acting on this imperfect information, Ambrose had decided on verifying the truth of the report by extending his inquiries to New York.

This extraordinary proceeding forced the suspicion on me that something had really gone wrong. I kept my doubts to myself; but I was prepared, from that moment, to see the disappearance of John Jago followed by very grave results.

The same day the results declared themselves.

Time enough had now elapsed for report to spread through the district the news of what had happened at the farm. Already aware of the bad feeling existing between the men, the neighbours had been now informed (no doubt by the labourers present) of the deplorable scene that had taken place under my bedroom window.

Public opinion declares itself in America without the slightest reserve, or the slightest care for consequences. Public opinion declared on this occasion that the lost man was the victim of foul play, and held one or both of the brothers Meadowcroft responsible for his disappearance. Later in the day, the reasonableness of this serious view of the case was confirmed in the popular mind by a startling discovery.

It was announced that a Methodist preacher lately settled at Morwick, and greatly respected throughout the district, had dreamed of John Jago in the character of a murdered man, whose bones were hidden at Morwick Farm. Before night the cry was general for a verification of the preacher's dream. Not only in the immediate district, but in the town of Narrabee itself, the public voice insisted on the necessity of a search for the mortal remains of John Jago at Morwick Farm.

In the terrible turn which matters had now taken, Mr. Meadowcroft the elder displayed a spirit and an energy for which I was not prepared.

"My sons have their faults," he said, "Serious faults; and nobody knows it better than I do. My sons have behaved badly and ungratefully toward John Jago; I don't deny that, either. But Ambrose and Silas are not murderers. Make your search! I ask for it; no, I insist on it, after what has been said, in justice to my family and my name!"

The neighbours took him at his word. The Morwick section of the American nation organised itself on the spot. The sovereign people met in committee, made speeches, elected competent persons to represent the public interests, and began the search the next day. The whole proceeding, ridiculously informal from a legal point of view, was carried on by these extraordinary people with as stern and strict a sense of duty as if it had been sanctioned by the highest tribunal in the land.

Naomi met the calamity that had fallen on the household as resolutely as her uncle himself. The girl's courage rose with the call which was made on it. Her one anxiety was for Ambrose.

"He ought to be here," she said to me. "The wretches in this neighbourhood are wicked enough to say that his absence is a confession of his guilt."

She was right. In the present temper of the popular mind, the absence of Ambrose was a suspicious circumstance in itself.

"We might telegraph to New York," I suggested, "if you only knew where a message would be likely to find him."

"I know the hotel which the Meadowcrofts use at New York," she replied. "I was sent there, after my father's death, to wait till Miss Meadowcroft could take me to Morwick."

We decided on telegraphing to the hotel. I was writing the message, and Naomi was looking over my shoulder, when we were startled by a strange voice speaking close behind us.

"Oh! That's his address, is it?" said the voice. "We wanted his address rather badly."

The speaker was a stranger to me. Naomi recognized him as one of the neighbours.

"What do you want his address for?" she asked, sharply.

"I guess we've found the mortal remains of John Jago, miss," the man replied. "We have got Silas already, and we want Ambrose too, on suspicion of murder."

"It's a lie!" cried Naomi, furiously—"a wicked lie!"

The man turned to me.

"Take her into the next room, mister," he said, "and let her see for herself."

We went together into the next room.

In one corner, sitting by her father, and holding his hand, we saw stern and stony Miss Meadowcroft weeping silently. Opposite to them, crouched on the window-seat, his eyes wandering, his hands hanging helpless, we next discovered Silas Meadowcroft, plainly self-betrayed as a panic-stricken man. A few of the persons who had been engaged in the search were seated near, watching him. The mass of the strangers present stood congregated round a table in the middle of the room. They drew aside as I approached with Naomi and allowed us to have a clear view of certain objects placed on the table.

The centre object of the collection was a little heap of charred bones. Round this were ranged a knife, two metal buttons, and a stick partially burned. The knife was recognized by the labourers as the weapon John Jago habitually carried about with him-the weapon with which he had wounded Silas Meadowcroft's hand. The buttons Naomi herself declared to have a peculiar pattern on them, which had formerly attracted her attention to John Jago's coat.

As for the stick, burned as it was, I had no difficulty in identifying the quaintly-carved knob at the top. It was the heavy beechen stick which I had snatched out of Silas's hand, and which I had restored to Ambrose on his claiming it as his own. In reply to my inquiries, I was informed that the bones, the knife, the buttons and the stick had all been found together in a limekiln then in use on the farm.

"Is it serious?" Naomi whispered tome as we drew back from the table.

It would have been sheer cruelty to deceive her now.

"Yes," I whispered back; "it is serious."

The search committee conducted its proceedings with the strictest regularity. The proper applications were made forthwith to a justice of the peace, and the justice issued his warrant. That night Silas was committed to prison; and an officer was dispatched to arrest Ambrose in New York.

For my part, I did the little I could to make myself useful. With the silent sanction of Mr. Meadowcroft and his daughter, I went to Narrabee, and secured the best legal assistance for the defence which the town could place at my disposal. This done, there was no choice but to wait for news of Ambrose, and for the examination before the magistrate which was to follow.

I shall pass over the misery in the house during the interval of expectation; no useful purpose could be served by describing it now. Let me only say that Naomi's conduct strengthened me in the conviction that she possessed a noble nature. I was unconscious of the state of my own feelings at the time; but I am now disposed to think that this was the epoch at which I began to envy Ambrose the wife whom he had won.

The telegraph brought us our first news of Ambrose. He had been arrested at the hotel, and he was on his way to Morwick. The next day he arrived, and followed his brother to prison. The two were confined in separate cells, and were forbidden all communication with each other.

Two days later, the preliminary examination took place. Ambrose and Silas Meadowcroft were charged before the magistrate with the wilful murder of John Jago. I was cited to appear as one of the witnesses; and, at Naomi's own request, I took the poor girl into court, and sat by her during the proceedings. My host also was present in his invalid-chair, with his daughter by his side.

Such was the result of my voyage across the ocean in search of rest and quiet; and thus did time and chance fulfil my first hasty forebodings of the dull life I was to lead at Morwick Farm!

Chapter 7

The Materials in the Defence

On our way to the chairs allotted to us in the magistrate's court, we passed the platform on which the prisoners were standing together.

Silas took no notice of us. Ambrose made a friendly sign of recognition, and then rested his hand on the "bar" in front of him. As she passed beneath him, Naomi was just tall enough to reach his hand on tiptoe. She took it. "I know you are innocent," she whispered, and gave him one look of loving encouragement as she followed me to her place. Ambrose never lost his self-control. I may have been wrong; but I thought this a bad sign.

The case, as stated for the prosecution, told strongly against the suspected men.

Ambrose and Silas Meadowcroft were charged with the murder of John Jago (by means of the stick or by use of some other weapon), and with the deliberate destruction of the body by throwing it into the quicklime. In proof of this latter assertion, the knife which the deceased habitually carried about him, and the metal buttons which were known to belong to his coat, were produced.

It was argued that these indestructible substances, and some fragments of the larger bones, had alone escaped the action of the burning lime. Having produced medical witnesses to support this theory by declaring the bones to be human, and having thus circumstantially asserted the discovery of the remains in the kiln, the prosecution next proceeded to prove that the missing man had been murdered by the two brothers, and had been by them thrown into the quicklime as a means of concealing their guilt.

Witness after witness deposed to the inveterate enmity against the deceased displayed by Ambrose and Silas. The threatening language they habitually used toward him; their violent quarrels with him, which had become a public scandal throughout the neighbourhood, and which had ended (on one occasion at least) in a blow; the disgraceful scene which had taken place under my window; and the restoration to Ambrose, on the morning of the fatal quarrel, of the very stick which had been found among the remains of the dead man—these facts and events, and a host of minor circumstances besides, sworn to by witnesses whose credit was unimpeachable, pointed with terrible directness to the conclusion at which the prosecution had arrived.

I looked at the brothers as the weight of the evidence pressed more and more heavily against them. To outward view at least, Ambrose still maintained his self-possession. It was far otherwise with Silas. Abject terror showed itself in his ghastly face; in his great knotty hands, clinging convulsively to the bar at which he stood; in his staring eyes, fixed in vacant horror on each witness who appeared. Public feeling judged him on the spot. There he stood, self-betrayed already, in the popular opinion, as a guilty man!

The one point gained in cross-examination by the defence related to the charred bones.

Pressed on this point, a majority of the medical witnesses admitted that their examination had been a hurried one; and that it was just possible that the bones might yet prove to be the remains of an animal, and not of a man. The presiding magistrate decided upon this that a second examination should be made, and that the number of the medical experts should be increased.

Here the preliminary proceedings ended. The prisoners were remanded for three days.

The prostration of Silas, at the close of the inquiry, was so complete, that it was found necessary to have two men to support him on his leaving the court. Ambrose leaned over the bar to speak to Naomi before he followed the jailer out. "Wait," he whispered, confidently, "till they hear what I have to say!" Naomi kissed her hand to him affectionately, and turned to me with the bright tears in her eyes.

"Why don't they hear what he has to say at once?" she asked. "Anybody can see that Ambrose is innocent. It's a crying shame, sir, to send him back to prison. Don't you think so yourself?"

If I had confessed what I really thought, I should have said that Ambrose had proved nothing to my mind, except that he possessed rare powers of self-control. It was impossible to acknowledge this to my little friend. I diverted her mind from the question of her lover's innocence by proposing that we should get the necessary order, and visit him in his prison on the next day. Naomi dried her tears, and gave me a little grateful squeeze of the hand.

"Oh my! What a good fellow you are!" cried the outspoken American girl. "When your time comes to be married, sir, I guess the woman won't repent saying yes to you!"

Mr. Meadowcroft preserved unbroken silence as we walked back to the farm on either side of his invalid-chair. His last reserves of resolution seemed to have given way under the overwhelming strain laid on them by the proceedings in court. His daughter, in stern indulgence to Naomi, mercifully permitted her opinion to glimmer on us only through the medium of quotation from Scripture texts. If the texts meant anything, they meant that she had foreseen all that had happened; and that the one sad aspect of the case, to her mind, was the death of John Jago, unprepared to meet his end.

I obtained the order of admission to the prison the next morning.

We found Ambrose still confident of the favourable result, for his brother and for himself, of the inquiry before the magistrate. He seemed to be almost as eager to tell, as Naomi was to hear, the true story of what had happened at the lime-kiln. The authorities of the prison—present, of course, at the interview-warned him to remember that what he said might be taken down in writing, and produced against him in court.

"Take it down, gentlemen, and welcome," Ambrose replied. "I have nothing to fear; I am only telling the truth."

With that he turned to Naomi, and began his narrative, as

nearly as I can remember, in these words:

"I may as well make a clean breast of it at starting, my girl. After Mr. Lefrank left us that morning, I asked Silas how he came by my stick. In telling me how, Silas also told me of the words that had passed between him and John Jago under Mr. Lefrank's window. I was angry and jealous; and I own it freely, Naomi, I thought the worst that could be thought about you and John."

Here Naomi stopped him without ceremony.

"Was that what made you speak to me as you spoke when we found you at the wood?" she asked.

"Yes."

"And was that what made you leave me, when you went away to Narrabee, without giving me a kiss at parting?"

"It was."

"Beg my pardon for it before you say a word more."

"I beg your pardon."

"Say you are ashamed of yourself."

"I am ashamed of myself," Ambrose answered penitently.

"Now you may go on," said Naomi. "Now I'm satisfied."

Ambrose went on.

"We were on our way to the clearing at the other side of the wood while Silas was talking to me; and, as ill luck would have it, we took the path that led by the limekiln. Turning the corner, we met John Jago on his way to Narrabee. I was too angry, I tell you, to let him pass quietly. I gave him a bit of my mind. His blood was up too, I suppose; and he spoke out, on his side, as freely as I did. I own I threatened him with the stick; but I'll swear to it I meant him no harm.

"You know—after dressing Silas's hand—that John Jago is ready with his knife. He comes from out West, where they are always ready with one weapon or another handy in their pockets. It's likely enough he didn't mean to harm me, either; but how could I be sure of that? When he stepped up to me, and showed his weapon, I dropped the stick, and closed with him.

"With one hand I wrenched the knife away from him; and with the other I caught him by the collar of his rotten old coat, and gave him a shaking that made his bones rattle in his skin. A big piece of the cloth came away in my hand. I shied it into the quicklime close by us, and I pitched the knife after the cloth; and, if Silas hadn't stopped me, I think it's likely I might have shied John Jago himself into the lime next.

"As it was, Silas kept hold of me. Silas shouted out to him, 'Be off with you! And don't come back again, if you don't want to be burned in the kiln!' He stood looking at us for a minute, fetching his breath, and holding his torn coat round him. Then he spoke with a deadly-quiet voice and a deadly-quiet look:

"'Many a true word, Mr. Silas,' he says, 'is spoken in jest. I shall not come back again.' He turned about, and left us. We stood staring at each other like a couple of fools. 'You don't think he means it?' I says. 'Bosh!' says Silas. 'He's too sweet on Naomi not to come back.' What's the matter now, Naomi?" I had noticed it too. She started and turned pale, when Ambrose repeated to her what Silas had said to him.

"Nothing is the matter," Naomi answered. "Your brother has no right to take liberties with my name. Go on. Did Silas say any more while he was about it?"

"Yes; he looked into the kiln; and he says, 'What made you throw away the knife, Ambrose?' 'How does a man know why he does anything,' I says, 'when he does it in a passion?'—'It's a ripping good knife,' says Silas; 'in your place, I should have kept it.' I picked up the stick off the ground. 'Who says I've lost it yet?' I answered him; and with that I got up on the side of the kiln, and began sounding for the knife, to bring it, you know, by means of the stick, within easy reach of a shovel, or some such thing.

" 'Give us your hand,' I says to Silas. 'Let me stretch out a bit and I'll have it in no time.' Instead of finding the knife, I came nigh to falling myself into the burning lime. The vapour overpowered me, I suppose. All I know is, I turned giddy, and dropped the stick in the kiln. I should have followed the stick to a dead certainty, but for Silas pulling me back by the hand.

"'Let it be,' says Silas. 'If I hadn't had hold of you, John Jago's knife would have been the death of you, after all!' He led me away by the arm, and we went on together on the road to the wood. We stopped where you found us, and sat down on the felled tree. We had a little more talk about John Jago. It ended in our agreeing to wait and see what happened, and to keep our own counsel in the meantime. You and Mr. Lefrank came upon us, Naomi, while we were still talking; and you guessed right when you guessed that we had a secret from you. You know the secret now."

There he stopped. I put a question to him—the first that I had asked yet.

"Had you or your brother any fear at that time of the charge which has since been brought against you?" I said.

"No such thought entered our heads, sir," Ambrose answered. "How could we foresee that the neighbours would search the kiln, and say what they have said of us? All we feared was, that the old man might hear of the quarrel, and be bitterer against us than ever. I was the more anxious of the two to keep things secret, because I had Naomi to consider as well as the old man. Put yourself in my place, and you will own, sir, that the prospect at home was not a pleasant one for me, if John Jago really kept away from the farm, and if it came out that it was all my doing."

(This was certainly an explanation of his conduct; but it was not satisfactory to my mind.)

"As you believe, then," I went on, "John Jago has carried out his threat of not returning to the farm? According to you, he is now alive, and in hiding somewhere?"

"Certainly!" said Ambrose.

"Certainly!" repeated Naomi.

"Do you believe the report that he was seen travelling on the railway to New York?"

"I believe it firmly, sir; and, what is more, I believe I was on his track. I was only too anxious to find him; and I say I could have found him if they would have let me stay in New York."

I looked at Naomi.

"I believe it too," she said. "John Jago is keeping away."

"Do you suppose he is afraid of Ambrose and Silas?"

She hesitated.

"He may be afraid of them," she replied, with a strong emphasis on the word "may."

"But you don't think it likely?"

She hesitated again. I pressed her again.

"Do you think there is any other motive for his absence?"

Her eyes dropped to the floor. She answered obstinately, almost doggedly,

"I can't say."

I addressed myself to Ambrose.

"Have you anything more to tell us?" I asked.

"No," he said. "I have told you all I know about it."

I rose to speak to the lawyer whose services I had retained. He had helped us to get the order of admission, and he had accompanied us to the prison. Seated apart, he had kept silence throughout, attentively watching the effect of Ambrose Meadowcroft's narrative on the officers of the prison and on me.

"Is this the defence?" I inquired, in a whisper.

"This is the defence, Mr. Lefrank. What do you think, between ourselves?"

"Between ourselves, I think the magistrate will commit them for trial."

"On the charge of murder?"

"Yes, on the charge of murder."

Chapter 8
The Confession

My replies to the lawyer accurately expressed the conviction in my mind. The narrative related by Ambrose had all the appearance, in my eyes, of a fabricated story, got up, and clumsily got up, to pervert the plain meaning of the circumstantial evidence produced by the prosecution. I reached this conclusion reluctantly and regretfully, for Naomi's sake. I said all I could say to shake the absolute confidence which she felt in the discharge of the prisoners at the next examination.

The day of the adjourned inquiry arrived.

Naomi and I again attended the court together. Mr. Meadowcroft was unable, on this occasion, to leave the house. His daughter was present, walking to the court by herself, and occupying a seat by herself.

On his second appearance at the "bar," Silas was more composed, and more like his brother. No new witnesses were called by the prosecution. We began the battle over the medical evidence relating to the charred bones; and, to some extent, we won the victory. In other words, we forced the doctors to acknowledge that they differed widely in their opinions. Three confessed that they were not certain. Two went still further, and declared that the bones were the bones of an animal, not of a man. We made the most of this; and then we entered upon the defence, founded on Ambrose Meadowcroft's story.

Necessarily, no witnesses could be called on our side. Whether this circumstance discouraged him, or whether he privately shared my opinion of his client's statement, I cannot say. It is only certain that the lawyer spoke mechanically, doing his best, no doubt, but doing it without genuine conviction or earnestness on his own part.

Naomi cast an anxious glance at me as he sat down. The girl's hand, as I took it, turned cold in mine. She saw plain signs of the failure of the defence in the look and manner of the counsel for the prosecution; but she waited resolutely until the presiding magistrate announced his decision. I had only too clearly foreseen what he would feel it to be his duty to do. Naomi's head dropped on my shoulder as he said the terrible words which committed Ambrose and Silas Meadowcroft to take their trial on the charge of murder.

I led her out of the court into the air. As I passed the "bar," I saw Ambrose, deadly pale, looking after us as we left him: the magistrate's decision had evidently daunted him. His brother Silas had dropped in abject terror on the jailer's chair; the miserable wretch shook and shuddered dumbly, like a cowed dog.

Miss Meadowcroft returned with us to the farm, preserving unbroken silence on the way back. I could detect nothing in her bearing which suggested any compassionate feeling for the prisoners in her stern and secret nature. On Naomi's withdrawal to her own room, we were left together for a few minutes; and then, to my astonishment, the outwardly merciless woman showed me that she, too, was one of Eve's daughters, and could feel and suffer, in her own hard way, like the rest of us. She suddenly stepped close up to me, and laid her hand on my arm.

"You are a lawyer, ain't you?" she asked.

"Yes."

"Have you had any experience in your profession?"

"Ten years' experience."

"Do you think—" She stopped abruptly; her hard face softened; her eyes dropped to the ground. "Never mind," she said, confusedly. "I'm upset by all this misery, though I may not look like it. Don't notice me."

She turned away. I waited, in the firm persuasion that the unspoken question in her mind would sooner or later force its way to utterance by her lips. I was right. She came back to me unwillingly, like a woman acting under some influence which the utmost exertion of her will was powerless to resist.

"Do you believe John Jago is still a living man?"

She put the question vehemently, desperately, as if the words rushed out of her mouth in spite of her.

"I do not believe it," I answered.

"Remember what John Jago has suffered at the hands of my brothers," she persisted. "Is it not in your experience that he should take a sudden resolution to leave the farm?"

I replied, as plainly as before,

"It is not in my experience."

She stood looking at me for a moment with a face of blank despair; then bowed her gray head in silence, and left me. As she crossed the room to the door, I saw her look upward; and I heard her say to herself softly, between her teeth, *Vengeance is mine, I will repay, saith the Lord*.

It was the requiem of John Jago, pronounced by the woman who loved him.

When I next saw her, her mask was on once more. Miss Meadowcroft was herself again. Miss Meadowcroft could sit by, impenetrably calm, while the lawyers discussed the terrible position of her brothers, with the scaffold in view as one of the possibilities of the "case."

Left by myself, I began to feel uneasy about Naomi. I went upstairs, and, knocking softly at her door, made my inquiries from outside. The clear young voice answered me sadly, "I am trying to bear it: I won't distress you when we meet again." I descended the stairs, feeling my first suspicion of the true nature of my interest in the American girl. Why had her answer brought the tears into my eyes? I went out, walking alone, to think undisturbedly. Why did the tones of her voice dwell on my ear all the way? Why did my hand still feel the last cold, faint pressure of her fingers when I led her out of court?

I took a sudden resolution to go back to England.

When I returned to the farm, it was evening. The lamp was not yet lighted in the hall. Pausing to accustom my eyes to the obscurity indoors, I heard the voice of the lawyer whom we had employed for the defence speaking to someone very earnestly.

"I'm not to blame," said the voice. "She snatched the paper out of my hand before I was aware of her."

"Do you want it back?" asked the voice of Miss Meadowcroft.

"No; it's only a copy. If keeping it will help to quiet her, let her keep it by all means. Good-evening."

Saying these last words, the lawyer approached me on his way out of the house. I stopped him without ceremony; I felt an ungovernable curiosity to know more.

"Who snatched the paper out of your hand?" I asked, bluntly.

The lawyer started. I had taken him by surprise. The instinct of professional reticence made him pause before he answered me.

In the brief interval of silence, Miss Meadowcroft replied to my question from the other end of the hall.

"Naomi Colebrook snatched the paper out of his hand."

"What paper?"

A door opened softly behind me. Naomi herself appeared on the threshold; Naomi herself answered my question.

"I will tell you," she whispered. "Come in here."

One candle only was burning in the room. I looked at her by the dim light. My resolution to return to England instantly became one of the lost ideas of my life.

"Good God!" I exclaimed, "What has happened now?"

She handed me the paper which she had taken from the lawyer's hand.

The "copy" to which he had referred was a copy of the written confession of Silas Meadowcroft on his return to prison. He accused his brother Ambrose of the murder of John Jago. He declared on his oath that he had seen his brother Ambrose commit the crime.

In the popular phrase, I could "hardly believe my own eyes." I read the last sentences of the confession for the second time:

> ... I heard their voices at the limekiln. They were having words about Cousin Naomi. I ran to the place to part them. I was not in time. I saw Ambrose strike the deceased a terrible blow on the head with his (Ambrose's) heavy stick. The deceased dropped without a cry. I put my hand on his heart. He was dead. I was horribly frightened. Ambrose threatened to kill me next if I said a word to any living soul. He took up the body and cast it into the quicklime, and threw the stick in after it.
>
> We went on together to the wood. We sat down on a felled tree outside the wood. Ambrose made up the story that we were to tell if what he had done was found out. He made me repeat it after him, like a lesson. We were still at it when Cousin Naomi and Mr. Lefrank came up to us. They know the rest. This, on my oath, is a true confession. I make it of my own free-will, repenting me sincerely that

I did not make it before.

(Signed) Silas Meadowcroft.

I laid down the paper, and looked at Naomi once more. She spoke to me with a strange composure. Immovable determination was in her eye; immovable determination was in her voice.

"Silas has lied away his brother's life to save himself," she said. "I see cowardly falsehood and cowardly cruelty in every line on that paper. Ambrose is innocent, and the time has come to prove it."

"You forget," I said, "that we have just failed to prove it."

"John Jago is alive, in hiding from us and from all who know him," she went on. "Help me, friend Lefrank, to advertise for him in the newspapers."

I drew back from her in speechless distress. I own I believed that the new misery which had fallen on her had affected her brain.

"You don't believe it," she said. "Shut the door."

I obeyed her. She seated herself, and pointed to a chair near her.

"Sit down," she proceeded. "I am going to do a wrong thing; but there is no help for it. I am going to break a sacred promise. You remember that moonlight night when I met him on the garden walk?"

"John Jago?"

"Yes. Now listen. I am going to tell you what passed between John Jago and me."

Chapter 9
The Advertisement

I waited in silence for the disclosure that was now to come. Naomi began by asking me a question.

"You remember when we went to see Ambrose in the prison?" she said.

"Perfectly."

"Ambrose told us of something which his villain of a brother said of John Jago and me. Do you remember what it was?"

I remembered, perfectly. Silas had said, "John Jago is too sweet on Naomi not to come back."

"That's so," Naomi remarked when I had repeated the words. "I couldn't help starting when I heard what Silas had said; and I thought you noticed me."

"I did notice you."

"Did you wonder what it meant?"

"Yes."

"I'll tell you. It meant this: What Silas Meadowcroft said to his brother of John Jago was what I myself was thinking of John Jago at that very moment. It startled me to find my own thought in a man's mind spoken for me by a man. I am the person, sir, who has driven John Jago away from Morwick Farm; and I am the person who can and will bring him back again."

There was something in her manner, more than in her words, which let the light in suddenly on my mind.

"You have told me the secret," I said. "John Jago is in love with you."

"Mad about me!" she rejoined, dropping her voice to a whisper. "Stark, staring mad!—that's the only word for him. After we had taken a few turns on the gravel-walk, he suddenly broke out like a man beside himself. He fell down on his knees; he kissed my gown, he kissed my feet; he sobbed and cried for love of me. I'm not badly off for courage, sir, considering I'm a woman. No man, that I can call to mind, ever really scared me before. But I own John Jago frightened me; oh my!

"He did frighten me! My heart was in my mouth, and my knees shook under me. I begged and prayed of him to get up and go away. No; there he knelt, and held by the skirt of my gown. The words poured out from him like—well, like nothing I can think of but water from a pump. His happiness and his life, and his hopes in earth and heaven, and Lord only knows what besides, all depended, he said, on a word from me.

"I plucked up spirit enough at that to remind him that I was promised to Ambrose. 'I think you ought to be ashamed of yourself,' I said, 'to own that you're wicked enough to love me when you know I am promised to another man!' When I spoke to him, he took a new turn; he began abusing Ambrose. That straightened me up. I snatched my gown out of his hand, and I gave him my whole mind.

"'I hate you!' I said. 'Even if I wasn't promised to Ambrose, I wouldn't marry you—no! Not if there wasn't another man left in the world to ask me. I hate you, Mr. Jago! I hate you!' He saw I was in earnest at last. He got up from my feet, and he settled down quiet again, all on a sudden. 'You have said enough' (that was how he answered me).

"'You have broken my life. I have no hopes and no prospects now. I had a pride in the farm, miss, and a pride in my work; I bore with your brutish cousins' hatred of me; I was faithful to Mr. Meadowcroft's interests; all for your sake, Naomi Colebrook—all for your sake! I have done with it now; I have done with my life at the farm. You will never be troubled with me again. I am going away, as the dumb creatures go when they are sick, to hide myself in a corner, and die.

"'Do me one last favour. Don't make me the laughing stock of the whole neighbourhood. I can't bear that; it maddens me only to think of it. Give me your promise never to tell any living soul what I have said to you tonight—your sacred promise to the man whose life you have broken!'

"I did as he bade me; I gave him my sacred promise with the tears in my eyes. Yes, that is so. After telling him I hated him (and I did hate him), I cried over his misery; I did! Mercy, what fools women are! What is the horrid perversity, sir, which makes us always ready to pity the men? He held out his hand to me; and he said, 'Goodbye forever!' and I pitied him. I said, 'I'll shake hands with you if you will give me your promise in exchange for mine. I beg of you not to leave the farm. What will my uncle do if you go away? Stay here, and be friends with me, and forget and forgive, Mr. John.'

"He gave me his promise (he can refuse me nothing); and he gave it again when I saw him again the next morning. Yes. I'll do him justice, though I do hate him! I believe he honestly meant to keep his word as long as my eye was on him. It was only when he was left to himself that the Devil tempted him to break his promise and leave the farm. I was brought up to believe in the Devil, Mr. Lefrank; and I find it explains many things. It explains John Jago. Only let me find out where he has gone, and I'll engage he shall come back and clear Ambrose of the suspicion which his vile brother has cast on him. Here is the pen all ready for you. Advertise for him, friend Lefrank; and do it right away, for my sake!"

I let her run on, without attempting to dispute her conclusions, until she could say no more. When she put the pen into my hand, I began the composition of the advertisement as obediently as if I, too, believed that John Jago was a living man.

In the case of anyone else, I should have openly acknowledged that my own convictions remained unshaken. If no quarrel had taken place at the limekiln, I should have been quite ready, as I viewed the case, to believe that John Jago's disappearance was referable to the terrible disappointment which Naomi had inflicted on him.

The same morbid dread of ridicule which had led him to assert that he cared nothing for Naomi, when he and Silas had quarrelled under my bedroom window, might also have impelled him to withdraw himself secretly and suddenly from the scene of his discomfiture. But to ask me to believe, after what had happened at the limekiln, that he was still living, was to ask me to take Ambrose Meadowcroft's statement for granted as a true statement of facts.

I had refused to do this from the first; and I still persisted in taking that course. If I had been called upon to decide the balance of probability between the narrative related by Ambrose in his defence and the narrative related by Silas in his confession, I must have owned, no matter how unwillingly, that the confession was, to my mind, the least incredible story of the two.

Could I say this to Naomi? I would have written fifty advertisements inquiring for John Jago rather than say it; and you would have done the same, if you had been as fond of her as I was. I drew out the advertisement, for insertion in the Morwick *Mercury*, in these terms:

> Murder.—Printers of newspapers throughout the United States are desired to publish that Ambrose Meadowcroft and Silas Meadowcroft, of Morwick Farm, Morwick County, are committed for trial on the charge of murdering John Jago, now missing from the farm and from the neighbourhood. Any person who can give information of the existence of said Jago may save the lives of two wrongly-accused men by making immediate communication. Jago is about five feet four inches high. He is spare and wiry; his complexion is extremely pale; his eyes are dark, and very bright and restless. The lower part of his face is concealed by a thick black beard and moustache. The whole appearance of the man is wild and flighty.

I added the date and the address. That evening a servant was sent on horseback to Narrabee to procure the insertion of the advertisement in the next issue of the newspaper.

When we parted that night, Naomi looked almost like her brighter and happier self. Now that the advertisement was on its way to the printing-office, she was more than sanguine: she was certain of the result.

"You don't know how you have comforted me," she said, in her frank, warm-hearted way, when we parted for the night. "All the newspapers will copy it, and we shall hear of John Jago before the week is out." She turned to go, and came back again to me. "I will never forgive Silas for writing that confession!" she whispered in my ear. "If he ever lives under the same roof with Ambrose again, I—well, I believe I wouldn't marry Ambrose if he did! There!"

She left me. Through the wakeful hours of the night my mind dwelt on her last words. That she should contemplate, under any circumstances, even the bare possibility of not marrying Ambrose, was, I am ashamed to say, a direct encouragement to certain hopes which I had already begun to form in secret. The next day's mail brought me a letter on business. My clerk wrote to inquire if there was any chance of my returning to England in time to appear in court at the opening of next law term.

I answered, without hesitation, "It is still impossible for me to fix the date of my return." Naomi was in the room while I was writing. How would she have answered, I wonder, if I had told her the truth, and said, "You are responsible for this letter?"

Chapter 10
The Sheriff and the Governor

The question of time was now a serious question at Morwick Farm. In six weeks the court for the trial of criminal cases was to be opened at Narrabee.

During this interval no new event of any importance occurred.

Many idle letters reached us relating to the advertisement for John Jago; but no positive information was received. Not the slightest trace of the lost man turned up; not the shadow of a doubt was cast on the assertion of the prosecution, that his body had been destroyed in the kiln. Silas Meadowcroft held firmly to the horrible confession that he had made. His brother Ambrose, with equal resolution, asserted his innocence, and reiterated the statement which he had already advanced.

At regular periods I accompanied Naomi to visit him in the prison. As the day appointed for the opening of the court approached, he seemed to falter a little in his resolution; his manner became restless; and he grew irritably suspicious about the merest trifles. This change did not necessarily imply the consciousness of guilt: it might merely have indicated natural nervous agitation as the time for the trial drew near.

Naomi noticed the alteration in her lover. It greatly increased her anxiety, though it never shook her confidence in Ambrose. Except at mealtimes, I was left, during the period of which I am now writing, almost constantly alone with the charming American girl. Miss Meadowcroft searched the newspapers for tidings of the living John Jago in the privacy of her own room.

Mr. Meadowcroft would see nobody but his daughter and his doctor, and occasionally one or two old friends.

I have since had reason to believe that Naomi, in these days of our intimate association, discovered the true nature of the feeling with which she had inspired me. But she kept her secret. Her manner toward me steadily remained the manner of a sister; she never overstepped by a hair-breadth the safe limits of the character that she had assumed.

The sittings of the court began. After hearing the evidence, and examining the confession of Silas Meadowcroft, the grand jury found a true bill against both the prisoners. The day appointed for their trial was the first day in the new week.

I had carefully prepared Naomi's mind for the decision of the grand jury. She bore the new blow bravely.

"If you are not tired of it," she said, "come with me to the prison tomorrow. Ambrose will need a little comfort by that time." She paused, and looked at the day's letters lying on the table. "Still not a word about John Jago," she said. "And all the papers have copied the advertisement. I felt so sure we should hear of him long before this!"

"Do you still feel sure that he is living?" I ventured to ask.

"I am as certain of it as ever," she replied, firmly. "He is somewhere in hiding; perhaps he is in disguise. Suppose we know no more of him than we know now when the trial begins? Suppose the jury—" She stopped, shuddering. Death—shameful death on the scaffold—might be the terrible result of the consultation of the jury. "We have waited for news to come to us long enough, "Naomi resumed. "We must find the tracks of John Jago for ourselves. There is a week yet before the trial begins. Who will help me to make inquiries? Will you be the man, friend Lefrank?"

It is needless to add (though I knew nothing would come of it) that I consented to be the man.

We arranged to apply that day for the order of admission to the prison, and, having seen Ambrose, to devote ourselves immediately to the contemplated search. How that search was to be conducted was more than I could tell, and more than Naomi could tell. We were to begin by applying to the police to help us to find John Jago, and we were then to be guided by circumstances. Was there ever a more hopeless programme than this?

"Circumstances" declared themselves against us at starting. I applied, as usual, for the order of admission to the prison, and the order was for the first time refused; no reason being assigned by the persons in authority for taking this course. Inquire as I might, the only answer given was, "not today."

At Naomi's suggestion, we went to the prison to seek the explanation which was refused to us at the office. The jailer on duty at the outer gate was one of Naomi's many admirers. He solved the mystery cautiously in a whisper. The sheriff and the governor of the prison were then speaking privately with Ambrose Meadowcroft in his cell; they had expressly directed that no persons should be admitted to see the prisoner that day but themselves.

What did it mean? We returned, wondering, to the farm. There Naomi, speaking by chance to one of the female servants, made certain discoveries.

Early that morning the sheriff had been brought to Morwick by an old friend of the Meadowcrofts. A long interview had been held between Mr. Meadowcroft and his daughter and the official personage introduced by the friend. Leaving the farm, the sheriff had gone straight to the prison, and had proceeded with the governor to visit Ambrose in his cell.

Was some potent influence being brought privately to bear on Ambrose? Appearances certainly suggested that inquiry. Supposing the influence to have been really exerted, the next question followed. What was the object in view? We could only wait and see.

Our patience was not severely tried. The event of the next day enlightened us in a very unexpected manner. Before noon, the neighbours brought startling news from the prison to the farm.

Ambrose Meadowcroft had confessed himself to be the murderer of John Jago! He had signed the confession in the presence of the sheriff and the governor on that very day!

I saw the document. It is needless to reproduce it here. In substance, Ambrose confessed what Silas had confessed; claiming, however, to have only struck Jago under intolerable provocation, so as to reduce the nature of his offense against the law from murder to manslaughter.

Was the confession really the true statement of what had taken place? Or had the sheriff and the governor, acting in the interests of the family name, persuaded Ambrose to try this desperate means of escaping the ignominy of death on the scaffold? The sheriff and the governor preserved impenetrable silence until the pressure put on them judicially at the trial obliged them to speak.

Who was to tell Naomi of this last and saddest of all the calamities which had fallen on her? Knowing how I loved her in secret, I felt an invincible reluctance to be the person who revealed Ambrose Meadowcroft's degradation to his betrothed wife. Had any other member of the family told her what had happened? The lawyer was able to answer me; Miss Meadowcroft had told her.

I was shocked when I heard it. Miss Meadowcroft was the last person in the house to spare the poor girl; Miss Meadowcroft would make the hard tidings doubly terrible to bear in the telling. I tried to find Naomi, without success. She had been always accessible at other times. Was she hiding herself from me now? The idea occurred to me as I was descending the stairs after vainly knocking at the door of her room. I was determined to see her. I waited a few minutes, and then ascended the stairs again suddenly. On the landing I met her, just leaving her room.

She tried to run back. I caught her by the arm, and detained her. With her free hand she held her handkerchief over her face so as to hide it from me.

"You once told me I had comforted you," I said to her, gently. "Won't you let me comfort you now?"

She still struggled to get away, and still kept her head turned from me.

"Don't you see that I am ashamed to look you in the face?" she said, in low, broken tones. "Let me go."

I still persisted in trying to soothe her. I drew her to the window-seat. I said I would wait until she was able to speak to me.

She dropped on the seat, and wrung her hands on her lap. Her downcast eyes still obstinately avoided meeting mine.

"Oh!" she said to herself, "what madness possessed me? Is it possible that I ever disgraced myself by loving Ambrose Meadowcroft?" She shuddered as the idea found its way to expression on her lips. The tears rolled slowly over her cheeks. "Don't despise me, Mr. Lefrank!" she said, faintly.

I tried, honestly tried, to put the confession before her in its least unfavourable light.

"His resolution has given way," I said. "He has done this, despairing of proving his innocence, in terror of the scaffold."

She rose, with an angry stamp of her foot. She turned her face on me with the deep-red flush of shame in it, and the big tears glistening in her eyes.

"No more of him!" she said, sternly. "If he is not a murderer, what else is he? A liar and a coward! In which of his characters does he disgrace me most? I have done with him forever! I will never speak to him again!" She pushed me furiously away from her; advanced a few steps toward her own door; stopped, and came back to me. The generous nature of the girl spoke in her next words. "I am not ungrateful to you, friend Lefrank. A woman in my place is only a woman; and, when she is shamed as I am, she feels it very bitterly. Give me your hand! God bless you!"

She put my hand to her lips before I was aware of her, and kissed it, and ran back into her room.

I sat down on the place which she had occupied. She had looked at me for one moment when she kissed my hand. I forgot Ambrose and his confession; I forgot the coming trial; I forgot my professional duties and my English friends. There I sat, in a fool's Elysium of my own making, with absolutely nothing in my mind but the picture of Naomi's face at the moment when she had last looked at me!

I have already mentioned that I was in love with her. I merely add this to satisfy you that I tell the truth.

CHAPTER 11

THE PEBBLE AND THE WINDOW

Miss Meadowcroft and I were the only representatives of the family at the farm who attended the trial. We went separately to Narrabee. Excepting the ordinary greetings at morning and night, Miss Meadowcroft had not said one word to me since the time when I had told her that I did not believe John Jago to be a living man.

I have purposely abstained from encumbering my narrative with, legal details. I now propose to state the nature of the defence in the briefest outline only.

We insisted on making both the prisoners plead not guilty. This done, we took an objection to the legality of the proceedings at starting. We appealed to the old English law, that there should be no conviction for murder until the body of the murdered person was found, or proof of its destruction obtained beyond a doubt. We denied that sufficient proof had been obtained in the case now before the court.

The judges consulted, and decided that the trial should go on.

We took our next objection when the confessions were produced in evidence. We declared that they had been extorted by terror, or by undue influence; and we pointed out certain minor particulars in which the two confessions failed to corroborate each other. For the rest, our defence on this occasion was, as to essentials, what our defence had been at the inquiry before the magistrate. Once more the judges consulted, and once more they overruled our objection. The confessions were admitted in evidence.

On their side, the prosecution produced one new witness in support of their case. It is needless to waste time in recapitulating his evidence. He contradicted himself gravely on cross-examination. We showed plainly, and after investigation proved, that he was not to be believed on his oath.

The chief-justice summed up.

He charged, in relation to the confessions, that no weight should be attached to a confession incited by hope or fear; and he left it to the jury to determine whether the confessions in this case had been so influenced. In the course of the trial, it had been shown for the defence that the sheriff and the governor of the prison had told Ambrose, with his father's knowledge and sanction, that the case was clearly against him; that the only chance of sparing his family the disgrace of his death by public execution lay in making a confession; and that they would do their best, if he did confess, to have his sentence commuted to imprisonment for life.

As for Silas, he was proved to have been beside himself with terror when he made his abominable charge against his brother. We had vainly trusted to the evidence on these two points to induce the court to reject the confessions; and we were destined to be once more disappointed in anticipating that the same evidence would influence the verdict of the jury on the side of mercy. After an absence of an hour, they returned into court with a verdict of "Guilty" against both the prisoners.

Being asked in due form if they had anything to say in mitigation of their sentence, Ambrose and Silas solemnly declared their innocence, and publicly acknowledged that their respective confessions had been wrung from them by the hope of escaping the hangman's hands. This statement was not noticed by the bench. The prisoners were both sentenced to death.

On my return to the farm, I did not see Naomi. Miss Meadowcroft informed her of the result of the trial. Half an hour later, one of the women-servants handed to me an envelope bearing my name on it in Naomi's handwriting.

The envelope inclosed a letter, and with it a slip of paper on which Naomi had hurriedly written these words:

For God's sake, read the letter I send to you, and do something about it immediately!

I looked at the letter. It assumed to be written by a gentleman in New York. Only the day before, he had, by the merest accident, seen the advertisement for John Jago cut out of a newspaper and pasted into a book of "curiosities" kept by a friend. Upon this he wrote to Morwick Farm to say that he had seen a man exactly answering to the description of John Jago, but bearing another name, working as a clerk in a merchant's office in Jersey City.

Having time to spare before the mail went out, he had re turned to the office to take another look at the man before he posted his letter. To his surprise, he was informed that the clerk had not appeared at his desk that day. His employer had sent to his lodgings, and had been informed that he had suddenly packed up his hand-bag after reading the newspaper at breakfast; had paid his rent honestly, and had gone away, nobody knew where!

It was late in the evening when I read these lines. I had time for reflection before it would be necessary for me to act.

Assuming the letter to be genuine, and adopting Naomi's explanation of the motive which had led John Jago to absent himself secretly from the farm, I reached the conclusion that the search for him might be usefully limited to Narrabee and to the surrounding neighbourhood.

The newspaper at his breakfast had no doubt given him his first information of the "finding" of the grand jury, and of the trial to follow. It was in my experience of human nature that he should venture back to Narrabee under these circumstances, and under the influence of his infatuation for Naomi. More than this, it was again in my experience, I am sorry to say, that he should attempt to make the critical position of Ambrose a means of extorting Naomi's consent to listen favourably to his suit.

Cruel indifference to the injury and the suffering which his sudden absence might inflict on others was plainly implied in his secret withdrawal from the farm. The same cruel indifference, pushed to a further extreme, might well lead him to press his proposals privately on Naomi, and to fix her acceptance of them as the price to be paid for saving her cousin's life.

To these conclusions I arrived after much thinking. I had determined, on Naomi's account, to clear the matter up; but it is only candid to add that my doubts of John Jago's existence remained unshaken by the letter. I believed it to be nothing more nor less than a heartless and stupid "hoax."

The striking of the hall-clock roused me from my meditations. I counted the strokes—midnight!

I rose to go up to my room. Everybody else in the farm had retired to bed, as usual, more than an hour since. The stillness in the house was breathless. I walked softly, by instinct, as I crossed the room to look out at the night. A lovely moonlight met my view; it was like the moonlight on the fatal evening when Naomi had met John Jago on the garden walk.

My bedroom candle was on the side-table; I had just lighted it. I was just leaving the room, when the door suddenly opened, and Naomi herself stood before me!

Recovering the first shock of her sudden appearance, I saw instantly in her eager eyes, in her deadly-pale cheeks, that something serious had happened. A large cloak was thrown over her; a white handkerchief was tied over her head. Her hair was in disorder; she had evidently just risen in fear and in haste from her bed.

"What is it?" I asked, advancing to meet her.

She clung, trembling with agitation, to my arm.

"John Jago!" she whispered.

You will think my obstinacy invincible. I could hardly believe it, even then!

"Where?" I asked.

"In the backyard," she replied, "under my bedroom window!"

The emergency was far too serious to allow of any consideration for the small proprieties of everyday life.

"Let me see him!" I said.

"I am here to fetch you," she answered, in her frank and fearless way. "Come upstairs with me."

Her room was on the first floor of the house, and was the only bedroom which looked out on the backyard. On our way up the stairs she told me what had happened.

"I was in bed," she said, "but not asleep, when I heard a pebble strike against the windowpane. I waited, wondering what it meant. Another pebble was thrown against the glass. So far, I was surprised, but not frightened. I got up, and ran to the window to look out. There was John Jago looking up at me in the moonlight!"

"Did he see you?"

"Yes. He said, 'Comedown and speak to me! I have something serious to say to you!"

"Did you answer him?"

"As soon as I could fetch my breath, I said, ' Wait a little, ' and ran downstairs to you. What shall I do?"

"Let me see him, and I will tell you."

We entered her room. Keeping cautiously behind the window-curtain, I looked out.

There he was! His beard and moustache were shaved off; his hair was close cut. But there was no disguising his wild, brown eyes, or the peculiar movement of his spare, wiry figure, as he walked slowly to and fro in the moonlight waiting for Naomi. For the moment, my own agitation almost overpowered me; I had so firmly disbelieved that John Jago was a living man!

"What shall I do?" Naomi repeated.

"Is the door of the dairy open?" I asked.

"No; but the door of the tool-house, round the corner, is not locked."

"Very good. Show yourself at the window, and say to him, 'I am coming directly."

The brave girl obeyed me without a moment's hesitation.

There had been no doubt about his eyes and his gait; there was no doubt now about his voice, as he answered softly from below—"All right!"

"Keep him talking to you where he is now," I said to Naomi,

"until I have time to get round by the other way to the tool-house. Then pretend to be fearful of discovery at the dairy, and bring him round the corner, so that I can hear him behind the door."

We left the house together, and separated silently. Naomi followed my instructions with a woman's quick intelligence where stratagems are concerned. I had hardly been a minute in the tool-house before I heard him speaking to Naomi on the other side of the door.

The first words which I caught distinctly related to his motive for secretly leaving the farm. Mortified pride—doubly mortified by Naomi's contemptuous refusal and by the personal indignity offered to him by Ambrose—was at the bottom of his conduct in absenting himself from Morwick. He owned that he had seen the advertisement, and that it had actually encouraged him to keep in hiding!

"After being laughed at and insulted and denied, I was glad," said the miserable wretch, "to see that some of you had serious reason to wish me back again. It rests with you, Miss Naomi, to keep me here, and to persuade me to save Ambrose by showing myself and owning to my name."

"What do you mean?" I heard Naomi ask, sternly.

He lowered his voice; but I could still hear him.

"Promise you will marry me," he said, "and I will go before the magistrate tomorrow, and show him that I am a living man."

"Suppose I refuse?"

"In that case you will lose me again, and none of you will find me till Ambrose is hanged."

"Are you villain enough, John Jago, to mean what you say?" asked the girl, raising her voice.

"If you attempt to give the alarm," he answered, "as true as God's above us, you will feel my hand on your throat! It's my turn now, miss; and I am not to be trifled with. Will you have me for your husband—yes or no?"

"No!" she answered, loudly and firmly.

I burst open the door, and seized him as he lifted his hand on her. He had not suffered from the nervous derangement which had weakened me, and he was the stronger man of the two. Naomi saved my life. She struck up his pistol as he pulled it out of his pocket with his free hand and presented it at my head. The bullet was fired into the air. I tripped up his heels at the same moment. The report of the pistol had alarmed the house. We two together kept him on the ground until help arrived.

Chapter 12

The End of it

John Jago was brought before the magistrate, and John Jago was identified the next day.

The lives of Ambrose and Silas were, of course, no longer in peril, so far as human justice was concerned. But there were legal delays to be encountered, and legal formalities to be observed, before the brothers could be released from prison in the characters of innocent men.

During the interval which thus elapsed, certain events happened which may be briefly mentioned here before I close my narrative.

Mr. Meadowcroft the elder, broken by the suffering which he had gone through, died suddenly of a rheumatic affection of the heart. A codicil attached to his will abundantly justified what Naomi had told me of Miss Meadowcroft's influence over her father, and of the end she had in view in exercising it. A life income only was left to Mr. Meadowcroft's sons. The freehold of the farm was bequeathed to his daughter, with the testator's recommendation added, that she should marry his "best and dearest friend, Mr. John Jago."

Armed with the power of the will, the heiress of Morwick sent an insolent message to Naomi, requesting her no longer to consider herself one of the inmates at the farm. Miss Meadowcroft, it should be here added, positively refused to believe that John Jago had ever asked Naomi to be his wife, or had ever threatened her, as I had heard him threaten her, if she refused.

She accused me, as she accused Naomi, of trying meanly to injure John Jago in her estimation, out of hatred toward "that much-injured man;" and she sent to me, as she had sent to Naomi, a formal notice to leave the house.

We two banished ones met the same day in the hall, with our travelling-bags in our hands.

"We are turned out together, friend Lefrank," said Naomi, with her quaintly comical smile. "You will go back to England, I guess; and I must make my own living in my own country. Women can get employment in the States if they have a friend to speak for them. Where shall I find somebody who can give me a place?"

I saw my way to saying the right word at the right moment.

"I have got a place to offer you," I replied.

She suspected nothing, so far.

"That's lucky, sir," was all she said. "Is it in a telegraph-office or in a dry-goods store?"

I astonished my little American friend by taking her then and there in my arms, and giving her my first kiss.

"The office is by my fireside," I said; "the salary is anything in reason you like to ask me for; and the place, Naomi, if you have no objection to it, is the place of my wife."

I have no more to say, except that years have passed since I spoke those words, and that I am as fond of Naomi as ever.

Some months after our marriage, Mrs. Lefrank wrote to a friend at Narrabee for news of what was going on at the farm. The answer informed us that Ambrose and Silas had emigrated to New Zealand, and that Miss Meadowcroft was alone at Morwick Farm. John Jago had refused to marry her. John Jago had disappeared again, nobody knew where.

Note in Conclusion. The first idea of this little story was suggested to the author by a printed account of a trial which actually took place, early in the present century, in the United States. The published narrative of this strange case is entitled *The Trial, Confessions, and Conviction of Jesse and Stephen Boorn for the Murder of Russell Colvin, and the*

Return of the Man supposed to have been murdered. By Hon. Leonard Sargeant, Ex-Lieutenant-Governor of Vermont. (Manchester, Vermont, Journal Book and Job Office, 1873.) It may not be amiss to add, for the benefit of incredulous readers, that all the "improbable events" in the story are matters of fact, taken from the printed narrative. Anything which "looks like truth" is, in nine cases out of ten, the invention of the author. W. C.

LEONAUR

ALSO FROM LEONAUR

AVAILABLE IN SOFTCOVER OR HARDCOVER WITH DUST JACKET

CAPTAIN OF THE 95th (Rifles) *by Jonathan Leach*—An officer of Wellington's Sharpshooters during the Peninsular, South of France and Waterloo Campaigns of the Napoleonic Wars.

BUGLER AND OFFICER OF THE RIFLES *by William Green & Harry Smith* With the 95th (Rifles) during the Peninsular & Waterloo Campaigns of the Napoleonic Wars

BAYONETS, BUGLES AND BONNETS by *James 'Thomas' Todd*—Experiences of hard soldiering with the 71st Foot - the Highland Light Infantry - through many battles of the Napoleonic wars including the Peninsular & Waterloo Campaigns

THE ADVENTURES OF A LIGHT DRAGOON *by George Farmer & G.R. Gleig*—A cavalryman during the Peninsular & Waterloo Campaigns, in captivity & at the siege of Bhurtpore, India

THE COMPLEAT RIFLEMAN HARRIS *by Benjamin Harris as told to & transcribed by Captain Henry Curling*—The adventures of a soldier of the 95th (Rifles) during the Peninsular Campaign of the Napoleonic Wars

WITH WELLINGTON'S LIGHT CAVALRY *by William Tomkinson*—The Experiences of an officer of the 16th Light Dragoons in the Peninsular and Waterloo campaigns of the Napoleonic Wars.

SURTEES OF THE RIFLES by *William Surtees*—A Soldier of the 95th (Rifles) in the Peninsular campaign of the Napoleonic Wars.

ENSIGN BELL IN THE PENINSULAR WAR *by George Bell*—The Experiences of a young British Soldier of the 34th Regiment 'The Cumberland Gentlemen' in the Napoleonic wars.

WITH THE LIGHT DIVISION by *John H. Cooke*—The Experiences of an Officer of the 43rd Light Infantry in the Peninsula and South of France During the Napoleonic Wars

NAPOLEON'S IMPERIAL GUARD: FROM MARENGO TO WATERLOO by *J. T. Headley*—This is the story of Napoleon's Imperial Guard from the bearskin caps of the grenadiers to the flamboyance of their mounted chasseurs, their principal characters and the men who commanded them.

BATTLES & SIEGES OF THE PENINSULAR WAR by *W. H. Fitchett*—Corunna, Busaco, Albuera, Ciudad Rodrigo, Badajos, Salamanca, San Sebastian & Others

AVAILABLE ONLINE AT **www.leonaur.com**
AND OTHER GOOD BOOK STORES

NAP-1

Lightning Source UK Ltd.
Milton Keynes UK
UKHW041054080422
401284UK00001B/60

9 781846 778216